1984

THE MAN WHO PLAYED GOD

The Man
Who Played God

ROBERT ST. JOHN

Doubleday & Company, Inc.
GARDEN CITY, NEW YORK

THE MAN WHO PLAYED GOD

PART ONE

1

The rays of the afternoon sun filtered through the thin curtains. Andor Horvath, lying comfortably on his back, felt the brightness attack his eyes and irritably turned over on his side. He stayed in this position for a few minutes, hoping for a return to that happy state of blankness from which the sunlight had jolted him. But the noises of Budapest's fashionable Váci utca below began to impinge on his consciousness, for despite the fact that this was March 1944 and the war had been going on for four years, the afternoon promenaders still took their customary stroll on the avenue. The problems that had faded away as he fell asleep in the early hours of the morning began to reappear and take shape. They didn't panic him, as they might have almost any other man. He had never been panicked by anything—anybody. That was his strength. The problems were now clear in his mind again, and he had no desire to avoid them. Still he was reluctant to leave the soft warmth of his bed. He sat up slowly and leaned his head against the bedstead. For several moments he remained like this, thinking. It was characteristic of him that he never moved quickly, a fact that occasionally gave him more than a little advantage over people who assumed—mistakenly—that the pace of his thoughts matched the pace of his movements. His actions were always deliberate and well considered. If he had a shortcoming it was that he did almost nothing spontaneously. There was, therefore, an apparent joylessness about him, but within his own self-imposed limits he took enormous pleasure in certain sorts of sensual experiences. Andor Horvath was essentially a creature of the night, a lover of the darkness when it was illumined by man-made lights, of public places if they were permeated with the aroma of distinctive tobaccos and fine liquors, of

3

salons and cafés filled with knowledgeable men and beautiful women. This was the world he had chosen for himself, and he had chosen it while he was still a boy.

In the small city of Pécs, about a hundred miles from Budapest, his father had owned a grocery store, and the family—Andor, his parents, and a sister—had lived in an apartment upstairs. Although most of the neighbors were Orthodox Jews, the Horvaths went to the synagogue infrequently. Andor grew up more occupied with the panorama of events in the material world around him and its exciting promises than with religion. Since he was the only boy, he became the center of life for his indulgent parents, especially his mother. She worked devotedly to make him a Hungarian gentleman. She would not allow him to wait on customers in the store. She bought him the best clothes to be had in town. Tirelessly she taught him to drink coffee gracefully, to click his heels and to kiss a lady's hand like an aristocrat, to play the piano more than passably well, and even to speak French. She skimped on her family's food to provide him with books that reproduced great works of art. Under her prodding he became a personable and ambitious young man, with great faith in his own abilities. If infrequently he doubted them, he was careful to behave so that others did not.

By the time he was sixteen he had acquired elegance of manner and fastidiousness in dress, enhanced by a handsome face and a moderately athletic physique. He gave every outward indication of being to the manner born. That same year he joined a Zionist youth group, not because he had any desire to go to Palestine—though he deeply believed that the Jews should have a homeland and that Palestine was rightfully theirs—but because he was fascinated by the bigness of the idea of Zionism and its political possibilities. He was certain that somehow the movement would provide him with the opportunity to become a leader of Hungarian Jewry. In the beginning the youth group had no meeting place of its own and very little money, but there was a well-to-do lawyer in the city who offered his house for their gatherings until, with his assistance, the young people could become self-supporting. Philip Kemeny was tall, gray-haired, and soft-mannered and lived in a stately white stone villa on the edge of Pécs that was filled with exquisite furnishings and art works from every part of the continent. To young Andor Mr. Kemeny and his estate represented everything that was desirable, and the boy worked diligently to emulate the behavior of his new-found idol. For his part, Philip Kemeny was delighted with his young worshiper. Like everyone else, he fell victim to the boy's charm and Andor became a frequent

4

visitor to the great stone house. The only unhappy fact of Philip Kemeny's life was that he had no son. But gradually over the years he began to look upon Andor as his protégé. When the boy was nineteen he sent him to the local university to study law. By this time he regarded him as his son and heir, and even thought of him as a likely husband for his frail, fair-haired Sarah, who was still only a child. He was unaware that long ago Andor had decided he would not be just a guest in the great house, but a member of the family and eventually the master. That the wide-eyed little girl who watched the youth meetings from behind the portieres might be part of this future made it only more enticing to Andor, for her delicacy and shyness inflated his ego and increased his feeling of strength and self-assurance.

In the intervening years most of it had come to pass. He and Sarah were married and lived here in the great city of Budapest, while Philip, now an old man, still maintained the villa at Pécs.

The sharp ring of the telephone in the living room startled him out of his reverie. He heard Sarah's muffled voice. A few moments later she appeared in the doorway, her small hands nervously clenched in front of her.

"It was Kurt Braun," she said. Despite Andor's frequent cautioning, in recent weeks she couldn't keep the fear and distrust out of her voice as she mentioned the German agent's name. "He wants to see you here immediately. Something urgent. I told him to come in half an hour."

"I'll dress right away." He said it matter-of-factly, to dissipate her fright, but she continued to stand there uncertainly. He thought, how like a young fawn she is. Her body was delicately formed in every detail, her wrists and ankles bone-slim, her fingers long and tapering. She had the sweet mouth of an innocent child, and her breasts were those of an adolescent. The complete helplessness and dependence she always exuded were multiplied now by her fear. Andor knew he must go further to reassure her, so he addressed her with the intimate form of the Hungarian word for darling. *"Drágaságem,"* he said, "don't be afraid. Everything is going to be all right."

Some of the tension left her and she gave him a simple, childlike smile. "If you say so, I believe it, Andor. I'll get your breakfast."

He sighed as he looked at the small blue porcelain clock on the night table: ten minutes after two. Braun must have bad news. Well, that would be no surprise. Was there any other kind these days? Sometimes he indulged in the luxury of dreaming about the life he would have when the war ended. The possibility that he might not survive it never occurred to him. Only rarely was he overwhelmed with the black feeling that there never had been peace and might never be again. He threw back the quilted, feather-filled *dunyha* and got out of bed, walked slowly to the dresser, and opened a drawer, examining as he did his reflection in the mirror on the wall. There were too many lines and shadows around his eyes for a man of thirty-five. He would have to stop this nonsense of so many all-night meetings of the Committee. He must take a stronger hand with them. Of course it was better for their morale if they thought the decisions were really their own, but he would have to get more rest. Going to bed at six in the morning was too much of a strain, even for him. He cocked his head to one side and bent closer to the glass to examine his temples. There were, as far as he could see, no new gray hairs. He moved his head back and surveyed his entire reflection and once more saw with pleasure the luxuriant dark hair, the straight nose, the firm, even mouth, and the confident eyes. Then, with one hand still on the knob of the open drawer, he began meticulously to select the clothes he was going to wear.

In the tiny kitchen Sarah prepared coffee and buttered *kiflis,* or breakfast rolls. While the coffee was brewing, she put a hemstitched white linen cloth on the small round table in front of the living-room window, then arranged the Limoges china and the service of heavy silver. She had tried to bring as much of the elegance of her father's house as possible to this modest, inexpensive two-room apartment and she had succeeded so well that it seemed to Andor a true miniature of the mansion in Pécs. She knew that in doing this she had pleased her husband greatly. She brought the large silver pot into the kitchen and filled it with coffee, wrinkling her nose in aversion as she smelled the fumes of the thick brown liquid. After four years she still was not used to this ersatz drink. She was just placing the silver pot, the buttered rolls, and a pitcher of milk on the table when Andor came in from the bedroom. She felt a surge of joy as she looked at him. She knew she did not possess him, but she did belong to him, and for her that was enough. It was enough to feel this belonging anew each day, as she felt it now.

Almost as soon as Andor sat down, there was a knock at the door. He was certain it was Braun, so he asked her to let him in. Then, seeing her hesitation, he patted her hand and said with a laugh, "He won't bite you, little goose. Not while I'm here."

When she opened the door, the tall German bowed decorously to her and wished her a *"guten Tag."* His bow was so deep that his short-cropped white hair almost brushed her breasts. She stepped back hastily and indicated the chair opposite Andor, poured two cups of coffee as the men greeted each other, then excused herself and left the room, as she always did when anyone came to see her husband on business.

"Now," Andor began as Braun sipped his coffee, "what is your urgent news?"

The German put down his cup and looked his host straight in the eye, his heavy, florid face grim. "Something you have been expecting for a long time. The German army will occupy Hungary within the next week." He took another sip of coffee slowly, his pale blue eyes still fastened on Andor, waiting for the enormous significance of the news to take hold of him.

Despite all the preparation he had made within himself for the possibility of this grim moment, Andor was plunged into despair. He was sure Braun was telling the truth, although he always suspected the German's motives. As casually as he could he lit a cigarette and inhaled deeply. Then, appearing to consider the matter with equanimity, he said, "Of course if what you say is true this would be a disaster for my people, but after all"—he smiled deprecatingly—"there have been such rumors before. Why should I believe them now?"

"Because I tell you it is so," Braun snapped, indignant that his competence should be questioned by this Jew. "Have I ever told you this before? In all our dealings have I ever misinformed you? In all the times I have carried messages back and forth to your Jewish Agency in Istanbul, have I ever failed you?"

"You've been well compensated for everything you've done."

"*Ach!*" Braun threw up his hands in exasperation but made no move to leave. Instead his mien became politely persuasive.

"The military situation has changed a great deal in the past year. Russian troops are now in front of the Carpathian Mountains and there have been serious rumors that the Hungarian Government is considering a surrender to the Western Allies before the Russians reach the Hungarian border." He smiled and brushed a nonexistent bit of lint from the lapel of his well-tailored dark suit. "Of course, you understand der Führer cannot permit such a surrender. For that reason there will be the occupation."

"All right," Andor said reasonably, "let us say I believe you. The Germans will control Hungary before another week has passed. Why have you come here to tell me about this calamity?"

Braun's features creased to a shrewd grin. "I've come to tell you how to *avoid* the calamity."

"Indeed."

"You see," Braun went on, his enthusiasm growing, "with the German occupation will come the SS. Of course, we in the Wehrmacht will still run things, but SS Colonel Wedemeyer will be in charge of the Jewish problem here. Now this is the important point: one of Wedemeyer's two aides is Baron von Klaussen. You remember that when Klaussen was in Czechoslovakia your people almost worked out a deal with him to save Jews. It was only the failure of your people to come through with the required amount of money that kept it from succeeding." He drained the last of his coffee, then leaned toward Andor in a conspiratorial manner. "I'm certain Klaussen can still be bought. When the German army moves in, I may be able to arrange a meeting with him for you. Then you could talk about a deal for Hungarian Jews."

Andor felt the terrible weight in his chest lighten, but he only said dryly, "I know you aren't going to do this for love. What's your price?"

"Twenty thousand dollars." The tone was complacent, final.

"That's robbery!"

Braun remained silent, adamant, his blue eyes fixed on vacant space.

"I can't give away Jewish money for nothing. What guarantee do I have that Klaussen will make a deal?" Andor demanded angrily.

Braun looked directly at him. "I can guarantee you nothing except a meeting," he replied coldly. "But I can tell you this: if you want to save your Jews you are going to have to pay and pay, from now on."

Andor rose. "I'll have to discuss it with the other members of the Committee. When we reach a decision, I'll let you know."

"I suggest you go about it quickly. There isn't much time." With that Braun got up and left.

As soon as the door closed, Sarah rushed into the room. "I heard everything. It's the end for us," she cried hysterically. "They'll drive us into camps like animals and then they'll let us die."

Andor put his arms around her. "Darling," he began softly, "we can't always believe what Braun says. We've heard these rumors before. Many times. But, even if they are true now, you must have faith that I can take care of us. Nothing bad is going to happen here in Hungary . . ."

She broke away from him, the tears streaming down her face. "They're going to kill us," she screamed. Over and over she repeated the words, her voice rising each time. "They are going to kill us."

He grabbed her by the shoulders and shook her hard. "Stop it, Sarah!"

She stared at him a moment, then collapsed on the sofa in a fit of quiet weeping. She looked so small and pathetic, he found it difficult not to comfort her, but he knew she had to come out of it alone. He sat down at the table by the window and began to watch the men and women promenading along Váci utca below, his thoughts on Braun's proposition. Some minutes later he realized with a start that there wasn't a sound in the room. He looked at the sofa. Sarah had fallen asleep. He glanced at his watch. It was four-fifteen. Damn! In all the consternation he had forgotten the four-o'clock meeting of the Committee at the Parisette. It would take him at least seven minutes to get there. Well, they would just have to wait. He looked once more at Sarah, considering whether to awaken her. Then he went into the next room, took the coverlet from the bed, put it over her gently, and left the apartment.

Downstairs he stood for a moment in front of the building and breathed deeply of the fresh March air. It felt good to be outside.

"I've been waiting for you," said a voice on his left.

He turned and saw the round, grinning face of Max Franck. For months there had been rumors that the plump little man whose sartorial splendor was always a little overdone was a counterespionage agent for the Hungarian police. This association Franck vociferously denied whenever he was confronted with it. Occasionally the Committee had hired him as a courier, for he had many useful connections and was able to move from one continent to another with extraordinary freedom. Andor regarded him stonily. "I am very busy this afternoon," he answered shortly, and started to walk away.

"I have something important to say to you," Max insisted.

"Then say it." Andor continued to walk toward the Parisette.

"The German army will take over Hungary in the next seven days." It was a flat pronouncement daring Andor to dismiss the bearer of such momentous news.

Andor stopped. "And that makes you, a Jew, happy?" he asked incredulously, misinterpreting the satisfaction in Max's voice.

"Who's happy? Why do you twist everything I say? I only wanted to tell you something you didn't know."

"I knew it."

Max looked at him disbelievingly.

"Braun came to see me today."

"Aha!" Franck cried triumphantly. "That fox. He's the one I want to talk to you about."

"Talk." Andor began to walk again.

9

"Well, I have been figuring. When the Germans take over, the SS comes in. Right? That means Braun and the others from the Wehrmacht will take orders from them. I think it would be smart to drop Braun and his gang and make some contacts in the SS. We should ride with the tide."

They walked almost a block as Max waited impatiently for some reaction. Finally he blurted out, "So, what do you think?"

"I think someday you will get an idea smart enough to put you in jail." Andor looked at his watch and quickened his pace.

For several seconds Franck stood staring after him, crestfallen. Then gradually his face took on an expression of derision. "Hah, the great moralist, the big-shot intellectual." He muttered the words to Andor's disappearing back. "Who needs you?" His ego repaired, he started happily in the opposite direction, his mind awhirl with schemes for the prosperous future of Max Franck under the new order.

2

The Parisette was a popular café on the Duna Korzó, that splendid, tree-lined avenue of expensive hotels and smart cafés and restaurants along the embankment of the Danube. Like the avenue itself and like the people who still thronged it, the Parisette was now but a shabby replica of what it had been before the war. The green canopy over the plate-glass windows facing the river was torn, and the letter *S* was missing from the sign. Inside, the soiled gray paint on the walls was chipped in places, and the black suits of the waiters were thin at the elbows and knees. Over all there was a sour smell that bore witness to the shortage of soap and the abundance of wine that had been spilled and never washed up. The air was heavy with cigarette smoke, even though cigarettes became scarcer every day. At some of the marble-topped tables men were reading newspapers fastened to long wooden poles so they could not be taken from the room either accidentally or on purpose. At other tables, covered with pieces of heavy felt, men were playing one or another of the many Hungarian card games: *alsós,* or *marias,* or the favorite of Budapest gamblers, *huszonegyes,* a Magyar version of 21. Several clients were writing letters with pen, ink, and paper supplied by the café. Others were just sitting, staring into the blue-gray cloud of tobacco smoke.

At a large marble-topped table in the rear of the room sat four men, members of the Budapest Rescue Committee, an oddly assorted lot, even to the casual onlooker. But if their differences in age, temperament, and background caused frequent friction among them, their diversified talents neatly augmented each other. They had fierce arguments but fiercer loyalties. For two years they had been working together. In that time they had become efficient at saving the lives of fellow Jews in the German-occupied countries of Europe. Some of them forged visas, passports, ration books, and miscellaneous documents. Others fed and clothed refugees from Poland and Czechoslovakia, kept in communication with the Jewish Agency in Istanbul and Palestine, and even established an underground railroad of partisans who guided across foreign borders into Hungary those Jews brave or frantic enough to try to escape from their persecutors. It was dangerous work. They were all risking their lives and knew it. Every day brought new problems, additional risks to be taken. But this afternoon they were especially worried. Yesterday two refugees and one of the Committee's guides had been captured crossing the Slovak frontier. This was the second incident of the week, a sign that there was probably a government agent among their trusted workers. They had discussed the matter last night and agreed to meet again this afternoon at the Parisette to conclude a plan of action. Now, at twenty minutes past four, they were waiting for Andor.

Impatiently Erno Gábor twirled the glass of *bikavér* on the table in front of him, fascinated by the circular motion of the ruby-colored wine. Then, for the tenth time, he looked at his watch. As he did, his eyeglasses slipped down until they rested on the tip of his nose. He was a thin man, about sixty, with sparse gray hair and bright blue eyes that darted toward the doorway every few moments. A retired manufacturer of ceramics, he was an ardent Zionist, with several friends on the executive council of the Jewish Agency.

"What is it," he said irritably, pushing back his glasses, "what is it that makes a man always late?" It was a rhetorical question, directed to no one in particular, and only Arthur Gruen acted as if he had heard it.

Gruen raised a large hand. "Don't get excited. He'll come. He always comes. And he's always late. Right now a few minutes aren't a matter of life and death. It's a little thing. Save your energy for the big things, Erno. You're going to need it."

It was said with some affection, but the attitude behind it annoyed

11

Erno, who had a continuous sense of urgency and unlimited energy, which he felt compelled to expend. The older he grew, the more Andor's habitual tardiness riled him, but he knew that any discussion of the point with Arthur Gruen would only end in an argument, as it usually did. "The *ganzer moccher*," he said to himself consolingly, "he knows everything," and went back to twirling his glass.

Arthur Gruen watched him, amused, his large leathery face creased in a half-smile. That was the trouble with little men, he reflected. They spent their energy on small matters and exhausted themselves in futility. Well, he had disciplined himself against such foolishness and he had been rewarded. When you go after something, go after something big. That had always been his motto. And it had paid off. Handsomely. To him each of his many lumberyards, scattered through the larger towns of Hungary, was a prize he had fought for and won. Deservedly, he was sure. He looked upon his wife, Elizabeth, and his two sons in much the same way. He cherished them all, without distinguishing much between them. They were the prizes of life, fairly won. They were visible proof to the world that he was a successful and happy man. A sudden jab in his left arm jolted him. It was the wood pole that held the newspaper Rachel, the secretary of the Committee, had been reading.

"Oh, Arthur, I'm so clumsy." She smiled at him impishly and with mock solicitousness rubbed his injured arm. Then she got up. "I think I'll see if there's a paper with some news that is a little more optimistic." She walked to the other side of the room, put the paper she had been reading on a rack, and took another. Several men in the café followed her progress with interest. Rachel Teller was not a woman who easily passed unnoticed, although in the past two years she had learned very well how to be self-effacing when necessary. Her carriage was proud, her bosom firm, her mouth had a soft fullness, and her compassionate eyes were framed by loose waves of chestnut-colored hair. As she returned, Arthur speculated idly, as he had done many times in the past, on why she had no man. If she did have, he would know it, for the lives of all of them were so intertwined that it wouldn't remain a secret for long. Was she in love with Andor? He rejected the idea almost immediately. She lived in the same apartment building as the Horvaths, but, after all, she had come from Pécs, Andor's home town, and she was in Budapest without her family; it was natural that the Horvaths would look after her. Still, was it a satisfying life for a young woman—even a very dedicated one—to devote all her energy to finding homes and cloth-

12

ing for frightened refugee women; to feeding and fondling other women's children? He doubted it.

The other two members of the group remained silent, each engrossed in a vital mental pursuit. Alex Peto, his sharp features twisted in frustration, his pale, gentle eyes desperate, was reading a small, tattered volume, *The Science of Military Strategy*. Occasionally with the palm of his right hand he smoothed down his unruly light brown hair, in an effort to regain his composure. What, he asked himself again and again, had possessed the Jewish Agency that they had instructed him to create a branch of Haganah, the underground Jewish army, here in Hungary? Why him? They trusted him, they said. Surely that was important. It was, in fact, the *sine qua non*. But was this reason enough to demand that he, a professor of physics, should be the one to try to build a secret resistance army? The idea was ridiculous. It was worse than ridiculous. It was insane. They knew him. They knew he had always considered the taking of life, even the life of an animal, a sign of basic bestiality, over which man had need to triumph if he was to make any pretense of being civilized. Then the war came, and friends argued with him that it was necessary to kill in order to put an end to the killing; that fire had to be met with fire. But he remained unconvinced. Then suddenly instructions had come from the Jewish Agency charging him with the responsibility for organizing an underground Jewish defense force. Until then his work with the Committee had been entirely concerned with relieving suffering and saving lives. But now he was to prepare to take lives, when necessary. His whole being rebelled, but despite his fervent objections Andor had insisted that he must accept the task. Finally he did, with many misgivings. So far all he had done toward organizing a Haganah unit was to study the manual the Jewish Agency had sent him. It had been brought from Istanbul by Max Franck weeks ago, along with a batch of confidential papers for Andor and the rest of the Committee. Like a good student, he had worked over the book, trying to memorize everything it contained. Whenever he would ask Andor to discuss the means of obtaining arms and ammunition for a Haganah unit, he was put off. Sometimes he felt Andor wasn't really interested in any organized military resistance. It occurred to him that maybe this was why Andor hadn't insisted on the appointment of someone else. Of course there was the problem of who else. Most of the young men of the community had been sent off to labor camps by now. He knew of no one really capable. "Except maybe you," he said half aloud as he looked across the table at the dark, intent face of Joe Nagel. "If only you weren't so young and headstrong, and if only you were a Hungarian."

The stocky youth was paying no attention to his colleagues. Instead he was watching the comings and goings of the Parisette's clients: Germans in mufti, Hungarian military officers in their elaborate uniforms, looking as if they belonged in a nineteenth-century light opera instead of in a twentieth-century war, businessmen with their ladies, and ladies alone, who might not really be ladies at all. Which of them were what they seemed to be? More important, which were not? Budapest had been infiltrated by foreign agents, refugees, and strange characters from many countries. Some had come to seek anonymity, some to make a profit from the war that now had engulfed the continent, some for more sinister reasons. Joe had become an expert in recognizing them all. Joe had been born in Poland and before the war had joined the *chalutzim,* the pioneers, that organization of youthful Zionists who were preparing themselves to work the land in Palestine, if and when the opportunity came for them to go there. When the Germans conquered Poland and began their persecution of the Jews, he and other chalutzim helped many Polish Jews escape to Czechoslovakia. After several months the Germans learned of his activities, so he fled Poland himself for Czechoslovakia, where he joined the chalutzim of that country and helped Slovak Jews escape into Hungary, often guiding them across the frontier himself. Then the time came when it was certain death for him to return to Czechoslovakia, and he came to Budapest. Through the Hungarian chalutzim he learned of the Budapest Rescue Committee and went to see Andor Horvath. Surely, he said, the Committee could use his experience even if he was not a Hungarian. Andor, as a test, gave him three difficult assignments, all involving getting Hungarian Jews across the frontier into Rumania. Joe carried them out so well that after several months Andor gave him a place on the Committee.

It was Joe, watching the figures entering and leaving, who first saw Andor and announced, "Here he is."

"At last!" Erno snorted. Andor greeted them with a cordial *"Jó napot"* and made his usual courteous apology for being late. *"Barack,"* he said to the waiter as he sat down.

"Now we can get to work," Erno began eagerly. "We must absolutely finish our plan today. I have had some second thoughts—" He interrupted himself as the waiter approached the table and put the apricot brandy in front of Andor.

Before he could begin again, Andor said solemnly, "There is something more important to discuss." They looked at him expectantly. Slowly he took a sip of brandy, enjoying the bite of the alcohol and the tangy flavor, and especially the attention of his Committee members. He put the glass down slowly, and then said, "The Germans are going to take over Hungary within the week."

For several seconds no one moved or spoke. They were as mute and motionless as if they were all cast in stone. Arthur was the first to recover.

"We'll mobilize all our people and meet the bastards head on!" he cried belligerently. "They won't get past the outskirts of Budapest."

Alex laughed bitterly. "Tell me, Arthur," he demanded cuttingly, "what will you use for weapons against German tanks and machine guns, kitchen knives? Or maybe that Hungarian ceremonial sword you're so proud of? And who will our soldiers be? Almost all our people who can bear arms have been forced into labor battalions. There is no one to fight and nothing to fight with." He slumped back in his chair.

"I can fight," Joe shouted at him. "And I am not above using a kitchen knife if it can kill a goddamn Nazi."

Rachel jumped to her feet. "Joe's right. All of us can fight, even the women."

"Quiet!" Andor's voice was stern, and suddenly they realized that some of the other clients were watching them curiously.

Rachel sat down, abashed.

When Andor spoke again his voice was soft and persuasive. "If we keep our wits about us we may be able to save our people without bloodshed." He told them of Braun's proposal. They listened soberly, relief slowly emerging on their faces as Andor talked. When he had finished, they agreed unanimously that he should let Braun arrange a meeting with Klaussen.

"Still, we should train as many of our people as we can, and organize them in small groups, in case of necessity," Arthur insisted.

"We *are* making such plans," Alex answered, his usually mild expression one of annoyance. He considered the remark an unnecessary reflection on his ability.

Joe intervened. "Don't be hurt, Alex. We know your job is an impossible one, but Arthur has a point—"

"I'm sure Alex knows what must be done and he will do it, when the time is right," Andor said in a tone that closed the discussion.

"I think we should write a report immediately on the whole matter for

15

the Agency and send it to Istanbul by one of our couriers," Erno suggested.

Andor agreed. "Besides informing them of what is happening here, it will give them an opportunity to tell the Allies of the coming invasion." He turned to Alex. "As head of Haganah, you will write the report."

"What about the Hungarian Secret Service?" Rachel asked. "Shouldn't we alert them? If we do, they might be more willing to protect us, in case our deal with Klaussen falls through."

"Bravo!" Andor patted her on the head affectionately. "You are becoming a real tactician. But I'm afraid the Hungarians have already been informed." He smiled wryly. "On my way here I was accosted by Max Franck."

A collective groan went up from the table.

Andor waited for quiet and then said earnestly, "Now we must examine the other possibility, namely that there will be no deal, either because Braun is lying, or because Klaussen can no longer be bought, or because the Germans are determined to destroy us. Whatever happens, we must make certain we'll be able to continue our work. We mustn't leave ourselves liable to arrest when the Germans take over. They probably know all about us, and what they don't yet know they'll learn from Braun."

The mood of determined optimism that had followed his account of Braun's offer disappeared. Arthur wearily wiped his face with a handkerchief and Erno asked impatiently, "What do you want us to do?"

"We'll go farther underground and keep working," Joe snapped at him.

Alex put a restraining hand on Joe's arm. "Go on, Andor," he said quietly.

"We should suspend our operations and keep out of sight until we know what the Germans are going to do here. We must find a place outside the city to stay in the meantime."

"That will be easy." Arthur slapped the table with satisfaction. "My father-in-law has a house at Budakeszi. He's offered it to me several times. It's vacant. Furnished but vacant. I'm sure he'll let us have it. Since he's not a Jew, we'll be safe there."

"Is it large enough to accommodate all of us and our families?" Andor asked.

"It could hold a regiment."

"Good. You make the arrangements. Of course"—Andor hesitated—

"one of us will have to remain under cover in the city to watch what goes on." He looked quickly around the table.

"I'll stay," Alex volunteered. "I'm alone now"—his face took on a melancholy aspect—"so it will be easy for me to move about unnoticed."

"Thank you, Alex." Unsentimental as Andor was, he regretted that Alex had been reminded of his loneliness. It was strange, he thought, that the passage of time did not seem to lessen Alex's grief over the death of Leah. Andor found it difficult to understand such absolute devotion to a woman, even to a living woman, let alone to the memory of a dead one, for it was completely outside his own experience. Still, in a peculiar, objective way, he admired Alex for it, and for the other qualities Alex had that he himself lacked, though he never admitted it to anyone else, and seldom even to himself.

He turned to the rest of them. "I suggest we meet at the Café Opera tomorrow at three to discuss Arthur's arrangements and to make our plans to move. That will be our last meeting until after the Germans arrive." He glanced around the table. "Does anyone want to add anything?"

There was a murmur of no's.

Arthur summoned the waiter and paid the bill. Andor handed the waiter a pengö and said, "I need twenty fillér for the phone." The others got up, took their leave, and began to depart. Andor put his hand on Rachel's arm. "Are you going home now?"

"Yes," she answered, then added, "I'll look in on Sarah. Don't worry. Will you be late?"

"Probably. I'm going to the Center to finish up whatever business I can before we leave the city." He sighed. "See if you can cheer up Sarah a little. She was very upset by Braun's visit this afternoon."

"I will. Don't worry," she said again as she left. "Sarah will be all right. She's really a brave girl."

With the coin the waiter gave him Andor went to the telephone booth in the back of the café and dialed Braun's number. "We have decided that you have a deal," he told the German.

"Your people have made a wise decision, Horvath." Even over the telephone the pleasure in Braun's voice was unmistakable. "I will call you as soon as I have some news."

"No, don't call me," Andor was deliberately curt. "I'll keep in touch with you." Before Braun could protest, he put the receiver back on the hook.

17

Outside the night was dark and cold as he walked toward the Center. He hoped Sarah was calm by now. Poor, defenseless little Sarah. The next few months—the next few years, perhaps—were going to be difficult. He must try harder to be kind and patient with her.

The Center was in a predominantly Jewish section of Pest, linked by an arcade with the city's largest synagogue, the twin spires of which were visible for a great distance in all directions. The Center faced on Sip utca (Whistle Street) while the synagogue was on Dohány utca (Tobacco Street). Theodor Herzl, father of Zionism, had been born on Dohány utca and although his dream of *The Jewish State* had not yet been realized, his birthplace already was an international Jewish shrine. The Center was a focal point of the cultural life of Budapest Jewry. The ground floor of the substantial three-story building was given over to offices and reception rooms. On the second floor there was both a great meeting hall and Goldmark Auditorium, named after the celebrated composer, in which plays and operas were frequently produced. Executives of the Jewish community had their spacious offices on the third floor. Andor had been given a small room on the ground floor as headquarters for his Rescue Committee. Tonight, as usual, there was a crowd outside his office, waiting to see him. He kept no regular hours, but they would wait until he came, even if it was long into the night. As he walked into his office, several people jumped up and began talking to him, all at once.

"I will see every one of you in turn," he told them. "Be patient." He nodded to a bald little man sitting nearest the entrance to his office. "Come in, Vajda."

The old man followed him and seated himself on the opposite side of the desk.

"You're looking fine these days," Andor began jovially.

"To look and to feel are two different things," Vajda replied irritably, determined not to be jollied out of his purpose this time. "Have you got me a certificate?"

Andor shook his head. "I'm sorry. So far I haven't been able to do it. There are a great many ahead of you. Since the war thousands want to go to Palestine. You know that."

"I know I have been coming here every month for ten months, and always the answer is no. Why? I am an old man. If I must wait much longer I will never see Palestine. I will die first. Do you care?"

For perhaps the hundredth time that week Andor explained, "The

18

British Government gives our Palestine Office here in Budapest only thirty-five certificates a month admitting people to Palestine. And I don't get all thirty-five. I have very little to do with saying who comes and who stays."

The last statement was far from the truth. He alone decided who received a majority of the thirty-five certificates. This was one of his sources of power in the community. It was true that the certificates didn't come directly to his office. The Jewish Agency had a representative of its own in Budapest who theoretically decided how to distribute the priceless certificates. But until recently most of the people who really wanted to go to Palestine to live were Zionists, and Andor was the dominant leader of the Zionist movement in Budapest. Moving to Palestine had had little appeal for Hungarian Jews. Even after the advent of Hitler, even during the early years of the war, most of the eight hundred thousand Hungarian Jews had a positive disinterest in emigration. They formed the most integration-minded Jewish community in Europe. While Yiddish was the language of Polish and Russian Jews, the Hungarian Jews prided themselves on their ignorance of Yiddish. In public and in private they spoke Magyar. In most other parts of Europe, Jewish communities held themselves aloof from the life about them. They had their own Jewish culture: their own literature, music, art, dances; their own opera and theater; their own writers, actors, playwrights, singers. Here in Hungary for generations the Jews had worked diligently to identify themselves with the national life. The number of Neologs, or reform Jews, was proportionately larger here than anywhere else, and a considerable percentage had given up the practice of their religion. The home of the Hungarian Jew looked completely Magyar, even to the piles of pillows and puffs on the beds, the colored tile stoves, the predominance of red in interior-decorating schemes. It was the knowledge that they *had* become so thoroughly integrated that gave Hungarian Jews their sense of security from persecution by the Germans. And so far they had been right. Many anti-Semitic laws had been passed and the fascist Arrow Cross party had a program of putting Jews in their place. But most Hungarian Jews took this for window dressing and were unafraid. They were Hungarians. If they suffered during the war, it would be because of their nationality; because Hungary, as in 1914, had chosen the wrong side to support, not because they were Jews. There were notable exceptions to these generalizations, but because this was the way they thought, very few of them had gone to Palestine and until now very few had even expressed a desire to go. For

19

that reason the minuscule number of certificates that arrived each month had been quite enough until recently. It was only lately that people who were not Zionists at all and who cared little about building a national homeland off in the Middle East were seeking certificates, as insurance policies. They cost nothing, so why not have a certificate in the pocket, just in case the situation, God forbid, should ever get really bad? Members of the Orthodox and Neolog communities began to put pressure on the Palestine Office, and Andor had to use all his talents to continue to get the lion's share of certificates. Abraham Kossuth, the Jewish Agency's official representative, several times in anger pointed out to Andor that he had never been either appointed or elected by anyone to leadership of the Rescue Committee, and that the Committee itself had no official status. It had grown out of necessity, that was all. Even though the Jewish Agency in Palestine and Istanbul did communicate with the Committee and had given it *de facto* recognition, it still had no official status in the community, except through Andor's bluffing and bullying.

When Kossuth talked this way, Andor would look at the dun-colored man condescendingly and say, "Abraham, I want thirty certificates this month, and I do not have time to argue." Usually he got them. He assigned them according to his own best judgment, seldom discussing the distribution even with members of the Committee. He gave preference to young people, men and women with vigor and purpose, who wanted to help build a Jewish nation and who had the strength to do it. But it would have been cruel to tell this to the old man who sat across the desk from him. There was no use hurting him more than he had to.

"This doesn't mean you should give up, Vajda. One of these days you will get your certificate," he lied.

"Who's giving up? I'll be back next month. And the month after. Maybe soon you'll give me a certificate just to get rid of me, eh?"

"It's a thought," Andor smiled, "but don't count on it."

As Vajda left, a middle-aged man entered. Could he have a letter delivered to his sister in Slovakia? After him came a thin, dark young woman. Could the Committee arrange to rescue her brother in Poland? How much would it cost? Then an older woman. Her husband was in a labor camp in the east. He was too sick and too old for the work. Was it possible to bring him back to Budapest? Their problems were myriad —some large, some small, but each caller was certain that Andor could help, that his Committee was all-powerful. He listened patiently, taking notes, smiling, trying to cheer them up with a warm grasp of the hand or a pat on the shoulder, promising them he would do whatever he could, sometimes promising much more than he knew was possible. Promising, occasionally, with no intention of doing anything at all.

At nine o'clock he went to a nearby restaurant for dinner. When he returned to the Center he wrote instructions about the cases he had heard and attached them to the notes he had taken during the interviews. These he would give to Alex, Arthur, Erno, Rachel, and Joe at the meeting tomorrow, and they would have to assign the various jobs to their workers immediately. Those cases that could not be handled during the week or so the Committee would be away from Budapest would have to be put aside. Toward eleven-thirty he packed all the confidential papers from his files and desk in a brief case and a cardboard box. He must remind the other Committee members to clean out their desks, too. At midnight he turned off the lights and went outside to hail a taxi.

When he walked into the living room, Sarah was seated on the sofa, her legs tucked up under her, the blue silk of her robe making a blanket that touched the floor. She always waited for him at night. But since he had formed the Rescue Committee she was especially nervous. The darkness of the night, the secret activities of the Committee, which he seldom discussed with her, and the tenseness created by the war filled her with dreadful images she couldn't shake off until she saw him walk through the doorway.

As he looked at her now, Andor could see no signs of the afternoon's hysteria. She was a little flushed, but the rosy hue of her skin was a becoming change from her usual pallor. He put down his packages and removed his coat. Then he went to the sofa and kissed her lightly on the cheek. She was warm and fragrant with a flowery cologne, but neither the touch nor the scent of her kindled any desire in him. He felt weak and depleted by the day's events. Wearily he went to the sideboard and poured a brandy.

"I'll join you," he heard her say. Masking his surprise, he poured another drink, returned to his place beside her on the sofa, and handed her the second glass.

She looked at him happily. "What shall we drink to?"

He lifted his glass. "To you, of course, darling." He colored the words with a gallantry he didn't feel. Then, keeping his eyes on hers in the old way of their courtship days, he sipped the brandy.

She kissed her index finger and laid it on his cheek. Gently he took her hand and pressed it to his lips, then put it back in her lap. "Did you see Rachel today?" He asked it casually, eager to turn the conversation into another direction without making it apparent.

"Yes, she was here about eight-thirty," Sarah replied indifferently. Then her small face became grave. "You know, I'm sorry for her. She's busy and important, and so many people come to her to be helped. But she has no one to love her, and no one to love. It is very sad to have no one to love." She murmured the words caressingly, lifting her small parted mouth to be kissed.

"You do love me, don't you? You are mine, all mine," she whispered, when they were in bed together.

"All yours, beloved." He uttered the easy lie and nestled his head against her cheek.

"Now I can tell you what I couldn't tell you this afternoon."

"What is it, darling?" he asked evenly, expecting some trivia, for she often exaggerated both her fears and her joys.

She raised herself on one elbow and faced him, her eyes shining. "We're going to have a child."

The shock was so great that for a moment he couldn't speak.

"Aren't you happy?" she cried shrilly, alarmed at his silence.

"Of course, darling." He put his arms out and drew her down to him. "I am—overjoyed." He knew he shouldn't have hesitated in saying the word. "Overjoyed." He repeated it with as much feeling as he could. "But after four years you can't expect me not to be surprised." Inwardly he was desolate. What a time to be born! What a time for anyone—but for a Jew! His child would come to an earth full of hate and death and tears. With all that, it would have a child for a mother. How contrary fate was. Four years ago he had fervently wished for a son. How proud he would have been to say "my son," and now . . .

"Are you sure?" He had to ask, but actually he knew the answer. She had planned too carefully how to tell him.

"Oh yes. I saw Dr. Hecht this afternoon. He said the baby will be born the last week in October, and I'm in good health." She snuggled closer to him. "I'm so glad, Andor, that you're happy. At first I was frightened about having a baby during a war and everything, but . . ." Her voice trailed off.

He felt a stab of guilt. "Don't be afraid, darling. Everything is going to be all right." His voice soothed her. He began to caress her hair, occasionally putting his lips to it, until he felt her supine against him.

"You know," she said dreamily, "I have a feeling it's going to be a boy."

"Of course it's going to be a boy."

In a few minutes she was asleep. A half-smile played about the corners of her mouth. But sleep wouldn't come to him. He lay very still, holding her in his arms through the night, listening to the melancholy sound of rain spattering against the windowpane.

3

Alex Peto paced up and down his dark little one-room hideout just off Dohány utca, impatiently waiting for the first light of morning. Occasionally he pushed aside the curtains just enough to see into the street below. It was Sunday, the nineteenth of March. "Six days," he said to himself, "since we received Braun's warning." Suddenly he had a fantastic thought. "Maybe the bastards aren't coming!" The very idea sent him into a dizzy spiral of elation, but he soon plummeted to earth again. "Alex," he chided himself, "you're going a little crazy here by yourself for so many days. Of course they'll come. Like rats bringing the plague they'll come."

Just then there was a sharp sound, like the noise of a car with a loose muffler. He parted the curtains and looked out. A yellow Mercedes was going slowly down the street, as if its occupants were looking for a particular house. After it passed, he saw that the rear license plate bore the letters POL. He knew what that meant. Grabbing his jacket from the chair, he rushed down the stairs, out into the street, and toward the Danube and the great Széchényi-Lánchíd, the stone bridge that crossed the river from the center of Pest to Buda. At first he kept close to the buildings, ready to slip into a doorway at the sight of a yellow car or a German soldier. He moved quickly, perspiring despite the early morning chill of the wind. As he approached the main avenue of Andrassy—the Champs Elysées of Budapest—he saw a yellow Mercedes coming toward him. There were two German soldiers in the front seat. It was too late to run for cover, so he merely slackened his pace and walked straight on, holding his breath but trying to feign unconcern, looking to neither left nor right. When the car was out of sight, he hurried again. In the murky half-light the handsome stone office buildings and the fashionable shops looked dreary, and the rows of tall trees that in summer shaded the wide street with their lush, green-leaved splendor were like ghostly sentinels, their stolid trunks dark and dry, their sharp bare branches like ugly, outstretched claws. Alex shivered and moved still faster. As he came within sight of the great cables of the Lánchíd, the sun came over the horizon. Almost at once the mist began to disappear. There was not a sound. There seemed to be no life anywhere, except for the throbbing of his own heartbeat and the noise of the pulse in his throat; no movement except the almost imperceptible ascent of the orange ball on the horizon and the shifting of the plump gray clouds above. He walked to the foot of the bridge and stood there, unable to fathom the stillness, staring at the great, tongueless lions of gray stone guarding the entrance. How fitting, he thought, as he gazed into their yawning, empty mouths. The enemy has come and we don't even murmur. He turned and started up the quay toward the Parliament buildings. He would prowl the streets awhile, cautiously, to see and learn what he could.

This quiet seizure of a nation was the climax of a series of events, some of them seemingly irrelevant. For months the Hungarian Government, guided by Prime Minister Kallay, had been secretly communicating with representatives of the United States and Great Britain, who had been requested to send British and American air missions to Hungary, with authority to negotiate on a high level. Fearful of invasion by the Soviet army, the Hungarians intended to propose that at the proper time their Regent, Nicholas Horthy, would go to Transylvania and announce the surrender of his country to the Western Allies. All this should have been kept a secret of the highest order, but somehow there was a leak and before long German intelligence learned that communication had been established between the Allies and the Kallay government.

By March the Soviet armies were perilously close to the Hungarian frontiers. They had crossed the mouth of the Dnieper River and begun to move northwest across the southern Ukraine; the German Sixth Army in this area had had a high toll of dead and wounded, and was badly disorganized. To the north Soviet troops reached Tarnopol in East Galicia. By the middle of the month they were west of the Dniester River in Moldavia, and a few of them managed to cross the Prut River on the Rumanian border. On several sides they were close to Hungary.

Nevertheless, Hungarian officials didn't order a general call to arms, despite their often-declared determination that no Russian soldier would ever penetrate their borders. Two divisions were ordered to mobilize and the Second Armored Division was alerted, but it was neither enlarged nor strengthened. These measures comprised almost the whole of the nation's preparation to resist invasion.

Otherwise Hungarian officialdom behaved as if there were no crisis. High society and the foreign diplomatic corps continued to give teas, cocktail parties, and dinners, all of them as elaborate and as gay as usual. After four years of war the mass of the people appeared both threadbare and hungry. The necessities of ordinary living were scarce, and prices were growing astronomical. Years of shortages, casualty lists, air raids, and dread uncertainty about the future had left their mark on people who had once been gay and high-spirited. But in the early spring of 1944 many of the Hungarians who lived in the sumptuous villas of Buda, on hills like Rózsadomb, still acted as if Budapest were an island of serenity in a sea of frightful nightmare. It was possible to see, sprinkled here and there through the drab populace on the avenues, these men and women who seemed to be from another world. The men carried themselves with ancient pride, and the women looked as if they had just come from scented baths and the hands of their *coiffeurs*. They were the people who kept the shops of Váci utca prosperous, apparently undisturbed that the prices of luxury items had been multiplied by ten or twenty. During the middle of the day boys on bicycles still delivered dinners in blue-enameled containers from the de luxe restaurants to private homes across the river. The kiosks and telephone booths bore advertisements of the opera and the theaters, with the casts' names in large red letters. There were ads inside and outside the trams, and on the backs of park benches, for the Sunday afternoon races, a symphony concert, and an art exhibition. Almost everyone was looking forward to the March 15 freedom-day festivities. They were to be followed five days later by a celebration of the fiftieth anniversary of the death of the great national hero, Lajos Kossuth. On Kossuth Day, Prime Minister Kallay was going to address Parliament. There were rumors that in his speech he would announce Hungary's surrender and the landing of the Anglo-American air missions.

March 15 was a happy day for most Hungarians. In the evening, promptly at seven-thirty, the curtain rose at the magnificent opera house on the première of a new work, *Petöfi*. Most of Budapest's distinguished citizens, as well as many foreigners, were there, in evening dress, with medals and decorations. Prince Regent Horthy and Prime Minister Kallay were in the audience.

Later that evening the German Minister, Von Jagow, called on Regent Horthy at the palace with a letter from Adolf Hitler. In it the Führer urged Horthy to come, with his Chief of Staff and Minister of Defense, to the palace of Schloss Klessheim, to discuss German-Hungarian problems. Since it was necessary for Hitler to be at his own headquarters on the twentieth, Horthy must come within forty-eight hours.

The next morning Horthy debated with Kallay and his ministers the wisdom of complying. It was finally agreed that he should go; that a refusal would only anger Hitler and make Hungary's already precarious position more difficult.

Horthy and his staff left Budapest by train on the evening of March 17 and arrived in Salzburg the next morning. Hitler, accompanied by his Foreign Minister, Joachim von Ribbentrop, and by General Keitel and other military leaders, was waiting at the depot to welcome them, but the greetings were formal. The atmosphere as they were driven to Klessheim was cold.

At the palace the guests were shown to their quarters, and a short time later Hitler asked for a private meeting with Horthy in his study on the main floor. No one was present except the two heads of state. Hitler seemed exceedingly nervous. He began the conversation by denouncing Italy's surrender to the Allies. He called it a "betrayal" and said it had put Germany in a disastrous position. He had been caught unaware by the "treachery," but this would not happen a second time. That was why he felt it necessary to take precautions to prevent Hungary from abandoning the Reich. He would not expose Germany to another stab in the back.

Horthy was enraged. He replied that in a thousand years the Magyars had never been traitors. Should events ever force him, in order to preserve Hungary's existence, to ask the enemy for an armistice, he would inform the Germans of his intention, honestly, beforehand. Hungary was certainly not planning any such action now.

Hitler replied that he had proof to the contrary. He accused Kallay and Hungarian legations in neutral countries of engaging in treacherous negotiations with the enemy, and he repeated that he had documents to prove it. Horthy challenged the validity of this proof. A heated argument continued for more than an hour.

The Regent declared that if Hitler meant "by taking precautions" an occupation of Hungary, a country that had made so many sacrifices for Germany, it would be a monstrous crime and would result in creating a great hatred for the Germans throughout Hungary. Finally Hitler announced bluntly, "I have decided to occupy Hungary militarily."

Horthy jumped to his feet, red-faced and furious. "If everything has been decided, it is useless to continue the discussions." He strode out of the study and headed for the stairs leading to his rooms. Hitler, distraught, ran after him, begging him to return. In the meantime Ribbentrop had had a discussion with Dominic Sztojay, Hungarian Minister to Berlin, during which the German Foreign Minister had asked the Hungarian whether he had forwarded to his government the German complaints addressed to him at their December meeting. He was unhappy that nothing had changed since that time, especially in connection with the Jewish question.

When Horthy reached his apartment in the palace he told his staff what had happened and they agreed that they should leave Klessheim immediately. The Regent asked that his private train be made ready without delay. Then he tried to telephone Kallay in Budapest. The line was dead.

A short time thereafter an air-raid alarm sounded and a message arrived informing Horthy that his train could not be prepared. Salzburg was under attack. This had disrupted telephone communications. As a precaution the Hungarian train had been driven out of the area. With this message there was an invitation for the entire Hungarian party to have luncheon with Hitler, and for Horthy to continue his discussion with the Führer afterward. The Regent was persuaded by his advisers to accept. A great oval table in the wood-paneled dining room was set with heavy linen and a sparkling array of thin crystal glasses; there were many courses of rich food, but little conversation. Hitler, obviously disturbed, toyed with what was on his plate, eating little. Throughout the meal the air was frosty. After coffee was served, Hitler and Horthy returned to the study. Again the Regent declaimed against the proposed occupation. If Hitler carried out this threat, the British and the Americans would bomb Hungary's munitions factories and communication lines, which were now functioning in the service of the Reich. Hitler replied that occupation was unavoidable. In that case, Horthy said, further conversation was futile, and left again. His Chief of Staff, Szombathely, trying to ameliorate the situation, sought an audience himself with Hitler. He found the Führer so incensed over Horthy's behavior that he was threatening to have him arrested unless he stopped being so "stubborn." Szombathely tactfully pointed out that such a blunder would be used to great advantage by Allied propagandists. He

27

said the occupation was really unnecessary, because Hungary was prepared and eager to defend her borders against the Russians. Hitler grew calmer and answered that all he wanted was a guarantee of military and political co-operation from Hungary; that if this was forthcoming German soldiers would move out of Hungary in two or three weeks. To prove his good will to Szombathely, he summoned General Keitel and asked whether the occupation orders could be rescinded.

Keitel replied that they could not be. The troops had already started to march.

Szombathely took this news quickly to Horthy, who descended from his rooms, sought out Hitler, and announced, "I shall, of course, lay down my office at once."

Hitler pleaded with him to reconsider. "I give you my word that the German troops will be withdrawn as soon as a new Hungarian Government that has my confidence has been formed."

Horthy said he would not make a decision immediately and returned to his quarters to consult his advisers. The diplomat, Sztojay, urged that they co-operate with the Germans, but that they bargain for the most favorable conditions possible. The others supported him, for they had meantime been warned by Hitler's aides that if Horthy relinquished his office, as punishment Hungary would be occupied not only by Germans but also by Slovaks, Croats, and Rumanians. This would be humiliation compounded.

Horthy finally decided that it was his duty to remain as Regent. He told himself that his resignation could not prevent a German occupation; that it would just give Hitler an opportunity to put the extreme, pro-Nazi Hungarian Arrow Cross party in power. So, reluctantly, he told the Führer he would remain at his post; he would dismiss Kallay and appoint a government acceptable to the Germans; he would put the entire strength of the Hungarian Army on the Russian front; Hungary would continue her complete economic co-operation in the production of war material.

Hitler then declared that a solution of the Jewish problem in Hungary was imperative. Specifically he demanded that a considerable number of Hungarian Jews be sent to Germany to work in war plants. Horthy agreed, later explaining that labor service was already required of Hungarian Jews who were not in the Army, and it should not matter to them that they would now be required to perform their labor abroad.

In return for these concessions Hitler pledged that the occupation would last only until a satisfactory government was installed; that

Slovak, Croat, and Rumanian troops would not be part of the occupying force; that the sovereignty of Hungary would be respected.

As soon as the agreement was reached, Horthy was eager to start for home. He asked that his train be made ready but was told that the air raid was not over yet. He waited for some time and then finally, at 7 P.M., hearing nothing more about the train or the raid, asked whether he was to consider himself a prisoner. He was assured that the alarm was now over and that his train would be ready in an hour. Chief of Staff Szombathely was asked to send a telegram to General Bajnoczy, his second-in-command in Budapest, saying that German troops would be "passing through" Hungary and should be "regarded as friends." This he did.

At eight o'clock Hitler accompanied the Hungarians to the depot at Salzburg. He was smiling and his good-bys were cordial. But just as the train started to move he said to Szombathely, "If one shot is fired at my troops during the occupation, the consequences will be boundless."

On the train there were, in addition to Horthy and his staff, several Germans, among them Von Jagow, Hitler's Minister to Hungary. The following morning, while the train was still en route to Budapest, Von Jagow informed Horthy that he had been recalled and that his successor, Edmund Veesenmayer, was on the train and would like to present himself to the Regent. Horthy consented and during their conversation Veesenmayer assured him that he wished to carry out his assignment in complete harmony with the Regent. It came out later that Veesenmayer had been given just three days in which to put into effect the agreement that had been reached at Klessheim.

In Budapest, Szombathely's telegram was received by General Bajnoczy soon after midnight. The message that German troops would be "passing through" did not alarm him, and he had it transmitted to the operational section, which notified all units of the armed forces, wherever they were stationed. By the time Bajnoczy received the message, the Germans had a strong foothold in the country. Shortly after twilight they had crossed the frontiers of Slovakia, western Rumania, and northern Yugoslavia. In the hours immediately after midnight the government began to receive reports from railroad stations and police at road posts that German troops were crossing the frontiers in trucks and trains. Many said the Germans were not passing through but instead were establishing themselves at strategic points. Military commanders telephoned to inquire whether they were still to treat the invaders as "friends." Some Hungarian soldiers on the frontiers, seeing the Germans detrain and arrange themselves in military formations, fired at them.

It was now plain to Prime Minister Kallay and his staff that the country was being systematically invaded from all sides. He sent for General Bajnoczy, the generals of the Army, and the head of the Regent's Military Chancellery. He had been informed that eleven divisions had already entered Hungary and would surround Budapest by 5 A.M. There had been no instructions—indeed, no message at all from the Regent— and he didn't know what action, if any, to take. His colleagues urged that until the Regent arrived and made known his wishes the Prime Minister should order an end to any resistance that had developed. After much discussion he agreed. An order went out for all Hungarian troops to withdraw to their barracks and remain on the alert, but not to attack or oppose the Germans unless they themselves were attacked.

At dawn airborne troops parachuted from German planes and took over airfields in the provinces. By now the German forces had Budapest encircled and were beginning to close in. At six o'clock the advance units were in outlying areas of the city, and by eight they had taken control of police headquarters, the radio station, the bridges, and many important government buildings. There had been almost no bloodshed, for when the orders prohibiting resistance were received they were scrupulously obeyed by almost everyone.

With the advance units of the German forces came the commander of the Gestapo and his squads. His first stop was the German Legation, where he was greeted by an out-of-office Hungarian politician who offered him the aid of his private organization of gendarmes. By eight o'clock, with these Hungarians guiding them through the streets, the Gestapo squads began to pound on the doors of their prospective victims. Their yellow Mercedes were darting into all sections of the city. Beside each driver was a young lieutenant with a list of names and addresses, neatly typed on sheets of blue-green paper. These were the suspected Communists, *agents provocateur,* and other enemies of the Third Reich who must be rounded up immediately, before they could fan a single spark of opposition into a fire of revolt.

Nevertheless, life went on almost normally in Budapest. Until they left their homes later that morning, most people didn't know that their nation had been occupied, and even when they saw armed German soldiers in the streets they expressed only mild annoyance or regret. They strolled along the sunny riverbank. They lingered in the restaurants and cafés, eating cakes and rolls and cold meats, and drinking coffee and soda water and wine. The races were crowded, although Gestapo agents mingled with the crowds, looking for the men on their lists. Busses and trams were filled with people making their usual Sunday visits to friends and relatives in other parts of the city.

At eleven o'clock the Regent's train, deliberately held up by the Germans until their occupation was accomplished, finally arrived. Prime Minister Kallay was at the depot to meet it and rode with the Regent to the palace, telling him on the way what had happened.

Simultaneously, across the river, just a few minutes before eleven, two of the yellow cars drove up and stopped abruptly in front of the Jewish Community Center on Sip utca in Pest. Each driver jumped out and opened the door of the car for his officer, then returned to his place behind the wheel. The two lieutenants, stiffly erect, fell in step with each other and strode side by side into the Community Center. For a few moments they stood in the entrance hall watching disdainfully through the open doorway perhaps fifty men and women talking, all at once, about the occupation, gesticulating excitedly, unaware of their visitors. Finally an old man glanced around and saw the German uniforms. With a look of fright he nudged the man next to him. This gesture was repeated by the second man and a third until, within a few moments, an ominous quiet filled the room.

"Who is your leader?" the older officer asked in German. The words were sharply bitten off and imperious.

There was no reply. They just stared at him.

He repeated the question even more sternly. Instead of an answer a babble of voices broke out. No one addressed the Germans. The people were all talking to each other again. Suddenly the younger officer pulled a large whistle from his pocket and blew into it fiercely. Before the blast died away, the people became silent again.

"*Achtung!*" he shouted, then nodded to his companion, who took from his brief case a sheet of paper with a large red seal near the bottom. Standing stiffly, with his heels touching, his toes pointed at a 45-degree angle, he read the paper:

" 'To the heads of the Jewish community of Budapest: Heil Hitler! You are hereby ordered to assemble for a meeting at the Jewish Community Center at 10 A.M. on Monday, March 20. Any heads of Jewish organizations unable to attend because of serious illness will delegate deputies to act in their stead. Organizations failing to send representatives will be dealt with in a severe manner. By order of Obersturmbannführer Walter Heinemann. Heil Hitler!' "

31

No one moved. No one spoke.

The lieutenant who had read the announcement reached into his brief case once more and extracted a hammer and a tin cigarette box from which he took several tacks. These he handed to his companion. The two men then reassumed their ramrod postures, marched across the hallway, and tacked the notice to the outside of the front door. As they approached their cars, the two drivers threw open the doors, saluted, then stood at attention. The officers seated themselves stiffly. Almost immediately the cars sped away.

Inside the Center there was a seething mixture of anger, defiance, courage, optimism, despair, and fear on the tongues and in the hearts of those who had heard and understood. After a few minutes they began to leave, singly and in small groups. By late afternoon there was hardly a Jew in Budapest and its environs who didn't know of the occupation and the meeting called for the next day. Alex, wanting to see the notice for himself, ventured to Sip utca at dusk. Straining to see in the shadowy light, he read the words with foreboding.

At nine-thirty the next morning he stationed himself in a dark doorway across the street from the Center. The Jewish leaders had begun to arrive. Many came with their wives and children. Some wore winter overcoats and mufflers, though the weather was mild. Some carried suitcases. By ten o'clock the corridors, the offices, and even the kitchen of the Center were filled with relatives of the two hundred men who sat on straight-backed chairs in the large assembly hall on the second floor waiting for the Germans.

At first they were tense and quiet, not daring to speak above a whisper. But when ten o'clock came and went and no German appeared and the minutes dragged on, the suspense became intolerable.

"What will they do?"

"What do they want?"

"Why do they keep us waiting so long?"

"How will it all end?"

They asked each other the questions nervously. There were many opinions but there were no answers. No one knew anything.

Shortly after noon four German soldiers with rifles and bayonets marched in formation into the assembly hall, followed by a civilian. Behind him walked two officers in immaculate, well-tailored uniforms, their boots of highly polished black leather, their gait military but easy. A hush fell over the assembled Jews, who gazed with combined awe and dread at these men in whose hands their fate lay. One was a lieutenant

32

colonel in his early forties, of medium height, stocky, with brown hair, a protruding jaw, and inscrutable hazel eyes. The second, a captain, appeared to be a few years younger. He was dark, tall, spare, with the air of an aristocrat. The entire group mounted the dais at the front of the hall. The four soldiers stood stiffly at attention. The civilian apparently was a stenographer. The colonel handed him a block of paper and told him to take down the name and address of every man present, and the organization he represented. It was a long, tedious procedure, for many spoke up timidly and had to be asked again and again to spell their names or repeat their addresses. The captain and the colonel sat back patiently surveying the scene, their eyes moving imperturbably from face to face. When each Jew had spoken his name and been listed, the colonel rose.

"You have been summoned to this meeting," he began, his manner firm but courteous, "as the first step in fulfilling the agreement that has been concluded between the Third Reich and the Hungarian Government concerning the disposition of the affairs of the Jewish people of Hungary. According to that agreement, from this day forward I, Obersturmbannführer Walter Heinemann, together with my associate, Hauptsturmführer Erich von Klaussen"—he turned slightly in the direction of the captain—"will direct the conduct of Jewish affairs, under the command of Obersturmbannführer SS Otto Wedemeyer.

"First, we wish you to understand that Jews will be permitted to pursue their religious and cultural activities as in the past. Of course, some restrictions will be imposed, but there is no reason for Jews to be fearful if they abide by the rules."

Taking note of the suitcases under the seats, he smiled. "Nobody is going to be arrested," he said placatingly. "There will be no deportations. No one will be abused simply because he is a Jew. We shall take into custody only those who are our political enemies or who in other ways are troublemakers. The German representatives on this dais will be responsible for the safety of Jewish persons and property. It is our desire to avoid any distress or panic among the Jewish population. Therefore we shall require you, the leaders of this community, to form a Jewish Council of not more than ten men whose duty it will be to transmit our instructions to your people, and to see that all such instructions are carried out.

"Now we recess this meeting for three hours"—he looked at his watch—"until 4 P.M., during which time you will choose the Council members who will represent you. At four o'clock we shall return and explain

33

in detail what their duties will be. At four o'clock we expect to find the entire Council seated on this platform." He smiled affably again, then added, "I remind you once more, there is no reason to be afraid as long as you obey orders." He stood up, and the procession moved out of the hall as it had moved in. Alex, watching them drive away, noticed that two German soldiers with fixed bayonets were left on guard in front of the Center.

At precisely four o'clock the Germans returned. Their order had been carried out. Ten men were seated on the dais. Near the center was the man who had been chosen president, Emmanuel Simon, representative of the large and very well-organized Orthodox community; elderly, balding, with a sharp-pointed white goatee. He was a wealthy manufacturer of textiles, an educated man of polished manners and discriminating tastes. On his left were two men who had been elected vice-presidents of the Council. Rudolf Tabor was about fifty, shrewd, aggressive, outspoken but kind; the publisher of a Zionist daily newspaper, the Hungarian *Gazette;* originally from Andor Horvath's home town, Pécs. Next to him sat Hugo Mayer, a lawyer, tall, thin, a member of the Hungarian Parliament, and the son of a traditionally wealthy family. He, too, was Orthodox.

Captain Klaussen, a dour smile on his gaunt face, called the meeting to order and told the clerk to make a list of the Council members. Each of the ten men in turn stood up and identified himself.

Colonel Heinemann then rose. "Herr Hofrat," he began, respectfully addressing President Simon by his new title, "members of the Council, and gentlemen: As I explained at our earlier meeting today, the Jewish people will be free to continue their religious and cultural life as before. Of this you can rest assured. However, the rigors of war have made it necessary to impose certain rules and restrictions upon the community. I wish to emphasize that these restrictions will continue only so long as the war lasts. When the enemies of the Third Reich have been defeated, there will be peace and good will, and all restrictions upon Jews will be lifted. In the meantime the creation and proper functioning of a Jewish Council is imperative.

"This Council will have various duties, but two will be basic: first, the Council shall provide us with concrete and accurate information on any matter that relates to the Jewish population. For example, we shall immediately require a list of all Jewish institutions and the names of their executives. We shall also require a statement declaring all real estate owned by Jews in Budapest. Second, it will be the duty of the

Council to inform the Jewish people of the regulations that are promulgated by us and to ensure that they are obeyed.

"I urge you men of the Council to make it plain to your people that everyone must obey your instructions; that such obedience is mandatory." He paused for a moment and then with an air of extreme reasonableness added, "Theoretically and practically I dislike the use of force, and I hope that it will not be necessary here. In the past we have used coercion only in those countries where Jews refused to abide by the regulations peacefully and themselves used force to resist." He paused again and then said with a show of regret, "Really, we had no alternative in those cases.

"However," he added, his voice hardening, "if there is any evidence of armed resistance in Hungary, we would again have no alternative but to restore peace by whatever means necessary, including the use of force."

Now he became very matter-of-fact. "For the time being, Jews are required to remain in their present places of residence. Also, they may not travel from one town or one province to another without our permission. These regulations must be strictly observed. Anyone violating them faces grave consequences." The Council members shifted nervously in their seats, but Heinemann appeared not to notice.

"To assure our victory and the defeat of our enemies in the present war, it is necessary to increase the productivity of those Hungarian industries that directly relate to the conduct of the war. Therefore it is necessary to increase the number of labor battalions now operating in the country. We request"—he stressed the word *request*—"that Jewish men between the ages of forty and fifty volunteer for this service. They will be treated in the same manner as other workmen, will partake of the same privileges, and will be paid according to the same wage scale. We hope that a sufficient number of men will come forward to take their places in the work groups. If they do not, unfortunately"—he paused—"unfortunately we shall have to draft enough men to make up the deficit.

"It is extremely important that the Council make a wholehearted effort to impress upon all their people that if they do their work—no matter what kind of work it is—efficiently and quietly, and obey orders, they will be safe and secure. I myself shall see that they are protected from molestation and from any infringement upon their legal rights. If there is any attempt to violate the safety or security of a Jewish person by anyone—even by a member of my own staff—I ask this Council to inform me of it immediately. Punishment will be swift and harsh."

It was almost possible to see the audience relax under these reassurances.

"I also invite the Council to come to me freely and speak candidly of other matters that may be causing concern or serious dissatisfaction. All such complaints will receive due consideration from me and an equally candid and unreserved reply. . . ."

In this spirit the meeting continued for another half hour.

Across the street, still keeping his vigil, Alex leaned against the inner wall of the doorway. His legs ached. Several times during the long wait he had sat on the floor to rest, hugging his knees so as not to reveal himself to the occasional passers-by, but especially to the guards who stood in front of the Center. Night fell, and still the meeting hadn't ended. No one had left the building. His anxiety began to be compounded by a feeling of lightness in his head and a weak sensation in his stomach that was slowly spreading to the rest of his body. He had eaten no food since before dawn, but the hunger he had felt in the early afternoon had given way to a general feeling of faintness. He sat down on the floor again; the darkness made it safe now. He tried to see the hands of his watch, but the dial was not luminous. Reluctantly he leaned his head against the wall and gave in to the exhaustion that overweighed him. Soon his head fell forward on his chest. For some time he remained in that position, dozing fitfully.

Suddenly there was the roar of motors revving up, then the sound of many voices, growing louder and louder, as if their owners were descending upon him. He jerked his head up and saw the German contingent step into their cars and drive away, the officers in their black limousines and the soldiers in yellow Mercedes. Through the open door of the Center streamed men and their families, chattering gaily, some of them laughing.

Alex could hardly believe what he saw. He ran across the street and joined the crowd, frantically searching for a familiar face. Just inside the door he saw the plump figure of Rudy Tabor and rushed up to him.

"Alex, my friend!" the newspaperman cried joyously. He clapped an arm around the smaller man's thin shoulder. "Where have you been these days? And why such a long face?"

Alex's pale eyes gazed at him incredulously. "What's happened here? What have they done to you?"

"Done? They haven't done anything. You worry too much. Everything is going to be all right. They only want to co-operate with us."

"Co-operate!"

"Come," Tabor said confidently, leading Alex out of the building, "we'll have coffee and I'll tell you all about it."

4

Alex was dispirited. He couldn't understand how the Germans had duped a man as clever as Tabor, and Simon and Mayer, too. Had they all lost their wits? To his protestations Tabor had answered, "Alex, the defeat of the Germans is now certain. The Russian army is only eighty kilometers away. It is a matter of a week, a month, several months at the most, before the Germans are through. In the meantime we'll go along with them and not create any difficulties for our people. The Nazis don't want trouble at a time like this. Under these circumstances it isn't logical for them to take Jews from Hungary and put them in concentration camps. They need every bit of their energy for more vital business than persecuting us. They need their trains and their personnel for military matters. All these fears you have, Alex, are based on stupid rumors and false assumptions. You must be logical."

Over and over again he told himself that Tabor was a shrewd man, but he was positive that this time the newspaper publisher was wrong. The Germans were being very clever. By this disarming attitude toward the Jews they were making certain that eight hundred thousand potential enemies inside Hungary would cause no trouble as they took over the country. Later, when they were firmly in control, they would probably start turning the screws and treating Hungarian Jews just as they had been treating the Jews of other occupied countries.

He was very tired. The coffee with Tabor had buoyed him up for a while, but its effect was gone now and he was consumed with weariness. His one desire was to lie down. Perhaps after he had slept a few hours he would be able to think more rationally. Then he must send a report to Andor and the Committee.

He entered his building and started slowly to climb the stairs. As he approached his own apartment, he saw a strip of light under the door. Panic surged through him. He turned and started to flee down the stairs. A strong hand suddenly reached out from the darkness and grabbed his arm. He found himself looking into the face of a Hungarian

37

policeman, who led him back to his own door. "You will go in, please, Mr. Peto."

Inside, sitting on a chair, was a German lieutenant, and standing next to him a burly German sergeant. Although almost everything was back in its proper place, Alex could see that the room had been carefully searched. After verifying that he actually was Alex Peto, the lieutenant informed him that he was under arrest.

"Why?"

"For planning an insurrection."

"An insurrection? Ridiculous! I am a professor of physics." He sat down in a chair opposite the lieutenant.

"Stand up when we are in the room," the lieutenant shouted, and the sergeant moved toward him. Alex jumped to his feet. The lieutenant, mollified, went on. "We know that you are the head of Haganah in this country . . ." Just then a bulge in Alex's coat pocket caught his eye, and he nodded to the sergeant, who removed a frayed book and handed it to the lieutenant. *The Science of Military Strategy,*" he read on the cover. "How careless of a military commander." He said the words with stinging iciness.

"It means nothing. I have wide interests. I read books on many subjects."

The lieutenant glared at him. "Don't take us for fools. That is one thing we will not tolerate. We know about the letter you wrote last week to your Jewish Agency in Istanbul. We know everything. Please respect our intelligence."

Alex gave up the pretense. It was no use. Desperately he thought of Andor and the others. How could he get in touch with them? It was impossible without placing them in danger. His body sagged. If only he weren't so tired.

"Anyway," the lieutenant was saying, "it is not my duty to explain to you the reason for your arrest, but only to tell you that you have ten minutes to pack a suitcase. And you had better take food with you."

Alex pulled a battered suitcase from under the bed and threw into it two sweaters, a jacket, pants, and a few underclothes. Then he began to rummage in his makeshift pantry. He found only some stale bread, *lekvár,* and a small container of ersatz coffee. These he wrapped in an old newspaper and placed the package on top of the clothes. Then he closed the suitcase and put on his overcoat.

"Let's go," said the lieutenant.

When they arrived downstairs, Alex saw a Mercedes at the curb.

Strange that he hadn't noticed it earlier. He had been too busy thinking about Tabor. Or too tired. What a fool!

The sergeant opened the door nearer the curb and then walked to the street side and took his place at the wheel as the lieutenant shoved Alex to the center and got in beside him.

They drove to a synagogue on the edge of Pest. In the unheated building there were at least a hundred and fifty men and about half as many women, all apparently Jews. A few of them had children with them. Alex's guards shoved him into the crowded room and closed the door again. The mothers had spread coats on the floor and were trying to put their babies to sleep. One of the infants was crying, a shrill, piercing wail of fright and frustration. In a corner several middle-aged men were praying aloud; next to them a woman sat on her suitcase, holding her head in her hands and rocking her baby back and forth to the rhythm of their chant.

Gingerly Alex picked his way through the jumble of reclining bodies to a tiny space against the wall. A plump gray-haired woman moved a few inches to make a little more room for him. He thanked her and sat down, asking her how long she had been there.

"Since late last night. I was one of the first." She waved her arm in a motion that took in everyone in the room. "They've been coming all day and all evening." After a moment she asked, "Your family? They left your family alone?"

"I have no family."

"You are lucky," she said. She explained that she had three daughters. She pointed to three young women sitting on the floor on the other side of her. "Rose, Lili, and Marcia," she said by way of introduction. The girls smiled feebly. They were all in their early twenties, dark-haired and thin, their eyes red and swollen from crying.

"We're from Debrecen," the mother said. Tears welled up in her eyes. "Yesterday morning my husband was arrested. They said he was a political enemy, a danger to the new order. Imagine, Nathan Pollack a dangerous man!" She shook her head at the utter incomprehensibility of it. "They took him away. We have no idea what happened to him. Where do you think they took him? Do you think we'll ever hear from him again?" She searched Alex's face for an answer. He told her there was no way of telling. She cried for a moment, then wiped away the tears with the back of her hand. "Yesterday afternoon they came back and took us. I guess they decided that the family of a dangerous political enemy might also be a menace, so here we are."

She decided to rearrange the contents of her suitcase. "Look at this. This is all we were permitted to take. Just these few things for the four of us. What will happen to everything we left behind? What will happen to my house? What is happening to the world? Is everybody going crazy?"

Alex wanted to comfort her, but no words of comfort came. Instead he reached over and gently patted her trembling hands. She smiled at him gratefully, but then a new wave of fright swept over her. "What do you think they will do with us?"

This was the question that all of them, sitting so fearfully in that cold synagogue, asked over and over, some of each other, some of the Lord, a few, like Alex, only of himself. He didn't know what would happen to them. They could be taken to a German prison and shot. That wouldn't be surprising. But seeing Mrs. Pollack's pleading eyes, he lied as casually as he could, "The Germans told me we would be taken to some place inside Hungary. I suppose that means to a labor camp." He smiled and added with an assurance he didn't feel, "That wouldn't be so bad, would it?"

She shrugged her shoulders and lowered her gaze to the floor.

"Mrs. Pollack, you aren't by yourself. Look around you. We're all in this together." Seeing that this got him no response, he raised his voice brightly. "I have an idea! Since I'm alone and you don't have a man with you, we'll adopt each other. We'll stay together like a family."

She smiled at him pathetically. That was something, a good sign. He plumped up his coat on top of his suitcase to make a pillow and prepared to lie down. "In the meantime it would be a good idea for us to get some rest." He stretched his legs out as far as he could in the compressed quarters. "Good night, Mrs. Pollack. Go to sleep and don't worry. We will solve tomorrow's problems tomorrow." His heavy eyelids closed.

Mrs. Pollack leaned her head on her suitcase and drew her coat over her. "You are a nice man," she said softly. "A very nice man, Mr. . . . ."

"Peto," he mumbled, his eyes still closed. "Alex Peto," and immediately he was asleep.

It seemed that he had slept only about an hour when he was awakened by a Hungarian policeman shouting for them to make themselves ready for a journey. He sat up quickly and looked around. In the doorway were several Hungarian police and a few soldiers of the German SS. He strained in the dim light to see the hands of his watch. It was four o'clock. The Hungarian shouted for them to file out of the synagogue and follow him. Frightened and half asleep, stumbling over each other and over their bundles, they walked after him. For a mile they walked in the early morning dimness, Hungarian police officers flanking them, the SS in the rear, until they reached a suburban railroad station. There they saw other groups of people like themselves, with a suitcase or a paper bundle apiece. On the tracks there was a train of freight cars, perhaps thirty of them, all empty.

Alex shuddered. Surely they wouldn't do this to them. How could the Hungarians permit it? When Mrs. Pollack saw the train she began to wring her hands and cry aloud. Her daughters put their arms around her, trying to comfort her. Alex started to go over to them, but just then the Hungarian police began separating the people who had come from the synagogue into three groups. He tried his best to get into the same group with the Pollack family, but the large arm of a policeman knocked him back. As soon as the synagogue people were divided into thirds, each group was shoved with dispatch into one of the freight cars. Some of the men balked, but the jab of a gun butt quickly convinced them that resistance was futile and therefore foolish.

Alex could see that those who had arrived ahead of them were being put into the rest of the cars. The quota seemed to be eighty persons per car. This didn't provide room enough for anyone to sit down. Eighty per car gave just room enough to stand, shoulder to shoulder. In the middle of the car were two pails, one filled with water for drinking, the other empty, for excrement. A putrid smell pervaded the car, as if it had been used for cattle.

As soon as everyone was inside, the door was sealed shut. At once it was black. Except for a tiny barred window near the ceiling there was no light at all. Alex felt as if he were going to suffocate. There seemed to be no air, and the heat from the close-pressed bodies caused the sweat to run down his face and his neck in rivulets until he was wet all over. A baby was screaming. Near him a young woman vomited. The car was filled with the sounds of weeping and cursing. At first he was unable to see in the darkness, but as his eyes adjusted to the dim interior he looked about, hoping that the Pollacks had been put in with him, but there was no sign of them.

The train moved out of the station slowly.

After about a half hour the people quieted down. The uniform click of the wheels seemed to have a soothing effect. Almost everyone appeared to be in a stupor. Only a few, in low nervous voices, were speculating on their destination. A large, thickset man named Koestler kept his eyes on the small patch of light that showed through the barred window near the ceiling. As it became brighter and brighter he said to Alex, "If I lift you so you can see outside, do you think you can tell where we are going?"

"I think so."

Koestler hoisted him up on his shoulders and Alex stared at the countryside. Immediately everyone in the car wanted to know what he saw.

"We're going toward Slovakia. I think we are near Miskolc now."

For two days they rode in this moving coffin. They were given no food and no more water. By the morning of the third day they had eaten the food they had brought, and they were desperate with thirst. On this third morning the train came to a halt and they heard voices outside speaking Polish. Everyone was excited. Alex, sitting on Koestler's shoulders, looked out the window. "It's Cracow station," he reported. "Who speaks Polish?"

"I do." Frantically a little man at the back of the car pushed forward to take Alex's place at the window. "Where are we going?" he shouted to someone on the platform. He strained his ears for the answer. Then he turned to the people in the car. "He says we are going to Oświęcim. Does anyone know where that is?"

The word was passed on by one pair of lips after another. Oświęcim. Oświęcim. No one had ever heard of Oświęcim.

A few minutes later the train started to move again. By now many of them, especially the older people and the children, were sick. The heat and the lack of oxygen and water had become nearly unendurable. They were all very weak. No one spoke.

At dusk the train stopped again, at a small station. Koestler hoisted the little Polish-speaking man to his shoulders once more. "Oświęcim!" he cried, reading the station sign. He said that underneath the name was translated: *Auschwitz.*

Suddenly the door of the car was slid open and three men in blue-and-white striped uniforms like pajamas jumped in, shouting in German, *"Hinaus—los!* Get out—quickly!"

"Where is this place?" Koestler asked one of them.

"Can we take our suitcases?" Alex asked another.

The men in the pajama uniforms ignored the questions and repeated their orders, pushing the passengers out through the door. Searchlights beat down on them as they stepped onto the platform. Alex glanced down the length of the train. The same scene was taking place in front of each car. Men, women, and children were stumbling onto the platform. Some were so exhausted they fell to the ground. The stench was worse than that of actual cattle cars. The deportees talked to the pajama men in every language they knew, but they received no replies.

They left the platform and were herded forward, without their belongings. The noise became infernal. Almost everyone was shouting or crying. When those who were too weak to move fell to the ground, guards roughly put them on their feet again and pushed them forward.

After walking a long distance in the dark they entered an opening in a barbed-wire fence that stretched so far they were unable to see where it began or ended. Suddenly, about ten yards away, Alex saw Mrs. Pollack and her daughters. He wanted to shout to them, to get their attention, but the din was so great that he knew they would never be able to hear him. He tried to hurry forward to catch up with them, but it was impossible to elbow aside those who were between them. Anyway, there was nothing he could do to help them. He realized that. Each must stumble on, in the direction of his fate, whatever it was. As they marched, more and more pajama-clad men surrounded them. "*Hinaus—los!*" they yelled over and over again.

About twenty yards ahead there was a spotlight illuminating a fork in the road. At this fork a man in an SS uniform stood on a small platform. Beside him were several soldiers holding bloodhounds on chains. The people from the train were being marched in a column five abreast. As they passed the man on the platform, he ordered some to go left down one road, some to go right down another.

As Alex approached the fork he again got a glimpse of the Pollacks. He saw the man on the platform motion to the mother to go left, the three daughters to the right. But they refused to be separated. They linked arms, all four of them, and defied the guards to tear them apart. One SS man grabbed Mrs. Pollack by the arm and tried to pull her out of this tangle. The daughters surrounded him, clawing and scratching at his face until it bled. They knocked off his hat and pulled at his hair. Finally he let go of their mother. But other SS men ran up to help him, shouting, "Jewish scum!" With their fists they beat the girls over the head. The screams of the Pollacks were terrifying. Alex closed his hands over his ears, but he continued to watch, hypnotized by the brutality of it. Mrs. Pollack slumped to the ground. Abruptly the screams stopped. An SS officer had the arms of each daughter pinioned behind her, with a hand over the mouth. The struggle was over. The three girls were taken down the road to the right, the mother down the road to the left. The column began to move again.

Alex was now only five feet from the man on the platform. He was tall, handsome, and blond and wore a tight-fitting SS uniform. How intelligent and distinguished-looking, Alex thought, staring up into the man's face. In one hand he held a baton. He looked like the conductor of an orchestra. With his wand he indicated the direction each prisoner was to take. When Alex's turn came, the baton was waved to the right. Most of the men were being sent in this direction. They were marched about thirty yards, guarded all the way by the SS with sub-machine guns and by the men in pajamas. By now their thirst was excruciating, and they begged in one language after another for water, but no one answered them. Instead, with rifle butts and clubs, they were pushed into a one-story, bare wooden building. "You will remove all your clothes and accessories," ordered one of the men in the blue and white pajamas.

When they were naked, they were herded into a large bathroom. There the pajama men sprayed them with a disinfectant. All hair on the body was cut off. With clippers they made a bare spot on each man's head, three or four inches wide, from the forehead to the nape of the neck. Then this band was shaved with a razor. The prisoners were disinfected again, and then each one was issued a blue-and-white striped uniform like the pajama men wore.

It was evening now, although no one knew the exact time because their watches had been taken from them. Through the windows they could see another lighted barracks, into which the women had been taken. There were no curtains or shades so they could see that the women were being treated just as they had been, even to shaving the strip down the center of the head.

When dawn came, they saw that the barracks extended for miles. As far as the eye could see. The buildings were all the same, a depressing gray-brown color.

Two SS men appeared and ordered them to line up outside the building. "Stand at attention until we return," one of them commanded. Then they disappeared. Just above Alex there was a young man in blue and white pajamas, replacing some damaged shingles on the roof. As he worked he asked them in Polish, "Who are you?" No one understood him. Alex looked around and realized that the little man from the train who spoke Polish was missing. The boy on the roof tried Yiddish, but his inflection was so strange no one could make out what he said.

"We're from Hungary," Alex shouted up to him in Magyar.

The boy jumped down from the roof. "So, your turn has finally come!" he said in Hungarian with a heavy Slav accent.

They crowded around him, bombarding him with questions.

"What happened to those who were sent down the road to the left?" Alex asked, silencing them with a wave of his arm. He was still worrying about Mrs. Pollack.

The boy pointed to a tall smokestack a few hundred yards away from which white-yellow smoke was billowing. "See that smoke? Well, that's your parents and your sisters and your children. Understand?"

Some of the men began to curse and threaten him. Others wept.

Alex turned his back on the boy and said under his breath to the others, "Don't believe him. I think he's a little crazy." Turning back to the boy, he asked, "How long have you been here?"

"Two years."

Alex turned to the others again. "See, he *is* crazy."

The boy heard and laughed. "So I'm crazy, am I? Well, in two or three days you'll see who's crazy." Then he climbed back up the ladder to the roof and ignored them as he went to work again replacing the damaged shingles. Fifteen minutes later he came down. This time he spoke softly to them. "You must believe me. I tell you the truth." Then he asked, "You need something?"

"Yes," Alex replied quickly. "Water. Please get us water."

But instead the boy went on talking. His voice was nervous again, and hard. He pointed to some buildings nearby. "Those are the gas chambers." Then he pointed to other buildings, with chimneys. "And those are the places where they burn the bodies. All those people who went to the left are being killed now by gas. They make them undress and they put them under shower baths, but instead of water, when they turn it on out comes the gas. Then they are cremated . . . burned to smoke, you understand?"

They listened, horrified, but few really believed him. He returned to the roof.

While they were still standing there, waiting for the SS officers to come back, a man appeared wearing a jacket with a wide red stripe down the back and elegant civilian trousers with a red stripe down each leg, and a beret, also striped red. "Do any of you speak Magyar?" he asked them.

They clustered around him, all talking Hungarian at once.

"I am a kapo," he announced. When he realized that this meant nothing to them, he explained, "Kapo is short for *Kamp Polizei*. I am a Slovak Jew. All kapos are Jews. We are prisoners, but we have been appointed overseers. I have been here a year. Almost everyone who enters this camp is killed, but I wanted to live. I wanted very much to live. I felt that I must survive." He looked away from them. "For this I agreed to be an overseer."

Koestler swore and lunged toward him but Alex and another prisoner held him back.

The kapo's voice became pleading. "We live here like in a jungle. The stronger you are and the cleverer you are, the better your chance to go on living." He glanced nervously in Koestler's direction. Seeing that the big man's anger had subsided, he said sternly, "Don't forget that you have been brought here to work and then to die. I am in charge of you. I will insist on absolute discipline. I will not hesitate to kill any one of you who disobeys me, for my own life depends on keeping order among you. And I want to live." Once more his manner changed, and in an imploring voice he asked them to understand. "I'm not bad by nature, and I am a Jew, like the rest of you, but above me are other kapos, and above them are the block elders, who are Gentiles, mostly Germans with criminal backgrounds, or Polish resistance fighters who are anti-Semites, and all of them also want to survive." Then he drew himself up to his full height and announced in an official voice, "In a few minutes there will be an inspection by the block elders." With that he walked away.

Soon afterward a tall, slender inmate appeared, scrutinized them, and left without saying a word. After him came an SS inspector. He walked slowly around the group, examined the men carefully, chose five of the strongest-looking, including Koestler, and took them away with him.

The boy who had been fixing the roof came scrambling down his ladder and almost gleefully said, "You won't see them again."

"Where are they going?" someone asked.

"Oh, they'll be put in a special unit, the Sonderkommando. That means the clean-up squad. They'll handle the bodies in the gas chamber and the furnaces." He laughed. "You'll see. I'm not crazy. It's everybody else that's crazy. The Jews who are kept alive do all the dirty work here. You'll see." He climbed back up the ladder.

In the days that followed Alex did see. Each man who had been sent to the right was given a job. The first assignment Alex drew was a simple one. Or it would have been if he had been able to anesthetize his mind. Each day one long railroad train filled with Jews arrived at

Auschwitz. The men, women, and children were marched up the road and most of them were sent to the left, for extermination. Alex's job was merely to see that when they undressed they obeyed orders. Their shoes were to be left in one place; their undergarments were to be stacked in a pile somewhere else; any jewelry was to be put in a steel box so that when it was full it could simply be locked and shipped off to the office in Germany that was concerned with this detail. All Alex had to do was to see that those who were about to die did nothing to prevent the orderly functioning of this well-worked-out scheme. He was to make sure that no one went in to the gas chambers wearing a wrist watch, a wedding ring, or a Mogen David on a chain around his neck.

Night after night lying on his cot, numb and exhausted, he told himself he couldn't endure the ugly reality of another day. Night after night he condemned himself for continuing what he called his "collaboration." Many times he went to sleep firmly resolved to throw himself at the throat of the first German officer he saw the next morning and die happy when the inevitable fusillade of bullets struck him. But he seldom saw a German officer. None of them had much contact with the SS. He often marveled that it took so few SS men to run such a vast extermination factory. His own immediate superiors were all kapos, who actually were doing no worse than he was. Like them he was possessed by a strong will to live. He hardly understood it, though he often thought about it. As a physics professor, he well remembered the rule about a body once in motion tending to remain in motion and a body once at rest tending to remain at rest. The Law of Inertia. So it was with life. There was a strange self-perpetuation about it.

Later he was given a much worse assignment. After the gassing he had to remove the gold teeth from the mouths of the dead. The first time he saw the bodies piled up like cordwood he felt the gorge rise in his throat and a cold clammy sweat spread over his body. His knees trembled. He was certain he was going to faint. The kapo in charge, seeing him blanch and then sway uncertainly, jabbed him in the ribs with his elbow half playfully and said, "You'll get used to it. When you look at them, be grateful that you're still alive." He prodded a body at Alex's feet with a stick he carried. "Better him than you. Remember that."

"No!" Alex tried to yell the word, but the muscles of his face seemed frozen, and his lips were stiff, and he couldn't force a single sound from his throat. He wanted to die. He was a slave of murderers. He was about to become a robber of corpses. These things he could not be. These things he could not do. He would lose his senses. His knees buckled, but the man alongside caught him and held him from falling. The kapo turned away in disgust.

The first day of the new assignment was the worst. Then gradually he did mechanically what they told him to do. He moved as if he were sleepwalking, putting one foot uncertainly before the other. He felt himself in a long nightmare.

Each prisoner received a pound of bread per day, and twice a day a bowl of watery soup. In the evening they were given something to spread on the bread, usually a bit of fat. The bread was the color of charcoal, and tasteless. Whenever they were able to manage it they would steal a few potatoes from the kitchens in which meals were cooked for the German soldiers. Day by day they grew weaker and thinner.

Each morning Alex had to walk two miles to his work. Each day for ten or twelve hours he played his small role in the death of hundreds of other human beings. Almost every day he saw some of his fellow prisoners die in the barracks or at work, their emaciated bodies and tortured souls unable to bear the grisly existence any longer. Maybe they and the ones who were killed were the lucky ones, he thought. Three or four times a week the kapos beat those who survived; any excuse was a good one. Some of the guards occasionally stoned them, for amusement, or made them get down on all fours and go through various antics, some of them salacious, pretending they were animals.

Weeks passed, then months. Alex became a dry-skinned skeleton, gray except for the pale burning eyes that stared out from hollow sockets. He felt barely alive now. Often at night, lying on his hard shelf of a bed, listening to the sobs, the nightmare noises, and the prayers of the wretched creatures in the tiers of bunks around him, he would decide to give up; to put this agony behind him. Sometimes he would lie there in the dark talking to his dead wife. He would imagine he was holding her hand as they climbed Gellért Hill late on a spring afternoon to their favorite restaurant. There they would eat dinner from an enormous wooden platter on which there would be three kinds of meat, garnished with a pickle, sweet red peppers, pickled cabbage, and a huge portion of potatoes. On the plate there would be a gaily colored penknife, a souvenir they would take home with them. After they ate they would watch the sun set and the lights of Budapest begin to twinkle as dusk fell over the city. White lights sparkled on the bridges. Red and green lights on the boats that moved up and down the Danube were multiplied as they were reflected in the night-black water. Sitting on the same side of the table, so close together that their elbows and knees touched, they would watch the lights come on in the Royal Palace, and in the villas of Buda, and along the ribbons of streets crisscrossing Pest, on the other side of the river. "Fairyland," she would whisper, squeezing his hand ecstatically, her own eyes sparkling more beautifully than any lights in Budapest, Alex thought. He remembered their summer days on Margaret Island—the rows of poplar trees that lined the paths, the riotous colors of the flowers, the smooth green lawns, and how they would bathe in the Strand baths and then lie in the warm, soothing sunshine, relaxed and lazy. He could almost feel the sweet and yielding flesh of Leah's body alongside him. But the dream always ended, and desperate reality impinged upon him once more, sometimes abruptly with the scream from a soul-tortured inmate, sometimes slowly as yesterday's scenes gradually faded away. Then he would whisper into the night's darkness, "I'm glad you are gone, Leah, my darling. The world is full of evil and horror. It's just as well that you cannot see it, beloved."

When he actually slept he would often dream of standing at one end of a corridor so long it seemed to go on forever. In the distance he would see the figure of Leah, her arms outstretched. She seemed to be calling to him, to join her. The horror of that dream was that no matter how much he struggled, he seemed unable to make any progress in her direction. If he ran, he either stumbled and fell, or Leah kept receding, despite the speed of his running.

These reveries, as he became weaker of body and foggier of mind, led to an obsession: he told himself he must start writing letters to Leah, or she would be worried about him. One morning he awoke with a strange look on his face. Everyone who encountered him that day noticed it. It was the expression of a man no longer normal. Before long they found out why it was. He wanted pencil and paper. For days he asked anyone who would listen to give him, lend him, sell him a pencil and a few scraps of paper. Finally a kapo said it could be arranged for a price. Alex had never been good at haggling, so with only a feeble protest he agreed to pay what was demanded. A stub of a pencil less than four inches long cost the obsessed man his bread allowance for three days. He was told he could have all the paper he wanted, at one day's bread allowance per sheet. The paper was a dirty gray, almost the shade of his own skin.

Alex sharpened the pencil by moving it rapidly back and forth on the stone of a wall. Now, after each day's work, he would sit on the edge of his bunk writing very painstakingly, in as small script as possible in order to economize on paper. He began each letter with the Hungarian word *Drágám* (darling) or with the more affectionate *Drágaságem*. He would never make any reference to where he was or what was happening around him. Instead, in delicate prose that at times was almost poetic, he wrote of his undying love for Leah, of how intensely he missed her, of the joyous times they would have together when they were finally reunited. He mentioned none of his troubles. Instead, he wrote of his worry about her. She must be strong and have faith that their separation would soon be over. Often he wrote of their past together. One night his letter began:

I remember so well, beloved, how after we had gone to bed together and had known that ecstasy I am sure no two other people in the world have ever experienced so intensely, I would doze off for a few moments, and then I would softly and slowly come back to full consciousness, as if floating through buoyant, warm air. I would know instinctively that you were still not far away, even though I might no longer be able to feel the warmth of your body or smell the sweetness of you. So I would stretch out a hand, slowly, gently. It would touch some part of you, and you would reach out your fingers and with them try to encircle my hand, and then, once more, with our fingers entwined, we would be in perfect union with each other.

Beloved, our love-making always was like a miracle to me, it was so breathtakingly beautiful, so intensely exquisite. It was something that seemed to pass human understanding. At least *my* understanding. Do you remember how often I would try to put it into words to you? I would ask the question, "Leah, darling, do you understand the miracle of it?" You would always smile, with the tolerance of a woman who knows that there are some things not to be plotted on a drawing board or analyzed in a test tube. You would smile and put your cheek against mine and only then would I stop trying to be so analytical.

You must remember all these things now, beloved. They must give you strength until this bitter separation is over. You must have faith that soon we will be creating the miracle again, and again, and again, locked in each other's arms. Oh, my darling, I can smell the exquisite fragrance of you as I write. I can feel the warmth of your body as I take you in my arms. How soft, how clinging, how wanting, and how wanted. Soon, beloved. Soon!

Writing these letters caused Alex to waste away physically much faster than the others, because of the price he had to pay for paper, but it gave him a new sort of inner strength. He now seemed to have a remarkable serenity that the others lacked.

Then one night he remembered a psalm he had learned as a child and had long ago forgotten. As a scientist he had been a religious skeptic most of his life, yet suddenly, lying in the dark on his hard wooden bunk in the extermination center of Auschwitz, the words came back to him, as if it were just yesterday that he had memorized them. Softly he said them to himself that night, and every night thereafter:

> *"Lord, how many are mine adversaries become!*
> *Many are they that rise up against me.*
> *Many there are that say of my soul:*
> *'There is no salvation for him in God.'*
> *But Thou, O Lord, art a shield about me;*
> *My glory, and the lifter up of my head.*
> *With my voice I call unto the Lord,*
> *And He answereth me out of His holy mountain.*
> *"I lay me down, and I sleep;*
> *I awake, for the Lord sustaineth me.*
> *I am not afraid of ten thousand of people,*
> *That have set themselves against me round about. . . ."*

5

At 1 P.M. on Sunday, March 19, after the German army had spread out over Hungary like a giant octopus, Regent Nicholas Horthy, just returned from his meeting with Adolf Hitler at Klessheim, called the members of the Crown Council to the palace. He looked old and tired as he recounted the details of Hungary's submission to the German dictator. He said that Hitler was angry because, among other reasons, the Hungarian Government had not yet begun to take the measures he considered necessary to solve the Jewish question. "We are accused of the crime of not having carried out Hitler's wishes, and I am charged with not having permitted the Jews to be massacred. . . ."

Dominic Sztojay, although only Minister to Berlin and not a member of the Council, was present and repeated Ribbentrop's warning to him: "He declared with extreme displeasure that nothing at all had been done with regard to solving the Jewish problem. I told him that if the Jews in Germany had made up as high a percentage of the total population as they did in Hungary, even Germany would not have been able to settle the matter so easily. . . ."

Ferenc Keresztes-Fischer, the Minister of the Interior, asserted his indignation at the sight of German soldiers directing Hungarian policemen, and the Gestapo arresting Hungarian citizens, whether they were Jews or not. "More than that, I will not allow one single Jew to be taken out of the city," he cried. But his was a lone voice.

Prime Minister Kallay offered his resignation, and the Regent, who felt he was now powerless in his own country, reluctantly accepted it and closed the meeting by saying, "I have complete faith in the future of the Hungarian nation and I believe that we will, by the grace of God, be able to survive the present crucial period." Then he left.

The next day the new German Minister to Hungary, Edmund Veesenmayer, summoned many right-wing Hungarian politicians to his legation and asked them to co-operate in creating a government that would be acceptable to Germany, Hungary, and the Regent. He told them that this new government would have three major tasks: to send more Hungarian soldiers to the eastern front, to give more economic aid to the Third Reich, and to achieve a radical solution of the Jewish problem. "Otherwise," he said, "someone will take my place who will treat Hungary as an enemy nation." His first choice for Prime Minister was Béla Imredy, leader of a small, extreme right-wing opposition party, and he persuaded the other politicians at the conference to agree. But when he sent Imredy to see the Regent the following day, Horthy rejected him on the ground that he had insufficient support throughout the country.

After interviewing many candidates the Regent finally chose the Hungarian Minister to Berlin, Dominic Sztojay, mainly because he was a professional soldier and therefore, in Horthy's estimate, a man of honor who would not violate the wishes of his commander, and also because he had spent many years in Berlin and was *persona grata* with Hitler. Veesenmayer agreed to approve Sztojay if the posts of Deputy President and Ministers of Defense and Interior were given to men selected by Heinrich Himmler, the SS Reichsführer. Horthy acquiesced and at 6 P.M. on March 23, just under the deadline set by Hitler, Horthy swore in Sztojay and the new members of the Cabinet in the Great Hall of the palace.

In the meantime, as SS Colonel Heinemann and Captain Klaussen were reassuring the Jewish leaders at the Sip utca Center, thousands of Hungarians, Jews and non-Jews alike, fearful of what the occupation might bring, hurried to the banks to withdraw their money. All day long they stood in queues that stretched for many city blocks.

The following morning the SS, having compiled a list of the names and addresses of all the Jewish lawyers of Budapest from the telephone directory, went from office to office and home to home taking them into custody. By the time they had seized about half the men on their list, the Minister of Justice, informed of this activity, registered a strong objection. The Germans, not wishing to create any unnecessary unpleasantness between themselves and the Hungarians at this time, gave up their hunt. Nevertheless, the men already in custody were taken to a college for rabbis on Rökk Szilárd utca, which the Gestapo had converted into a prison, and were detained as hostages.

At the same time all public meetings were forbidden. The festivities planned for Kossuth Day were canceled. Radio programs were revised to eliminate all political speeches. Listeners heard popular music hour after hour. Armed German soldiers were stationed in front of all government buildings. Parliament met on the twenty-second, but the Speaker merely declared the legislature in session and then proposed that it recess indefinitely.

Despite such developments, the significance of which was not yet known to most of the people, the Germans were determinedly polite to everyone and seemed especially eager to mitigate the apprehension of the Jews. The Jewish Council was assured by the Germans that deposits in Hungarian banks were absolutely safe and suggested that the Council pass on this assurance to the Jewish population. The Council did, and accordingly thousands of trusting people obediently paraded back to the banks and redeposited their savings.

On Tuesday the Jewish Council made its first request of Hungary's new rulers. Hundreds, perhaps thousands, of Jews had been apprehended and had vanished. The Council had information that they were being held in an internment camp at Kistarcsa, on the outskirts of Budapest. In return for all the co-operation it had already shown, the Council would appreciate it if the Germans would order the release of these people, they said. Two days later all men over sixty, women over fifty, and children under sixteen were released. The Council members took this as proof that it was going to be possible for them to get along amicably with the Germans.

Rudy Tabor was bitter over the German order closing down all Jewish papers. This meant that he and his whole staff were suddenly out of employment. But the rule was amended to permit publication of one daily, to be called the *Magyar ZsidokLapja,* the *Newspaper of the Hungarian Jews,* and Tabor was appointed manager. On Tuesday, on behalf of the Council, he painstakingly wrote an article in which the Council transmitted to their people the first instructions they had received from the Germans.

". . . we herewith announce the rules to be observed . . . and the behavior obligatory to everyone concerned. Everyone must remain at his post . . . and must devote his full energy to the work required of him by the authorities. We wish it to be known, on the basis of a definite statement to this effect issued by the competent authorities, that the commercial, cultural, and social life of the Jew is to continue as before. This announcement should reassure everyone. . . . A Central Jewish Council has been formed to represent the Jews. It will have the right to appoint subcommittees to perform specific tasks. This Council is the only authorized . . . body representing the whole of Hungarian Jewry and is the body commissioned to maintain contact with the German authorities.

"It has been stated that no one will be arrested because of his Jewish origin. Should arrests prove necessary, these will be owing to entirely different reasons. Jews may not go outside the boundaries of the capital, nor may they change their address. Provincial Jews may not travel to Budapest. . . . Applications for travel permits . . . must be submitted to the Central Jewish Council. The attention of all concerned is emphatically drawn to the necessity for the strictest and most conscientious observance of all these regulations. Only if the regulations are observed carefully can it be guaranteed that everyone will be able to live a normal life. . . ."

In the many-towered, stone Parliament building on the Pest embankment the new Cabinet of the Hungarian Government held its first session. Prime Minister Sztojay told his colleagues, "The Germans are demanding the issuance of an edict requiring Jews to wear a distinguishing emblem. They also enjoin us to separate the Jews from the rest of the Hungarian population. . . . Veesenmayer recommends that the Jews should be placed in ghettos in the towns and in internment camps in the provinces. The property of the Jews should be confiscated by the state. He also declares that the Germans do not want a pengö of this for themselves; everything will go to the Hungarian state."

To his Ministers of State and Interior he said, "You will outline plans to implement these policies as they fall within your respective jurisdictions and draw up the proper decrees. Henceforth such decrees will be approved by me in conjunction with Dr. Veesenmayer. The Regent no longer wishes to have decrees submitted to him for approval. He apparently does not want to sanction our new policies."

At the Sip utca meeting on Monday the Germans had told the Jewish Council that from time to time they would present the Council with documents of requisition for articles they drastically needed. The Council would be expected to provide these articles promptly and willingly. Of course, the Germans said, they would pay for them, either in cash or in kind. The following day Council headquarters received from the office of Heinemann's adjutant an order for eight hundred blankets. The president, Emmanuel Simon, regarded the request as excessive. He knew, and he felt the Germans also must have known, that after four years of war and shortages there were hardly any blankets left in Jewish hands that weren't in use. Still he assigned a committee of Council members to try to get the blankets from the Jewish community.

By Wednesday noon the committee reported it had been able to collect only four hundred. Simon, reluctant to irritate the Germans so early in their relationship, told Hugo Mayer to accompany the committee on a second round of calls on institutions and private homes to persuade people to give up blankets they were not actually using. An hour later the German adjutant sent two officers to the Center to inquire why the blankets had not yet been delivered. They were received by a Council member who told them that unfortunately so far it had been impossible to fulfill the quota of blankets. "They are very precious," he explained. "Since the war people just don't have them to spare."

The taller of the two officers whipped his revolver from its holster and thumped it down on the desk. "If the blankets are not in our possession in three hours, we will have those who are responsible shot. Now dare to tell me again that it's impossible." He picked up his gun and stalked out, followed by his companion.

The committee went from house to house, begging, demanding, urging people to give up blankets. In two hours they managed to collect the required number, mostly from families whose men had been sent to labor camps and from the Jewish Hospital. Shortly before the expiration of the deadline the blankets were delivered to the Germans.

As the days passed, the demands of the occupying forces increased. Besides supplies for the Army, such as mess equipment, brooms, and bedding, they requisitioned typewriters, silverware, radios, automobiles, and even women's silk undergarments and cologne. Young German officers were constant callers at the Center, always with lists in their hands. Gradually the Council members grew to expect them and to oblige them without comment, no matter how extraordinary their requests.

But not all the Jews of Budapest adapted themselves so readily. Daily more and more of them came to the Center with complaints. At railroad stations Gestapo agents and Hungarian detectives were demanding to see the identity cards of anyone they suspected was Jewish. Any Jews found in the vicinity of a depot were arrested. Women, some almost hysterical, came to the Center to report that their fathers, husbands, and brothers, especially those thought to be wealthy, had been routed out of their homes or stores or offices by the Gestapo and detained without explanation.

President Simon, alarmed at hearing these reports with such frequency, discussed them with the Council, and it was decided that Hugo Mayer, the acknowledged diplomat among them, should request an audience with Heinemann.

In his offices in the elegant Hotel Majestic on the suburban hill called Svábhegy, which the Gestapo had requisitioned for itself, the colonel received Mayer cordially and invited him to be seated. A civilian secretary was the only other person in the room.

"Now, Herr Mayer, what is it you wish to see me about?"

"I come, Herr Obersturmbannführer, as a representative of the Council on a matter that has been causing us some anxiety. It has come to our attention that several of our people have been requested to produce identity cards in the vicinity of the railroad stations and when they did they were arrested. It has also come to our attention that the number of arrests of our people has been increasing. Most of the arrests have seemed to be for no real cause at all. It is our desire to keep order and peace among our people and to co-operate fully with representatives of the Third Reich in discharging this function. But"—he smiled and raised his hands in a gesture of helplessness—"these seemingly inexplicable measures taken by your subordinates have brought our people rushing to us in agitation, and it has become very difficult to convince them that these measures are indeed necessary. I am certain that you understand that the position of the Council in this matter is not an easy one. If perhaps you could assure us that some of these practices will be modified, or reconsidered, it would help allay the fears of our people and enable us to carry out your instructions more successfully."

The German colonel listened to Mayer's cool, carefully chosen words without moving, his expression unfathomable. Then his face broke into a smile. "I am glad you have come with your complaints, Herr Mayer. That is the way it should be, frank and open. About the arrests, naturally they cause anxiety, but you can tell your people that they have no reason to worry. Most of those who have been detained will be released in a very short time. When we have separated them from the real scoundrels!" He chuckled as if he had made a joke. "You, in turn, surely understand that we have enemies and we must be careful to see that they are not free to cause us trouble. As for the arrests near the railroad station, I think your informants are exaggerating the situation. Of course"—he shrugged his shoulders slightly—"it may be that the Hungarian police in this case are letting loose their venom on your people. I am not sure how much we can do about that, but you have my word: we shall try to alleviate the situation." He stood up. "Please convey my reassurances to your colleagues. In future if there are any more problems, I hope you will bring them to me. Good day, Herr Mayer."

Hugo Mayer returned immediately to the Center, where Emmanuel Simon, Rudy Tabor, and the other Council members were anxiously waiting for him. He repeated his conversation with Heinemann, stressing the colonel's ingratiating manner. The others heard him with relief. Tabor, noting Heinemann's remark about the Hungarian police and his apparent reluctance to interfere with them, ventured, "This may mean one doesn't always know what the other is doing. It's quite common with gangsters. So maybe we should inform the Hungarian Government of these restrictive measures that are causing us so much trouble. In a sense it is our duty, isn't it?" he asked with a shrewd grin.

Several members objected that it might be dangerous, but after some discussion most of the Council sided with Tabor. That afternoon he and Simon went to the Ministry of Justice and requested an appointment with the Secretary.

What was the nature of the matter they wished to discuss?

They explained their mission to the clerk, who disappeared into an anteroom. In a few minutes a fair-haired young man came into the room and introduced himself as the First Undersecretary of State. What, he asked, could he do for them? Simon told him in detail the purpose of their visit.

When he had finished the Secretary replied, "I am truly sorry, gentlemen, but we cannot act upon your complaints, justified though they may be." Seeing the resentment in Tabor's eyes and the unhappiness in Simon's, he added, "Hungary is no longer a sovereign nation. Our army has been forced to submit to an occupying power. Even our gracious Regent has two armed German soldiers posted at all times outside his door. There is nothing we can do."

They walked out of the building slowly, almost aimlessly. Simon, dejected and tired, stroked his white goatee silently. He was not eager to face his colleagues with an account of the afternoon's failure. For several minutes even Tabor was quiet and thoughtful. Then he muttered, "So it isn't time yet to play one against the other. But it will come. It will come."

"In the meantime," Simon said pointedly, "we wish to protect our people, so we will co-operate."

"We will co-operate," Tabor agreed wearily.

During the week before the German army entered Budapest, Andor and Sarah Horvath, Erno and Esther Gábor, Arthur and Elizabeth Gruen, Joe Nagel and Rachel Teller moved into the house of Gruen's father-in-law in the village of Budakeszi, just west of the capital. They were reasonably comfortable. Each married couple had a room, while young Joe slept in the attic and Rachel downstairs on a cot in the study. Most of them did not venture outside, for fear of causing gossip among the neighbors about their presence in Budakeszi. On Friday, two days after they had moved in, Alex telephoned Andor from Budapest. Everything was quiet, he said, but there was a rumor that the Regent was going to Austria to see Hitler. As soon as he knew more he would phone again.

Saturday passed slowly, a gray, murky, depressing day. Arthur Gruen went, as he did each day, to the center of the village to buy newspapers. It was all right for him to circulate because he had often visited his father-in-law and was known by the villagers. When he returned with the papers, he and the other men read every word in them, but they found no hint of German occupation. In the afternoon and evening they took turns listening to the radio, but they heard nothing extraordinary: there was a dramatized story about Kossuth, popular music, some news from the war fronts. Gábor's sweet-faced, chubby wife, Esther, did the cooking. Elizabeth Gruen shopped for the food and managed the household. Sarah Horvath, always frail and now often nauseated because of her pregnancy, spent most of the day in her room, not even coming downstairs until dinnertime. Rachel watched over her and kept her amused with recollections of their girlhood in Pécs. The evening meal was generally pleasant, considering the nervous uncertainty of their lives. Esther Gábor was a good cook and enjoyed preparing *halászlé* (a fish soup) and other typically Hungarian dishes.

After dinner they listened to the radio again. As soon as the early news report ended, Arthur Gruen and Erno Gábor generally played a game of backgammon at the far side of the living room, banging the checkers as they made their moves and giving each other threatening looks, as if they were playing a game of life and death. The women usually retired early. The last man up the stairs was always Andor. It was well past midnight when he undressed in the dark and slipped in quietly beside Sarah. She never actually awakened but in a half sleep knew he was there, and when he was settled she moved with warm pleasure into the curve of his arm. Then he would kiss her forehead gently and they would both soon be sound asleep.

A banging on the front door woke Andor. As he struggled to get his bearings, it seemed to him that the racket had been going on for some time. Sarah was sitting up in bed, immobilized by terror. In the upstairs hall he could hear a jumble of arguing voices. As he rushed out, Joe grabbed his arm. "It's the Gestapo. I saw them from the window. The occupation must have begun!"

Elizabeth Gruen was pleading with her husband. "Let me go, please. I'm the only one who won't arouse suspicion."

Two others backed her up.

Arthur exploded. "You're asking me to hide like a coward behind the stairs while my wife faces those bastards?"

"Don't have so much false pride. She's right," Joe said.

"What do you know, are you married?"

The banging became more insistent.

"Let her go, Arthur," Andor commanded.

"All right, but if anything happens . . ."

Andor ignored the remark and took Elizabeth's hand firmly in his. "Greet them as calmly as you can, and don't tell them any more than you have to."

She nodded, then turned, walked down the stairs, and opened the door as sedately as she could.

Before her stood a German lieutenant and a Hungarian policeman.

The Nazi seemed disconcerted at seeing Elizabeth's blue-eyed blondeness. He glanced quickly at the list in his hand. Then he looked at Elizabeth again.

"Your name is Hirschon?"

"No."

"You live here?"

"Yes."

"Your name, please."

"Láng. Elizabeth Láng." She gave her maiden name, and he wrote it on the paper.

"This is Number 34 Lázár utca, Frau Láng?" he asked, glancing at the gold band on her finger.

"It is Number 32."

"I see. Do you know the Hirschon family?"

Under his questioning it was becoming harder and harder for her to hide her nervousness. Behind her she could faintly hear excited whisperings, and she was terrified that in a moment or two her interrogator would hear it also.

She shook her head.

"You don't know your neighbors?" His tone implied that she was lying.

"We have lived here only a short time," she replied, and was immediately frightened that he might probe in this direction. But she needn't have been, for he had apparently received this kind of answer before. He regarded her simply as one of those misguided Christians who were thwarting the representatives of the Third Reich in the performance of their duty by trying to protect their Jewish neighbors and friends. Well, they would soon feel the penalty for such stupid behavior. However, this morning his task was to round up Hirschon and the others on his list. Besides, she was pretty . . . He pointed to the house on the left.

"That is 34?"

"Yes."

He clicked his heels together and bowed, then, with the Hungarian tagging along, went to the next house. Elizabeth closed the door. For a long moment she stood there, her hand still on the doorknob, her eyes shut. She was dizzy with the aftermath of fright. Her throat was dry. As she opened her eyes, the others came trooping down the stairs and surrounded her, loud in their congratulations.

"Come," Andor called out, walking to the dining-room window. "Let's watch them."

They saw a man open the door at Number 34. The German spoke to him. The man answered and then opened the door wider to permit the two officers to enter. For five minutes they peered from behind the curtains but neither saw nor heard anything more. Then the door opened and three men emerged, Hirschon in the middle. They entered a small yellow car, which immediately sped away.

Andor was filled with apprehension, and he knew the others were, too.

"Why doesn't Alex call?" Erno Gábor asked with some asperity. "What can he be doing? He must know how crazy we are to hear what's happening."

"Yes," Sarah added. "If they decide to come back here, we may not be so lucky again." She turned to Andor. "We've got to get out of here."

"Darling, we are as safe here as anywhere," he answered soothingly. "They won't be back. They have too much big game to look for in other places. No one knows we're here. But," he said to the men, "I am beginning to worry about Alex. It's not like him to be irresponsible. I wish I knew what was going on in the city."

"Maybe we could phone him," Arthur said, eager to do anything that would put an end to the waiting.

Andor shook his head. "If he's in trouble, it would be too dangerous. They might trace a call from here. We'll wait until tomorrow night. If we haven't heard from him by then, I'll call Braun from a pay station in the village and I'll find out about the deal with Klaussen at the same time. Meanwhile let's stay close to the radio."

But there was nothing on the radio except routine news, and by Monday evening there was still no message from Alex. About ten-thirty Andor walked to a small café in the village and phoned Braun. There was no answer. He went to a table and ordered a glass of *aszu*, a Tokay-type wine, then lingered over it for almost a half hour. When he dialed Braun's number again there was still no answer, so he walked back to the house, worried and frustrated.

He had always been a man of action. He liked to make quick decisions and carry them out at his own pleasure, generally without anyone's advice or consent. Also, he was a city man. He liked the noise, the confusion, the bustle of Budapest. Here in suburban Budakeszi he was nervous and restless. As he walked down the country road that led to Number 32 he decided that he had made a minor error in agreeing to this hide-out plan. Of course, it was keeping the women safe. Also, now that Sarah was pregnant he owed her some special consideration.

Yet he believed he had larger responsibilities, whatever his feeling was for his wife and their unborn child. If the Germans really had already occupied the country he must devise some plan immediately to save Hungarian Jewry. Until now the Budapest Rescue Committee had been working mainly in the interests of Slovakian and Polish Jews. Now it was their own Hungarian Jews who were in peril, eight hundred thousand of them. In what other country of Europe, except possibly Russia, were there still eight hundred thousand Jews? He walked with his arms swinging vigorously, breathing deeply of the crisp March air. Eight hundred thousand Jews. They were a very special breed of men. He was one of them, he should know. Hungarian Jews were different from Jews anywhere else in Europe. Anywhere else in the world. This was why it would be difficult to convince them that they, as Jews, were in special danger, now that the Germans were in occupation. Or were they in occupation? After all, one yellow Mercedes and one German officer with a list of Jews in his hand didn't constitute proof of what Braun had predicted.

Eight hundred thousand Jews. If the Germans were here in force, what stood between them and degradation and death? Their rabbis? The staid, conservative community leaders like Emmanuel Simon? The few Jewish politicians there were? Andor asked the questions silently as he strode along, and answered them with a vigorous shake of his head, as if he were on a public platform. The only answer was the Budapest Rescue Committee. The eight hundred thousand, of course, didn't know this. But whether they yet knew it or not, his Committee was their only hope. And he, Andor Horvath, *was* the Committee. Alex—what could have happened to Alex? Alex had done some good work setting up the underground railroad by which they had smuggled Jews from the north down into Hungary and eventually into Rumania. But Alex was too soft to stand up to the brutal emergencies and exigencies of war. In war a man must develop a certain ruthlessness. But there was no trace of ruthlessness in Alex. In war a man must learn to adapt to the situation. It was, of course, impossible even to try to meet fire with fire, but at least they could meet cunning with greater cunning. Alex was too gentle, too moral, too poetic a person to deal with Nazis. Joe and Rachel were tough, all right, but they were both too headstrong. They needed to be held in check. Erno was a valuable man. His continuous sense of urgency and his boundless energy were great assets. But they were in a situation now that called for patience and adroitness. These were qualities Erno completely lacked. Then there was Arthur, a successful businessman. He had grandiose ideas. He was aggressive. His sense of values might be open to question, but he knew how to get what he wanted. Yet it was impossible to deal with the Nazi organization as if you were dealing with a rival businessman you were trying to force to sell out to you.

He had a good Committee, all right, but they needed a strong leader who could make decisions for them; a man who knew how to connive, to intrigue, to bluff when need be, to stay always one jump ahead of the opposition, to outthink them at every move.

A man passed in the dark and Andor said *"Jó estét kivánok"* to him cheerfully. At this point he was feeling like himself again. He needed, at frequent intervals, to recharge the self-esteem that sparked all his activity.

But his wave of euphoria was quickly blighted by the realization that while the Germans apparently had been surging across Hungary, he was off here in the country, out of contact with everyone and doing nothing to safeguard his fellow Jews. So far he had not even succeeded in laying the groundwork of the negotiations with Klaussen, if the occupation was an actuality. He was a fish out of water. Why in hell hadn't Alex called? And where was Braun? If Braun failed him, he would have to look for a new avenue of approach to the Germans.

Early the next morning he went back to the village and phoned Braun again. This time the guttural reply of the German was a welcome sound to his ears. When Braun understood who was calling, he cried, "Where are you? I have some good news for you."

Andor answered cautiously, "I'm not in the city but—"

"I thought it was strange that I hadn't seen you or your people around town. But of course you will come back now. Everything is going smoothly."

"Not immediately. I'm waiting to hear from one of my men first."

There was a long silence, as if Braun were trying to make up his mind about something. Finally he said, "You mean Peto?"

"How did you know? Has something happened to him?"

There was another pause.

"Be frank with me, Braun. I'll find out soon anyway."

"Peto was arrested by the Gestapo last night and deported."

"Why?"

It was a cry of distress as much as a question, although Andor tried to keep emotion from intruding into his voice.

"Because of his Haganah connection. It had nothing to do with your Rescue Committee," Braun added hurriedly. "That wasn't even mentioned."

Was Braun telling the truth? It was difficult to know. "Where was he sent?"

"I don't know. It could have been to any place—to Mauthausen, Auschwitz, maybe to Theresienstadt."

"Can you find out?"

"Now, Horvath, you know that that would be too risky, even for me. But perhaps you would like to do something about it."

"As soon as possible."

"Well, when you see Klaussen—"

"You have arranged a meeting?" Andor felt a rush of joy.

"That is what I have been trying to tell you. Klaussen is here, and he has agreed to meet with representatives of your Committee on April seventh at his apartment on the Svábhegy." He gave Andor the address. "I will see you there—unless you will be coming to the city before that?"

"No. I will meet you at Klaussen's apartment."

A few days after the German occupation began, the newspapers of all opposition political parties were suspended. Those papers that continued to be published reported little domestic news, except the decrees of the government. But by reading these official pronouncements carefully the members of the Jewish Council were able to anticipate the troubles they would begin to have in the next day or so, for most of the decrees during the last half of March imposed new restrictions on the life of the Jews, and as soon as the Hungarian police and the SS began putting them into effect new crowds gathered at Sip utca to lodge their protests, to ask whether they should obey, to demand protection, and to insist that their leaders get the new edict rescinded.

On the last day of the month the morning papers carried Decree 1240/M.E. It was signed by László Endre, Undersecretary of State in the Ministry of the Interior, who was known by them all as one of Hungary's most violent anti-Semites.

When Emmanuel Simon arrived at the Center with a morning paper in his hand, he found the three-story building vibrating with indignation. Crowds had not yet started to gather in the streets, but the other members of the Council were all there, and each one was surrounded by a cluster of gesticulating, angry, loud-talking people, some of them clerks and stenographers employed at the Center, others the vanguard of those who would be coming all day long.

"We must have an emergency meeting of the Council at once," President Simon announced.

One by one his colleagues extricated themselves, made their way to the second-floor assembly hall, and took their places at the oval table around which the Council always met. Simon usually presided sitting down, but this time he stood at one end of the table as he solemnly addressed the meeting.

"My friends, this is a sad day for us. I shall not read the decree to you. I'm sure you all know it by heart. This order—that every Jew in Hungary must wear a six-pointed star made from canary-yellow silk or velvet on the left breast of his outer garment—is modeled on the decree that was issued in Slovakia, which in turn, of course, was based on the original German law.

"Many of us never expected to see the day when such humiliation would be imposed on Hungarian Jews. But this day has come." He paused. The strain of the past two weeks had already left its mark of bitter exhaustion on his face and on the weary way he carried himself. After a moment, he asked, "Does anyone else have anything to say?"

Every one of them did. Who would be required to wear the star? The decree said every Jew over six years of age, regardless of sex, and it said that the Nuremberg racial laws were to be used as a basis for determining who was a Jew. There would be few exceptions: veterans of World War I who had received high decorations for valor and men or women with at least a seventy-five per cent physical disability.

"The decree says the punishment for any violation will be six months' imprisonment," said a member at the far end of the table, "but it also says something about internment in a concentration camp. Do you suppose they really will go as far as that?"

One of the younger members jumped to his feet. "I say we should boycott the order. We should defy the Germans and their Hungarian imitators as well. The Mogen David is our holy emblem. But we are about to permit them to turn it into something for the Nazi-lovers to spit on. If all eight hundred thousand of us refuse to wear it, what can they do? They can't put us all in jail for six months, can they?"

The president motioned for him to sit down. Then, standing at the head of the table and rubbing his thin hands together slowly, he spoke in a low voice.

"Gentlemen, my friends, it is not so easy as that. How can we, a handful of leaders, organize all eight hundred thousand of our brothers into such a campaign of defiance? Who will go from house to house, street to street, city to city with the instructions? We have no freedom of movement. We are now all being watched. How can we print the leaflets that would have to be distributed by the tens of thousands into every corner of the country, calling on our people to make this defiance? We are opposed by a militarized Hungarian state and by the German army."

He looked down at the younger man at the far end of the table. "Our friend's suggestion is a noble one. As much as anyone, I would like to see a campaign of passive resistance, or civil disobedience, or whatever you wish to call it. But here and now it would be very impractical. No, I am afraid we are forced to comply."

The question still remained as to what advice the Council should give to the Jews of Hungary about wearing the star. After President Simon again declared that there was nothing to be gained by resistance except the imprisonment of hundreds, perhaps thousands, of offenders, the Council voted to publish a communiqué advising all Jews to obtain yellow stars of the prescribed size—ten centimeters in diameter—and to wear them carefully sewn to the outer garments. After President Simon declared the motion passed he said, "If we are going to wear the Mogen David, then let's wear it proudly, not with embarrassment or apology. As for myself, I'm going to wear two, one on each side of my coat, just to show them how I feel about being labeled a Jew."

On April 3 there was a severe American air raid on factories and an oil refinery in the suburbs. Many people were panic-stricken. It was the first large air raid Budapest had had. Some Jews, as they ran from their homes for air-raid shelters, forgot the coats or jackets on which their yellow stars were sewed. After the raid was over and the all clear had sounded, they were arrested on their way back to their apartments. That night the relatives of many of them stormed the Center, begging for help in locating the victims. People also came with eyewitness accounts of Hungarian detectives making the rounds of factories and businesses that employed Jews and if they found a man or woman without a star, no matter what he was doing, that person was promptly arrested, even though his star might be firmly sewn onto the jacket or coat he wore out-doors. One man told the story of his friend who worked beside him in a factory. He was sitting on a toilet seat when a Hungarian detective pushed open the door and arrested him although the yellow star was on his jacket, which he had momentarily taken off and had hung on the inside of the toilet door. Other detectives, the Council members were told, were roaming the streets, and if they saw a star not sewed onto a garment firmly enough to please them, or a star of a shade of yellow that didn't conform to their idea of "canary yellow," they would rip the star off and take the offender away for internment.

In a working-class area of Pest someone organized a campaign of defiance. Several hundred Jews decided to engage in mass disobedience. When the report reached Sip utca that the entire area had been cordoned off by Hungarian police and that the offenders had been hauled away in a convoy of trucks, Simon sat for a long time with his elbows on his desk, his head in his hands. Finally he looked up and said, "This is just what I was afraid of. The Council is not a totalitarian organization. We cannot order our people to do or not do anything. But we must find some way to persuade them that we know what is best; that they must obey our directives."

In the Dohány utca Synagogue adjoining the Center a sermon was delivered by Rabbi Ferenc Hevesi, who said:

"The yellow star does not humiliate us, but those who have pinned it on our breasts. It brings humiliation and shame on the Hungarian people, who stand by indifferently and watch Jews being branded who have rendered many a sterling service to the Hungarian nation. . . . It would be the duty of every church to advise its flock to pin a yellow star on their own breasts, too, as a demonstration against the unbrotherly treatment of the Jews and thus frustrate the branding and endangering of the Jews. The yellow star will be removed from us, but a mark of humiliation will always show on the breasts of those who forced us to wear this star and those who by their indifference permitted this to happen."

The indifference was general, although not unanimous. The Papal Nuncio, even before Decree 1240/M.E. was issued, demanded to see the Regent to protest against the new anti-Semitic laws being promulgated each day, especially those affecting Jews who had been converted to Christianity. After 1240/M.E. was announced, some Protestant clergy, as well as the Catholic authorities, raised their voices, particularly in the interests of their own flocks. The six-pointed star was an emblem not of the Jewish race but of the Jewish religion, and therefore to force Jews who had become Christians to wear it was a contradiction and, in effect, was forcing these converts to renounce their Christianity, they said. The government backed down to the extent of publishing a supplementary decree exempting priests and nuns of Jewish origin. But the protests went on until at last the new Prime Minister himself was forced to issue a statement saying:

"In the opinion of the Royal Hungarian Government, the Star of David does not represent a religious symbol, but merely a necessary means of marking, from the administrative point of view, members of the Jewish race. Nevertheless, the Government will raise no objections if Jews of Christian religion, without awaiting special orders to that effect, wear a cross on their clothes in addition to the Star of David."

On Friday, April 7, Andor and Erno Gábor drove in Andor's small car to the Svábhegy. Because they had been in hiding for so many days, the trip was full of surprises. They saw that many Jewish shops had been closed. In some sections of Budapest almost everyone wore a yellow Mogen David on the left breast, even children. They had read all the regulations in the newspapers, but it was quite another thing to see how thoroughly the regulations had been imposed. Gábor alternated between explosive anger and silent dejection. Andor gripped the steering wheel tighter, furrowed his forehead, and sank into contemplative silence.

The Svábhegy, just five kilometers from the heart of Budapest, was a predominantly green hilltop section of resort-type hotels, expensive restaurants, and massive villas, with here and there a sanitarium for the treatment of ailments peculiar to a certain class of society. For generations the aristocracy and the traditionally wealthy had flocked there to escape the heat, the noise, and the congestion of the metropolis. The Svábhegy was reached either by a cog-wheel railroad or by a winding road originally built for carriages.

As Andor pulled his car up in front of the address Braun had given him—a rococo house set in a private park of close-cropped grass and formal flower beds—he muttered, "Naturally, they take the best for themselves."

Inside, a maid in a trim black uniform ushered them into a salon furnished in Louis XV style, with a pale Aubusson rug that covered the entire floor. Braun was waiting. He greeted them pleasantly, almost too pleasantly, Gábor thought.

On the long wall, behind a blue velvet sofa, there was a small Renoir painting in a heavy gold frame. Andor left Gábor and Braun making idle conversation and went over to look at it more closely. It evoked in him not only delight to see such an excellent example of Renoir's *nacré* period, but a fierce desire for possession and all that possession signified. He stood before it entranced.

68

In a few minutes Klaussen came into the room, followed by a junior officer. Braun and Gábor rose. Andor turned his back on the Renoir and bowed slightly. Braun introduced the two guests. As they greeted each other Andor took the measure of this man who might have the power of life and death over him and all the eight hundred thousand Jews of Hungary. He was in his late thirties, tall and broad-shouldered, with a trim, lean figure. He carried himself with an assurance obviously bred into his bones, rather than with the arrogance of so many young German officers whose importance was clearly first-generation. He had a small scar on his left cheek, a souvenir of his youthful fencing days— as much a mark of distinction to a German officer of the old school as a monocle to an Englishman of a certain class.

"I think I can do business with him," Andor told himself as he finished his scrutiny. Aloud he said, "We are most happy to have the opportunity to pay you this visit, Herr Baron." He gave a slight emphasis to the last word, sure that his knowledge of Klaussen's title would make an impression.

Klaussen smiled, visibly pleased, and waved his hand to indicate that they should all be seated.

Andor began, "We have learned of the discussions that took place in Slovakia between you, Herr Baron, and our people there. It is regrettable that they weren't able to raise the money needed to conclude the negotiations. However"—he leaned back in his chair expansively—"that is something of the past. This is another time, another place. This is Budapest, 1944, and we are ready to talk business."

A mask of reserve covered Klaussen's slender features. "What is it you wish?"

"For the sum we are prepared to pay, we want four guarantees. First, that there will be no formation of ghettos or concentration camps. Second, that there will be no pogroms or large-scale executions. Third, that there will be no deportations. Fourth, that Jews who have certificates from the British Government authorizing them to enter Palestine will be permitted to go there."

For some time Klaussen sat silent, considering the demands. Then he asked, "And the price? You are willing to pay what the Slovaks offered, two million dollars?"

"We are willing to pay one million," Andor replied firmly.

Klaussen stood up. "There are eight hundred thousand Jews in Hungary. The minimum amount I can even discuss is two million dollars.

If you decide you are willing to pay this sum to guarantee the safety of your people, you can let me know."

His tone indicated that he considered the meeting over. His aide started toward the door.

Erno Gábor, still thinking of the closed shops they had seen and the sad faces of the people with the yellow stars sewn to their coats, jumped up. "We can pay it! We are ready to meet your demands."

Andor tried to catch his eye, but Gábor was staring at Klaussen, waiting for his answer. Hiding his irritation behind a diplomatic smile, Andor said, "We are, as Herr Gábor declares, ready to meet your demands, provided you are ready to meet ours."

Klaussen sat down. "Good. Now as to the guarantees you wish. For the first, I can assure you that the Germans have no intention of creating ghettos here." He said it blandly. "But for the security of your people I think you would be wise not to object to the setting up of Jewish communities of about ten thousand."

Andor raised his eyebrows skeptically. "What kind of *communities?*"

Klaussen shrugged. "Ordinary communities, like those they have been living in. Of course, they may be a little more crowded. As you know, there have been two air raids on munitions plants in Pest by the Americans and the British. No housing was damaged, but if it happens in the future, even the Hungarians may have less room."

"Will they be ordinary communities?"

"Quite ordinary. In such large groups your people will be safe from harassment by troublemakers. And after all, that is what you want, isn't it?"

Without waiting for Andor to reply he went on, "Concerning your second request, it is our aim to maintain order and to prevent violence, so we shall hardly encourage pogroms, or any other disruptive activity. On the other hand, we are fighting a war, and I cannot counsel the use of our troops to protect Jews. You could hardly expect me to do that, gentlemen.

"As for the third point, we promise that no Jews will be deported out of Hungary.

"Your fourth request . . ." He inhaled deeply on the cigarette in his amber holder before continuing. He seemed to be planning his answer carefully. "I regret that I cannot grant it."

Gábor looked disconsolately at Klaussen and then at Andor. The latter's face showed no reaction. He was waiting.

Klaussen went on, "It would be a complex undertaking to let a small group of Jews leave Hungary. But if you could present us with an emigration plan by which we could get rid of a large number—say at least a hundred thousand—that might interest our Reichsführer Himmler. Discuss it with your colleagues and bring your proposals to me. I will transmit them to Berlin. But I warn you to decide quickly, before the Hungarian fools find out what is going on. We cannot let them think we have come here to protect Jews."

Andor agreed to discuss the emigration proposal with the rest of the Committee and return for another meeting within the week. "But, Herr Baron, there is something that disturbs me. Many of our people are being picked up by the Gestapo almost at random and carted off to detention centers. Have we any guarantee that this will stop?"

"Such activities are inevitable," Klaussen said casually. "They are part of all revolutionary changes. This will level off. The innocent will be freed. It is really nothing to be concerned about. If there are a few people you would like to have released, bring me their names and I will see what I can do."

"That is most kind, Herr Baron. There is a man named Alex Peto."

Klaussen stiffened. "The Haganah leader?" His tone was one of incredulity.

"Yes."

"Impossible! I cannot release the commander of a resistance army. However, I will, as I promised, try to release the others whose names you submit." Then he added sternly, "Provided there is no serious charge against them."

He lit a fresh cigarette and his voice was more pleasant as he said, "Now, about the terms of payment. So that we can begin to put the plan into effect as soon as possible, we shall require an advance payment of ten per cent—that is two hundred thousand dollars—within two weeks. If you cannot pay the entire amount in dollars, we will accept pengö, calculated, of course, according to the black-market rate of exchange. Is that agreeable to you?"

"Calculated at the black-market rate increases the total payment considerably," Andor demurred.

Klaussen smiled warily. "Come, Horvath, you know as well as I do that this is the only realistic basis of exchange."

What he said was true, and it was futile to argue. Andor knew he had to give in. "All right, we'll make the first payment to you within two weeks."

"I am happy to see that you are a man who knows how to make a decision quickly," the captain said. "Now let us seal the agreement." He turned to his aide. "We will have the brandy." The lieutenant filled five glasses from the decanter on the table beside him. Each of the Germans and Andor took one. Gábor stood up with them, but he didn't move toward the table. "You will excuse me if I do not drink," he said quietly.

They stared at him. His face was a blank. Andor shot him a look that said, "We are here to make a life-or-death deal. Don't doom it at the beginning." But Gábor lowered his eyes and said nothing.

Braun, fearful that he might not be able to collect his twenty thousand dollars if anything went wrong, glanced nervously at Klaussen to see the effect of Gábor's act, but the captain merely smiled as he raised his glass and said, *"Prosit!"*

When they finished their drinks, Gábor and Andor prepared to leave. As they walked to the door, Andor took a box wrapped in brown paper from his overcoat pocket and handed it to Klaussen.

"I have a friend who occasionally finds a way to get Swiss chocolates to me. These are excellent. I especially recommend the ones wrapped in foil."

Klaussen thanked him and the two visitors left. As soon as the door was closed behind them, the baron removed the brown paper wrapping and opened the box. Among the chocolates were four in gold-colored foil. As Braun watched enviously, he chose one and unwrapped it. Between his well-manicured fingers he held not a piece of candy, but a magnificent hard blue sapphire.

"Good God!" Braun exclaimed.

Klaussen took a handkerchief from his pocket, wiped the stone, and examined it carefully. "Not bad," he murmured. A broad grin spread across his thin, aristocratic face. "This may be a very profitable venture."

He offered the box to Braun with mock generosity. "You like chocolates? Have one."

The Wehrmacht agent looked quizzically at Klaussen, then put his blunt fingers on a piece wrapped in gold foil.

The baron laughed. "Not that kind, Herr Braun. It might give you indigestion."

Andor drove back to Budakeszi silently, planning the strategy he would use in negotiating with Klaussen. The captain had been polite, though his terms were less than satisfactory and his promises questionable. But all that would be altered. He had the full measure of the man now, and he was certain that in any deal he would come out with more than the German intended to give. His self-confidence gave him a feeling of strength, almost of buoyancy. After all, Klaussen was an intelligent man, a crafty negotiator, and a baron besides. It would be stimulating to match wits with him. It would be a real triumph if he could succeed in getting the better of him. He wished he could have seen Klaussen's face when he found what was in the foil wrappings.

Alongside him Gábor fidgeted, alternately watching Andor's changing expression and the passing scene. When he could stand the silence no longer, he blurted out, "You're angry with me. I don't blame you. But I couldn't drink with them. I just couldn't."

Startled, Andor looked at his friend's pleading, myopic blue eyes behind the thick lenses. He had almost forgotten there was anyone else in the car.

"Angry? No, I'm not angry. But we can't let that kind of thing happen again. From now on, Erno, you'll have to remember, you may be rude to your friends, they'll forgive you; but being rude to your enemies is a luxury, and we can't afford such luxuries at a time like this."

"I know, I know."

Neither of them spoke for a while. Then Gábor asked, "Where did you get the chocolates for Klaussen?"

"From Arthur's father-in-law. But they weren't just chocolates."

"They weren't?"

"No, there were four sapphires among them."

"Sapphires! Jewels for the murderers! Why? Aren't we going to pay them their ransom?"

"Of course we are going to pay them—if we have to. But today's gift was the cheese to tempt the rats. As long as they think they can profit by keeping us alive, we're safe—and only that long."

"Why didn't you tell me about this before?" The edge of his voice was rough with resentment.

"Would you have agreed?"

"No."

"That's why I didn't tell you."

"Who decided on this plan?"

"I did, and Arthur offered to get the jewels."

"Nobody else?"

"No."

"Since when is the Committee run by one man who doesn't think he has to let the rest of us even know what he is doing?"

"Since right now!" Andor shouted. "This is no longer a debating society. Someone has to negotiate for the lives of our people. It's a dangerous job, and I will not be accountable to you or anyone else for every gesture I must make to save your skins." He slammed the gears into second as they approached the Jánoshegy, and the car began to climb the hill. But his anger subsided as quickly as it had flared up. He laid his hand on Gábor's arm. "Trust me," he said quietly. "I will know what to do."

The next day the members of the Budapest Rescue Committee and their wives left the house at Budakeszi and went back to their homes in the city.

Andor and his colleagues now faced what was for them a unique task. It was a fact that the Committee had no authorization from anyone to act for the Jews of Hungary or even the Jews of Budapest. It was not even empowered to represent the small Zionist minority in the country. From the start Andor had been the undisputed leader of the Committee, but no officers had been elected; no minutes were kept; parliamentary procedure was ignored. Frequently there were differences of opinion and many hours were spent in wrangling over methods and tactics, but the others always eventually yielded to Andor's will. Six months ago they had established contact with the Jewish Agency, which had been created under the terms of the British Mandate over Palestine to represent the Jews of that area in their dealings with the British Government but which had come to have a much broader scope and influence. In the eyes of Zionists it was the shadow government of the Jewish state that would someday be created in Palestine.

During its existence the Committee had saved the lives of hundreds of Polish and Slovak Jews by smuggling them across frontiers, hiding them, passing them from family to family on a sort of underground railroad. Now it was confronted with a much more mundane problem, yet one of staggering magnitude and desperate urgency: how to raise two hundred thousand dollars immediately, and after that the rest of the two million they had promised Klaussen.

At a special emergency meeting in Andor's apartment they discussed the problem late into the night. Gábor wanted to appeal to the Jewish Agency without delay. Time was too short, Andor replied. It might take days to get a message by courier to the Istanbul office of the Agency, and it would be difficult to explain by letter the urgency of their situation. Finally, at Andor's suggestion, it was decided to go to Emmanuel Simon. He was wealthy and he had important contacts. They knew he hadn't been sympathetic to the activities of their Committee. He had always been punctilious about observing not only the letter but the spirit of the law. He was no intriguer. However, there seemed to be no alternative. Simon was a Hungarian gentleman and a man of high principle, but he was first a Jew.

Emmanuel Simon received Andor and Gábor in his villa. His manner was gracious, but his mood somber. He listened gravely as Andor told of the meeting with Captain Klaussen until the German's demand for two million dollars was mentioned. At this point he jumped to his feet, exclaiming, "But they promised us!" His visitors looked startled but said nothing as he paced back and forth across the thick Turkish carpet, his fragile little figure trembling. "Why should we pay them a fortune when they have already agreed to treat us properly?"

His astonishment seemed so great, his anger and distress so intense, that Andor was disturbed. He had arranged the meeting feeling that everything depended on winning the help of this old man who obviously wanted to believe with his heart what he knew in his mind was not true: that the Germans would keep their word. If they couldn't make him give up this fiction to which he was clinging so desperately, the deal with Klaussen would be off and the consequences for all of them might be disastrous.

Andor bowed deferentially. "That is so, Mr. Simon; they have promised. But have they kept their promises anywhere else? Even here, are they keeping them now? They have arrested many of our people on ridiculous charges. They have forced thousands out of their homes."

Simon stroked his sparse white goatee thoughtfully, staring at the empty space on the wall where his favorite painting, a small Renoir in a heavy gold frame, had hung until two days ago, when it was commandeered by a German lieutenant who appeared at the Center with an official requisition ordering the Council to supply a certain number of art works for villas and apartments now being occupied by high-ranking SS officers. The order said they would, of course, be returned after the "final victory." Simon sighed. "I suppose you are right," he said to Andor, and wearily sat down again.

Encouraged, but careful not to press his argument too energetically for fear Simon would be offended, Andor went on, "If we can keep them hoping they will receive money from us, we may be able to get concessions. As long as they are convinced that doing business with us will be profitable I'm sure we can protect ourselves from what they really want to do with us."

Simon shook his head. "I doubt that even your plan will save the Jews of Hungary. However, we can't reject the slightest chance of rescuing them, no matter how improbable its success. We don't dare," he muttered to himself. Then he addressed Andor briskly: "So what is it you wish me to do, young man?"

One week after the appeal had been made to him Simon telephoned Andor, saying he had collected the stipulated sum of two hundred thousand dollars, mostly in pengö. He suggested that when they came for the money that evening they bring a large suitcase.

At 8 P.M. the elderly textile manufacturer was waiting for them in his study when they arrived. After greeting them he locked the door of the room, slipped the key into his coat pocket, and led them to the far wall, which was covered by a tremendous Flemish tapestry. At one side hung two silk cords. He pulled one of them and the tapestry moved slowly on an overhead rod until it revealed a piece of steel two feet square, flush with the wall. Simon manipulated the combination of the wall safe deftly with his tapered fingers until the door sprang open and then from the interior began to extract neatly tied bundles of bank notes. He handed them, one bundle at a time, to Gábor, who packed them into the suitcase he had brought.

"That last bundle makes it the equivalent of two hundred thousand dollars, at the latest black-market quotation for pengö," Simon said, closing the safe door and pulling the tapestry back into place.

Andor looked at the little white-haired patrician with a feeling of gratitude that he found difficult to put into words. Seeing this, Simon took his hand gently.

"I know you will put this wealth to good use. Some of my friends and I have worked very hard to acquire it."

"I promise," Andor replied fervently.

Tears filled the old man's eyes. "May your venture be blessed," he said.

By the time the two men returned to Andor's apartment their spirits were so high that even Sarah was caught up in the gaiety. Andor picked her up and kissed her resoundingly as they entered. She flushed with happiness. Attention from him always raised her spirits, but when, rarely, he was affectionate, she was overjoyed, though she understood that what put him in such a mood was not a wave of feeling for her at all but some personal triumph that fanned his ego.

"Now," he said as he put her down, "I must phone Klaussen."

The captain wasn't there, his maid replied. However, she would relay Herr Horvath's message.

An hour later Klaussen's aide called to say that the captain would see them that night at eight.

Promptly at eight they were admitted by the black-frocked maid and led into the salon again. They waited for half an hour and still Klaussen didn't appear. Gábor began to be nervous. "Maybe we should ask the maid," he whispered, getting up and walking toward the door.

"Be patient. It's probably just a psychological trick. He may think we'll be easier to handle if we're anxious and worried. Remember, *we* must outsmart *him,* so relax."

But Gábor was not the relaxing type. He opened the door stealthily and peered down the hallway. There was no one in sight. At this moment a door opened on the other side of the salon and in came a German lieutenant colonel of medium height, stocky, with a protruding jaw and an inscrutable expression. He was followed by a young lieutenant.

"They never trust themselves alone," Andor muttered as he gazed curiously at the two men.

The colonel introduced himself as Obersturmbannführer Walter Heinemann. He carefully looked over the two visitors and then addressed Andor: "You are Horvath." It wasn't a question. It was a statement. He turned to Erno. "And Gábor." They nodded.

"Listen to me," he began. "I have been authorized by the head of the SS, Reichsführer Heinrich Himmler, to conduct the negotiations with your Committee concerning the disposition of the Hungarian Jews." He went on to say that the negotiations were a state secret of the Third Reich and that any hint of them to Hungarian authorities would be punished by death to the betrayer. He said all this quickly, as if he had learned it by rote. He paused, then asked gruffly, "Now, you have brought the money?"

Gábor lifted the suitcase onto the table, unlocked it, and opened the lid. For a split second all four men stared down at the mass of bank notes. With exaggerated casualness Heinemann picked up a bundle, flipped the bills in a patently halfhearted manner, then tossed the bundle back into the suitcase. "Good, we will have it counted and the exact value assessed."

Gábor began to shut the suitcase. So far he hadn't spoken, but now, quite suddenly, he turned on Heinemann and let loose a torrent of words: "Yes, we have collected it; the full amount asked for. Two hundred thousand dollars. But unless our conditions improve, there will be no more. Our people are frightened. They hear horrible things, from the provinces. At Mukačevo. Do you know what happened at Mukačevo? They ransacked houses. They stole money and jewelry from our people. They jammed thousands of them into brickyards. No roof over their heads. No beds. No cots. No place to sleep. No place to—no hygienic facilities. No doctors. No drugs. Almost nothing to eat. They die like flies. Like—" He stopped to catch his breath.

Andor felt sick. He saw a flicker of annoyance sweep across Heinemann's face. But the colonel covered it with an unctuous smile. "That's just a lot of evil gossip. No harm has been done to your Jews. We have given strict orders that all brutality is to be avoided and that Jewish lives should be carefully safeguarded. If there have been occasional unfortunate incidents, it is regrettable, but didn't Klaussen advise you that your people would be better off in larger communities, where the Hungarians cannot molest them?" His tone held a suggestion of reproof.

"However, we wish to be just." Then he repeated to them what he had said to the Jewish Council: "If in future you have any complaints, you may bring them to me here. I assure you that every legitimate complaint will be investigated, every injustice, if any, righted."

Andor was satisfied. Because of their prompt payment of the money Heinemann had felt forced to give them this invitation. Now he broached another matter: "Has the SS agreed to the four proposals we made to Captain Klaussen?"

The question seemed to put Heinemann at ease. He explained that he had discussed their requests with Captain Klaussen. "And," he added in a tone that told his visitors they should be very impressed, "I have also discussed them with Colonel Otto Wedemeyer, who, as you should know, is head of Section 4B, the Judenkommando. Obersturmbannführer Wedemeyer has transmitted to Berlin your idea of an emigration of at least a hundred thousand people. However, before approval can be granted, we will have to be certain that there actually is a place where so many Jews would be accepted."

Gábor shifted nervously in his chair. Andor felt his own muscles grow tense. Heinemann was looking at him coldly and waiting for a reply. There was no alternative but to bluff. It was the only way they could possibly delay the negotiations long enough to work out a feasible emigration plan. Right now they had no plan at all. The truth was that each month Budapest received from the British Government, by way of the Jewish Agency, thirty-five immigration certificates for Palestine. So far, the Budapest office of the Jewish Agency had been unable to get any more than that allotment. If German intelligence was good, they knew this. But he had to take the chance, so he assumed as nonchalant a pose as he could and told Heinemann, "The British have agreed to allot us the entire thirty-five thousand certificates they promised in the last White Paper. Since each certificate can be used for a whole family, considerably more than a hundred thousand Jews will be able to emigrate."

The colonel seemed surprised, but he said only, "Just how do you propose to do this?"

"We haven't worked out all the details yet. That will take a little time. But when we have, with your permission we would like to contact the Jewish Agency in Istanbul. There are many points that will need their approval." He hoped this all sounded plausible.

"I see no reason why you cannot contact Istanbul," Heinemann replied, "but I must warn you, as Hauptsturmführer Klaussen has done, that it is extremely important to get these negotiations started just as soon as possible, so don't dally, if you want to see your Jews safely out of the country. We will give you no support if the Hungarians hear about this."

"We understand, Colonel," Andor said placatingly.

"There was another matter we discussed with Captain Klaussen," Gábor put in. "The release of some friends—"

"Have you brought the list?"

Gábor handed it to him and he glanced at it. "All right. They will be freed tomorrow." He wrote something on the paper and gave it to the lieutenant.

Andor and Gábor left the building and walked down the tree-lined avenue to where Andor had parked his car. "Take it easy, Erno," he said, apprehensive as the elderly little nervous man pranced like an excited race horse beside him. "They may be watching from the window. Take it easy until we get into the car."

But Gábor was too elated to control himself. "You did it, Andor! You pulled it off! We've got them eating out of our hands."

Andor couldn't help smiling at the old man's antics. Actually he was pleased with himself, yet behind that feeling was a small ineradicable fear. As he started the engine his expression became serious. "I think we fooled them, but I wonder if they're playing the same game with us as we are with them."

Very soon it began to look as if Andor's fear was justified. Day by day the harassment of the Jews increased. A few brave men, refusing to wear the Star of David as a badge of dishonor, were fined as much as seven thousand pengö each, and when they could not pay—as most could not, because of the economic measures taken against Jews—they were imprisoned. Those who did wear yellow silk stars were jeered at on the streets by men of the Arrow Cross, the Hungarian fascist party. Arrests for disobeying the new regulations became so frequent that the Council felt it imperative to publish a warning in the *Newspaper of the Hungarian Jews:*

BROTHERS: The Council cannot permit orders to be ignored . . . It cannot allow individuals to disregard published instructions. Such a course would result in disaster for the entire Jewish population. On receiving orders from the Council, every person must carry them out to the letter . . . The existence of the community depends on the regulations being heeded by everyone. . . .

In spite of this warning, crowds gathered outside the Center in protest against the restrictive orders. A few men were angry and daring enough to stand on makeshift platforms and try to persuade the others to resist with force. Sometimes they were applauded, but they were regarded by most of the other Jews as dangerous threats to the safety of the Jewish community. Usually they ended up in the hands of the Hungarian security police, who habitually kept a discreet distance from the Center but moved in speedily whenever they saw sufficient excuse for making an arrest. Throughout the city there were many suicides, mostly old people. They used gas, razor blades, and stout pieces of rope.

Increasingly the mass of Jews lost faith in the Council's ability to protect them, and so all day long and late into the night, more and more of them jammed the office of the Budapest Rescue Committee asking for help. Arthur Gruen, Erno Gábor, Rachel, and Joe worked in shifts. At no time during the twenty-four hours was the office unstaffed. At least one of them was always there to help the hungry, the sick, the terrified, and those wanted by the police. The Committee gave them food, hiding places, forged identity papers, or guides to take them to the Rumanian frontier. Every case was different, every case was urgent, many were a matter of life or death. The Committee members were forced to develop an exterior of seeming imperturbability and callousness.

The number of restrictive orders directed against the Jews had grown so large that now it was difficult to remember them all, let alone obey them. Jews were required to declare all their possessions; to turn in all gold and jewelry; to report the contents of safe-deposit boxes and private safes, which were then sealed so the owners couldn't get into them again. Bank accounts in excess of a thousand pengö were frozen. No Jew was supposed to possess a total of more than three thousand pengö. Radio sets were confiscated. Telephones were disconnected. Jewish organizations were dissolved and all their holdings seized. Jews were given special yellow ration cards entitling them to far less than other people received. They could buy only three ounces of beef or horse meat a week. They received no butter or other fat, no rice, no milk. Only the rich could buy food in the black market, and even if one had the money it was risky. Worst of all were the rumors from the provinces: that ghettos were being established; that everywhere Jews were being herded into inadequate enclosures of various kinds, apparently with indifference to the fact that most of them would die of cold, disease, and hunger.

6

One morning, near the end of April, as Andor was having breakfast, a courier arrived at his apartment with a letter from his comrades in Bratislava, the Slovak capital. As he opened it, his eyes fell on the words ". . . saw the first train packed with Hungarian Jews crossing . . . on their way to the extermination center at Auschwitz. . . ."

"What's the matter, darling?" Sarah had come in from the bedroom. She rushed to put her arms around him as she saw the shock on his face.

He extricated himself gently. "Nothing is the matter," he replied quickly. Making a feeble attempt at sarcasm, he added, "Nothing more than usual. The people in Bratislava want more money to take care of refugees, that's all."

"Oh." She was relieved. "My Andor will find a way to get the money for them." She caressed his cheek. "Don't worry so much about everything, darling." Her gray eyes searched his face lovingly. "I wish you didn't work so hard. You look very tired."

"I'm fine," he said crisply, eager to be free of her scrutiny. "I have a strong constitution, but you—you must take care of yourself and the baby." He lifted her chin and kissed her lightly. "Now I must go. There are probably a thousand people waiting at the office."

After leaving the house he telephoned Gábor from a public booth and told him to round up the others for a meeting at the Parisette Café in an hour.

A little after eleven o'clock, as he made his way through the late morning crowd in the Parisette to the corner table where they generally met, he was happy to see that everyone was present. Without any of the usual preliminaries, he read the letter to them.

"Those bastards!" Joe ejaculated.

Arthur Gruen turned to Gábor angrily. "I thought Heinemann promised you and Andor that this wouldn't happen. A fine deal you made! This is what we get for two hundred thousand dollars."

Gábor's blue eyes twitched. He folded and unfolded his hands nervously as he mumbled to himself, "Auschwitz, Auschwitz!"

Rachel had a bitter look. "When I think," she said, to no one in particular, "of all the people I know who may have been on that train . . ." Her voice died away, but a second later she added softly, "Maybe Alex." She looked off into space, trying to choke back the tears.

When they had all calmed down they agreed that Heinemann must give them an explanation. The meeting adjourned with Andor authorized to see the colonel as quickly as possible.

He made several attempts during the next three days to get through to Heinemann, but each time he was put off by a secretary. It was not until the fourth day that the colonel finally received him.

The atmosphere was frigid. Heinemann sat stolid, unsmiling, as Andor, with barely concealed anger, related the news he had received from Bratislava.

"I want to know, Colonel, what this deportation means," he demanded.

"Calm yourself, Horvath. It has no ominous meaning at all. Some of you people are beginning to let your imaginations run away with you. Someone mentions Auschwitz and you automatically say 'extermination.' Auschwitz? What is Auschwitz? It's a town in Poland. We have a labor camp there. Besides, how does anyone in Bratislava, who sees a train crossing the frontier, have the gall to inform you that it's going to Auschwitz? How does he know? Who told him? The engineer of that train didn't even know where those people were being taken. We change engineers two or three times on every run, just so no one person will know. But your Jew in Bratislava knows! The trouble with you Jews is that you think you're all so goddamn smart. You always know everything. Now let me tell you something, Horvath."

He leaned forward in his chair and fixed his inscrutable eyes on his visitor. "It so happens that I know all about this train you mention. It *did* cross the Hungarian-Slovak frontier. It *was* loaded with Jews. But would you like to know where they were going?"

He paused to let his anger cool. When he continued, his voice was less belligerent, almost condescending, except for the overtone of sarcasm.

"I'll tell you. To a labor camp in Germany. We needed some extra help, quickly, so we gave a trainload of your people the chance to do some constructive work for us, under quite pleasant conditions. Now, do you see how stupid you were to believe that piece of gossip you have in your hand?"

Andor was not yet ready to surrender. "Can you prove all this?"

"Prove it? Why should *I* have to prove anything to *you?*"

Before Andor could answer, he decided to change his tack. "I'll make you a prediction, Horvath. I predict that the families of the people on that train will begin receiving mail from them in a very few days. Wouldn't that prove it?"

"Where will they write from?"

"From Waldsee, the place they were taken to work."

"Waldsee? Where's that?"

"In the southwest of Germany, near Lake Constance. Anyway, we have taken only qualified workers—"

"What do you mean, qualified workers?"

"Those who are capable of learning a trade in the Reich."

Exasperated by Heinemann's bland manner, Andor exploded. "Colonel, I am not here to play games. I want to know where we stand. Less than a month ago in this very room Klaussen assured Gábor and me that you Germans had no intention of deporting Hungarian Jews."

Heinemann rose. "I have told you all I can."

"It's not enough. I want to see Klaussen."

"Klaussen is no longer in Budapest."

"Where is he?"

"In Pécs."

"Then I wish to have a permit to travel to Pécs."

Heinemann shrugged. "You may have it." He turned to his young aide. "See that Horvath receives a pass." Then he stalked from the room.

"Come with me!" the lieutenant said to Andor.

When Andor returned to his apartment that evening and told Sarah he was going to their home town, she begged to go along. She hadn't seen her father and her old home for more than a year. Besides, he would be away overnight and she didn't want to be in the apartment alone. He explained patiently that he had only one pass and that it wasn't possible for both of them to travel on it. Stroking her honey-colored silken hair, he promised to have Rachel stay with her and to bring back a souvenir from the old villa.

Her eyes brightened. "The little Sèvres vase on my dressing table!"

"You shall have it, madame." He bowed solemnly as she giggled, then playfully patted her buttocks. "Now would you like to help me pack?"

Early the next morning he boarded a train at the East Station and settled himself for the five-hour journey to the southwest. He had taken a book with him and bought a newspaper, but as the train rumbled out of the city and into the suburbs he sat with his hands folded, staring out the window at the trees and bushes budding under the warmth of the sunshine, as he reflected with anger and frustration on the events of the past month, desperately trying to conjure up a way to outwit the Germans in this dangerous charade he and they were playing. He sat immobile for two hours, thinking, oblivious of his fellow passengers and the scenery outside. Suddenly the train screeched to a halt. He looked to see if they were at a station, but there were only level fields, a mixture of dry winter brown and the moist green of spring. Well, perhaps there was a crossing up ahead. After several minutes the passengers became restless; some of them opened the doors of their compartments and stepped outside to see what was happening. Finally Andor went outside, too. In front of the train, about a hundred yards ahead, a road crossed the tracks. It was crowded with people, all going in the same direction. They were jammed close together, moving at a snail's pace. As he walked closer he could see that they all wore yellow stars. Some sat precariously perched on horse-drawn carts piled high with odd pieces of furniture, mattresses, suitcases, paper-wrapped bundles. Most of them walked in the road; old men and women struggling to keep up with the procession; weary mothers dragging tearful children by the hand; some carrying babies. Their faces were pale and full of an unutterable terror. Alongside them strode German soldiers with fixed bayonets who occasionally jabbed the needlelike points of their weapons into the backsides of those who dropped by the wayside in exhaustion.

The blood pounded in his temples. "The bastards! The bastards!" Over and over the epithet repeated itself in his brain.

He had no idea how long he stood looking at the dismal parade or whether he said the words aloud, but suddenly he felt a sharp jab at his shoulder. He turned and saw a soldier with a bayonet motioning for him to get back into his compartment.

When he left the train at Pécs, he began to walk along Szabadság út, which led into the center of town. He wanted to stretch his legs and clear his head in the fresh air. Before he met Klaussen he must shake off the uncomfortable drowsiness he felt after such a long, dreary ride. He passed the neo-Romanesque Reformed Church and then turned into Rákóczi út, staying on it until he came to the Majláth tér, where he stopped to gaze at the old Moorish-style synagogue, then on to the busy shops along Király utca, and at the corner on the right the Town Hall, with its roof of gay-colored tiles forming geometric patterns and its cobbled courtyard. Everything here in this town of his youth was so familiar. If it weren't for the war and the problems troubling his mind, his visit would revive many happy memories. He entered the yard and walked into the building.

Hauptsturmführer Klaussen was not especially pleased to see him. He greeted him with a sour smile. But Andor was too filled with the anguish of what he had seen only a few hours ago to notice or to care.

He wasted no time on amenities. "Last month in Budapest you guaranteed me that there would be no ghettos and no deportation," he said sharply. "Your people accepted our money for those guarantees. Now you have gone back on your word. I want to know what is going on."

Klaussen lifted his slender hands in a gesture of helplessness. Slowly, reluctantly, he replied, "After my first meeting with you, Wedemeyer pushed me out of the negotiations. Perhaps he thought I was too friendly with you. Then he assigned me this dirty work: to direct the transport of Jews to the ghettos."

Andor repeated the words bitterly: "To the ghettos."

Once more the aristocratic hands brushed the air in a gesture of resignation. "You see, Horvath, I am a soldier. I have been a soldier all my life. Therefore I must obey orders. I have done my best to soften the fate of your people, but Secretary of State Endre, one of your own Hungarians, is determined to persecute the Jews, and certainly Colonel Wedemeyer will not stop him."

He sounded in earnest, but Andor couldn't be sure. He leaned forward in his chair. "Colonel, I want you to tell me plainly, are we on the verge of a general deportation or only of those who are qualified to work?"

"I don't know. Frankly, I don't know. It's been some time since I left Budapest. But I must go there next week, and I will talk to Wedemeyer. Give me a call after I get there. I will see what I can do."

Andor thanked him, feeling it was useless to press him any further, and then asked if there was a ghetto in Pécs.

"No. Not yet. . . . Ah, you are thinking of Kemeny, your father-in-law. He is at home. No one has disturbed him."

Andor thanked him again and left.

Outside, the late afternoon sun was still bright, but he felt chilled. He buttoned his coat against the slight breeze, hired a carriage, and rode to his father-in-law's villa at the edge of town. The old tree-lined street and the large stone house looked as serene as ever. How long would they remain that way? he wondered glumly. He paid the driver and went up the walk.

Ancient Maria, Philip Kemeny's sole servant these days, admitted him with a cry of delight and took his hat and coat. He had always been one of her favorites. Behind her Kemeny hurried to greet him, his dignified figure a little stiffer, but his gray hair bristling and his brown eyes alight as always. He embraced his son-in-law happily.

"How wonderful to see you, Andor! Come, let's be comfortable while you tell me all the news." He led Andor into the salon which was larger, by far, than the entire Horvath apartment in Budapest.

They seated themselves on the sofa, and Kemeny lifted the stopper from a crystal decanter on the low fruitwood table before them.

"How is Sarah?" he asked as he poured white Tokay into two glasses.

"Well—very well," Andor answered absently.

"Good." He handed a glass to Andor and raised the other. *"Lechaim!"*

"Lechaim." Andor emptied his glass in a single gulp.

The older man looked at him intently. "Things are bad?"

Andor nodded.

"Worse than I know?"

He nodded again, then reached for the decanter, filled his glass, and began to tell Kemeny about the negotiations in Budapest and his visit to Klaussen at the Town Hall. His father-in-law listened without interrupting, careful to hide his growing dismay. He was alarmed by the news, but his alarm was doubled by Andor's manner of telling it. For the first time in all the years he had known Andor he saw that the younger man was letting his emotions possess him. "I wouldn't have thought it possible," he said to himself, "but that shows how little we know other people, even those who are closest to us." A sigh escaped him.

"It's intolerable," Andor fumed. "They say one thing, do another, and then smile. It makes me feel like a fool." He struck the table with his fist and the glasses rattled. "So far it's been their game, every move, and yet *I'm* supposed to be the smart one." He leaned against the back of the sofa, exhausted, and wiped his forehead with the palm of his hand.

Kemeny gave him a few moments to regain his composure, then said quietly, "This is a crisis for our people, Andor, and saving them will take cleverness and strength. You have those qualities in abundance. It is partly because of your cleverness and strength that I have been proud to have you for a son-in-law—proud to feel you even closer—to consider you as my own son. I know that sometimes the burden of such a task as you have undertaken becomes too much for a man. But not for you, Andor. You can make yourself master of any situation, as long as you don't lose your head in anger. An angry man is seldom a clever one; remember that."

In spite of himself Andor chuckled. "You are right, Philip. You are always right." Now that he had recovered, he was ashamed of his outburst, although inwardly he still felt the searing anger and humiliation of the past few days. Slowly he looked around the room, at the paintings, the beautifully carved furniture, the Aubusson rug. "You may have to give all this up and move to a cold, filthy, crowded ghetto. How can you regard such a prospect so calmly?"

"Not so calmly, my son." Kemeny smiled wryly. "But I think that with your help perhaps we won't be forced into ghettos." His expression became grave. "However, if we are we must remember that possessions, as hard as it is to give them up, are only possessions. Inanimate objects are always replaceable. We have lost our possessions before. If we lose them now, we will get them back—or we will start over again. It isn't really important. All that matters is that our people survive. For more than two thousand years we have been persecuted, murdered, dispersed—but we are still here!" His voice was triumphant. "We have always survived, and we will this time, too. Remember that, Andor, my son."

The two men talked until it grew dark. Gradually, in the quiet and beauty of the old house, the wisdom of Philip Kemeny's counsel reached Andor and became balm for his hurt pride and a spur to his purpose. Later, in the walnut-paneled dining room, Maria served dinner. If there was a remnant of the angry uncertainty in him it was dissipated by his pleasure in the fine linen, the crystal, the soft patina of the silverware, the delicacy of the Meissen china, and the excellence of the food.

Afterward, in the salon, they drank their coffee leisurely. As Andor sipped his with evident enjoyment, his father-in-law said, "It's good, isn't it? I will give you some to take home tomorrow."

"Can you spare it?" Andor asked incredulously.

A slightly roguish expression came over the old man's dignified features. "I still have a few connections," he said, smiling.

On the day Andor was in Pécs, an elderly man wearing not only the inevitable yellow star on his left breast but also a prayer shawl over his shoulders, came to the Committee office while Joe was on duty.

"Please," he said plaintively, "let me tell you. It was like this. We were all sitting around the table in the big room of the flat. We had just eaten dinner . . ."

Joe and the other Committee members were accustomed to this sort of narrative. Inconsequential asides, innumerable irrelevant details. It was often difficult to get the narrator to come to the point. In this case, Joe finally learned, the man's son, his daughter-in-law, and their five children had been taken away one night last week by the SS.

"Then we heard nothing. Nothing. It was like they had been swallowed by the sea. What had they done? Tell me, what had they done? Where did they go? Why *my* son? Why not somebody else?"

He asked the questions as if he expected answers, but he didn't pause long enough to get any, even if there had been answers.

Finally his face brightened a little. "Today this came." He reached into a pocket and pulled out a post card. "It's from a place called Waldsee. It says— Here, you read it." The old man's hand trembled as he passed the card across the desk.

Joe read it carefully. It was written in Hungarian. There were just four short sentences: "We are well. We have plenty to eat. We are working hard. We send our love to all of you."

Joe handed the card back with a smile. "What's your problem? Why have you come to us?"

The old man grew very agitated. He handed the card back. "This is from my son. My only son. I know it is him because I know his handwriting. But look how he signs it. His name is László, but he signs it in Hebrew. You read Hebrew?"

"Yes."

"Then read it and don't ask me foolish questions. 'What is my problem?' Ach! He signs it Liebalmush. Liebalmush! Who is Liebalmush? His name is László. What's wrong with my boy? Maybe these Nazis give our people Hebrew names now? Liebalmush! I don't like it. And where is Waldsee? That's why I came. My wife drives me crazy asking, 'Where is Waldsee?' How do *I* know where is Waldsee? Waldsee! Liebalmush! She says to ask you. She says you people know everything." He dropped his voice to a whisper and looked furtively around the room. "You fixed up my wife's brother. His name is Herman. Remember?"

Joe nodded automatically. He was staring at the Hebrew signature. The old man, seeing a peculiar expression cross his face, demanded nervously, "What's the matter?"

Joe hastily relaxed his expression. "Nothing. Nothing at all. I don't think you have any cause for worry. I think your son took a Hebrew name just to show that he is still a good Jew. He's a brave young man. You must be very proud of him." The father smiled. "About Waldsee, I'll look it up. We have an atlas in the next room. Wait a minute while I look."

A few minutes later he returned with a large book. Pointing to a spot on the map, he said, "Here it is. Waldsee. See? In the southwest part of Germany near Lake Constance." He closed the book and put a hand on the old man's shoulder. "You go home and tell your wife not to worry. Tell her that the next card will probably give more information. Tell her to be happy that her son and his family are in good health and have plenty to eat. That's more than a lot of people can say these days."

The old man grasped Joe's hand in both of his own and pressed it to his chest in a gesture of affection and gratitude. "You are a good boy. My wife was right. You know everything. *Shalom.*"

The instant he was gone Joe ran to Rachel's desk. "Tell me quick, what does the Hebrew word *liebalmush* mean?"

Rachel looked up at him curiously. "You aren't making any crude suggestions, are you, Joe?" She grinned.

He was in no mood for jokes. "What does it mean?" he barked. "It means 'without any clothes on.'"

As Rachel pondered the oddity of men, he walked away, mumbling, "That's what I thought. The sons of bitches!"

So many other people came after the old man that Joe forgot about the Waldsee mystery until, late in the afternoon, his secretary admitted a frail, pinch-faced young woman, with deep-set eyes. She was dressed all in black. She seemed so close to collapse that Joe immediately gave her his chair.

Her first question was simple and to the point. With no self-introduction she asked, "Do you read Hebrew?"

Joe nodded.

"Then look at this."

She opened a worn black handbag. Joe saw that there was nothing in it but her identity papers, her yellow ration card, a soiled handkerchief, and the post card that she pulled out and handed to him.

He knew it by heart now. "We are well. We have plenty to eat. We are working hard. We send our love to all of you." He skipped over the Hungarian words quickly to the signature. It was, as he had expected, in Hebrew, but he had difficulty reading it. He turned to the woman. "Excuse me a moment, I must get someone to help me translate the signature." As she held up her hand to stop him, he noticed that the sleeve of her coat was so torn that her elbow protruded. "It's not necessary. I know Hebrew perfectly. My husband has written those Hebrew letters in a way he used to write when he was courting me and we wanted no one else to know. It's not ordinary Hebrew. Would you like me to tell you what it says?"

Joe was tired. It had been a long day. It was becoming increasingly difficult to help all the people with their problems. His job took a strong stomach, a stout heart, and a callousness that he was beginning to think he didn't have, after all. But this woman seemed like the personification of tragedy itself. Why did she have to be so melodramatic? "Yes, please tell me what it says."

"It says, 'Don't believe a word of it.'" She stood up, put the card back in her handbag, and said sharply, "I just thought you ought to know what is happening to *some* Jews while *you* Jews sit here in your fine office, being important."

The words stung Joe. He started to hurry after the departing figure, then suddenly realized that even if he caught up with her there was nothing to say. She was right. What the hell *were* they doing there?

"Andor thinks we're outsmarting them," he said to himself. "They're fooling us at every turn. Waldsee! I'd bet my last pengö the train never went near any place called Waldsee."

The next morning a few more people came with Waldsee cards in their hands. There was nothing different about any of them. They bore the identical four sentences, written in the hand of the missing person. The signatures on the cards today were merely the names of the senders, in Latin script. But in the afternoon a man appeared with a card that was peculiar in one respect. In the upper right corner there were two postmarks. One said "Waldsee" quite clearly. The other was really three postmarks, one on top of the other. By studying them carefully Joe could see that two bore the word "Waldsee." The third was almost blotted out. It looked as if those two Waldsee stamps had been put there with a great deal more force than the one that was illegible. They were blacker and the lines of the letters were thicker. Perhaps, he theorized, the postal clerk had been trying to obliterate something.

"Do you mind if I keep this card of yours until morning?" Joe asked the man across the desk from him. "You see, I have a friend whose brother was on that same transport. I think it will make him very happy if I can show him that they are all well and happy."

That night Joe spent an hour lying on his cot studying the postmarks with a powerful magnifying glass he had borrowed from one of the Committee's expert forgers.

The next day, when Andor called them to the Parisette to report on his trip to Pécs, Joe said to him in a low, bitter voice, "Remember your conversation with Colonel Heinemann about Waldsee? Well, I have news for you. Waldsee is Auschwitz. They are exterminating your Hungarian Jews in the gas chambers and the crematoria of Auschwitz, and if you don't believe it I've got the proof."

7

Early one morning during the week after Andor returned from Pécs, Braun, the German agent, appeared unannounced at the Váci utca apartment. He had obviously dressed in a hurry. His tie was slightly askew and his usually well-brushed gray hair looked sleep-rumpled. "I have something important to tell you." There was urgency in his voice, and he strode into the living room without waiting to be invited.

Andor, in dressing gown, his own hair uncombed, followed him grumpily and sat down, indicating the chair opposite for Braun. From the small table beside him he took a cigarette, lighted it, and inhaled deeply. Then he leaned against the back of the chair. "Now, what the hell brings you here at the ridiculous hour of eight in the morning?" he asked with a touch of annoyance, suspecting Braun had come looking for more money. They had paid him the twenty thousand dollars he had demanded for arranging the interview with Klaussen, but he knew that Braun was a man who was never satisfied.

"Wedemeyer!" Braun threw out the explosive word and waited for the reaction.

"Wedemeyer?" Andor repeated the name almost stupidly, unable to conceal his amazement. It was one of the few times in his life he had ever blurted out anything without due consideration. "What does Wedemeyer want?"

"He wants to see you in one hour at his office." Braun suppressed a smile as he saw how well he had upset the aplomb of this egotistical Jew.

Andor studied him a moment, then gave a short laugh, knowing very well what Braun had been thinking. "Well," he mused, drawing deeply again on his cigarette, "we are really dealing at the top now, aren't we?" There was more than a hint of satisfaction in his tone.

Irritated that Andor had recovered his composure so quickly, Braun hastened to add, "There is something else, but it must not be known that I have told you—"

"Of course, of course. Get to the point." The game was beginning to irk him. It was much too early in the morning.

"Total deportation has been decided upon. . . ."

Andor was stunned. Braun seemed to recede before his eyes. He watched the German's lips move as he explained the details of the deportation plan, and he listened to the words, but he didn't hear them. He was thinking of the Hungarian Jews he had promised himself he would save.

Gradually Braun's face came back into focus and what he was saying began to take on some meaning.

". . . So I would advise you to do everything you can to meet the conditions the Germans set and to use your influence with the Jewish Council, too. This way you may be able to gain some time." He got up. "I must go now." He walked toward the door, then stopped and looked at his watch. "In twenty minutes an SS car will drive up. You are to wait for it in front of the house."

Eighteen minutes later Andor emerged from his building, freshly shaved, his hair neatly brushed, wearing his best suit, and carrying gray gloves. He had never hurried so much, nor had he ever, since moving to Budapest, been so smartly on time. Two minutes later a black Mercedes drew up to the curb. A young corporal stepped out and approached him. "Are you Horvath?" When he said yes, the German told him to get into the car. He sat in the rear, alone. He was keyed up, and the excessive speed of the Mercedes nauseated him. As they drove up the Svábhegy, the shops and cafés were a shifting blur. The car stopped abruptly before the Hotel Majestic. The corporal opened the rear left door. "You will get out and follow me," he said to Andor.

They walked into the hotel lobby, past two saluting German guards, and then up a flight of stairs and along a heavily carpeted hallway until they came to a door on which was printed JUDENKOMMANDO. They entered a room with several desks, all of them occupied by junior officers of the SS. Some were reading official-looking papers, others were talking to civilians, mostly Jews. A low hum of voices filled the room, occasionally punctuated by a sharp word that rose above the discreet babble. In converting this room of the luxurious hotel for their use the Germans had stripped it of all ornamentation except the great crystal chandeliers, which now looked rather incongruous.

"You will wait here!" the corporal said, and went into an inner office.

Andor stood gazing about him, not daring to jeopardize his situation by taking the liberty of sitting down in one of the chairs lined up along the wall. After a few moments his palms began to feel moist. He was angry with himself. What was the matter with him? He could deal with this man. He could deal with any man. It was just a matter of the right technique, playing the cards shrewdly, bluffing when it was necessary.

"Horvath, you will come in." It was the corporal addressing him from the doorway to the inner office.

Slowly and deliberately, mustering all his self-assurance, he walked to the threshold. Before him, sitting at a huge walnut desk in the center of the room, was a slight, fair-haired man in his late thirties with a thin face and large ears, wearing the uniform of a colonel. Next to him, standing, was a young captain in a tight-fitting uniform. Just inside the door sat a civilian stenographer, his pencil poised. On the walls of the room were half a dozen oil paintings that looked like old masters.

"You may sit down, Horvath," the colonel said. Andor chose a chair that did not force him to look directly into the bright light from the window.

"Do you know who I am?" the colonel asked, with seeming ingenuousness. His voice was high-pitched and nasal, and he spoke rapidly.

"Indeed, Colonel Wedemeyer, your name is well known here," Andor replied with a smile, trying to keep out of his voice the dreadful implication of his answer.

"Good. Nevertheless, to keep the record straight, let me tell you that I am the personal representative of SS Reichsführer Himmler. I directed the solution of the Jewish problem in Germany, Poland, and Czechoslovakia. Now it is time to do this in Hungary." He paused for a moment to let his visitor get the full significance of the remark. He looked down at the papers on his desk, then once more fastened his hard blue-eyed gaze on Andor. "I have brought you here to make you a proposition," he said slowly. "I have received a great deal of information about the international Jewish body known as the United Relief Organization. It is more than solvent. It is in command of vast amounts of money. It has the support of all the millionaire Jews of America." He smiled slyly. "I have also heard that the American President, Roosevelt, has broadcast a speech in which he expressed concern about the lives of Hungarian Jews. Well, I want to make it possible for him to do something for them." He paused, then added deprecatingly, "Oh, I know of your negotiations with Heinemann and Klaussen, but all that is small stuff." He waved his right hand as if to brush it away. Then he leaned forward. "I now offer you a really important deal, a great opportunity—a chance to save a million Jews!" By the time he finished the announcement his voice had risen to a new high pitch. He seemed very pleased with his offer.

At his words Andor's heart leaped, and he felt the vein in his temple throbbing. But he sat motionless, hoping Wedemeyer wouldn't notice.

"I am prepared to sell you a million Jews for goods," the colonel continued enthusiastically. "You may take them from any country you wish—from Hungary, from Poland, even from the camps at Auschwitz. You may save whom you will—men who can beget children, women who can bear them, old people, young people. Whom would you like to save?"

"It isn't for me to say who shall live and who shall die, Colonel. I want to save all my people," Andor answered quietly, trying to keep his tone reasonable. "We are willing to ransom them. You have only to say how much money you want."

"Come, Horvath, be realistic. I cannot sell you all the Jews in Europe. Not now, anyway, even if you could pay enough. But I can sell you a million. For goods, not money," he added emphatically. "I need war material, especially trucks. So I will make you a fair proposition: for every truck you deliver, you can have a hundred Jews. For a million Jews the price is ten thousand trucks, new and completely equipped."

Andor was dumfounded. After several moments he said, "I would do anything to save my people, but what you are asking is impossible, Colonel. Who do you think will sell us such vital war material under these conditions?"

"That is your problem, Horvath. However, in both our interests, I am willing to make the solution as easy as possible for you. I shall permit you or one of your Committee to go abroad to meet with your own leaders and with representatives of the Allies. You may calm their apprehensions by assuring them that we promise on our honor to use the trucks only in the east, not in the west. You will return with a detailed proposition. If it is satisfactory, we shall release your Jews. If it is not, you will face the consequences." With these words Wedemeyer's thin face took on a predatory look.

Andor was certain that if he failed to satisfy this man whom Hitler had placed in charge of the Jewish problem, the consequences would be catastrophic. He was just as certain, without even putting out any feelers, that the Allies would never sell trucks to anyone, knowing that they were going to end up in German hands. Still, there might be some solution. Meanwhile he must stall for time.

"Colonel," he said politely, "I am sure you will keep your promise, but my people abroad are certain to ask me, 'What guarantee do we have that a million Jews will really be saved?' How can I answer them?"

"If you return with a concrete plan for working out an agreement, I shall close Auschwitz and bring a hundred thousand Jews to the frontier. You can take them away and then deliver the thousand trucks to me. That will be our procedure—a thousand trucks for every hundred thousand Jews. That's more than fair, isn't it?"

"It's quite fair," Andor acknowledged, showing his pleasure a little too openly.

"Now tell me where your representative will go, so we can begin to make arrangements for the journey," Wedemeyer said briskly.

Andor tried to think quickly. Edward Schoen of the United Relief Organization was in Switzerland. His own Zionist comrades, however, were in the Jewish Agency at Istanbul. They would understand the situation best. They had direct links with the Allies in Jerusalem and Cairo. But more important, the Rescue Committee had been maintaining an unbroken connection with the Agency for months.

"Our representative will have to go to Istanbul, Colonel."

"I will give you three days to talk this proposition over with your Committee and decide which of you is going. You understand, of course, that whoever goes must leave his family behind. After all"—he smiled wryly—"I must be certain that the man will return."

"Of course."

"One more thing. I warn you it will go very badly for you if any of this leaks out to the Hungarians," he said ominously.

"I assure you there will be no leak, Colonel."

Wedemeyer then turned to the captain who was standing beside him. "Have the Jew brought in."

Almost immediately Max Franck appeared in the doorway, his bald pate gleaming with perspiration under the brilliant light from the chandeliers. He looked pale and unhappy.

"You know each other, of course," Wedemeyer began, amused at the obvious fear of the one and the animosity of the other. Without waiting for an answer he said to Andor, "I have decided that Franck will accompany your representative. He has traveled a great deal—many times to Istanbul, I understand. He is also a shrewd observer. So it will be interesting for us to hear what he has to say when he returns from this mission." Then the craftiness disappeared from his demeanor and he said abruptly, "That is all for now. Just remember, I expect you back in three days with your representative, Horvath."

As soon as they were outside the building and beyond earshot of the guards at the door, Andor wheeled on Max. "How can you do it?" he began furiously. "How can you spy on us, your own people, for those murderers? How flattering it must be to you that they trust you! Have you no shame? What kind of a Jew are you, anyway?"

"Stop it!" Max yelled, raising his arms in protest. "I'm a good Jew and you know it. Haven't I brought many of our people across the border from Slovakia? Haven't I carried your messages to Istanbul and risked my life to do it?"

"For money!" Andor spat on the sidewalk contemptuously and

quickened his pace, as if to escape from the presence of something vile.

"No!" Max's pudgy legs almost collapsed beneath him as he tried to keep up with Andor. "Not just for money. I took those who couldn't pay, too."

Andor, regretting his outburst as undignified, slowed his steps. Max was relieved. "It isn't nice you should talk to me like that," he said plaintively, looking up at Andor to see what effect his words were having. "Those Nazi swine routed me out of bed at six this morning and kept me waiting, facing the wall, for four hours. Not even a cup of coffee I had. Now they tell me, 'We have decided you are going to Istanbul.' Could I say no?"

Andor stopped walking and stared at the pleading little man before him, suddenly aware that unsavory as he was, he was telling the truth. Gradually his anger disappeared and a feeling of exhaustion came over him.

"No," he answered slowly, "you couldn't have refused. But see that you don't serve them too well. Remember, they aren't powerful enough to kill all of us." With that he turned on his heel and walked away.

8

Despite her anxiety, Sarah began to feel drowsy. Sitting on a hassock in a corner of the living room, she alternately knitted on a small white sweater and watched her guests through the haze of tobacco smoke that filled the room. They had been talking for hours, discussing over and over again the same problems.

For the twentieth time Erno Gábor pushed his glasses back on his thin nose. "I'm still not convinced that it is right for us to supply the Germans with trucks," he said stubbornly. "After all, trucks are war material. The more war material they get, the more military strength they'll have. The more military strength, the more of a chance that they may win the war. How would we feel if we had to live with the thought that the trucks we supplied them were the straw that tipped everything in their favor? How would we feel if we had to live the rest of our lives in a Nazi world?"

Joe waved his finger impatiently at Gábor. "Erno, you miss the whole point. The Germans have offered to free a hundred thousand Jews *before* we deliver a single truck. There'll be months of negotiations with the countries our people will be sent to. There'll have to be negotiations with the countries they will travel through in transit. When these matters have all been settled, we will have to arrange railroad and ship accommodations for them. By that time the Nazis will have been defeated and we won't have to give them any trucks. But meanwhile we will have saved one hundred thousand of our people."

Arthur Gruen added, "Besides, Wedemeyer has guaranteed he will close down Auschwitz if Istanbul agrees to the deal. If he does, it's not likely that after months of negotiations, when the German situation is certain to be even worse than it is now, the Germans will have the spare manpower to reopen the camp."

"Well, perhaps you're right," Gábor admitted. "But while we sit around here talking about big plans our people are being herded into ghettos in the provinces and sent to their death. We can't just talk for weeks and months. We must do something to stop the deportations, and do it now."

"What can we do?" Rachel asked dolefully. "Our workers have warned people. We have begged them not to report to the deportation centers when they're called. But most of them don't listen to us. They listen to the Council. The Council tells them to obey all orders—"

Andor interrupted. "Erno's right. We must try to make it a condition of the deal that the deportations stop immediately. When I go back to Wedemeyer with our answer, I'll put it to him that way." He looked at the faces around the room. "But do we all agree that we should transmit Wedemeyer's proposal to Istanbul?"

There was a murmur of assent.

"I think I should tell you," he continued, "that I don't believe for a minute the Allies will be willing to meet the German demands. But it is absolutely necessary for us to get some kind of counterproposition from them. We must make this very clear to the Agency. Negotiations with the Allies must not be allowed to be broken off for any reason, and it will be up to the Agency to keep them going. Only so long as the Germans see the possibility of some kind of a deal, with our help, only so long can we pull strings to save lives. Whoever goes to Istanbul must try to come back with a proposal that the Germans will be willing to consider."

"Do you think they'll be willing to accept money or other goods instead of trucks?" Rachel asked.

The question started a new discussion, which Andor brought to an end by saying, "I think we should decide now"—he looked at his watch and then at Sarah, who was nodding over her knitting—"because it's getting rather late, which one of us is going to Istanbul."

"You are the cleverest diplomat," Rachel said, putting her hand on Andor's arm. "You're the one who should go."

"No!" Sarah jumped to her feet. Skeins of white wool fell in a tangle around her dark skirt, and she almost tripped on them as she rushed to her husband's side. "He can't go. Our people need him here. And so do I."

The others gaped at her in astonishment. She had been so unobtrusive they had forgotten she was in the room.

"Sarah, sit down." Andor's voice was kind but firm. He wasn't disturbed over her not wanting him to go. He had never considered choosing himself as the envoy, and he had no intention of permitting himself to be persuaded. Someone else would have to go. His place was here, where he was, at the head of the Committee he had created and made into a powerful organization. Even Hugo Mayer and Emmanuel Simon wanted him to negotiate for their Orthodox groups. He had an opportunity now that he had worked for since his youth in Pécs, and he wasn't prepared to surrender it to anyone. That his chance to become the most powerful leader of Hungary's Jews had come at a time like this and under such unhappy circumstances was an act of fate over which he had no control. Nevertheless, the opportunity was here, and it was his. Besides—he looked around the table at the expectant faces turned toward him—not one of them was capable of taking his place.

Aloud he said modestly, "If most of you want me to go, of course I will go. But I think we should send the person the Jewish Agency knows best, the man they will have confidence in, the man whose judgment they know and trust. That person is Erno. I think he should be the one to go."

"He gets my vote," Arthur said with finality. "He can explain our desperate situation to them so they'll understand, and they'll know that he isn't exaggerating. That's more important than anything else, because we must have their help."

Joe agreed. And then Rachel. So it was decided that Gábor would make the journey to Istanbul. A large smile spread across his lined face. He was enjoying the adulation of his colleagues.

"Unfortunately you won't be traveling alone," Andor said to him. "The Germans have decided to send Max Franck with you."

Arthur groaned in disgust.

Gábor pushed his glasses back angrily. "I won't do it," he snapped, his blue eyes bright with indignation. "I don't want such a person for a—"

"Now, Erno," Andor said soothingly, "Max isn't a companion any of us would choose, but we really have nothing to say about it. Besides, wouldn't it be worse if you had to travel with a German, a real Nazi?"

"I hadn't thought of that," the older man said with resignation.

Andor laughed to see the suddenly subdued mien of his friend. "It won't be so bad, Erno," he said affectionately. "Don't let it worry you." He shifted the papers on the table before him and put a blank sheet on top. "Now let's prepare a cable to Istanbul. . . ."

Within a few days the Rescue Committee received a reply from Istanbul. The Agency considered Gábor's journey imperative and was eagerly awaiting his arrival. Andor hurriedly thrust the message into the pocket of his jacket, called for Gábor at his apartment, and drove him up the Svábhegy to the Hotel Majestic. There he introduced him to Colonel Wedemeyer.

"Our colleagues have decided that Herr Gábor should represent us in Istanbul," he explained. Taking the crushed cable from his pocket and holding it out to Wedemeyer, he added, "This morning we received this saying the Agency is ready to receive him."

"So." The colonel carefully surveyed the gray-haired, myopic man before him, holding out his hand for the cable but continuing to scrutinize Gábor until the retired ceramics manufacturer squirmed in discomfort. "You understand the risks of this journey?" he asked.

"Yes."

"You know that you must leave your family here as a guarantee that you will return?"

"Yes, but I understand that in my absence they will be under your protection, and I have your assurance that they will be safe. Is that true?"

"That is true. I give you my word."

"In that case I'm ready to go."

For the first time Wedemeyer smiled. "Well then, we don't want to waste time." He banged on his desk, and a young sergeant appeared. "Take these men to Colonel Heinemann and tell him to order the travel documents for Gábor." He turned back to his visitors. "The day after tomorrow Gábor will be picked up at his home and driven by car to Vienna. Colonel Heinemann will accompany him that far, see that he receives his travel permits, and that he boards the plane for Istanbul."

Andor said urgently, "Herr Obersturmbannführer, our people are most eager for Herr Gábor to return with an answer that is acceptable to you. We greatly desire the success of his mission. For this reason we wish the proposition you have offered to be presented to our Agency under the best possible circumstances. But the continuing reports of deportations in the provinces will most certainly be a hindrance. By now our people in Istanbul have heard about them, and it is doubtful that they will regard your offer as put forth in good faith if the deportations continue. Therefore we earnestly ask you—so the negotiations will not fail—to stop the deportations."

Wedemeyer stared at him coldly. "The deportations will continue. Each day twelve thousand Jews are being moved out of Hungary, and each day twelve thousand will continue to go. However, I will make one concession. Instead of sending them to Auschwitz I will send them to Austria. They will remain in Austria until Gábor returns with a satisfactory answer; then they will be transported to the frontier of any foreign country that will accept them." Then, facing Gábor, he said, "Of course, if you fail to return or if you return with an unsatisfactory proposal, these transports will be sent to Auschwitz, and I assume you are aware of what that means."

Gábor paled. "Colonel, you are almost dooming the negotiations before they start."

Two angry red spots appeared on Wedemeyer's thin cheeks. "Do you take me for a simpleton, Gábor?" His nasal voice rose to an ear-shattering pitch. "If I stop the deportations, the negotiations will without a doubt also stop. If your people think that the Jews of Hungary are safe, they'll never conclude a deal. I know what I'm doing. So if you want to save your Jews you had better return quickly—let us say within two weeks—and with a positive proposal."

"But suppose the Agency and I have to deal with the Allies directly? It may take longer than two weeks to get them to agree to the plan."

"Then you must send me a cable and I will hold up the deportations. You may travel to any city you please if you think it is necessary in order to conclude the agreement, but I must be informed first of any travel plans beyond Istanbul."

"I am firmly resolved, Colonel, to bring you a definite proposal, but I beg you to reconsider and stop the deportations now." Gábor put all the feeling he possessed into the plea.

Wedemeyer ignored it. "I suggest that you start at once preparing for your trip. You realize that you will leave in just two days." Then, to indicate that the interview was over, he picked up a report from his desk and began to read it. Suddenly he looked up at his visitors again and said, "Don't dally in Istanbul, Gábor. I can't keep your Jews on ice indefinitely."

In a modest flat on Palotas utca, Esther Gábor sat on the small wine-colored sofa in her living room and for the twentieth time checked the items in the suitcase that lay open beside her. Erno, sitting at the little round mahogany table near the window, sorted some papers he was taking with him and from time to time glanced at his wife anxiously.

Finally she brushed a wisp of gray-black hair from her forehead and turned to him. "I think I've put in everything you'll need. Now a cup of tea, maybe?" she asked, trying to smile.

"Esther, dear Esther," he said, rising and going over to her, "everything has been there since you packed it the first time, at nine o'clock." He sat down and put his arm around her. "I don't want a cup of tea. I want to spend these last few minutes with my wife by my side, full of hope, as I am." He turned her face toward him and kissed her gently on the cheek. It was wet and tasted of salt. He drew her close to him and murmured, "My golden one, you must be brave. In two weeks I will be home again." The sturdiness of his arms calmed her, and she stopped crying.

"I know, and I'm ashamed to be so afraid. But I think of all the terrible things that could happen to you and how much the Germans hate us." She wiped the tears from her cheeks. "There is no life for me without you," she said, looking up at him with eyes full of love. "You know that, don't you?"

He stroked her hair. "Not for me either, without you. That's the way it has always been between us, and that's why you can be sure I'll come back." A wonderful excitement came into his voice. "Remember, when this is all over we'll go to Palestine, and there everyone will be like us, and before the end of our lifetime our old homeland will belong to us again. I'm sure the British will give it back to us, as they promised. It will be *our* land, Eretz Israel, only ours, and it will be a happy place, and we will grow old there without problems any more."

His spirit and his strength became hers, and she smiled at him. "I believe you, my Erno."

"So," he said, getting up, "you have water on the stove?"

She nodded.

"I think a cup of tea would taste good now."

"To me, too." She brewed the tea strong and black and set her best white and gold china cups and saucers on the mahogany table.

They sat down together, and Esther poured the steaming, fragrant liquid. Erno lifted his cup. "Next year in Jerusalem." It was a promise, the way he said it.

Suddenly there was a sharp rapping. Esther felt her heart stop. Erno put down his cup and went to open the door.

A young German sergeant stood before him. "You are Erno Gábor?"

"Yes."

"I am here to take you to Obersturmbannführer Heinemann."

"I am ready," Gábor replied, going to the sofa and picking up his suitcase. He went over to Esther, who all this time had stood numbly by the little table, unable to move or speak, and kissed her fervently on the lips. She grasped his empty hand with both of hers. "I will be back soon, my dear one," he said, "and with good news. You'll tell that to the children, won't you?" and with his eyes he begged her to have courage.

She released his hand and nodded that she would, afraid to trust her voice. He kissed her once more and followed the sergeant out the door and down the flight of stairs to the street.

From the hallway Esther watched until he was out of sight and then went back into the apartment. On the coat tree just inside the door she saw his old raincoat. Grabbing it, she ran down the dark stairs, calling him. As she reached the sidewalk, the black Mercedes was moving away through a drizzle of light rain. Panting and panic-stricken, she raised her voice and called louder, but the car kept going, gathering speed as it moved down the road. Through the back window she could see the bald head of Max Franck and the iron-gray hair of her beloved husband, moving farther and farther away from her.

"Erno, Erno," she whispered, the tears streaming down her face. She stood there, a forlorn little figure in the rain, holding an old coat against her body, watching the car disappear.

9

Spring came to Hungary as if nature were determined to compensate for all the ugliness that man was creating. The countryside had never looked lovelier. First, the greens appeared: the delicate yellow green of the willows, the darker green of new grass, the mottled green of the forests with their black-looking firs and spruces, interspersed with the deciduous trees, so pale by contrast. Against this background the fruit trees suddenly burst into bloom. One morning they were covered with buds that were tight and seemed reluctant to open and expose the beauty they held. Then a warm sun caressed them and by twilight they unfolded, converting the landscape into a spectacular scene of pink and white beauty. The fields were carpeted with wild flowers, yellow, blue, pink, all delicately pastel-colored. Everywhere nature was in harmony. There wasn't a discordant note.

Then suddenly the roads of Hungary were crowded with people wearing yellow stars. Their eyes were on their feet, not on the exquisite fruit blossoms. Their bodies were wasted. Most were dirty and wore rags. The country air, fresh and heavily scented with the perfume of the peach and plum blossoms, began to be polluted with the acid-sour smell of unclean bodies and the stench of human excrement as columns of Jewish prisoners trudged along the roads. Many had been given no opportunity to bathe for weeks. Some had severe dysentery, but the guards who kept them moving in orderly procession gave them no chance to relieve themselves. Anyone who tried to stop beside the road was goaded back into the slow death march with the jab of a bayonet.

Nature was putting on her annual miracle play, exemplifying the glorious renewal of life, but these people knew that for them the end of life was rapidly approaching: that in another hour or another week they would be herded into freight cars and transported to some strange place to die. Word had spread across Hungary that everywhere in the provinces where there were Jews ghettos were being established, and the purpose of the ghettos was at last understood: they were nothing more nor less than places to assemble men, women, and children for deportation. Only the most naïve still thought that the trains were taking Jews to labor camps. Almost everyone now knew about Auschwitz.

When the roundups in the provinces first began, the Hungarian security police conducted them in the early morning, before daylight,

104

to prevent the local Christian population from seeing them. Later, when Undersecretary of State for the Interior László Endre ordered the pace quickened, the Jews were often driven through the streets of the towns in the middle of the day. Onlookers who protested or even showed compassion for the victims were arrested or threatened.

To stave off the growing complaints, a secretary in the Ministry of the Interior declared publicly, "Nobody intends to exterminate, annihilate, or even torment the Jews. . . ." Few who heard the statement believed it.

In several towns Christians who had obtained authority to enter ghettos volunteered to act as couriers for the Jewish Council of Budapest, taking money and messages to the restricted Jews. This was hazardous, for being apprehended meant arrest, torture, or even confinement in the ghetto itself.

As frantic reports poured into Budapest, the Jewish Council wrote letter after letter begging the Minister of the Interior to permit the Council to ameliorate the conditions of the Jews in the provinces. The Minister transmitted each of these requests to his anti-Semitic Undersecretary Endre, who replied, "The measures adopted have been carried out by us in a humane manner and with due regard for moral considerations. . . ."

With a determination born of desperation, the Council rejected this reply and demanded an interview. Peremptorily Endre's aide answered, "The Secretary has no time to receive Jews." When they persisted, he barked, "It is only the fate they deserve that has finally caught up with the Jews. Just the same, the horrible stories about the ghettos are lies, and if the Council members continue to insist on repeating them, they will be treated like any other malicious rumormongers."

Holding tenaciously to a last small hope, they went to see Colonel Otto Wedemeyer. That hope died as the head of the Judenkommando said indignantly, "Not a single word of what you tell me is true. I should know. I have just returned from an inspection tour of the provincial ghettos. The living quarters of the Jews there are just as good as those of German soldiers during maneuvers. The fresh air will improve their health. You Jews don't ever get enough of it."

They tried to wring some admission from him by citing names, dates, and places, but he was unmoved. "If there were any abuses," he replied evenly, "they cannot be laid to the Germans. It is the Hungarians who are to blame. Endre wants to devour the Jews with paprika."

There were protests from other quarters. A Roman Catholic bishop in eastern Hungary whose parishioners complained to him of the floggings and other indignities inflicted upon Jews in their area wrote a letter to Endre. Shortly thereafter the Jews were removed from the town and were never seen again. The bishop received no other reply to his letter.

In the south another bishop wrote to the Minister of the Interior: "I raise my protesting voice and hereby hold you responsible before God, Hungary, and history for all the sickness and death, for all the hatred and contempt that will come in the wake of your policies."

The Minister, through one of his aides, sent the bishop a warning: "If he does not keep quiet and stop criticizing the decisions made by me, I will have him interned."

Instead of keeping quiet the bishop wrote to Prime Minister Sztojay, asking him to curb the activities of his ministers. Sztojay did not reply.

The Papal Nuncio and Cardinal Seredi, the Catholic Primate, intervened frequently with government authorities. The results of their efforts were polite promises that were never kept.

The doyen of the bishops of the Protestant churches *did* receive an audience with Sztojay. He protested the tortures and inhumane treatment inflicted on the Jews and presented a petition drawn up by the Universal Reformed Assembly asking for an alleviation of the conditions in the provincial ghettos. Sztojay acknowledged that he had heard there was some brutality, adding that he of course deplored it and had ordered the ghettoization to be effected without the use of force.

"But," he said pointedly to the bishop, "the Jews are a race, so the solution of the Jewish problem is not a question of religion but of race." He promised that baptized Jews would be allowed to wear a badge indicating their Christian faith, although they must still wear the Star of David.

None of the interventions, Christian or Jewish, had any real effect. A few lives were saved. Brutality was sometimes temporarily lessened. The physical conditions of existence for people on their way to death were improved a little. But the roundups and the deportations went on.

Endre, determined that a few sentimental Christians should not interfere with his program to rid Hungary of all Jews, persuaded the Minister of the Interior to order all mayors to make public the names of Christians who had helped the Jews in any way, and the security police were ordered to arrest at once anyone conspiring to obstruct the government's regulations concerning Jews.

Still, in many towns Christians continued to sabotage Endre's operations. In one area an officer in the Hungarian Army warned the Jews to hide their valuables a week before they were put into a ghetto. In another place a policeman hid the money of his Jewish neighbors in his own home. The mayor of still another town permitted a Jewish family to remain outside the ghetto on the excuse that the man was needed to supervise a farm providing the town with grain. A Jewish university student was discovered in a Catholic seminary wearing the cassock of a theological student. A policeman was interned for taking photographs of deportations at a railroad station. A teacher, together with his whole family, was arrested because he protested against the deportation.

Many such stories reached Andor and his Committee in Budapest. But the zealousness of the Hungarian security police in ferreting out those who obstructed their program discouraged any widespread resistance by the non-Jewish population.

Some of the Jews in the provinces escaped to Slovakia or Rumania with illegal travel permits furnished by local Jewish councils. Some obtained documents saying they were Christians and with such papers in their pockets made their way to Budapest. But the journey to the capital was fraught with danger. Policemen in uniform and others in plain clothes stalked the railroad depots, both in Budapest and in the provincial towns. At any time a person might be asked for his papers. Sometimes an entire train was raided. If a man carrying a Christian identity card was suspected of being a Jew, the police would demand that he recite the Lord's Prayer. If he could not—and almost no Jew could—he was arrested as an impostor.

Yet many people from the provinces and thousands from Budapest itself appeared at the Center or at Andor's apartment to ask for help. They came streaming in every day. The Rescue Committee was their final resort, their last chance, and the Committee knew this. The burden of Andor's work became almost unbearable. In addition to handling the growing number of people who asked for help each day, he and the remaining members of the Committee had to take on the duties of Alex and Gábor. Often they worked eighteen hours out of the twenty-four. Rachel learned to forge identity cards and passports when she wasn't caring for refugees. The arduous days put smudges of gray beneath her once bright eyes and an uneven haste to her once sprightly movements. The flesh on Arthur's large frame seemed to melt away, his body sagged, and the ruddy hue of his complexion faded until it was sallow and mottled. Each night Elizabeth watched worriedly as he shuffled papers on the dining-room table and entered figures in the Committee's account books.

Only Joe looked the same. His tough young body was as resilient as ever, and the dark, rugged features of his face were alive with the old eagerness. He talked continually about the day the Russians would cross the Carpathian Mountains into Hungary and free them all, as if the wish, uttered ardently and often enough, would in some mysterious way hasten the reality.

Andor's face took on a slightly haggard aspect. It was not unbecoming, for it made him look like a rather dissipated matinee idol, but its attractiveness escaped Sarah's notice. Each day she grew more anxious, as the depressing reports came in from the provinces. Andor tried to keep them from her, but she heard others talk, and she knew. He was working longer and longer hours. She knew, too, that he was unwilling to admit his own exhaustion; that he was riveting all his attention on trying to satisfy the increased demands made on his truncated Committee.

As the situation in the provinces became more desperate, Andor realized that he and his Committee would now have to organize a different sort of action. It would not do simply to rescue the few hundred people they could smuggle with false documents across the Rumanian frontier, while they were waiting for an answer from the Agency in Istanbul, for it appeared now that the Germans had worked out a plan they were following with precision: to remove the Jews near the frontiers of the country first, then to draw the circle in, closer and closer. Gradually the circle was approaching Budapest. Eventually, of course, when all the other Jews of Hungary had gone, even those in the nearby suburbs, the same "solution" would be found for those concentrated in the capital.

As the deportations were stepped up, he thought with a stab of painful fright that if the Germans were certain they were losing the war they might decide to destroy all the Jews of Hungary before the Reich finally surrendered. Perhaps they had already reached this decision. It might explain the long lines of railroad trains to Auschwitz, Theresienstadt, Bergen-Belsen, and Mauthausen. It was ten days since Erno had left, and they had heard nothing from him or from the Agency. This worried Andor more than he wanted to admit to anyone, even to himself. Of course, there were many possible explanations. Some of them he disliked thinking about.

After several days of self-deliberation Andor decided that the thing to do was to cable Istanbul. He hoped that a reminder of the dreadful situation they faced would spur his colleagues down there into some sort of action. But what to say in the cable? He was not so naïve as to think that he could communicate secretly with Istanbul. The Hungarian telegraph office certainly turned over every message, incoming and outgoing, to the Gestapo. Any cables he sent would find their way to Wedemeyer's desk, and it wouldn't do to antagonize the colonel at this point by mentioning atrocities.

Finally Andor decided on a simple, two-word message: DEPORTATIONS INCREASING. After he had sent it he telephoned Arthur and told him to call the others for a meeting at the Parisette at nine that evening.

When Andor entered the Parisette at nine-fifteen, he had a small wild flower in his buttonhole. His secretary, Zipora Nayari, had put it there. As he glanced at it, he told himself she was probably in love with him, in a remote, hero-worshiping way. Hardly a day went by without her indicating this, in a look or a word. He was flattered and pleased, nothing more. It wasn't unusual for him to inspire, or think he inspired, such feelings. Women of all ages were impressed by him. The romanticist in them was attracted by the grace with which he kissed a lady's hand, or bowed from the waist during an introduction, or lit someone's cigarette, or crossed his legs carefully when he sat down so the crease in his trousers would not be ruined; by his seeming ability to rise above the petty and mundane; by the impression he gave of being a true man of affairs, accustomed to dealing with big problems and making critical decisions.

He knew he affected most people this way, especially women, and he drew strength from the knowledge. His ego was an important part of the machinery that drove him, enabling him to go on almost indefinitely without sleep, without food, without cigarettes or alcohol, when necessary, to achieve his goal. As he approached the table where his colleagues were sitting he saw how tired they looked. He was tired, too, but a small wild flower from a young woman had given him a renewed sense of purpose, and confidence in his own importance.

He quickly called the meeting to order and told them of the cable he'd sent. "Naturally we're all worried because there's been no news from Istanbul," he said, "but we must hide this from Wedemeyer. Somehow we must convince him that we think the negotiations are progressing satisfactorily."

For some time they discussed how they would deceive the colonel. Joe sat in his usual seat facing the entrance of the café. No matter who was talking, or how important the conversation, he always sat in that same seat with his eyes on the door. Even when he himself was talking, he never ceased taking note of everyone who came or went.

Suddenly the others noticed Joe's fingers tighten around his glass until the veins stood out. The muscles of his jaw were tense. Rachel, who also was facing the door, looked up and saw six Hungarian security police standing just inside the door, looking over the customers. The sound of tinkling glasses and the babble of conversation faded away as the people in the crowded café stared curiously at the uniformed men, waiting to see what they would do. After a few seconds the Parisette owner left his cash register and scurried over to them. The leader of the group, a sergeant, whispered something to him. The owner replied in a whisper, turning toward the Committee's table and nodding at Andor.

"Sit where you are and say nothing," Andor softly commanded as the police approached.

Under Joe's strong fingers the stem of his glass abruptly snapped. Rachel clenched her fists and looked into her lap.

Arthur pretended to be fumbling with an evening newspaper.

Andor nonchalantly took the wild flower from his buttonhole, picked off a broken petal, and was replacing it in his buttonhole when the sergeant barked, "Horvath, you and your *associates* are under arrest." He said the word contemptuously, grabbing Andor by the arm. His assistants, having surrounded the table, followed his example with the other three. Joe tried furiously to shake off the one who had seized him. Andor asked in a calm voice, "What's the charge?"

"Sabotaging the Jewish regulations." The sergeant tried to pull Andor to his feet, but he refused to move.

"What regulations?"

"You'll find out at the station." Turning to the policeman beside him, the sergeant said, "Give me a hand with this bastard."

There wasn't a sound in the smoke-filled café. Not one of the patrons or waiters moved. When the two men began twisting his arms, Andor gave up and, seeing this, the others did also. The police hustled them outside, pushed them into two cars, and drove them out of the city, to a jail in the suburbs.

For two hours Andor's angry demands to know why they were being held were answered only by a loud "shut up!" from the guards. The cell in which the four of them had been locked was small, about seven by nine feet, with a brick floor and a barred window near the ceiling, blacked out by heavy curtains against the Allied air raids that had begun in April. In one corner stood a battered tin pail that gave off the acrid stench of stale urine. Outside, it was spring, but in the cellar of this dank building they felt cold. Rachel shivered in her light coat, walking back and forth and hugging herself to keep warm. There were no chairs, not even a cot. Arthur, his legs tiring under the burden of his large body, finally sat down on the grimy floor, resting his back against the wall and sighing with relief. Joe, like a restless cougar, paced the cell on the opposite side from Rachel. Andor leaned against the wall beneath the window, his eyes half closed, trying to think of some way to get them out. They had stopped talking to each other. It not only was useless to speculate on the cause of their arrest, it was also risky, Andor had said, for they might unwittingly give away information about their activities that the police—if they had wired the room—could use against them. Actually the Hungarians might have nothing on them. This detention could simply be a way of inducing them to incriminate themselves.

A guard appeared and unlocked the door. "Lieutenant Darvas wants to see you," he said to Andor, and led him to a small, brightly lighted room. A young, pleasant-faced police lieutenant sat behind a table. The sergeant who had arrested them at the Parisette stood glowering at Andor as the lieutenant told him to sit down. Seeing the look that passed between the two men, the lieutenant laughed shortly. "Sergeant Halasz has perpetual dyspepsia," he said, then abruptly asked, "Do you know a man named Chaim Szind?"

Andor felt his heart plummet to the bottom of his stomach, but he answered calmly, "No."

"That's strange. He says he knows you." Darvas' voice was friendly, although his smile was wry.

Andor shrugged. "I don't know him."

"He not only says he knows you, but that he works for you." There was still no hint of irritation in Darvas' voice, but he picked up a folder and began thumbing through its pages.

Andor knew that Darvas expected him to try to see what was in the folder. It was difficult to resist the impulse, but he sat back, pretending unconcern, and answered, "He's lying. He doesn't work for me."

"It took some time for us to persuade him to talk."

"After so much persuasion he would probably tell you any story that came into his head."

Darvas took from the folder four passports. Andor recognized them immediately as documents that had been forged on his instructions. With a sinking feeling he wondered if all eighteen had been caught, but to Darvas he said in a disinterested, impatient voice, "What do these things have to do with me?"

"Szind says you ordered him to forge them. He says he forged passports for eighteen Jews who tried to cross the frontier into Rumania."

"He's a liar." Silently he begged Chaim's forgiveness.

"Don't be foolish, Horvath. We've caught all eighteen of them. They'll all talk before we're finished with them. It'll save both of us a lot of time if you'll admit your part in this matter."

"How can I make such an admission? I don't know these people and they don't know me." It was true. At least the last half. Fortunately the eighteen didn't know the source of the assistance that had been given them.

Darvas' patience seemed inexhaustible. He nodded toward the rear of the building. "Your friends in there may tell a different story."

Andor knew it was inevitable that the police would question Joe, Rachel, and Arthur separately. If they told conflicting stories they were all in trouble. But even if they didn't give themselves away, this gentle treatment wouldn't last. When the Hungarian authorities saw that they weren't going to co-operate, stronger methods would be used.

"Lieutenant," he said with a weary smile that was meant to indicate this was all a tiresome and foolish business, "sitting here, I can't prove to you that my friends and I aren't guilty. But if you will allow me to make one telephone call, I think the whole matter can be straightened out promptly."

"Really?" Darvas feigned surprise. "All right, Horvath, you may make your call." He pointed to the telephone on the table and then rose, motioning to the sergeant to follow him. "We'll be back in a few minutes," he said, and they left.

Andor sat there for a moment trying to get his bearings. The lieutenant was a reasonable man. Too reasonable. Of course they would listen in on his call. He wondered whether they had any information about his negotiations with Wedemeyer. If they did, it would explain why Lieutenant Darvas had so readily given him permission to telephone. Well, they wouldn't get anything from him.

He dialed his own number. He knew that Sarah would be worried by now. She might panic when he told her he was in jail, but he was counting on his own firmness to reassure her and make her understand that if she called "the fixer"—their long-time sobriquet for Kurt Braun—everything would be all right. He heard one ring . . . two . . . three . . . She must be asleep. That was a good sign. Maybe being pregnant had something to do with it. The phone rang again . . . Then again. Still no answer. He let it ring several times more, unable to believe that she wasn't home. Where could she be? He looked at his wrist, then remembered that his watch and the contents of all his pockets had been taken from him by the police. It must be after 3 A.M. A wave of ominous fear swept over him. He must get out of here and find her. He must get the others out, too. Unless he did they were all finished. It wouldn't take Darvas long to build an open-and-shut case against them. He hated to give away his German connections, especially if the Hungarians already suspected them, but he had no choice. Ruefully he dialed Braun's number.

In a room at the end of the hall Lieutenant Darvas carefully wrote down the first number Andor dialed and gave the slip of paper to his sergeant, who immediately set to work to check the name of the subscriber. When there was no answer to the first call, Darvas' face lighted up. He knew there was nothing like frustration to make a man desperate, and a desperate man was always reckless. He waited. Horvath must be worried. By now he would be wondering how much of a chance to take. There was the clicking of another number being dialed. Darvas wrote the figures on a piece of paper and handed it to Sergeant Halasz. This time there was an answer. A thick German voice came on, the gruff voice of a man annoyed at being awakened in the middle of the night. Gradually it became calmer, even appeasing, as Andor explained what had happened.

"I will take care of it as early as possible in the morning. Don't worry. It will all be over soon," the voice promised.

When he heard Andor hang up, Darvas removed his earphones and turned to Sergeant Halasz.

"I checked the numbers," the sergeant said. "The first was his home. The second was Kurt Braun, a Wehrmacht agent."

Darvas rubbed his chin reflectively. "Put a tail on Braun right away."

"Yes, sir." Halasz picked up the telephone and gave the order to his men. Then he watched Darvas make notes on the conversation he had just heard. "What do you think it means, Lieutenant?"

"I'm not sure, but I intend to find out. We probably have only a few hours to work over Horvath and his bunch and try to get the truth out of them. Come on, let's go."

10

At 1 A.M. Sarah stopped knitting. She carefully wrapped the partially finished baby cap around the needles and put them in the workbasket beside her on the floor. Then she picked up a pair of white bootees and patted them flat, thinking how beautiful her child would look in the ensemble. She sighed contentedly, for the moment forgetting the frightening world outside. She laid the bootees in the basket, which she put in the deep drawer of the serving table, out of sight. Andor disliked signs of middle-class domesticity strewn about. Then she went to the bedroom to make herself ready for him. This ritual was the greatest pleasure of her day. It was an incomparable reward to see her desirability confirmed in his eyes as he looked at her. She glanced at her watch. He would be home soon.

She sat at her little white dressing table and with deft fingers quickly tinted and powdered her fair skin and rouged the curves of her small pink mouth. Then she brushed her fine hair until the honey-colored waves glistened under the lamplight. Satisfied with the vision she saw in her mirror, she went to her clothes closet, opened the door, and stood there, undecided which gown to wear. She chose the sleek-fitting rose damask. It wasn't her favorite, but Andor seemed unable to resist its charms.

She stood before the mirror on the closet door, moving one way and then another, scrutinizing her image. She passed her hands over her breasts and blushed. They were fuller now, the breasts of a woman, and that pleased her, though they were hardly abundant. The seams of the rose silk strained at the melon-sized bulge of her stomach. Reluctantly she took off the gown and hung it back in the closet, choosing instead a wide-skirted one of soft green voile. She knew that the reflected color made her eyes intriguingly catlike. She glanced at her watch again: a quarter to two. He would be home any minute now. To her ear lobes she applied a few drops of the rose-and-jasmine cologne her father had sent her, almost spilling it in her haste, then, taking a final look at her reflection in the mirror, moved a rebellious strand of pale hair into place and surveyed herself with satisfaction.

She turned off the light and went into the living room to wait, arranging herself carefully on the sofa. For a few minutes she watched the door eagerly. She glanced around the room, making certain that everything was in its proper place. There must be nothing to annoy him. The little Cézanne looked slightly askew. She got up and painstakingly moved it the infinitesimal part of an inch. Then she sat down again and waited. A cold feeling of uneasiness crept over her. She rebuked herself for being foolish. Maybe someone had come to his office needing help right away and he had been too busy to call her. Or maybe he and Arthur were talking and he had just forgotten how late it was. Didn't they often? She went to the bookcase and picked out a novel. For several minutes she read, then suddenly realized she had reread the last page three times. It was impossible just to sit and wait. She had to do something. Maybe Rachel was home. She might know what had happened. She tiptoed out into the hall and knocked on Rachel's door, loud enough, she hoped, for Rachel to hear but not so loud as to awaken the neighbors. There was no answer. She knocked again, a little louder, and waited. Still there was only silence. Disheartened, she went back to her own apartment. The dreadful fears she had choked back day after day began to overwhelm her. Perhaps the Hungarians had discovered the Committee's illegal office and had arrested Andor and all the rest of them. That would account for Rachel not being home either. Perhaps an unfavorable reply had come from Istanbul and the Germans had thrown them all into prison. She tried to put down the panic rising within her. Maybe Elizabeth Gruen knew something. She dialed the Gruens number, letting it ring eight or ten times before she replaced the receiver. "Elizabeth is probably at her father's house, since the boys are living there now," she told herself with a desperate reasonableness. But why wasn't Arthur at home?

Her hand trembled as she dialed Andor's office number. No one answered. She started to dial the number of the Parisette, then put down the receiver. He disliked being called at a public place. If he was there, he might be angry with her. Tears filled her eyes and dripped down onto the green gown, making spots of deep emerald over the bodice. Well, it didn't matter even if he was angry. She had to know that he was safe. Defiantly she dialed the Parisette number. It rang only once.

"Hello," said a masculine voice, in slurred syllables.

"Is this the Parisette?" Sarah asked, afraid she had the wrong number.

"Yes, it is, darling. What can I do for you?"

Sarah ignored the lecherous tone. "Do you know if Andor Horvath is there?"

There was a short silence. Then he asked, "Who?"

"Andor Horvath, *please*." She was becoming very nervous.

"Never heard of him, but—"

"Can I speak with Mr. Stern, the owner?"

There was another pause. Then the man came back on the phone. "I don't see him around. Look, darling, if your friend hasn't shown by now, you'd better give him up. Why don't you come here and join me? Or, better yet, I'll come and join you. You sound very charming, like a blonde. Are you a blonde?"

She banged down the receiver and ran into the bedroom, pulling off her gown as she went. From the closet she seized a dress, not caring which one. She pulled it hastily over her head, grabbed her purse from the dresser, took her coat off the rack just inside the front door, and rushed out of the apartment. He must be at the café. He had to be.

When she stepped out of the building onto the sidewalk the utter darkness almost made her turn back. Since the start of Allied bombings the blackout was being rigorously enforced. The only light came from the moon, which, she saw gratefully, was bright tonight. For perhaps a half minute she stood still, letting her eyes become adjusted to the dark. The streets were watery from a rainstorm that had ended only an hour before. She noticed that where the moonlight fell on the pavement its brightness was reflected in the gleaming wetness, making a fair path to guide her. Still, the silent blackness that was everywhere else seemed treacherous and her heart was faint as she put one foot before the other, telling herself over and over that she had only to go six blocks in a straight line and she would be at the café. As she walked, the outlines of the buildings and doorways and trees became clearer, and the tenseness that had all but paralyzed her began to abate. At the third intersection she stepped off the curb into a stream of moonlight that flooded the street. Ahead, two policemen watched her curiously, then started toward her. When she saw them she was panic-stricken. Though they were in the shadows, she knew they were men, for she could see dimly the separation of their trousers. She also knew they were in uniform because of the outline of their capes. She turned hastily and started to flee back toward the apartment. She looked around once. They were running after her. Now she could see that they were Hungarian police. Their swords swayed and hit their legs as they ran. Hysterical at the very thought of being caught by them, she tried to run faster. Perspiration was pouring in rivulets all over her body. Her damp hair clung to her wet face. Several strands had fallen over her eyes, making it difficult to see where she was going. The soles of her shoes slipped perilously on the wet sidewalk. She could hear the policemen's heels against the pavement coming closer. Without slowing her pace she turned to look over her shoulder again. At this instant she came to a street crossing, and as she stepped from the curb onto the road she lost her footing and plunged forward. She screamed in terror as she sprawled full length on the cobblestones. A searing pain ripped through her belly. Then everything was black.

The policemen stood over her, but she didn't move.

"Perhaps she hit her head," one of them said, bending down and cradling her head and shoulders in his arm so he could see. "There doesn't seem to be any injury," he added after a closer look.

"Let's see who she is," the other said, taking her purse. "Maybe that will tell us why she's prowling the streets at this hour." He walked into the shadowy hallway of the nearest building and lit a match to examine the contents of the purse while his partner tried to bring Sarah back to consciousness. He was still bending over her when the first officer returned, holding the purse in his hand. "A Jewess," he said, "and she lives in the big apartment house on Váci utca."

"Should we take her to the Jewish Hospital? I can't seem to bring her around."

"No. Why should we bother? We can take her home in a minute." He looked down at the small still heap. "What do you suppose she was doing out here, anyway?"

"Who knows? Maybe with the new laws against Jews and everything she went a little crazy. They're like that—cowards except when it comes to swindling you out of your money."

Sarah started to moan and move her arms. Then she was quiet again.

"Let's get her off the street," the first policeman said.

The other picked her up easily and carried her toward the apartment, followed by his partner, still holding the purse. "She's certainly skinny for a grown woman," he said scornfully, feeling the thinness of her thighs against his arm.

Early the next morning Obersturmbannführer Walter Heinemann, having received a telephone call from Kurt Braun, went immediately to the apartment of Colonel Wedemeyer and told him of the arrests. The thin blond colonel, propped up against the pillows in an immense carved and gilded bed, looked apprehensive. "The damn Hungarians," he muttered. "Demand that the prisoners be transferred to our custody at once and don't, for any reason, accept a refusal." He pounded the rumpled bedding with his fist to emphasize his order. "We can't afford to leave these Jews in a Hungarian prison. If Istanbul hears about it, it will be very embarrassing. Besides, Jews have no backbone. They're all a bunch of jellyfish. They'll talk if the Hungarians get rough with them, and we can't allow the secret of our negotiations with them to become known. The Hungarians might become very intractable."

Two hours later Andor and his colleagues were at Wedemeyer's office in the Majestic. After assuring the colonel that they had told the Hungarians nothing, they were freed, disheveled and with a few sore limbs, souvenirs of their night with the Hungarian police.

Outside the hotel they separated, Arthur and Joe getting on one bus and Rachel and Andor on another. Rachel, exhausted, put her head on Andor's shoulder and was asleep in an instant, but he remained awake, impatiently looking out the window as they came closer to home, anxious about Sarah. They left the bus a block from Váci utca and walked hurriedly to the apartment house. As they entered the building, Mrs. Herczog, who operated the pastry shop across the street, was just coming down the stairs. They said good morning to her and she returned their greeting, but she looked at them a little strangely. Just then the concierge's door opened, and an untidy gray head emerged.

"Ah, Mr. Horvath, I'm so glad you're home," the wife of the concierge began, stopping as she saw Mrs. Herczog standing near the outer door, gazing curiously at them. "Good morning, Mrs. Herczog," she said brusquely. "You're late this morning, aren't you?"

An expression of disdain on her face, Mrs. Herczog turned and left without replying.

Andor grabbed the flabby arm of the concierge's wife. "What's happened? Is my wife ill?"

"Come inside," she said, opening the door wider to admit them. Then she explained that two policemen had brought Mrs. Horvath home about three-thirty. She was unconscious. She had been hurt, but the doctor was upstairs with her now. He had been for some time.

Without a word Andor raced up the stairs and into his apartment, with Rachel following. Dr. Hecht was sitting on the sofa in the living room, staring at the wall in front of him. He rose as the two came in.

"Is she all right? I want to see her." Andor started to brush past the doctor, but the old man put a restraining hand on his shoulder. In his eyes Andor read the awful, irrevocable answer.

"When?" he whispered.

"Just a few minutes ago."

Andor buried his face in his hands.

"I'm sorry, Andor. I couldn't do anything for her. The injury was too severe."

"Injury?" He was bewildered. "What happened?" he cried in anguish.

"I'm not sure." The doctor repeated what the policemen had said. "She must have been very frightened," he added. "Anyway—"

"But why was she outside at that hour?"

The doctor hesitated, obviously undecided whether to say more. Andor grabbed the lapels of his suit. "If you know you must tell me!"

Rachel, on a hassock in the far corner of the room, watched them, unable to hold back her tears.

Dr. Hecht released himself gently and said, "Sit down, Andor," at the same time seating himself on the sofa again. "Sarah wasn't conscious all the time, so not everything she said made sense."

"But why did she go out? She was so afraid of the dark, and she was so afraid of the police."

The doctor hesitated again.

"Please . . ."

"She said she was going to the Parisette."

"The Parisette!"

"I had the impression she tried to go there to find you." His voice was barely audible as he said it.

Andor covered his face with his hands. Then he got up and turned his back to the doctor. "I want to see her alone," he said, and walked into the bedroom, closing the door behind him.

She was completely covered by the sheet. He lowered it slowly and looked down at her. The cold northlight fell across her face. He gasped as he saw the signs of her suffering written so plainly on her countenance and dropped to his knees beside the bed. With his hand he smoothed her forehead and stroked the silky pale brown strands of hair that spilled over the pillow, as if with that loving gesture the agony on the little face would disappear. For several moments he continued to do this, and gradually she became again for him the wide-eyed girl, hardly more than a child, who had come to him a virgin, innocent, sweet, and adoring. Two large tears fell from his eyes. He was overcome with his own guilt and his own grief. He took the delicate ivory hand and held it gently, kissing each slender finger, then laid his head upon the sheet and pressed her to him. He remained for a long time like this, murmuring soft words as he held her.

11

Late one morning at the beginning of June, as Andor was leaving the apartment, the concierge brought him a cable. With trembling hands he opened it and read the message. A preliminary agreement had been worked out. It was signed by the head of the Jewish Agency in Istanbul. There was no mention of Gábor.

Well, he told himself, it was better than nothing. It might enable him to stall Wedemeyer for a while. But he was confused and angry about the silence from Erno. It was almost three weeks since he had left. Surely Erno knew from the cable he had sent to Istanbul that Wedemeyer had accelerated the deportations. What in hell was he doing?

He read the message again, trying to regain his calm, then telephoned the others to tell them the news. After that he drove to the Majestic and asked to see Wedemeyer. He was aware that German espionage agents had probably made copies of the cable and that Wedemeyer undoubtedly had seen it already, but there were certain unstated rules in this game they were playing, and it would be stupid to ignore them. So when he was admitted to Wedemeyer's presence he eagerly offered the cable to the colonel, asking, "Have you heard the good news, Herr Obersturmbannführer?"

After Wedemeyer had read the message, Andor said brightly, "It means things are progressing satisfactorily. It should be only a short time before we receive the text of the provisional agreement." Without giving Wedemeyer a chance to reply he rushed on, "In view of this promising situation, I ask you once more to halt the deportations."

Wedemeyer shook his head even before the last words were out. "There is no question of it. The deportations will continue without pause."

"But it will mean stopping them only for a little while," Andor pleaded, pointing to the cable Wedemeyer still held in his hand.

120

The colonel dropped it onto his desk disdainfully. "Anyone can send a cable. It means nothing."

"Then there is nothing more to say. Good day, Colonel." Infuriated and overwhelmed with disappointment, Andor strode out of the office and down the hall to Heinemann's quarters. There he recounted the interview to Wedemeyer's deputy and added, "Colonel Wedemeyer has kept none of his promises. Apparently neither reason nor pleading will change his mind. Therefore I feel obliged to tell Istanbul that I think there is no point in continuing the negotiations."

Heinemann's stolid countenance betrayed no alarm as he listened. Despite Andor's threat he was sure that the Jew had come to him precisely because he was still looking for a way to continue the negotiations. So he said blandly, "Wedemeyer is in a bad mood today. I'll talk to him later and get in touch with you."

With that promise Andor left.

The next day Heinemann's aide telephoned to say that there would be a meeting in Colonel Wedemeyer's office at 2 P.M. and Herr Horvath was requested to attend.

Promptly at two o'clock he was led into Wedemeyer's office. Already there, seated on Wedemeyer's left, were Heinemann and Klaussen. On the other side were a handsome colonel and a sallow-faced young captain. Andor had never seen either of them before. No introductions were made, so he merely nodded, first to Klaussen and Heinemann and then to the two strangers. Wedemeyer, his usually pale face flushed, was obviously in a rage. "You may sit down, Horvath!" he bellowed.

Andor sat opposite him, silent. It was wiser to wait until Wedemeyer's temper had cooled before speaking, he told himself. He knew the outcome of this meeting was crucial. If Wedemeyer couldn't be persuaded to stop the deportations, everything was lost. All the money they had already paid the Germans would have been for nothing. Hungarian Jewry, and whoever else found out about it, would brand the Budapest Rescue Committee a pack of crazy men. Perhaps even traitors.

Wedemeyer launched into a lengthy exposition of his activities as Commissioner for Jewish Affairs in Austria and Czechoslovakia. At one point he leaned across the desk and said to Andor, "Once I had a great deal of sympathy for Zionism. I was convinced that a homeland was the proper solution of the Jewish problem." But this sympathy had been destroyed by the Jews themselves, he added. As for the deportations, it was impossible to stop them or even provisionally to suspend them. He would not be dictated to by Jews. They would do well to realize that his patience had limits. With that warning he abruptly asked Andor, "Exactly what do you want from me?"

"I want a guarantee that our agreements will be respected," Andor said quietly. "You promised that our people marked for deportation would be sent to Austria and kept there in safety during the negotiations. You haven't kept this promise. You're sending them to extermination centers."

"It is you and your people who have failed to keep your promises. Gábor was supposed to be back here in two weeks. Why hasn't he returned? Can you tell me that? I said that if he did not return within the agreed time the deportations would continue. I keep my word. They continue."

Andor stood up. "Under those conditions I see no point in carrying on this conversation."

Wedemeyer was stunned by this "insolence," but he recovered quickly. A mock solicitous expression came over his face. "Your nerves are overworked, Horvath. I think I will send you to Auschwitz for a little convalescence."

"That wouldn't help you," Andor snapped. "There would be no one to negotiate in my place."

Wedemeyer sprang to his feet, furious. "Try to understand me, Horvath," he shouted. "I must dispose of the Jewish garbage that has been contaminating the Hungarian provinces. No argument and no complaint will make me change my mind." He paused, then continued in a somewhat calmer voice, "If you really believe that the text of the agreement will arrive soon, why all this fuss about the few Jews who will be deported in the meantime?"

"Every Jewish life is important to me. But aside from that, it isn't only these few, as you call them, who are involved. Developments in Istanbul are not taking place faster because you are intensifying the deportations. If you want our Agency to take your offer seriously, you must give them some evidence that it is being made in good faith."

The German officers sitting on either side of Wedemeyer listened to the discussion in impassive silence. Wedemeyer's mood changed several times. Twice it seemed as if he might be on the verge of giving in, then in a new fit of temper he would bang the desk and say that he refused to hear any more argument.

Suddenly his eyes lit up. "Horvath, I will make you a proposition. I will give you a chance to save a thousand Jews, if you have that many with certificates for Palestine."

It was an announcement that caught Andor completely unprepared, but he tried to hide his pleasure as he said quickly, "I accept the proposition. We could send them to Palestine by way of Rumania, then by ship from Constanta down the Black Sea, through the Dardanelles, and finally to Haifa."

Wedemeyer held up his hand. "Not so fast. The Grand Mufti of Jerusalem is an ally of the Third Reich. I can hardly afford to offend him by sending a thousand Jews into his part of the world. Besides, right here in Hungary I must avoid playing the role of a Jew-saver. I promised Endre that not a single Jew would remain alive in Hungary. However, there is a way around that."

He sat in his chair with his head tilted back, the fingers of his left hand lightly touching the fingers of his right hand. After several seconds of contemplation he turned to the aristocratic captain on his left. "Klaussen, you will tell Police Colonel Ferenczy that we have discovered a country-wide Zionist plot. Tell him that we plan to isolate these plotters from the rest of the Jews as fast as we can catch them. When they are all rounded up, we will deport them as a group. We must make this look like a special deportation to Ferenczy and the other Hungarians."

Andor listened carefully to the plan. The idea of an escape disguised as a deportation didn't appeal to him, but there was no sense in spoiling a chance to save even as few as a thousand Jews.

"If they won't be permitted to go through Rumania," he asked, "how do you propose shipping them to Palestine?"

"I said nothing about shipping them to Palestine!" Wedemeyer roared. "I shall transport them to Germany and put them in one of the camps at Bergen-Belsen."

"Bergen-Belsen!" Andor repeated in a shocked whisper.

"I must send them there so it will look like a real deportation. But after several weeks they can leave for Lisbon via France and Spain. From Lisbon they can embark for West Africa. However, all that is up to you. What happens to them after they leave Bergen-Belsen is your problem and no concern of mine."

Of course it was an insane plan. Andor realized that. But wasn't insanity the order of the day? Was there any better alternative? While he was gambling on trying to save vast numbers, he might as well make sure of saving a thousand. The man across the table, who sat there waiting for his answer, had the power of life or death over all of them.

"All right, I accept your offer," he said crisply. Then he had a brilliant thought. "You mention the figure of a thousand. It so happens that there

123

are fifteen hundred of our people who have British immigration certificates for Palestine. If it's a big Zionist plot, surely as many as fifteen hundred would be involved."

It was a bold lie. The number of Hungarian Jews with British certificates was very small. Perhaps a few hundred at the most.

The colonel slapped the desk impatiently. "Fifteen hundred then. But let that be the end of it." A crafty smile crept across his face. "Actually the greater the number of your people I sell you, the better it will please Colonel Weber." For the first time he turned to the blond officer on his right. Then he turned back to Andor. "You will, of course, pay for these fifteen hundred Jews at the rate fixed in our original agreement, one motor truck for each one hundred men, women, or children."

"But I can't possibly produce trucks until the negotiations in Istanbul have been concluded," Andor said, adding, without knowing at all how he would get the money, "However, we are prepared to pay the monetary equivalent, that is, one hundred dollars per person."

Wedemeyer dismissed the suggestion with a peremptory wave of his hand. "I made it very plain to you, Horvath, that we do not need money. We want goods."

"Be reasonable, Herr Obersturmbannführer . . ."

But Wedemeyer ignored him as Colonel Weber leaned over and whispered in his ear. After a short conversation Wedemeyer sat back in his chair and addressed Andor again. "Colonel Franz Weber is head of the SS Economic Division. He is the man to whom you will make your payments," motioning for Weber to take up the conversation.

Andor looked intently at the handsome colonel. He had an inkling that this man was going to play an important role in the Committee's future business with the Germans, so it was important to know where his strength and weakness lay. He had a pleasant face, with none of the hard lines that Wedemeyer's had. He seemed much more like a successful businessman than a professional army officer. When he spoke his voice was matter-of-fact, neither cruel nor ingratiating.

"Horvath, for a payment of two thousand dollars per head we will permit your fifteen hundred Jews to go."

Andor looked astonished. "But that is twenty times the agreed price!" he cried in an aggrieved voice.

Wedemeyer, apparently surprised by the intensity of this outburst and not wishing to jeopardize the new deal, said hastily, "Well now, Colonel Weber, perhaps we could compromise at a thousand?"

With apparent reluctance Weber agreed but added firmly, "It is understood, Horvath, that you will pay one third immediately and the rest before the rescue train leaves Budapest."

Andor shook his head. "If we pay the entire sum before the fifteen hundred people leave, how do we know that they will ever get out of the Reich alive? I suggest, instead, that we pay the last two thirds into a bank in a neutral country, say Switzerland, the money to be released to you as soon as the rescue train reaches Lisbon."

Wedemeyer leaned over his desk and looked at Andor coldly. "Horvath, for a man in such a spot you are a hard bargainer. But that's a Jewish trait." He leaned back as he uttered the last sentence, talking more to his associates than to the man before him. Then he bent forward again. "All right, I'll agree to that, but no member of your Committee will be permitted to leave on the train. After all, we must have some assurance that you will pay the last two thirds."

Andor nodded his assent, then said, "But we must have one guarantee: that the people on the train will be moved in unsealed cars and that they will be permitted to take luggage with them."

"I will order the cars left unsealed, but I cannot give you an unrestricted luggage allowance," Wedemeyer replied irritably. "I told you this must have the appearance of a deportation, not a pleasure trip." Then he concluded the conference by telling Andor to draw up the list of fifteen hundred names as promptly as possible. When he received it, he, Wedemeyer, would order the people rounded up for shipment to Bergen-Belsen. "I assume you will be choosing some from the provinces, so we will bring those from outside the capital here to Budapest. After all, we cannot have the rescue train traveling around the country. But while they are waiting here, it will be up to you to feed and shelter them."

With more assurance than he felt, Andor said his people would take care of this matter. At the moment he had not a single idea how fifteen hundred men, women, and children could be housed and fed by the Jews of Budapest, so many of whom were already in need themselves. More important, he had no way of knowing whether Wedemeyer really intended keeping his promise this time. But he was happy as he left the Majestic. He was playing a reckless gambling game against an astute and professional opponent. The stakes were lives. In the past hour he had won, by playing his cards cleverly, at least the promise of fifteen hundred.

Outside the hotel, squatting on the sidewalk against the stone wall of the building, a gypsy girl hailed him. She was sitting in the center of a great mass of cut flowers in tin cans. Andor was impressed by her mass of jet black hair, her immense gold earrings, and her bronze breasts, almost completely exposed by the décolletage of her blouse. Her smile was almost a leer. "Flowers, mister?" Andor tossed her a ten-pengö piece, took one white daisy from a bouquet, put it into his buttonhole, broke the stem off short, waved aside the change, and went down the street, whistling.

That night the Committee met in the Horvath apartment. Andor had changed nothing in the apartment since Sarah's death, but the absence of a woman was obvious to the other three members the moment they entered. The neatness and order Andor had always wanted in his home were gone. There was a necktie over the back of a chair, a pair of shoes on the floor in a far corner of the room, and newspapers scattered about.

They took their places around the living-room table, as they had always done, and while they talked they smoked or drank *barack* from small glasses, as usual, but they missed Sarah's quiet presence.

When Andor told them of Wedemeyer's rescue offer, their reactions were mixed. Arthur slapped him on the back, then took his hand and pumped it vigorously. "Andor, you're a genius. It's wonderful! Imagine that Nazi butcher making such a concession."

Rachel was less enthusiastic. "Andor," she said, "there will be many problems."

Joe was suspicious and scornful. "I have a lot of questions," he said bluntly.

With a gesture of resignation Andor signaled him to go on.

"I was in favor of sending Erno to Istanbul on Wedemeyer's promise that he would release a hundred thousand of our people and close up Auschwitz. But the son of a bitch has broken his word to us on both counts. Why should we make any more deals with him? I think—"

"You're talking the way I do when I argue with the Germans," Andor interrupted. "It's all right to try to confuse *them*. That's part of my technique. But let's think clearly ourselves. Actually Wedemeyer said he would deliver a hundred thousand Jews to us and close Auschwitz after we brought him a concrete proposition from Istanbul. We have received nothing to date from Istanbul except that vague cable. Therefore Wedemeyer has broken no promise."

Joe's eyes flashed angrily. "I didn't think I'd ever sit here and listen to you making excuses for the goddamn Nazis!"

"I'm not making excuses. I'm trying to reason objectively."

Joe took a new tack. "Do you still trust those bastards?"

"Of course not. But whom are we to trust? The British and the Americans? What have they done to help? The Nazis are *exterminating* us. That's a hard word to say, but we've got to face reality. We are being exterminated, and the rest of the world seems to be swept by a great, overwhelming indifference. So we've got to look out for ourselves. No one else even cares. Maybe not even our own people abroad. Consider what wonderful co-operation we've had from Istanbul!"

"He's right," Rachel said grimly.

Andor bent across the table and waved his cigarette in Joe's face. "If we deal with the Germans, maybe we can reduce the daily deaths of our people by a half, a quarter, a tenth. I don't know how much. Maybe we can save no more than the fifteen hundred. But do I have the right to say no to any proposition that comes up? If the devil himself offered me fifteen hundred people in return for my soul, I'd bargain with him."

Joe returned to the attack. "All right, and if it works, how can you possibly persuade fifteen hundred frightened people voluntarily to board a train they know is going to Bergen-Belsen, a German concentration camp? They won't do it. Maybe *you* are willing to take the word of the SS, but can you persuade fifteen hundred other people to have such faith in them?"

Andor drew a long puff on his cigarette. "Yes, I think I can handle that part of the problem without much trouble."

But Joe wouldn't be convinced. "How can you possibly pick fifteen hundred Hungarian Jews to be saved out of eight hundred thousand? That's less than a quarter of one per cent!"

"What's the alternative? To save no one?"

Joe shrugged and lapsed into silence.

"Let's get on with it," Arthur said impatiently. "Who are we going to pick?"

"I think Andor should make up the list," Rachel said quietly.

"But all of us should discuss what categories of people are to go," Arthur insisted.

"Even the great Solomon never had such an awful decision to make," Joe grunted. "We're putting Andor—or he's putting himself—in the position of that Nazi officer who stands at the crossroads in Auschwitz, so I hear, and tells some Jews to go left, some to go right; some to the gas chambers, some to labor camps. I'm glad my name isn't Horvath."

Andor looked at him quickly. Joe smiled and touched his forehead in a mock salute.

"If we are going to help Wedemeyer in his pretense that these people are Zionist plotters," Arthur suggested, "then we should pick people who have devoted their lives to working for a revival of Eretz Israel."

Andor agreed and made a notation on a sheet of paper.

"I think," Rachel said, "that preference should be given also to women whose husbands have been taken away to forced labor camps, and to children, especially orphans."

Andor nodded and made another notation.

There was a quarter of an hour of talk about the list, and then they turned to the second urgent matter on the agenda, the problem of finding a place to house the hundreds of people who would be brought to Budapest from the provinces.

Arthur spread his hands out in a hopeless gesture. "First they confiscate all the real estate owned by Jews, then they give us a problem like this!"

"Be constructive, Arthur, think!"

They sat around the table for several moments obeying Andor's order, until Rachel suddenly said, "I have it! The Jewish school for the deaf and dumb on Columbus utca. It's been closed for a long time. The buildings are so old no one wants them. But with a little work they can be made suitable for at least a thousand people, if they don't have to stay there too long."

"A fine idea," Andor said, reaching over and patting her hand. "I appoint you and Joe as the housing committee. You'd better start right away putting the buildings in shape." He paused as he lit a fresh cigarette, then added, "And in your spare time, Rachel, you'd better get someone to help you forge at least fifteen hundred British immigration certificates for Palestine. It's too bad we've lost Chaim Szind. I don't think Wedemeyer will demand to see the certificates, but we'd better have them ready, just in case."

As Andor filled their glasses with *barack,* Arthur, with a timidity not customary, said to him, "I hate to put a damper on all this constructive talk, but I'm a businessman, and I'd like to know how we're going to pay those crooks in the Majestic the one thousand dollars per head you promised them. That comes to a million and a half dollars. Where do you imagine you are going to find a million and a half dollars? Growing on a tree over on Margaret Island?"

Andor smiled. "Let's go slow, Arthur. First, our immediate problem is to raise only one third of the amount. That's half a million dollars."

"All right, and where do you get that first half million dollars?"

Andor rubbed the palms of his hands together, a look of self satisfaction on his face. "I think I'm going to sell places on the train."

The other three stared at him in amazement.

"You don't make any sense, Andor," Arthur objected. "We've already agreed that most of the passengers will be Zionists—old-time Zionist workers, plus some women and children. These people won't have money. Not that kind of money."

"I don't intend to get money from them. I have another idea. To-morrow I'm going to call on Hugo Mayer. Perhaps there are some rich members of the Orthodox congregation who aren't averse to being saved."

At Mayer's office the next morning Andor explained about the rescue train. The elegant leader of the Orthodox community was startled, but he didn't appear as antagonistic to the idea as Andor had thought he might be.

"Why have you come to me?" he asked as his visitor finished.

"To offer you a hundred places on the train at five thousand dollars each."

"Why, that's half a million dollars!" Mayer gasped.

"Exactly. This is the down payment Wedemeyer requires."

"But why should all the money be extracted from my community?"

"If I may quote Karl Marx, Mr. Mayer: 'From each according to his ability to pay.' Your people are the only Jews in Budapest with this kind of money. If I have to pass a hat for pengö I'll be from now until doomsday collecting the equivalent of a hundred dollars."

As Mayer hesitated, Andor urged, "If you'll undertake to sell these one hundred places to people able to pay, I'll let you choose twenty others to board the train without payment."

Mayer stroked his long thin nose reflectively. His mouth was pursed. Finally he said, "No, I couldn't possibly sit as a judge and pick just twenty people. What's twenty people? Why do you give me so few? It's not fair. You know very well that the Orthodox community numbers more than ten per cent of the total. Therefore, in all justice, we should have at least ten per cent or a hundred and fifty places, not twenty."

"I am offering you a hundred and twenty, not twenty. Twenty free, one hundred to be paid for," replied Andor patiently.

Mayer was unimpressed.

Andor decided that unless he used larger bait he might make no catch at all, so he said, "Mr. Mayer, I want to be very fair, and I want your co-operation, so I will make a large concession. You sell the hundred places at five thousand dollars each, in cash, and I will give you not twenty places but an extra fifty, free, plus ten places for members of your own family. These will not be counted in the quota."

Mayer replied quietly, "Of course you know that I won't go on the train myself. The Germans have made me agree to make no attempt to leave the country. If I do, they say there will be reprisals against our people. However, I am happy for the opportunity to save ten members of my family. But it will be an agonizing task to select the ten." He paused, as if already making the list mentally, then continued, "I don't envy you, Horvath. You have a much greater problem of selection. I only hope you choose wisely. You are aware, of course, that those you omit from your list you may be condemning to death."

Andor left the office annoyed by Mayer's last remark, and also by the fact that not once had Mayer congratulated him for making the deal. But there would be time to enjoy recognition later. What was important now was that Mayer had agreed to act as the salesman for the one hundred paid places.

During the next few days Andor spent almost all his waking hours working on the list. He went without sleep and skipped many meals as he added name after name, first from provincial towns and then from Budapest. Subtracting the places he had promised Mayer, he had 1340 places left. When he finally completed his list and made a count, he found he was more than a hundred names over the quota. The problem of elimination was much more difficult than the problem of selection had been. He tried not to think that when he drew his pencil through a name it might mean he was condemning that person to death, as Mayer had said. He kept telling himself that this was a sentimental way of looking at it—a negative attitude, quite contrary to his usual manner of thinking. Instead he must have the positive feeling that every name on the list meant a life saved.

That same week Joe and Rachel began to prepare the Columbus utca buildings. They hired carpenters, bricklayers, glazers, and other workmen who repaired both the interior and exterior and constructed several flimsy new barracks. They had the entire place disinfected and cleaned. Many beds had to be installed in tiers so there would be accommodations enough for fifteen hundred people. A central kitchen and a mess hall were created on the main floor. A high fence was erected around the entire camp.

Eight days after their previous conversation, Andor met with Hugo Mayer again.

"I have been very successful," the lawyer announced after he had locked the door of his private office. "Here is your first list." He handed Andor five sheets of legal-size paper, stapled together. "Those are the names of the one hundred passengers. You'll notice at the top twelve members of Emmanuel Simon's family. They are his sons, his daughters, and his grandchildren. He has paid us more than anyone else: sixty thousand dollars. As soon as I had him signed up, I had no trouble getting the rest, except that many of them, of course, didn't have dollars. As you must know, it is almost impossible to buy dollars on the black bourse any more, so I had to accept whatever kinds of money people had. Without a doubt I have collected the oddest assortment of coins and bank notes anyone ever saw outside a numismatist's shop." He laughed shortly.

Andor smiled. "I trust that the pengö and all the foreign money were figured into dollars at the prevailing black-bourse rate."

"Naturally. I didn't presume that your German friends—I mean the German officials with whom you are negotiating—would accept any other rate." He pointed to two suitcases beside his desk. "It's all in there. You will find them rather heavy, because some people paid in actual gold, and then there were a few who desperately wanted to go on your train but had no money of any kind. They paid with jewelry. Attached to each article you will find an assayer's tag, giving the weight of the gold and an estimate of the value of each jewel. We have tried to be systematic enough to please the Germans. I will have my servant accompany you to your apartment and carry the suitcases for you. I'm sure you don't want to let them out of your sight. Half a million dollars is not easy to come by these days."

Andor thanked him and was starting for the door when the attorney stopped him.

"Perhaps it isn't of great importance to you, but here are two other lists you must have. The first is the list of the fifty members of the Ortho-dox community whom we have picked, after careful consideration, for free passage, in accordance with your agreement. I say 'we' because I wish you to know that I raised the half million dollars much more quickly and easily than I compiled this list, even though I enlisted the assistance of at least a dozen leaders of the Orthodox community to help me in making the selections."

Mayer then handed him another piece of paper. "These are the ten members of my own family. When they go, everything in life that is important to me goes. And if your German contacts harm a single hair of their heads—" He turned on his heel without finishing the sentence and left the room. A moment later his servant appeared and followed Andor down the stairs, carrying the two heavy suitcases.

Andor spent that evening and most of the night making a final revision of his own list and adding Mayer's names to it. It was getting light when he went to bed for a few hours' sleep. This was one of the few times in his life he was nervous. He had locked the two suitcases in the hall closet, but until they were delivered and he had a receipt for them, he would be uneasy.

At 10 A.M. he took a taxi to the Majestic. The guards at the entrance knew him well by now, but they looked suspiciously at two suitcases that could make even so robust a man sag under their weight.

Colonel Weber greeted him pleasantly. Andor tried not to show his apprehension over presenting the odd assortment of wealth. He put the two suitcases on the large flat-topped desk. Mayer had closed them with sealing wax. Curious as Andor had been, he hadn't opened them. Weber broke the seals and lifted the two lids. Both men stood staring at the glittering contents. There were piles of bank notes neatly tied in bundles, several small bars of gold, a box of gold coins, and a large assortment of jewelry: tiaras, rings, brooches, necklaces; articles of gold, strings of pearls, diamonds, and sapphires. Weber assumed a nonchalance obviously designed to camouflage his astonishment.

"We shall have it counted and appraised, Horvath," he said. "If it comes to the correct amount, we shall accept it as your first payment. I will have my secretary give you a receipt for two suitcases. We shall say on the receipt, 'Value *approximately* five hundred thousand dollars.'"

From Weber's office Andor went down the hall to see Wedemeyer. The colonel was in a better than usual mood and had him admitted at once.

"I have kept my word, Herr Obersturmbannführer, and delivered to Colonel Weber the half million dollars," Andor announced. "Also we have barracks on Columbus utca ready to receive the people of the transport, and here is the list of the fifteen hundred we have chosen to go." He handed Wedemeyer a folder of neatly typed names and addresses.

"Good," the colonel replied. "But prepare accommodations for an extra one hundred, because we have one hundred Jews of our own choosing who will also go on the train."

Andor wanted to ask who they were and why the Germans were interested in saving them, but after a second's hesitation he decided to wait and find out later, in his own way.

"I will turn this list over to Captain Klaussen," Wedemeyer said, "and he will start getting your people rounded up and delivered to Columbus utca. Now let's see . . . Today is June the eleventh. I think we shall have the train start for Bergen-Belsen on the twentieth."

Andor nodded his agreement, then said, "While our people are waiting at Columbus utca, it is to your interests as well as ours that the Hungarian authorities not bother them. Therefore may I suggest that an SS guard be placed around the camp to prevent anyone entering, even Hungarian officials?"

Wedemeyer's reply was to order Klaussen to have a half dozen SS men assigned to guard duty there at once.

That night Andor worked with no sleep at all composing a letter to be sent to each of the fifteen hundred chosen to be rescued. He had two worries: either the people chosen would be afraid to go, as Joe had said, or, even worse, they would be so confident they would survive, while those left behind would die, that they would try to take along with them relatives and friends. The letter must cover both points.

He began by announcing that this was an official communication of the Budapest Rescue Committee. (This would quiet the fears of most of them, for most of them knew about the Committee.) He said the recipient had been chosen because of the special conditions of his case. (This was vague, but it had to be, to cover orphans, Zionists, women with men in labor camps, and even Mayer's Orthodox people.) It would be dangerous for everyone concerned, if the recipient showed this letter to anyone else. (Andor knew human nature in general and his own people in particular well enough to realize that this order wouldn't be universally honored, but some, anyway, would probably obey it.) If any discussion was necessary, if there were any questions, the recipient was to consult ————. (Here a blank was left, to be filled in by Andor's secretary in ink, with the name of the one person in each town whom Andor was putting in charge.) The recipient had been selected by the Rescue Committee for passage on a train that would soon leave Budapest for abroad. (He purposely made no mention of Bergen-Belsen. That would have had the very effect Joe predicted. Also, he omitted mentioning that the ultimate destination was Palestine, knowing that Wedemeyer would not approve of putting this in a letter.) All passengers for the train would be assembled in Budapest. They would be called for in a few days by SS squads. This was necessary for their own protection, and they were not to be alarmed. (He did not dare say that the SS would protect them from Hungarian interference.) They could bring one large suitcase apiece containing anything they wished, but some food should be included. Bedding would be provided at the Budapest reception center. Because it was impossible to add any other names to the list, the recipient was asked not to discuss additional names except with the person mentioned above. If the recipient was not in possession of a British immigration certificate, he could obtain his certificate from the person named above.

Andor finished the final draft of the letter just as his secretary, Zipora, appeared for work. While she was making a stencil, he began to compose letters to the twenty men he had chosen to direct the operation in the twenty provincial towns and cities from which the people of the transport would be coming. Each had to be a personal letter, because he could take some into his confidence more than others. A few—men like Leo Strauss, in his home town of Pécs—had been close friends since boyhood. Others were rabbis who, he hoped, could control the people of the community better than anyone else.

In the letters he emphasized the need of avoiding panic on the part of people who might refuse to go, or people not on the list who insisted on going. With each of the twenty letters he enclosed the proper number of British certificates, without mentioning the fact that they had been forged by other members of his Committee. He authorized each of the men to substitute the names of worthy people to take the places of any men, women, or children who refused to go, or whose departure was made impossible because of sickness, death, or previous transportation to a deportation center. But such substitute names must be transmitted at once to Budapest, so the Committee could give them to the SS authorities in charge of the roundup. In the letters he said the best argument the twenty local leaders could give, if their people were afraid to go, was that while officers of the Jewish Council of Budapest and members of the Budapest Rescue Committee were forbidden by the Germans to leave the country, the transport would include many members of their families, and this surely was proof of the confidence the Council and the Committee had in the plan.

While his secretary was transcribing the twenty letters, Andor went to the Majestic and obtained the necessary permits so three messengers could go to three different regions of Hungary delivering them. He argued that it was to the Germans' interest that there be as little confusion as possible, in order not to arouse the suspicions of Hungarian espionage agents, and the Germans readily agreed. He also asked for and obtained their agreement that the roundup would not commence for another week, in order to give him time to make any necessary revisions in the list, due to death or—he smiled wryly as he said it—"to enforced absence, for whatsoever cause."

Before he left the Majestic, Andor learned that the Hungarian authorities had already been informed of "the extensive Zionist plot" the SS had uncovered and that a Hungarian officer would probably accompany the SS men as they collected the people on Andor's list.

In Nagybathely, in the west of the country, a Hungarian and two SS officers came to the large white house of Jesse Vogeler, a young Orthodox rabbi, now jammed with members of his congregation, living like rabbits in a hutch because their own houses and apartments had been commandeered and local authorities had made no provision for their rehousing. Reading from a list he held in his hand, an SS lieutenant called out ten names.

"Those present will come forward," he ordered. Four men and three women separated themselves from the frightened crowd and pushed their way to his side. He asked them to identify themselves, and as each did he made a check mark after the name on his list. Then, louder than before, he said, "Rabbi Jesse Vogeler, wife, and child." He paused. There was silence. "Where is Rabbi Vogeler?"

The eyes of most of the people who swarmed the hallway and a staircase leading to the floor above turned in the direction of a slim, black-bearded man standing in a far corner. The SS lieutenant followed their glances and shouted, "Are you Rabbi Vogeler?" A thin voice said, "I am."

"Then why have you not stepped forward?"

The answer came in such quiet words that many in the room barely heard them. "I ask to be permitted to remain here with my people. They need someone. At least to care for the sick and bury the dead."

The Hungarian officer stared at the slim figure in astonishment, then, laughing, turned to the SS lieutenant. "Since when do we ask a Jew if he wants to go?"

The lieutenant did not return the jocularity. His expression became a stony rebuke to the Hungarian. To Rabbi Vogeler he said in a flat, official voice, "Our orders are to take everyone on the list." It was courteous, formal, but final. Then he told the other seven clustered around him to pack one suitcase apiece and assemble as quickly as possible in the garden.

Amidst much whispering and excitement the people packed their few belongings and went, some singly, some with their families, into the garden to wait. A few were cringing with fear. Most were joyous, sure that Andor Horvath had saved them. But they all had threadbare clothes, battered suitcases, and emaciated figures. They stood in the bright sunlight, patiently waiting. One young woman went from rosebush to rosebush smelling each flower, as if she had a premonition it might be a long time before she would be able to enjoy such odors again.

Within the hour several more Hungarian police and SS men appeared, to escort the group to the railroad station. Rabbi Vogeler, waiting with his wife, Deborah, and their infant son, stood beside a baby carriage holding his phylacteries. A Hungarian strode over and seized the carriage and the sacred boxes. "You're not permitted to take these," he growled. "You're no different from anyone else here."

Immediately an SS man retorted, "Oh, let him take them. What's the difference?" The Hungarian retreated sullenly.

Such consideration from the SS astounded Rabbi Vogeler, but he and the others were to be surprised again. The conduct of the Germans on the way to the railroad station was nothing if not polite. A sergeant even carried the suitcase of a frail, elderly man. It was almost as if they had been ordered to treat their charges humanely.

In Pécs, Andor's native town, the Jews had been moved into a ghetto many weeks earlier. The morning of the roundup there was a great deal of activity and much visiting back and forth in the tents that had been put up on the grounds of the brickworks, for a large number of families had been told to prepare to leave. In one tent Leo Strauss sat on the edge of a cot, holding his infant daughter and listening to the chatter of her eight-year-old sister as he watched his wife pack. He was a big man, with a florid face, close-cropped brown hair, happy eyes, thick, sensuous lips, massive shoulders, large hands, and a warm manner.

He was never happy unless he was with people—the greater the number, the better. He was more exuberantly cheerful this morning than his wife had seen him since the start of the war. His large body fairly bounced on the cot as he talked to her about Andor.

"I knew he would get us out, Vera. Didn't I tell you a hundred times? He's a great fixer. Even when he was a young man he was clever.

Always knew the right people. Always knew how to manipulate them. Remember Greenberg, who owned the restaurant?"

Vera nodded and went on with her packing. In her dark eyes there was the happy satisfaction of seeing her husband once more full of his normal vigor and enthusiasm.

"Well, one night Greenberg's son Moshe came to the newspaper office where Andor was working—you remember that Tabor gave Andor a job while he was studying at the university. Anyway, this night Moshe showed up very excited. The police had arrested his father, he said. Why? Because he had kept the restaurant open after closing time. The police accused old Greenberg of resisting arrest and assaulting an officer. Moshe was frantic. He begged Andor to come help his father. But Andor was only a university student and a cub reporter. What could he do? Well, he picked up the telephone and asked for the captain of police of the district. He told the captain he would appreciate it if Greenberg was released in his custody. The captain said no, it was a very serious case and Greenberg would have to be tried in court. So what do you think Andor said then?" He slapped his thigh in glee. "He said to the captain, 'Just send for this man Greenberg and take a look at him, then you look at the policeman he's accused of hitting. If you really think this little Jew could have hit that big policeman, then you send him to prison for life.'"

"So what happened?" Vera prodded.

"What happened? The captain hung up. But after a while the phone on Andor's desk at the newspaper rang. It was the captain's office saying Greenberg had been released. We had a good laugh over that one. Andor didn't even know what the policeman looked like. He might have been half the size of Greenberg. But somehow things always work out for Andor." There was a touch of wonderment in his voice, but then it changed. "They're going to work out right for us, too, now that he's dealing with the Germans." He said the words with great conviction.

In another tent, on the opposite side of the grounds, Andor's sister Rena watched anxiously as Philip Kemeny clumsily tried to pack his suitcase. His fingers were stiff. Since Sarah's death he had become sick and old beyond his years, and there was a perpetually sad, faraway expression in his eyes.

"Sam," Rena whispered, tugging at her husband's sleeve to get his attention, "should I help him?"

"No. It's better to leave him alone. Then he doesn't have to pretend."

"I don't think he can make it to the station."

"He won't have to walk. I heard from Leo that a truck is going to take those who are old or sick."

She sat down on a cot, relieved, then looked around vainly for her small son. She jumped up frantically. "Where's Dan?"

"He must have run outside." Sam opened the tent flap and looked out, then poked his head back in. "He's just watching the soldiers. I'll get him."

She sat down again, filled with an apprehension she had been hiding from Sam. I wonder what's going to happen now, she thought, and glanced over at Philip Kemeny's thin, brittle figure. What more can happen to him? To any of us? If this is a fraud—if someone has played a trick on my brother—we could all die. She shivered in terror at the prospect as she thought of Dan. To die at the age of three? It was too fantastic. It won't happen, she reassured herself. My brother Andor is too clever to let it happen. . . .

12

Andor and his committee were plagued by a thousand problems. No one had thought about a supply of milk for the babies at Columbus utca. Tomorrow was the Sabbath and no provision had been made for tonight's services; the religious element was greatly disturbed. Rabbi Jesse Vogeler had sent word he preferred to return to Nagybathely, where he felt he was needed. There was constant quarreling about accommodations and frequent charges of favoritism shown to one group or another. No word had yet come from Gábor. Day after day Wedemeyer threatened to break off negotiations. They pleaded with him and stalled him with half-truths. They cabled Istanbul again, begging for something more definite.

There was another crucial problem. Deportations were taking place in every part of the country except Budapest. One of the messengers who had been sent out to deliver some of the fifteen hundred letters came back saying he was unable to find a single Jew in one large town to which he had been sent. The two hundred thousand Jews of the capital, learning what was happening elsewhere in Hungary, feared that the pattern would soon be repeated in Budapest, so many of them frantically sought ways to obtain Christian identity papers or hiding places. As the desperate activities of these frightened people grew more

and more feverish, some of them heard a rumor that there was un-
assailable safety behind the fence of the Columbus utca camp; that
those inside had been given the promise of an eventual voyage to Palestine. The camp was so safe, they heard, that not even the Gestapo
could enter without a permit. They heard reports that Andor Horvath's
Rescue Committee had selected those to be saved, and so they besieged
Andor and his colleagues at their Sip utca offices, jostling and elbowing
each other as they swarmed through the rooms, sweating and shouting,
pleading and threatening, pushing at the Committee their money,
jewelry, silverware, anything of value they had hidden, and begging to
be taken to the camp. The chaos was uncontrollable, the cacophony
earsplitting, but they wouldn't be dissuaded. Each day additional hundreds appeared. In the middle of the madness that was Hungary, the
serene and peaceful island on Columbus utca seemed to be their only
hope.

On the day the train from Pécs was to arrive, bringing the people
chosen from that city for rescue, Andor attended to his usual duties at
the Center, but at least half his thoughts were far away—with the members of his family and the old friends he would soon see. When Rachel
announced that they had arrived and were being installed in Columbus
utca, he struggled through the throng that jammed his outer office and
rushed eagerly to the camp.

Leo was waiting for him just inside the gate. Until today the camp
had been without a leader, but from the moment Leo arrived his boom-
ing voice was everywhere, giving orders, assigning tasks, settling disputes, and keeping everyone else quiet so he could be heard. He and
Andor embraced with a show of affection that neither tried to camouflage. As soon as word spread that Andor Horvath was there, most of
the others from Pécs ran to greet him, some who were strangers, some
who had known him since he was a child. They slapped him on the
back and shook his hand. Many of the women kissed his fingers and
expressed their gratitude with smiles and tears. Those who couldn't reach
him shouted their greetings and thanks. Everyone talked at the same
time.

Andor was inflated with happiness. These people were closer and
dearer to him than any others on earth. He was proud to be the agent
of their deliverance. He held up his hands for quiet and told them this.
When he had finished, they pressed close around him again, but Leo
stretched out his great arms and forced them to make an opening to
the building, saying, "It's enough for now. Leave him alone. You'll see

him tomorrow. You'll see him the next day. What do you want, to wear him out? He's a man, not a machine. Make way there. Lady, he can't kiss your baby now. Make way, everybody!"

First Andor went to see Rena. She and Sam and little Dan shared a room on the second floor with another family. Altogether there were eight people living in the small quarters. The cots were stacked three high, to save space, but the occupants looked ecstatically happy. Rena ran to him and kissed him impulsively, something she had never done. They were brother and sister, but being very different, they had never been close, except in the routine externals of family life. Now as she gave him this sign of genuine affection and gratitude, he felt happy out of all proportion to the gesture, and a flood of love for her swept over him, the first feeling of love for anyone or anything he'd had since Sarah's death. It gave him a sense of exhilaration and, in a way he didn't quite understand, of freedom. He hadn't realized how severely he had been punishing himself for what had happened to Sarah by denying to himself a need that was common to every living man: freedom to express love. Rena's affectionate outburst had released him. He returned her kiss with fervor and then gaily picked up Dan and raised him high, to the small boy's squealing delight.

Afterward he and Sam retired to a corner and talked. He could tell from the serious expression in his brother-in-law's dark eyes, even when he smiled, that he was worried about Rena. He didn't say so, but it was plain in the uneasy way he watched her as she attended to Dan. Poor, sensible, goodhearted Sam, Andor thought. How did you come to choose such a nervous woman as my sister? But he simply put an arm around Sam's shoulder as he left and said reassuringly, "By the end of the month you'll be out of here, and before the end of the year in Palestine. You keep telling her that." He glanced toward the bed where Rena was drawing the blanket up over Dan.

Sam nodded and shook his hand gratefully.

At the door Andor stopped. "By the way, where is Philip? I thought he would be here with you."

For the first time an unclouded smile came over Sam's homely features. "He's in the next room." He pointed to the right. "He doesn't need us any more. He has much better service than we can give him."

"What are you talking about?"

Sam Breslau's eyes twinkled with amusement. "You'll see. Go in."

Mystified, Andor walked down the hall and entered the next room. It was like the one he had just left except that here he saw only a man and woman with two little girls who bobbed their heads at him as he came in. At the far side a white cotton sheet was draped over a rope that had been strung across the room, closing off about a third of the space.

"Mr. Kemeny . . . ?" he asked.

The man pointed to the sheet. "In there."

Andor lifted the thin white partition slightly and bent to go under the rope. There before him, asleep on the bed, lay Philip Kemeny, a gray pallor on his face, his eyes sunken, his lips twitching as he slept, his thin hands covered with taut skin that was dry as parchment. Andor's heart suddenly ached to see the disintegration of this gentle patrician who had been his boyhood idol . . . Suddenly he heard a movement behind him and wheeled around. Standing in front of the sheet holding a tray of food was a young woman. With restrained deference she greeted him by name and set the tray on the small bureau next to the bed. He was awe-struck at the sight of her and couldn't turn his eyes away. Her hair, jet black and abundant, was pulled back tightly from her forehead, exposing her ears, and then was wound in two large coils at the nape of the neck, making her look almost masculine. She wore no make-up, and her dress was dark and shapeless. The first impression she gave was of severity and primness. But as Andor's glance took in more details he found contradictions. Even without cosmetics her skin was a lovely olive shade and was without blemish. Her mouth, although a little too wide, was soft and full. Her severely done hair was in slight rebellion, for several strands had escaped the coils on the neck and had curled themselves in an extremely unmasculine manner. But it was her eyes more than anything else that gave the lie to the first impression. They were sapphire-blue, as brilliant as jewels, but they seemed partially shrouded by a cloud of some sort. Andor decided that eventually he must discover what it was that was behind this conflict. He scrutinized her figure. Her shoulders were small, her breasts delicately rounded. Her well-fleshed hips undulated as she crossed the room. He watched, fascinated, as her strong, slender fingers placed the tray on the bureau.

"Will you sit down?" She said it politely, even graciously. Her tonal register was essentially pleasant, but Andor thought he had never heard a voice that sounded so disembodied, so cold and lifeless. The words came as if from across a great abyss separating two worlds. She went on quietly, apparently trying not to awaken Philip. "The trip was quite an ordeal for him. But he will probably be awake soon."

Andor thanked her and sat on one of the two chairs beside the bed, vaguely disquieted. He realized that this woman was having an almost hypnotic effect on him. Her features bore a candid expression, yet there was about her an impenetrable reserve and an absence of any feminine desire to please. This irritated him. If he had been honest, he would have called it indifference. He was accustomed to being treated in many various ways, but never with indifference. This was the only attitude he could not tolerate in others. Yet he now sat here hypnotized by it. Most irksome of all, he felt awkward before her—he who had never felt awkward before anyone. If she was aware of it, she gave no indication.

"I'm greatly indebted to you for nursing my father-in-law," he said, somewhat condescendingly, trying to place himself in the dominant position, the only one in which he could be happy. "It is very kind of you."

"It isn't kindness," she replied with chilling bluntness. "He is alone and I am alone." She paused and her attitude became pensive. "After all, I must do something to justify my being alive." It was a remark Andor ordinarily would have answered with a gallant Hungarian proverb about a beautiful woman needing no justification for her existence. He had used it a hundred times on Sarah and on countless other women. But this time the words wouldn't come. Instead, in an effort to put the exchange on a less reserved basis, he said, "I don't even know your name."

"I am Jessica Hoffmann."

"Are you from Pécs?"

She gave him a smile that said it was a foolish question. "My father was Joseph Werner—"

"The famous lawyer!" He said it too quickly, eager to show her he was impressed. "I am sorry about your husband," he added more quietly. Everyone knew that Werner's son-in-law had been executed by the SS for hiding two young Slovak Zionists wanted by the Gestapo. It was because of this that Mrs. Hoffmann's name was on the rescue list. How foolish of him not to have realized sooner who she was.

She made no reply but looked down at the gold band that ringed the third finger of her left hand and twisted it slowly around and around, nervously. The old man on the bed stirred. He opened his eyes and looked about slowly, as if he were not quite sure where he was. When he saw Andor, his face brightened and he raised himself with some difficulty to grasp his son-in-law's hand. It had never occurred to him to blame the younger man for Sarah's death. In his gentle heart there was

142

still only affection for the boy he had guided to manhood as he would have his own son. He pressed Andor's hand between his own.

"It is good to see you," he said warmly.

The quavering sound of his voice was a shock. But with a pretense of joviality Andor replied, "It is good to see you, Philip," at the same time propping the old man up against his pillow. Once again he felt a terrible burden of guilt pressing down on him, not only because of Sarah, but because of her father, too. "I see you have a new friend," he said with feigned cheerfulness, turning to Jessica.

"Yes. Isn't she wonderful? And I have discovered that she is just as beautiful in here"—he put his hand over his heart—"as on the outside."

She flushed. "I've brought you some biscuits and a bowl of soup." She removed the cover from the dish and took the tray to the bed. "You missed your lunch, so you'd better eat now—if Mr. Horvath doesn't mind." She looked at Andor with distant politeness, but Philip broke in.

"You are very thoughtful, my dear, but I will eat later. I want to visit with my son now."

"Eat, Philip," Andor said quickly. "I'll sit here and talk to you."

The old man accepted the tray, and Jessica smiled at him affectionately. Then she gently tucked a napkin under his chin and kissed him on one cheek. Andor watched her ministrations enviously. When she talked with Philip, she seemed to open one small gate in the dam she had built around her emotions. He watched the way she put a gentle hand on the old man's arm; how the cloud that covered her face lifted when she looked into his eyes. There was an understanding of sorts between these two people who were so different in so many ways. As she prepared to leave the two men alone, she kissed her patient on the forehead, patted his arm, and said, "I'll be back in a little while." Then she turned toward Andor. The mask was back in its place. She bowed her head slightly to him, without saying a word. Her eyes met his for a small part of one second. They said nothing. He stared after her as she held up the sheet and bent to go under the rope. For him her hair was the symbol of her. If he could only undo those hard ugly knots and run his hands through the black hair and swirl it into a soft frame around her face— A surge of desire and conceit swept over him. If he could hold her in his arms and make love to her, he was certain that with gentleness and passion adroitly combined he could break down the wall she had built.

For some time he talked with Philip, staying long past the hour when he should have been back at the Center, his only excuse the urgency of his desire to see her again. Still she didn't return, and finally, knowing he must leave, he told Philip he would try to find Jessica and send her back.

The older man brushed aside the suggestion with a feeble hand. "She'll be back soon. She is just giving us some privacy." He chuckled. "This is one of her prime virtues. She understands the value of privacy. So few people do." He pointed to the hanging sheet. "After you have lived in a ghetto, you know how priceless it is."

Andor almost answered that if it meant shutting out the world, it was more dangerous than priceless, but he closed his mouth hard on the words.

When he left the room, he took the longest way through the corridors, glancing everywhere, even into open rooms, hoping for a glimpse of her. But she was nowhere to be seen.

13

Captain Ely Farber was just as handsome in a pair of khaki shorts, a white shirt open at the neck, and a pair of sneakers—the costume he habitually had worn during his five years in Palestine—as he was now in the uniform of a captain in the British Army. He was twenty-eight years old, slim, wiry, brown-skinned, with black wavy hair that was the envy of most young women who saw it. His eyes were keen and alert, the eyes of an intense man, who was daring but not reckless, fearless but not unaware of the presence of danger, and intelligent without being pedantic. No subject was uninteresting to him. He volleyed a tennis ball, rode a horse, drank whisky, played poker, listened to serious music, or discussed philosophy with equal animation and enjoyment. He was essentially happy. He could laugh without self-consciousness, be carefree on occasion, and savor every experience to the final moment.

Five years earlier he had left his native Hungary and immigrated to Palestine, a young, idealistic chalutz, or pioneer. He had labored on co-operative farms under the fierce heat of the sun until his muscles bulged and his skin became a glowing brown. He had stood watch against Arab marauders during the dark nights. He had known agonizing thirst and weakening hunger. He had been afraid of neither work, hardship, nor the occasional threat of death.

When the war began in Europe, he immediately volunteered in the

British Army, believing that freedom and dignity were the right of all men and that Britain's enemies were threatening them. His extraordinary qualities soon became apparent, and he was given a commission, rising rapidly to the rank of captain. When he discovered that the Inter-Allied Organization was an intentionally innocuous name for a spy and counterespionage project with ambitious plans for creating chaos behind German lines in occupied southeastern Europe, he volunteered and was sent to organization headquarters in Cairo, Egypt, for training. For months he and his colleagues were taught the tactics of espionage, sabotage, and guerrilla warfare. They were given courses in the detailed geography of the particular area in which each was to specialize. They were trained in the use of radio transmitters, a course they couldn't pass until they had learned how to take a transmitter apart and put it together again in the light of a fountain-pen flashlight held in the teeth. Then they received their assignments.

His mission was to drop by parachute into northern Yugoslavia with three comrades. They would then make contact with the Partisans of General Tito, who would guide them across the frontier into Hungary. There they would put into effect a well-laid-out plan for organizing resistance against the Germans, with the assistance of Haganah in Budapest. They would also establish an escape route over which British fliers who had been forced to bail out of their damaged planes on the way back to Mediterranean bases from missions over occupied Europe could reach friendly territory. At this time it was taking Britain so much longer to train replacement crews than to build replacement planes that high priority was given to trying to rescue airmen who were stranded in Europe, yet not actually in prison camps.

It was an assignment any adventure-loving young man would have liked. It suited Ely Farber perfectly. Magyar was his first language, even though he had been using Hebrew exclusively these past five years. Just before going to Palestine he had spent an entire summer near the Yugoslav-Hungarian frontier in the very area in which they were now going to be dropped, and during that time he had learned enough Serb to be able to conduct a limited conversation. In Cairo he had done some tutoring and found it came back easily. It was an ideal assignment for other reasons. He and most of his fellow Jews back in Palestine, as well as the British in Cairo, by now knew about Auschwitz and the other extermination centers. They knew that even if an Allied victory came soon, it might find few of Europe's Jews still alive. So far his people had gone to their death with what looked at a distance like resignation. Until now there had been almost no organized resistance. In Palestine and Cairo they realized that there were many extenuating circumstances to explain it. They knew that the power and organizational ability of the SS had concentrated on preventing, by every possible means, any opposition. But in Cairo, sitting around their barracks, he and other members of the Jewish Brigade had often argued that as long as death by gassing and cremation was inevitable, why make the exit from life with such resignation? Why make it so easy for the exterminators? Why not leave fighting? If enough of them resisted, it might cause such confusion inside Hitler's Europe, and make such demands on the German military machine to suppress it, that the Allied victory would be hastened. This in turn might result in many more Jews being alive at the end. These were the arguments they advanced to each other in their barracks. The contention seemed irrefutable.

Recently they had received word that the Germans were beginning to apply what they called the "final solution" to the Jews of Hungary. Ely had contended to his superior officers that the situation in his native country was certainly ripe for resistance. The Russians were pressing close on two sides. The Americans were stepping up their bombing attacks. There were signs that the Hungarian Fascists were growing nervous. Other Hungarian Aryans were putting out peace feelers. What mystified Ely, as well as the Inter-Allied Organization in Cairo, was why Haganah in Budapest was not in action. If it were, surely some reports would have leaked out. But intelligence messages received in Cairo indicated that hundreds of thousands of Jews in the provinces of Hungary were being shipped to Auschwitz with even less display of resistance than Jews in other countries had shown at a time when Allied troops on all fronts were in retreat.

Ely thought of all these matters as he sat on a hard wooden bench in the bomb bay of the British Lancaster, his chute strapped to his back, while the plane thundered its way at high altitude across the Mediterranean and up over Yugoslavia.

In a few minutes he and his companions would plunge into a cold, alien sky, and when they hit earth they would be in a foreign land, among professed friends whose loyalty, in the nature of the situation, must be suspect.

Sitting there, he told himself that he had never in his life really been afraid, and he was not afraid now, for himself. But this was the first time he had ever assumed the life-or-death responsibility for any other person. With a chill he realized that what he did from this moment on would determine the fate of all four of them.

The other three looked preoccupied, sitting on the edge of the bench on the other side of the bay, each with his own private thoughts. Naomi's black curls were disarranged, falling onto the collar of her khaki shirt. For the first time since he had known her, her onyx eyes had not a brittle gleam but a soft shine. He wondered if she was thinking of how it would be to see the land of her birth. She had been in Palestine twice as long as he had: since she was a girl of seventeen. Ten years ago she had left her sister in Budapest and had set out to put her youthful idealism into action. The pioneering group of which she was a member was the most active of all the chalutzim in establishing new agricultural settlements, always in the most dangerous spots in the country. As soon as one was going well and the settlers were beginning to enjoy a few of the basic amenities of a civilized life—such as outdoor privies and enough water to permit daily washing—the hard core of old-timers would load a truck with tents, a few simple agricultural tools and enough provisions to last a short while, and—like the amoeba—would multiply by dividing, going off onto the desert somewhere and starting another new kibbutz in some remote and unlikely place. For ten years Naomi had lived this way; always picking for herself the most difficult job; taking the dreariest and longest watch; asking no consideration because she was a female. She had become tough and competent and unyielding. Yet tonight the excitement of their enterprise had brought a becomingly soft glow to her face. There was a dreamy slackness to her mouth instead of the usual intensity. Even in her khaki trousers and shirt she seemed a woman. Her breasts were large and firm, her hips wide and sensual. Her hands were efficiently big. Her gait when she walked was resolute, and easy for a man to fall in step with. As Ely stared at her, she suddenly checked the straps holding her portable radio transmitter, and in that instant the dreaminess was gone and her whole mien became purposeful again.

Beside Naomi, Aaron Jaffee nervously shifted his thin legs and stuck out a bony wrist to look at his watch. His uniform seemed to hang on his wiry frame as on a scarecrow, and his watery brown eyes were anxious as he looked up at Ely.

"Five minutes?" he asked, checking his timepiece.

"Five minutes."

Ely realized that Aaron might be their problem. He was the only one who wasn't a Palestinian. "An international Jew," he called himself. Rather foolish. Weren't all Jews international? He said that his parents, who were Transylvanians, liked to joke about how they were born in the Austro-Hungarian Empire, were married in Rumania, and had almost been killed in a pogrom in Hungary, yet never in their lives had been out of the same village. This was because Transylvania had changed hands so many times. Aaron himself had lived not only in Hungary but in four surrounding countries: Yugoslavia, Rumania, Austria, and that part of Czechoslovakia called Ruthenia. He could pass for a citizen of any nationalistic division of that part of Europe, so great was his linguistic ability. He had arrived in Cairo by a circuitous route, after many brushes with death. The Inter-Allied Organization tests had proved that he was a man without what is conventionally called fear, yet he was such a bundle of nerves that Ely worried that he might crack unless everything went exactly according to schedule.

Sensing Aaron's anxiety, Martin Klein, who sat on the other side of him, leaned over and put an arm around Aaron's sloping shoulders. "Everything's going to be okay. Right, Ely?"

"Right."

The sight of Martin's bright, eager face buoyed Ely, too. "He's going to be a blessing on this mission," he said silently.

The noise of the plane prevented him from hearing what Martin was saying to Aaron, but watching from across the bomb bay he could see Aaron's tension gradually subside as the fair-haired, blue-eyed Martin encouraged him.

Martin was the youngest of them, only twenty-one. His shoulders were square, his firm jaw was an advertisement of his defiance, and from the way he walked it was obvious to anyone that here was a man who did not want favors from anyone but at the same time would not take "special treatment" from the society in which he lived. He was cynical for a man so young, but if he had had to explain it he would have called it "a sense of reality." He questioned everyone's motives and had no use for maudlin sentiment, religions that refused to face the verities of actual life, defeatism and resignation, or obedience for its own sake.

He had been in trouble many times in Cairo with his British superiors. Nevertheless he still managed to hold his commission as a lieutenant, because of his brilliance and the British need of him. He and Ely had been friends since they first met, more than a year ago, and when plans for the present mission were discussed he was the first man Ely picked to go along.

Ely looked at his watch and then, in the voice of a military commander, shouted above the roar of the plane's four engines, "Attention, everyone. In a couple of minutes we'll be leaving this crate. Before we do, I want to remind you that our mission is a sacred one. Our mission is not just to organize effective resistance against the goddamn Nazis but to help save our people from annihilation. This is a high honor and a great responsibility. I'm not good at making speeches or delivering sermons, but the Agency and the British Army have placed their trust and confidence in us. Let's make certain we don't fail them." Then his tone became businesslike. "Have you two got your radios strapped tight?"

As Naomi and Aaron answered "yes" the voice of the pilot on the intercom announced, "Bomb-bay doors open."

Ely shouted as he moved into jumping position, "This is it!" Then, over his shoulder, he said, " 'Happy landing' to all of us," and disappeared.

The other three followed him in quick succession. They floated down gently, after their parachutes opened, into a vast wheat field, shimmering yellow even in the murky predawn gloom.

Almost immediately a small truck that had been parked on the road several hundred feet in the distance ground its way across the field to Ely. The occupants were a stocky Yugoslav Partisan major and two noncommissioned officers. They took note of Ely's British uniform and asked him to identify himself.

"Bohinjka-Bistrica" Ely replied, giving them the agreed-upon password, the name of a summer resort in the Slovenian part of Yugoslavia.

They welcomed him enthusiastically.

Martin was grinning when they came to him. "What a beautiful drop! I never had such a great ride! And this grain! I felt as if I were coming down into a field of pure, eighteen-karat gold."

Naomi was combing her hair when they reached her. The three Yugoslavs looked her over as if they hadn't seen a female in years. When they found she could speak a little Serb, they all talked to her at once. Ely interrupted to remind them that there was a fourth parachutist.

They found Aaron hopelessly entangled in the ropes of his chute. It took all six of them to set him free. Aaron was afraid he had fractured one ankle, but after a little exercise it seemed usable again.

The Partisan truck drove them to a farmhouse about a half mile to the north. There each one was given a suit of civilian clothes. When it came to outfitting Naomi, the major, whose name was Vidovich, said gallantly, "Male or female clothes, mademoiselle? Which do you wish?"

Naomi gave him a half-smile, then replied sharply, "A pair of pants and a shirt. The darker and more inconspicuous, the better."

After they had changed into the clothes the Yugoslavs gave them, Ely held an inspection. "If I were to meet the three of you on a dark road, I'd head for the woods," he laughed. But the truth was that Naomi, now that she had tied around her head a bandanna she had brought along, looked much more feminine than before.

Ely pointed to the pile of British uniforms on the floor and said to Major Vidovich, "We'll leave these for you. Who knows? Someday they may be very useful."

The major accepted them eagerly. "We're not oversupplied with clothing these days, Captain. And we'll be proud to wear uniforms once worn by British officers." Then he gave them a briefing on the frontier situation.

"It's bad," he said. "The border is sealed off so completely that it's difficult to make any contact with our friends in Hungary, and as you know, it's two hundred and fifty kilometers to Budapest. The railroad stations are heavily guarded all the way. However, we know a group of Hungarian soldiers working underground against the Germans. We permit them to come and go freely across the border. I think they'll be willing to help the four of you get into Hungary."

Ely wasn't happy over the briefing. He was reluctant to offend Vidovich, yet he wanted to make sure that the members of his mission didn't fall into a trap.

"Major," he said politely, "do you know for certain that these Hungarians can be trusted?"

"Definitely," came the quick answer. "I'm willing to vouch for them. They have helped us in several sabotage operations along the frontier. They are very keen to organize a partisan force in their own country, like ours."

Ely still looked unconvinced.

"I'll take you to see them this afternoon," Vidovich continued. "You can judge them for yourself. You don't need to tell them anything more about your plans than you wish to."

Ely agreed to that, and after they had eaten a breakfast of brown bread and local cheese, washed down with several glasses of strong *šlivovica*—a drink Aaron couldn't swallow despite his Balkan experiences —Major Vidovich and a noncom drove them several miles to a town adjacent to the border. There in a small house on the outskirts they were received by a Hungarian captain named Dobos and a lieutenant who greeted the Yugoslavs cordially. The major introduced Ely and his companions simply by name, but Ely himself volunteered that he was a captain in Tito's army and that the other three were also Partisans. He noticed that Vidovich raised his bushy eyebrows slightly at the bare-faced lie. The four of them were on a secret mission to Hungary, Ely continued. Major Vidovich had brought them here in the hope that they might receive some assistance.

"A secret mission . . ." mused Captain Dobos. "Well, we may be able to help you. Major Vidovich has been most co-operative with us. But . . ." He hesitated and then with an enigmatic smile said, "Secret or not, if we are to have any part in it, we will have to know something about your mission."

"Of course," Ely said hastily, hoping to put the Hungarian at ease. "We wish to go to Budapest to make certain arrangements. For this we have two pressing needs. First, we must have false papers. Second, we will need guides to take us across the river."

"I see." Captain Dobos lowered his glance and drummed his fingers on the table in front of him. Ely held his breath, not daring to look at anyone else in the room. Finally Dobos sat back in his chair and gazed directly at Ely. "It is possible to get papers for you," he said, "but in order to do this I must present my superior officer with some proof of your identity and your intention. Your friendship with Major Vidovich is good, but it is not enough." He stopped short and faced Vidovich. "Pardon me, Major, but any of us can be fooled."

"Of course, caution is necessary," Ely admitted, adding, "On all sides." He wasn't certain yet how far he should trust this man. Vidovich was probably all right. Cairo had vouched for him. But should they trust anyone Vidovich vouched for?

The others in the room were staring at him, waiting for him to go on. What could he say? Unfortunately they had only one choice: to confide in this Hungarian group or try to cross the frontier on their own. The latter would be suicide. He reached into his pocket and produced a memorandum on heavy official-looking stationery—but without a heading or signature—that had been prepared in Cairo and was addressed in Hungarian: "To Whom It May Concern." It asked that all courtesy be extended to the bearer and his party, who were engaged in attempting to create a pocket of resistance in Budapest, in co-operation with Haganah.

Dobos read it slowly and then looked up with suspicion written across his face.

"Who wrote out this memorandum?" he asked sharply.

"My superiors," Ely replied evasively.

"No one in the world would put such a matter as this into writing but the British," he said bitingly. "However, it should satisfy my superior officer."

Ely flushed with embarrassment. "I had no intention of carrying that paper any farther than this," he declared. "There wouldn't have been any danger of it falling into enemy hands—unless I had been killed in the—before now."

"Do you know the leader of Haganah in Budapest?" Dobos asked.

Ely, glad the subject had been changed, replied easily, "Yes. He's Alex Peto, an old friend of mine. He'll vouch for me."

"Good. I have no doubt that we will assist you. Now we need photographs for the identity papers."

Ely pulled out four—one of each of them—from his pocket and handed them to Dobos, who studied them, matched them with the four faces in front of him, and then, satisfied, put them in his own pocket. "We shall have the identity papers ready for you the day after tomorrow. If you return in forty-eight hours we will also be ready to guide you over the border."

Two days later Major Vidovich again drove them to the small house near the frontier. There, waiting, were Captain Dobos and two soldiers. Dobos had the papers for them. Ely examined them carefully and was pleased to see that they were excellent forgeries. He distributed them to Martin, Aaron, and Naomi. Then he told the captain they were ready to leave. The two soldiers, they learned, were to be their guides. It was mutually agreed that it would be wise for them to split up. The first group would go over just after dark at a point about forty miles to the northeast. Major Vidovich said he would drive them there. The second group would go over just north of the place where they now were. Ely decided that each group would take one of the radio transmitters. "Don't forget," he cautioned, "that we have two-way radio contact with Cairo whenever we need it." He decided that Aaron and Naomi should go together. She had enough guts for the two of them. Aaron, he knew, was sure-footed and fast as a deer when he needed to be. They would be a strong combination. He and Martin would go together. They were so compatible they could almost read each other's thoughts, no small advantage if they got into a tight spot.

Naomi was eager to get started and begged to be allowed to go first. Her black eyes were bright with impatience.

"No," Ely said flatly. "It's better that Martin and I go first and see what the risks are. If nothing happens to us, you two can follow."

He couldn't have said anything worse. Naomi jumped to her feet. "Look, Ely, we agreed before we left Cairo that you would forget I'm a woman. You promised. This means in *all* ways. So if there's any feeling-out of the situation to do, if there's any more danger in going now than later, Aaron and I are the ones to take it. We're much more expendable than you and Martin. This is a rugged business and we all know it. You and Martin are the key figures. It's vitally important that you two don't get caught. You'll excuse me, Captain Farber, for defying a superior, but Aaron and I are going first."

Ely knew it was useless to argue with her. If he pulled rank and commanded her to go later, she'd obey, but it would dampen her ardor, kill her enthusiasm, and besides, she was right.

As dusk began to dim the countryside, Naomi and Aaron, accompanied by Major Vidovich, prepared to leave by truck. Each carried a rough haversack containing pieces of a radio transmitter, covered over with foodstuff the Yugoslav Partisans had contributed: dark peasant bread, several heads of garlic, some local cheese wrapped in vine leaves, and a few raw potatoes. The Partisans had apologized that there was no meat to be had.

"*Srécan put!*" Ely said as he grasped their hands. He used the Serbo-Croat words intentionally. Then as he put an arm over the shoulder of each of them he added, "Good luck."

As the sound of the truck faded he started to pace the floor of the farmhouse. Martin tried to lower his tension. "Stop stewing, pal. Take it easy."

"I'm sorry," Ely replied, "but, God damn it, Martin, I wish we'd gone over first. Why in hell did I let that girl talk me out of it?"

"So we didn't."

Ely wheeled around on him. "Did you ever take into your hands the responsibility for a human life? Can you understand how I feel? God damn it, I wish I'd stayed a private so I could just take orders!"

Martin persuaded him that they should try to get some rest in order to be fresh for their own problems in the morning and set an example by curling up on a cot with all his clothes on. In three minutes his heavy breathing indicated he was asleep. Ely lay down on a cot on the opposite side of the otherwise barren room, but although he closed his eyes he remained wide awake. Every hour or so he raised his wrist and glanced at the luminous figures on the dial of his watch. At midnight he thought surely Naomi and Aaron were across the river by now. At 1:30 A.M., if

153

they had encountered no trouble, they might have found a place to sleep for the rest of the night, so why shouldn't *he* sleep now? But he remained awake.

At 3 A.M. Janos, the imperturbable Hungarian who was to be their guide, came in to tell them it was time to get started.

"Any report from Major Vidovich?" Ely asked, hardly able to wait for the reply.

"No."

"That's good news, isn't it?"

"Yes. If there had been any trouble we'd know about it by now."

"Good." Ely felt a little relieved.

The three of them walked to a point on the shore of the Drava River where Janos had hidden a rowboat. It was as quiet as death, and although they moved stealthily each footstep seemed to resound in the stillness. Every dry twig they broke underfoot sounded like a burst of rifle fire. But they were fortunate: there seemed to be no one around at that time of the morning.

Janos slipped the canoe easily into the slow-moving water and paddled it swiftly to the opposite shore. In their relief and gratitude at landing safely on Hungarian soil, they clapped Janos on the back, but he only stared at them blankly, then grunted an acknowledgment. He carefully hid the green-painted boat in a cache of fallen branches, then led them along a road in the chill morning to the railroad station in the next town, Barcs.

To Ely it was almost unbelievable that they could be behind enemy lines, in German-occupied Hungary, two Jews, both British officers. Ely studied the people around. They were all peasants, with the look and the smell of the earth about them. They appeared no different than he remembered them years ago when he spent a summer in this general area. On the other side of the Drava the people spoke mostly Serb; on this side Hungarian. Their costumes and some of their customs were different. But they all raised cattle, poultry, onions, beans, potatoes, corn, wheat, peppers, and the same sort of flowers. They all fertilized their fields with the same sort of manure, the smell of which clung to them, and they all lived just about the same sort of primitive existence, no matter which side of the river they were on.

At Barcs they took a local train to Pécs, where they got off and waited for the express to Budapest. By now it was late morning. The heat of the sun was warming the buildings and the cobble-stoned streets. It shone brightly on the many-colored tile roofs. In Palestine he had greatly missed these typically Hungarian roofs with their geometric patterns. It was a pleasant morning, he thought, on which to be alive. He looked past the station, at the city, with mingled curiosity and nostalgia. This had once been his city. He wondered how much it had changed in the years since he had left. He would have liked wandering the streets to see. As he looked around at the people on the platform, he thought about Rachel. She was his only sentimental tie to the city. He pictured her round softness and remembered the warmth of her body against his when they used to lie side by side in a canoe on a summer night. He thought, too, of the cruel tearing apart when they had separated five years ago, the day he left for Palestine and she disappeared from his life. They had never corresponded, yet he had not forgotten a single detail of what they had been to each other.

In an effort to collect himself he talked to Janos about the city, but the Hungarian guide maintained his impassive expression, answering most questions by saying dully that he didn't know. The only thing he did know was that there were no more Jews left in Pécs.

"No more Jews?" Ely asked incredulously.

"No. It's finished. They've all been taken to the camps." He said the words tonelessly.

Of course, to the camps. To Auschwitz. To the gas chambers. Ely doubled up as if a knife had been plunged into him. Maybe she had left Pécs in time. Maybe somehow she had escaped. But all the people he had grown up with, what of them? He abruptly turned away from Janos and walked toward the other end of the platform. Martin, who had been gazing down Szabadság út, the street leading to the station, followed him.

"Look!" he said, tugging at Ely till he turned around again. Janos was standing where they had left him, but a man in a gray jacket had approached him and was engaging him in a low-voiced conversation. As they watched, Ely and Martin saw the stranger's glance dart at them with what seemed like unusual interest. He looked away quickly when their eyes met. Apprehensively they started back, trying not to show their haste, but before they reached Janos the stranger had retreated into the station house.

With seemingly idle curiosity Ely asked, "Who was that?"

Janos shrugged. "A man."

"What did he want?" The pretense was falling away.

"He wanted to know if the train to Budapest had arrived yet and I told him no." The answer was gruff, but the last part of it was lost in the rhythmic din of the oncoming train. With obvious relief Janos saw them board it, then left, as inscrutable as he had been from the start.

On the train Ely watched out the window and Martin paced the interior to see if the stranger was aboard, but there was no sign of him.

"I don't like it," Ely muttered when he returned. "He didn't have to ask Janos about the train. That's what the stationmaster is for."

"Maybe we're getting too nervous, imagining things that don't exist," Martin replied. "Let's eat; we'll feel better." He opened the package of food and offered a piece of dark bread and a head of garlic to Ely, who refused with a shake of his head but grinned at Martin.

"When you're young, eating is a cure for everything. . . ."

"I haven't eaten since last night, and neither have you."

"I'll live." Ely settled back and closed his eyes.

Martin shrugged good-naturedly and bit into the bread with gusto.

14

It was midafternoon when they arrived in Budapest. Despite its wounds of war it excited them. It was a big, vibrant city, and there were Magyar characteristics about it that even the Germans had been unable to spoil—the beauty and grace of the Danube bridges, the bustle of life on the river, the elegance of the Korzó, the majesty of the Parliament buildings, the green of the Buda hills.

Ely looked at the contact names and addresses he had been given in Cairo and decided to call first on Alex Peto, since he was the head of Haganah. He dialed the number from a public booth. It rang several times, but no one answered. Next he phoned the number he had been given for Andor. A woman's voice came on at the other end. Yes, this was the Horvath apartment. No, she said, Mr. Horvath wasn't there. She had no idea when he might return. Ely gave her the password. She sounded puzzled. He asked about Alex and Erno, but she said she had never heard of them. Bewildered, he hung up. At the other end the wife of the concierge, who happened to be in the apartment, shook her head, equally nonplused, and replaced the receiver.

Disappointed, the two men decided to walk to the Sip utca Center and explore the area on the way, hoping to meet someone they knew. As they walked they noticed that Jews were restricted to special houses marked with yellow stars. There were many Jews on the streets, but they, too, wore the emblem of David.

At the Center the reception room was full of people, most of them wearing the yellow star. Ely immediately went to the receptionist and asked to see Andor Horvath.

"Your name please?"

After a wait of about a half hour he was shown into Andor's office.

"What can I do for you?" Andor glanced at him briefly, without recognition, preoccupied with some papers he was removing from a filing cabinet. Ely noticed that he didn't wear a yellow star.

"Don't you know me?"

Andor looked at him again, more closely this time, and shook his head.

"I'm Ely Farber, from Pécs."

Andor stared in stupefaction. "Are you crazy!" he cried. "What the hell are you doing here?"

Ely went to the door and called Martin from the reception room. Together they explained their mission in detail, but said nothing about Aaron and Naomi. It had been Ely's idea to keep them a secret until it was certain they were safe.

Andor was stunned by what they told him. Pale and shaken, he seemed almost eager to be rid of them. From time to time he glanced nervously out of the window, his agitation mounting by the minute. Finally he said to Ely, "Look at the doorway across the street. See those two men standing there? They're detectives. You and Klein had better get out of here quick. Something's brewing. Come back later. In the meantime I'll try to find you a place to stay."

Ely knew they looked suspicious or at least unusual. They weren't wearing yellow stars, and they didn't have the harassed look of the rest of Budapest's Jews. Besides, he thought, by now Andor should be a better expert in this game than I am. For the time being, anyway, maybe I should follow his lead.

But downstairs in the lobby, disheartened by their reception and plagued by the certainty that all was not well, they decided to try to contact the other people on their list. Ely would go to Erno's and Martin to Alex's. If they found they were being followed when they left the Center, they would split up immediately, then meet again later back at the Center.

157

As they walked outside and slowly ambled down the street, Ely noticed that the two men moved out of the doorway across the street and started in the same direction. They kept pace exactly, but always remained just twenty feet to the rear.

He nudged Martin. "Don't turn around, but they're tailing us. At the next corner I'll turn right. You keep walking straight ahead. We'll meet at the Center at 7 P.M. In the meantime keep your eyes and ears open. And make sure you lose that tail before you go near Alex's apartment."

At the corner Ely ducked into the side street, but the sharp footsteps on the pavement behind him continued to make a tattoo on his ears. Ely stopped suddenly and looked in a shop window. The clicking stopped, too. When he resumed his walking the clicking began again.

He led his shadow on a long walk. He especially wanted to tour Váci utca. He saw that a bomb—probably American—had landed in Váci utca recently, but most of the elegant shops were still open. Many people were drifting down the street in twos and threes, talking and window-shopping. He had hoped the crowd would be large enough so he could lose himself in the confusion, but it wasn't. Gradually he became aware that there were no Jews on the street. At first he was puzzled, then he realized there must be a daily curfew. He was lucky to have Christian identity papers and no yellow star on his jacket.

Just ahead of him he saw a German security-police officer standing in a doorway. He sucked in his breath as he walked by, but the officer glanced at him without interest and fixed his gaze on other passers-by. However, he knew that the Hungarian detective was still behind him. Even on this busy street he could hear the rhythm of the clicks.

He had to make a move to lose the bastard. He went to a newsstand and bought a paper with Magyar money Cairo had supplied him, then stood near the curb, idly scanning the headlines but watching from the corner of his eye for the approach of a trolley. All this time he felt the remorseless scrutiny of the detective, standing just twenty feet away, staring with pretended interest into a shop window but watching in the plate glass the reflection of every move Ely made. For several minutes they played this game, then a trolley screeched to a stop at the corner. The detective watched Ely closely, ready to pounce if he made a move, but Ely stood where he was. The driver closed the doors of the trolley, and it started to move. For the first time the detective dropped his guard. Ely bolted for the moving vehicle, caught onto the handle of the door, and pulled himself up onto the step. The driver cursed, opened the door enough to let him in, and kept going. As Ely paid his fare and sat down, he glanced back through a window. The detective was frantically trying to flag down a taxi.

Ely remembered that there had been a cheap cinema on a side street about five blocks ahead. When the trolley reached it, he got off and hurriedly made his way down the narrow street. The theater was still there and in business. He bought a ticket and went in, tense and hardly believing he had shaken his pursuer.

He stayed in the protection of the darkened theater for several hours. At ten minutes to seven he mussed his hair, put his jacket over his arm, carried his hat in his hand, and left with a group of people who were going out of the theater, careful to stay in the middle of the cluster.

There was no evidence that he was being followed so he went to Gábor's address. He would be late in arriving at the Center, but he had to find out what was going on. Maybe Gábor could tell him. Andor had acted so strangely. As he reached Gábor's house he noticed that it bore no yellow star. A plump, gray-haired woman answered his knock. She didn't seem to be Jewish. Nevertheless, he asked for the Gábors.

"Mrs. Gábor doesn't live here any more." Her manner was abrupt and she moved to close the door, but Ely stepped forward.

"Please, do you know where she has moved to?"

She shook her head and closed the door in his face.

His spirits sank still lower. The woman had said "Mrs. Gábor." Where was Erno? He was frustrated and incensed. He resented the fact that he and Martin had had to split up because Andor wouldn't even try to give them some security. He was torn by conflicting emotions. In a nostalgic way it was good to be back in this city that always had had so many fairyland qualities. It was good to see men bowing graciously and behaving like gentlemen. It was good to see on Váci utca women who apparently were still making a lifework of being beautiful, despite the war. It was strange, after Cairo, to walk down the same streets with Nazis. It was surprising to find out how normally, on the surface at least, life was going on inside Hitler's Europe.

But transcending all these other reactions were his feelings about his own personal situation. He and Martin, by any standard, were heroes —two men who had risked death to drop onto an enemy continent. They had, furthermore, succeeded in crossing a well-guarded international frontier and in reaching Budapest, an enemy-occupied city. And yet look how they were being treated! Surely they deserved a different welcome than the one they were getting. . . . Still, these were incredible times, he told himself, desperately holding on to hope. Strange things happened during a war. Maybe there was an explanation, and maybe before long Andor would give it to them.

He was somewhat calmer when he reached the Center. It was almost nine o'clock, but Andor was there, waiting. There was no one with him.

"Where's Martin?" His voice rose in alarm.

"He hasn't returned. Why are you so upset? Didn't you lose the detectives?"

Ely told him what had happened and how he had sent Martin to Alex Peto's apartment.

"You didn't!"

"Sure I did. Why the hell shouldn't I?"

Andor sat down wearily and held his head in his hands. "Because Alex has been deported. They know about Haganah . . ."

Ely rushed to the door. Andor jumped up to restrain him.

"You can't go there. It isn't safe. I'm sure they have the place watched."

"I don't give a damn. We've got a job to do, this kid and I. Besides, I sent him there. It's my responsibility. I can't let anything happen to him."

"Wait a minute." With an expression of resignation Andor pulled a set of keys from his pocket and gave one to Ely. "If you must go, you'll need this. Come to my apartment tomorrow morning. There's a great deal you don't understand." He gestured toward the key in Ely's hand. "And tonight, be careful."

Ely turned the key in the lock and let himself in easily. As he opened the door, the light from the hallway filtered into the living room and he could see that the curtains were drawn. He closed the door and stood in the blackness for a moment, afraid to switch on the light. Instead he lit one match after another and explored the rest of the small apartment. At one side of the living room was a closetlike windowless kitchen, and in the cupboard he found some candles, lit one, and placed it on top of the table. It gave enough light for him to find his way around the living room, but not enough to be seen from the street, he hoped. Lighting another candle, he went into the next room, which was minuscule and contained only a large bed and a dresser. Together they filled the entire space. Off the bedroom there was a toilet.

Suddenly he felt very tired and hungry. It had been a long, discouraging day. He hadn't eaten anything except some fruit Martin had urged on him in the train. That train ride seemed weeks in the past, so much had happened. He searched the kitchen; Alex hadn't left even an old crust of bread. Well, there was no place to get food now. He turned on the faucet and let the fresh cold water run over his wrists and then splashed some of it in his face. It felt so good that he removed his jacket and shirt and took a bath from the waist up. He dried himself with his handkerchief and went back to the bedroom. The plump softness of the eiderdown *dunyha* looked irresistible, and he succumbed, half sitting, half lying on it, while he assured himself he would remain awake to listen for Martin.

About twenty minutes later there was a barely audible knock on the door. He got up and removed his shoes, careful to make no sound that could be heard from the hallway outside, then took the revolver from his hip pocket, released the safety catch, and walked into the living room. After turning the key in the door, he opened it slowly.

There in the doorway, standing uncertainly, was Rachel. His brain reeled. Rachel, in a thin summer dress of sky blue. In the candlelight he could see she was fuller now, and her hair was short. But she had the same large velvet-brown eyes and soft, generous mouth. It was impossible. He couldn't believe it. He had to touch her.

As he stepped from behind the door, she gave a little gasp and almost dropped the paper bag she was carrying. He pulled her into the room and locked the door, then stood staring at her. As the flickering light played on the full curves of her face and the fuller curves of her body, he was engulfed in a great wave of desire, but he constrained himself and became politely formal.

"Let me help you." He took the bag from her and put it on the cupboard.

"I've brought some food for you and your friend Martin," she said evenly, taking her cue from him. If she had expected a different welcome, she didn't show her disappointment. She began to take cheese and bread and a package of adulterated coffee out of the large bag.

"What are you doing here? I mean in Budapest." He was unable to control his curiosity any longer, though he tried to keep his tone casual. "How did you know about this apartment?"

"Budapest is a long story," she replied. "I'll tell you later, after you've eaten." She didn't look at him as she said it, but he was sure he heard a break in her voice.

She cut the cheese and bread dextrously, then filled a pot with water and put it on the stove to heat. "Andor told me you were here."

"Did he tell you why?"

"Not exactly. Anyway, I didn't understand it. He seemed very upset, and that's unusual for him."

They ate their simple meal in the quiet dark, not speaking, both of them uneasy, she because she couldn't tell from his face what was in his heart, and he because he was perplexed and bewildered by the strange events of the day, including her sudden appearance. Despite the tenseness of the situation Ely could not help bolting down a lion's share of the food. When they had finished, he asked her softly, "What's going on here, Rachel? Why was Andor so unhappy to see us?"

She sighed. "It's not you. It's the idea of resistance. He thinks it will destroy his plans."

"What plans?"

"I can't tell you. I wouldn't explain them properly. He'll tell you tomorrow. He wants you to know all about them so you'll understand."

"Do you believe in these plans?"

"Yes."

He was silent for a few moments, then suddenly he looked at her intently. "What's it like here in Budapest, living with Nazis?"

"Like some horrible nightmare." She leaned toward him. "What's it like outside—outside this prison they have made of Europe?"

He gestured vaguely with his hands and looked away from her. Suddenly he could no longer control the thoughts and emotions that had been pounding at his heart and mind. The lovely sound of her low voice and the blurred vision of her gently rounded body brought back the familiar overpowering passion and the wild, angry heartbreak.

"Why?" He shouted the word at her, forgetting everything else but this question that had been gnawing at his vitals for five years.

Terrified that they would be overheard, she rushed to him and put her hand over his mouth. The pressure of her flesh against his lips melted his fury. He lifted her hand away and looked into her eyes. "Why?" This time it was a whispered plea, full of grief.

She lowered her eyes. "I was afraid." The words were almost inaudible.

"Afraid!" His incredulous whisper filled the room. "Of me?"

"No—of a strange land and strange people." She looked up, begging him to understand. "Remember, Ely, I was only eighteen."

"Why didn't you tell me? Didn't you think I loved you enough?"

She shrugged helplessly. "At first I was going to keep my promise and follow you to Palestine. I told myself it would be all right. But at the last minute I lost my courage. I was terrified, and at the same time I was ashamed of my fear. That's why I didn't answer your letters. It was impossible to explain. Then in a short time the war began. Andor came here to Budapest and formed the Rescue Committee, and gave me a job as Committee secretary."

"And you weren't afraid to be part of a dangerous underground?" There was a touch of scornful disbelief in his voice.

She laughed bitterly. "Oh yes, I was afraid. I'm still afraid. I was afraid to come here tonight." Her eyes were clear and candid as they met his. "But I had to prove to myself that I could do it anyway. Don't you understand?"

He reached out and with his fingers caressed her smooth cheek. "I still love you."

"I know." She raised her face to his, and in the sweet, moist meeting of their lips everything but their awareness of each other was obliterated. They kissed again and again, muttering endearments, their arms around each other, their bodies pressed together, straining until their limbs trembled from the power of their mutual desire.

"I want to belong to you." The words were muffled as he pressed her head against his shoulder.

In the bedroom he undressed her slowly, gently kissing each part of her that he made naked. Her body quivered with excitement. He removed his own clothing, garment by garment, without letting her out of his clasp. When he, too, was naked he took her in his arms, and for a long time they stood like this, feeling their passion mount. Then she slipped away from him, and lay on the bed, her arms opened. He lay down beside her. In the shadowy light they embraced with a desperate tenderness, and all the bitterness of the intervening years dissolved away. . . .

Exhausted with happiness, he slept. In the dimness she lay close, studying him. His strong features were blissfully relaxed, his black hair tousled on the white pillow. His hand still clasped hers. Occasionally his fingers tightened. Exaltation for the present, regret for the past rose within her. "This time I'll go with you, my darling," she promised silently. "I love you. I always have. Only you." She leaned over and put her lips lightly on his cheek. Without awakening he gathered her to him and nestled her within his arms, then she slept, too.

They were roused by an insistent but low scratching noise at the lock of the door. With a jolt Ely remembered Martin and jumped from the

163

bed pulling on his trousers hastily and at the same time telling Rachel not to be frightened. He had almost reached the doorway when he abruptly turned and walked back to the bed. Cupping her chin in his hand, he bent down and whispered, "I am part of you now. Remember that." Then he hurried to the outside door. Pistol in hand, he opened it stealthily. Under the dismal hall light he saw a disheveled Martin, his blue eyes bloodshot, his ring of passkeys in his hand.

"Couldn't get the damn thing open," he mumbled.

"Where the devil have you been?" Ely asked as he lit the candle.

"Around." Martin's tongue was thick. "Around and around." He made a circular motion with his hand. "Been to every café in town. Couldn't lose that bastard."

"But you did lose him?"

"Guess so. Got to sit down." He shuffled to the sofa and dropped onto it.

"What the hell do you mean, you guess so?"

"He didn't come out of the last place, so I figure he's still there. I either drank him under the table or he's tireder than I am. Too tired to give a damn any more."

"You need some coffee."

"I need a bed."

"First the coffee," Ely insisted, but Martin was no longer paying attention to him. His eyes were riveted on the doorway to the bedroom, where Rachel stood, her face radiant above the thin blue dress. Even in his half stupor Martin marveled at the brightness of the brown eyes, the glow of her cheeks, and the upturned corners of the soft mouth.

"I'll make coffee for all of us," she said, smiling at them as she walked toward the small kitchen. But her eyes lingered a moment on Ely, and the look was not lost on Martin. For a moment he felt envy, the envy of a healthy young male. But then his good nature asserted itself. He loved Ely too much to be jealous of him. Actually he felt an increased respect for his friend. "Aren't you going to introduce me?" he asked with a mock leer.

A little self-consciously Ely presented him. Rachel acknowledged the introduction warmly, then turned to her task at the stove.

As they drank their coffee the men told each other what had happened since they separated in the afternoon. Rachel listened and said nothing, but a dreary despondency came over her.

It was almost daylight. Martin stumbled off to bed for a few hours' sleep. In the small kitchen Rachel washed the cups and saucers and the pot, occasionally glancing into the living room at Ely, who sat pondering the situation in which he and Martin found themselves.

15

At 10 A.M. they went to Andor's building on Váci utca, Martin still groggy despite several cups of coffee. The apartment was shuttered, and it was dark inside. There was only one small light in the living room, where Andor took them. They noticed that he looked harassed and thin and moved too quickly, not at all the suave, self-possessed man Ely had known in Pécs.

With pressing eagerness he began to tell them what had happened to the Jews of Hungary. It was obvious to Ely what he was trying to do. Most of the Jews, he said, had been deported already, except those in Budapest. As he talked he watched his two guests, measuring their reaction to his words. Martin occasionally gave away his feelings with a look of incredulity or a gasp of astonishment. Ely returned Andor's gaze stolidly, determined not to give him the comfort of knowing when he had scored a point.

"However," Andor continued, "my guess is that at least three hundred thousand of the original eight hundred thousand are still alive, and it is these people we're going to save, I and my Committee."

"How?" Ely asked bluntly.

Andor smiled patiently. "I'll tell you." Then chapter by chapter he related his negotiations with Wedemeyer and Erno's mission to Istanbul, mentioning several German names that were strange to Ely and Martin. While the negotiations over the Jews for trucks were going on, he added, Wedemeyer had agreed to hold up the deportations in Hungary.

Martin looked impressed. Ely gave no visible reaction. Andor was careful not to mention that, as far as the Rescue Committee knew, the deportations and exterminations were going ahead, at full speed, despite the negotiations.

All this time Andor had been pacing the floor of his living room, gesticulating frequently to emphasize the points he wanted to be sure they understood. Neither young man had interrupted, but now Ely jumped to his feet, unable to contain himself any longer.

"I think you're mad!" he shouted. "How could an intelligent man like you be taken in by a bunch of Nazi butchers? Is the air here so poisoned that even an intelligent Jew can't think straight?"

Andor started to answer, but Ely went on, "Can't you see that this truck proposition is just a scheme to try to divide the Allies? The Nazis win whatever happens. Istanbul is swarming with agents from all countries. As soon as the agents of the Soviet Union learned that a Hungarian Jew was approaching the Western Allies and representatives of American Jewry with a proposition to trade Jewish lives for war material—"

"The agreement was that the trucks wouldn't be used on the western front."

"And that proves to the Russians that in the middle of a war our side is double-dealing," Ely yelled. "But we aren't. Neither Britain nor the United States nor any body of Jews anywhere will fall for this deal of yours. No one is going to give a cake of soap to the Germans, let alone ten thousand trucks."

"It isn't my deal," Andor said quickly.

"So it isn't yours, but look at the service you're performing for the goddamn Nazis by being so gullible."

Andor was beginning to get angry. He wasn't accustomed to taking such talk from anyone. Ely was young, inexperienced, and not very shrewd. He had demonstrated that already. But he was in a position to wreck all the Committee's plans, so Andor controlled his fury and let him go on.

"My friend," Ely said, talking more quietly, "can't you see the tragic error you're making? What if it were possible for you to consummate the deal? Can't you see that this would prolong the war? If it's trucks the Nazis want, then they must be desperately in need of trucks, so we should concentrate on trying to destroy the trucks they have. Can't you see that the quicker the Allies win, the better for all of us?"

"I don't give a damn about the Allies or an Allied victory," Andor exploded. "The Allies have let us rot. All I care about is whether our people live or not."

"You don't make sense. The longer the war goes on, the more successful Hitler will be in the great ambition of his life: to do away with us. The sooner we can bring about an Allied victory, the more Jews will be alive when the shooting stops."

He put his face close to Andor's. "And that is why I am here. I and Martin." He turned and smiled at his companion, who had said hardly a word so far. "We're here to organize resistance: to find men with

166

guts, men who would rather die with a gun in their hands than die licking the boots of the sons-o'-bitching Nazis. You make your deals. We'll organize the underground. We've got our orders from the Agency and from the British Army."

As soon as he heard the word Agency, Andor reached his hand into a breast pocket and pulled out the cable he had received from Istanbul. "Read this," he said, handing it to Ely, who read it quickly.

"It's an impossible hope, Andor," the younger man said as he returned the cable. "If everything is going so well in Istanbul, why isn't Erno back?"

Instead of answering, Andor decided to play the card he was certain would save the situation for him. He leaned back in his chair, lit a cigarette, and began calmly, "I haven't mentioned anything personal up to now, because with me—as I know it is with you—this is a matter of principle, but let me tell you what happened in our home town."

Then, in almost too casual a tone, he gave an account of the formation of the Pécs ghetto, the mistreatment of the Jews there, and their final shipment to an extermination center. He included stories of incidents that had taken place in other parts of Hungary, but he justified this to himself with the reasoning that they *might* have taken place in Pécs. He mentioned the names of many people he was sure Ely knew, even the names of several of Ely's relatives.

He turned to Martin. "When did you last hear from your parents?"

The boy leaned forward nervously until his chair was balanced on its two front legs. "It's been a long time. More than a year. A friend in Switzerland brought me indirect news."

"Let me tell you what's happened to them. My Rescue Committee was able to get them from their town of Cluj here to Budapest just before a ghetto was established in Cluj. They're still safe, but not for long, unless you persuade your"—he hesitated, as if weighing how much sarcasm to put into the words—"your commanding officer here to adopt a more humane, a more Jewish attitude toward this whole situation."

"What in the hell do you mean, Horvath?" Ely cried resentfully.

"Let's keep our tempers under control," Andor cautioned. Then he told them the story of the rescue train, ending with a description of the haven in the Columbus barracks.

"What's this have to do with Martin?" Ely asked impatiently.

"Simply this," Andor replied quietly. "His parents are in the barracks, waiting for our train to get under way. And the one thing that certainly will keep the train from ever going will be for you two ambitious young

Englishmen"—he stressed the word—"to insist on carrying out a stupid military order."

Back in Cairo the Inter-Allied Organization, with years of experience in espionage, had prepared them for every contingency their instructors could imagine. But this was a situation no one in Cairo had ever envisioned. They had been conditioned for a clear, clean hatred. But now everything was getting mixed up. Now Ely was faced with a situation in which whatever he did would be wrong: a problem for which there was no sharp definitive solution. Until now there had been nothing inconsistent in being both a Jew and a British officer. In this war all the right, he felt, was on the side of Britain. The enemy, the Nazis, were the personification of evil. It was the Nazis who had gone in for trying to kill off a whole people. It was the British who were trying to defeat them and save the Jews. Heretofore it had been simple and clear. But now, sitting across from him, was a fellow Jew, a man he had respected since he was a boy, who had just about convinced him that he was on a futile mission and that he should disobey orders for which the punishment might be execution.

He was a British officer, he kept telling himself, and his only honorable course was to carry out the task that had been assigned to him. But if he did and the train never went and those sixteen hundred people were put to death, how could he live with himself?

"So, what am I supposed to do?" Ely asked aloud.

"I am asking you to drop your plan and do nothing to organize either an escape route or resistance inside Hungary." Andor's tone made it obvious that he knew he was once again master of the situation.

Ely's answer was low-pitched and somber. "We are British officers. You are asking us to commit a crime as terrible as treason."

"I am asking you not to sentence the rest of your people in Hungary to death."

"You ask me to make a frightening decision. You must give us three or four hours to think it over."

Andor nodded. "Good. I'll expect you back here in four hours."

Shortly after Martin and Ely left, a pair of Hungarian plain-clothes men appeared at the Horvath apartment and demanded to know the whereabouts of the two men from Palestine.

Andor denied any knowledge of them.

The larger detective snorted, "Don't be stupid. We tailed them to your office yesterday. We know all about them. Ely Farber and Martin Klein."

He pulled something from his pocket and handed it to Andor. It was a photostat of the false identity papers that had been made on the Hungarian-Yugoslav frontier for the two men. "You see," the detective said, "we'll find them—with your help or without it. It's up to you, Horvath." A grin spread across his face, but the words were touched with menace.

Andor shrugged. "They were here, but they went away. I don't know where."

For some time the detectives questioned him, but finally, convinced that he didn't know where Martin and Ely were, they left.

The rest of the morning passed slowly for Andor. When the four hours were up, neither Ely nor Martin had reappeared. He was worried. Another hour went by. He decided they must have been arrested. What should he do? It would be disastrous for the rescue train if the Germans found out about them from the Hungarian police. The solution was for him to tell the Germans first. If *he* gave them the news, it would throw them off guard. Also it would give him a wonderful alibi in case anything happened. But of course he mustn't tell the Germans the whole truth. He would change the story just enough to suit his purpose.

He hurried to see Colonel Heinemann at the Hotel Majestic and explained to him that two emissaries from Palestine had arrived in connection with the Wedemeyer truck deal and had disappeared. They probably been picked up by Hungarian authorities. Would the colonel inquire into what had happened to them? If they were in prison would he use his good offices to get them released? Andor repeated that they had come in connection with the negotiations. He hoped this would make Heinemann eager to free them.

The colonel was annoyed. "You Jews are always complicating matters. You're always getting yourselves into trouble, and then you come to us and want us to get you out of it." For several minutes he continued his lecture on what he termed "stupid Jewish conniving," then grudgingly said he would look into the matter. "However, if Farber and Klein have not been arrested by the Hungarians, you must deliver them to me just as soon as they show up," he added stonily.

Andor took a taxi to go back to his apartment. Three blocks away, as he was glancing casually out the window, he saw Ely and Martin walking in the street. He told the driver to stop, got out, and brought them back to the taxi. Then they drove around aimlessly for a half hour while Andor told them what he had done.

"I'm afraid I acted a little prematurely," he confessed.

Ely was thunderstruck. It was inconceivable to him that a Jew would turn in another Jew to the Nazis. "What the hell happens now?" he asked.

"I haven't figured it out yet."

They were all silent.

There was no question but that something had gone wrong. The visit of the Hungarian detectives was proof of that.

"Where do you suppose they got the photostats of our false papers?" Martin asked.

No one answered.

Maybe all that had happened was for the best, Ely told himself. "Are you sure you know what you're doing in these negotiations?" he asked Andor.

"Of course." Once more Andor was the man of boundless confidence. He had the Germans practically in his pocket, he explained to them, if no more unexpected incidents occurred.

Ely's tone was less certain. "I had an important mission. Now I've got myself involved in a spy story—like something in a movie. Maybe the thing for me to do is to disappear."

"If you really want to," Andor said, "I'll help you escape to Rumania. Of course"—he shook his head unhappily—"I don't know what effect this would have on our rescue train. It's supposed to go in about a week."

Ely sighed. Always the rescue train. Sixteen hundred people. His people. Sixteen hundred people against military honor. It was as bad as trucks for blood. How could anyone equate such disparate things? Horvath knew him well enough to be sure that he had him in a corner every time he mentioned that damned train. . . .

Andor's voice was rambling on. "Also, I don't know how your case is going to affect my negotiations with the Germans for more trains." He laid a comradely hand on Ely's arm. "I have no right to dictate to you what you should do. Your conscience will have to decide." Then, seeing the compassion in Ely's eyes, he added, "But I must tell you that Colonel Heinemann has asked me to take you to him. If I fail to produce you, it will be very embarrassing for me."

Once again there was a long silence as Ely considered the alternatives. Finally he said solemnly, "All right, I'll play your game."

For the first time since they had entered the taxi Martin spoke. "I'll give myself up with you," he said quietly to Ely.

Ely slapped him on the back and smiled affectionately, but almost immediately he became grave. "No, you can't. It would be too dangerous. They would certainly question us separately, and if we didn't tell exactly the same story they'd know we were all lying to them."

After some discussion they decided Martin would have to escape. Andor thought for a moment, then told the driver to go to the Columbus camp. "You'll stay there with your parents," he said to Martin. "When the train leaves, you get on it and go with the rest of them."

Martin agreed, but then suddenly turned to Ely. "I can't let myself be saved while you—"

Ely stopped him. "We'll meet in Tel Aviv as soon as it's over, and I don't think that will be long. You've got to stay alive, because I want you as a witness at my wedding. Don't forget it. And as for having a guilty conscience about disobeying orders, remember I'm your superior officer and whatever happens, whatever you do from here on in, you swear before God and man that you did it on my specific orders. Understand? *Lehitraot!*"

A few minutes later Andor delivered Martin to big Leo Strauss with the warning that the young man's presence was to be kept as quiet as possible.

"I've got just the place for him," Leo boomed, "on the top floor, with two old people who are both deaf and dumb. You know them. The Horowitzes from Pécs."

Andor went back to the waiting taxi and told Ely that now they were going to the SS on the Svábhegy in Buda.

Before they were out of Pest an air-raid alarm sounded. They jumped from the car and made for the nearest shelter. For more than an hour they heard the whine of falling bombs and the heavy thud as they landed. Several times the walls around them trembled. But they were almost oblivious to their surroundings as Andor repeated again and again the details of the negotiations, so that when Ely told his story to the SS he wouldn't be trapped in any contradiction. As soon as the all clear sounded, they went up into the street again and hailed another taxi. As they rode along, Ely took a small pad from his coat pocket and wrote a note. Then he folded it and handed it to Andor. "Will you give this to Rachel?"

As usual, Colonel Heinemann's broad face was inscrutable when Andor presented Ely. He didn't acknowledge the introduction. He just turned to the young aide sitting beside him and said, "Captain Mueller, escort Horvath to Room 20. I will see him later."

Andor was surprised, for he hadn't expected to be held or even questioned. He hesitated as the captain started from the room, but seeing Heinemann glare at him, he thought better of it and followed Mueller.

As soon as the door was closed, Heinemann's face returned to its normal inscrutability. The tall, slight sergeant at an adjacent desk turned to a blank page in his notebook, his pencil poised.

The colonel was exceedingly polite as he began the interrogation. "Who sent you here, Herr Farber?" he asked in a voice that said the question was routine.

"The Jewish Agency."

"Were there any others sent with you?"

"One. A young man named Martin Klein."

"Where is he now?"

"I don't know."

"You don't know! Come, Farber, surely you don't expect me to believe that."

Ely, trying to maintain a calm and courteous manner, explained about the Hungarian detectives following them and said they had split up. After that, he added, he hadn't seen Martin.

Heinemann dropped the matter. "Are there any others coming later?" he asked.

"Not that I know of."

"Why were you sent here?"

Ely repeated the story about coming to negotiate, the story Andor had coached him to tell, hoping desperately that the shrewd colonel would believe it. But Heinemann's face remained impassive.

"Tell me, Farber, how did you get into Hungary?"

At this point Captain Mueller returned to the room and sat down. Ely hesitated, but Heinemann ignored the interruption and motioned for him to get on with his answer.

Ten days ago he had been in Palestine, he replied, and had been flown over in a British plane and dropped by parachute into Yugoslavia, dressed as a British officer. "Some uniforms and sub-machine guns were also dropped, to give us a cover—an excuse—an alibi," he added, still unable to tell whether his story sounded plausible. "Then we bribed a British colonel working with the Partisans to let us pass through their lines."

Heinemann smiled for the first time, but his dark eyes were hard and bright. "How clever you and your companions were."

Ely gave an involuntary start at the word "companions." Did Heinemann know about Aaron and Naomi?

The colonel's smile grew broader as he became certain he had trapped his quarry. "Aaron Jaffee is dead," he said flatly. "Now do you want to tell us the truth? It will go hard with you if you don't co-operate."

Ely started to protest that he had told the truth, but Heinemann cut him short. "Captain, take the prisoner into the interrogation room," he ordered Mueller, bestowing a sardonic glance on his victim.

Two hours later, in the basement that the Germans had converted into a prison, the guard held onto Ely as he swayed along the corridor.

"Here," the German said, stopping before a cell and unlocking the door.

Ely stumbled inside and fell on the cot. His face and hands were puffed and bruised. One eye was closed. He was drenched with his own sweat, and his mouth felt as if it had been stuffed with cotton. He had a maddening thirst, but before he could gather strength to say so, the guard left. He lay in a half stupor exactly as he had fallen. He had no idea how long he remained like this, but some time later the sound of footsteps and the clanging of the door of the adjacent cell roused him. The guards were bringing in another prisoner. When the door had been slammed shut and locked, they stood outside it, talking about a Jewish girl from Palestine who had been captured on the Yugoslav frontier.

Ely's wounds throbbed, and the pressure in his head was unbearable. Naomi . . . they had caught Naomi. . . . It was all over.

With his swollen fingers he painfully pried loose a coil from the steel spring of his cot. It was rough and rusty. Holding it firmly in his left hand, he rubbed his right wrist against it, in a sawing motion, back and forth, back and forth. He felt only the first jab of pain as the rusty steel cut through the skin, then the nerves, and finally the veins. He sat on the edge of the cot, hypnotized as he watched the blood flow in a red velvet stream. How abundant it was. He began to feel very weak. Too weak to sit up any longer. As he put his head down the room became a beautiful bright red: the walls, the floor, even the ceiling. It would be pleasant to live in a place painted such a happy color. Then the room began to recede in all directions. The ceiling was so distant that he could hardly see it. The floor seemed as far away as the sea had been when they were flying over the Mediterranean. The walls were hardly visible at all. Everything was getting blurred and dim. He looked at his slashed wrist. It was impossible to tell whether the blood was still flowing. How very peaceful it is here, he thought. He closed his eyes. He could go to sleep now, the nightmare was over.

In another part of the underground prison Andor waited most of the night before Captain Mueller appeared to lead him back to Heinemann's office. Despite the hour the colonel was sitting stiffly upright at his desk, the back of his thick figure to the door as Andor entered.

"Where is Klein?" he asked abruptly, not turning around.

"I don't know," Andor answered.

Heinemann wheeled about, choleric with rage, and shouted that he knew all about the parachutists' mission and that he wouldn't tolerate such trickery by anyone, especially not by Jews. His voice rose to an almost deafening crescendo.

When the storm of abuse abated, Andor, ignoring it, tried to offer a placating explanation. He told himself, with an all-consuming dread, that the lives of the people in the camp on Columbus utca, among them his friends and family, were now really in danger. This was the time for him to use every grain of intelligence, every trick he could think of.

"Colonel, I believe I can prove my good faith, in spite of the circumstances that must seem suspicious to you," he began quietly. He had known nothing about the parachutists until Farber and Klein appeared at his office, he continued soothingly. After that he had lied about their purpose only to prevent their arrest. It was never his intention to help them in any way in the mission they had come to perform. Surely that was clear now, since he had persuaded Farber to drop his plan and had delivered him to the colonel.

Heinemann fixed a beady eye on him. "Farber has not been co-operative." Then he turned to Mueller. "Have him brought in." While they waited, he said to Andor, "We shall see now, Horvath, how good *your* powers of persuasion are."

After a few minutes Ely was half led, half carried into the room by a guard. He was unable to stand without support. His face was white, his undamaged eye glazed and unseeing, the bruises on his face purple. His right wrist was heavily bandaged.

The guard shoved him into a chair and apologized to Heinemann for the delay. "The prisoner tried to kill himself," he said with some contempt, "and we had to bandage him."

Andor rushed over and put his arms around his friend. "Don't worry, Ely," he whispered frantically. "Everything is going to be all right." He wasn't sure Ely heard him, for the young man gave no sign of recognition. His one eye stared straight ahead. Andor was desperate. "Listen to me, Ely," he begged. "Just co-operate. Everything will be all right. Don't do anything foolish again."

Heinemann watched in silence. He realized Farber was in no condition to be questioned further. "Take him back, but watch him," he barked at the guard. "I want him alive." As guard and prisoner left he turned to Andor. "Now for the last time, Horvath, where is Klein?"

Unable to think of a way out of the trap, Andor stalled for time. "At the moment I don't know," he said cautiously, "but if you will free me for a few hours, I'm sure I can find him."

"I'm sure you can." The derision in Heinemann's voice was palpable. "So I will give you exactly three hours. If at the end of that time you do not return to my office with Klein, Farber will be shot and your people at the Columbus camp will be sent to Auschwitz."

Andor went directly to the camp. It was early morning, and except for the SS sentries who stood guard no one was stirring. Fortunately Leo had told him where he was going to house Martin. He tiptoed through the quiet corridors until he came to the right room. From the door he could see Martin's blond head. He shook the boy's shoulder gently, at the same time whispering so as not to awaken anyone else. Martin sat up sleepily. Andor told him that the Germans wanted him. The young face took on an uncomprehending, incredulous expression.

"Listen to me," Andor said, tightening his grasp on Martin's arm. "You can go free if you wish. It's up to you. But I must tell you that Ely has been arrested and has been beaten badly. The situation now is this: the Germans have faithfully promised me that nothing will happen to you if you go to them with me, but if in three hours you have not presented yourself at headquarters Ely will be shot."

A look of pain came over Martin's face. He blinked several times and then rubbed his eyes vigorously, as if this whole scene were some ugly mirage that he could wipe away if he rubbed hard enough.

"There's also the rescue train to consider," Andor urged. "If you don't go with me, the Germans threaten to send it to Auschwitz."

All this was said in breathless undertones. Martin was still only partly awake, but gradually the reality of the situation forced itself upon him. I'm in a box, he thought in despair. Here is a guy who says my best friend will be shot and that everyone in this camp, including my mother and father, will go on a death train, instead of being rescued, if I don't give the right answer. How the hell did we ever get in this box, Ely and I? What did we do wrong? His throat tightened as he thought of Ely. If in three hours he didn't present himself at headquarters, Ely would be shot. He looked up at Andor. "I'll go to the Germans with you," he said slowly, then mechanically began to put on his clothes.

Just outside the camp gate they were met by Captain Mueller. He wore a wide grin as he opened the door of the SS car. "May I offer you a lift?" Andor was not really surprised to see him. He knew by now how efficient the SS was. It was even possible, he thought, that they had known all the time that Martin was in hiding there.

At SS headquarters Martin was put in the same cell as Ely. Horrified at the sight of his battered friend, he began to sob. Ely, though he was almost consumed by pain and desolation, managed to put his uninjured hand on Martin's arm and slowly tighten the fingers in affectionate pressure.

The following day they were transferred to a regular prison in the city. It was crowded with more than two thousand inmates. New suspects were brought in every few minutes. Several were added to Ely and Martin's cell, mostly Jews who had tried to escape to Yugoslavia or Rumania. From them they learned that Naomi was in another part of the same prison. The story of her capture had been spread by word of mouth until almost everyone in the prison knew it.

On their third morning the cell door opened and Major Vidovich, red-eyed, haggard, and dirty, was shoved in with them. Amazed to see him and eager to know what had happened, they bombarded him with questions. Their military mission was over now, and whatever had gone wrong was of only academic interest, but they wanted to collect every detail of the story of their agonizing defeat.

Vidovich's thick fingers rubbed the dark stubble on his tired face as he talked: "When we came near the border, we realized it was heavily guarded. There were Hungarian soldiers at every point where we might have crossed. So we split up. Miss Naomi insisted on going alone, with a Hungarian guide. She is a very strong-min—" He stopped and smiled. "She's a very stubborn girl. But we finally persuaded her to let us go first, so that if we got caught the Hungarians would be diverted and then maybe she could slip in. But our luck was bad and we were ambushed by a couple of guards. They found part of the transmitter on your man Aaron. Right away they wanted to know where the rest of it was. They were very rough with him. Still, he didn't tell them anything about Naomi."

"Good for Aaron," Martin interrupted.

"But they weren't fools. One of them knew a lot about radios. He told his companion there were parts missing and if neither of us had them there must be someone else who did. One of them stayed with us while the other went to organize a searching party. I guess they combed the woods until they found Naomi."

"Did you see her again?" Ely asked.

"Yes, they brought her back, and we were all there together. They said they were turning us over to the Germans. That's when Aaron started to break. At first he got very nervous. He kept muttering that he was sure they would force him to talk. He was afraid they would force him to tell what he knew about you two."

"But what happened to him?" Martin asked impatiently.

"When one of the guards turned his back, Aaron grabbed his revolver and shot himself in the head. He died almost immediately." After a pause the major added, "But he didn't talk."

There was silence in the cell for several moments, and then Vidovich said, "We didn't know it then, but several of Captain Dobos' men were members of the Hungarian counterespionage, so they—and through them the Germans—knew all about your mission." He raised his arms in a helpless gesture. "I am sorry."

"Your sergeant and the car—what happened to them?" Ely asked, almost choking with anger and frustration. "Didn't you even try to get away?"

"The sergeant was hiding the car among some trees when they spotted us," Vidovich answered in a voice whose dreadful monotony made plain how greatly he was struggling to keep it under control. "We were perhaps a hundred feet away from it, too far to reach it, even if we ran. But the driver started the engine and moved toward us. They saw, and they blew him and the car to hell with a grenade." He passed his hand over his face at the recollection.

For a few more minutes no one said a word. Then Martin asked quietly, "What do you think they will do with Naomi?"

The big Yugoslav's laugh was short and bitter. "The same as they'll do with the rest of us. For them we are all spies. Goddamn spies." When he saw the revulsion on Martin's face he added soothingly, "But the war's going badly for them. Who knows? It may end before they get around to dealing with Naomi. Or with any of us."

The afternoon sun was bright, and the sky was clear and blue, only sparsely festooned with billowing white cumulus clouds. As she walked among the well-dressed strollers along Váci utca, Miriam Berg pretended that everything was as it had been before the war, when her husband was alive and they were wealthy. Each day, between one and three, the hours when Jews were permitted to move freely about the city, she took this walk. It was play-acting. Paradoxically it was both her escape from reality and the means by which she gathered strength to face the dreary and ominous circumstances of her present life. She was a slight, fair-haired woman with a pale complexion and rather docile eyes, eyes from which all hope had been crushed, except during the brief revival each day on Váci utca.

As she passed a fashionable millinery shop, a Gestapo officer stepped in front of her, blocking the way. A pang of fear contracted her heart.

"Are you Frau Miriam Berg?"

"Yes," she whispered, panic-stricken.

"You will come with me, please." He led her into one of the ubiquitous little yellow police cars, gave an order to the driver, and they sped away to the prison where the parachutists from Palestine were.

She was taken to a small room and seated opposite two SS officers who proceeded to question her in detail about herself and her family. For some time, bewildered and frightened, she couldn't imagine why they had brought her to this place nor what the aim of their questions was. Then one of them said, "You have a sister named Naomi Loeb?"

She nodded.

"Where is she now?"

"She is living on a kibbutz—a farm—south of Tel Aviv, in Palestine."

"Are you certain?"

"I haven't heard from her in months, but—"

"Your sister is here, in this prison."

She gripped the arms of the chair, feeling as if she were going to faint.

"Your sister is involved in a very serious crime, and she refuses to tell us about her accomplices." He looked Miriam straight in the eye. "You love your sister, Frau Berg?"

"Oh yes."

"Then you would not want her to die?"

"No," she exclaimed in a horrified whisper.

"Of course not." He was all sympathy. "I am going to take you to see her. You must persuade her to tell us everything she knows about this crime. If she doesn't, you will not see each other again. Do you understand?"

"Yes." Her lips felt stiff and unwilling as they pronounced the word.

He led her down the corridor to a small cell. Even before the iron door was unlocked to admit her, she recognized her sister. It had been several years since they had seen each other, but Naomi had often sent

178

photographs that showed how healthy and happy she was in Palestine. Now she seemed many years older than she actually was, and her face wore the look of a cornered wildcat. Her expression softened slightly as she recognized her sister. They fell into each other's arms and kissed tearfully. Then Naomi pulled away and looked at her fragile sister sadly. "Forgive me, Miriam. I didn't mean to do this to you."

Miriam brushed aside the apology and then was struck by a terrifying thought. "Is this all my fault?" she asked. "Did you come back to Budapest because of me?"

"No, dear Miriam." Naomi rushed forward to put her arms around her sister again, but the officer stepped between them.

"Whispering is forbidden. Whatever you say must be said aloud."

In Naomi's eyes there was a veiled glint of fury, but she made no reply.

Miriam repeated everything the German had told her, but she added nothing, neither persuasion nor plea, and Naomi understood.

"I've told them all I'm going to tell them," Naomi said to her with finality. Then to the Gestapo man: "You can release my sister now. She can't persuade me to say anything, and she knows nothing herself."

Abruptly he motioned to the guard to unlock the door and took Miriam back down the corridor. But he didn't release her. Instead she was taken to a cell in another wing of the prison. The Gestapo had other plans. Despite what had been said, they intended to make certain that the sisters did meet again, often. Eventually the strong-willed one would tell the other her secrets. Of this they were certain. Then it would be no problem to get them from Frau Berg.

Each day, for an hour, the inmates were permitted to exercise by walking in the prison courtyard. It was during this daily walk that the sisters met. The second day Naomi noticed the yellow star on the breast of her sister's dress. She pointed to it.

"Why are you wearing that?"

"We all have to wear it. It's a symbol of the degradation forced on us."

"You don't really believe that!" Naomi said furiously. She bent down swiftly and drew a large Mogen David in the courtyard dust as Miriam leaned over her, anxiously watching.

"What are you doing?"

As Naomi finished the six-pointed star, she stood and shouted to the guards, "Come and see the Star of David. It is the pride of the Jews, not their shame. This is something you're going to learn."

The guards came running, and so did many of the other prisoners.

Confusion and disorder spread through the yard. The guards blew their whistles for attention. One of them fired a shot into the air. Two of them grabbed Naomi, and another contemptuously rubbed out the dust-made star with his shoe. She spat at him, and he slapped her hard on the face. As he did, Miriam let out a cry of terror. Other guards seized her. Then, as she watched in horror, Naomi, kicking and cursing, was half dragged, half shoved back to her cell.

It was a week after that before Naomi appeared in the courtyard again. When she did, Miriam noticed that the life and color were gone from her cheeks, which were now thin and sunken. Her black hair and eyes had lost all their luster. Only her lips seemed as firm as ever, firmer perhaps.

Day after day they took their exercise in the grim courtyard. Each day Miriam asked Naomi hopefully whether she had received any news from her friends outside. The answer was always no.

"I'm sure they don't know I've been caught," was her unchanging explanation, mostly to herself. Miriam's heart was filled with pity for her brave sister, but she made no comment.

In this way Naomi spent days, then weeks. She was questioned periodically and forced to submit to minor tortures and major indignities, but she defied her imprisoners, clinging tenaciously to a hope.

16

The work of the Budapest Rescue Committee continued as it had before the arrival of the parachutists, but Andor noticed a change in his colleagues. Since Ely's imprisonment Rachel had become fearfully quiet. She moved like a wraith among the women and children who were her charges. Her hands were still gentle and comforting, and she smiled with her lips, but there was a blank look in her eyes, and she rarely spoke, except when it was necessary.

One afternoon when the Committee office was crowded with people, Rachel suddenly turned to Andor and said, "I must speak to you."

"In a few minutes. As soon as I finish this—"

"No, now!" Her tone made him put down the paper in his hand and go at once with her to a far corner of the room.

Her eyes were desperate. He was used to desperate people. For weeks, months, years, he had been dealing with them. But Rachel's eyes were somehow different. They held him a prisoner. They kept him from looking anywhere except at her face.

"What is it, Rachel?" he asked, eager to get it over.

"Andor, I have been your most loyal supporter."

"Of course."

"I've defended you on many occasions against many people."

"I'm grateful, my dear."

"I've always said you could do anything you wanted to, as long as you wanted to do it enough."

He smiled. "That's a bit of an exaggeration." But the way he said it made it evident that he didn't really disagree.

"Andor, there is one thing you've got to do."

"If you mean—"

"Listen to me, Andor. You must go to the Svábhegy and get them to release Ely."

He started to speak, but she interrupted before he was able to utter a syllable. "I know all your arguments, all your excuses. But I don't accept them. This time I am against you. This time you are wrong. You know in your heart you haven't done all you could for him." Her voice was loud now and her words staccato. "You must help him, Andor. I beg you. Oh, Andor, I beg you."

She burst into sobs. He put his arm around her shoulders. Her head sank against his chest. He could feel her body trembling. Over his shoulder he signaled to his secretary. When she came, he turned Rachel over to her, saying softly, "I think some strong coffee, Zipora. Then maybe she could lie down for a while on the cot in the first-aid station. She's very much overworked."

The next morning he noticed that Rachel's eyes were bloodshot, but they were still aflame with righteous indignation. He never again looked into her face without seeing this accusing expression.

Joe, too, had changed. He went about his tasks with the same energy and thoroughness as before, but he was no longer the volatile, plain-spoken opponent of ideas he didn't like. Now he wouldn't express an opinion, even if pressed to do so. He had become a receiver of orders, which he carried out with a brooding efficiency. Nothing and no one seemed to reach him. Only occasionally would his eyes light up, when he forgot himself for a moment and spoke aloud his cherished hope: that the day would soon come when the Russians would enter Budapest and set the city free. But each time, as soon as the words were out, he caught himself and pursed his lips to shut them tight, like a trap that had inadvertently sprung open.

Even Arthur was subdued. The driving force that had made him rich and powerful, and had won him a beautiful aristocrat for a wife, this dynamism in him was dying. He knew it, and he knew the dying had begun with the imprisonment of Ely and Martin. He had stepped on a great many people in his time. Some of them he had used, and others he had ruthlessly shunted aside to get what he wanted. He had justified this jungle behavior to himself by saying they were weak. If they weren't, they would have done to him what he had done to them—their goals were the same as his. So there was no reason to be conscience-stricken over them. But sacrificing Ely and Martin was different. It was two for sixteen hundred, he told himself over and over, but the nagging sensation of guilt wouldn't go away. To hide it, and because he dreaded the possibility that the whole matter might be brought up for discussion again, he began to be very careful about what he said, not only to Andor, but to the others as well.

Andor noted these unhappy reactions among his colleagues with dismay. But he wasn't discouraged by them for long. His supreme confidence in his ability to manipulate people with his charm and shrewdness bolstered him. He was certain that eventually he could put the relationship between himself and the rest of the Committee back on its old friendly, trusting basis. But in the unlikely event that he couldn't—and he must consider this possibility, for he was a man to whom all things were possible—they would have to follow his lead anyway. Any other course would be sure disaster for all the Jews still in Hungary, and they knew it. Besides, he was the undisputed spokesman for the Jews now, and they knew that, too. This rescue train was his great mission, the fulfillment of the promise he had felt within himself since he was a boy. Once the world was shown that he could accomplish this almost unbelievable feat—the first mass transport of Jews out of German-occupied Europe with German approval—perhaps then the world would be willing to help him deliver others to freedom the same way. Though he had little faith in the rest of the world—the Allies, even the Jewish Agency and his own people in Hungary—he had unlimited faith in his own destiny and in the response of the rest of the world to his success—to anyone's success. So, once again in favor with the SS officers on the Svábhegy after having delivered the two parachutists to them, he continued to make plans with Wedemeyer for the transport of the rescue train.

The discussions turned to the date of departure. Day after day Wedemeyer stalled, insisting that a preliminary agreement from Istanbul must be in his hands first. But with persistent diligence Andor finally convinced him that the best way of getting some real action from the JA was to let the train go. The original plan was for the sixteen hundred people to go to Bergen-Belsen for several weeks and then leave for Lisbon by way of German-occupied France and Spain. From some Spanish port they were to embark for West Africa, and then eventually for Palestine. The JA sent a cable saying the Spanish and Portuguese governments had granted consolidated visas for all sixteen hundred passengers and that representatives of the International Red Cross would meet them at the Spanish frontier. These assurances dissipated Wedemeyer's fear that no country would accept the refugees and that eventually they would be thrust back into his hands again. He fixed the departure of the transport for June 30.

But on June 6 the Allies had invaded France. A thousand planes and gliders dropped paratroops onto the Normandy peninsula. More than three thousand American and R.A.F. bombers attacked fortifications along the coast. Tens of thousands of assault troops landed on the beaches. By now, late in June, there were almost a million Allied soldiers in Normandy, and the Americans were making a push for Paris. German communication lines were undergoing constant bombardment. The Allied bombings of bridges and other installations delayed the reinforcement of German troops. Equipment and ammunition now had to be sent to the front by a circuitous route.

As soon as it appeared certain that the invasion forces were not going to be driven out of France, both Andor and Wedemeyer were aware that it would be hazardous for the rescue train to travel the route originally laid out—through France to Spain—and each, for different reasons, reconsidered it.

Wedemeyer regarded the sixteen hundred as a pawn. He knew how many prominent Jews were on the list and the esteem in which many of them were held by Jewish leaders abroad. This made him certain he could use them to blackmail the JA. That was why he had been so pleased with the selections, including so many wealthy Orthodox Jews who had bought places on the train. That was the reason for his preoccupation with their safety.

"What will happen if the train is hit by an American or English bomb, or if it's derailed in the middle of its journey?" he asked Andor during one of their meetings.

This gave Andor the lead he was looking for. "Wouldn't it be possible to provide the train with some sort of air cover?" he said quickly.

This was a little too much for Wedemeyer. With a burst of acid indignation he snarled, "Surely you don't think the Reich has nothing better to do at this moment than to protect Jews!"

Andor made a gesture with his hand as if to dismiss the suggestion he had made. "Let the people leave on the train as planned. We'll take all the risks," he said calmly. But the darting vivacity of the colonel's cold blue eyes and the sleek cunning of his manner suddenly put Andor on his guard again and caused an ugly suspicion to cross his mind. It was within the realm of possibility that Wedemeyer was planning to blow up the train and blame it on an Allied bombing. He mustn't allow himself and his people to get caught in this trap, so he added, "Since we both are eager for the train to arrive at its destination safely, perhaps it would be wiser to detour it to Switzerland."

Wedemeyer clicked his tongue speculatively and replied that he wanted to think it over. Andor got no more from him that day, but the next morning Wedemeyer acquiesced. At once the Budapest Rescue Committee applied to the Swiss Government to permit sixteen hundred people of the rescue train to take refuge in that country until they could get passage to Palestine. The permit was received almost immediately. When it came, Andor told himself with great self-satisfaction that all his intriguing and conniving were about to pay off, and he hurried to the Columbus camp with the good news.

It had become his habit to go there every afternoon, ostensibly to oversee the activities of the camp and to drop in on his father-in-law, but he was willing to admit to himself that his visits were much more frequent than they would have been had it not been for Jessica.

Even with all the tension of the past several weeks, Jessica haunted him night and day: her sad-sweet face, the black hair pulled back so defiantly, the delicately rounded breasts. Day after day he tried to penetrate her wall of reserve, but he made almost no progress. She treated him with marked courtesy and respect, but with chilling indifference. Worst of all, whenever they were in the same room, or out in the corridor together, she was still, always, the master of the situation. This was one of the challenges she posed for him. Somehow, he told himself, he must find a way to break down her dominance and make her subservient to him.

But it was more than that, and he knew it. He wanted her physically, too. He wanted to prove to her with passion and affection that her great need—the lack of which made her so brittle—was the love of a man she could respect and to whom she could give herself completely. As yet he still was not able to force her to give even a smile when he wanted it.

Thinking about it, he realized he had never been so timid with a woman before. But with Jessica he had been disciplining himself so strictly in her presence that he had never even made any verbal advances to her. Yet surely, being a woman, she was astute enough to see and comprehend. Or was her grief so intense, her indifference to life so complete, that her intuition had been dulled?

Often when he was away from the camp he would wonder if this was not the first time in his life he had really been in love, despite his many experiences with the pretenses of love. Or was it just because this was the first time he had ever been frustrated?

One proof he found of the influence she was having on him was his frequent debate with himself as to whether or not he should go on the train. Until Jessica's arrival he had not even given a single thought to the idea. His place was in Budapest, making more and more deals, trying to save not a few hundred or even a few thousand but tens of thousands of Hungarian Jews. But in the quiet of the night, when he would lie on the rather uncomfortable cot in the living room, he would often think of the future. There were two possible futures: the future as it would be after she was gone, and there was no camp to visit any more, and there was no one to excite him with a toss of the head or a half-smile grudgingly given, or the future as it could be if he went with her and they were together in Switzerland and then possibly Palestine. If she left without him, her bitterness might harden into something no man could ever break.

But he said none of these things to Jessica. Instead he played the role of dutiful son-in-law and man of affairs—the latter the only role he had ever really thought befitted him. He was gracious and charming. Every day he brought her a gift—some small luxury the three of them could share. Sometimes it was uncut tea, or a few Hungarian pastries that were now rare, or a bottle of real *barack,* or sugar, almost as valuable as gold.

Gradually her distant manner changed, and with the delicacies he brought she would arrange a little party that they all enjoyed. Gradually he learned how to amuse her. He was a good storyteller, and while Philip drowsed he would regale her with preposterous tales of his mischievous adolescence, hungrily watching for her tight-held lips to part in amused relaxation. Sometimes he told her about his negotiations with

185

Wedemeyer, and then her sapphire eyes would fasten on him intently and grow large with admiration, but when it was all over she was again the epitome of polite decorum, distant, impersonal, almost forbidding. He found it maddening and more often than not left Columbus as much infuriated with his own helplessness as with her obstinacy. Love had always come to him. Women had always found him difficult to deny. But Jessica apparently found it easy, and he couldn't bring himself to use on her the artifices with which he had so blithely seduced others. He had a fierce desire for her to love him, to want him as he was. That she seemed not to be aware of such a possibility was a blow to him as a man that drove him almost to despair. Yet, the next day, as full of renewed hope as a youth struggling through his first love affair, he would return to watch her and be tortured again.

June 30 was a rainy day. Intermittently a soft summer drizzle fell on the Columbus camp. But no one minded. By noon all the inhabitants had their bags packed and were waiting in the courtyard to go to the railroad station. They had been told they were to provide their own food for the trip. As a result the thirty kilos of luggage that each was permitted contained mostly edibles, plus a few valuables they refused to leave behind and some pieces of clothing. Those who were sick or aged—about forty—were loaded onto a truck, Philip Kemeny among them, although he protested that he could walk the distance easily. The rest marched five abreast to the station—not the large main terminal of the city, but a small one on the outskirts. By the time they arrived it was midafternoon.

Andor had co-operated with Wedemeyer's office in working out the details of the trip so there would be as little confusion as possible. It was agreed that instead of any other pieces of legitimation, each person would identify himself whenever called upon to do so by producing a British immigration certificate bearing his name, age, sex, and place of birth. These certificates, forged under Rachel's direction, had already been distributed to the sixteen hundred.

Andor volunteered to make the loading of the train quick and efficient by assigning each person a place in one of the twenty-eight baggage cars that would comprise the train. So that no one would forget his car number, it had been written by Andor's secretary with a red pencil in the corner of each British certificate.

He tried to be humanitarian in the assignments. An average of fifty-seven persons would have to ride in each car. In the first three cars he put Hugo Mayer's Orthodox people and in the cars immediately following other people from Budapest. In the center of the train were cars containing the large contingent from Pécs. The cars at the rear of the train were filled with people from other provincial towns and with refugee Zionists from Slovakia and Poland. In this way, he reasoned, families and friends would be all together and morale would be improved.

There were about twenty rabbis on the train, but instead of grouping them together, he decided they should travel like everyone else.

He isolated the one hundred passengers chosen by the SS in cars 27 and 28. He hadn't had time to make a personal investigation of these people and didn't yet know why Heinemann's office had decided that they should be saved, but he had warned Leo Strauss to keep an eye on them, especially after the train reached Bergen-Belsen.

At the end of the train were two cars loaded to the roof with food and a coach for the use of the German military in charge of the train. The cars of food were another tribute to Andor's genius at negotiating. Just three days ago he had made a trip to the Svábhegy and argued that the JA in Istanbul would be impressed if he were able to report to them that Colonel Heinemann personally had permitted the people of the transport to take along a freight car or two loaded with food to supplement their rations at Bergen-Belsen. At first Heinemann stormed his refusal. But when Andor said that his Committee would buy the food, transport it to the depot, and load it themselves, and that he, Heinemann, could have all the credit for it, as far as Istanbul was concerned, the colonel agreed. The food was purchased in the black market at exorbitant prices, but Andor felt certain that his sixteen hundred fellow Jews would someday bless his name for this final proof of his thoughtfulness. The only meat he could find was bacon, but he knew that some of the nonreligious people on the train would relish it, and perhaps even Orthodox rabbis would find a loophole to permit its consumption by their followers in such an emergency as this. He had also purchased a large quantity of cheese—a variety that would improve rather than deteriorate with age—and a great deal of tinned goods.

Most of those in the marching column were footsore by the time they reached the railroad siding where the rescue train stood. As soon as some of them saw the baggage cars with their sliding wooden doors, they began to protest loudly that no one had told them they were going to "travel like cattle." They expected coaches, they said. Others expressed their quiet amazement that there were only six SS guards to watch over sixteen hundred people.

Andor was standing on the railroad platform with a sheaf of papers in his hand. Rachel and Joe were near, ready to assist in an emergency. Already the forty sick and aged who had come by truck had been helped into their cars. Here and there a wizened or ghostly pale face could be seen peering out an open car door. In the door of the tenth car stood Philip Kemeny, looking anxiously with his watery eyes into the crowd of new arrivals for Jessica. When he spotted her, his face creased in a gentle smile and he made a ceremonious little bow from the waist to her.

Andor supervised the loading of the train. He stood at the door of first one car, then the next, calling off names from his list. As each person responded, he was required to show his British certificate to the SS agent standing beside Andor, then was permitted to throw his luggage up into the car and to climb in after it.

Fortunately there weren't many farewell scenes. Andor had specifically ordered that if any relatives or friends wanted to say good-by they must do it at the Columbus camp, and even this was virtually ruled out by the curfew that made it illegal for Jews to be on the streets of Budapest except during two hours every afternoon.

"We'll have problems enough without the emotionalism of good-bys," he had said to the Committee.

Arthur Gruen was present at the depot in his capacity as a member of the Rescue Committee, but his first task was to see that his fragile Elizabeth and their two boys were safely aboard. He annoyed the SS man standing beside Andor with his interminable instructions as he helped his family into their car.

"You remember, Elizabeth, where I packed the medicine for your throat, don't you, dear?" She assured him that she did.

"Keep an eye on that infection on Jacob's foot, and if it gets worse . . . And don't let the boys eat all the cheese I put in the brown suitcase the first day."

The SS man lost his patience. "Get these people into the car. You're holding up the whole line."

Tears were streaming down Arthur's florid face as his wife's golden head disappeared into the darkness of the car. Then he turned away, wiped his eyes dry, and began to help the other passengers. He saw the elderly parents of Martin Klein waiting their turn and picked up the heavy suitcase Mrs. Klein had already carried so far. She thanked him warmly as he lifted it up into the car. Then she laid a thin, dry hand on his arm and looked up at him imploringly. "You will help Martin, please?"

He nodded, not trusting his voice. If he had spoken, he wouldn't have known what to say.

When Andor got to Car 10 the first names he called out were those of Leo and Vera Strauss and their two daughters. As he checked them off his list, he said, "Leo, after you get your family aboard, I have a job for you. You know most of the people on the train. Go from car to car and get them to organize a committee in each one, to take charge and run things in an orderly manner. Someone on the committee should stand watch in each car during the night, in case of an air raid. If there is an attack, the train will stop, but someone will have to direct the people and get them into the woods or away from the tracks. Pick men for the committees who are likely to act calmly in an emergency."

Leo nodded, then whispered, "But the doors? They'll all be sealed, won't they?"

Andor looked at his friend with a smile of self-satisfaction. "No. This was one of the many concessions I was able to get from them. The cars won't be sealed. They won't even be locked. You'll be as free as the wind. That's the agreement."

As Leo hurried down the platform to carry out his commission, Andor went back to checking the passengers into Car 10. Next on his list were his sister and her family. He kissed Rena, and she held onto his arm until he released himself from her frightened grip. He embraced little Dan, shook Sam's hand firmly, and assured all three that they would have a safe journey. "Please relax and try to be happy," he said to his sister, patting her arm and kissing her once more as he left.

He had put Jessica's name at the very bottom of the Car 10 list, so she would be the last aboard and therefore near the door. Finally he came to it. He tried to read it in an entirely normal voice: "Mrs. Jessica Hoffmann."

"Present," she said. He looked at her and smiled. While the SS officer was inspecting her immigration certificate, he said softly, "You get up into the car and I'll come back to say good-by as soon as I check the rest of the train."

"That would be very kind of you." Her face softened, and her eyes smiled at him for a fraction of a second.

Suddenly there was a commotion and the sound of high-pitched yelling at the rear of the platform that was so loud it could be heard all over the station, even above the babble of hundreds of passengers and the crying of a few children. Andor started to move toward the disturbance, but as he did he saw big Leo elbowing his way in the same direction, so he stopped and returned to his checking.

Leo pushed his way through a circle of curious but frightened spectators and found a Gestapo guard holding by the scruff of the neck a small, wiry young man with a mass of curly black hair and bushy eyebrows. The prisoner was squirming violently. The more he twisted about, the more firmly the guard fastened his grip. They were shouting at each other, the German almost apoplectic with rage. Beside the young man was a battered brown suitcase, and around him on the ground were several pencils and an open sketchbook.

"He was drawing pictures," a woman whispered, as Leo pushed his way to the center of the scene.

The German, who fortunately had been one of the guards assigned to the Columbus camp and therefore knew Leo, began to explain that he had found this man sketching the scene at the station. "It's against the rules!" he exploded, and thereafter punctuated every other sentence with this remark.

"The rules, the rules . . ." The bushy black head of the artist wagged with disgust as he mimicked the guard.

Leo shot him a warning glance, then apologized to the German, adding that he would see to it that everyone obeyed all the regulations, without question, from now on.

Mollified, the German left, and Leo wheeled on the unrepentant little man. "How come it's always you who makes trouble, Moshe? Why can't you behave like other people?"

"Because I'm not like other people. I'm an artist. I'm a free soul!" As he warmed to his subject, his voice took on a sonorous quality. "This society"—he waved his arms to include everyone on the platform—"is fettered with uncountable repressive regulations and tyrannies that strangle the creative spirit of man—"

"All right, all right," Leo bellowed. "I'm sorry I asked. Just remember this"—he shook a thick finger in Moshe's face—"I'm not going to let anybody's creative spirit endanger the people on this train. You cause more trouble, the Gestapo can have you." With that he walked away, shaking his head. "Philosophy he gives me at a time like this. Artists!" he spluttered contemptuously.

At the rear of the platform Andor finished with cars 27 and 28. Turning to Rachel, who had remained beside him most of the time, he said, "I think we deserve to take a bow, my dear. Every one of our passengers is present and accounted for, except, of course, old Mr. Rosenthal."

"What happened to him?" she asked in the dull monotone in which she talked most of the time these days.

"He had a stroke this morning in the barracks. He was dead by the time a doctor reached him. So that brings our total down to fifteen hundred and ninety-nine. It's too bad we haven't someone to put in that empty place. By the way, where did Joe disappear to?"

"He told me a few minutes ago that he had a job to do. I don't know what it is."

"You'd better see about that woman who's sick in 18," Andor said, folding the sheaf of papers and putting them in an inside coat pocket. "I must go back to Number 10."

Rachel made no comment. She knew about Jessica and the effect she was having on Andor. In one way Rachel resented it. This woman with whom he was so obviously in love was about to go off to safety. The man she loved with an intensity Andor couldn't possibly understand was in prison, and Andor had refused even to lift a finger to save him. His excuse was that he mustn't do anything to jeopardize the departure of the train. Maybe, Rachel kept telling herself, once the train was under way she could persuade him that he was risking nothing by using his influence to try to obtain Ely's release.

As Andor approached Car 10, he saw first Philip Kemeny's gaunt face. The old man was sitting on his suitcase in the open doorway. Behind him stood Jessica with a china cup in her hand. She handed it to the old man. "Drink it while it's still warm. It will do you good," she said.

Andor gripped the doorjamb and pulled himself up into the car. "How do you feel, Philip?" he asked.

"Like a very fortunate man." As Philip smiled philosophically, Andor was reminded of an ancient Hebrew prophet. The thought flashed across his mind that if all went well and the Germans kept their promises, most of the people on this transport might eventually reach Palestine and have a good life after the war ended, but there was little likelihood that Philip Kemeny would be one of those fortunate ones. Even all of Jessica's attention would probably not be enough to keep him alive. Andor leaned down, put his arms around the thin shoulders, and gave his father-in-law a final embrace. "Have a good trip, Philip. Next time we meet it will be under happier circumstances."

The old man took Andor's hand and held it tightly in both of his. "Thank you, my son. Thank you for everything."

As Andor straightened up, he found himself looking directly into Jessica's face, the face of the woman who for him was the most important person on the train. He was ready now to admit this to himself and to her—if he could find the words and if she would listen.

He noticed that she had on the same shapeless dark dress she'd been wearing the first time he saw her. Her black-fringed sapphire eyes looked at him questioningly. He forgot the ugly dress, the tightly drawn hair, the wall he had not yet been able to breach. He was sure her eyes were trying to make some sort of a response.

Andor knew that the people on his rescue train had a better chance of surviving the war than any other Jews in Europe, perhaps than any people at all behind German lines. He was sure of this. Yet now that the moment had come to say good-by, he realized there was a chance he might never see Jessica again. Even if the train arrived safely in Germany, even if the passengers eventually got out of Germany and to some safe haven, there was always the possibility that he himself wouldn't survive.

He realized more than ever that he wanted her. He wanted her desperately—for the rest of their lives.

He took her left hand, raised it slowly to his lips, and kissed it, gently at first, then with more and more ardor.

She drew back a little in astonishment and searched his eyes with hers. She was trembling a little; he could feel it in her hand. He stepped closer. "Jessica, please listen to me." He pronounced her name caressingly.

"Yes?" Her eyes were soft, and she seemed receptive, but he couldn't find the words to tell her. Instead he said, "You are not to be afraid on this trip. You are not to worry. You are going to live. Someday—" Suddenly he cupped her chin in his free hand and put his face close to hers. "Someday you're going to be very happy again."

She looked surprised but made no movement to free herself from either his hands or his gaze.

He bent his head slightly as he raised her hand to kiss it for the last time. He hoped she would feel in the pressure of his lips all he hadn't said. When he lifted his head and let loose her hand, he saw that there were tears in her eyes. "Remember all I've said and all I wanted to say but haven't yet said," he whispered. Without looking back he jumped to the station platform and hurried off to find Leo Strauss.

At Sip utca Andor was just locking the list in a small steel office safe when Joe appeared, looking hot and tired.

"What happened to you at the railroad station?" Andor asked with a trace of annoyance. "I could have used you."

Joe eased himself up onto the edge of a desk, crossed his legs, lit a cigarette, then asked, "Did you know that while you were loading your people into their cars, another train pulled into the station, on the very next track?"

"There were so many trains coming and going I didn't notice. Why?"

"This other train was hidden by ours—it was beyond ours, on the next track. No one paid any attention to it because it was just thirty or forty cattle cars, all of them locked—with padlocks. But I went around to the opposite side of our train, and at the little windows near the top of each car in that other train I could see faces—faces I knew belonged to Hungarian Jews. They were too terrified, I guess, to do any shouting."

"What's the point, Joe?"

Despite Andor's impatience, Joe was silent for a long moment, then in a cold voice he asked, "How many were on your train, Andor?"

"Fifteen hundred and ninety-nine, because of that death we had early this morning."

"Well, Andor, when you take credit for saving all those people on your rescue train, make the number sixteen hundred and seventy-nine."

"What are you talking about, Joe?"

"One of the ways I prepared for my work on your Committee—I told you once, but I guess you've forgotten—was to take some instruction from a locksmith. In addition to the lessons he gave me a few tools of the profession." As he spoke Joe pulled from his trousers' pockets a collection of master keys and half a dozen instruments that looked as if they might have come from a dentist's office.

"You mean you picked the lock on one of the cars in the other train?"

"Yes."

"My God, Joe, how many people were in the car?"

"Exactly eighty."

"What did you do with them?"

"I opened the doors on the far side of three cars in our train and put one third of them in each."

"Joe, you shouldn't have done this without asking me."

"Without asking you? Are you crazy, Andor? Our train was about to start. There was no time to call a meeting and hold a debate." His voice was bitter.

"But, Joe, that means there are almost ninety people in each of those three cars!"

"I picked cars 24, 25, and 26 because I knew they were full of mostly Polish and Slovak refugees. Most of them are chalutzim. Nearly all are men. They're tough or they wouldn't have gotten this far. Also, they know how to share."

Andor leaned back in his chair. "Maybe when the train stops somewhere—"

Joe interrupted. "I thought of that, so just before the train got under way I looked up Leo Strauss and told him what I had done, and I suggested that as soon as he got an opportunity he spread them out a little more evenly. After all, it means an average of only two or three extra per car."

"Who were these people? Did you find out?"

"Yes. They were from towns in Transylvania. I guess this was one of the last provincial transports. The people seemed to know they were going to Auschwitz, and they knew very well what was going to happen to them when they got there. That's why there was no arguing about it when I told them that our train was taking people to safety."

"But did they have any papers?"

"No. You know very well, Andor, the goddamn Nazis are not bothering any more with papers for the people they are sending off to be gassed and cremated."

"But these eighty people of yours will be spotted the minute they get to Bergen-Belsen because they won't have British immigration certificates, like all *our* people have," Andor said nervously.

Joe broke his last cigarette into two pieces, put one half in his breast pocket, and lit the other half. Then finally he answered.

"When Rachel and her forgers were making the false certificates, I had them make an extra hundred for me. I took them with me when I went to the railroad station. I thought maybe someone in your transport might have lost his certificate. I even brought along the red pencil your secretary used in marking the car number in the corner of each certificate, remember?"

Andor nodded.

"Well, when I said good-by to Leo, I gave him all hundred of the certificates, as well as the red pencil. I told him it would give some of the members of his train committee something to do, filling in the name, the age, and the other details on the eighty certificates. The other twenty certificates I told him to keep. Who knows? Somehow they may come in handy."

17

It was dusk as the train moved out of Budapest. Leo had explained to the committee in each car—then the committee had explained to the rest of the passengers—that the doors were all unlocked and when the train stopped to take on fuel or water they could get out long enough to fill their canteens or empty their bladders. But it was Leo's idea that they should keep the doors closed the rest of the time. It would obviate the danger of children or careless adults falling out when the train went around sharp curves, or the greater danger from Hungarian secret police in towns through which the train would pass, who were accustomed to Jews being shipped in sealed cars and who might try to make trouble if they saw sixteen hundred Jews riding across the countryside in cars that weren't only unsealed but had wide-open doors.

However, that first night as they were leaving Budapest for what many believed might be the last time, it was too great a temptation for them not to open the doors a few inches and take turns getting a last glimpse of their city. They stared, without much conversation, at the city's sky line until finally the dusk grew thick. Then they shut the doors and everyone but the lookouts settled down to get some rest. Those who took turns listening for the moan of air-raid sirens or the drone of bombing planes noticed that the train stopped and started frequently during the night. It seemed to be standing still more often than it was in motion.

When morning finally came, one of the watchers cried out with excitement that they were in the marshaling yards on the edge of some large city. Others looked out in amazement, and there was a heated discussion about what city it was. Then someone else shouted: "What idiots we are! It's Budapest."

He was right. The train had been shunted around all night, from one yard to another, and now they were back within a mile or two from where they had started. Leo went to one of the SS guards and asked what the trouble was. The guard said he was as puzzled as they were. Even Leo

was nervous until a half hour later, when the train finally got under way
—this time in earnest—and they took another last glimpse of Budapest.
In a short time they were speeding westward across the Hungarian countryside.

Late that day they arrived at Magyaróvár, near the Austrian and
Czechoslovakian frontiers. Here there was a long wait. The German
commander of the train, accompanied by two of his SS men, went off to
talk with the chief of the Hungarian border patrol. There seemed to be
some question whether the transport would be allowed to leave Hungary. Everyone was apprehensive. Leo had issued strict instructions that
the passengers must do nothing to complicate the situation by getting out
of their cars or even leaving the doors open. The committees had difficulty enforcing the order. After several hours the German commander
returned with a Hungarian captain, who remained outside the coach at
the rear of the train until the German reappeared with a large document.
In a mixture of good German and stumbling Magyar, he explained his
transportation order. The people in Car 28 heard part of the conversation. Horrified, they insisted to those in the adjacent car that the
German had said he was escorting the train to Auschwitz.

The dreadful whisper was passed from person to person, car to car.
By the time it reached Car 10 and Leo heard it, panic had seized the
passengers. Their faith in Andor Horvath had melted away. Some wanted
to jump off the train at once. Others began calling on God for deliverance.

Leo decided that there were two possibilities: either the men in Car
28 had misunderstood or the German commander had been trying to
allay Hungarian suspicion by assuring the captain of the frontier guard
that these Jews, like all the others, were destined for the gas chambers of
Auschwitz. He himself was certain they were on their way to Bergen-
Belsen and to eventual safety, as Andor had told him, but he had to
convince the others. Suddenly the name of a Czechoslovakian village
flashed through his mind: Auspitz. He and Vera had stayed there once,
years ago, when they were on a holiday.

He clapped his hands for attention, and when the car was quiet he
said, "If anybody knows an ear doctor, send him back to examine that
man in Car 28 who started this story. Auschwitz, he says. I happen to
know where we are going. And I don't get my information by secondhand grapevines. Listen to me. We are going to a place called Bergen-
Belsen. A camp. That is in Germany. To get there we cross Czechoslovakia, yah? On our way across Czechoslovakia we stop, maybe, at

Auspitz. Listen to me. Auspitz. Not Auschwitz, Auspitz. Ask my wife. She knows Auspitz. It was 1934 we were there, eh, Vera?"

It was almost possible to feel the tension in the car subsiding. But Leo wasn't finished.

"I tell you now a joke. Do you know the difference between where we are going, Auspitz, and where we are not going, Auschwitz? Well, I tell you. The first, Auspitz, is like *Tzion,* and the other, Auschwitz, is like *tzian.*" The Hungarian word for Zion, land of the Jews, is *Tzion;* the Hungarian word for cyanide gas is *tzian.*

It wasn't a joke to cause any belly laughs, but it was repeated from car to car, along with the story that they were going to Auspitz in Czechoslovakia, not Auschwitz in Poland, because Leo Strauss said so, and wasn't Leo Strauss nearer to Andor Horvath than anyone else, and besides, wasn't he an honest man?

When the train was under way again, Leo sat on his suitcase in a far corner of Car 10 and leaned against the side of the car. He was very tired. How many more times before it was over would he have to put down rumors and keep up morale? Then he thought:

I could write a book about Auschwitz, even though I have never been there. It was never an important place in Poland. We Hungarians had never even heard the name until some Polish refugees got to Budapest and tried to tell us what was happening there. They told us about gas chambers and the crematoria, but we refused to believe. The idea that millions of Jews were being gassed and cremated at Auschwitz or anywhere else was beyond the capacity of our comprehending, despite all our twenty centuries of persecution and conditioning.

There's a difference between hearing and comprehending, between knowing and believing. Maybe it's a shield that human nature provides for us. You hear someone tell you the truth, but it doesn't sink in. You hear but you don't believe, because you don't want to believe. If you believe and comprehend, you're finished; it's the end. So you dismiss the stories and say maybe he made a mistake. Maybe he got it secondhand. Maybe he exaggerates. But even if it is true, it can't happen to me. We immunize ourselves against the idea of death—of death for us personally.

So then the Hungarians establish a ghetto and you say to yourself: This I will be able to survive. We will live in a ghetto, yah? So there will not be so much food any more, and some people will die. But people die every day. Even in a place like New York they die. Maybe they take some of us to work in labor camps. So what? They can get from

197

us only so many hours of work a day. Maybe even twenty-four. But no more. If they want us to do hard work they must give us decent food, or we will not have the strength to do the work they want. Maybe some of us will die. But some of us will always die.

In Pécs there was a small resistance movement of young Jews who said we were all going to die in Auschwitz, so why not die fighting, with a gun in the hand? But most of our people kept saying, maybe there is no Auschwitz, maybe I won't be sent there. If I am sent there, then maybe something will happen before I arrive. Maybe someone will bomb it. Or maybe the war will end. If I do arrive there, maybe I will be one of those sent to the right, at the fork in the road, to work. If I am sent to the left, maybe . . . Always, always "maybe." It is the "maybe" that makes it possible for all of us to go on. That is why we hear but we refuse to comprehend.

But now suddenly someone says Auschwitz, and I have to argue the other way. I have to tell them it's all a lie. Maybe it *is* a lie. How do I know? But maybe tonight the train turns north and tomorrow we will be on our way to the real Auschwitz. Not Auspitz. Auschwitz. I could write a book about Auschwitz, even if I never get there.

During the night they reached the edge of Vienna. The train circled the city and stopped at a railroad yard on the outskirts. In the morning a German military doctor came aboard to treat anyone in need of medical attention. Several doctors who were passengers on the train were resentful, feeling this was a slur on their professional ability, but Leo brushed them aside impatiently. "This is one more concession our friend Horvath obtained for us. Be grateful, and hope that we live long enough to thank him for all he's done." There was no serious illness on the train, so within two hours it started on its way again.

The next stop, later that day, was Linz. Here, the passengers were told, they would be escorted into town, where they could take hot showers in the public baths. Many were delighted. Because of the poor quality of coal the railroads used, the locomotive had been continuously showering the twenty-eight boxcars with soot and belching black smoke, most of which ended up in the ears, eyes, and nostrils of the passengers. Hot water and soapsuds would feel good. But a minority, still nervous because of the Auschwitz scare, were reluctant to leave the train. Hiding their real fear, they said they were afraid someone would loot their baggage. Leo answered that by assigning one person in each car to remain as a guard. He chose people who were indisposed, aged, or for some other legitimate reason felt unable to make the trip in to town on foot.

The others all marched, men and women separately, in wide columns to the public bathing center. As the women paraded through the outside yard and began to disappear into the buildings, Rena, who had been especially agitated, suddenly felt her fears mushrooming into an overpowering hysteria. Still she moved forward, step by frightful step, with the others. But when it was her turn to enter the building, she couldn't raise a foot to cross the threshold. Hastily she picked up little Dan, turned around, and blindly began to push against the tide of humanity entering the baths.

Jessica, just behind her, seized her by the arm, knowing well what the trouble was, for she, too, had had a momentary impulse to flee, as she was sure many of the others had.

Rena tried to shake her off. "They are going to kill us. There's no hot water in those showers, only gas—gas!" she screamed as she pushed against the crowd.

The pressure of the oncoming women strained Jessica's arm until she had to let go. As she watched Rena's retreating figure with compassion, all at once she felt possessed by a great calm. She was certain Andor had known what he was doing. So far everything had gone as he had planned. The thought of Andor was comforting. She realized that this was strange, because when she had first met him he seemed to her egotistical, vain, and self-centered; more show than substance. She hadn't liked him at all. But during the weeks at the Columbus camp that impression of him had changed. He was capable and kind and warm. . . . She entered the baths serenely.

At the end of two hours everyone emerged clean and refreshed from the showers and returned to the train. For the rest of the journey the travelers were in high spirits.

One week after the train left Budapest, on the afternoon of July 7, the 1,679 passengers arrived at the Bergen-Belsen railroad depot. Just as at Budapest, the sick and the elderly were driven to the camp in trucks. The rest marched in a disorderly column, each person carrying his own luggage. Because so much of the weight had been in food, which by now had been nearly all consumed, their burdens were considerably lighter. The German guards who met the train apparently had not been informed that these Jews were in a different category than others. They were short-tempered and rough with them, repeatedly urging them to quicken their pace and accenting their orders with sharp taps of a rifle barrel on the legs.

Bergen-Belsen was a large place, larger than any of them had imagined. It was miles from any prewar community of houses and shops, but it was a city in itself. The one-story wooden barracks stretched as far as the eye could see, in all directions. There were murmurs of "So clean and neat!" and "It isn't at all as I thought it would be." Most of them were not unaware that in this camp thousands of their people had been put to death, but they were astounded that such an evil place could look so deceivingly beautiful. They were taken to a group of empty barracks, no different from hundreds of others. They were clean and smelled strongly of disinfectant. The men and women—even husbands and wives—were housed in separate buildings. This caused a great many tears and, here and there, some hysteria.

Each person received a straw mattress and two half-wool blankets. The beds were three-tiered. The men and women were told they would eat together in a large communal dining room and be allowed to use the same recreation yard. During the day they could go freely from one set of barracks to another and intermingle as they pleased. In their section of the camp they had internal autonomy. Within a few days Leo was unanimously considered their "president" and their intermediary with the Germans. No question was raised about how he had acquired his position. Without asking for or receiving a mandate from anyone, he set up a benevolent despotism, although he gave it the semblance of democracy. He chose a council of ten friends to advise and consult with him, but as with Andor and his Budapest Rescue Committee, Leo often found that emergencies required him to act without the luxury of consultation.

Andor had given Leo a copy of the list of the original 1,599 passengers to which Leo had added the eighty additional names. The morning after their arrival at Bergen-Belsen he went down the column that gave occupations and made a list of all the lawyers. There were nineteen, and he appointed them members of a permanent court to settle disputes. Minor arguments could be resolved by a single member of the court. In a major dispute a decision by any ten of the nineteen would be binding and would not be subject to appeal.

Then he went down the column showing ages and chose the fifty youngest men to serve in a militia to keep order, so the Germans would have no excuse to interfere with their internal activities.

Next he made a list of all the doctors and asked each of them to write after his name his barracks number and the field of medicine in which

200

he specialized. This list was posted on an outside wall of a centrally located barracks so anyone could consult it.

By word-of-mouth inquiry he obtained the names of ten Hebrew teachers who agreed to conduct daily courses in conversational Hebrew. When some of the older, non-Zionist people asked why they should learn to speak Hebrew, Leo responded sarcastically, "When you get to Palestine you think they'll all talk Magyar, yah?"

Then he appointed an educational committee of men and women who had had some general teaching experience to set up a school for the children.

Gradually, as the internal affairs of the group became more organized, almost everyone had a task to perform or a role to play in this self-governing community. But the dominating force was energetic Leo Strauss, who seemed to be everywhere, directing, planning, encouraging, appointing, supervising, or criticizing.

The inmates of the camp had a regular and unvarying daily routine. After rising in the morning they washed with cold water. Then two or three men from each barracks would go to the camp kitchen with large tin buckets to get the black liquid the Germans called coffee. They also brought back large chunks of dark bread. Breakfast, as well as the other two meals, was eaten at long wooden tables in the mess hall. Although Leo made no rule about it, they continued to group together almost as Andor had arranged them on the train, according to where they had come from.

After breakfast they lined up in front of the barracks in which they slept for *Zählappell,* or roll call. Sometimes they would have to wait two or three hours, even in the rain, for the German officers to arrive. The Germans didn't call out names, they merely counted their prisoners. If there were fewer in front of any barracks than there should be, the officers went inside and counted the number who were sick in bed. If there was a suspicion that someone was merely pretending to be ill, a German doctor was sent for. The rule was that anyone able to stand on his feet must attend the roll call.

In Jessica's barracks there was a woman from a mountain village near Cluj whose passion was knitting. Instead of food she had brought in her suitcase innumerable balls of wool, obtained, she explained, by unraveling any old knitted garments she had been able to lay her hands on. She always took her knitting to *Zählappell,* and while the others just stood she knitted. This infuriated the Germans, who each morning, al-

201

most as if it were part of the routine, would stand in front of her heaping insults on her. "Woman, you are mad!" they would shout, but she never looked up from her knitting. The louder they cursed her, the faster her needles moved, until finally they would depart.

After *Zählappell* they cleaned their barracks. Then some would read or write letters. The women sewed and washed clothes. Some taught classes. Others worked in the kitchen. But they all spent a great deal of time worrying.

Leo obtained permission for the establishment of a synagogue in a corner of one of the barracks, and here the rabbis took turns conducting prayers. They had torahs and prayer books but so few that the rabbis ordered them cut in half so that twice as many people could use them.

For the first four weeks they lived fairly well. The war had been going on for almost five years, and they were accustomed to short rations. Many of them had been living in ghettos before they left Hungary; by comparison with ghetto fare the food wasn't bad. The two carloads of edibles Andor had sent to supplement what the Germans gave them were stored in empty barracks, to which Leo assigned a round-the-clock guard. Sick people were given preference in the distribution of these reserves. At first they received bacon or other protein once a day. By the first of August the two carloads of reserves were gone and hunger began to spread in the camp. Cigarettes and any item of food, even crusts of bread, became the community's currency, and lively bargaining often took place. As the situation became more severe, Leo received complaints that the people of the transport were stealing from each other. It was only with enormous effort that he and his council were able to keep order. They were driven by the fear that unless they did, the Gestapo would take internal control away from them. What depressed Leo was the discovery that those who had had something before the German occupation of Hungary—wealth, position in life, a profession—were the worst offenders. Men who had been rich were the first to become thieves; doctors and university professors suffered a collapse in morale, abandoned their principles, and reverted to the law of the jungle even before others did. Or so it seemed.

To help keep their minds off their troubles Leo encouraged them to form an amateur dramatic society and give frequent plays. Gradually the subject of food began creeping into the dialogue on the stage, even if the play had a philosophical or religious motif. Because of the effect on the audience, Leo issued a flat order: no more mention of food from the stage.

Many people started to steal from the Germans, especially those who had entry to the kitchen because they worked there. Leo and his councilmen took drastic steps to stop this, too, not out of respect for German property, but because they knew the entire community would be punished if the pilfering became apparent and because they realized it actually was self-looting. The German commissariat delivered so many pounds of foodstuff a day to the community kitchen for the 1,679 of them. If ten men stole a pound of food apiece on a certain day, it meant that each of the other 1,669 had a little less than usual to eat that day.

Most of the camp prisoners discovered that their hunger pains were the worst at night. It was difficult to fall asleep with the stomach rumbling because it was so empty and paining because of the hunger contractions. In the women's barracks housewives who had prided themselves on their culinary ability lay in their three-tiered bunks in the dark praying in vain for sleep to give them some surcease. Then they began talking, softly at first, to the women across the narrow aisle or in the bunks above.

"Did you rub the chicken with garlic before you put it into the oven?"

"How did *you* make *tzimmes?*"

"Would you like my recipe for *kneidlach* . . . ?"

Sometimes they would lie there in the dark for hours, torturing themselves with the memory of meals they had served their families in the days when food was plentiful and eating was one of their principal pleasures.

In the camp, dinner—the main meal—consisted of a single bowl of thin vegetable soup. One day as Leo was leaving the dining hall after finishing his dinner, old Mr. Klein hurried up to him and held out his empty bowl with trembling hands. Tears filled his eyes.

"There has been a catastrophe. I was pushed as I got my soup, and it fell from my hands to the floor, and I am so very hungry. . . ."

There were about five hundred people in the dining hall at the time. Leo rapped on a table for attention. He explained what had happened and asked if some of them would share their soup with Mr. Klein.

Complete silence fell upon the hall. No one ate. No one moved. Leo waited for a full minute, then he shouted, "Have we sunk so low we can't give up one coffee spoon of soup apiece to keep an old man from going hungry? What are we, animals? Even animals take care of their own!"

In the back of the hall Moshe Hahn stood up. The bushy-haired artist was skinnier than ever. He had half finished his soup, but he came forward with what was left and dumped it into the bowl in Mr. Klein's shaky hands. The old man thanked him piteously. A relieved sigh spread through the hall, and then a hum of activity as the five hundred people began to eat and talk again.

Moshe brushed aside the old man's gratitude and walked out of the building back to his own barracks, where he tried to resume work on an oil portrait of Jessica. Her impenetrable serenity had intrigued him, as it had Andor, and he had felt compelled to try to capture it on canvas. But after a few minutes he laid aside his brushes. The hunger pains in his stomach were too distracting. Unlike the others, he had brought no food with him. His immense brown suitcase had been filled with as many brushes, pencils, tubes of paints, water colors, papers, and canvases as he had been able to cram into it. So for weeks he had been existing on less than subsistence rations, and now he was desperately hungry—"like an animal," he said to himself, recalling Leo's tirade in the dining hall. "When I get out of here, I'm going to eat all day long until I burst," he promised himself. He began to pace the barracks. He had to do something to get rid of this voracious craving. Maybe he should make believe, the way the others did. They were always talking about food, the men bragging of what wonderful things their wives used to cook and the women exchanging recipes, as if tomorrow they could make some new dish. Well, he could do better than they. He rushed back to his corner, put a blank canvas on his easel, and began to sketch a still life: roast goose, peaches, strawberries, grapes, and on the far right of the canvas a bottle of wine. He worked feverishly for hours, oblivious of his surroundings and the people who stood behind him gazing wistfully at the objects he was putting onto his canvas. By curfew time the goose looked brown and succulent and the fruit so lusciously real he could almost smell its fragrance. At the signal for lights out he reluctantly cleaned his brushes and screwed the caps onto his tubes of oil paint. He left the canvas on the easel in such a position that the light from a street lamp coming through the window illuminated it as if it were on display in an exhibition. He lay on his bunk staring at it. Tomorrow he must make the skin of the goose a little browner and accentuate the drops of fat oozing out of it. And the strawberries should be a little deeper red. In a few minutes, overcome by weakness and exhaustion, he was asleep.

The next morning people gathered around to gaze at the painting as soon as they finished breakfast, even people from other barracks who had heard about it when they went for their coffee at the camp kitchen. They left only when they were summoned to *Zählappell*.

The day was sunny and warm, and Moshe stood through the long check-up impatiently, eager to get back to his work. When they were dismissed, he hurried toward his barracks. As he reached the doorway, he noticed that his canvas was still on its easel, but there was something wrong. Someone had taken a knife and slashed it twice, from end to end. With a cry of agony he ran and picked it up, holding it at arm's length and staring at it, unable to accept what he saw. Then he turned and rushed back into the yard with it. He held it high, so everyone could see it, and yelled, "Here, *this* is how low some among us have sunk. . . ."

There were shocked murmurs among the crowd. Philip Kemeny leaned on Jessica's arm. He was heartsick. "To destroy a work of art!" Tears welled up in his eyes. Under his breath he said, "Maybe it was the Germans who did it." He was fighting off the suspicion that it could possibly be one of his own people. For him the most precious thing in existence, next to human life, was a painting, because to him it represented at least some small part of the artist's soul. "How terrible! How terrible!" he kept mumbling.

"It serves you right," a man on the edge of the crowd shouted at Moshe, "for torturing us with such a picture."

As others mumbled their agreement, the wiry little artist dropped his ruined canvas and made for the man. Rabbi Vogeler stepped in front of him. "Don't compound one evil with another," he pleaded.

Moshe shoved him out of the way. Just then Leo Strauss, steaming with exasperation, stepped into the melee. "Why is it—" he began, then stopped abruptly, remembering Moshe's kindness to Klein the day before, and started over again. "What's the matter?"

Everyone began to talk at the same time.

From the side lines Rena and Sam watched. Dan, sitting on his father's shoulders, jiggled with excitement as the violence threatened to spread over the entire yard. Sam held onto him tightly, but his own feelings were growing hotter. "Only a maniac could do such a thing. Only a maniac!"

"That's not true," Rena replied. "Whoever did it should be thanked. It was an act of kindness to the rest of us." Her voice was shrill and full of indignant self-pity.

Sam put his son on the ground. "You have lost your mind!" Then suddenly a look of apprehension came into his eyes. *"You* didn't . . ."

Her laugh was short and bitter. "Not me, but I wish I had."

He gazed at her, searching her face for the truth, then slowly it came to him. "You know who did, don't you? Rena, you have to tell." He shook her angrily.

Little Dan looked up from one parent to the other, bewildered by this exchange, and began to cry.

"See, now you've frightened him," she snapped.

Sam ignored the accusation and picked up his son. "Everything's all right," he said soothingly. "Look." He leaned over and kissed Rena on the cheek, and she forced herself to smile.

"You have to tell," Sam whispered as he left her to go to his own barracks. Rena stared straight ahead, without answering, a bright vindictiveness in her eyes. She had seen who it was, all right, but nobody was going to make her tell, least of all Sam.

The person who slashed the painting was never found out. In a few weeks the scandal was forgotten. But it served a purpose. On second thought the act of violence seemed to have shocked even those who at first had applauded it. It shocked them into a realization that they were destroying themselves without the help of the Germans. After that the camp grew more quiet and orderly, and a sense of unity returned to the inmates. If their spirits weren't joyful, at least they weren't bitter.

18

The early summer of 1944 was a time of crisis for the Nazis of Germany as well as for the Jews of Budapest. On the western front British and American troops were making spectacular advances against the Wehrmacht. In the east the Russians captured Vilna and encircled Lwów. A thousand U. S. Fortresses and Liberators were going off from British bases every twenty-four hours to bomb German cities. The Luftwaffe's secret weapon, robot bombs, had failed to destroy London's morale. Germany's allies were growing nervous. In Hungary the movement for a separate peace was gaining new adherents by the day. But for Hungarian Jews the greater the German military reverses, the more precarious their situation. There was strong evidence that someone—Hitler, Himmler, or Wedemeyer, no one was sure which—was determined that even if the military defeat of Germany was inevitable, as few Jews as possible should be left at the end.

With mathematical precision and cold efficiency they had started in the most remote corners of the country. Drawing the circle smaller and smaller, they had caught, deported, and executed first the Jews of the provinces, then the Jews of the suburbs of Budapest, and now they were ready to deal with the Jews left in the capital itself.

But at this critical moment the survivors of Hungarian Jewry began to acquire champions and supporters abroad, principally because of a document that came to be known as the Auschwitz Protocol. Two Slovak Jews, who had somehow managed the almost impossible feat of escaping from the Polish extermination camp, wrote a sixteen-page factual report on what the place was like, gave an approximation of how many had been executed there so far, and told the rate at which new arrivals were being gassed and cremated.

The Jewish Council of Budapest made many copies and tried devious methods of getting the report into circulation. Thanks to the Swedish and Swiss diplomats stationed in Budapest, who were willing to violate the technicalities of diplomatic protocol in a higher interest, the report was sent out of the country in diplomatic pouches and soon was being circulated around the world. Newspapers in Geneva and Lausanne printed articles based on the Protocol, and news agencies cabled excerpts from these articles abroad.

In many circles there was a profound shock at the realization that millions of people had gone to such a horrible death with so little action or even protest on the part of any substantial percentage of the population of Germany, Hungary, the neutral countries, or even those nations at war with the Germans. The sense of guilt was alleviated somewhat by the knowledge that there was still a chance to do something constructive—that there were at least two hundred thousand Jews alive in Budapest and, despite rumors that their extermination was imminent, none had yet been moved into deportation camps. Accordingly, many voices began to be raised.

Swiss university professors and scientists signed a manifesto of protest. Churches in many countries held days of mourning. A debate broke out in the British House of Commons over what should be done. The Papal Nuncio, on behalf of Pope Pius XII, had already, in a note to the Hungarian Prime Minister, expressed shock that a Christian nation— a nation overwhelmingly Catholic as well—could behave so inhumanely toward human beings and went so far as to say: "The fact that persons are persecuted because of their racial origin is in itself a breach of the laws of nature. If God Almighty has given them life, nobody has the right to take this life or the means of its sustainment, unless some crime has been committed." When this note was ignored a stronger one was sent, specifically demanding "humane treatment for all Jews" and an end to deportations. President Roosevelt threatened round-the-clock bombing of Hungarian towns and cities if the deportations weren't halted. B.B.C. broadcast a message from the Archbishop of Canterbury appealing to Hungarians to behave in a Christianlike manner. Then, as if aware that stronger inducements were needed, B.B.C. threatened massive retaliation by British bombers and reminded the Hungarians that "every day the Red army gets nearer to the heart of Hungary." The King of Sweden sent Admiral Horthy a personal message asking him to "save what remains of this unfortunate people," and in London, Foreign Secretary Anthony Eden declared the actions of the Hungarian Government had filled the British Government with "abhorrence."

Taking courage from this sudden external interest in what was happening to Hungarian Jewry, the Budapest Jewish Council addressed an official communication to Admiral Horthy, listing, district by district, the 427,400 Jews of the provinces who had been deported and presumably exterminated.

"Therefore it cannot be surprising," the appeal added, "that we are filled with a great anxiety by rumors now circulating, according to which the deportation of Budapest Jews is about to begin and Hungary is going to be completely rid of Jews."

Meanwhile both Hungarian anti-Semites in the government and Wedemeyer's office stepped up their activities. They knew they were racing against time. New restrictions were issued: Jews henceforth could not receive visitors in their quarters; they could not converse with a passerby through an open street window; they were denied access to all public parks; they had to use the last car on tram lines; half a million books by Jewish authors were consigned to the pulping mill at a public ceremony; the curfew was extended so that even between the hours of 2 P.M. and 5 P.M. Jews could leave their homes only in case of dire necessity.

The mail of Budapest Jews was cluttered with post cards from relatives and friends bearing the once mysterious "Waldsee" postmark, but now almost everyone knew of the hoax, so when such postals were received, saying "I have arrived safely and all is well," religious Jews would often say the prayers for the dead. In houses marked with the yellow star the talk these days was all about deportation: how soon will our turn come? In many houses the Jews organized a guard system, so they could spread the warning when Hungarian gendarmes made a sudden night raid. Most of those required to wear a yellow star—women as well as men—no longer undressed at night.

Admiral Horthy became so concerned that he came out of his self-imposed retirement. Summoning his Crown Councilors, he told them of the protests he had received from Pope Pius XII, President Roosevelt, and the International Red Cross. He sharply reproved the commander of the gendarmerie for the brutal tactics of his men, but the commander insisted not his men but the Germans were responsible. At this, Prime Minister Sztojay rose to defend the Germans. The Regent, infuriated by the quibbling and blame-shifting, ordered Sztojay to cancel all plans for the deportation of Budapest's Jews, which he had been secretly informed was about to begin, and to relieve Secretary of State Endre, that zealously anti-Semitic head of Jewish affairs, of his duties.

At the very time this meeting was in progress, in another part of the city Wedemeyer, the Hungarian chief of police, and Secretary Endre were in conference working out details of their plan for the deportation of Budapest's Jews. One decision they reached was that a ghetto would be established. In normal times the two hundred thousand Jews of the capital lived scattered around the city in apartment houses and villas. Months ago Hungarian authorities had marked twenty-six hundred of these buildings with large yellow stars and announced that henceforth Jews could live only in these places: Jews in the other seventy-four hundred apartment houses and villas would have to abandon them and double up with those already inhabiting the twenty-six hundred yellow-starred buildings. But Wedemeyer and Endre were now planning to concentrate all of them in even fewer buildings in one particular area. From this ghetto in a few days shipments to Auschwitz would begin. The plan called for the last Jew to be out of Budapest at the end of a week.

When Wedemeyer received confidential reports of Horthy's order, he made two quick decisions: to get rid of a considerable number of suburban Jews he still had on his hands, and to encourage a clique of Hungarian gendarmerie officers to put into action at once a plan they had devised, with SS assistance, to stage a *Putsch* against the Horthy government and put Endre in as Prime Minister. To make it appear an entirely Hungarian uprising Wedemeyer decided that the SS would take no part in the affair openly. As soon as Endre was in power, the deportation of Budapest Jews would begin.

During the first few days of July sixteen hundred gendarmes were brought to Budapest from provincial towns, and another three thousand were concentrated just outside the city. The excuse was that they were "gathering information concerning the Jewish situation."

Andor watched these developments with growing anxiety. He was in a peculiar position. If the pressure from abroad was great enough and if Admiral Horthy was able to seize control of the situation, Wedemeyer's power might be clipped; he might even be forced to leave Hungary. This might save the two hundred thousand Jews of Budapest from deportation. But what of the 1,679 people of the transport? They were in Germany now, hostages. He was responsible for having sent them there. If Wedemeyer left, with whom could he bargain to obtain their release? If Wedemeyer left, Weber and Heinemann and the rest of the SS staff would probably go, too. That would put an end to any chance of further bargaining for the lives of the cream of Hungarian Jewry now at Bergen-Belsen. If the Hungarians forced Wedemeyer to leave, his first move, after he got back on German soil, might be to send all the people of the transport to their death in retaliation. But even if Wedemeyer stayed on in Budapest, it was going to take more astute bargaining than before to win concessions from him, a depressing prospect since he had so few cards of any bargaining value left in his hand.

When reports reached Sip utca that the last few thousand suburban Jews were being concentrated at the towns of Budakalasz and Monor for deportation, Andor made two trips to the Majestic to try to persuade Wedemeyer that this would further hamper the deal with Istanbul.

"Istanbul!" Wedemeyer screamed at him. "I don't want to hear that word from you again. From now on, in my dictionary, Istanbul is just another word for Jewish procrastination, Jewish lying, and Jewish double-dealing. Don't talk to me any more about Istanbul."

That night Andor cabled the Agency in Istanbul that the situation was desperate and begged that Erno be sent back.

Two days later, on the morning of July 7, as Andor was looking over the day's schedule at his desk in the Sip utca office, a messenger arrived with a thick envelope that had come by diplomatic plane from Istanbul. Andor hurriedly tore it open and read the message. As he finished he could hardly contain himself for happiness. The Agency had sent the provisional agreement. They agreed to supply the Germans with foodstuffs and money in exchange for lots of ten thousand Hungarian Jews, delivered to the frontier of a neutral country.

He shouted across the corridor to Arthur, who was sitting in his own office. Laughing and talking at the same time, he waved the letter in the air, as Arthur, astounded by this extraordinary performance, rushed across the hall to find out what had happened. Andor embraced him gaily, pressed the agreement into his hand, and picked up the telephone to call SS headquarters at the Majestic Hotel.

When Andor arrived at Wedemeyer's office, he found that Colonel Franz Weber, the handsome director of the SS Economic Division, was also there. He handed the Istanbul letter to Wedemeyer and addressed both officers triumphantly: "You see, this is proof. Our friends in foreign countries *are,* after all, willing to conclude a large-scale commercial agreement with you—provided, of course, that your demands are not unreasonable . . ."

Weber listened to him without expression, but Wedemeyer continued to read the letter, never lifting his eyes from the page. Then he looked up. "So, Gábor is not coming back—"

"But they've explained," Andor said hastily. "Gábor must stay there to participate in our negotiations with the Allies."

"Humph!"

"They offer to send someone else to Budapest in his place."

Wedemeyer waved his hand for silence and continued to read. When he had finished, he gave the paper to Weber, who perused it just as carefully, then laid it down and glanced at Wedemeyer. The Obersturm-bannführer nodded his head affirmatively and Weber said, "I think the agreement will be acceptable to Berlin, Horvath."

Encouraged by this quick compliance, Andor pressed his advantage. "Is the SS willing to send an emissary to a neutral country to discuss the means of putting the agreement into operation?"

Weber nodded.

"And will this emissary be authorized to discuss not only the fate of the Hungarian Jews, but the fate of all Jews under German domination?"

"I think Reichsführer Himmler will be favorably disposed toward that proposal."

Wedemeyer's thin lips curled disdainfully, but Andor didn't notice. His attention was fastened on Weber, who seemed to have considerable authority and whose attitude was much more amenable.

"Unfortunately"—Andor's voice was politely apologetic—"foreign nations from which we must get help may look on expressions of Germany's good will with some suspicion as the deportations—"

"There you go again with your malicious lies!" Wedemeyer shouted. "See if you can tell the truth for once. Just for once."

Weber ignored the outburst and asked him to go on.

"You see," Andor explained, "Gábor's mission was bound to fail because those same Hungarians who were to have been rescued in the exchange have already been gassed at Auschwitz. This is generally known. Our negotiations abroad will be considered seriously now only if the people who were sent to Bergen-Belsen arrive in a neutral country before the negotiations get under way. Then and only then will our friends be certain that the Germans mean to carry out their part of the agreement. On the other hand, the negotiations will most surely be doomed if the Jews of Budapest are deported in the meantime."

He tried to see in Weber's handsome face what impression he had made. He was gambling for big stakes—for the lives of hundreds of people he loved—his own sister, Philip, Leo, Jessica—and also for the lives of the rest of the surviving Hungarian Jews, two hundred thousand of them, who might be doomed to an early death unless he succeeded this afternoon. . . .

"I agree with you in principle that it would strengthen your hand if deportations were halted. We shall request authorization for this change of policy from Reichsführer Himmler," Weber replied.

Andor smiled his thanks. "As for the Bergen-Belsen transport," Weber continued, "I am prepared to recommend that they be shipped to a neutral country as soon as you have paid the one million dollars you owe on that deal."

Andor felt a sinking sensation at the thought of having to raise a million dollars now. As he tried to think of a way to stall, he suddenly remembered something. "Of course we have already paid seven hundred thousand dollars."

"Five hundred thousand," Weber corrected.

"No, seven, with the two hundred thousand we paid in the first place to Obersturmbannführer Walter Heinemann."

Weber looked at Wedemeyer with some perplexity.

Wedemeyer instantly grew angry again. "May God strike me dead if I ever have to have any business dealings with a Jew again! You are all cheats! You know very well, Horvath, that the two hundred thousand was an entirely separate deal. It has nothing to do with your train. Colonel Weber is right: if you want those people to leave Bergen-Belsen, you'd better raise the million dollars in a hurry."

But Andor wasn't going to give up so easily. With perfect poise he

212

said, "May I remind you gentlemen that when *this* deal was made the agreement was that the remaining two thirds would be placed in an account in Switzerland and released to you only when the people of the transport were safe on the soil of some neutral country?"

Weber smiled deprecatingly. "It is foolish for you to try to bargain with me this way, Horvath. You have promised us the million dollars. As far as I know, you have made no progress toward raising this money, yet you come here and ask for the release of your people from Bergen-Belsen. I tell you now that the account must be closed—the money paid —before we can discuss anyone leaving Bergen-Belsen."

Andor needed time to work his way out of his corner, so he decided to acquiesce for the moment. "The money will be paid," he announced simply.

"Then you may cable Istanbul that we are ready to negotiate the details," Wedemeyer snapped, and the meeting was over.

Andor sent the cable that night, adding an appeal for one million dollars to save the Bergen-Belsen hostages. It was late in the evening when he left the cable office. He was extremely tired and therefore decided to go home instead of returning to the office on Sip utca. Before he talked to anyone, even Arthur, he wanted to think things through. It had been a peculiar meeting. He wondered why Wedemeyer had been so willing to let Weber take over. But that was all right. Weber wasn't a bad sort. He almost liked him. He was courteous, even-tempered, and, unlike Wedemeyer, he seemed to have no maniacal drive to send Jews to their death. Still, it was strange for Wedemeyer to take a back seat. . . .

He was awakened early the next morning by the wail of sirens. He drew the curtains aside and opened the windows, but looking out, he could neither see nor hear anything in the sky resembling airplanes. He turned on the radio and waited for the warning that was always given during an air-raid alert, but there was no announcement, just dead air. He tried the telephone; it was also dead. A very odd situation, he thought. He looked out the window again. There wasn't even one of those ever-present yellow Mercedes in sight, although now he did see Hungarian policemen here and there, dotting the scene, ready to arrest anyone who violated the law and tried to circulate during a raid. If he went down to the basement shelter, Rachel might be there. He had no desire to talk to her just now. It would be much better to remain here in the apartment and work. He had to figure out, among other things, where to get a million dollars quickly. Also what his next move should be in this game he was playing with Wedemeyer and Weber. But it was impossible even to think. For five hours the sirens kept up their mournful wailing. There was no sound of planes, no shrill whine of dropping bombs, no dull thud of explosions. In all the years of the war nothing like this had happened before.

Late in the afternoon the wailing stopped. A few minutes later the telephone rang. It was Rudy Tabor, the stocky, aggressive former newspaper publisher, now a vice-president of the Jewish Council.

"Good news!" he shouted happily.

Andor moved the receiver away from his ear.

"The coup has failed!" Tabor yelled.

"What coup?"

"I thought you knew everything. Four thousand gendarmes were supposed to seize power, take the capital, kick out the Regent, and put the bastard . . . you know who I mean . . . in as P.M."

"So what happened?"

"Horthy's army has won. The gendarmes are leaving the city and returning to their stations."

"Is that why the sirens were going all day?"

"Of course. To keep everyone off the streets in case there was a battle. . . ."

While the people of Budapest huddled in their homes and shelters that day, wondering what was happening, Prime Minister Sztojay had an audience with Cardinal Seredi, the Catholic Primate of Hungary, to whom he made a solemn promise, with his hand on a Bible, that Christians of Jewish origin would be protected and that no Jew who had been baptized would be deported. But the Regent decided that that was not enough. He summoned Sztojay and categorically issued an order: the deportation of all Budapest Jews was to stop, and the Prime Minister would so inform the Germans.

That night Colonel Wedemeyer paced his office in the Hotel Majestic. The glittering light of the two large crystal chandeliers that hung from the gilded ceiling illuminated the small bald spot on the top of his head as he strode back and forth. The failure of his carefully planned coup was humiliating. Under his breath he was cursing the stupidity of his Hungarian conspirators when his orderly entered and handed him a message from Prime Minister Sztojay: Effective immediately, the deportation of Budapest Jews must cease.

He stared at the note, his frigid eyes glazed with astonishment, then

214

crumpled it in his fist and sank into a chair. "I can't believe it," he murmured. "I can't believe it." The note dropped to the floor, but he ignored it. The bewildered orderly picked it up and put it on the desk. "Will that be all, sir?"

Wedemeyer looked up at him blankly, as if he had forgotten who the boy was.

As soon as the government's new policy toward baptized Jews became known in the city, thousands besieged the churches, begging for baptismal certificates. There was a long-established rule that conversion must be preceded by three months of ecclesiastical instruction. Serious religious teachers undertook to hold speed-up courses, often in the basement of air-raid shelters of buildings marked with the yellow star. Some religious denominations contended that the sacred rite of baptism would be profaned if the period of dogmatic instruction was shortened. But many Catholic priests and Protestant ministers waived the regulations and baptized Jews in masses, on the ground that they thus were saving the lives of human beings who otherwise were in danger of almost immediate extermination. In some streets in front of parish houses the queues of people seeking baptismal certificates were longer than the lines of hungry people waiting for the day's ration of bread. The fever of conversion led to some cruel exploitation on the part of a few pseudo-priests and other impostors who swindled Jews out of large fees on the promise of short-cut conversions without the necessity of any instructions at all. Those seeking baptismal certificates were also preyed upon by disorganized mobs of young Hungarian Fascists in Arrow Cross shirts who would go down a queue beating up Jews indiscriminately and loudly denouncing them for their cowardice in attempting to escape extermination.

In other ways the desperate condition of the Budapest Jews improved slightly during July. They were given a little more food and a little more freedom of movement. Red Cross representatives were permitted to enter internment camps. Newspapers were ordered to modify the virulence of their anti-Semitic pronouncements. By decree of the Regent six hundred Jews who had distinguished themselves in the arts, science, and business were given certificates releasing them completely from the necessity of obeying any of the anti-Jewish regulations. The consulates of Switzerland and Sweden began giving out safe-conduct visas in considerable numbers.

These developments infuriated Wedemeyer. He could boast that to date he had shipped off for extermination almost a half million Jews from Hungary and that the Hungarian countryside and even the capital's suburbs were more nearly pure Aryan than any similar area on earth, but in July 1944 he was a very unhappy man. With angry frustration he had watched his power dwindle, but despite Horthy's increasingly firm stand against him and the Crown Council's decrees, he was determined to deport the Jews of Budapest. With the help of the discredited Endre and some of his followers, Wedemeyer planned to begin the deportation secretly on July 10. Outwardly he assumed a conciliatory and reasonable manner toward the Hungarian Government. He would content himself, he said, with "cleaning" a few sections of the city, and he asked the government to permit the deportation of the Jews living in the seventh, eighth, and ninth districts of the capital. The request was refused. Then he asked for "just ten thousand" Jews whom the Reich urgently needed for work necessary to the war effort. This request was also denied.

Wedemeyer was furious. Horthy would pay for this someday. The old idiot would learn that no Hungarian puppet could give orders to one of Adolf Hitler's most trusted obersturmbannführers and get away with it. He summoned Endre, and together they worked out secret arrangements for deporting the fifteen hundred inmates of the internment camp at Kistarcsa on July 14.

Through a tipster Rudy Tabor heard of the plan and told the other officers of the Jewish Council. At a hastily summoned meeting they agreed that Regent Horthy's office should be informed.

The Regent, after verifying the rumor, ordered the Minister of the Interior to have the deportation stopped. If the train had already left, he said, it was to be halted wherever it was and brought back to Kistarcsa —by force if necessary. A company of gendarmes was sent to execute the recall order. They found the train just outside the town of Hatvan, about forty miles northeast of Budapest. That same evening they escorted it back to the capital, with its fifteen hundred passengers unharmed.

When Wedemeyer learned of this rebuff, his amazement was exceeded only by his rage. Far more important to him than the fact that Jews were being saved was that the dominion and prestige of the SS were being undermined. This was intolerable. He told Endre that he must ferret out the source of the leak without delay.

Early the next morning Wedemeyer received a report from Endre. As soon as he had read it, he issued an order that Emmanuel Simon,

Hugo Mayer, Rudy Tabor, and the rest of the members of the Jewish Council were to appear at his office at once. When they arrived, all of them curious and nervous as to why they had been summoned, Wedemeyer, Heinemann, and Captain Mueller took turns issuing new instructions to them and presenting "urgent problems" for discussion. It was even suggested that the morale of Budapest Jews might be improved if cinema performances were held for them. All morning and all afternoon the Jewish leaders were kept there, restless and perplexed. While the pointless talk went on and on, a large contingent of Gestapo agents surrounded Kistarcsa. The fifteen hundred inhabitants, including the staff of the X-ray laboratory at the Jewish Hospital, were holding a "freedom celebration," congratulating each other on their deliverance. The German agents loaded the bewildered men and women into trucks and drove them to the East Station, where they were again put into freight cars for deportation. The train departed shortly before 7 P.M. At 7:40 P.M., when Wedemeyer's headquarters received confirmation that it was well on its way, the leaders of the Jewish Council were dismissed, still unaware of the real reason they had been summoned to the Svábhegy.

Wedemeyer's happiness was short-lived. On the afternoon of July 20, Andor received a telephone call from Captain Mueller, who said Colonel Wedemeyer wished to see him immediately.

When he arrived, Wedemeyer didn't even wait for him to be seated before he began a prolonged outburst of invective. In his hand Wedemeyer held a newspaper, which at last he threw across the desk. Andor picked it up. It was a copy of *The Times* of London, with the headlines:

A MONSTROUS "OFFER"

GERMAN BLACKMAIL

BARTERING JEWS FOR MUNITIONS

The article described the terms of the offer and then said:

The British Government know what value to set on any German or German-sponsored offer. They know that there can be no security for the Jews or other oppressed peoples of Europe until victory is won. The Allies are fighting to achieve that security; and they know, as well as the Germans, what happens when one begins paying blackmail. The blackmailer increases his price. Such considerations provided their own answer to the proposed bargain.

. . . the German "offer" seems to be simply a fantastic attempt to sow suspicion among the Allies.

"Do you know what has happened?" Wedemeyer screamed. "The British have arrested Gábor and Franck. That's how your friends in Istanbul have carried out their part of the bargain."

When Andor had recovered from the shock, he tried to persuade Wedemeyer that the Agency had acted in good faith, in spite of what had happened. "After all," he pleaded, "they shouldn't be held responsible for the acts of the British—"

Wedemeyer's skinny fists pounded the desk until the knuckles were white. "The deportations will be speeded up. All the Jewish garbage in this city will be removed—and disposed of." He gave Andor a look of contempt, then added, "And don't delude yourself; that old fool in the palace won't be able to protect them."

The cords of his neck were distended and bulging. Andor studied them, fascinated. For the first time in his life he had the urge to kill a man. His fingers itched to entwine themselves around that bloated throat, to press the life out of it, to silence that ugly voice forever.

"You are not listening, Horvath!"

"Oh yes I am, Herr Obersturmbannführer." Andor forced himself back to reality. He couldn't save the remainder of his people except by continuing to negotiate with Wedemeyer, revolting as that now was. With Weber he had gone a short way toward the goal. But to go further he had to have help from abroad. There was no possibility of raising the money Weber demanded here in Hungary. The Jews who remained had little left but the breath of life and the will to exist. As for getting the million dollars from Istanbul, that now appeared to be wishful thinking.

"Of course I was listening, Herr Obersturmbannführer," he reiterated, "but I was also thinking that our negotiations need not come to an end because the British refuse your proposition. There is another avenue open, the Americans. I'm sure we can do business more easily with them."

"Do you mean with the American Government?" Wedemeyer asked, showing some interest.

"No. I was thinking of something else," Andor replied, full of self-confidence again, now that he felt control of the situation returning to his hands. "There are five million Jews in the United States. Some of

them, as you know, are not only very wealthy but have great influence."
He thought he could see a glimmer of avarice in the colonel's face so he
went on. "There is an organization financed by American Jews that
is supposed to spend its money assisting European Jews. Its name is
the United Relief Organization, but it is usually referred to as the
U.R.O."

"And what is your suggestion?" Wedemeyer was getting impatient.

"The U.R.O. has a European representative in Switzerland named
Schoen—Edward Schoen. He's a retired Swiss banker. I think there's a
very good chance we could get money for you from this source. Would
you be willing to send an emissary to Herr Schoen to discuss this matter
and to permit me to go along as a representative of the Hungarian Jews?"

As Wedemeyer started to reply, Weber burst into the room, not at
all the calm, reserved SS colonel. Wedemeyer shot him a look of annoyance. Ignoring it, Weber bent down and whispered a few words into
his ear. Suddenly Wedemeyer's pale face turned chalk white.

"Wait! I will go with you," he said as Weber turned to leave.

In about twenty minutes Wedemeyer returned and resumed the conversation where they had dropped it, but he seemed uneasy and dis-
tracted, and he wasn't nearly so belligerent as he had been before the
interruption. "What makes you think you can get money from the
U.R.O.?" he asked.

"It's rich, very rich. Besides, at this point I'm sure that the American
Jews are extremely eager to help their European brothers." He hesitated,
then added, "Those few who are still left." Wedemeyer scowled, but
Andor continued, "The U.R.O. has worked with the War Refugee Board
of the American Government to help Jews before this. I'm sure we can
count on their assistance."

Wedemeyer toyed with a clip of automatic-revolver bullets he used
as a paperweight, then after some consideration said, "All right, I will
ask the Reichsführer for authorization to make the arrangements."

"Of course it would be a great spur to the negotiations if the people
at Bergen-Belsen were permitted to go to Switzerland," Andor put in
quickly. "That really would be proof of German good will."

"Enough!" Once more the skinny fist banged the desk. "I'm tired of
hearing about German good will. It is the Jews and their friends who
have shown not one small particle of good will up to now." He leaned
across his desk. "Remember, Horvath, the people at Bergen-Belsen are
hostages. Do you understand what a hostage is? They don't move until
the one million dollars you owe us for them is paid and the terms of

219

the tentative agreement with Istanbul is acted upon. This is the last time I am going to tell you."

As Andor got up to leave he realized that, for all the bombast, Wedemeyer seemed like a shaken man. His anger appeared to be less than genuine—an act put on to intimidate his adversaries. Andor was puzzled.

When he returned to his office at the Center, Joe was waiting for him, his body taut, his black eyes gleaming with excitement. He closed the door quickly after Andor had entered. "You won't believe it!"

Andor sat down wearily. "Joe, don't play games. I'm tired. *What* won't I believe?"

"There's a report that some of the generals of the Wehrmacht tried to kill Hitler today!"

"Did they succeed?"

"No, but—"

"So what makes you happy? Now he knows who his enemies are. The failure will only make him stronger." Suddenly he remembered Wedemeyer's white face as Weber whispered to him. He leaned back in his chair, put the tips of his fingers together, and said slowly, "In return for your news, Joe, I'll tell you something I found out this afternoon."

"What?"

"Wedemeyer is frightened."

"Is that good or bad? I mean for us."

"I wish I knew."

Wedemeyer discussed with Franz Weber Andor's proposal to approach the Jews of America through the United Relief Organization. The young colonel thought it sounded like a promising idea and took a plane for Berlin to present it to Himmler. On August 2 he returned to Budapest and met with Andor and Wedemeyer at the Majestic. He was beaming. Reichsführer Himmler was still prepared to exchange Jews against goods, he reported cheerfully. The only condition he imposed was that the liberated Jews must not stay in Europe, since he wished that after the war not a single Jew would remain on the continent. A broad smile brightened his well-proportioned features. "Now here is the best news of all for you, Horvath. The Reichsführer has agreed to permit the Hungarian Jews at Bergen-Belsen—the people of your train —to be released."

Andor's heart pounded.

"However, at first only a group of three hundred can leave. The others will be permitted to go later. You will discuss the details with Colonel Wedemeyer. He has already received orders on this matter from the Reichsführer himself."

Wedemeyer nodded, but his displeasure was plain. "You understand, Horvath, that I will not give the order for the departure of the three hundred until the date of the meeting between Colonel Weber and the representative of the United Relief Organization is fixed," he said sourly.

They discussed a suitable time and place for the proposed meeting, and Andor was authorized to make the necessary arrangements with Edward Schoen by telegraph. But there was one matter uppermost in Andor's mind. As soon as he had an opportunity he asked, "What will happen to those who remain behind at Bergen-Belsen?"

Wedemeyer glared at him. "I have told you a hundred times before: they will go when the one million dollars you owe us is paid. That is my final word on the subject."

"How are the three hundred to be chosen?"

"You may pick any three hundred you wish, so long as you do not include any Zionist leaders. They will have to wait."

"Will members of my own family be allowed to go?"

"You know better than to ask such a question. Neither yours nor Gruen's." He seemed to take intense pleasure in saying it. Then with a derisive smile he added, "But if you trust your friends to keep their bargain, there is no reason to be afraid of what will happen to those who remain behind, now is there, Horvath?" The cold blue eyes danced maliciously.

Two days later, after receiving a telegram from Schoen, Andor went to the Hotel Majestic to report that the meeting was set for August 21 at St. Margrethen, on the Swiss-German frontier. As he walked out of the cool, sumptuous interior of the hotel into the blinding summer sunshine toward his car, he thought uneasily of the possible results. Would the U.R.O. help them? It was difficult to tell. The million dollars he needed desperately wouldn't be an overwhelming sum to this organization which had the support of so many wealthy American Jews. But would they be suspicious, as the Agency and the British at Istanbul had been? No one yet knew what had really happened to Erno. He hadn't dared tell Esther what Wedemeyer had said about his arrest. The changing military situation also worried him. As the Allied armies advanced on both the eastern and western fronts, city after city was being liberated. Whatever Jews remained in these places were now finally out of all danger. But at the same time there were fanatics among the German leaders, like Wedemeyer, who would be deterred by nothing—not even the imminent military defeat of the Reich—until they had rid the territory they controlled of all Jews. It was an insane attitude. What difference would it make to them how many Jews were left after the defeat of Germany and their own death—for surely few if any of them would survive? In 1939 there had been seven million in Europe. But as the German Operation Night and Fog relentlessly moved across the continent, their numbers decreased by the hour, by the minute. How many were left now? Who knew? Perhaps a million. Maybe only a few hundred thousand.

He opened the door of his car and got in. The air was suffocatingly hot and still. He lowered the windows, started the motor, and drove off quickly, eagerly inhaling the breeze created as the car sped along. He tried to turn his thoughts into more hopeful channels. He must write a letter to Leo about the people who were to be released.

As soon as he reached his office he took paper and pen and began:

Dear Leo,

On the basis of the negotiations I have had it has been decided that three hundred of the transport will be sent soon to Switzerland. We would not like to decide here in Budapest exactly who will go; we wish only to give you a general guide in making the choice. Families and small children should get preference. I think it is only fair that the three hundred places should be distributed proportionately among the different categories that compose the transport. The chalutzim and Orthodox and Pécs people must all have their percentages. Also the Zionists. But no Zionist leaders will be permitted to go. This is Colonel Wedemeyer's order. (I leave it to you to judge who is a leader, but that should not be difficult. If you have any doubts whether a man should be considered a leader, do not put him on the list. This is very important; we do not want this rescue operation delayed for any reason.) No members of my family may go, nor Gruen's. Unfortunately you and yours must also remain. Please let all the rest of our friends know that we hope their turn will come soon.

The proper offices will permit me to receive an answer to this letter. I ask you to give me a detailed report of the events of the past few weeks and of the general feeling of the people of the camp. Of course we are very much interested in knowing how they are.

As he put down the pen, he thought of Jessica. He had tried to keep her out of his mind these past five weeks. He needed all his energy, all his time, all his power of concentration for the job at hand—trying to save lives—but at night when he lay in bed, trying to slow down his brain enough to make sleep possible, he could divert his thoughts from his problems by imagining that she was beside him. He had forgotten not a single detail of her appearance: her sapphire eyes and olive skin, her soft voice, the way she walked, the tilt of her head, the shiny black tight-bound hair.

Coming out of his reverie abruptly, he realized he must tell Leo to put her name on the list of the three hundred. He picked up the pen, then put it down again. To order her release would single her out. It might be dangerous for her, and it would give the Germans another weapon they could use against him any time they wanted to, for they would certainly read his letter before delivering it. Besides, Philip Kemeny couldn't go, being both a member of his family and a Zionist leader, and he knew that Jessica would never go and leave the sick old man behind.

He had almost finished the letter when Arthur walked in briskly. "It's getting late. How about closing up and going to Molnar's Delicatessen for dinner? Maybe tonight the *gulyás* will have something in it that tastes like fresh meat for a change."

Andor laughed in spite of himself. "You're libeling Molnar. He's one of the cleverest black marketeers in the city. If there's any fresh meat within a hundred kilometers, he'll have it." He turned back to the paper on his desk. "I just want to finish this letter, then I'll be ready to go. I'll take it with me. I want you to see it. You'll be surprised, Arthur. Very surprised."

The dinner turned out well. The *gulyás* was made of fresh beef and was redolent of herbs and spices, and the *rakott káposzta,* that wonderful sour cabbage, was just tart enough. For the *pièce de résistance* Molnar himself brought two *almás rétes,* an extraordinary luxury these days.

Arthur ate his slowly, savoring the thin, delicate pastry and the sweet rich filling of apples and nuts. It had been a meal to satisfy both the palate and the soul. Only the knowledge that Molnar had served them such a meal because he knew they had dealings with the Gestapo lessened Arthur's enjoyment. He sometimes wondered if Andor was bothered by such thoughts. Surely he knew why they—two Jews—were treated so well. He studied his friend across the table, but he saw only an elegantly dressed, darkly handsome man leisurely sipping *barack* with the critical attitude of a connoisseur. Some things about Andor irritated him. "Where's the letter you were going to show me?" he asked abruptly.

The shortness of his manner didn't escape Andor. He looked up from his glass quizzically and, seeing the chilled expression in Arthur's eyes, slowly took a package of expensive Turkish cigarettes from his pocket, removed one, lit it, and inhaled deeply before replying, "Some of our people in Bergen-Belsen are going to be released to Switzerland in a few weeks."

"You're sure?"

"Himmler has agreed." Andor put the letter on the table.

Arthur ignored it. "Elizabeth and the boys—will they go?" he asked urgently.

"No. Unfortunately no one from your family, or mine, will be allowed to leave until the deal has been completed."

Arthur slumped in his chair. "I might have known."

"Don't be like that. This isn't the time for such a negative attitude. The date for the talks has been set. We're on our way to saving not only the people at Bergen-Belsen but a great many others. Maybe all that are left."

Arthur gave him a reproachful look. "You're an incredible optimist," he said caustically.

Andor slept fitfully that night, occasionally grunting angrily in his dreams as he heard Arthur's bitter words again. All the dreadful possibilities of failure assailed him, as he turned from one side to the other of the disarranged bed. As the hours passed, he began to feel an oppressive weight on his chest. He sat up, brushed the hair out of his eyes, and stared stupidly at the opposite wall. He had to do something. He couldn't just wait calmly for the talks on the Swiss frontier to begin. Schoen must be told beforehand how he and his colleagues felt and what they expected. He got up, put on his robe and slippers, pulled aside the blackout curtains to let in the gray morning light, then went to the small walnut desk, and began to write:

. . . the development of the catastrophe suffered by our people has been unequaled in the history of any nation. We cannot describe it to you in detail, but we are sure you know it well. Despite the new policy of the Hungarian Government the patterns that lead to deportation continue. . . . We are steadfastly depending on you to do everything—without qualification—to provide us with the means of rescuing our brothers. . . . We fervently believe you will see to it that those of them who still live are not betrayed. . . .

224

19

It was extremely hot, even for mid-August, the morning Franz Weber and Andor Horvath set out for the Swiss frontier, but the SS colonel had thoughtfully requisitioned a large limousine so they would be comfortable on the long trip. They were driven by Weber's youthful adjutant, a Captain Erhardt.

Andor was in an ebullient mood. There was a good chance, he felt, that the meeting between Colonel Weber and Edward Schoen would give him an opportunity to engage in some top-level negotiating that might affect the future of all the Hungarian Jews who still survived. This in itself was enough to excite a man for whom diplomatic bargaining was the greatest pleasure in life. But also the Germans had arranged for the Bergen-Belsen train to reach the Swiss-Austrian frontier simultaneously with their own arrival. It would be dramatic justice for him to be present when the first lot of the Hungarians he had saved left the nightmare of Hitler's Europe and crossed over into the comparative peace and calm of neutral Switzerland. It would be a joy to see the faces of three hundred men, women, and children who owed their lives to him.

Travel was slow, because the roads of both Hungary and Austria were being used for the movement of heavy military equipment, but they had allowed plenty of time, so there was no need for concern. They stopped for their meals and for occasional glasses of beer in villages along the way. Colonel Weber's SS uniform got them special attention everywhere, but interested glances were cast in Andor's direction. He smiled to himself and thought that not even the most imaginative of these idly curious people would guess that he was the spokesman for —perhaps, if all went well, the deliverer of—Hungarian Jewry. They would never believe that he, a Jew, and this German colonel together were engaged in an attempt to save Jewish lives.

Wherever they went—even when they were in the car, out of the range of curious glances—Weber maintained a dignified reserve, never becoming very personal, yet Andor had a strong feeling that if circumstances were different they might have become friends.

They stopped overnight in the picturesque Austrian town of Imst, where each had a separate small room in the best hotel. After a short drive the next morning they reached Bregenz, a city of thirteen thousand war-weary inhabitants, at the extreme eastern end of Lake Constance. Captain Erhardt told them the frontier of Germany was four kilometers to the North, the frontier of Switzerland eleven kilometers to the southwest. Under an international agreement Swiss railroad trains were permitted to cross those eleven kilometers and discharge or pick up passengers at the Bregenz depot.

The bells of an immense gray stone church on a hill dominating the city were ringing as they drove through the center of the business district, because on the Catholic calendar this was St. Bernard's Day. At the railroad depot, which was on the edge of the lake, there were two sets of tracks. On one stood a train of day coaches, which had just arrived. Although the day was hot, the windows were closed and uniformed guards patrolled the right of way to see that they remained closed and that no one left the train. As soon as the limousine stopped, Andor jumped out and hurried in the direction of the depot. He could see faces pressed hard against the windows. From the markings on the side of each car he knew it was a German train.

Just then the stocky figure of Colonel Heinemann emerged from a special car in the middle of the train. This confirmed it. He was relieved. The Germans had kept their promise. Heinemann's black boots gleamed in the sunlight. His jaw seemed to protrude more than usual. As Andor walked half the length of the train to greet him, he studied the people in the windows. Word had obviously spread among them that he had arrived. Many of them waved eagerly; several women blew him kisses. He smiled back at them. He was searching for one special face when he heard his name spoken in guttural German. "Horvath, the list of the passengers." Heinemann was holding out a sheaf of papers.

"Thank you, Colonel." Andor accepted the papers. He was pleased to see that with Germanic efficiency they had arranged the list alphabetically. He thumbed the pages until he came to the *H*s. There was no *Hoffmann, Jessica*. He felt a pang of disappointment. Of course he had no right to expect her. . . .

Heinemann's thick voice was saying, "You will check the list with your people on the train. Then you will give me a receipt for three hundred Jews."

At that moment they saw smoke and heard the noise of a Swiss train approaching from the southwest.

The transfer of passengers and baggage was orderly and swift. In less than an hour the German train had been emptied and was on its way north. A few minutes later the train for Switzerland got under way.

Standing on the platform, he watched the Swiss cars pass by. The people he could see through the windows were laughing, shouting, waving joyously. The happiness he saw in their faces was reward enough for all his work. He put his cigarette to his lips and puffed in deep satisfaction. Individual Jews had been escaping from Hitler's Europe for years, but this was the first organized, wholesale shipment, and he was responsible. He had argued, fought, lied, pleaded, even gone to prison to get them out. Listening to the click of the wheels as the train gradually picked up speed, he decided it was beautiful music. Then abruptly he threw the butt of his cigarette to the ground and stamped it out. This was no time for self-adulation. Those three hundred Jews, who in a few minutes would be safe in Switzerland, were only the first small wave. More trains must follow. Whether they did depended on Weber, and Weber's attitude in turn depended on what happened tomorrow morning at their meeting on the frontier. He wished it were today. Patience was not one of his virtues.

Edward Schoen was a tall, spare, white-haired man with ascetic dark eyes, thin tight lips, a determined chin, and inflexible principles. A retired banker and onetime president of the Swiss Jewish Federation, he lived with his wife in a comfortable but inelegant villa in St. Gallen, a medium-sized Swiss city about a hundred kilometers from the spot where Germany, Austria, and Switzerland come together. He was a respected member of the business community and personified the qualities of honesty, integrity, thrift, scrupulous attention to minute detail, and general conservatism. He suffered, like most of his neighbors, from a lack of imagination. One story they told about him in St. Gallen was that as a young man he had dreamed of the time when he might become successful enough to afford a different suit of clothes for each day of the week, and when he finally achieved the financial position where this was possible, he had his tailor make him seven suits—but all of the same material, so no one would know he was so extravagant as to have seven suits. It was indicative of the feelings Edward Schoen inspired in others that the nickname by which everyone called him, even his own wife, was the cold, impersonal, yet rather dignified "E.S." Few people, either to his face or behind his back, referred to him in any other way.

Since the start of the war E.S. had devoted himself exclusively to assisting the beleaguered Jews of the countries surrounding Switzerland. He was only the director of the Swiss branch of the United Relief Organization, but gradually, as the Germans conquered country after coun-

227

try, his office became headquarters for the entire U.R.O. European operation.

E.S. and Andor Horvath were both Jews. Otherwise they were as unlike as two men could be, except that each had a committee and the committee theoretically made all the decisions, while in practice, in each case, the chairman was virtually autonomous. E.S.'s colleagues were so busy with their personal affairs they were willing to permit him a free hand. Being retired, he could devote his full time to the work. Also, most of his committee members were reluctant to be connected too closely with actions that might compromise Swiss neutrality and thus bring down on their heads the displeasure of the Swiss Government. Besides, the nature of E.S.'s rescue activities was such that quick decisions often had to be made, without the possibility of committee meetings and prolonged debate. U.R.O. headquarters in New York trusted E.S.'s judgment and gave him almost unlimited freedom of action.

Some of his work was with Jews fortunate enough and daring enough to have escaped from German-occupied countries to Switzerland. If the U.R.O. agreed to support them with money from America, the Swiss Government would usually permit them to remain, even though they had entered illegally. But E.S. also sent money, medical supplies, and food to Jews in France, Belgium, Holland, Slovakia, Bulgaria, Rumania, and even Poland, sometimes openly through the International Red Cross, sometimes secretly through underground organizations.

For all this onerous and dedicated work he accepted no remuneration, either from the U.R.O. or any other source; not even reimbursement for the considerable expenses he incurred in getting help to so many thousands of people. "The Americans give this money for relief and rescue; every penny of it must be spent on relief and rescue," he would say flatly.

In his book-lined study were three shelves filled with ledgers containing detailed and exact records of every transaction. Every penny he had received was accounted for; even the illegal dealings were included. Every night before he went to bed he committed to writing in a journal notes on all his conversations of the day, along with comments on his problems. On the wall behind his desk hung a large plaque bearing three stark letters: O.P.M. His friends knew that the letters stood for "Other People's Money" and that he had put the plaque there mainly for his own benefit, so he would be constantly reminded that he was handling funds contributed by people who, he often said, were entitled

to scrupulous honesty and careful disbursement of their money by him
and everyone else whose hands touched it.

There was no unanimity of opinion, even in Jewish circles, about
E.S. Many men who were risking their lives to smuggle refugees out
of dangerous areas and to run supplies into ghettos and concentration
camps were scathingly critical of what they called his "bookkeeper
mentality." They accused him of being "stingy" and declared that this
was no time to count pennies or argue over technicalities. But others
said the U.R.O. had never been so fortunate as when it persuaded E.S.
to be its Central European representative and the disburser of its
funds.

Sunday, August 20, was hot, but the sky was gray and the atmosphere
heavy as E.S. climbed into his small, four-cylinder automobile and drove
across St. Gallen to the home of his friend Isaac Singer, a member of
the Swiss Jewish Federation, a corporation lawyer, and E.S.'s adviser on
all legal matters.

"I hope the storm misses us," Singer said as they started back across
St. Gallen to get to Route 148. Many people in the streets on their way
to church were carrying umbrellas.

Singer was a small, thin, middle-aged man with gray-black hair and
an air of patient complaisance.

"I don't quite understand why you want me to go with you, E.S.," he
said, as soon as they were out of the range of the church bells that had
made conversation in the center of the city almost impossible.

"I'm suspicious of this whole matter," the older man replied, frowning.
"Horvath operates in a most unconventional manner. I've already had
some reports from New York about him. He sent one of his people
down to Istanbul to try to get military equipment for the Germans in
return for the freeing of a certain number of Jews from detention camps.
A very questionable operation. They were suspicious in Washington as
well as in London. Now that his Istanbul operation has failed, he is
turning to us."

"Whom are we meeting, besides Horvath?" Singer asked.

"An SS colonel named Franz Weber. I went to the expense of paying
someone in Berne to give me a report on him. He's the head of the SS
Economic Section. He has a decent business background. Probably a
very shrewd man. We must be careful not to say anything in his presence
that he can use to embarrass the U.R.O. or, in turn, the government in

Washington. Also, we must remember that we are Swiss. I am sure they would be nervous in Berne if they knew about this."

"I understand about Berne, but how can we possibly embarrass Washington?" the lawyer asked.

"It's very complicated, Isaac. There are people in the United States who think that the mission to Istanbul arranged by Horvath was not at all a serious attempt to trade Jews for trucks, but a way of sowing seeds of suspicion in Russian minds that the West was playing a double game."

"You mean this was Wedemeyer's objective?" Singer asked.

"Yes. Now about our meeting today. I'm sure it will be reported to Moscow before many hours have passed, and Moscow may think that we are acting as intermediaries between Washington and Berlin in some new attempt at double-dealing. I'm afraid that despite his motives—which I do not question, mind you—Horvath is doing the Allied cause and in that way the Jewish cause a great disservice."

"But I heard that a train arrived just yesterday in Basle loaded with three hundred of our people that this same man Horvath succeeded in getting out of Hungary. Is this true?"

"Yes," Schoen replied.

"That's an amazing accomplishment."

"Yes, but the whole matter is not clean-cut. I have been warned to be cautious. Actually I have no stomach for the matter at all. My wife is angry that I have even agreed to meet with a Nazi officer. She thinks this is something no good Jew should do. I told her she was being emotional. You know Paula! She is always inclined to let her heart rule her mind."

"There are worse crimes than that, E.S."

Just then a Swiss soldier at a check point waved the car down and demanded to see their identity papers.

A slow, steady drizzle was falling as Captain Erhardt drove through the last Austrian village, Höchst, and continued on another half mile to a steel bridge, just wide enough for two vehicles, crossing the Rhine seven miles upstream from where the river flows into Lake Constance. The bridge formed the only international link in this area between Switzerland and Austria. He parked the car at the side of the road, and the three men got out. The Austrian soldiers guarding their end of the bridge snapped to attention when they saw Weber's uniform and insignia. Three hundred feet away, at the far end of the bridge, Andor could see a cluster of Swiss soldiers. As he watched, two men in civilian clothes detached themselves from the group and started toward the center of the bridge. After a few words with the captain of the Austrian guards, Weber motioned to Andor to follow and they, too, started across the narrow bridge.

The four men met exactly in the center of the span. Technically they were not in either country. Andor introduced himself to Schoen and Singer. They seemed to be looking him over critically. He felt no instinctive bond of union with them. He presented them with stiff formality to Weber. No one shook hands.

"Have you provided us with Swiss visas so we can hold our conversation somewhere out of this rain?" Andor asked.

"No," Schoen replied in an unapologetic tone. "I made application, as you requested, but the visas did not arrive."

Weber seemed annoyed, but he said affably to Schoen and Singer, "We can't very well talk here, so I invite you two gentlemen to come over onto Austrian soil. At least we can sit in our car and talk, or go to a café in Höchst."

"Thank you, no." Schoen's voice was clipped and cold. Singer made no answer.

Weber waited a moment, as if undecided how to handle the situation. Then he drew himself to his full height and in an official voice announced, "I am the authorized representative of Reichsführer SS Heinrich Himmler, with full powers to discuss the situation of the Jews under German jurisdiction with representatives of the Allies and world Jewry. These negotiations, of course, will be based on a commercial agreement, the final approval of which must be given by the Reichsführer himself. I suggest we begin by discussing the Hungarian Jews. Orders have already been drawn for the deportation of the two hundred thousand Jews of Budapest. What happens to them depends on what sacrifices Jewish organizations abroad and the Allies are ready to make for them. Now I ask you, Herr Schoen, are you ready to fulfill the German demands that have been transmitted to your Jewish Agency in Istanbul?"

As Weber finished everyone looked at Schoen. A flush had turned his face pink, but his voice was calm and even as he answered, "I am first and primarily a Swiss citizen. I have not come here as a representative of the United Relief Organization but as president of a Jewish rescue organization in Switzerland. I know nothing of any German demand, and therefore I cannot take any position on this subject. Besides, I have no connection with the Jewish Agency or anyone in Istanbul. As for the deportation of Budapest Jews, this is in itself not such a great misfortune, if you mean they are merely to be moved out of Hungary. But if you mean there is a possibility that they will be taken to extermination camps, I have something to say on this subject. If the Germans wish to have a single gram of good will left in the world, if they expect decent people even to talk to them, let alone negotiate about anything with them, then they must put an end once and for all to such inventions as gas chambers, and not because they are being paid or bribed to do it."

Andor was shocked. He glanced quickly at Weber to see how he had taken this rebuke, but Weber's expression indicated that he was in complete control of himself.

Actually the German colonel was extremely irritated, but assuming Schoen's words were a bargaining tactic, he replied, "If our negotiations are successful, it is possible that such actions against Jews as you mention will cease. As a matter of fact, we have already shown our good intent by letting a group of three hundred Jews from Bergen-Belsen enter your country only yesterday. Now we want to hear what you offer in return."

Schoen's face turned a deeper pink. "I refuse to have anything to do with the bartering of human lives." Then he added icily, "Before we can engage in any other form of negotiating, the Germans must exhibit some humanitarianism. They must plainly show a change of heart."

Weber snapped angrily, "Come now, Herr Schoen, you are talking a lot of empty words. You are a banker and a man of affairs. Let us get down to business."

"In any case," Schoen replied stiffly, "I have no power to promise anything. I must first consult the competent authorities."

Weber wheeled on Andor. "You have brought me here on false pretenses! There are no visas, the other side is totally unprepared to negotiate, and its representative has the audacity to lecture me on humanitarianism, as if I were responsible for everything that has happened."

At this Singer intervened with the suggestion that Schoen get in touch at once with the competent authorities and that another meeting be held at a later date.

Weber, having regained his composure, agreed and proposed that the discussion should be resumed in ten days.

When they separated, water was dripping from their hats and the shoulders of their jackets were soaking wet. Weber ordered Captain

Erhardt to start at once for Budapest. For a long time neither of the men in the back seat spoke, each deep in his own thoughts. But during the long drive the dismal failure of the first contact began to gnaw at Weber. He reproached Andor again.

Though it was difficult for Andor to explain away what had happened, especially since he himself was angry with Schoen, he made a determined attempt. Schoen was a representative of the U.R.O. even if he denied it, Andor said, and when he talked of consulting the competent authorities he was thinking not only of the U.R.O. but also of the American War Refugee Board, which was a part of the United States Government. The Board's authority was necessary to any plan for converting the dollars of the U.R.O. into Swiss francs.

"I know that in many ways Schoen is a difficult person," he continued. "But the very fact that he is a hard-bitten, penny-pinching Swiss banker makes him all the more important to both of us. He is going to take some handling, but when we once get his word that he'll meet our demands, you can be sure that he'll deliver what he promises."

He talked on and on, choosing his words carefully, trying to be just patronizing enough without letting it become obvious; flattering his listener now and then; using all his charm to placate and persuade.

When they stopped for the night, Andor asked if he could have the privilege of being the host and choosing the dinner. He held a long consultation with the *patron*. The meal that eventually was produced was fit for a gourmet. Also, they had a 1911 Château Rothschild that Weber admitted was the best red wine he had ever tasted.

By the time they reached Budapest the next afternoon, Andor and the colonel were again on relatively friendly terms.

For a month events in Hungary, sharply influenced by the rapid military advance of the Allies in other parts of the continent, had been moving toward a precipitous climax. Squadrons of Allied planes bombed her cities, demolishing homes and factories and crippling communications. The northeast section of the country was invaded by partisans from Czechoslovakia. In the south Tito's men infiltrated from Yugoslavia. The relatively few Hungarian gendarmes available for patrolling highways and transportation lines were unable to control the influx into Budapest, which was now overrun by refugees, deserters, thieves, spies, and escaped prisoners of war. In an effort to maintain at least some internal security and order, the government restricted public activities and even imposed a curfew for all inhabitants in many areas.

The decline of Germany's military and diplomatic position was an

233

undeniable fact. If the Hungarians had had doubts before, they had none now. In Finland pro-German President Ryti had been forced to resign. Turkey broke off diplomatic relations with the Reich. Allied troops swarmed over France, took Falaise, and closed the Argentan gap, where a hundred thousand Germans were killed or captured. There were rumors, privately circulated, that the Rumanian Government was negotiating for a surrender to the Allies.

With these changes of fortune Horthy, now certain that Germany had lost the war, decided that Hungary's wisest course was to remove herself from the conflict just as soon as it was safe to do so. In the meantime he and his government resisted the demands of the Germans more stubbornly. Wedemeyer, alarmed, decided to speed up the Jewish extermination before it was too late and announced that the deportation of Budapest Jews would begin on August 27, under the supervision of the SS. For this purpose several additional SS detachments were brought into the capital. Panicky, and having no faith in Andor's negotiating, Emmanuel Simon, on behalf of the Jewish Council, appealed to the Regent's son, Nicholas Horthy, Jr., to oppose the deportation. The reply was depressing: Budapest was defenseless, except for the palace bodyguard, and there was no way to bring Hungarian troops in from the provinces without a fight, for German soldiers had the capital encircled.

To frighten the Hungarians into continued submission, the Wehrmacht staged a gigantic military parade through the streets of Budapest. Then preparations were begun for the application of the final solution to the Budapest Jews. Hundreds of trucks were brought to the edge of the city. Captain Erich von Klaussen and his subordinates appeared at the brick factory of Békásmegyer, which they began to convert into an assembling center for the prospective deportees.

But on August 20, Rumania suddenly withdrew from the war. When Horthy heard the news he told his friends that for Hungary this was a sword that cut two ways: while it made Germany's defeat more certain, it left Hungary's eastern borders defenseless and open to invasion by the Soviet army, a prospect that filled him with revulsion. He had hoped for sufficient time before Germany's collapse to arrange a surrender to the Anglo-Americans, while defending the eastern frontiers against any further Russian advance, with the assistance of the Rumanians as allies. Nevertheless he acted quickly. He dismissed the Sztojay government and appointed a new Prime Minister, General Lakatos, with instructions to restore Hungary's sovereignty as completely as possible within the framework of the German occupation, to bring an end to all anti-Jewish actions immediately, and to plan secretly to take Hungary out of the war.

In Berlin, Himmler, re-evaluating Germany's position and prospects, sent a message to the Hungarian Government retreating from his previous stand on Jewish affairs and offering to discuss a new solution. In reply he received a demand that Germany return all control of Jewish affairs to the Hungarian Government and put an immediate stop to any anti-Jewish activities of its own on Hungarian territory.

While this exchange was going on, Regent Horthy was using the services of a trusted English-speaking friend to contact the Americans and British in Italy over a secret radio transmitter hidden in the royal palace.

On August 25, Budapest heard that Paris had been liberated by American and French troops.

At eight o'clock that evening Captain Erich von Klaussen telephoned Andor at his apartment and asked him to come immediately to his villa on the Svábhegy.

The maid ushered Andor into the Louis XV salon, where he found the aristocratic captain as meticulously attired as usual but surrounded by disorder. There were several large packing cases in the center of the room and around them on the floor piles of crumpled newspapers and excelsior. On a large center table were porcelain and silver *bibelots* that had decorated various niches in the house. All the chairs in the room were heaped high with books, many in fine leather bindings. On the floor leaning against the far wall were several oil paintings of assorted sizes. Andor glanced quickly at the wall where the small Renoir in the heavy gold frame had been. It was no longer hanging there, over the blue velvet sofa.

Klaussen greeted him with a forced smile. "Well, you have won. Our headquarters is withdrawing."

Andor was taken by surprise, for he'd heard only a vague rumor that this might happen. He decided to be cautious. "What has happened?" He tried to keep his voice neutral.

Klaussen picked up a bottle of Courvoisier from a potpourri of objects on a card table, poured the contents equally into two large brandy glasses, and handed one to Andor. Then he put the empty bottle back on the table. His movements were unhurried. "Everything comes to an end." He lifted his glass. *"Prosit."*

Andor returned the toast. The mellow liquid soothed his tense insides, but he wished Klaussen would get on with whatever it was he had to say.

The finely chiseled features of the captain relaxed in a somewhat sardonic grin. "I shall come directly to the point, Horvath. The Reichsführer has taken into consideration the Hungarian Government's demands concerning the Jews. Since the Rumanians have defected he deems it more *prudent*"—the way he said the word it was obviously a euphemism—"not to irritate the Hungarians any further. So he has ordered Colonel Wedemeyer and his entire Sondereinsatzkommande to leave Budapest."

Andor's first impulse was to shout with joy. If Wedemeyer and his gang left Hungary, if Horthy was able to wrest even partial control of the situation away from the SS and make a separate peace with the Allies, or if the Russians came in soon and drove the Germans out, then Budapest's two hundred thousand remaining Jews would be saved. But there was another aspect of the situation that gave him a sharp jab of pain. With Wedemeyer gone there would be no one to negotiate with for the people at Bergen-Belsen, unless . . .

"Will Colonel Franz Weber be going, too?" He tried to make his voice sound casual.

"I assume so. We are all going."

By now Andor knew these Nazi officers well enough to be certain that there was purpose in his having been sent for and treated so well. He tried to enjoy his brandy while he waited to learn what it was.

Klaussen slowly put his empty glass on the table and looked down at his slender, well-manicured fingers. "I am glad, in a way, that I never soiled my hands, either literally or figuratively, with blood. The final solution has never really been to my liking. Now that I am leaving I do not mind telling you this. In a way I'm very fortunate." His voice took on a slightly confidential tone. "I am one of the few who have a completely clear conscience about what has been done to the Jews of Hungary."

Andor smiled to himself. It was clear now why he was here.

Klaussen looked up and in a friendly tone continued, "I wanted to have this final drink with you before I left and tell you that I am perhaps much more responsible than you have ever realized for the fact that you personally and many of your friends have escaped what unfortunately has happened to so many of your people. You do realize this, don't you, Herr Horvath?" It was the first time any of the German officers had addressed him as "Herr Horvath." Klaussen's voice was well modulated and ingratiating.

Andor put his own glass on the table and stood up. "For what you have done, we are, of course, grateful," he said, trying to be polite and still not commit himself in any way.

What neither Captain Klaussen nor Andor knew was that Secretary of State for the Ministry of the Interior, László Endre, had convinced Wedemeyer the overthrow of Horthy and the installation of a friendly regime was so imminent it would be foolish for him to leave the country.

"I have a castle at Velem, close to the Austrian frontier," Endre told Wedemeyer. "Come and relax there as my guest for a few days, and then, as soon as Horthy is liquidated, you can return to Budapest and together we will clean up what's left of the Jewish garbage—if I may steal that wonderful expression of yours."

Since returning from the Swiss frontier Andor, controlling his animosity toward Edward Schoen, wrote two long letters to him, which he persuaded a friend in the Swiss Consulate to put into the diplomatic pouch, thus avoiding both German and Hungarian scrutiny.

Several days after the departure of Wedemeyer and his Kommando, he learned that the one officer left behind was Colonel Weber. After all, he was an "economic expert." It was fortunate that he had not gone, because a new crisis had arisen. Late in August an anti-German insurrection had broken out in Slovakia, and the Germans were holding the Jews responsible. As soon as Wedemeyer heard of it, he asked Berlin for permission to go to Bratislava and accomplish the liquidation of the remainder of Slovak Jews. The authorization was granted. Andor was immediately swamped with appeals to try to prevent the extermination. His workers operating along the Slovak frontier, couriers who still succeeded in making occasional trips between Bratislava and Budapest, and refugees who managed to escape to Hungary—all brought reports that left no doubt about the seriousness of the situation.

Although Andor had little hope of dissuading the Germans, he and Arthur went to see Weber. They were received politely, but the colonel rejected their plea for help. "How can you expect me to intervene on your behalf with the Reichsführer after what happened at the St. Margrethen bridge?" He shook his head. "It's impossible. The Jews in Slovakia—or anywhere else—can be saved only if Schoen and the organization he represents are ready to conclude the agreement we discussed with the Jewish Agency."

237

As they left the Majestic Hotel, Arthur threw up his hands angrily. "What is it that makes a man act like an enemy of his people when they're being slaughtered? What does Schoen have in his veins, seltzer water?"

Andor sighed. "I've tried hard to understand him. He insists that first the Germans must prove they are softening their policy."

"In other words, we should teach the nasty Germans good manners. Until then he won't help."

"It's not as simple as that, Arthur. The Nazis disgust him, as they do us, but our attitudes are very different. And for a simple reason. He and those like him are on the other side of the fence, safe and secure. We, on our side, are in constant peril for our lives. They can afford to discourse on ethics; we only fear death. They pity us and think we are powerless. We want to live, and so we think that rescue ought to be possible. This is the gap between us, and we must find a way to bridge it."

For a moment they walked along in silence, then Andor's mood changed. "I'm going to send Schoen a telegram. I think the Slovak situation may move him."

Every day for a week Andor wired more details. At last he received a reply. Schoen agreed to make "a reasonable payment" in return for a guarantee that not another Slovak Jew would be harmed.

Andor put on an air of optimism he didn't really feel as he placed the telegram on Weber's desk. "See, the old rascal has come through, after all!"

The colonel read it twice before replying. "No, Horvath, it won't work. In the first place, it is much too indefinite. Those words 'reasonable payment' could mean anything—or nothing. Besides, I was informed this morning that the liquidation of the Slovak Jews is now a necessity, for military reasons. Colonel Wedemeyer has absolute proof that they were the ringleaders in the recent insurrection."

Andor didn't even try to hide his reaction. His shoulders sagged as he slumped into a chair opposite Weber. Suddenly he looked very tired.

Weber changed his tone to one almost of friendliness. "However," he said, "I think your man Schoen should be given some encouragement in return for his willingness to be realistic, so you may tell him that I am ready to go to Switzerland and confer with him about saving the rest of the Jews of Europe, on condition that he will agree in advance to a businesslike discussion of payments, and no lectures on humanitarianism."

"I'll telegraph him at once," Andor said, his hopes rising again as he picked up his hat to go.

Weber held up his hand. "One other condition. Tell Schoen that we will not even leave Budapest until he informs us that he has procured Swiss visas for us. No more of this nonsense of standing in the middle of a bridge. And this time my adjutant will go, too, so ask for three visas."

20

As Miriam Berg walked out of the German prison into the chill October air, she shivered slightly. She had on the same flowered cotton dress she had been wearing the day they arrested her almost four months ago. This morning they had returned her clothes and her handbag and told her she was free. The autumn breeze loosened a strand of her pale hair. She pushed it back in place and smiled inwardly. It had done them no good to keep her locked up all summer. They had learned nothing. She and Naomi never mentioned the parachute mission. They spoke about Palestine only during moments of their exercise period when they were positive no one else was close enough to hear.

With the flat of her hand she tried to smooth out the wrinkles in her skirt. It was hopeless. She started away from the prison, opening her handbag as she went to see whether they had taken her money. It was all there. She would walk to the bus, she decided, and go straight to Andor Horvath at the Sip utca Center. He was the only one with influence enough to get Naomi out of prison. Actually, she mused, it was strange that he had made no move to help her. Naomi had said he was supposed to be one of her contacts. Surely he knew . . .

Miriam's thoughts were broken by the earsplitting wail of air-raid sirens. She looked around quickly for a shelter. In the next block several people were rushing into a doorway a half flight below street level. She hurried toward it and ran down the steps.

It seemed like a rather small room. There was a hum of voices, and in the half-light she could see vague outlines of men and women moving about, but her eyes couldn't adjust immediately to the darkness. The air was thick with tobacco smoke. She coughed and wiped her smarting eyes.

"My lady, let me help you."

A stocky, brown-haired man in some kind of a uniform rose from the desk in front of her as he spoke the exceedingly polite words. Suddenly she saw clearly the crossed green arrows on his arm band. A scream began to take form in her throat, but she killed it before it escaped. She pressed her handbag to her breast to cover the yellow star.

The officer, noticing her consternation, pointed to the people still coming down the stairs and said, "It's all right. You see, our party headquarters is often mistaken for a shelter. You can stay here until it's all over. Sit down." He gave her his chair.

She sat down meekly.

Before her, on the desk, was a large street map of Budapest with markings here and there in red, yellow, and green. In one corner, in large letters, were the words: THE HUNGARIAN ARROW CROSS PARTY. He saw her glance at it. Looking confidentially into her blue eyes, he grinned, tapped the map with his index finger, and said, "You see, sister, with or without Horthy's consent we are going to get rid of the Jews. All of them, including those who pretend they are not Jews." He rolled up the map and walked to a cabinet to put it away. As he crossed the room, another officer approached him and they began to talk in low tones.

She looked around covertly for a way out. There was only one small door besides the entrance she had come through. She made her way to it as inconspicuously as she could. From the corner of her eye she could see that the two officers were still engrossed in their conversation. Opening the little door quietly, she slipped into the room. It was a water closet. Trembling with fear, she locked herself in and leaned against the door. For an hour or more she remained there, afraid to make a sound. When the all clear came, she let herself out, careful to mingle with the others, and walked up the stairs to the street.

At the Center the receptionist told her Mr. Horvath wasn't in.

It was a cruel disappointment.

"Would you like to see someone else, Mr. Gruen, perhaps?"

"No, it must be Mr. Horvath." She was not going to be put off. "Please, when will he be back?"

"I can't say exactly."

"Then where can I find him? I must see him. It's desperately important."

The receptionist looked up at her wearily. "I know," she said in a soft voice. It was always desperately important. But her words promised nothing except compassion.

Miriam felt tears pressing against her lids and fought to keep them back. "Please try to understand. My sister from Palestine is at the German prison. They are holding her as a British spy."

The receptionist blinked in astonishment, but she kept her voice matter-of-fact. "I'll try to get in touch with Mr. Horvath for you. Just write your name and address on this and I'll call you as soon as Mr. Horvath can be reached." She held out a slip of yellow paper.

Miriam wrote the information and handed the paper back to the girl. "Will you try to contact him right away?" she persisted.

"Right away. Go home and wait for our call." The girl picked up the piece of paper, glanced at the name, and then gazed speculatively at Miriam's receding back, unaware that Arthur, who had just come in, was doing the same thing.

"Who was that?" He pointed toward the door.

" 'Mrs. Miriam Berg,' " she read from the yellow slip. "She says her sister from Palestine is being held at the German prison as a British spy."

"Not another one!"

"She wants to see Mr. Horvath."

"He won't be back for another two or three days." If he ever gets here at all, he said to himself. Going to Slovakia to bargain for what Jews were left there was foolish and dangerous, even with Weber's permission; even for a clever manipulator like Andor.

"Will this business keep until he returns?" the receptionist asked.

"I'd better look into it myself tomorrow." He took the yellow slip and read aloud the notation, " 'Mrs. Miriam Berg, 16 Akácfa utca, Apartment 24,' " and put it in a vest pocket.

Miriam went to the tiny apartment she had shared with Sandor Kaplan, his wife Anna, and their adolescent daughters, Rebecca and Dora. Mr. Kaplan was a tailor; "the best," he always said bluntly. He was a baldheaded, voluble little man with a quick temper, an indestructible zest for life, and effusive generosity. When Miriam walked in, Sandor and his daughters were seated at the table and Anna Kaplan was dishing out their supper of cabbage soup and potatoes. The little tailor jumped up, almost upsetting the ladle in his wife's hand.

"Look who's here!" he shouted happily. "Everybody look!" He threw his arms around Miriam, lifting her so that her feet no longer touched the floor, and swung her in a complete circle before he put her down. By that time he was too out of breath to say a word, but he continued to pat her arm and touch her, as if to make certain she was a real, live person.

"It is the happiest moment of my life!" he finally blurted out.

The whole family crowded around Miriam, kissing her and all talking at once.

"Come, you'll sit down and eat; you'll talk later," Mrs. Kaplan said as she set another place at the table.

"It's a celebration!" Sandor cried. "Mamma, didn't I tell you things are getting better?"

"You told me. Now come and eat your soup, everybody."

But the little bald-headed tailor was too excited. "Who is eating, at a time like this?" he asked. Seeing someone return from a German prison camp—for when anyone disappeared for months that is where he was always assumed to be—released his long-suppressed natural ebullience. "We have to have music." All radios owned by Jews were supposed to have been confiscated long before this, but the Kaplans, like many others, had risked arrest by not turning theirs in. Always they played it very softly, with their ears close to the speaker, so not even the people in the next apartment would know. Sandor went to a clothes chest and from under some blankets extracted a small radio.

Suddenly the gay strains of the "Emperor Waltz" filled the room.

"Sandor! Sandor! Turn it down or we'll all go to prison." Mrs. Kaplan started across the room for the radio herself. Her husband motioned her away. "It's a celebration, Mamma! To hell with the Nazis!"

It had been a long time since Miriam had heard any music, especially such happy music. A flood of memories rushed at her. Then suddenly she felt she couldn't bear to hear the joyous, majestic melody in the shabbiness and tragedy that now surrounded her. At the same time she thought of Naomi. She gripped her spoon hard and lifted the soup to her lips.

Sandor came back to the table and began to eat, humming occasionally in tune with the radio, despite his wife's disapproving look. Between bites he told Miriam what had happened in the community while she had been away. Rebecca and Dora interrupted frequently to joke about some ridiculous situations that had resulted from all the stupid regulations.

"Every time there's another air raid, it's us that loses houses even if the bombs don't hit our houses," Mr. Kaplan said.

Because Miriam seemed perplexed he went on and explained. "You see, if a Christian house gets hit, they move the Jews out of some building with a yellow star and give it to the *goyim*."

Rebecca laughed. "But sometimes it's fun. Chaim and Shoshana—

you remember them, Miriam—they had a lovers' quarrel and weren't speaking. Then one night there was a bombing, and a lot of our people had to double up because their apartments were taken away from them, and guess what? They put Chaim's family and Shoshana's family in the same apartment, and now they're going to get married!"

No one asked Miriam what had happened during her long absence. She thanked them all silently for that. Soothed by their kindness, she laughed at their stories and let herself be drawn to them, but Naomi was never out of her consciousness. Behind the sweet, grateful smile she gave the Kaplans was a constant heartache for her wan, dark-eyed sister, alone now in the cold cell of an enemy prison.

The next day was Sunday. At one o'clock, having just finished their midday meal, they were sitting around the table listening to the radio announcer read the weather bulletin and the Danube water-level report. Suddenly the melody of the "Rákóczi March" blared from the speaker.

Mr. Kaplan looked at the small clock on the mantel. It was ten minutes after one. "Why do they play the station signature now?" The others were as puzzled as he.

The entire march was played. Then it was repeated from the beginning. Halfway through the second time the music stopped and the announcer said, "Attention. Attention. We are about to make a momentous announcement. Hungary is seeking an armistice. We will now read the Regent's proclamation."

The five people in the squalid little room sat motionless, as if they hadn't heard or couldn't believe, while the announcer's voice read out Horthy's words: "I am informing the representative here of the German Reich that we are concluding a preliminary armistice with our enemies and are ceasing all hostilities against them." Then followed an order of the day to the Hungarian Army.

All at once there was a great commotion throughout the building. People were rushing up and down the corridors passing the news along, shouting and laughing. A man ran into the Kaplans' room, grabbed Anna, and led her round and round in a frantic dance. That broke the spell. Rebecca and Dora kissed each other and their father, then Miriam. At the height of the bedlam Miriam joyously cried out Naomi's name, but the room was jammed now with hysterically happy people and what she said no one heard. Now they all ran to the street, and the younger people began dancing a *csárdás*. Crowds were streaming from all the houses on Akácfa utca, everyone in a frenzy of ecstasy. Miriam, caught up in the gaiety, was whisked about in the exultant dance and embraced by strangers.

Sandor, red-faced and perspiring, tore the yellow star from his jacket and threw it into the air. "We are no longer 'Jewish scum.' We are people again, Mamma," he shouted to his wife, reaching for the emblem on her dress.

People up and down the street were ripping stars from coats and jackets and dresses. Miriam pulled at hers, then stopped abruptly as she remembered the Mogen David drawn in the dust of the prison courtyard and Naomi's defiant cry: "It is the pride of the Jews!" She smoothed the yellow patch back into place and drew herself up a little taller.

In many apartments radios, which until today had been hidden carefully, were left on as the people poured into the street. Through open doors and windows the announcer could be heard reading again the Regent's proclamation and the order of the day. But no one was listening.

Just before one o'clock Arthur left his apartment on Dalnok utca and walked toward the address Miriam had left at the Center. The usual Sunday strollers were out by the thousands, gossiping and enjoying the bright, brisk October day. As he walked along elegant Andrassy út, he saw sadly that the leaves of the great trees had turned from brilliant red to dull, dry brown. Masses of them skipped along the sidewalk, chased by the wind, crackling as passers-by stepped on them.

He noticed, too, that the avenue was beginning to fill up with an extraordinary number of people. They were coming from all the side streets leading into Andrassy, some of them laughing and shouting, but most of them just standing about in small groups, silent and uncertain, as if they were waiting for something. More and more of them streamed in, until the avenue was almost a solid block of humanity.

A burly man pushed his way through the throng. Shoving his face in front of Arthur's, he yelled, "Hurrah for peace!" A few people timidly echoed his words, and an elderly woman cried in an unsteady voice, "Hurrah for the Regent!" But most of them stood around, quiet and aimless, perplexed. As the burly stranger started to elbow his way down the avenue again, Arthur grabbed him.

"What happened?"

The man looked at him incredulously and then shouted with laughter, "*You* don't know? You and your people are safe now, my friend. Hungary is out of the war. We are going to join the Allies. You Jews have nothing to worry about now." He slapped Arthur on the back with a powerful arm and moved on, shouting in the faces of people in his way, "Hurrah for peace!" as if to sting them out of their lethargy.

When Arthur reached Akácfa utca, the scene was quite different. Here, in front of the yellow-starred houses, there was riotous rejoicing. Three times he was kissed and twice drawn into a line of dancers as he tried to make his way to the end of the street. By the time he reached Number 16 he, too, had been infected with the delirium, though he tried to caution himself against premature optimism. He knew better than the naïve celebrants around him the frequency of cross and double-cross in war and politics . . .

In front of Number 16 he asked a girl if Mrs. Miriam Berg was around. Rebecca gazed at him diffidently for a moment, then glanced over the crowd. "There she is." She pointed to Miriam's slight figure leaning against the wall. There was a bittersweet look in the pale blue eyes as they watched the rejoicing. She was part of it and yet not part of it at all. For her the terror wouldn't be over so long as Naomi was a prisoner.

Arthur went to her and introduced himself. He had to shout above the noise to be heard. "Is there some place where we can talk?"

She nodded and led the way to the apartment. The radio was still on. The announcer was reading the proclamation for a third time.

Although she was grateful to him for coming, she said, she hoped Mr. Horvath wouldn't be away much longer. "They say he can get anything from the Germans. Not that I think there will be any trouble now," she added hastily. "Naomi *will* get out, won't she?" There was a note of pleading in her voice.

"Oh, she has a much better chance as things are now," he answered with exaggerated heartiness, though he thought, if the girl is really a British spy, who knows what they will do with her, even now? "As for Mr. Horvath," he said aloud, "it looks as if he may be delayed for some time, and I don't think it would be wise to put off seeking help for your sister." He realized with a start that there was a strong possibility that Andor might not return at all. It would be a miracle if the damned Nazis allowed him to come back, now that Hungary was an enemy country. Or at least neutral. There would probably be fighting on the Slovak frontier, and no one would be able to cross in either direction.

Without warning the radio was silent. They looked at each other, surprised. Then it came to life again with the strident sound of a military march. After several seconds the music faded and the piercing wail of air-raid sirens beat at them.

Miriam clasped and unclasped her hands nervously. "Do you think the Germans are going to bomb us?"

Arthur grinned. "Maybe the Hungarian Government just wanted to get all these noisy crowds off the streets. They've tried that trick before, and it always works. Nobody wants to die. I guess that's one thing we all have in common—Jews, Christians, Germans, Frenchmen, even dogs and cats, I suppose. We don't want to die."

He stuck his head out the window. "They're all coming inside. I think we'd better go down to the shelter, too, just in case it's the real thing. It would be foolish to get killed now that it's about over, wouldn't it?"

He took her arm, smiling at her reassuringly, and led her to the basement. There, in a tightly packed corner surrounded by the other tenants of the apartment house, Miriam told him about Naomi.

At twenty minutes past three the all clear sounded and people went back upstairs, much subdued. Radio Budapest began to broadcast again, but just Hungarian military music. The neighborhood was quiet. Some people wandered out into the streets to see what was happening, others hung out of windows. The rest, like the Kaplan family, sat by their radios, hoping to hear more good news. Arthur was saying good-by to Miriam, having promised that he would immediately set about trying to obtain Naomi's release, when they heard several muffled shots that seemed to come from the next building.

Suddenly their own building was in an uproar. The noises of stomping boots, crashing furniture, and the curses of angry men came from the floor below. A woman screamed. From the stair well rose the shout of a military order given in a harsh Hungarian voice. They all stood rooted to their places, even Arthur. The hard clack of the boots on the wooden steps came closer. Then the door was thrown open and there stood two men in Arrow Cross uniforms.

Miriam stared with terror at the stocky figure and brown hair of the older one. It was the man with the map. Her legs felt weak, and she began to shake. But the officer wasn't looking at her. He was watching Sandor and Arthur, as he ordered the young man with him, "Search the place!"

"For what?" Sandor objected. "You have taken everything already."

The older officer reached out a brawny arm and hit him in the face, knocking him against the wall. Anna gasped and ran to her husband's side.

"For weapons!" The Hungarian spat out the words. "You Jewish scum have killed one of our men. We're going to make sure it doesn't happen again. Do you have any objections?" He asked the question with mock politeness as Anna wiped the blood that trickled from her husband's mouth.

Miriam had moved several steps until she was behind Arthur, almost out of sight of the two Arrow Cross men. Arthur could feel her trembling so violently against his back that he stepped aside and put his arm around her shoulder, unwittingly exposing her to view.

This time the stocky Hungarian noticed her. A mean grin spread across his face as he walked toward her. "So! What do we have here? A Jewess who tries to pretend she isn't one! Such smart people you all are!" There was a loud crack as his hand left a stinging imprint on her face.

Arthur swung his fist and hit him squarely on the jaw. The blow dazed him for a moment, but his young partner drew his pistol from its holster and Arthur felt the sharp muzzle in the small of his back before he could turn around. Sandor took three quick steps, flung open a closet door, reached under some clothing, and pulled out an old-fashioned revolver. Raising it to shoulder height, he took quick aim at the younger Arrow Cross man and pulled the trigger. The shot went wild. As Anna screamed, the intended victim brought the butt of his gun down on the bald head of the little tailor, who slumped to the floor. Arthur made a dive for the revolver Sandor had dropped, but the Arrow Cross commander was too quick for him. He pushed Arthur's heavy frame out of the way with his shoulder, picked up the gun, and shoved Arthur back against the wall. The four women in the room all tried to go to Sandor's help, but they were ordered to stand back. As they watched with fear in their eyes and a horrible premonition in their hearts, the two Arrow Cross men prodded Arthur and Sandor out of the room and down the stairs.

In front of the building, surrounded by Arrow Cross guards, were at least thirty men and boys. Arthur and Sandor were ordered to stand with them. For the better part of an hour they remained there, while more and more prisoners were added to the group. Sandor had difficulty standing. Blood from the cut on the top of his head was trickling down the back of his neck, and one eye was almost closed.

Finally they received an order to face to the south and to "forward march." From a side street they swung into Rákóczi út. The shops that lined the thoroughfare were all closed, because it was Sunday, but there were thousands of window-shoppers promenading the broad sidewalks.

In the distance there was a roar. The throngs on the sidewalks turned their attention from the shop windows and the motley parade of Arrow Cross prisoners to watch what was coming down the wide thoroughfare. Arthur strained his eyes to see. The Germans! The goddamn Germans! Their Tiger tanks and armored cars were moving slowly but with a noisy relentlessness down the avenue. Fury and anguish gave Arthur the urge to shout defiance at them, but the words were strangled in his throat. All he could do was to mutter to himself, "The goddamned Nazis!" No one else in that vast watching crowd lifted a voice, either. Most of them just stared blankly at the plodding vehicles.

Arthur laughed bitterly at the insanity of the whole scene.

Sandor looked up at him. There was bewilderment on his swollen face. "This is a time to laugh?" He wondered whether the big man had lost his mind.

Arthur's large, florid features took on an awesome soberness. "I laugh to keep from crying." He looked straight ahead as he said it. From then on he walked like a man in a dream. His gaze took in neither the German armed might that was still rumbling down the street in the opposite direction, nor the little tailor beside him, nor the confused people milling around him, nor the arrogant young Arrow Cross guards, who kept shouting insults and ordering them to move faster. He had no idea where they were being taken, but he had a strong premonition what was going to be done to them. Yet something suddenly had anesthetized him. He walked with his head high, his large shoulders thrown back.

The guards led their prisoners down the length of Rákóczi, across Kossuth Lajos utca, and toward the Danube. When they reached the quay, the Hungarians ordered them down to the docks under the Elizabeth Bridge. Here they tied each man's hands behind him with a length of stout rope. Then, at last, even the most optimistic of them knew. Out of the mouths of many came the rhythmic sound of prayers, echoing against the under side of the bridge.

Arthur Gruen didn't pray. "Speak the holy words with me," Sandor begged him, but he didn't hear.

The men and boys were marched out onto a landing stage and lined up single file. At one end the guards began to fire their pistols, and the prisoners dropped into the river like wooden ducks in a carnival shooting gallery, their falling bodies causing the muddy water to splash in great showers on the men and boys who still stood helplessly on the pier.

One by one they fell, and then it was Sandor's turn. He lifted his face to the sky. "O Lord, let not my unprovoked enemies rejoice over me . . ."

Arthur felt the river water splatter in his face as the little tailor fell forward. Now it was his turn. He heard the resounding noise of a pistol shot behind him, and a flash of searing heat spread through his stomach. Everything went dark. Then suddenly he was cold, so very cold. He was in the river. Foul water was filling his mouth, his nose, his ears. He stretched his neck and kicked his feet furiously to keep his head above water. He didn't want to die. They couldn't kill him if he didn't want to die. He struggled with passionate frenzy against the sucking force of the water, unmindful of the excruciating pain in his abdomen.

"I will not die!" he shouted. "I will not . . ."

A guard on the pier took careful aim. The bullet struck him between the eyes.

"Cut it out!" the commander yelled from the other end of the line. "We don't have ammunition to waste."

In the squalid apartment on Akácfa utca Miriam and the Kaplan women clustered around the radio, listening to endless military marches and waiting desperately for some hopeful news.

At twenty minutes to ten the announcer came on with a bulletin. "As a result of the Regent's disgraceful treason," he said, "the Chief of the Hungarian General Staff has issued the following order of the day to the Hungarian Army: 'Every Hungarian detachment must continue the war as before and with all its strength.'" Then came an angry voice that announced a "proclamation to the nation by the Arrow Cross party, Hungarist Movement." The "conspiracy of interests of the internal enemy has been removed from Hungary's path . . ." it said, and followed the proclamation by a vitriolic attack on the Jews.

Rebecca jumped up angrily and turned off the radio.

Anna Kaplan looked a thousand years old. "Papa's not coming back," she said quietly.

Rebecca went to her, took the work-worn hands in her own, and held them tenderly.

Little Dora began to cry. Miriam put her arms around the girl and murmured comfortingly to her. She hardly knew what she said, for her own heart was swollen with grief.

"Darling Naomi, what can we do now?" she cried silently to her sister.

21

All day Sunday and throughout the following night, unknown to the people, three forces in Budapest were engaging in a desperate struggle for power: the Horthy government, the Arrow Cross party, and the Germans. At the start the Regent seemed to have the advantage. The Hungarian Army Chief of Operations had explained to him and his Crown Council that the Russians, already at Debrecen, could not be stopped by the Wehrmacht. Before long Budapest would be encircled; the great city that was the pride of every Hungarian might be converted into a mass of rubble if the Germans insisted on trying to defend it. The councilors and the Regent were impressed.

The Arrow Cross party on its side had a powerful ally: fanaticism. The worse the war news became, the more difficult it was for the leaders—even if they had wished—to keep the aggressive young Fascists in check, so strong was their desire for power.

The German Minister, summoned unexpectedly to the palace and informed of the armistice negotiations, had a diplomatic weapon. He told the Regent that his son, Nicholas Horthy, Jr., was a prisoner of the Gestapo. He also had a military weapon: he told Horthy that at that moment Budapest was surrounded by four Wehrmacht divisions. To help create temporary chaos, the Germans were distributing arms to Arrow Cross members and encouraging them to behave as they pleased.

At 6 A.M. on Monday the Regent himself was made a virtual prisoner by the Germans, after being informed that Berlin had sent orders that he and his family were to be given sanctuary in Germany. At noon an SS man knocked on the door of the room in which he was being held and announced that the Prime Minister had come to see him.

"Admit him," the Regent ordered.

In walked Ferenc Szalasi, Hungary's most uncompromising anti-Semite and supporter of Nazi ideology.

"Prime Minister!" Horthy exploded. "Who said you're Prime Minister?"

That afternoon German soldiers began to loot the Royal Palace. That night Horthy signed a document drafted in the German Legation handing power over to Szalasi and declaring that the Sunday proclamation had been an error; his signature, the document said, had been misused. Several days later he and his family—excepting his kidnaped son —were safe in Germany.

Joe Nagel approached Sip utca cautiously. When he saw that crowds of men and boys with Arrow Cross arm bands were milling about in front of the Center, he circled the neighborhood and entered the grounds by a garden in the rear. Each member of the Rescue Committee and the Council had a key to the cellar door, for use in just such an emergency.

Andor had not yet returned from Slovakia. Erno Gábor was in Istanbul or somewhere in the Middle East, apparently still in British custody. Arthur Gruen was dead; during the night Joe had received a report from one of his non-Jewish informants on what had happened. Rachel was caring for some orphaned children and wouldn't be at the office until tomorrow. Today he and he alone would have to be the Budapest Rescue Committee. And, he added under his breath, it looked as if there would probably be plenty of rescuing to be done.

As he started up the cellar steps, he could hear the mob trying to break down the front door. It sounded as if they were using a heavy timber of some kind as a battering ram. Without making any attempt to be quiet, he ran to the Committee's office, twirled the dials on the office safe until he heard the tumblers fall into place, flung open the door, and hurriedly filled two large wastebaskets with the contents: money and valuable papers. These he took to the basement, put them in an empty corner of a coalbin, and with a few quick motions of a scoop shovel covered them with coal.

Then he ran back to Andor's office and picked the telephone from its hook. There was no use calling Colonel Weber; these were Hungarians battering at the door. He dialed the office number of Lieutenant Colonel László Ferenczy, chief of Hungarian gendarmes and liaison officer with the Gestapo, who had recently been appointed by the Sztojay government to handle all Jewish matters. Since the German occupation Ferenczy had been one of the Jews' worst Hungarian enemies. They had nicknamed him "the ghoul of the deportation" and "the cruel bloodhound."

Just as the number began to ring, Joe heard the noise of splintering wood.

As soon as a secretary answered, Joe said quickly, "I must speak with Colonel Ferenczy. It is urgent."

"Who is calling the colonel, please?"

"Just tell him, from Sip utca. He'll understand."

Joe hoped the bluff would work. There was perhaps one chance in a

251

hundred, no more. From the hallway he could hear the noise the invaders were making as they began to storm through the building.

"This is Colonel Ferenczy. What is it?"

As the abrupt voice came over the wire, the door of the Committee office was thrown open and a half dozen fanatic-looking young men with crossed arrows on their arms rushed in. Their leader held a revolver in his right hand, pointed directly at Joe. Above the noise coming from the hall, Joe said into the phone, "Colonel Ferenczy, this is the Jewish Community Center on Sip utca." As he said the name, the Arrow Cross leader half turned to his followers and held up his hand for silence. They stood in a semicircle listening while Joe went on with his telephone conversation.

"Our premises have just been entered by the Nyilas (the popular name for the Arrow Cross men) and we were wondering whether this was done with the authorization or permission of your office."

The words that came back over the wire were sharp and venomous. "What arrogance! How dare you ask me such questions?"

Joe pressed the receiver close to his ear, hoping to keep the others in the room from hearing.

"I'm very glad you said that, sir."

"Said what? What in hell do you mean?"

"Do we have your permission, then, to tell our visitors you disapprove of their actions, in view of your agreement with us?"

As he glanced up, Joe could tell from the leader's expression that the ruse was working. He pressed the receiver more tightly to his ear to muffle the roar that was coming over the wire.

"You can tell them that they have my permission to do anything they damn well please to you or your building. You Jews are going to get what has been coming to you for a long time."

The receiver at the other end was banged down so violently that the receiver in Joe's hand trembled. He hung it on the hook gently and stood up. With complete self-assurance he said to the Nyilas leader, "Colonel Ferenczy asks me to tell you he's guaranteed this building against any trouble. He has his own reasons. He said he will come personally with a unit of his gendarmes unless I phone him back in ten minutes that everything's okay."

Joe held his breath, waiting for the reaction. Instead of replying, the leader consulted with one of his subordinates. Then a whispered order was passed along to those in the hall. In less than two minutes the building was deserted.

Joe put the somewhat splintered front door back in place as best he could, then returned to the office. Dropping into Andor's upholstered chair—the only upholstered chair in any of the offices—he lit a cigarette, inhaled deeply, and growled, "What a hell of a time for you to be away, Horvath!"

One of the first calls Joe received after the departure of the invaders was from Rachel. He advised her to come by the back way, and bring hammer and nails to fix the front door, and plenty of cigarettes.

It would have taken ten switchboard operators and a hundred complaint clerks to handle the appeals of all the people who tried to call the Center during the next several days. Joe and Rachel did what they could, alone. Fortunately there were some emergency food rations in the building, so they didn't go hungry. But it was a dismal, exhausting vigil they kept.

One of the first acts of the Szalasi regime was to seal all houses marked with a yellow star. No Jew was permitted to enter or depart, even in the case of emergencies. Jewish doctors were told they could no longer leave their homes to visit patients, and the sick weren't permitted to leave their homes to call at doctors' offices. The dead were denied burial; the corpse couldn't even be removed from the building where death had occurred. Those who had no food in their larders had to find people in the same building who did have and were willing to share. Some of the new regulations also affected non-Jews. Henceforth it was illegal for more than three persons to be together in the same place, except at a trolley stop.

Late Tuesday afternoon Rachel put down the telephone and blew her nose in a strange manner that told Joe something was wrong.

"So what is it?" he asked in his usual gruff manner.

"Do you believe in God, Joe?"

He looked at her sharply. She must have been crying quietly to herself, for her eyes were red. "Why?"

"How could a god permit it? Even the most calloused, impersonal, bitter god?"

"Cut it out, Rachel."

"But Joe—"

"Cut it out. This is no time for thinking."

"Do you know what that last woman said?"

"No. Do I have to hear?"

"Five people in her building have committed suicide already today. It's like an epidemic in her building."

253

"So what's her problem?"

"She wants to know isn't there something they can do with the bodies."

Instead of answering, Joe said, "I've talked to the Budapest Volunteer Ambulance Service three or four times. They say the Nyilas won't let them stop at any place with a yellow star. They say they've had fifty or sixty calls about suicides already. They say— Who the hell cares what they say!"

He put his head in his hands for a moment, but soon he was busy answering calls again.

One afternoon those who had radios, and dared use them, heard the broadcast of a statement by the new Arrow Cross Minister of the Interior, Gábor Vajna:

". . . I do not differentiate between Jews belonging to the Catholic, Protestant, or Israelite churches. I deal only with the Jewish *race*. I will not acknowledge the validity of any safe-conducts or foreign passports issued to a Hungarian Jew. At present all Jews living in Hungary are subject to the control and direction of the Hungarian State. And we will not tolerate interference from anyone, in Hungary or abroad."

Andor was dejected when he left Bratislava. He'd had one brief audience with Wedemeyer, late on Saturday, at which the colonel was more than usually difficult.

"You'd better forget about Slovaks and worry about your own Hungarian Jews," he growled.

As Andor left his office, he added, "Tell my friends in Budapest that I'll be back there soon. Don't let them think that Hungary is going to be another Rumania for much longer. And when I do come back—" The threat was unmistakable.

Sunday morning Andor started for Budapest, having failed to save a single Slovak life. At the last railroad station before crossing over into Hungary, the train was stopped.

"The frontier has been closed," a German soldier on the platform told them.

"Why?"

"Some kind of a revolution's going on in Hungary. That's all we know."

It was Tuesday afternoon before the frontier was reopened for normal traffic and Andor returned to Budapest.

On Wednesday morning, while he was enjoying the first sound sleep he'd had in a week, his telephone rang. It was a summons to come immediately to Colonel Wedemeyer's office in the Majestic. He dressed so hurriedly he forgot the pearl stickpin he always wore in his dark necktie. On the way up the Svábhegy he speculated on whether Wedemeyer had actually returned. Perhaps it was Weber or someone else who wanted him. He hoped so.

Wedemeyer's face was etched with hate as he looked up from the papers on his desk. "I wanted you to be one of the first to know of my return, Horvath."

Andor tried to look nonplused.

"We shall be working in close co-operation with the Hungarians, now that there's a government here sympathetic to the principles of the New Order in Europe," the colonel went on. "I have returned with instructions from the Reichsführer to accomplish the deportation of Budapest's Jews as quickly as possible. This time, however, they will go on foot." He said it with unpleasant intensity. "We need our rolling stock for other purposes. Of course, if you and your friends were able to provide trucks—"

It wasn't clear from the truncated sentence what would happen if trucks were provided, and Andor didn't dare ask. On the way to Sip utca he wondered. Did Wedemeyer mean he would use the trucks to transport the Jews of Budapest to the Austrian frontier, or was he referring obliquely to Erno Gábor's mission and the SS offer to sell Jewish lives for trucks?

That night Andor wrote a letter to Schoen, thanking him for his offer of a "reasonable payment" but explaining why it had failed to save the Jews of Slovakia. Then he tried once more to give him a picture of the impossible conditions of life in Budapest for their people. He told him of Wedemeyer's threat of deportation on foot; the possibility that a few trucks might at least make the last hours of many Jews not so harrowing. "Most of those who remain are women and children, and the aged," he wrote. "If they are required to walk all the way to the Austrian frontier, there will be suffering worse than death."

The rest of the letter read:

Wedemeyer is in an extremely frustrated mood. If we do nothing to change his attitude, I am certain he will consign the people of our transport at Bergen-Belsen to the gas chambers. If this happens we—as well as the Germans—will have to bear the responsibility. There are more than a thousand people in this group still being held as hostages. They represent the cream of Hungarian Jewry. They were the leaders of our community in this country. Colonel Weber has insisted on the payment of the million dollars I had promised him before he will release them. Even if he receives the money in hand, it may now take considerable bargaining and cajoling on my part to get these people out of Germany, because of the changed situation. You made it clear at our meeting on the bridge how you feel about trading in human lives, but there is now no alternative. Therefore I urge that you agree to the payment of this sum before it is too late.

About the Jews still here in Budapest, if you could go so far as to agree to try to supply a considerable number of trucks, I might be able to continue my bargaining for the entire two hundred thousand souls whose chance of surviving now begins to appear very slight. I know that Wedemeyer is not going to stand for much more equivocation. There is evidence that he is planning to start the deportation from Budapest quickly, before the advance of Russian troops and other developments of the war make it impossible. Therefore it seems to me we have a dreadful choice to make: Do we offer a great many trucks—hundreds of them —in return for Jewish lives, or do we offer a few, to transport our people in some degree of comfort to what will probably be their extermination, or do we stand aloof and permit the old, the sick, women, and children to be driven down the roads of Hungary to their death like cattle?

I am not trying to be dramatic, Herr Schoen, but I could not any longer consider myself an honorable Jew unless I made this final appeal to you and the people you represent, in the starkest possible terms.

I have had no reply to my telegram in which I told you that Colonel Weber says he will meet with you on Swiss soil if you will obtain visas for us.

I beg you to inform me immediately by telegraph what you are prepared to do in this final hour of crisis for the remnant of Hungarian Jewry.

Forty-eight hours later Andor received a telegram from St. Gallen:

SWISS VISAS ARE WAITING FOR YOU AT FRONTIER POST STOP EAGER FOR DEFINITE NEGOTIATIONS SOON AS POSSIBLE STOP SUGGEST MEETING ZURICH AT YOUR EARLIEST CONVENIENCE STOP CAN ALSO ARRANGE MEETING FOR WEBER WITH PERSONAL REPRESENTATIVE OF ROOSEVELT WHO IS ON AMERICAN WAR REFUGEE BOARD

The Savoy was Zurich's oldest hotel. The four-story white stone building in the heart of the business district a few steps off the main street, Bahnhofstrasse, faced on the Paradeplatz, a small square that seemed to be full of pigeons at all hours of the day and even at night. Many of the Swiss people looked as if they were suffering from food shortages, even though their country had succeeded in remaining neutral, but the pigeons seemed fat and healthy. The small lobby of the Savoy was crowded as Andor, Colonel Weber and Captain Grimme, all in civilian clothes, came through the door. There was a frayed Gobelin tapestry on one wall and facing it an immense Rubens painting. The babble that filled the lobby was compounded of the singsong Swiss-German dialect, high German, Italian, French, Russian, a little Spanish, and a great deal of Magyar, for the Savoy had always been a favorite rendezvous of Hungarians living in or passing through Switzerland's largest city.

Edward Schoen was waiting for them. With him was a tall, blond American who appeared to be about the same age as Andor and Weber —in his middle thirties. Although Weber and Schoen merely bowed slightly to each other in greeting, the American, Cornelius Trench, shook hands with Andor, then Colonel Weber and Captain Grimme, as he was introduced to them. Because it was lunch time, they began their conference at a round table in a remote corner of the hotel dining room, just off the lobby. The maître d'hôtel apologized for the limited variety of dishes on the menu with the word "rationing," but Andor's gourmet instincts were delighted by the chance to linger over the choice between *truite saumonée Reine Marie, paupiettes de veau Fontanges, suprême de volaille Auvernaise.* . . .

At the other tables there were men who looked like bankers and real estate brokers, manufacturers and men of affairs. They were in earnest conversation, about matters which they undoubtedly considered of grave importance, but as Andor looked at the American and the German facing each other across the table he had a sudden sense of the historic importance of this meeting. Here were a personal representative of the democratic government of President Roosevelt and a man who had the right to speak in the name of the oligarchy of Adolf Hitler. At this moment in other parts of Europe Germans and Americans were killing each other, but at this table, for the first time, perhaps, since Pearl Harbor, spokesmen for each side were about to confer. And he, Andor Horvath, until so recently an obscure newspaperman from a provincial town in a minor country of southeastern Europe, had brought it about.

Before they left this table they would have settled the fate of hundreds —perhaps many thousands—of human beings whose lives at this moment hung in the balance. He thought of the sad, thin face of his father-in-law, Philip Kemeny; of his ailing and neurotic sister, Rena; of his ebullient friend, big Leo Strauss, and of Jessica. He sipped the dry white Johannesburg wine from the Valais that Schoen had ordered for them and thought how pleasant life could be if the end of the war—which surely must not be far off—found all of them alive and well.

After a few formal pleasantries Colonel Weber said, "Let me review the situation, gentlemen. The Slovak Jews have been punished because they were ringleaders in a revolt. The Budapest Jews are soon to be deported to the Reich because they are needed there, as laborers. As for other Jews—the Bergen-Belsen group in which Herr Horvath has such an interest and the Jews in concentration camps scattered around Europe—the Reichsführer is willing to negotiate for their release under certain conditions. What Germany wants in return is goods, principally textiles, medicines, and foodstuffs."

The blond American leaned forward in his chair and began to speak in a soft, pleasant voice, but with firmness and conviction. Everyone else at the table watched his face intently. "I must point out, Colonel Weber," he began, "that not only in my country but in most of the civilized world people have been deeply shocked as they learned of the excesses of the Nazi regime, especially of the attempt to exterminate the Jews of Europe. As we have been informed of the tortures, the gas chambers, the crematoria—as we have begun to get an idea of how many million Jews have been put to death in a campaign that amounts to genocide—our feeling of horror has increased. We are aware now that your regime has raised the cold-blooded murder of noncombatants—even women and children—to the rank of state policy."

Weber looked annoyed. "May *I* point out, Herr Trench," he replied, "that your country and its allies even as we sit here are murdering innocent noncombatants by bombing the residential quarters of our German cities. You speak of millions of Jewish women and children. I tell you that millions of our women and children have been the innocent victims of your bombs."

Trench reacted quickly. "I can answer that by pointing out that it was your Luftwaffe that began the practice of indiscriminate civilian bombing."

Andor was getting nervous. This was just the sort of "moralizing" that had made Weber so angry last time. "Gentlemen," he said, "we are here to discuss the exchange of goods for a certain number of Jewish lives."

But again Trench seized the initiative. "I am not a Jew, as you all

258

know, but I resent the idea implied by both Colonel Weber and Mr. Horvath that the lives and safety of innocent Jews are a currency of exchange, to be used in purchasing goods someone may want or need."

Schoen, emboldened by this remark, added, "I also refuse to discuss the barter of human lives."

Andor felt the meeting getting out of hand. "We are quibbling over words, my friends," he said in as authoritative a voice as possible. "Let us talk merely about payments and counterpayments. Now what can we do, Herr Schoen, to provide the payments of goods Colonel Weber asks for?"

The man from St. Gallen sat nervously clasping and unclasping his hands as he replied, "The United Relief Organization has authorized me to make twenty million Swiss francs available. The first problem is that permission of the United States Government must be obtained before the money can leave America."

Trench added, "I am authorized to say that this consent will be forthcoming on one condition. After all, Colonel Weber, I hardly think you can expect Mr. Schoen or his people to act as purchasing agents for you, so the money will be placed in a Swiss bank account. Surely you have representatives, people connected with your government or your military force, who can purchase here in Switzerland the goods you want. But our condition is that I reserve the right to control what can and cannot be purchased with this American money."

"There is also a question of not doing anything to compromise Switzerland's neutrality," Schoen interjected. "As you know, Colonel Weber, no goods can leave my country without the permission of the Swiss Government."

"I will take the responsibility for intervening with the Swiss to obtain all the exit permits that are needed," Trench said.

There was a long pause, broken by Andor, who said, looking directly at Weber, "Now what are we to get in the way of counterpayment for all this?"

"What is it you wish?" the colonel replied with a slightly ironic smile. "Your friends here do not seem to care to talk about barter agreements. What is it you wish?"

"First, the release of the rest of the people of my train."

"There was a previous agreement on that subject involving a million and a half dollars, of which only one third has been paid. When the remaining one million is delivered, we will start shipping your Bergen-Belsen people to the Swiss frontier."

"I am not willing to pay money under these conditions," Schoen declared. "When you inform me through Herr Horvath that all the people of the transport still in Bergen-Belsen have been put on a train and the train has started for Switzerland, I will go myself with the money to the frontier and pay it to your representative."

Weber whispered to his adjutant and then replied, "I think that will be quite satisfactory. I cannot at this moment give you a precise date for the movement, but—"

Andor interrupted. "Let's be quite frank with each other, Colonel. There are several reasons for speeding this up as much as possible. You want the million dollars. We want to save these people. Winter is coming on, and they are not prepared to remain at Bergen-Belsen after it starts to get cold. Also, the events of the war are moving so rapidly that at any time the escape route for these people may be cut."

"We will arrange it as quickly as possible," Weber promised.

As Andor leaned back, satisfied, Trench spoke up. "In return for the supplies you will purchase with the rest of the money that these people are agreeing to pay you, Colonel, I think they have a right to demand respect for human life in the future. They have a right to ask, in return, that civilians who have committed no offense be treated humanely, whatever group they may belong to. They have a right to demand—and the whole civilized world will back them up—that you discard your policy of extermination and genocide; that you respect the rights of people, whatever religion they wish to practice; that you stop persecuting people because they belong to a minority."

Weber didn't reply. Andor tried to read his mind. Obviously he couldn't make such blanket promises. But there was no use annoying either the young humanitarian or the old banker by trying to buy a specific number of Jewish lives with twenty million francs. Perhaps it would be better to leave it all very vague for the moment. As soon as the money started to flow in, he could do some real bargaining with the Germans, the sort of bargaining they understood.

"How long do you think it will be before the money starts becoming available?" Weber asked Schoen.

The Swiss said he thought within not more than a week or two. Weber announced that he would leave Captain Grimme in Switzerland to be on hand to make the cash purchase of supplies as quickly as the money was paid.

It was after 2 A.M. when the meeting broke up. The dining room was deserted. In the little lobby a Swiss army officer lay sound asleep on a sofa under the Gobelin tapestry. The concierge, whose limp indicated he probably had a wooden leg, showed Andor and the two Germans the rooms that Schoen had reserved for them.

As Andor undressed he felt tired but content. The evening had gone far better than he had imagined it might.

22

The Germans and Hungarians went from district to district, street to street, house to house, systematically. If the building was marked with a yellow star, they hammered on the door until it was opened, then went from room to room until they found every male inhabitant between the ages of sixteen and sixty. If a man was sick they pulled him from his bed. If he could stand, this proved conclusively that he was not really sick at all. Sly damn Jews; you can't ever trust them; always full of tricks. Some of the men claimed they were seventy, seventy-five, eighty. Unless their backs were bent in a curve, unless they were toothless and decrepit, they were presumed to be lying. If a twelve-year-old boy was a little tall for his age, he went along, too. Certificates by medical officers were either waved aside or glanced at and then torn into pieces. It was not easy for the women either; it was not easy for them to stand by and see the men they loved pulled from their sickbeds. It was not easy to watch some arrogant SS officer or his pimply-faced young Nyilas "assistant" destroy a medical document they thought would save their men from being taken away. Some of the women cringed and wept quietly. Others, hysterical, prostrated themselves at the feet of the Germans, begging them to let their men stay. A few, unable to contain their fury, threw themselves at the officers, clawing and biting. The least they received in return were slaps across the face or blows with riding crops.

The official order said that each man was to be given one hour to prepare for a long trip. He was to be informed that he should bring food to last three days. That was all he and his family were told about what was to happen to him. But the Nyilas were such ambitious young anti-Semites, so full of enthusiasm for their work, that they had little patience. Why should it take a Jew an hour to get ready for a trip? How long did a Jew need just to say good-by to a wife and a few children? So they hurried them and harried them. They took many without coats or hats. Those who had foresight put on the heaviest shoes they owned, but others came in flimsy footwear that would be full of holes in a very short time.

The roundup began at dawn. By noon fifty thousand men and boys had been herded together at the two places of assembly, the old race course on the grounds of the Students' Sports Association and the new race course. There they were formed into companies and told they were going to be marched to a certain place some distance from Budapest, where they would dig trenches for the defense of the capital. As soon as the columns got under way, the lame and the sick, the cripples and invalids began to fall.

It was Friday, October 20. To Joe and Rachel the Sunday of the Horthy abdication seemed like a day in the dim past. All week they had worked with little sleep. Neither had even been out of the Center.

As soon as the roundup began the switchboard at the Center became constantly illuminated with small red lights. As fast as a call was answered another came in. Most of the callers were Jews, desperately appealing for help, for advice. ("I will kill myself this very hour unless you do something to save Isaac. He is so sick! You understand? The beasts, they took him from his bed. Do something quick!") But there were a few calls from Christians living along the route down which the trench diggers were being marched. They said they thought someone at the Center should know that those who fell by the side of the road, the ill and the feeble, were being left there to die, unattended. Wasn't there someone who could come and collect the corpses and the near-corpses?

Joe called the Jewish Hospital. Every bed was full. The operator said the halls were so packed with cots that the nurses could hardly move. The hospital no longer had a single motor vehicle of any kind.

Joe called the Budapest Volunteer Ambulance Service. It was now down to a single ambulance and had nineteen emergency calls to make, with more coming in all the time.

One of the Council members knew where they could rent some horses and carts, but the price was exorbitant. "You could buy a horse a month ago for what they are asking now for the hire of one for a single day!" But there was no alternative, so five horses and five carts were engaged to follow the march of the trench diggers, at a discreet distance, and pick up the bodies that were left behind.

By night of that dismal Friday the Center had been turned into a hospital. In the courtyard, stacked up like cordwood, were the bodies of nineteen men. Not one of them looked to be under sixty-five.

On Sunday enormous yellow posters went up all over Pest announcing that all Jewish women between eighteen and forty must report the next day for compulsory labor services. Also any men who had been missed in the Friday roundup. Andor, who had returned the previous night, went to the Majestic to investigate and returned with the news that it was not a deportation. The women were also going to be used to dig trenches, somewhere near the town of Kispest, under the supervision of Arrow Cross police. The military situation, he learned, was critical. The Russians were pressing closer and closer to the capital. He was told that this was no time for him to make complaints.

By Monday the chaos and panic that had begun to sweep through the two thousand buildings in Budapest marked with yellow stars was multiplied by the indiscriminate raids of the Nyilas. With sub-machine guns under their arms, they went from building to building, robbing, looting, pillaging. Some were boys as young as thirteen. They hauled away in carts anything that pleased their fancy: clocks, radios, bicycles, furniture. At party headquarters on Andrassy út the loot was divided.

The Papal Nuncio assumed the lead in trying to combat the insanity of the situation. Besides calling many meetings of the neutral diplomats to plan collective action, he took several dozen religious buildings under his protection and permitted as many Jews as could jam themselves in to hide in these places.

Raoul Wallenberg, a Christian businessman from Stockholm, obtained special diplomatic accreditation from the Swedish Government and issued nearly five thousand documents to Jews stating, falsely of course, that they were the owners of valid Swedish passports and therefore were entitled to the same treatment as other Swedish nationals.

The most active of the neutral diplomats was Swiss Consul Charles Lutz, Chief of the Division of Foreign Interests of the Swiss Legation in Budapest. In this capacity he was handling the interests of Great Britain, the United States, Belgium, and six other governments. Until the British Legation was leveled by bombs, he hid in its spacious cellars, as well as in the American Legation building, hundreds of Jews who were being hunted by the Gestapo. Thousands of other panic-stricken Jews besieged his office each day, seeking his protection.

For reasons of prestige the new Arrow Cross government wanted the official diplomatic recognition of Switzerland. Consul Lutz saw this as a bargaining instrument and agreed to try to obtain such recognition in return for the right to protect some fifty thousand Budapest Jews, which permission was finally given to him after tedious negotiations with both German and Hungarian officers. In the heart of Pest he rented a three-story glass warehouse that the Jews nicknamed the Glass House and staffed it with twenty-five clerks, many of them Jews, who issued Swiss documents declaring that the bearer was under the protection of the Swiss. They were emblazoned with the Swiss emblem—a white cross on a red background—and were stamped with a rubber stamp reading "Legation de Suisse, Budapest."

To give actual physical protection to the holders of protection certificates, Consul Lutz persuaded the Hungarian authorities to clear seventeen large apartment houses of all their inhabitants and turn the buildings over to him for housing the people under his protection. Three hundred gendarmes were assigned to guard every door of every one of the buildings to prevent anyone from entering except certificate holders.

When Joe and Rachel found that the certificates were actually being honored by the Nyilas, they put their forgers to work. Soon thousands of false Swiss certificates were being distributed by the Rescue Committee. Unfortunately the man who made the rubber stamp used on the counterfeits left the *i* out of Suisse. Eventually the Gestapo discovered the error, and thousands of Jews who held the false papers lost their protection and were sent to extermination camps for having engaged in trickery.

Consul Lutz knew that at night many hundreds of Jews—those who had still been in line when the office closed—slept in the Glass House rather than lose their places. What he may not have known was that the Glass House was being used for another purpose. By now, with Joe's help and without Andor's approval, an underground partisan fighting force had been organized among the chalutzim, those young men who had been trained for work on the land in Palestine. Their most difficult task was to keep out of sight, for no young man had any right to be in Budapest now. Non-Jews were all in the Hungarian Army, on the fighting fronts. Jews either had been sent to extermination camps, were in labor battalions, or were digging trenches on the outskirts of Budapest. The partisans organized themselves in what they called *Bunkers,* the German word for underground strong points, but a bunker in the partisan sense meant any relatively safe hiding place. The principal bunker was the Glass House. Three chalutzim were on Consul Lutz's staff, and so they had keys to the building. They converted an unused cellar into their headquarters, using one room for a munitions dump, a second for nonexplosive supplies, a third as a factory for manufacturing false papers.

Their greatest need was for uniforms. They had one complete SS outfit obtained by chance. Several partisans one night saw on a lonely street an SS officer so intoxicated he was almost unconscious. A slight blow on the head induced oblivion. Then they stripped him of every item of his clothing. By good fortune the uniform was the correct size for a young chalutz born and raised in Germany who was so fair he was often mistaken for an Aryan. His German was perfect. Supplied with plenty of German marks, he made a number of trips to a German supply depot where Nazi soldiers could buy articles of clothing. Each time he took along a list of the sizes of "some of the men in my outfit who asked me to pick up new uniforms for them." The partisans supplied themselves with Hungarian army uniforms by a simpler procedure: bribery. Arms and ammunition were obtained in the same manner.

About this time Consul Lutz received the Hungarian Government's permission to issue four collective passports, each containing the names of two hundred and fifty Budapest Jews who would be permitted to leave the country as soon as the four documents had been completed. This meant attaching to them the photographs of all one thousand Jews. One of the partisans on Lutz's staff offered to handle the collection of photos. He divided the names and addresses among the thirty partisans who had SS uniforms. Each night they would make their rounds, banging on doors of Jewish apartments, and when they were admitted and the door was closed behind them would whisper in Hungarian, "Consul Lutz has sent me for your picture for the collective passport."

One night one of the partisans, known as Timmy, who worked on Lutz's staff, left the Glass House in civilian clothes, carrying under his arm a brief case containing two hundred false passports that had been manufactured the night before in the basement forgery department. He was to deliver them to two hundred Jews who lived in a building in a remote part of Pest.

An hour later word reached the Glass House that Timmy had been arrested and beaten so badly that he had been taken to the Jewish Hospital. No one knew what had happened to the brief case. If it was not retrieved, the two hundred Jews whose pictures were in the passports were in danger of arrest and probable death. Three partisans put on SS uniforms and went to the hospital, which had been under constant Nyilas guard since the change in government. This time, however, the guard was a Jew. He recognized the three callers in spite of their uniforms and told them where to find Timmy. By an odd stroke of luck the wounded man had never let go of the brief case, and his assailants had ignored it. It was with his clothes on a chair beside his hospital cot. As the partisans were leaving with Timmy and the brief case, the young Jewish guard begged them to reconsider. He was certain he would be shot for having permitted the kidnaping. The objection was answered by also kidnaping the guard.

One night on a deserted street two SS military policemen accosted two partisans in SS uniforms and demanded to see their papers. The partisans knew they were cornered, so what they pulled from their pockets instead of papers were revolvers. When the two MPs dropped, they both happened to fall face forward. One of the partisans had a piece of brown wrapping paper in his pocket. He hastily wrote across it in large German letters:

THIS IS WHAT HAPPENS TO JEWISH SWINE WHO STEAL
SS UNIFORMS AND POSE AS GERMAN OFFICERS

After pinning the sign on the two dead bodies and stealing the MPs' guns, they fled. A week later the bodies were still there, for no one had dared touch them.

23

Four months. It seemed impossible to Ely Farber that they had been locked up that long, but the marks on the wall proved it: thirty-one for July, thirty-one for August, thirty for September, and thirty-one for October: one hundred and twenty-three scratches in the plaster. Martin was keeping score. One day early in July, Ely, with mock formality, had appointed him official bookkeeper, timekeeper, and historian of the cell. Martin's handicap was that he had neither pencil nor paper. They had asked the guards several times for some sort of writing material, but asking the guards for anything was a waste of breath; they learned that the first week. Still, there was always the handle of a mess kit. It was of aluminum and could make a deep scratch in the plaster. So the whole history of their imprisonment was there on the wall, for anyone to read. The one hundred and twenty-three scratches just over Martin's cot indicated the length of their incarceration. Each of the ninety-five scratches near the cell door stood for an execution that had taken place down in the courtyard. Ten men were usually shot at one time, so they had heard the dispatch of almost a thousand human lives.

By now Ely had a bushy black beard and a sizable mustache, for in this prison no one was given the chance to shave or even use a pair of scissors. Those in charge were taking no chances. Martin's beard was blond and soft, and his mustache hardly more than fuzz.

During most of July there had been two other prisoners in the cell with them. Sometimes they would stay a day or two, sometimes a little longer. When they were taken away there was no way of telling what would happen to them. To keep up Martin's morale, Ely always insisted that they were just being transferred to another prison, but in his heart he knew. The Yugoslav major had remained with them only two days.

July had not been a bad month. Although it was suffocatingly hot in the cell, because their side of the building got the full afternoon sun and there was not much ventilation, the stream of men who came and went through the door of Cell 167 brought news. But on the first day of August the extra two cots were taken out of the cell, and since then the two Palestinians had lived alone.

Ely was weathering it better than his young friend. The wound on his left wrist had not healed well and still caused him considerable pain. However, his morale, after that first suicidal depression, had remained good.

Their daily life was like that of two caged animals. Daylight coming through a small window near the ceiling of their cell woke them up. At 7 A.M. there was the rattle of a four-wheeled cart in the corridor, and then two mess kits just wide enough to go between the iron bars of the cell door were poked at them. Breakfast was dark bread and a cup of a muddy brown liquid, always only lukewarm. The other two meals were at noon and 7 P.M. and consisted of more dark bread and a watery soup.

In one hundred and twenty-three days they had not been out of this ten-foot-square room. Other prisoners had duties: emptying the tin pails in the cells that served as toilets; filling the smaller tin pails with water that could be used either to drink or splash over the body in a pretense of bathing; doing kitchen duty; cleaning the corridors; digging graves in the prison compound. But Ely and Martin were confined to their "cage," as they called it, apparently forgotten.

"That's what I think it is," Martin said earnestly one day. "They've just forgotten us. Forgotten we're even here. Maybe they lost the record of our case. Maybe we'll just rot here—die of old age."

There were cells on both sides of the corridor, but no two doors faced each other; they were staggered. This made it impossible to see the

267

prisoners in any other cell. But at night when there were fewer guards on duty, a wireless telephone system went into operation. New inmates were questioned in whispers by the men nearest to their cells—by men whose faces were pressed against the iron bars, hungry for some word of what was happening in the outside world. The answers were flashed from cell to cell, sometimes by word of mouth, sometimes by tapping out information in a dot-and-dash code on the steel bars. In this way Ely and Martin learned of Horthy's abdication and departure for Germany and the take-over by the Arrow Cross.

The day the Nyilas came to power, new prisoners started pouring in, all of them Budapest Jews with stories of the Nyilas terror. Martin was so disturbed that he spent much of his time pacing the cell, his hands behind his back, his head bent in thought. One day Ely put his arm around the younger man's shoulder and said, "Martin, I know that no one can control what goes on inside the head of any other person, but do me a favor and cut out the walking, will you?"

"Why? Does it bother you, Ely?"

"No. It's you I'm thinking of. You're burning up energy. It's all right for a lion to do this. He gets raw meat that gives him strength to waste. But we've got to conserve every bit of energy we have."

"What for?"

"You never can tell." Ely tried to make his tone sound optimistic.

The executions were always just before the four-wheeled cart came rattling down the corridor with breakfast. Each morning when they heard the hobnailed boots of the firing squad clacking across the cobble-stoned courtyard, they would stand on the edge of Ely's cot and stare out the window. The victims were always put up against the prison wall, directly below their cell, so all they could see of the execution was the behavior of the firing squad. The squad always consisted of four privates and an officer. They used regulation rifles. As soon as they had fired their volley, they were marched away. Then a detail of prison inmates, in charge of two guards, would come with stretchers to get the bodies. It was then that the young Palestinians could see how many had been executed.

When Ely realized what a depressing effect this almost daily routine was having on Martin, he suggested that they make a solemn pact not to attend any more executions. There was nothing they could do to keep the sound of the rifle fire from reaching their ears through the open window, but there was no reason to stand on the cot and torture themselves with the sight of the grizzly procedure. After the end of July whenever they heard the officer barking, "Fire!" and the simultaneous crack of four rifles, they would observe a moment of silence and then talk about something else.

One morning about two weeks after the Arrow Cross take-over, Ely was splashing cold water on his body when they heard the hobnailed boots in the courtyard. Several moments later the small cell was suddenly full of a girl's voice: "I'll show you how a Jew dies!" The cry was in German, with a distinctly Hungarian accent.

Ely stopped rubbing himself with his towel and looked at Martin. Occasionally during the four months someone lined up against the wall prison had let out a curse or a cry for mercy, but this was the first woman's voice they had heard. It was coming from below, clear and defiant: "You swine!"

Martin screamed out, "Ely! It's Naomi!"

With a wild look on his face he jumped onto the cot and stared down into the courtyard. Ely climbed up beside him. They could see the firing squad taking up its customary position. But the voice had not stopped.

"If only you knew how the world hates you! Someday you will pay for all this. Someday decency and respect for human life will return to earth, and then—"

"Fire!" shouted the German commander.

"*Shalom!*" the girl screamed.

The four rifles cracked.

As the shots rang out, Martin stifled a cry and dug his nails deep into Ely's arms.

The execution squad marched away. Two men in prison uniforms came with a stretcher. For no more than half a minute they were out of sight, directly under the window. Then they appeared again. Naomi's black hair hung down on one side of the stretcher. It was so long it brushed the ground. The steel bullets had torn her breasts to shreds. The stretcher was tilted slightly from front to rear because one soldier was so much taller than the other. A steady stream of blood ran from the stretcher down the front of the uniform of the shorter man and then splattered on the gray cobblestones.

Martin flung himself on his cot, face down, and began to cry. Ely sat down on the floor beside the cot and put a hand on his shoulder. For a long time he did not speak. Finally in a quiet voice he said, "I knew her very well, Martin. She was quite willing to give her life for what she believed in. Now you and I *have* to live, so we can pass on the story of how bravely she left this stinking world."

269

But Martin was certain their turn would come next. "It's not that I'm afraid to die," he said, "or I wouldn't have volunteered for this mission. I wouldn't mind dying in battle. I wouldn't mind shooting it out with one of these Huns. But to have my hands tied behind my back and be stood up against a wall— Damn it, I don't want to die that way."

For days they hardly said a word to each other. Then one night word came along the prison grapevine that a new prisoner had said the Russians were at Debrecen and that a large-scale battle was going on there. Ely was excited. "Do you realize how close Debrecen is?" he asked Martin. "It's only a hundred and thirty miles the way a bird flies. A plane could cover the distance while we're talking about it. If they only forget us a little while longer . . ." He hardly dared put the hope into words.

One week after Naomi's execution a prison guard came to Cell 167 late in the afternoon and ordered Ely into the corridor. He relocked the door and growled, "Follow me." There was no time for Martin and Ely even to say good-by, but five minutes later Ely was back. In his arms he had a small cardboard carton, which apparently had already been opened for inspection. He was bursting with excitement.

"I was taken to the assistant warden's office and there was a young fellow—Swiss, I think. International Red Cross."

"What's in the box?" Martin interrupted, tugging at it.

"Wait a minute. He said he'd been trying for weeks to get permission to bring me a package. He said it's a standard Red Cross package like all war prisoners get. Several times he mentioned someone named Lehcar. He spelled the name: L-E-H-C-A-R. He said it was impossible for people on the outside to send letters to anyone in this prison, even through the Red Cross, otherwise I would have heard before this from Lehcar. Who in hell is Lehcar?"

Martin shrugged. His eyes were on the box. "Let's open it," he said, folding back the lid.

"Look at this stuff, Martin!"

"A sweater!"

"Good. We can share it. It'll be good when it really gets cold. You can wear it every other day. A box of crackers and a bar of chocolate! I'd forgotten such stuff exists. And a cake of soap. Maybe we can get rid of some of the smells now. I'm damn tired of stinking like a—like a garbage dump."

They sat on Ely's cot handling the articles as if they were jewels. When the carton was empty, Martin suggested they tear it into several pieces. They could lay one piece over the drain in the center of the floor to keep out the sewage smell. The rest they could use in the window, which had no glass. The nights were getting cold, now that it was late autumn.

As Martin was ripping the carton into pieces, he suddenly whispered, "Ely, look!" In his hand he held a small but very strong-looking hack saw.

"Where the hell did that come from?"

"There must have been a false bottom in the carton. The saw was glued between two pieces of heavy cardboard. See? These two pieces."

For hours they sat on one of the cots whispering. Who could have sent it? How would they use it? The window near the ceiling was too small for either of them, emaciated though they were, to get through. Should they try to cut one bar of the door?

At last they decided to hide it for the time being. Once a week the cells were thoroughly inspected, so no place was really safe. Martin suggested that they unravel a little of the sweater and use the yarn to tie the saw to the inside of his left leg, as high up as possible. During inspections they had never been required to take off their two-piece uniforms, and Martin's was loose-fitting, so the slight bulge wouldn't show. Ely finally agreed. They used a small piece of the cardboard to prevent the teeth of the saw from digging into the flesh.

That night they were too elated to sleep. Several hours after lights out Ely called softly, "Are you awake?"

"Yes."

"Good. I've just thought of something."

He got up and went to the other cot. "I know who Lehcar is," he whispered. "Spell it backwards, Martin. Of course, she's the one who sent the package to us."

Martin leaned up on his elbow. "Rachel . . ."

"Who else would have cared that much?" Ely murmured, half to himself.

Late the next morning a guard unlocked the door and ordered them out into the corridor. In a few minutes they were joined by thirty other prisoners, then all of them were taken to the courtyard.

It had been four months and a few days since Ely and Martin had been outside the walls of that ugly gray stone building. The sunlight was so bright it almost blinded them. Ely covered his eyes with his hands and breathed deeply of the crisp autumn air. Martin stared at the prison wall, looking for a window covered with a piece of brown cardboard. Finally he found it. His gaze traveled down the wall and rested for a long time on a low wooden platform below the window with the cardboard. It was of plain boards but was covered with large dark stains.

"Ely, you don't think they're going to—" he began in a voice half wondering, half fearful.

Ely took his hands from his eyes and stared at his friend. When he saw where Martin was looking he said, "Don't be foolish. It's always much earlier than this; always before breakfast. Forget it. Let's not worry until we have to."

Just then a truck drove into the courtyard. They were loaded aboard and taken to a suburban railroad station, where a train of thirty or forty freight cars stood on a siding. Each sliding door was locked with a padlock. There was no sight of human life. Martin and Ely noticed that every car seemed to be steaming. Small clouds of white vapor poured through the cracks and came from the small steel-barred window near the top of each car.

The German prison attendants turned the thirty-two men over to a Hungarian officer of gendarmes who seemed to be in charge of guarding the train and drove away. Just then Ely saw a small automobile make a tour of the station square and park in a narrow street just opposite where they were all standing. Two men in SS uniforms got out and approached the platform. One, a youth with black hair showing under his military cap, held a paper in his right hand. He approached the Hungarian gendarme officer.

"I have an arrest order for two men here, Ely Farber and Martin Klein," he said in Hungarian. There was a stir among the cluster of prisoners. Martin looked at Ely with a questioning expression.

The Hungarian officer called out the two names. Ely and Martin stepped forward. At that moment the Gestapo captain in charge of the train came out of the heated waiting room.

"What's this all about?" he demanded.

As the Hungarian officer handed him the arrest order, the Gestapo captain shot a quick glance at the two prisoners and the two SS men, who had started to walk away. A flicker of recognition lit up his face.

"Wait a minute!" he shouted. The four men stopped. "You—" He pointed to the SS officer with the black hair. "I know you. *Gott in Himmel!* Joe Nagel!" Half turning to the Hungarian beside him, he commanded, "Arrest him! He works for the Jew Horvath."

Joe and his companion started to run. The Gestapo captain whipped a revolver from his holster and was just taking aim when Ely, who had come up behind him, knocked his arm down and tried to grab the gun.

Martin took the lead from Ely and made a flying tackle of the Hungarian officer. The four were rolling around on the ground when a shot suddenly rang out.

"You bastard!" Ely clutched his left side as he said the words. For a few seconds he writhed in agony, then suddenly stiffened and lay still. The Gestapo captain, seeing that the gendarme officer now had Martin's arms pinioned behind his back, put his revolver back in its holster and was brushing the dust from his trousers when he was almost bowled over by a girl in trousers and a khaki shirt. Martin had seen her leap from the parked car the instant the shot was fired and run across the station square as Joe and his companion escaped.

She threw herself on the ground beside Ely. Cradling his head in her arms, she stroked his forehead. "Ely. Ely, my darling. I'm here. I'll never leave you now, beloved, never."

There was no response.

She bent down and put her lips on his and kissed them passionately, again and again. His blood was staining her shirt, but she was unaware of it. She was unaware of everything, even the restraining hands of the Gestapo captain, who finally in disgust said to one of several Hungarian gendarmes who by now had appeared on the scene, "Such a heroine as this deserves a reward. Let's see that she gets it. Put her on board with the rest of them."

Her grief and fury had given her superhuman strength. It took four stocky gendarmes to tear her away from Ely's body and push her into a freight car that already seemed full. Martin and three other men from the German prison were put in after her. The rest of the thirty-two were added to the steaming human cargo in other cars.

The original passengers in the car had been able to see nothing because the door had been closed, but they had heard the shot and now they saw the blood on Rachel's shirt. They questioned her, but she hung her head on her chest and refused to speak. Martin answered a few of their questions in monosyllables, but he also was too shocked to talk or want to talk.

The train got under way almost immediately. In a few minutes it was out of the yards and picking up speed. The rhythmic clicking of the wheels over the rail joints served to calm the turmoil inside Martin's head, and slowly hate began to take the place of fear; an overpowering hate, accompanied by a feeling of tenderness toward Rachel. He could hear her sobs coming from the far end of the car. It was not easy to get to her side. There were probably eighty people packed into this small space. Almost half were women; many were old. But the other passengers seemed to understand and made way for him as best they could.

For a long time he stood beside her, saying nothing. He was not certain she even knew he had been put into the same car. After a while her sobbing stopped and she lifted her head. Her eyes were red and swollen. As she saw Martin, a slight look of recognition flickered across her face, but nothing more.

He kept his silence. He had not yet figured out what he could possibly say. The train lurched around a curve, and suddenly he felt the teeth of the hack saw in his leg. In the fight with the gendarme officer, the piece of cardboard must have slipped out of place. Feeling the saw teeth gave him an idea. He looked up at the window near the top of the car. A normal-sized person could just about get through it, once the single steel bar in the center was out of the way.

He took one of Rachel's hands and placed it against his leg so she could feel the saw. She did not look directly at him, but her eyes indicated she understood.

"That Gestapo captain—do you know who he was?" she asked. Her voice was dead, devoid of emotion.

Martin shook his head. "I'm sorry, I don't."

There was silence for several moments, then, fumbling for something to say, he added, "Please try not to dwell on what has happened. Think of the future. This hack saw—"

"I *am* thinking of the future. I want very much to live."

There was feeling in her voice now, the sharp sound of metal striking against metal.

"Good," Martin said as cheerfully as he could.

She seemed not to have heard him. "I want to live long enough to see that Nazi bastard die the way Ely died." She paused, then added, "Even if I have to kill him myself."

"To do that, you have to escape."

"Yes."

"The saw—*your* saw—"

He pulled up the left leg of his prison uniform and untied the two pieces of yarn. When the other passengers saw him extract the saw, a murmur of excitement spread through the car.

Martin picked two tall young men who stood not far from him and explained his plan: he would try to cut the window bar if they would let him stand on their shoulders. If he succeeded, they could all escape, one at a time, when the train was going slowly. The two men agreed to help.

His arms and legs were sore from the tussle he had had with the gendarme officer, but he was living on nervous energy. No one knew where they were going or when they might suddenly reach their destination, so there was no time to be lost.

The rasping sound the saw made was drowned out so completely by the noise of the train that few people even in his car could hear, but for several hours, as he cut through the bar in two places, top and bottom, every neck was craned. At least they all had something to talk about now.

"This is very dangerous," one old man said. "If they find out they may kill all of us."

"And what do you think's going to happen to us anyway?" his wife whimpered.

"Well, I'm taking my chances and staying right here," the husband replied. "Nobody's going to make me go through that little hole and maybe get hit by another train."

"Who said you have to go?"

In another part of the car someone pointed out that the only way to get to the window was by standing on someone's shoulders. They could all escape like that except the last man, on whose shoulders the next-to-the-last man would have to stand. How should they pick who the last man was to be?

It was beginning to grow light when Martin gave a sigh of accomplishment and climbed down, with a twenty-inch piece of steel bar in his hand.

"Somebody take this," he said, holding it out. "It'll make a very good weapon, if any of us get a chance to fight for our lives."

One woman turned to another and angrily said, "He shouldn't talk that way. He'll scare everyone. Fighting for our lives! Imagine!"

No one in the car realized it, but a great change had come over Martin. The tragedy at the Budapest station had matured him, hardened him, all in the course of a few minutes. Gently but firmly he said to Rachel, "I've noticed that sometimes the train goes along slowly for five or ten minutes. Maybe they do that because of signals. Anyway, the next time it slows down, I'll jump. As soon as I'm out the window, you get onto their shoulders and look back at me. I should have something to wave as a signal that it's okay for you to jump, too."

Rachel dug into one of her trouser pockets and pulled out a man's white handkerchief.

"Take this."

275

"Good. I'll wave it as a signal, then you jump. I'll run ahead along the tracks until I find you."

"All right," Rachel said, a chilling determination in her tone.

He turned to the two young men who had helped him. "After her, you two can follow. Then, after you, whoever else wants to take the chance."

He looked around the car. From the expressions he saw, he was certain there would not be many who would want to. They were mostly old people; they all looked either sick or feeble and emaciated. Few appeared to have the strength even to climb onto someone's shoulders.

The first light of morning was transforming dark objects along the way into trees, cottages, and telegraph poles when the engineer gradually decreased his speed. Martin took Rachel's hand and said quickly, "Whatever happens, remember that we both loved him. Now don't jump until you see me wave the handkerchief. *Shalom!*"

He scampered up onto the shoulders of the two young men and poked his head out the window. He was relieved to see that they were not in a railroad yard or going through a city. There was a deep-looking ditch beside the tracks, and then open fields.

"Shalom!" he said to the others, then eased himself out the window and jumped. He tried to twist his body so he would land on his shoulder rather than his head. Dead branches lashed his face, then his body hit the ground. His shoulder felt as if it were broken. Water filled one ear and forced him to close his eyes. When he opened his mouth, it began to fill up with mud. He struggled to raise his head. Finally he was able to open his eyes. He could see, now, that the ditch was half full of water. As he listened to the wheels of one car after another go clicking by, he realized the train had suddenly picked up a great burst of speed. The handkerchief! He reached into the breast pocket of his uniform for it. By the time he had it out and began to wave it, the last car of the train was rounding a slow curve; in another second it was out of sight.

He stood there in the ditch, water up to his knees, for a long time, too stunned to move. His shoulder hurt. He looked blankly at the curve around which the train had disappeared. Rachel couldn't possibly have seen him wave the handkerchief, and surely she wouldn't have been so foolish as to jump after the train had picked up speed, but he must keep his promise. He struggled to work his way out of the muck that was sucking his feet deeper and deeper into the ditch. He reached the tracks, but walking was difficult because his legs were heavy with water and mud.

When he reached the curve he was disappointed to see no sign of life.

On the side of the right of way that the window had faced was a steel-and-wire fence, at least twenty feet high, topped with a coil of barbed wire. It was very close to the tracks and extended as far ahead as he could see. Now he knew for certain Rachel could not have jumped. A sharp thought suddenly impinged itself on his tired mind. This fence, the tall towers at frequent intervals . . . He remembered photographs of German prison camps he had seen. Then he saw a guard with a machine gun walking around a platform at the top of one of the towers. As slowly and quietly as he could, he retreated back down the tracks, around the curve, then across the ditch and into a field. This was a dangerous sort of landscape to be crossing in daylight, but in the distance he could see trees, so he made for them. When he reached them, he discovered they were not part of a forest, as he had hoped, but formed two lines, one on either side of a well-paved road. He was standing cautiously behind a tree when he heard the sound of a motorcycle coming from the direction of the fenced-in camp. He threw himself on the ground and covered his body as best he could with some of the dry brown leaves that were everywhere under the trees. The motorcycle was approaching at a peculiarly slow speed. As it came near, he discovered why. It was leading a column of men.

Martin gasped as he saw that the several hundred figures straggling along the road toward him were wearing the same German prison garb he had on. Their hair, like his, was long, and they also were unshaven. With few exceptions they looked old and extremely emaciated. At last the motorcycle passed. Now came the shuffling of the prisoners' feet. Martin tried not to move a muscle although his injured shoulder felt hot and painful. At least some of the men were Jews. Maybe all of them. He could tell partly from their appearance, partly from the occasional words they spoke. Now most of them had passed his hiding spot. He could hear the sharp sound of the hobnailed boots of the soldiers bringing up the rear. Now he could see them. Six men in SS uniforms. Four were walking on the pavement, one in the ditch at each side of the road. The one on his side—

Martin tried to swallow the scream of pain that swelled in his throat as the hobnailed boot stepped squarely on his injured shoulder.

"Verflucht noch einmal!" the soldier shouted as he pitched forward.

He picked himself up quickly and turned to kick the object he had tripped over. Suddenly he shouted, "Look! How the hell did this man escape?"

Two of the other guards came running and lifted Martin to his feet. "Smart, eh? Well, we'll give you a treat for being so clever. We'll let you be the last."

Martin did not understand. All he knew was that his shoulder felt as if it had been torn into shreds. The pain was excruciating. A guard gave him a blow in the stomach with the butt of a rifle, and his whole body became one searing mass of agony.

They made him run to catch up with the tail end of the column. The other prisoners looked at him strangely. He dared not ask questions. What good would it have done? Probably none of them knew the answer to the primary question. The guard's words pounded inside his head: "We'll let you be the last." He tried to stop thinking about them and let his mind dwell, instead, on Rachel and Ely. He wondered whether his parents had really escaped and were safe. He thought of Andor Horvath and how skillful Horvath had been in persuading him to give himself up to the Germans that night he had come to the Columbus camp. He had agreed in order to save Ely. But now Ely was dead.

They were turning into a brickyard. A horrible stench was in the air. An SS captain lined up the men, twenty abreast. By the time Martin and the others at the tail of the column were placed in the formation, there were eleven lines of twenty.

The first line was given an order to march ahead to the edge of a pit. Martin was too far back to see much, but he heard the fusillade, and then an order barked in German for the next twenty to advance.

Only a few of the prisoners awaiting their turn showed any emotion, but a man in the row ahead of Martin screamed wordlessly. It was like sandpaper on Martin's raw nerves. It was worse than the terrible pain in his shoulder. He wanted to shout at the man to stop.

It was time for the row just ahead.

"March!" the captain shouted.

The twenty men advanced to the edge of the cliff. Now Martin could see how it was done. Twenty soldiers took up positions just behind the twenty prisoners. When the order was given, they raised their rifles and fired. The infernal screaming stopped. Twenty bodies tumbled into the abyss, then the captain shouted to the next line, "March!"

Martin held his head as high as his injured shoulder would let him. For the first time in months he suddenly felt a strange calm and peace.

They were not permitted to stop until their feet were at the very edge of the cliff. Some looked down, and what they saw made them try to flee, but just behind them were the twenty German soldiers with rifles raised to their shoulders. One man yelled, "No, no, no!" Martin looked straight ahead. He had not wanted to die. But he was no longer afraid.

"Fire!"

It felt like a red-hot needle entering his neck and coming out through the left eye. He teetered on the rim, then the body of the next man struck him, and they plunged forward together.

It was a long fall, for the pit was deep. When he landed, it was on his injured shoulder again. The body under him moved slightly, then was still.

Thought and feeling began to recede. First the stench went. Then the pain. Then he began to float. Then he was in a warm, warm bath. It was delightfully relaxing. Then he was—nowhere.

It was dark. Or was it because he was unable to open his eyes? His left eye was on fire, but slowly he succeeded in opening the lid of his right eye. He must be alive, because he could see a quarter moon in the sky, and stars. Millions of stars. Somehow he was on his back now. The salty taste must be blood. By moving his head an inch or so he could see the top of the pit. The Germans must have left. There was no movement up there. There was no movement down here, either. The execution squad had done its job well. All except for him. But if he lay still he would soon be dead, too. The sensation of floating had been so pleasant. What had broken it? Why had he come back? Then he heard a sound that seemed to be coming from a great distance.

"Is there anyone else alive? Answer me, please. Is there anyone else who wants to live?"

It was a firm voice, speaking Hungarian.

Martin gathered all his strength to answer, "I am alive." The effort cloaked him in sweat.

"Speak again, so I can find you. Say something, anything."

All Martin could think of was the familiar old wish, "May you live to be a hundred and twenty." He said it with profound gratitude.

In a few moments he felt strong arms lifting him.

24

Andor was conferring with two members of the Jewish Council when his secretary, Zipora, informed him that a Swiss courier who had just arrived from Cairo by way of Istanbul wished to speak to him. Curious as to what news the man might have, Andor quickly excused himself and followed Zipora into the anteroom.

"I have a verbal message for you," the Swiss said without introducing himself. "In view of the nature of the news, I could hardly refuse to bring it, although I preferred not to use the telephone. As you know, Herr Horvath, there is hardly a line in the city that is not tapped; especially yours and ours, I am afraid."

"Very good of you to come," Andor said politely.

"The news is that your colleague, Erno Gábor, is dead. He was arrested by the British, as you probably know, when he was crossing into Syria. They took him to Cairo. The British were extremely suspicious of him, I was told, especially because of his traveling companion, a man sent along with him by the Germans. Also, the British said they felt they had to arrest him to show the Russians that they were not engaged in a double cross."

"I have heard all this. But how did he die?"

"The British were not holding him under lock and key. He was living in a hotel, but under—shall we say surveillance. As far as anyone knows, death was from natural causes. He had a heart attack in his sleep the other night and was dead by the time a doctor arrived. Your people down there wanted me to get this news to you at once. He was buried in the Jewish cemetery of Cairo."

After the courier left, Andor went to his private office, locked the door on the inside, opened the bottom drawer of his desk, and from under a pile of papers extracted a bottle of brandy and held it up to the light. There were two or three good drinks left. He found a water tumbler and emptied the contents of the bottle into it.

There had been times when the members of the Committee annoyed him, and sometimes he decided they were more of an encumbrance than a help. Their tedious arguments had often kept him at the Parisette half the night, and although eventually he always had his own way, the debating-society atmosphere of so many of their meetings irked him. But now that he had no Committee he had a queer feeling of loneliness. Never before could he remember that he had ever felt lonely. The apartment was lonely; he actually hated to go there. The wife of the concierge kept the place clean, but she never polished any of the silver and she had spoiled Sarah's arrangement of the furniture. The office was lonely; he missed Joe and Rachel and their cold efficiency. Tipsters had brought him the news of the incident at the railroad station, but of course there was nothing he could do about it. For several days he had worried about what Weber or Wedemeyer might say, but the matter was never mentioned. Apparently Joe was alive and in Budapest, and each day Andor expected that he might get a message from him, but no word had come. He missed blustering, forthright Arthur, too. He hadn't been of much practical help to the Committee, but he had been a sounding board, an alter ego for Andor. As for Erno, by now Andor had grown used to doing without his usually sage advice, but he missed the old man. He even missed his impatience and his kindly scoldings. They were all gone. He was all there was to the Budapest Rescue Committee now, and his people were in greater peril than ever.

He took a long drink of brandy, and as he began to feel its warming effects he decided that he must take a new grip on himself. He alone had done all the bargaining up to now, and he had to go on doing it. He put the empty bottle in a wastebasket, drained the last drops in the glass, unlocked the door to the outer office, and asked Zipora to get Colonel Weber on the phone.

Weber had been very impressed by the progress of the negotiations at Zurich. He had made this evident to Andor on the long trip back to Budapest. The moralizing of young Mr. Trench had annoyed him, but this was more than balanced by the fact that he would be able to boast to Reichsführer Himmler that he had personally made contact with a special envoy of President Roosevelt. Andor had been impressed, too. Perhaps, he thought, this might be the first step in a negotiated peace between Germany and the Western Allies. If so, he might have made for himself a place in history he hadn't even contemplated. Weber had also been pleased by a cable Schoen let him read, from the American Secretary of State, authorizing the U.R.O. to transfer five million dollars to Switzerland. This, he felt, was proof that big money was available and that they were fishing in the right pool.

Since the Zurich trip Andor had thought often of the arguments Cornelius Trench had advanced. He had been more articulate, more convincing than Schoen had been at the meeting on the bridge, but there was still the great gap between the reality that those in the swirl of events had to face and the theorizing those in safe places could indulge in. It had been good to hear this young man express the revulsion of all mankind toward the German atrocities against the Jews, and it had been interesting to watch Weber's face when Trench attacked the Nazis' master-race theory. But he was naïve if he thought he could re-educate Weber, and through him Himmler and Hitler, by such lectures, or save any Jewish lives this way. There was only one way to save Jewish lives; that was by bargaining. This had been his own creed from the start, and he must pursue it.

On the basis of the Zurich agreement, Andor sent word to Leo Strauss that the rest of the people of the rescue train would soon be on their way to Switzerland.

Every day or two he called Weber to ask if Wedemeyer had fixed a date for the departure from Bergen-Belsen, but despite the terms of the Zurich agreement Wedemeyer continued to imply that the departure was contingent on other matters.

"I warned you long ago," he said to Andor one day, "that I was going to start deporting the Budapest Jews on foot unless you supplied trucks to move them. Where are the trucks? The deportation begins November 8. This is your last chance."

With Wedemeyer's permission Andor telephoned St. Gallen. Schoen said the U.R.O. had the money, but the State Department in Washington would not permit it to be used for the purchase of trucks for the Germans, even if the trucks were to be used to buy the lives of Jews or to transport them. Trucks, Washington said, were pieces of military equipment.

Several days later Wedemeyer called Andor and demanded two freight-car loads of animal skins. Andor learned that the kind of skins required were available in Bratislava, and he arranged for them to be bought with U.R.O. money and delivered to Wedemeyer. Then the colonel said he had to have thirty thousand pounds of coffee immediately. Again Andor arranged for the purchase to be made with U.R.O. money that had been earmarked for ransoming the Bergen-Belsen transport. Almost every day there was a new demand. In one way Andor did not object. He told himself he was buying time—postponing further exterminations. As long as Wedemeyer and his Nazis had desires that he and the U.R.O. could satisfy, they were in business.

But early in November, Wedemeyer began to round up Budapest

Jews by the thousands and concentrate them in suburban brickyards. Panic spread through the buildings marked with yellow stars. Some tried to bribe their way into the seventeen apartment houses Consul Lutz had taken over, but they were already packed with humanity. Even the Glass House was jammed to the doors. Then some of the terrified people thought of the camp on Columbus utca. Hadn't it been an island of safety for the people Horvath's Rescue Committee had chosen? They flocked to Columbus utca until there were nearly four thousand people living in quarters that had seemed crowded when inhabited by the sixteen hundred people of the Bergen-Belsen transport. Andor, hearing one day that the SS was about to collect all four thousand and take them to a brickyard for deportation, persuaded Red Cross officials to put their red and white flag over the camp and assume charge. Wedemeyer made the next move. He offered to send the four thousand to Bergen-Belsen, to be "put on ice," as he enigmatically explained, if Andor would supply him with enough trucks to transport them. Trucks seemed to be his mania. Again Andor telephoned to St. Gallen, but Schoen replied, "I gave you my answer, Herr Horvath, when you asked for trucks last time."

Zipora Nayari had been Andor's secretary since the formation of the Rescue Committee. She was happy in her work partly because it was neither monotonous nor stereotyped, but mainly because of her feeling for her employer. In her opinion there was no man in Budapest—perhaps not in the whole world—who was at the same time so handsome, so intelligent, so fearless, and so much a gentleman. Andor might easily have taken advantage of this situation, for he knew that she would have responded to any request with the same unquestioning loyalty she gave him when he asked her to work half the night or come in to the office on Shabbat. But in the early days of the Committee he needed the hero worship she gave him much more than romantic opportunities.

Zipora never failed to compliment him if he used an especially well-turned phrase in a letter, or gave some arrogant Hungarian politician a sharp retort, or demonstrated once again his ability to twist a German colonel around his finger. After a time they developed so great a rapport that she could congratulate him by just a glance, without saying a word.

Zipora was beautiful in a dark, Sephardic way. She had a mass of curly jet-black hair, deep olive skin, and almond-shaped brown eyes that gave the impression of perpetual mystery. In the beginning she had been a constant source of temptation to Andor, who had never been oblivious to physical charm, but he was wise enough to know that if he began to treat her as he might have treated any other attractive young woman, the spell would be broken and she might begin to treat him like any other attractive man.

Zipora, along with everyone else working in the Center, had a document issued by the Hungarian Ministry of the Interior and countersigned by the Judenkommando, which stated that she was exempt from most of the restrictions imposed on Jews, although she did have to wear a yellow star. When the roundup of Budapest Jews for deportation began, Andor and members of the Council, in the course of some intensive bargaining with the Judenkommando, agreed to set up soup kitchens and try to feed the people assembled in the various brickyards. But, they pointed out, it would take a small army of workers to cook and distribute the food. They asked for a thousand special passes, stating that the bearer was employed by the Judenrat, in work considered essential by the SS, and therefore was not to be shipped out of Budapest. These passes were first distributed to all the regular employees at the Center, including Zipora, then to men and women chosen by Andor or the Council for this special exemption.

When Andor handed Zipora her pass, she did not look pleased, as he had expected she would, but instead her eyes became clouded and she turned her back while she put the pass in her handbag silently.

When she went home that night, her mother began talking almost before she had closed the door of their minuscule, one-room apartment.

"Zipora, they are taking Budapest people now. Mrs. Kohn in the next street called me on the phone. They took fifty people from her building this afternoon. She says they are being taken to Austria to work. But they are taking old people. How can old people work?"

Zipora tried to quiet her fears or at least stop the flow of questions and entreaties, but it was useless.

"Zipora, if they come after me, you wouldn't let them take me, would you? If they *did* take me, you wouldn't let me go alone, would you, darling? I would die before I got to the end of the block. You promised when your father passed on that you would take care of me, remember? You wouldn't leave me, would you?"

Her voice was growing more hysterical as she became the victim of her own words. She clutched her daughter's arm frantically, tears streaming down her face.

Zipora led her to a sofa and sat down beside her. "Mamma, I promise that we will never be separated, whatever happens. Haven't I been faithful to you all these years since Papa died? What makes you think I would let them take you away from me?"

Mrs. Nayari stopped sobbing and looked up at her daughter. "I've never felt jealous of anyone except that man you work for. If it was a choice of him or me—"

Zipora closed her eyes for a second and swallowed with difficulty. "Mamma, we won't be separated. Please stop worrying," she pleaded.

As she went about the work of getting supper, she thought of the pass in her handbag and realized that she must not mention it or let her mother see it. All day long employees at the Center had been asking about passes for their relatives. A few had been given out so that husbands and wives would not be separated, but the line had been drawn there. As for children and parents, Andor had permitted word to be passed around that on his return trip from Zurich he had extracted a promise from Colonel Weber that if a deportation of Budapest Jews did take place, he (Weber) would persuade Colonel Wedemeyer not to take small children, invalids, or the aged. Therefore it would be wasting passes to use them for any of these categories.

Two nights later, while Zipora and her mother were clearing away the supper dishes, there was a commotion on the staircase and then a loud banging, first on the doors of the other apartments on the same floor and then on theirs.

When Zipora opened the door, a man with an arm band of crossed arrows snarled at her, "Fifteen minutes to get ready for a long trip." As he turned to climb to the next floor, she said, "I understand that old people and invalids are exempt. My mother is—"

The Hungarian looked at her with contempt. "There are no exemptions. Both of you get ready, and be quick about it."

Zipora shut the door and ran for the telephone to call the Center. She jiggled the hook nervously. The line was dead. She knew that if she ran fast enough she could get to Sip utca and back before the fifteen minutes were up. She put on a coat, then threw open the window and looked down. Two soldiers were standing at the entrance to the building, and although she couldn't tell from this distance what uniforms they wore, she could see that each had a sub-machine gun cradled in his right arm.

Mrs. Nayari had ripped two blankets from the bed and spread them on the floor. Onto them she was piling all the articles she didn't want to leave behind. As she worked she kept up a semihysterical monologue. "Zipora, get ready quick. He said fifteen minutes. We have a lot of packing to do. Where do you think they'll take us? Should we carry sheets as well as blankets? Mrs. Kohn said—"

"Mamma, you and I are going to have to carry those blankets and everything you put in them," Zipora interrupted quietly.

"Carry them? Surely they'll have wagons for our baggage!"

Zipora had never failed to appear for work before. Andor, suspecting what had happened, went to her apartment, but the building was deserted, except for a gang of Arrow Cross boys systematically looting the apartments. He knew that by now tens of thousands of deportees were in the suburban brickyards. Even if he could argue his way past the guards, it would be futile to try to find one small, black-haired young woman in that mass of humanity, so he went back to Sip utca, hoping that at any moment she might appear. He wondered why, if she was involved in a deportation, she hadn't used her exemption pass. She couldn't have lost it; it wasn't like Zipora to lose things; in all the time she had worked for him she had never even misfiled a letter.

The road from Budapest to Austria northwest through Györ to the Hungarian frontier city Hegyeshalom was wide enough for twenty soldiers to march along it shoulder to shoulder, but these people were not soldiers. With few exceptions they were the sick and the feeble, the very young and the very old, those who had neither the money, the energy, nor the wits to escape into Rumania or to get into the Columbus utca camp or the protected houses of Consul Lutz. It would have pleased the SS officers in charge of the movement if they had walked in an orderly, organized manner; it would have satisfied their sense of neatness and their desire to get them to the Austrian frontier as quickly as possible. But instead they straggled all over the road. Some victim of exhaustion would drop the bedroll he had been carrying on his back and the rope would break and whatever had been rolled up in the blanket would scatter over the road, and then there would be the confusion of trying to pick up all the articles and tie them in the blanket again. While this was happening the entire column, perhaps for miles back, would be held up. A mother would lose her child and run up and down the line of march, screaming for it. When an invalid collapsed and groaned that he could go no farther, Arrow Cross guards would come on the run and beat him, shouting for him to get on his feet and start moving again. A few would try, but usually the beating finished off the man. To discourage this behavior the guards took to shooting any who loitered or were obstinate.

It was the coldest, dampest November anyone could remember. The wind took the icy rain and used it as a whip across the faces and hands of the marchers.

The organizers of the march had set thirty kilometers a day as the minimum to be covered. That would get the head of the column to the frontier city of Hegyeshalom in seven days. But with all their boasted efficiency, the organizers had not counted on enteritis, typhoid fever, dysentery, the rain, or the inability of limbs that were seventy or eighty years old to move so rapidly, even if prodded.

The forty or fifty thousand people in the march formed a column that seemed to those who were in the middle to have no beginning and no end. As far as they could see in either direction the sight was the same: a wide road packed solid with a colorless mass of figures, the backs nearly all bent from age or the loads they carried, the feet sometimes hardly seeming to move at all, and on each flank angry, impatient guards, harrying their prey like rabbit hounds.

After days in the suburban brickyards only a few people had any of the food they had brought with them left. Those who did have could demand almost any price if they wished to sell.

"Who will give me a piece of bread for a blanket?" someone suffering from hunger pangs would shout. After he had made his offer again and again, perhaps for hours, someone might finally respond, "A blanket and what else?" Then the bargaining would begin.

In one town they passed through, the Hungarian inhabitants, apparently moved to compassion by the spectacle of so many hungry-looking people, ran into their homes and returned with food of all sorts, even pastries and tarts. The Nyilas guards took the gifts, assuring the donors that they would "distribute it fairly." They did—among themselves. As soon as they were outside the village, they ate everything.

That first day, whenever the column halted, many of the marchers would scramble into fields adjacent to the road and try to find an ear of corn, a potato, or something else that had been overlooked in the harvest. At first the Nyilas merely shot their guns into the air to frighten them back into the road, but later in the day, when the marchers, aware that no one was being hit, continued to scrounge in the fields after such a volley, they began to shoot in earnest.

All that first day it rained.

During the afternoon Zipora and her mother heard an SS officer on a motorcycle reprimand the Nyilas guards because the column was moving so slowly. After that if someone stopped for as innocent a matter as tying a shoelace he was likely to be shot.

That first night, when the order was passed along to halt, most of the people dropped right where they were. Those who had strength enough untied their blankets and used them as protection against the cold, damp ground. They huddled close together to conserve the natural heat of their bodies. Some sections of the column were in places where the mud was so deep it was impossible to do anything but stand up all night, leaning against each other for support and trying to sleep in that position.

Rain fell most of the second day. The problem of survival was now growing by geometric progression. Everyone had less strength, yet more weight to carry, for the blankets and everything else that could absorb water were rain-soaked and therefore much heavier than before.

That day as they were passing through a large town, a baker in his white apron and cap, with flour all over his arms, stood in the doorway of his shop, watching them go by. When he saw a Nyilas captain approach in the sidecar of a motorcycle, he stopped him and, loud enough for the marchers to hear, offered to bake five hundred loaves of bread in the next few hours if he would be permitted to distribute them himself to the marchers.

"You want to use good Hungarian flour that's so scarce to feed Jews?" the captain asked in amazement. "It would be better if you threw it into the mud or gave it to pigs to eat."

All day it rained.

Early in the afternoon the column went through the heart of a town with narrow, twisting streets. The sidewalk before the shop fronts was no more than two feet wide. What food there was in the windows made the gnawing in everyone's stomach worse. Zipora happened to look up just as a young man in a Hungarian officer's uniform came out of a bakery with a large loaf of bread under his arm, loosely wrapped in a newspaper. He stopped short as he saw her, staring down into her dark eyes, then in a sudden impulse handed her the loaf of bread. She gave him in return what he could not have known was the first smile that had crossed her face in many days. She hid the loaf under her coat. Just beyond the town the column stopped for a few minutes, and she began to break the bread into small pieces, each no larger than her smallest finger. Thus she was able to share her gift with almost a hundred of her companions.

It was still raining hard when the column stopped for the night.

Zipora and her mother, along with several thousand others, camped on the rough cobblestones of a village square. At least the pavement sloped in such a way that there was no standing water to bother them. That night, while her mother slept, Zipora decided to lighten their load. On the first day Mrs. Nayari had carried one blanket, nothing else, tied to her back, but on the second day even this was too much for her so Zipora had had to shoulder the burden of everything her mother had insisted on bringing, and everything was waterlogged. Her own strength was giving out. So, without consulting her mother, she went through their possessions, eliminating such weighty objects as a silver teapot that had been her mother's favorite wedding present, many other articles of a purely sentimental value, and several tins of food they had no way of opening. In the morning it was with difficulty that she got her mother into the line of march without her seeing all she had jettisoned. As they left the square, Zipora glanced back. Hundreds of other marchers must have had the same idea. The cobblestones were littered with an incredible assortment of articles.

It rained most of the third day. Soon the extra weight of the water that the blankets absorbed made Zipora's burden feel as heavy as it had been the day before.

That third day all the pretenses of civilization began to disappear. Men and women alike performed their natural functions in full view of everyone else, without shame. The odor of human excrement hung over the entire line of march. Everyone was dirty and ragged. Many were walking barefooted, their shoes having broken or worn out. Some were troubled by lice and fleas, others by dysentery.

"We're becoming worse than gypsies," someone said, and the whole column took up the dirge: "We're becoming worse than gypsies."

The third day was marked by two important events. About noon the column was halted, and the officer in the motorcycle sidecar went up and down its length ordering the guards to collect all children under ten at the side of the road. A woman near the head of the column asked those around her, "Are they going to shoot the poor things right here on the spot?" The whisper was passed from person to person. Before it had gone far, it was changed from a question to a statement of fact: "Up ahead they say the children are all going to be shot, right here on the spot." The terrible news traveled down the column like fire along a gasoline-soaked path.

When the Nyilas started to collect the children, some of the mothers fought them with the little strength they had left. Other women, trying to be cleverer, took blankets and wrapped them around their young so that not even a hair of the head showed. Then, when the danger was past and they unwrapped the blankets, many of them screamed for God's help in bringing life back to the children they had smothered to death. Eventually more than three thousand children were judged to be under ten and were loaded into trucks and taken in the direction of Budapest. The noise of the engines was almost drowned out by the wailing of mothers who had lost their offspring.

Later in the day other trucks came from the direction of the capital and terror swept along the line of march. But there were audible sighs of relief when it was seen they were marked not with swastikas, but with red crosses on a white background or the blue and white flag of Sweden. Officials in charge of the convoy had been given permission to distribute to the marchers a vegetable stew that was in large steel containers aboard the trucks. It was dished out in tin cups. Though it had been hot when it left Budapest, it was now barely lukewarm. There was hardly enough to give a cupful to everyone.

That third night Zipora and her mother were in the center of a small Hungarian village when the order came to halt. It was dark, and the populace had cautiously barricaded itself in its houses, with the shutters drawn so tight no light showed anywhere, but in the market place there were several flimsy wooden sheds where the farmers of the district sold their produce on market days. Zipora led her mother to a corner of one of the sheds, put both blankets around her shivering form, and sat close to her, trying to comfort her. By chance one hand that was on the ground touched three small, hard, round objects. She shook her mother. "Look, dear, what I have found; potatoes! Eat them; they'll give you strength for tomorrow."

Mrs. Nayari gently pressed her daughter's hand. "They're for you, Zipora. For me there isn't going to be any tomorrow. I feel the life going out of me. I am very tired. Lie close to me, darling. You have been such a faithful daughter. I want to sleep now."

As she held her mother in her arms, Zipora gnawed on one of the potatoes. It was almost dawn when, only half asleep, she felt a shudder convulse her mother's fragile figure, then the body stiffened. She reached under the blankets and felt for a pulse beat, but there was none. She began to sob. Her years of sacrifice were over, but now there was no future. She was alone and on the road to Hegyeshalom, alone with a body in her arms that already was beginning to grow cold.

A short time later the order came to start moving. When the guards finally pulled Zipora away from the still figure, she saw that her mother would not be alone. Scattered around the market place were at least twenty other bodies, also being left behind.

There were bitterness and fear in Budapest as news of the forced march trickled back to the capital. When Andor heard there were several thousand small children in the line of march, he went to the Majestic and accused Weber of having broken a promise. The colonel tried to placate him.

"It is not my fault, Horvath. I spoke to Colonel Wedemeyer when I returned from Zurich, and I obtained his agreement not to take the children. I will speak to him again at once." He picked up the telephone and asked for Wedemeyer's office.

At the end of a short conversation Andor heard him say, "In that case, Colonel, I feel I shall have to call the Reichsführer and get his opinion." There was a long silence on Weber's part; then he smiled and said, "Thank you very much. I am glad you agree." He turned to Andor. "You may relax. He is issuing an order for all children under ten to be returned to Budapest immediately."

Several days later many truckloads of children arrived in Budapest. Having been torn from the arms of their parents in many cases, they were victims of hysteria as well as hunger, cold, and exposure, but before they could be properly accommodated and cared for, the Center had a new problem. The Swedish Legation and the International Red Cross had rented all available vehicles and sent them along the Hegyeshalom road to pick up among the human debris anyone with a spark of life left. By the time the vehicles returned to Sip utca, however, they contained mostly corpses. The scarcity of doctors and the lack of medical supplies prevented much being done for those still barely alive. Holes were dug on the grounds of the Center for the burial of the dead.

Eight days after the start of the forced march, a high-ranking official of the SS, General Juettner, and the commandant of the camp at Auschwitz arrived in Budapest. They had driven over the same road being used for the deportation, although traveling in the opposite direction. For years they had both been occupied with the extermination of Jews, yet they were horrified by what they saw. Told that Colonel Wedemeyer was temporarily out of the city, General Juettner ordered other officers of the Judenkommando to discontinue immediately sending Jews down the road on foot. By this time fifty or sixty thousand had been dispatched. If Wedemeyer's superiors had seriously wanted these people for manual labor in the Reich, the operation was a fiasco, for hardly any were arriving at the frontier physically fit for even light work. If it was a sardonic trick to kill off Jews without the expense of gas or fuel, bullets or explosives, it was a brilliant success, for every kilometer of the way was strewn with corpses.

The third day after discontinuance of the forced march, which was a Shabbat, Wedemeyer returned, called members of the Jewish Council to a meeting, and announced that a closed ghetto would be set up at once in Pest. He showed them on a map where it would be—seven city blocks long by three wide. The twelve thousand non-Jews residing in the area would be moved out. The Jewish Council must supply them with apartments at least as commodious as those they were leaving. Thirty-three thousand Jews now living outside the area would be moved in. This meant a congestion of fourteen persons per room. The thirty-three thousand could bring from their present quarters only what they could carry. The ghetto would be enclosed by a stout wooden fence. The Jewish Council must buy the lumber and supply the labor. There would be only four gates, one at each point of the compass.

That same day Wedemeyer ordered a resumption of deportation on foot, along the road to Hegyeshalom. When Andor heard the news, he went to see Weber, but before he said a word the economic expert declared angrily, "I have just had a message from my aide, Captain Grimme, in Zurich. He says he is convinced that the U.R.O. has no intention of making any substantial payments. He says your man Schoen avoids him; that he refuses even to answer telephone calls. He says he sees no sense in his staying in Zurich any longer."

Andor tried to make excuses, but Weber was out of patience. "In the morning I am going to Berlin to see the Reichsführer. I can no longer take responsibility for such nonsense as this. I am certain that when Herr Himmler learns of this interminable equivocation and the insulting treatment my aide has received, he will order an end to negotiations." He paused, then looked straight into Andor's eyes. "And that will also eliminate any possibility of saving the rest of your people at Bergen-Belsen."

The next morning when Andor learned that Weber had not been bluffing and actually had gone to Berlin, he decided the situation demanded bold action. Without wasting the time to try to communicate with Schoen, he went to Weber's adjutant and said, "I have a vitally important message for the colonel. Do you suppose you can get it through to him at once?" Then he handed the adjutant a sheet of paper bearing the message:

> Schoen apologizes for the delay, which has been due solely to difficulties of a technical nature. He says the twenty million will be at your disposal by the time you return. Schoen and all others involved are working day and night to wipe out the final difficulties.

When Weber came back from Berlin, he called for Andor. Wedemeyer also was present at the conference. It was obvious now that there was smoldering antagonism between the two colonels. The economic expert was cheerful and friendly. "I have won all along the line for you, Herr Horvath, thanks to your message. The Reichsführer has ordered an immediate cessation of all extermination proceedings. The gas chambers at Auschwitz will be dismantled, if our negotiations are consummated. As the first evidence of his good faith he has ordered that your transport at Bergen-Belsen be sent to the Swiss frontier at once."

As Andor began to thank him, he held up his hand. "Of course—upon payment of the rest of the million dollars that is due."

Then Wedemeyer interrupted. "There is something else you had better bear in mind, Horvath. If the money is not immediately forthcoming, I, in my capacity as head of the Judenkommando in Hungary, will take all the Jews left in the country and exterminate them like vermin."

Weber ignored the remark and turned to Andor. "The train from Bergen-Belsen will arrive at Bregenz on the frontier on December 6—that's next Wednesday—sometime in the afternoon. I have instructed Captain Grimme to be on hand to receive the money. I think it would be a good idea if you were there, too, to see that the money is paid. After all, you have much more of an interest in that transport than"—he hesitated and smiled—"than, say, someone in Switzerland might have."

Wedemeyer leaned forward and fixed a cold, hostile glare on Andor. "I am sure, Horvath, you will seize this opportunity to try to slip through my fingers. Therefore I plan to hold back all the members of your family in Bergen-Belsen."

"I have no intention of going to the frontier or to Switzerland to try to get money for you on those conditions," Andor snapped, hoping the threat would work. "If I do go, I will return to Budapest without such a club being held over my head."

"Your man Gábor promised *he* would come back, too, remember?" Wedemeyer retorted.

"You have several hundred thousand of my people in your hands here in Budapest, Colonel," Andor replied. "If you think I would risk anything more happening to them by not returning, then you are not aware, after all these months we have known each other, of my character."

Wedemeyer seemed to be weakening, but he made one last threat: "I promise you this, Horvath: if you try to double-cross us, the Jews of Budapest will feel the full fury of my revenge."

25

Andor, Schoen, and Captain Grimme sat in a café facing the railroad tracks so they would be able to see the train as soon as it arrived. It was a gelid December afternoon; an icy wind that swept in from the lake whipped noisily around the building. Schoen, for whom a special visa had been obtained so he could cross the frontier to Bregenz, was in as disagreeable a mood as the weather. Captain Grimme, who seemed to bear no grudge now that matters were reaching a satisfactory conclusion, wanted to start counting money and finish with the formalities while they were waiting for the train. Schoen refused.

"My agreement is that I will hand over the money when the people of the transport have been delivered to us," he said. "I shall do this when they are all in a Swiss train and the train is ready to start."

"But, Herr Schoen," the German captain replied, "don't you trust me enough to tell me at least in what form you have the money?"

Schoen's expression stiffened. "Trusting doesn't enter such negotiations. I keep my agreements. I expect others to do likewise."

His last words were muffled by the rumble of an approaching train. It was covered with ice, and the steps of each car were packed with snow. The windows were frosted, so that it was impossible to see any sign of human life inside. A man stepped from the first car. It was Obersturmbannführer Walter Heinemann, who had also accompanied the previous train. He greeted Captain Grimme, who saluted briskly, and then nodded to Andor, who introduced Schoen. Heinemann nodded curtly to the banker. At Captain Grimme's suggestion they returned to the café to continue their negotiations.

Heinemann ordered a double schnapps.

"Now, Schoen," Grimme began, "the amount due is one million dollars."

"Minus the amount we have paid for the two carloads of skins from Bratislava and the coffee," Schoen interrupted. He had it all tabulated on a sheet, with a carbon copy, which he handed to Captain Grimme. Then he went on. "Now in payment of the balance, I have here—" He reached into the small satchel on the floor beside his chair. As Heinemann saw the piles of bank notes, he instinctively looked around the café, which was deserted except for the barmaid, then put his revolver on the table, anyway.

For the next two hours they counted money: Swiss francs, English pounds, American dollars, German reichsmarks, Austrian shillings, Hungarian pengö. There was even some South American money. Schoen and Grimme each had a conversion table showing the current black-bourse rates for the various currencies, but their tables were not in agreement. This resulted in tiresome bickering over the actual value of the foreign notes. The way Grimme figured it, Schoen was sixty-five thousand dollars short of the amount due.

"I'm sorry," he said with a look of apology in Andor's direction, "but I am absolutely forbidden by instructions I received just yesterday to permit the people of the transport to leave the Reich until the full amount has been paid."

Schoen was equally adamant. "The instructions from my people are that I am to make a settlement at the rate of exchange prevailing this morning in the bourse at Zurich. I am unable to compromise in any way. This is other people's money!"

Heinemann drank his schnapps and watched stolidly. Andor tried to figure out a loophole. One city block from where they sat the train, his train, was on a siding, waiting. Aboard it were *his* people, and among them was Jessica. Suddenly he broke the gloomy silence by calling the young barmaid who had been watching the counting of the bank notes with wonder and disbelief. "Four more schnapps, please," he said, and then to Schoen, "Let me see that balance sheet."

While the other men concentrated on their drinks, he studied the columns of figures. Suddenly he put the paper down. "Gentlemen, the joke is on us! Someone has forgotten to enter a credit for the housing of the transport at Columbus utca."

"As I remember," Heinemann retorted, "that was to be an expense of your Committee."

"The food, yes, Colonel, but it was agreed that we would be credited eighty thousand dollars for the expense of constructing new barracks on the Columbus utca grounds." Without even pausing to permit a debate of the bald-faced lie, Andor went on, "Now sixty-five from eighty is fifteen, so actually we have overpaid you by fifteen thousand dollars."

Schoen was beaming. Grimme looked disturbed. Andor took the lead again. "Gentlemen, we are all tired, and unless we conclude this business quickly we are going to have a great many new problems on our hands: feeding the people on the train; paying the Swiss railroad system for waiting time for the Swiss train, which I presume is out there now on the siding. I'm sure that my colleague, Herr Schoen, will agree, in a spirit of compromise, to overlook this slight overpayment." He glanced at the banker, who seemed perplexed by this new gambit, but before Schoen had a chance to say a word, Andor declared, "Yes, he agrees. So, gentlemen, it's a deal! Now let's have a bottle of champagne to celebrate. Waitress, call the *patron*. Certainly in the cellar of such a well-known establishment as this there is a bottle of fine old champagne —say a Piper Heidsieck 1937—that has been saved for just such an occasion as this."

With her fingernails Jessica Hoffmann scratched a hole in the thick frost on the window large enough so she could see where they were. It was a bleak-looking town. The hotel opposite the station was boarded up. In the next block there was a café; each time the door opened to let someone in or out she could see how brightly lighted it was. Otherwise Bregenz was as blacked out as every other place in Hitler's Reich.

"What do you see, my dear?" Philip Kemeny's voice was like a soft summer breeze that made almost no vibrations at all on the ear, but Jessica was accustomed to it by now.

"Nothing, Philip. A town. A few people. But they tell me that on the other side—on the lake side of the railroad yards—a Swiss train has arrived, empty. It must be for us, Philip, only I wonder why they are keeping us waiting so long here."

"Have faith. I'm sure that Andor is here, and if he is he will arrange everything."

During the many hours the train was in the Bregenz yards, Leo went from car to car trying to keep up morale, answering the hundreds of questions people put to him with replies that were more ingenious than truthful.

"Why are we here so long?" one man asked.

"Where would you rather be, in Bergen-Belsen?"

When a man in the next car asked the same question, he replied even more sharply, "So long? How many times have you crossed from Austria into Switzerland? This is a big frontier. There are always complications. Papers. Affidavits. You act as if you were going from Buda to Pest."

People laughed, and Leo moved on to the next car.

It was 10 P.M. by the time the negotiators emptied the bottle of champagne.

"Now if you will sign here, Herr Horvath," Heinemann said. "It's just like the receipt you signed last time. It says we have delivered to you the remaining 1,359 people of your transport."

Andor took the pen Heinemann held out and was about to sign when he suddenly put the pen down. "As I recall, the number left at Bergen-Belsen after the three hundred came out was 1,379, not 59."

Heinemann smiled. "You don't forget anything, do you, Horvath? When you board the train and talk with Strauss, he will tell you that twenty old people died, all of natural causes. That leaves 1,359."

Andor put his signature to the paper and addressed Grimme. "I assume you will order the passengers transferred to the Swiss train immediately?"

"Naturally," the captain replied.

"In that case, may I give you both my sincere thanks and say good-by until we meet back in Budapest." He shook hands with Heinemann and Grimme. To Schoen he said, "Let's go now. I must find some friends of mine on the train."

The faces of the passengers were flushed with happiness as word spread that their wait was over and that they should prepare to move their belongings to the Swiss train on the next track.

Leo guided Andor from car to car, his pride plain on his face, in his voice, in every gesture. In some cars where there were young people, Andor was cheered. In every car people wanted to shake his hand, embrace him, or just touch him. Leo stayed close, reminding him in confidential whispers of the identity of people whose faces he might have forgotten ("You remember Moshe Hahn, the artist."), or telling him news he might not have heard ("Mrs. Gruen is in the next compartment with her back to us. She's been very ill, so we haven't told her yet about what happened to Arthur."), or warning him of problems he might wish to sidestep for the moment ("Those people in the aisle at the far end of the car are the parents of Martin Klein. They'll certainly ask whether you've had any news of their boy.").

As Andor noticed how thin and gaunt everyone had become, he began to worry about Jessica. Had she aged and become as forlorn-looking as some of these other people? When he came to his sister, Rena, he hardly recognized her, her cheeks were so pinched and her complexion so gray. They embraced but did not kiss. He noticed that her hands shook as if she had palsy. Her husband, Sam, was strangely nervous, though he tried to smile.

On their way to the next coach Andor suddenly thought of the twenty people who had died. He seized Leo's arm. "My father-in-law— is he all right?"

Leo grinned. "Sure. He's in the compartment at the front of this car we're coming to. But if you don't mind, Andor, I think I'll see if we can start moving the passengers onto the Swiss train now. I'll come back in a few minutes."

Andor, certain Leo had deliberately left him alone at this moment, hurried to the foremost compartment. Through the half-open door he saw the back of her head. She was looking out a peephole in the frost on the window. On the opposite seat there were four sleeping figures, their heads on each other's shoulder. Philip was next to the window, directly opposite Jessica. His cheeks were hollow and his white hair very sparse, but his expression was serene. Andor's gaze returned quickly to the back of Jessica's head. She had not changed the way she wore her hair. It was pulled back as tight as ever. At last she must have felt his presence, for she turned around slowly and looked at him. A soft smile brightened her face. She made no effort to get up. She said simply, "I'm very happy to see you."

The next instant he was on the seat beside her. He put his arms around her and whispered, "Not nearly so happy as I am to be here with you." She made no reply, but she was not struggling to get free. She was warm and pliant; he could feel her breasts against his own body. "I love you," he whispered, bending to kiss her lips. She gave a short gasp and slipped out of his arms. "Philip is waking up," she said, nodding at the old man, who had begun to stir. "He's been living for this moment when he would see you again. He has had such faith in you. He will be so very happy, as I am, too," she added, softening the rebuff.

26

Before the war Caux had been a Swiss mountaintop summer resort much in favor with wealthy vacationers from other parts of Europe and the British Isles. It was reached by a regular railroad train to Montreux, with its castle made famous in Byron's *Prisoner of Chillon* and with a white stone statue of Queen Victoria on the main thoroughfare, erected by the British. From Montreux the trip to Caux was made by an autobus that went around and around in a series of circles that seemed to be without end, or by a cog-wheel railroad that gave the impression of ascending at about an 85-degree angie.

For the passengers on the rescue train who had never been in high mountains before, Caux, at nearly four thousand feet, was exhilarating; it seemed as high up as a man could possibly get, but the morning after their arrival, when they looked toward the sun, they saw the Rochers de Naye, a snowcapped mountain towering another three thousand feet above them.

Through the good offices of the Jewish community of Switzerland almost a thousand people of the transport were housed in the six-story Palace, one of Europe's grand hotels built in the nineteenth century—when it was mainly the aristocracy that traveled abroad—and the rest in a hotel that at various times had been called the Grand or the Regina, or the Grand Hotel Regina. The three hundred who had arrived months earlier were scattered through several smaller hotels on the same mountaintop. Leo had a delicate task deciding who should get the de luxe rooms facing the lake and who should share what accommodations with whom.

"Just like Bergen-Belsen!" became their standard remark whenever they wanted to comment about something. They said it to each other when they first saw the crystal chandeliers and the gold leaf on the salon ceiling, and when they found that although most of the elevators were out of service because of the electricity shortage, one was maintained to carry the ill and the feeble back and forth between their rooms and the dining hall. They said it when they saw there was real toilet paper in the marble-lined bathrooms. They said it many times every day, until it became their favorite remark.

One week after their arrival a party was held in the main dining room of the Palace for all the people of the transport, financed partly with funds provided by the Jewish community of Switzerland, partly with money some of them had had on deposit in Geneva or Zurich. The dinner menu was the most elaborate any of them remembered since before the days of wartime shortages. There were several amateur musicians among them, and a few professionals. During the week a number of instruments had been procured, so there was music throughout the dinner, the only music many of them had heard in a long time. It was the first day of Chanukah, so the ceremony of lighting the first Chanukah candle was performed, and each child received a small gift. After dinner Leo Strauss got up to make the speech of the evening. Everyone had eaten well, and there had been a glass of Swiss white wine for every adult. Now they all sat back, content and hoping to be entertained. A transformation had already begun to take place in them. The gauntness and grayness were disappearing. Andor looked down from his place at the head table and smiled at Rena. He had not seen her like this since before the war; she actually seemed to be enjoying herself. Everyone was quiet, waiting for Leo to begin.

After a long, formal opening, during which he tried to mention everyone of importance in the hall, he paused, made a sweeping gesture with his large right hand toward the tables that had not yet been cleared, and said, "Look at you! So much food you leave it on your plates! Just like Bergen-Belsen, yah?" Andor saw nothing very amusing about the remark, but the others all laughed. It was their own little joke.

Leo went on, "Who would have thought a month ago that tonight we would be here, safe, sleeping in regular beds, drinking wine, having music, and—leaving food on your plates!" Again they laughed. "Tonight we lit the first Chanukah candle. We do this remembering the Maccabees and how they made such a big victory over the Egyptians."

Vera was tugging at his coattail. He tried to brush her hand away and go on with his speech, but she continued to tug so he bent down to hear what she wanted to whisper. Then he straightened up and smiled. "The victory was over the Greeks, not the Egyptians, yah? My wife knows the Book better than I do. She goes to temple for both of us."

Now he had the audience relaxed and receptive.

"The Maccabees maybe were great people, but that was not the last Jewish victory. Tonight we are paying our respects to the man who brought *us* out of *our* bondage, out of *our* land of exile, and fortunately he is with us to hear what we think of him. Andor Horvath! Stand up, my friend!"

More than a thousand pairs of eyes turned toward Andor. His dark suit had been carefully pressed for the occasion, he had a crisp white handkerchief protruding slightly from his breast pocket, he wore a new blue silk tie, and in his buttonhole there was a small flower Jessica had put there just before they came into the dining room, whispering, "This is my Chanukah present to the man I love." Andor wondered where she could possibly have obtained such a flower on a mountaintop in the middle of December, but she gave him no chance to ask. In her embarrassment at her own boldness, she turned quickly and fled. Now, as he stood up, he caught her eye. She was sitting beside Philip at the next table. Both of them were smiling proudly at him, and in recognition he gave them a small wave of the hand.

The audience started clapping, then someone cheered. Soon they were pounding their feet on the floor and making a great din.

"Stand up on a chair, Andor; they can't see you in back," Leo commanded, and when Andor hesitated, forced him to do it. That caused an acceleration of the enthusiasm. Finally Leo waved his massive right hand for silence and helped Andor down. Reaching under his chair, he produced a large package wrapped in white tissue paper. The people of the transport wanted the man who had saved them to have a permanent memento of their appreciation, he said, so they had made this huge book for him, three or four times the size of an ordinary book, and on every page there were pictures—"real pictures done in real oil paint, by our own camp artist, Moshe Hahn." The pictures, he explained, were mostly of their life at Bergen-Belsen.

"Stand up, Moshe!" Leo commanded, and at a far table the skinny bushy-haired artist rose. "I am very happy—" he began, but he got no further, for Leo bellowed, "Moshe, I told you to stand, not to talk. *You* make the pictures, *I* make the speeches! Now sit down."

The audience guffawed, then Leo continued, "Moshe had been working day and night all this week making the pictures for you, Andor. He has hardly slept at all, and he has hardly eaten at all—not more than three or four times a day." Everyone laughed again.

After the speeches there was dancing in the great salon, with its cut-crystal chandeliers, gilded cupids, and air of dusty elegance. Most of the time Andor was surrounded by a cluster of people, but when the orchestra began a Viennese waltz, he excused himself, found Jessica sitting in a Louis XV gilded chair beside Philip, bowed low, and said,

"May I?" Holding her in his arms as they glided around the room was an intoxicating experience. Her hair was still pulled severely back off her ears, but her face had begun to grow softer. The touch of her hand on his arm seemed very gentle.

"You were charming when you made your speech," she said. "Philip was so proud, as he'll tell you when he gets a chance."

It was late when the orchestra stopped and the musicians began to pack up their instruments. Jessica was just starting up the long circular marble staircase to the second floor when she felt a hand on her arm. "May I walk with you?" At first they discussed what a happy evening it had been for everyone, then Andor said, "Do you know there's a full moon tonight?" She shook her head. "My room," she said, "is on the back and I get lots of sunshine in the day, but the moon I never see."

Andor laughed. "Leo insisted on giving me what I'm sure must have been the bridal suite in the old days. Anyway, from my windows I can see the moonlight making the snow glisten like mounds of white diamonds, and if I stretch my neck a little I can see one corner of Lac Léman. It's a beautiful scene. Would you like to see it?"

"I would love to see it."

During the week they had been at Caux they had seen little of each other. To Andor it seemed that every person in the transport wanted to consult him about something. People followed him everywhere, asking for appointments, begging for "just a minute of your time." They wanted to know about friends and relatives left behind in Budapest, about how long he thought it would be before the war ended. The Zionists wanted to discuss plans for getting to Palestine; the non-Zionists wanted to know whether he thought they would ever be able to return to Hungary, or how about emigrating someday to America.

But now, at last, he was alone with Jessica. They stood for a long time looking out the large windows of his sitting room, their arms linked together, their fingers entwined.

"It's too beautiful to try to put into words," she said softly. "Where is Montreux and the lake?"

He pointed, and they craned their necks until they saw it, glistening in the moonlight, so far away that although it was one of the largest lakes in Europe it looked like an elongated pearl under a bright light.

"I have a Chanukah gift for you," he said, leading her away from the window. From an end table near the door he lifted a shiny white cardboard box tied with a pale blue ribbon and handed it to her.

Although they had not turned on the lights, in the moonlight he could see her face brighten in a smile. She sat down on the sofa covered with chartreuse velour, opened the package, and slowly lifted out a negligee. It was white and silk, trimmed with delicate Swiss lace.

He couldn't decide whether she was pleased or shocked. "I went down to Montreux this morning to get it," he said. "I wanted something very feminine. I hope it fits."

"It's very lovely."

Unable to restrain himself any longer, he took her in his arms, and kissed her passionately.

Andor stroked Jessica's hair slowly. "Darling, you know I love you. I have shown how much I love you. But I must tell you this: soon I have to leave this paradise. I have to go back to Budapest."

She gave a sharp cry of pain. "No, no! I won't let you go." She began to sob heartbrokenly.

He tightened his arms around her tense body. "Try to understand, Jessica," he pleaded. "I must make an attempt to save some of our people left in Budapest. There are several hundred thousand of them. I can't just let them be murdered. There is a possibility that I may be able to outwit the Nazis—a little. I have a chance of saving a few. If I'm lucky I may be able to save many more. I'm not conceited, Jessica, but in some ways I *am* a man of destiny. God has picked me to be His instrument in salvaging something out of this chaos. You must have faith in me. You must help me. Be strong, as I try to be strong. Give me courage, don't take my courage away from me. And when I have done all I can, I will come back to you, and then we will enjoy the happiness we have earned. . . ."

As he talked he felt the stiffness in her body slowly disappear.

27

Soviet armies were advancing on Budapest from three sides; every hour the escape corridor grew narrower. All eight bridges over the Danube had been mined, and Geman demolition experts stood at each one, ready to throw a switch. Not a day went by without an air raid. For months American planes had attacked by day, the R.A.F. by night; now it was Russian bombers. Although they seemed to be aiming at military targets—especially transportation facilities—a majority of their bombs fell on dwelling places, and nearly all the dead were civilians. Almost everyone believed that the fall of Budapest was unavoidable, and many were enraged that their city, the most beautiful in all Europe, was being slowly, systematically destroyed, for no obvious reason, except to postpone the inevitable.

In this doomed place there was disorganization and despair. The civilian population went to sleep listening to the thunder of distant shelling; they were awakened by the scream of air-raid sirens, the whistle of falling bombs, and finally the dull noise of crumbling buildings. There were screams in the dark and terror by day and by night. Only the reckless ventured into the streets, and they often found their way blocked by debris.

In the ghetto life was still uglier. Surrounded by the tall wooden fence were a hundred thousand Jews, barely alive. Diphtheria, scarlet fever, and typhus had broken out in the tight-packed buildings. There were Jewish doctors but no medicines. Rules of hygiene were no longer observed. People slept on stairways, in cellars with neither natural nor artificial light, in passageways, or in any empty corner they could find. Many were sure that at the last moment the ghetto would be either dynamited into oblivion or bombed by German planes; there was a widely circulated story that Colonel Wedemeyer had ordered: "No Jew must come out alive from the ghetto."

On December 22 someone at the Majestic telephoned an order to Sip utca for members of the Jewish Council to assemble at the Center on the stroke of nine that night. The message was taken by a sister of the porter who out of fear or confusion failed to tell anyone about it. At 9 P.M. three large Mercedes drew up at the door and several SS men with sub-machine guns entered the building. On learning that the Council members had not been summoned, they beat the porter and threatened him with death if the Jewish leaders were not on hand at nine the next morning.

The next day the encirclement of Budapest was complete except for a gap of thirty miles. During the previous night Wedemeyer and his staff had suddenly decided it was too dangerous to remain in the city, and they hastily left for Vienna. At 9 A.M. the Council members assembled at the Center, convinced they were either going to be killed off because they were no longer needed or taken as hostages, but no one came for them.

On Christmas Eve, Russian tanks were just five miles west of the city.

On Christmas Day the last railroad line out of the city was cut and the Soviet arc was within nine miles of being a complete circle. The Russian shelling was taking many victims. Rockets were demolishing whole rows of buildings.

Each day in the chaos of the situation the Arrow Cross found new ways to prey on the Jews. They would demand to see the protection pass of any Jew they found outside the ghetto, and when he presented it they would pocket it and then sell it to some other Jew they found without a pass, thus creating a self-perpetuating market for their machinations. A few minutes after a Jewish Council vehicle delivered food to a Jewish-occupied building, an Arrow Cross vehicle would appear, the food would be demanded, and the truck would drive off with it. In a six-story building on Pozsonyi ut, occupied by nearly two thousand Jews, there seemed to be no way to prevent starvation on the top two or three floors, because whatever food arrived and was not confiscated never was sufficient for those above the first few floors.

A few minutes before noon on December 28, Andor left a Swiss train at Bregenz, entered the depot, and asked for a first-class ticket for the rest of his journey. When he said "Budapest" the stationmaster looked up in surprise. "Don't you know?" he said. "Budapest was encircled two days ago, when the Russians captured Esztergom. That's a fortress on the Danube about—"

"I know where Esztergom is," Andor interrupted. "Give me a first-class ticket to Vienna."

Joe Nagel had been living in the bunker in the cellar of the Glass House since his unsuccessful attempt to free Ely and Martin. He had never been, by nature, lighthearted, but the shooting of Ely and the capture of Rachel had increased his cynicism and bitterness a hundred-fold and now he was a man with an obsession for revenge. For months he had argued with Andor that what they were doing was not enough; that negotiations on the surface should be combined with secret preparations for armed resistance; that when the battle for Budapest finally took place every Jew strong enough to hold a gun should assist in the liberation.

After the disaster at the railroad station he decided to spend every waking hour of life that was left to him killing or planning to kill the enemies of the Jews.

In the bunkers there were no ranks, but each man took an oath: "I promise to die with honor, as I have promised to live with honor, in order to avenge the injustice that has been done to my people."

Every man among them was anesthetized with the narcotic of hate. They took chances that a few weeks earlier would have seemed suicidal. They had a half dozen stolen automobiles and motorcycles, and a large store of firearms. They all wore Arrow Cross, Hungarian army, or German uniforms. They had one radio in their bunker that they kept tuned to Moscow. From military communiqués issued a thousand miles away in the Russian capital they learned what was happening in the suburbs of their own city.

Late one night Joe shuffled into the Glass House basement, tired from distributing arms to chalutzim in some of the protected houses. As he stretched out on the floor for a few hours' sleep, Moscow Radio was announcing that two Red Army emissaries carrying a white flag had tried to present an ultimatum calling for the surrender of Budapest by the German defenders but were killed before they could deliver it.

"The goddamn bastards!" Joe growled. "I'd like to pump hot steel into their stinking bellies right now."

The youth who was operating the radio looked over his shoulder. "Cheer up, Joe," he grinned. "Before the end of the week we'll be dancing with our Soviet friends along the Korzó."

SS headquarters, Vienna, were in the Grand Hotel, not far from the old Imperial Palace, the Hofburg. Some of the German officers stationed in the Austrian capital were living in commandeered apartments and villas scattered around the city, but more than a hundred had rooms, as well as their offices, in the once elegant Grand. Andor had learned this from a German officer with whom he shared a compartment on the long ride from Bregenz, so he took a taxi directly from the depot to the Grand.

When he learned that Colonel Weber and the entire staff of the Judenkommando had arrived in Vienna and that Weber already had established an office at the Grand, he decided that fortune was smiling on him. But he was less than happy when he was finally admitted to Weber's presence and saw the expression on his face.

"Horvath," Weber said curtly, "you have made life very difficult for me. We kept our bargain with you to the letter. We let all the people of your transport—even your family—go to Switzerland, and yet we have received not a dollar of the additional money you promised us. We have not had a single communication from Schoen."

It took a long time to pacify him, but before the conversation was over Andor had the impression that Weber—and possibly Himmler, too —was actually more interested now in establishing a postwar alibi for himself than in receiving more money. This pleased him, for it gave him a new bargaining instrument.

"Anyway," the colonel ended, "as long as you agree to continue to keep the negotiations open, I shall look out for you. There is a billeting officer on the next floor. I'll take you to him and get you a room here in the Grand. Even though you have a German passport, I do not advise you to do much roaming around the city. Here in this hotel, at least, you will be safe."

By the end of December life no longer had much meaning for anyone in besieged Budapest. There was no water, no electricity, no gas, and no food, except for the meat of horses that had been hit by shells or had dropped dead in the streets. Sleep was impossible; all the ear-aching noises of war echoed across the Danube. The area in Buda held by the Germans was under constant shelling. In Pest there was hand-to-hand combat—house to house, street to street. Budapest was such a sprawling metropolis, six thousand square blocks in the city proper, that it took the Russians until January 8 to get possession of just one third of it. Each day radio bulletins from Moscow told exactly how many more city blocks had been liberated.

Joe and his fellow chalutzim roamed the streets, creating as much additional chaos as possible. Each day, dressed in their SS uniforms, they went to prisons or hospitals and with fake military orders "arrested" Jewish patients or prisoners, whom they took to their bunker. The liberated men, unless they were too weak, were given weapons and German or Hungarian uniforms and sent into the streets to harass Budapest's defenders in any way they could contrive.

Dead bodies and overturned motor vehicles littered almost every street, but there was no stench yet, because the corpses were frozen solid.

Captain Klaussen's apartment was not far from the imperial-yellow Schönbrunn Palace, with its fourteen hundred rooms, in which the Emperor Franz Josef was born. The apartment was furnished with old Viennese elegance, each piece looking as if it had been selected with as much thought as a jeweler might put into choosing the diamonds for a queen's necklace. The salon was done entirely in gold and white. Beyond it was a walnut-paneled library. How many rooms there were Andor had no way of telling. A few hours earlier he had seen Klaussen for the first time in months as they had passed each other in the lobby of the Grand, and the German baron had invited him to spend the evening over champagne and a little caviar at the apartment.

When Andor asked who owned the furnishings, Klaussen replied, "Everything is mine; every book, every single object. You see, I love beauty." He picked up a delicate piece of cloisonné from a table and fingered it affectionately. "And so I moved many of the things I have collected over the years here to Vienna, to have them as near to me as possible." He paused, then added, with slightly raised eyebrows, "I am glad I had a hunch about not moving them to *your* charming city."

Andor was only half listening. He noticed on the bookshelves volumes by Arnold Zweig, Emil Ludwig, Lion Feuchtwanger, the sociologist Arthur Ruppin, Albert Einstein, and many other undeniably Jewish authors. As his host observed his interest and apparent surprise, he said, "You must realize, Herr Horvath, that all of us who wear German uniforms do not necessarily think exactly alike. Naturally we are all loyal to the Führer, but— For example, you can see plenty of indications in front of you of my feeling about Jewish intellectuals." He paused again. "And that brings us to the matter I wish to discuss with you."

For the next hour the suave German baron told his guest, as they sipped their champagne, of the conflict that now existed between Himmler, who had decided the time had come to put a quick end to the extermination of Jews, and Wedemeyer, who still argued that the more imminent an Allied victory appeared, the more they ought to speed up the work of the Judenkommando, because—and the baron said these were Wedemeyer's exact words—"The minute we are forced to sign an armistice, our attempt at a final solution of the Jewish problem will come to an end."

Finally the whole purpose of the evening began to come out.

"Do you remember, Herr Horvath, the forced march from Budapest to the Austrian frontier? Well, I was at the border town to receive your people. The International Red Cross and the Swedish Legation registered protests, so I agreed with them not to take for forced labor those who were either sick or otherwise incapable of work. I agreed to ship them back to Budapest, whence they had come. Well, when Wedemeyer heard of this he threatened to have me court-martialed. Since then he and I have barely been on speaking terms."

Walking slowly back and forth across his thick rugs, with his champagne glass held gracefully between his long aristocratic fingers, the baron told his guest that he was a man of honor and integrity, having nothing in common with those who had behaved toward Jews in such a bestial manner. He was sure that Herr Horvath was already aware of this. Then he filled their glasses again.

Just before dawn on January 8, Joe went back to the Glass House after all-night patrol duty. The young radio operator looked up as he came into the cellar and shouted, "Hey! Warsaw has just fallen! Damn, I wish I had a drink. We ought to celebrate. Do you know that it's taken five years, three months, and twenty days?"

Joe smiled. "We'll have something else to celebrate soon. I think our Russian friends are going to try to liberate the ghetto today. At least that's what I hear from the other side of the lines. This is one fight I want to be in, so excuse me if I catch a little rest before the fun begins."

Three hours later, somewhat refreshed, he opened one eye, looked at his watch, stretched several times, and got to his feet. He had slept in his greatcoat because the basement was almost as cold as the outdoors. Now he slipped it off and hung it over the door. From the next room, where the munitions were kept, he took six hand grenades and put one in each pocket of his trousers and jacket. Then he tied ten more together with a piece of rope, which he fastened around his waist. As he went back to the next room, the radio operator looked at him glumly. "If you get hit by a bullet, you'll go up like a sky rocket."

"So what?" Joe put on his overcoat. Fortunately it was too large for him. He only hoped the bulges wouldn't show.

The guard at the Dohány utca entrance of the ghetto saluted him respectfully as he entered. Joe had a carefully worked-out plan in mind. This was the side from which the Russians would attack. At intervals along Dohány utca the Germans had established defense points by stacking sandbags in a semicircle to a height of about ten feet and then lining them with large sheets of heavy steel that would deflect anything short of artillery shells. Inside each of these strong points were twenty or thirty German soldiers equipped with machine guns and enough ammunition to withstand a long siege. Joe had figured out that if just one of these miniature forts could be taken by the Russians they would be able to attack the others from the rear and capture them easily. The largest and most formidable of the German defense points was directly opposite the entrance to the ghetto. Inside the ghetto fence and facing the fort was a three-story building. Joe entered it determinedly, as if he were on official business.

As he climbed from floor to floor of the ghetto dwelling, he had to make his way around the men and women sleeping on the staircase. Seeing his SS uniform, they hastily moved aside for him. One word came to Joe's mind as he climbed over them: cringing. An ugly word, he thought. Slaughter was an ugly word, too. But cringing was worse. This was what had been happening to a proud people: they cringed or they were slaughtered, or maybe both. Maybe they were slaughtered because they cringed. He wasn't sure about these things, but he knew that for him death was better than cringing. By sundown he might be dead. It was the gamble he was taking. Damn the stinking bastards! He hated their guts. He hated the look of them, the smell of them, the sound of them. Jew-haters, all of them. Even the best of them. Fucking bastards!

On the second-floor landing an old man with a beard jumped up from a lying position and began to scream in broken German, with his face no more than a foot away from Joe's, "You swine! You Nazi swine! You're starving us to death. My wife is so hungry she can't stand on her feet. You Nazi swine!"

The others on the landing drew back in terror. The old man was left there, alone, trembling with rage, shaking his small fist, and screaming, "Nazi swine!"

Joe laid his hand gently on the old man's arm. Quietly he said in Hebrew, "Shalom. Shalom aleichem." There was a gasp of astonishment from the other people on the landing. But he continued his climb, saying nothing more.

On the top floor there was a ladder leading to the roof. He mounted it and slowly pushed open a trap door. Around the edge of the roof there was a parapet about three feet high. He had observed it from the street and knew it was ideal for his purpose.

The wait was not so long as he had expected. After less than an hour he could hear the Russians approaching. They were being fought house by house, but the sound of battle kept coming closer and closer. Soon he could see darting figures less than a block away, taking shelter in doorways, blazing away with their guns, then moving irresistibly forward. The Germans inside the semicircle of sandbags and steel kept up a rapid fire with their machine guns. Joe could see them picking off the Soviet soldiers as fast as they exposed themselves and came within range.

He took off his greatcoat, laid it on the roof, and kneeled on it. Then he took off his SS jacket. He was in a white shirt now. The day was bitter cold, but he was full of too much inner fire to care. On the left breast of his shirt there was a large yellow star. He piled his grenades on the roof close beside him. This was the moment he had been living for. Now everything made sense. He took one of the cold steel grenades in his right hand and stroked it lovingly. With his left hand he pulled the pin, then threw it like a ball, aiming carefully. It was a perfect shot. It landed in the very center of the German fort, putting one of the three machine guns out of commission. At least two of the soldiers were wounded by fragments of the grenade. Joe ducked behind the parapet, but apparently the Germans had no idea from what direction the surprise attack had come.

In the next quarter hour he used twelve of his sixteen grenades. The last two put the only remaining machine gun out of action and either killed or wounded the only German soldiers in the fort not already dead or dying. Now the way was clear for the Russians to swarm in and overpower the other defense points, one by one, from the rear.

He let out a shout of victory, then ran like a madman in his white shirt with the yellow star down the stairs to the street, at the same time pulling from his trouser pocket a bright red cloth almost two feet square. He dashed from the building to the entrance of the ghetto through which Russian soldiers had begun to swarm. In the lead was a young officer with a revolver in his hand. Joe waved his homemade Soviet flag, pointed to his yellow star, and threw an arm around the officer's shoulder. "Welcome, Comrade!" he shouted in Russian.

The officer gazed at him coldly. With his free hand he reached up and pushed Joe's arm away. As he did he noticed the gold watch on Joe's wrist. Deftly, he put his revolver into its holster, held Joe's arm with his right hand and unfastened the watch with his left, put the watch around his own wrist, drew the revolver from its holster again, pushed Joe aside impatiently, and then motioned his men to follow him into the ghetto.

311

28

Warsaw had fallen, Budapest was surrounded, Berlin's days were numbered, with Russian troops only fifty miles away, and Vienna was under daily aerial attack.

Andor found it strange to be a Jew in Vienna in January and February of 1945. This city, which gave the world Sigmund Freud, Stefan Zweig, and many another great Jew, before the war had had a Jewish population of nearly two hundred thousand, one in every eight people. Today there were said to be only about two hundred of them left. Nowhere else in Europe had the exterminators done their work so thoroughly. The old Hapsburg capital was now 99.9 per cent pure.

Frustrated in what he had returned to do—save the lives of a few more Hungarian Jews—Andor began to negotiate for any Jews who still remained in German hands. It was obvious that Hitler's Third Reich was collapsing, but those at the top might try to pull down with them into the swirling chaos of defeat all those Jews who had not yet been obliterated.

Colonel Weber flew back and forth frequently between Vienna and Berlin. It was clear to Andor that he enjoyed the confidence of Himmler and that Himmler, although angry about the failure of the U.R.O. deal, might be pressured into making new concessions in order to appear less like a villain after the war was over.

Never before had Andor felt so intensely that he was in an historically important position and that so much depended on how keen-minded he remained, and how clever he could be at handling these SS officers, who were beginning to be confused by the inevitability of the master race's defeat. Weber, he knew, was the one instrument he could use to accomplish this purpose, and so whenever American planes showered Vienna with high explosive bombs, his prayer was that he and Weber would be among the survivors.

Each time the colonel came back from Berlin he related to Andor what he had achieved.

Himmler had ordered cessation of Jewish exterminations elsewhere in German-held territory.

Himmler had given him a promotion; he was now Standartenführer (full colonel) Franz Weber.

Himmler had given permission for the transport of four hundred Bratislava Jews to Switzerland, as requested by Herr Horvath.

Himmler had agreed with the principle that any money already paid to the Germans for the release of Jews should be returned in full after the end of the war.

Only once did Weber come back from Berlin with a frown on his face. That was the day he said Himmler was angry because just before the fall of Budapest a group of young Jews had assisted the Russian besiegers by forming a fifth column inside the city and harassing the two SS divisions that were encircled there. Andor could only shrug his shoulders. "It isn't always easy, Colonel, to keep people under control, especially if they are young and without leadership," he said suavely. "If I had been there—"

Weber brushed aside the explanation with a curt wave of his hand and said, "My big problem is not Himmler but Wedemeyer. After all, the Jewish question is supposed to be his province, not mine, and he continues to pressure the Reichsführer. He thinks we should liquidate every last Jew we can get our hands on, the quicker the better. Perhaps even you." He smiled wryly.

Andor returned the smile. "My life isn't important, except that the lives of so many other people depend on me." He leaned forward intently. "Colonel, there is one order you must persuade Himmler to issue. If Wedemeyer has his way and if the advancing Allied troops find the camps full of Jewish corpses, I am certain that the smell of the rotting bodies will be nothing compared with the smell of the crime in the nostrils of the rest of the world." He paused, then, seeing that Weber was impressed, went on. "You remember our meeting in Zurich with that young American, Trench, who was sent over by the White House. You remember how much he talked about humanitarianism. The Americans are dedicated to that sort of thing. If Himmler is at all interested in conciliating America at this point, he must be persuaded that the camps should be turned over intact; that the commandants must take no action against the inmates, on pain of severe punishment."

Weber made no promise that night, but the next morning he left for Berlin again. He was gone several days, and when he returned he sent for Andor.

"You and I are going on a long trip, Herr Horvath," he announced enigmatically, lighting a cigarette and settling back in the chair behind his desk. Trying not to let the extent of his curiosity show, Andor lit a cigarette of his own and waited.

"The Reichsführer was impressed with your argument about the camps—so impressed that he has given me a special assignment to make a tour of all the camps still remaining in our hands. I have written orders"—he tapped his breast pocket—"instructing all commandants that their camps are to be turned over in good order to whatever Allied force approaches, that no installations are to be destroyed, and that no inmate is to be put to death, under any conditions, or for any reason. What do you think of that?"

Andor leaned back and sighed with satisfaction. "It was my dream to accomplish this," he said emotionally. "I hope you encounter no difficulties on your trip, Colonel."

Weber smiled. "Not my trip, Herr Horvath. Our trip. The Reichsführer made it very clear to me that he wanted you to accompany me, so you can see how much in earnest we are about this."

They went by automobile, just the three of them: Weber, his driver and aide, and Andor. They traveled from camp to camp, talking to the commandants, showing them the written instructions from Himmler, listening to their objections, answering their arguments, and leaving with the definite understanding that the extermination of Jews was over—that not another execution would take place.

It was too late to do anything about the vast network of extermination centers at Auschwitz, in which so many thousands of Hungarian Jews had been gassed and cremated. It had already fallen to the Russians as they swept across Poland. The Germans had had time at Auschwitz to destroy by fire and explosives much of what was on hand, but they carelessly left behind such odd pieces of evidence as 293 bales of female human hair. At Auschwitz the Russians found the ashes of hundreds of thousands, perhaps millions, of Jews, but in Vienna Andor heard that at the last moment fifty-eight thousand Jewish inmates of Auschwitz had been transferred to camps scattered around Germany that had not yet been liberated. This made their mission even more important.

The trip was without serious incident. In one camp in the south of Germany the commandant was difficult. He had his own plan: as soon as his camp was in danger of being taken, he was going to put all his Jewish inmates on river barges and sink them in the nearby Danube. When Weber told him this was exactly the kind of action Himmler was forbidding, the commandant said his area of Germany was now under General Kaltenbrunner's direction and that Kaltenbrunner approved of the barge plan. It took only one phone call to Berlin to convince the commandant that he must obey the order conveyed by Weber.

At another camp on the edge of an extensive coal-mine area the commandant proudly told them how he was going to march all his inmates into the galleries of the nearest mine as the enemy approached and then seal them in and bury them alive by setting off charges of explosives that already were in place and wired to a central switch in his office. It took a great deal of persuasion to convince him that this was in violation of Himmler's orders.

Early in March 1945 the American First Army became the first invading military force to cross the Rhine since 1805. At the same time Berlin was winning the distinction of becoming the most heavily bombed city in the world.

Late in March, Vienna began to fill up with wounded German and Austrian soldiers, as units of the Soviet Army reached the city's eastern suburbs.

During the first week of April, Bratislava fell, and the Russians began to shell Vienna. Gestapo Chief Himmler issued orders that every German town and every house must be defended to the last man; those disobeying would be subject to the death penalty. The American and Russian armies were now closing in on Berlin.

By mid-April on all European fronts the forces of the Allies were sweeping ahead. More than two million German prisoners had been taken in the past few months. Everyone realized that the war in Europe could not last for many more weeks. Perhaps not even for many more days.

In one corner of a small Austrian café Weber and Andor sat with their heads close together, talking, two large steins of beer on the table in front of them. Everyone else was listening to the radio. A German voice announced details of the death of Franklin D. Roosevelt and then read bulletins describing the fight still going on between Germans and Russians for the northern sector of Vienna.

"I am going to do three last favors for you, Herr Horvath," Weber said above the noise of the radio. "First, I am going to have Colonel Heinemann assigned to drive you from here to the Swiss frontier. I assume that your friends in Switzerland will be able to arrange for your admittance. Naturally, Heinemann will not be able to cross over with you, but his instructions will be to leave you within walking distance of the border, if possible."

Surprised, Andor thanked him. "And the other two favors?" he asked.

The colonel smiled. "You will find out about them in the due course of events, if all goes well."

29

Mauthausen concentration camp was built to accommodate a hundred thousand inmates, without crowding. It had both a Jewish and a non-Jewish section. In the area reserved for Jews the killing was done as efficiently as at Auschwitz, by gas, and the bodies were disposed of in two crematoria. The non-Jewish section was for political prisoners, among whom the best known were some of the generals who had plotted the assassination of Hitler.

In January, as the Russians swept across Poland, thousands of Jews were transferred from Auschwitz to Mauthausen, most of them walking skeletons, with hollow chests, spindly legs, concave stomachs, and sallow complexions. One of them was a tall, thin man whose skin was a dirty gray and whose deep-sunken eyes seemed to be staring at something far away. When the roll was called, he answered to the name of Peto.

In the past nine months at Auschwitz, Alex had handled almost a hundred corpses a day. He had been forced to look into the faces of more than twenty-five thousand dead men and women, faces twisted in suffering and fear. His duty had been to pry open the jaws and extract the gold teeth. Gold for the Nazis. Gold to buy Swedish ball bearings. Gold to keep the war going until the master race triumphed.

The hatred of the Nazis he had acquired at Auschwitz for what he called "the monstrosity" had now swelled until it was a hatred of everyone around him: all Germans; his fellow prisoners; even of himself. The ordeal of the past months was etched in his features. His was the face of a man who despised the world and would be pleased to leave it. Why he hadn't gone voluntarily, as so many others had, he couldn't explain, even to himself. Suicide was such an easy way out, yet despite the agony of his daily existence he made a conscious effort to keep the spark of life burning.

For three months he and the other men from Auschwitz worked

fifteen hours a day in the nearby stone quarry, but each day their number grew less. How the commandant chose those for extermination neither Alex nor anyone else had been able to figure out.

At Mauthausen the Nazis were no longer using gas; now the usual method of execution was by injecting gasoline into the veins.

On the day that the Nazis' shrine city of Nuremberg fell, the one friend Alex had in Mauthausen was called to the political department and never returned. Several hours later the overseer of Alex's barracks, a German political prisoner, pointed to smoke coming from the chimney of one of the crematoria and said in a matter-of-fact voice, almost as if he were discussing the weather, "Your friend."

Alex did not sleep at all that night. The next morning while standing at roll call he suddenly felt weak and fell to the ground. As the others were marched off to work, the overseer told him to go back to the barracks. Several hours later a guard appeared and said he was wanted at the political department. He knew what this meant. It was just as well, he thought. He was no longer of any use to them, or to himself, or to anybody. On the way to the political department he wondered whether it would be by gasoline injection. He had heard that this was an extremely painful way to die. But what was pain? You could bear it or you couldn't. If you couldn't, you fainted. If you could—well, you could, so why worry? The long sleep would be good. It had been many months since he had had a good night's sleep.

"What's your number?" the man behind the desk demanded.

Alex spoke out his number.

The officer checked it against a number written on a paper, then said, "You are being transferred to Section A."

That was all. The guard gave a sign that the prisoner was to follow him, out of the office. Alex was confused. Section A was the area for non-Jewish prisoners. Those men received special SS rations; they weren't required to salute the guards; they didn't have to answer roll call; they lived in more commodious barracks and slept on more comfortable cots, and they didn't have to work in the quarry.

In Section A he still had to wear his soiled and ragged blue-and-white striped pajamas that marked him as a Jew, so he was shunned by the other prisoners, except those who asked him who he was and why he had been transferred to their elite section. When he shook his head dumbly, they decided he was either lying or was an idiot and turned their backs on him.

Eight days later he was taken to the main office. Three men were there: the camp commandant, his deputy, and a very handsome blond colonel.

The colonel pulled a silver cigarette case from his pocket, opened it, and extended it to Alex. "Would you like to smoke?"

Alex made no answer. What was this game they were playing with him? Was this the preliminary to some new kind of torture? He glanced at the commandant, who indicated with a movement of his eyes that Alex was to take one of the cigarettes. After several moments' hesitation he did. It would be the first cigarette he had had since his arrest that night in Budapest, back in March. He thought of it as he put the cigarette between his lips. It was only about a year ago. It seemed a thousand years ago. The colonel, seeing his hand shake, lit the cigarette for him. He inhaled the first puff deeply and immediately felt so dizzy he wanted to sit down, but the only chairs in the room were occupied.

"Why were you arrested?" the colonel asked in a matter-of-fact voice.

Alex took the cigarette from his mouth. "Because I was accused of trying to organize a resistance movement in Hungary."

After several more questions that seemed perfunctory the three officers held a whispered conversation, then the commandant announced, "You will be transferred this afternoon to Block One. You will be provided with a complete outfit of civilian clothes and will be free to go anywhere in the camp you wish."

Alex knew about Block One. Everyone knew about Block One. It was the section of de luxe prison quarters. At one time Italian Marshal Pietro Badoglio's son had been held there, and later it was used to house the prostitutes serving the officers of the camp.

During the next ten days he lived in a world of complete bewilderment. No one would explain anything to him. The clothes they issued to him were the best he had ever owned, and his meals were as good as his normal, prewar fare.

On May 4, the day half a million German troops surrendered in Northwest Germany, the Netherlands, and Denmark, two SS officers appeared in Block One and said they had come to take him away, but first he must have an overcoat. They led him to the camp tailor. The coat finally chosen for him looked as if it might have been made by the best tailor in Budapest. It seemed to fit perfectly, but one of the SS officers said, "I don't like the way it hangs." While they all waited, the tailor moved the entire row of buttons a half inch.

Alex was dumfounded. For months he had been watching SS officers supervise the extermination of Jews by the millions; now they were ordering that the buttons on a Jew's overcoat be moved over a half inch so the garment would hang nicely.

At the camp gate a limousine was waiting. For a half hour they drove in silence. Alex could see fires here and there on the horizon, and he realized that they meant the liberators were not far off, but where was he being taken, and why? If he had been permitted to remain at Mauthausen he might soon be safe, set free by the military force of one of the Allies, but in the hands of these two SS officers, anything might happen.

"Where are we going?" he finally asked.

"You will see, if we aren't hit by a bomb before we get there," one of the officers replied. They both seemed exceedingly nervous.

After several hours they arrived at a town bordering the Danube, and the limousine was driven onto a wharf. He was told to go ahead of the two officers, up a swaying gangplank. When he reached the deck of the boat, one of the officers told him to wait there, and both disappeared. There was no place to sit down, so he slowly paced back and forth, torn by curiosity, as well as being hungry, thirsty, nervous, and uncertain whether he should try to escape.

An SS guard with a sub-machine gun passed by occasionally. After some time Alex asked him, "Where am I?"

"Shut up!" the guard growled, and walked on.

In the morning a new guard was posted, and when he saw Alex he put his gun into firing position and shouted, "Who are you? Give the password!"

By this time Alex's impatience was beginning to win out over his discretion and common sense. "I'm a Jew," he replied brusquely.

The guard recoiled. "What are you doing here?" he demanded.

Alex shrugged. "I don't know." The guard started angrily across the deck toward him, but at that moment the colonel Alex had seen in the commandant's office at Mauthausen appeared from below.

"Herr Doctor, haven't they served you breakfast yet?" he asked cheerfully.

Alex shook his head.

"My apologies," the colonel said. "This is a terrible pigsty of a place." Thereupon he ordered an elaborate breakfast for both of them, which they ate sitting at a table in the stern of the boat, on the open deck. When they had finished, he took Alex to his cabin. There, at last, he introduced himself.

"I am Franz Weber," he said, "Standartenführer Franz Weber. You were, I am told, a member of the Budapest Committee headed by Andor Horvath?"

Alex nodded. He was beginning to understand.

"We do not have time to discuss the past, but Horvath and I have done certain favors for each other. I saw to it that he got to the Swiss frontier some days ago. As a favor to him, I wanted to ensure your safety also. I wanted to get you to Switzerland, but unfortunately in the past several days the French have occupied the Swiss-Austrian frontier. I could have left you at Mauthausen and perhaps nothing would have happened to you, because I issued orders that the camp is to be turned over to the Allies without trouble. But who can tell? There might be some foolishness despite the orders, so I thought you would be safer with me. That is why I took you out of the camp." He offered Alex a cigarette and then asked, "How about papers, documents—do you have any at all?"

"No," Alex replied. The colonel disappeared. He was gone about ten minutes. When he returned, he had a formidable-looking document in his hand. It read:

COMMANDER OF COMBAT ARMY SS

Movement Order

Dr. Alex Peto has received movement orders from Camp Mauthausen. Destination: Andor Horvath, Switzerland. All SS personnel are to render every possible assistance to the bearer.

The order bore the signature of an SS general, which gave Alex the idea that the boat was being used as secret SS staff headquarters.

"This," said Weber as he handed Alex the paper, "should save you from any difficulty as long as you are behind German lines."

That morning they set out by car to see how close they could get to the Swiss frontier, Weber and Alex in the back seat, a uniformed aide driving. As they started, Weber pulled from his pocket a sizable bar of dark chocolate, broke it in the middle, and gave half to Alex. It was the first chocolate he had seen in more than a year. Chocolate in any form had always been one of his weaknesses. He smelled it, eagerly. Weber laughed. "It's to eat, you know." Alex hesitated, but after the first taste he gobbled the rest ravenously. Soon he was doubled up with stomach cramps, which made him realize that after what he had been through, he must return to a normal life slowly. For a long time he would not be able to indulge in even the simplest pleasures.

Not far from Salzburg, high in the mountains, they came to the health resort of Bad Ischl, famous for its sulphur springs, ice caves, mud baths, and cures for many maladies. Even this high up and this early in the year, there was a touch of spring in the air, but Alex was still in pain, little interested in either the weather or where they were. He only half heard Weber say that he wanted to try to locate some friends and might be gone for some time. Alex was tired after standing all night on the deck of the river boat, and when his ache abated he fell asleep. About an hour later he was awakened by a babble of Yiddish. He opened his eyes and sat up. In a field just opposite from where the car was parked were four or five adults and several children. The men were pitching a tent. He walked into the field and began a conversation with the strangers. They were refugees from Salzburg, and when they learned that he had been in a camp and had no plans, they offered to share their meager food with him and let him sleep under their tent. But by now Weber had reappeared and was beckoning to him from the road.

"I have some very exciting news, Herr Doctor," he said. "I have been given permission to use a hunting lodge not far from here but a little higher up in the mountains. It's a wonderful place. I know, because I have been there before. Hermann Goering's sister used to live in it. It's really a castle. We'll be very comfortable there."

Alex shook his head. "If you don't mind, I'd rather spend the night here in the field with my own people. I'm not really accustomed to castles."

"Remember, Doctor, you are still a prisoner and you must obey orders." But Weber smiled as he said it. He opened the door of the car and pointed to the rear seat. Alex decided it was wiser to obey and got in.

It was a strange night for him. The lodge was staffed with many servants and was, as the colonel had said, almost a castle. The bedroom assigned to him was at least four times the size of his entire apartment in Budapest. The bed was of deeply carved dark wood and was hung with a canopy. The sheets were white and crisp. The pillows were enormous and fluffy, and on top of the bed was a mountainous duvet. On the bedside table were several books bound in rich green leather and a delicate Bohemian glass decanter of water. The rugs looked oriental, the huge oil paintings on the walls were magnificent Flemish art, and the crystal chandelier made the room dance with spots of reflected light.

For more than a year he had been sleeping on concentration-camp cots. Suddenly this happened. It wasn't easy to make the adjustment. As he climbed into the bed, he began to think about his host. The young colonel was exceedingly courteous and considerate. He kept asking, "Is your coffee hot enough?" or "Don't you want more sugar?" But he wore an SS uniform. Standartenführer Franz Weber represented a system he had grown to hate violently. Yet now that he had a chance—now that he could jump on him as they climbed a staircase together and strangle him with his bare hands—he no longer had the desire. For months he had planned what he would do when the opportune moment came, yet here it was, and what was he doing? Sharing a castle with a standarten-führer. Putting his own body between the very sheets that Hermann Goering's sister might have used last month. He reached over and pressed the button that turned off the bedside lamp. Through the half-open window he could hear sounds of gaiety from the dining room downstairs. The mattress was cloud-soft. His stomach no longer ached, but his head was full of confusion.

The next morning a servant brought his breakfast on a silver tray. The coffee was in a huge china pot, and there was a dish of *Schlag* (whipped cream), and hot rolls, butter curled into fancy shapes, and strawberry jam. The servant also brought the news that during the night American troops had entered Bad Ischl.

Alex was finishing the last roll when there was a knock on his door. Weber entered. He was wearing a dark blue silk dressing gown, with a light blue ascot around his neck, and carrying a lighted cigarette in a long holder.

"I trust you slept well, Herr Doctor," he said briskly.

Alex had not slept well. Tossing around in the large, soft bed, he had wondered whether he would ever sleep well again. He no longer had hunger pains, and the cramps caused by the chocolate orgy were gone. He knew that nature might eventually heal the damage to his body. It wasn't physical pain that kept him from sleeping now; it was the ache in his soul. It was remembering. How long, he wondered, would it take to forget? Could a man ever forget? A man is composed of everything that has ever happened to him, and what had happened in the past year would be the chief ingredient of his own composition from now on.

The colonel thought Alex had not heard. "I trust you slept well, Herr Doctor," he said again.

"The bed was very comfortable," Alex replied. "Thank you."

Without further niceties the colonel got down to business. "I believe you left Budapest before your chief, Horvath, began entering into negotiations with us for the release of some sixteen hundred Hungarian Jews. There is no time now for me to explain all the details, but we permitted these people to go to Switzerland in return for a certain sum of money. A great deal of it was contributed by men and women who actually were on the rescue train. It came to us in the form of coins and bank notes of various countries, also a considerable amount of gold bullion and some jewelry. This wealth was eventually turned over to me, because I am the economic officer of the SS, in charge of such matters. Everything we received during these negotiations with Horvath was put in a steel chest, which I brought along in the luggage compartment of my car and which was under my bed last night—and still is."

He began to walk up and down the room, several times parting the curtains and looking out the window.

"The future of all of us, Doctor, is very uncertain at this point, even more uncertain, I might say, than it has been during the long war. I trust that you will recover quickly from your experiences, and I hope that my life will not be too unpleasant. But one never knows."

He paused and inhaled deeply from his cigarette. "Anyway, not many weeks ago I told Horvath in Vienna that what was paid for his transport would probably be returned to your people. You are the one who will have to see that it is. There will, of course, be many problems for you. The chest itself is very heavy, so I will transfer the contents into two suitcases I have procured that are equipped with stout locks. As soon as they are ready, I will have one of the servants bring them to your room."

He looked out the window. Something he saw made him nervous. He turned hastily to Alex and said, "I hope you will remember our little experience together with some pleasure, Herr Doctor, and that when you find your friend Horvath and turn over the suitcases to him, you will remind him that I did three considerable favors for him. *Auf Wiedersehen.*"

An hour or so later two servants appeared, each half carrying, half dragging a suitcase. As they gave Alex the keys and quickly departed, he heard a strange noise in the courtyard. Looking down from the window, he saw two khaki-colored jeeps loaded with soldiers. His first instinct was to get the suitcases out of sight, so he pushed them under the bed. His next instinct was to get out of sight himself. He was fairly sure the visitors were Americans, but there was no use taking a chance. Besides, how could he explain to Americans what he, a Jew from Budapest, was doing in a castle that had once belonged—perhaps still belonged—to the sister of Hermann Goering? Thinking about it, now that he had the colonel's full explanation, Alex himself felt that the story was incredible.

The windows were really french doors, hung with heavy dark drapes and then lighter curtains. Alex placed himself between the draperies and the curtains, hoping that if the house was searched he might not be noticed. Also, from this position he could watch what was happening in the courtyard without being seen.

After several minutes he saw Colonel Weber and his aide leave the house guarded by soldiers who held revolvers in their hands. The two Germans were placed in the rear seat of one of the jeeps. Then he heard an officer shout in English, "I think this is all of them, but better make a quick search of the rest of the house."

Hobnailed boots echoed on the bare staircase leading from the floor below. Then one door after another along the hallway was thrown open and banged shut. Finally they came to his room. He was grateful that his breakfast tray had been removed and his bed made. Seeing them at close range, there was no longer any question in his mind about whether they were Americans. They were in and out of his room quickly. The suitcases under the bed had not interested them.

In a few minutes he saw the jeeps start up and drive away. As soon as they had gone, an old servant appeared and said to him, "Colonel Weber left this envelope for you, and he also said to tell you that if his car is still in the courtyard there is no reason why you should not use it."

After the man left, Alex opened the envelope. There was no letter, just five one-hundred reichsmark bank notes.

Alex was much happier in the small village hotel into which he had moved than he had been in the hunting lodge, except for his worry over the suitcases. German was his second language, so he had no trouble making himself understood among the villagers. He knew a little English, too, and if the American soldiers asked questions he could explain that he was a Jew who had escaped from a concentration camp. But if they found the suitcases and opened them, how could he explain the contents? The colonel had mentioned no figure, but judging by the weight, there must be a great fortune.

Alex worried so much that he spent most of his time in his room guarding the treasure. He even asked if he could have all three meals served in his room, but the innkeeper said that because of the shortage of help he would have to eat lunch and dinner in the dining room. Alex found that by sitting on the right side of a certain table he could see the only stairway leading to the floors above, so he asked to have this place reserved for him. If a stranger entered the hotel, he was nervous until the man left, and he irked the young chambermaid by refusing to leave his room while she made the bed. At night it was not difficult to stay half awake. Sleep was not a habit with him any more. The slightest noise at night caused him to sit up in bed, until he figured out where it came from and what it was.

He was surprised that officially no one paid any attention to him. The American Army, apparently, was too busy with more important matters than questioning the inhabitants of a small village. There was still confusion everywhere in Europe, as far as he could gather. The village gossip was that Hitler and Goebbels had committed suicide, that Goering had given himself up, and that the war in Europe was over except for scattered fighting in such places as a Baltic island and a pocket or two in Czechoslovakia.

On the fourth day after he moved into the inn, handbills signed by "The American Military Government" were distributed in the village. They stated that anyone who had received property from the Nazi party, or from any officer of the German Army, must hand over such property to occupational authorities immediately. Failure to do so would subject the offender to the death penalty.

The automobile he had driven down to the village from the hunting lodge had disappeared during the first night, so he had no concern on that score. But the two suitcases worried him. It would be ironic, after all he had lived through, if he were to be summarily executed by the liberating American Army because of two suitcases turned over to him by a German colonel.

Each day he had made inquiries about the communications situation. Mail service in and out of the village had not been resumed. There was no railroads operating in Austria except for military business, and crossing the frontier into either Switzerland or Hungary was still out of the question and probably would be for a long time. As a result of this situation, there was no way for him even to start looking for Andor or to get in contact with Joe, or Rachel, or Erno, or Arthur back in Budapest.

On the fifth day he heard that the American Military Government had intelligence headquarters at Bad Ischl, and he decided to go there with his problem. He was nervous about leaving the suitcases unguarded, but he was even more afraid of hiring someone to watch over them or putting them in the care of the innkeeper. Finally he decided to take a chance and leave them where they were, under his bed.

He hitchhiked a ride in an American military car to the health resort and found intelligence headquarters in an office in one of the large hotels. There were three Americans seated at desks as he walked in hesitantly, hat in hand. The man at the desk on the far side of the room was dark, and Alex decided he might be Jewish, but a large Aryan-type blond who sat nearest the door looked up and asked gruffly, "What do you want?"

"I have a big problem," Alex said slowly in his broken English. Then he asked hopefully, "Do you speak, maybe, some language not English?"

The American shook his head.

Stumblingly Alex tried to tell the story of his release from Mauthausen and the two suitcases. When he finished, the blond officer snapped, "That's your story. Now let's have the truth!"

As Alex was protesting that he had told the entire truth, preposterous as it might seem, the other two officers picked up their caps and started from the room.

"See you at the mess hall in a little while," the blond said to them. As soon as the door was closed, his attitude changed. Turning back to Alex, he said in Hebrew, "Now that we are alone we can talk freely."

"Why did you create such difficulties for me?" Alex asked. "Why did you make me try to talk English?"

The officer smiled. "Because of my colleagues. This is not a matter for the American Army. It's entirely a Jewish affair. We must get these suitcases into the hands of the Jewish Agency."

Alex tried to protest. "I think they should be turned over to Andor Horvath, if we can find him. Those are my orders."

"The Agency will find him. The main thing is to get the suitcases into the Agency's hands. I'll drive back to your hotel with you and take the stuff off your hands."

On the way Alex was wet with nervous perspiration, worrying whether the suitcases would still be under his bed. When he found them, he sighed with relief.

"You say there's jewelry and money in both of them?" the officer asked.

"How do I know?"

"You mean you've had these suitcases for almost a week and you haven't opened them?"

"No, why should I?"

"You're a goddamn queer man," the American said. "But I'm not. I can't wait to see what's in them. Let's have the keys." He sat on the floor as he tried first one key, then the other. At last he flung open the lid of the large suitcase.

"Great God!" he gasped as he saw the array of diamonds, sapphires, pearls, gold coins, gold bullion, and bank notes. He gave a low whistle and ran his fingers through the mass of wealth. More to himself than to Alex he added, "Holy cow, there must be a million dollars in this one suitcase! A million dollars!"

Alex just stood and stared. All he could see in the suitcase was the gold. He hated gold, the color of it, even the feel of it. He hated everything about gold. He would be glad when this American drove away with the suitcases. He'd done his duty. Tonight, maybe, for the first time in more than a year he would be able to sleep a little.

PART TWO

30

In Jerusalem, several city blocks from the King David Hotel with its European-type luxury and the Y.M.C.A. with its twin domes and tall tower, stood a four-story building in which the Ministry of Supply and Rationing of the Government of Israel had its main offices. It had been built as a de luxe hotel, but the year it opened, 1936, was the year of Arab troubles so sanguinary that they frightened away most tourists. The British then took it over to house the Agriculture Department of the Mandate government. During the Israeli War of Liberation it stood empty, but after the armistice the State of Israel commandeered it and in its high-ceilinged rooms established first one ministry, then another. Having never been remodeled, it was an unlikely place for government offices. There were white curtains on the french windows, parquet floors, crystal chandeliers, gilt and glamour. Many of the stenographers had their offices in tiled bathrooms, rooms so large that it was unnecessary to remove the plumbing fixtures to make space for the desks and filing cabinets.

Andor's office was on the second floor and faced onto a large Arab graveyard. Each time he walked through the marble lobby and into his white and gold office, he experienced a sense of exhilaration. Although it was furnished simply, in keeping with the austerity of the times, there was an air of magnificence and grace that appealed to his aesthetic sense. It was a far cry from the cluttered editorial rooms in which he had worked in his younger newspaper days and his stark office at the Sip utca Center in Budapest. Here he had many proofs of status, from the gold lettering on the door—Andor Horvath, Director of Rationing—to his name and title on stationery, documents, official orders, and press releases. Often when he had a moment for reflection, he told himself that he was well along the road to the success he had been sure would be his, here in the land of his ancestors. The first step had been the job they gave him in the Tel Aviv office of the Jewish Agency when he and Jessica first arrived. That had been six years ago.

After their reunion in Switzerland they had stayed on there for two years, first to help the people of the transport with their manifold problems. Some insisted on going back to Russian-occupied Hungary to search for relatives they had left behind, or possessions they felt they could not live without, or because they were so Hungarian at heart that they feared they could never be happy very far from the Danube. Others, enamored of Switzerland, decided to remain in this place of high mountains and the tranquillity so many of them craved. A few had friends in America who would see that they were admitted under one immigration quota or another. But the majority of the men and women Andor had picked for his transport were Zionists, and the one place they wanted to live out the rest of their lives was Palestine, where they felt they would no longer be strangers, as they were everywhere else, tolerated at best, perhaps despised.

Andor and Jessica were married quietly in Geneva and rented a two-room apartment. He had a report to write for the first, postwar Zionist Congress, which was to be held during the summer of 1946. Her only responsibility now was to make him happy, for shortly after Andor's return to Switzerland, Philip Kemeny had died one night in his sleep, his hands folded on his chest, a look of peace on his face. He had left a will, although he had almost nothing to bequeath anyone, except a small, diamond-studded gold watch that had belonged to his wife—this he left to Jessica—and a well-worn copy of his favorite Hungarian book, bound in rich brown leather, that he left to Andor. But the will was much more than a legal document; it contained a gentle essay on the potential nobility of man, contrasted with the savagery in which man often indulges. In it the aged lawyer compared the selfless work of his son-in-law with the viciousness of the exterminators. Swiss law required that the will remain on file with the cantonal authorities, but Andor had two photocopies made; one he sent to Leo, who by then was in Palestine, and the other he kept in a wallet that he always carried. Occasionally he showed it to some newly made friend, as if it were a passport or a visa; often he would read it over to himself, acquiring strength from this post-mortem praise by the only man in the world he had ever admired and respected completely, without reservation.

332

Andor spent hours every day on his report. Technically, he was not obligated to make a report to anyone, for the Budapest Rescue Committee had been his own creation, and he had acquired his position as its chairman by self-appointment, but at this Zionist Congress there would be the remnants of the leadership of world Jewry; they would be discussing the holocaust in all its phases, and it might well further the ambitious plans he had for his future to let them know the details of his negotiations and manipulations in the campaign he had waged to save Jewish lives, and so the report grew from thousands to tens of thousands of words, and eventually to more than a hundred thousand. Each night, after the supper dishes had been cleared away, Andor would sit under a floor lamp on a sofa close beside Jessica and read her what he had written that day. Occasionally when she complimented him on a phrase she liked, he would think of his secretary, Zipora, back in Budapest. He occasionally wondered what had happened to her. She had fed his ego well in those harassing days, and he would always be grateful to her, but Jessica was all Zipora had ever been, plus a great deal more. She had Sarah's ability to create beauty, even out of such mediocre surroundings as this Geneva flat. She would spend a Swiss franc or two for an armload of wild flowers and arrange them so that they made the whole apartment inviting. She would watch the sales in shops along the Rue de Confederation and buy at bargain prices pieces of bright-colored cloth she turned into covers for cushions or drapes for the windows. She was physically exciting, too. Every time she entered the room he was in, desire stirred within him.

The Zionist Congress was held at Basle, in the German-speaking part of Switzerland. In some ways it was a sad gathering; most of the old faces were missing; for the first time delegates from the New World dominated the meetings. The Horvath Report, as it was promptly labeled, was received with acclaim by most of the delegates, although there were a few critics who thought there should be a more exact accounting of the money disbursed by the Budapest Rescue Committee. Andor answered with a remark that was loudly applauded and widely quoted: "I had to choose between being a bookkeeper or a rescuer of Jews."

In the weeks following his return to Geneva he received frequent letters from Leo urging him to wind up his affairs in Switzerland and join his Zionist friends in Palestine, but it was not until 1947 that he felt free to go.

In March they went by ship from an Italian port. The night before they were due at Haifa, Andor talked to the captain and found they would be sighting land about five in the morning, so he suggested to Jessica that they leave an early call.

The morning was soft, the air still, the sky cloudless as they stood side by side at the rail staring hard at the horizon. Jessica was the one who saw it first. It began with a faint black streak where sky met sea, then it grew and grew until they could see the hill of the Carmel rising behind the city and the crescent shape of the bay.

They still had the deck to themselves, except for a few sailors, which was the way Jessica had hoped it would be. She had enjoyed the voyage because she had had her husband entirely to herself most of the time, but she knew that once they were ashore she would have to share him again with the hundreds of people who would ask his advice, make demands on his time, and continuously be stealing him away from her; so for her this last hour had a reverent quality.

"It's just like I have always imagined Naples to be!" she said ecstatically, staring across the ever-narrowing strip of water that separated them from Haifa.

Andor laughed. "They say, 'See Naples and die,' but I say, 'See Haifa and live.'"

"Do you really think we'll find peace here, Andor?"

"I'm sure of one thing," he replied. "Our people have waited for many centuries to reconstitute Israel, and the time is almost here when the dream will finally become a reality."

"But the Arabs, Andor? Will Jews and Arabs always have to fight each other? I'm so tired of fighting and suffering. I love the Hebrew word *shalom*. Do you really think we'll find peace here?"

"Eventually, yes, although we may have some rough times first."

For Jessica it was not much reassurance, but their conversation was interrupted by a faint noise that sounded like a cheer. On the dock, about a thousand feet away, they saw several hundred people. Some had binoculars to their eyes, and all were waving. Now they could make out one man in front of all the rest; a large man, waving his hat vigorously and leading the cheering.

"Leo!" Andor exclaimed.

The minute the gangplank was down, the big man came rushing aboard. How he had arranged to be granted precedence over the British customs men, the port doctor, and all the other officials was a mystery, but there he was, his skin sun-browned, his eyes sparkling, more effervescent and voluble than ever.

"Welcome to the Promised Land!" he shouted, throwing his arms around Andor's shoulders, then kissing Jessica. Before they could say anything he added, "I think you arranged it for the ship to come in at 6 A.M. just to find out if we cared enough about you to get up in the middle of the night, yah?"

Andor laughed and said yes, he had arranged it that way.

"Well, you see in a couple of minutes how many people cared!" Leo replied, then beckoned to a ship's photographer to take a picture of the three of them together, arms entwined.

After the formalities they started down the gangplank, to be greeted by prolonged cheering from the reception committee. Andor's eyes grew moist. Not everyone coming to Palestine, he told himself, got such a reception. He could see in the crowd his sister, Rena, and Sam, and the boy, Dan, only he was hardly a boy any more. Towering a little over the others was the gaunt face of Alex Peto. Andor greeted them all, one after another. In a restaurant close to the water front that Leo had taken over for the occasion there were speeches of welcome, and wine from one of the Rothschild vineyards to drink, and plenty of food. Leo was the toastmaster, and as a climax to the festivities he handed Andor a key.

"You think this is just an ordinary, everyday key, yah? Well, it isn't! This is the key to happiness, for Mr. and Mrs. Andor Horvath. All your friends here and everybody else on the train who lives in Palestine helped to pay for this key, each according to his ability. Now Moshe over there"—he paused and looked around for Moshe Hahn—"Moshe painted a big oil painting and sold it to get the money for his contribution. So with all the money, Andor, we bought an apartment for you in Tel Aviv. Why Tel Aviv? Because, Andor, this is the first Jewish city since the dispersal. All Jews, could you believe it! No *goyim!* No ghetto! This is the key to the front door, yah? You must carry your bride across the doorstep. And now we drink the toast to life. *Lechaim!*"

They all stood up and raised their glasses. Jessica's eyes were filled with tears. She leaned over and whispered to Andor. "If only Philip were alive . . ."

Leo drove them from Haifa to Tel Aviv in his own car. It was an American make, many years old, and it sounded as if it were functioning on no more than three of its four cylinders, but it was large enough to take all the Horvath baggage, and even if it rattled it moved along at a good speed. Leo was an excited guide as he pointed out historical spots. Jessica was fascinated by the Arab villages they passed. The long white cotton garments the Arabs wore, which Leo told her were called *galabiyas,* intrigued her, but she was nervous at the way they stared. "Do they really hate us?" she asked.

"Not really," Leo replied. "Of course they can cause a lot of trouble when they get worked up, but we try not to do anything to work them up."

Along with acting as guide and chauffeur, he gave them bits of news. He told them how this man had opened a law office; another had taken his family to a religious kibbutz; there had been a few deaths but many births; as for himself, he had borrowed some money and opened a shop on Jaffa Road in the New City of Jerusalem.

"Business must be good; you look prosperous," Andor remarked.

Leo chuckled, pleased with himself. When the war suddenly ended, he explained, the British Army had been left with a vast quantity of khaki shorts and bush jackets on its hands, and through a friend in London he had bought, with borrowed money, a small shipload of this surplus property at ridiculously low prices. Today almost every Jew in Palestine was wearing khaki shorts and a khaki bush jacket, because they were cheap and practical.

"Now if I could only get the Arabs out of the *galabiyas* into shorts and bush jackets, I'd be a millionaire!" he concluded.

For Andor the most important piece of news was that Leo had obtained a position for him with the Jewish Agency in Tel Aviv.

"Someday, Andor, when we get our Jewish state, the leaders of the Agency will become the leaders of the country. It's what the British call a shadow government right now. That's why I want you in the Agency. I'm going to push and pull until I make you a Prime Minister. Nothing less!"

Tel Aviv amazed them: the bustle of a big city so close to the desert; the lines of trees along Rothschild Boulevard; the sidewalk cafés giving the business section such a Parisian atmosphere; office buildings that rose to a height of six or eight stories. Tel Aviv had none of the Old World charm of Budapest, and it had no Danube, but as Leo drove them along the sea front Jessica clapped her hands together in excitement: they would be able to swim and to sun-bathe on the lovely soft-looking sand and forget the chaos of Europe.

"Yes, and you can walk to the sea front from the apartment we bought for you," Leo told them.

The building on the Street of the Palms was modern, of reinforced concrete, four stories tall, with an entranceway flush with the street.

Their apartment was on the second floor: two small rooms facing the street, a minuscule hallway, and behind it a third room, a kitchenette, and a bath. Andor knew that he should be extremely grateful. He was aware that even such modest accommodations were expensive in postwar Palestine, but he kept thinking of his old Budapest apartment and of the elegance of Váci utca. The apartment he and Sarah had had was small, but at least it had charm. This one was like something that might have been designed by a child playing house. But Jessica was radiant. It was more than she had anticipated, and after Leo left she told Andor that, given a little time and a little money, she could make it into a real home for them.

Then, having read his mind, she asked mischievously, "Did your apartment in Budapest have such a nice little balcony as we have?"

"What bothers me more," Andor confided, "is being in Tel Aviv at all. The Agency's headquarters are in Jerusalem. That's where the Mandate government is. That's where everything centers, except business. Leo should be over here; I should be in Jerusalem, instead of in a branch office in Tel Aviv."

Jessica threw her arms around his neck. "Darling, don't be so impatient. This is a wonderful start, a home and a position. If I know you, in a few months you'll be helping to run the country."

When he smiled at her, she went on, "Palestine is a place with tremendous possibilities. It's an old part of the world. Our people were here two thousand years ago. But at the same time it has all the possibilities of a frontier country. I'm sure from all you've told me that it's going to start growing fast, now that the war is over. Think of the millions of Jews who may soon be moving here. It's like America was two or three hundred years ago. This is the perfect place for you, Andor. They are going to need great men, men like you, darling."

That had been years ago. How much had happened since then. . . . At first Andor and Jessica had concerned themselves with illegal immigration—with trying to outwit the British and hide Jews who were brought secretly to the country on ships that had run the gantlet of the British Navy. They laughed and celebrated when they succeeded; they went into temporary mourning when they suffered reverses. There were the "Arab troubles," too, as they were called by old-time Palestinians, who were inured to them; for the newcomers who had hoped to find their *shalom* in the Promised Land the conflict with the Arabs seemed a dreadful thing.

Many of the people of the transport who were well enough and young enough joined one of the underground armies, happy over the feeling of dignity it gave them to be part of a real defense force that was training for the day when Israel would be re-created as a state and the Jews would once more become a people with a nationality as well as a religion. Alex Peto, who had suffered so much because he had been a Haganah leader in name only, now became a Haganah leader in fact. Others joined Irgun, the underground organization that was trying to pressure the British to give up their mandate over Palestine by acts of terrorism.

On the November day that the United Nations Assembly approved the plan to partition Palestine into an Arab and a Jewish state, Andor brought home so many friends to help celebrate that the small apartment on the Street of the Palms was full to bursting. The guests overflowed into the back room that Jessica had made into a study for Andor and into which no one was normally admitted, and out onto the balcony, from which they could see young people in the street below singing, dancing the *hora,* and running wild.

In May, Israel was declared a state, the British left, and the armies of neighboring Arab countries invaded.

After several temporary cease-fires a permanent armistice was declared, and although no peace conference had yet been held, the Israelis were devoting all their energies to trying to build the kind of country that they and Jews everywhere could be proud of. Immigrants were pouring in; housing was desperately needed; people were working ten to fifteen hours a day; there was a shortage of almost everything, except enthusiasm.

As Director of Rations, a less astute man than Andor might have made himself the most despised person in all Israel, but so far he had managed to remain liked by everyone who came into contact with him and at the same time to do his job well. This, he told himself over and over again, was step number two. At the next election he would get himself put up as one of the candidates for a seat in the Knesset. Then someday he would graduate into the Cabinet, and after that— He had never forgotten the remark Leo made the day they arrived at Haifa. He had made no comment at the time, even to Jessica, but Leo's prediction was not beyond his own conception.

He and Jessica had been happy during these years, but there were some things about this new life that troubled him. It was so different from Europe; especially from Budapest. Here the men dressed in khaki shorts—Leo's surplus army goods—or in long trousers, with a shirt open at the neck; no tie, no jacket, except maybe one of Leo's bush jackets.

Few of the women seemed to make the effort he felt they should to look chic. It was in many ways too casual a society, and he felt that the heat alone was not enough excuse.

He was also troubled by how direct people here were. There was none of the ceremonial courtesy there had been in Hungary; no preliminaries to bargaining; none of the niceties in which a polite society indulges. He remembered with anger and humiliation last week's reception for a new Minister who had been appointed to the Cabinet to fill a vacancy caused by a death. When he entered the reception room and paid his respects to the Minister and his wife, he lifted the lady's hand, said *"kezëit csókolom,"* and touched his lips lightly to her finger tips. Some of the people standing around snickered. The Minister's wife paled and murmured coldly, "Please don't ever do that again!" The Minister, as if to make up for her reprimand, shook Andor's hand heartily and darted a disapproving glance at his wife, but as Andor moved on he heard her plaintive voice behind his back: "I'm sorry if I offended him, but he should realize he's in a democratic country now, where such gestures of aristocracy have no meaning." Well, he would have to change, but it would be difficult. He had been trying for a long time now, without much success. They were so outspoken here, so blunt, and he suspected that some of his associates in the government didn't completely trust him because they felt he held things in reserve; that he didn't say everything he thought. They were right, but it had always seemed to him stupid to be too openmouthed. No good bargainer should ever show all the cards he held in his hand.

The door opened and a black-haired girl of about nineteen entered with a pile of letters, most of them already opened, which she put on Andor's desk.

They exchanged *shaloms*.

"Would you like your coffee before we begin?" she asked.

He gave her his most charming smile. "If you please, Nira."

As she hurried downstairs to the buffet on the ground floor, Andor turned his attention to the mail. Besides the official government correspondence, he received about a hundred letters a day from the public. There were all kinds but mostly requests for extra allowances, and complaints; for rationing in Israel, as everywhere else it had ever been imposed, was very unpopular. Sticking out of today's pile was a scrawled note. He picked it up curiously and read:

339

Dear Sir:

I am going to be married in twelve days. In Bombay, where I come from, for a week we have a feast of rice, curry, raisins, fruit, and other delicacies. Please tell me where and how I can get these things to eat. It may ruin my whole life if I do not have the right kind of a wedding feast . . .

Nira came in with a brass tray on which there was a cup of Turkish coffee and a glass of water with a spoon carefully balanced across the top of it. As she put the tray on his desk, she grinned, seeing the note in his hand. "She'll probably invite you to the wedding if you give her a few extra ration cards."

"Then by all means we must see that she gets them," he smiled back at her. As Nira made a note to send the extra cards, he sipped the thick, sweet coffee, then washed it down with half the glass of cold water. "Now let's get to work," he said briskly.

For an hour and a half he dictated, much of the time pacing the floor and occasionally glancing out the window at the queer-shaped stones marking the Arab graves across the street. Memoranda to the enforcement division of the division, press releases for the newspapers, notes to the Minister on how the program was going, and finally answers to a few of the letters from the public that Nira had selected as important. The rest she would answer herself.

Andor's duties were complicated and exacting: to tell people how much food they could have—and what they could not have. Yet he must manage to give them at least the minimum amount and sufficient variety for good health. He had to make the Minister realize how the public felt about the restrictions and keep him cognizant of the state of mind of the housewife standing in a queue. He had to ascertain, for instance, whether it would be better to increase the ration of marmalade or sugar. He had to convince the recalcitrant part of the population that less meat, eggs, and sugar meant more weapons for defense, tools for farms, machinery for industry, more homes for new immigrants. Many of the people still could not speak Hebrew, so despite the fact that it was the national language, Andor decided his division must speak to them in their own mother tongues. Accordingly bulletins were printed in Yiddish, Arabic, Polish, German, Russian, Hungarian, English, and several other languages. He sighed aloud, thinking of the difficulties of communication.

Nira glanced at her watch. "It's eleven o'clock. The press must be here. Will you see them in the conference room?"

340

"In a minute. Tell them to wait." As she left, he picked up a pencil and wrote a note to himself, then stuffed it into his breast pocket behind the fresh white linen handkerchief he so carefully arranged as he dressed each morning.

Every day at 11 A.M. reporters from the three leading afternoon papers appeared in the conference room down the hall from his office. No matter what they had written about him the day before, he always received them enthusiastically. His policy, he was fond of saying, was "an open door at all times for the press." As a result his public relations were very successful. Like all ambitious men, Andor made his activities serve two purposes: his employer's and his own. Since he had arrived in Israel, he had spent a great deal of time building up connections that would provide a smooth path for him to high-bracket politics, and he never forgot that the press could be an invaluable ally. He wanted power and influence at any cost, and he believed that the time was approaching for him to make a real bid for them. In Hungary he had proved he could get people's confidence; that they would listen and follow him. He was beginning to do it here. Some people's lives were closely tied to his. Many people owed their very existence to him. Surely they would be grateful.

That afternoon in the same conference room he had a meeting with the heads of the four sections of his division of the Rationing Ministry: food, industry, prices, and enforcement. The four men had myriad problems. One of them began by reiterating a theme on which he had been persistent for weeks: "I must say again, gentlemen, it is becoming increasingly important that we reduce the number of items rationed. There should be fifteen, at the most. More than that makes enforcement almost impossible."

Andor took out a package of cigarettes, removed one, tapped it several times on the back of his hand, then put it in his mouth and held it there. After several moments he removed it from between his lips, tapped one end again on the back of his hand, returned it to his mouth, lit it, and inhaled deeply, seeming to get intense pleasure as he slowly exhaled the smoke. He took the cigarette from his mouth, held it between his thumb and forefinger, and stared at it. All this had become a ritual. It gave him time to calculate the temper of his subordinates, to think out an adequate reply—a defense or an attack, as was necessary —to the problem posed. When the speaker finished, he slowly and deliberately put down the cigarette, still gazing at it, then finally turned his attention to the four waiting men.

"There seems to be a misunderstanding of what the purpose of this department is," he began quietly, "and it is past time that it should be cleared up. It is not our duty to adjust rationing policies to the tastes of the people. It is our job to decide what it is necessary to ration, for the welfare of the entire nation, and then to *persuade* the people—or force them, if that is the only way—to obey the rules we lay down.

"Apropos of persuasion, I want to say we are not making our plans interesting enough to the press. They have given us a lot of publicity, most of it favorable, but I want to see their interest increase. The enthusiasm of the press is the most effective way for us to put over our program with the public."

Another department head brought up the difficulty with the Yemenites. These people from the Arabian Peninsula were not accustomed to a European diet, so it was futile to give them a ration of such items as eggs and margarine, which they were not used to eating, he said. It might be all right in principle to try to force them to adopt a European diet this way, but what they did was to sell the ration tickets they neither needed nor wanted and use the money to buy *arak,* an alcoholic drink they liked. The problem was becoming acute, and something had to be done about it soon.

Thus the discussion continued until two-thirty o'clock, which was the end of the working day for most government offices. By that time the clerks and stenographers, as well as the officials, had worked seven hours, having started at 7:30 A.M. and taken no lunch hour. Andor, still possessed by many of his old habits, could not bring himself to begin work before nine-thirty, but at two-thirty, when the staff conferences ended, he would go back to his office and usually work until eight or nine at night. This was his schedule in Jerusalem four days a week, Sunday through Wednesday. By special allocation he had a small gray car, and each Wednesday night he drove the forty-five miles to Tel Aviv, then on Thursday and Friday he worked in the division's branch office at Sarona, the former German Templar development on the edge of Tel Aviv. On Saturday he celebrated the Sabbath by spending the entire day with Jessica. The half week in Tel Aviv was always a happy time. The change from the Judean hills to the seashore was stimulating. More important, it was exciting to have this weekly reunion with Jessica. The enforced separation for four days out of each seven made their desire for each other all the more intense. There was always so much to talk about on Wednesday nights; small household affairs, gossip Jessica had heard in Tel Aviv, news from Budapest, and then all the important matters Andor would want to discuss—the raw material of his hopes and ambitions. Jessica marveled at the way ideas gushed out of him in a continuous flow. When he occasionally dwelled upon the frustrations of political life in the capital, she gave him understanding, encouragement, and inspiration. Each Sunday, his tension eased by the gentle affection and the passion she lavished on him, and his ego bolstered by having been able to talk freely of his problems and his triumphs, he returned to Jerusalem charged with fresh enthusiasm, confident that his shrewdness and strength would catapult him into the position of prominence he deserved among the leaders of the new nation.

His days and nights in Jerusalem were crammed with work. Since it was impractical to drive to Tel Aviv each night, he decided to rent a room in the capital. Leo lived with his wife and two daughters in what was for this time and place a spacious apartment on Gaza Street, and they had a spare room, which Andor quickly accepted when Leo offered it to him, for he was not a man who could live alone pleasurably; he had discovered this after Sarah's death. He needed an audience, preferably an appreciative one. His old friends Leo and Vera, and especially the two girls, Hannah, now seventeen, and Deborah, nine, were delighted to provide it for him.

Vera was a plump, motherly woman, patient and gentle. She was used to the antics of her ebullient husband, and the addition of Andor's relatively calm presence to her household was welcome. He kept Leo busy. Usually he arrived at nine or nine-thirty in the evening. Vera would serve him dinner in the small dining alcove off the kitchen, while Leo sat and listened to him talk about the problems of the day. Then both men would have coffee in the living room and before long would be deep in one of their endless discussions on the nature of justice, or why the Germans lost the war, or some other conundrum. When Andor returned from the office early, the girls would still be up and usually pounced on him gleefully as he entered. He gave them the affection he might have lavished on children of his own, and they gave him in return both love and respect. With them he talked about music, art, and history, imparting to them some of his own wonder and fascination at the magnitude of the universe and the importance of man's role in it. Occasionally, when Deborah pestered, he would play a game of cards with her and watch with feigned surprise as she discovered triumphantly that she had won. All the while Hannah would sit in ill-disguised impatience, waiting for Debbie to be sent to bed so she could have her idol all to herself. Then she would bring up some controversial question, such as she had overheard her father discuss with him. One night, her thin, eager face bright with excitement, she began to talk about the position of women in Israel and how different it was from what her mother had told her about women in Hungary and what she had read in books.

"That's true," Andor said. "Women are really independent here. They are equal citizens with men, and they are equal in everyday life, too. However"—he paused—"I'm not sure this is an entirely good thing. Giving woman equal power can be dangerous." He grinned wryly as he saw her bristle and deliberately went on teasing her. "You know, women are great intriguers. Much more than men."

"They are not!" Hannah's hurt showed in her face.

"Indeed they are. Do you know the famous story of Medea? She was an ancient sorceress who intrigued with a stranger, Jason, to steal the Golden Fleece from her father, the King of Colchis, and then ran away with him to Corinth. When he tired of her and left her for the Princess of Corinth, she practiced her sorcery again. She sent a fine gossamer robe with beautiful embroidery as a present to the princess. When the girl put it on, it burst into flames and she was burned to death before Jason's eyes." He shrugged. "That's only one story. There are many others. Lucrezia Borgia, Catherine the Great of Russia—"

"I don't know about them," Hannah cried, "but I do know that men are more treacherous than women could possibly be. I know about Laban, who fooled Jacob by giving him his daughter Leah at night in marriage, instead of Rachel, whom Jacob loved. And Absalom, who invited his brother Amnon to a feast so he could have him murdered. When Amnon was drinking wine with the rest of his half brothers, Absalom ordered the servants to kill him. That was the same Absalom who sent spies into all the tribes and took up arms against his own father, David the King. And these things are told in the Scriptures, which are holy and are older than any of your silly stories." Her voice was shrill, but she was plainly trying to hold back angry tears of disappointment. In her innocence she had taken Andor's words to apply to herself, and the thought was intolerable.

Realizing this, Andor felt a surge of compassion. "You are right, of course, my dear Hannah," he said as if she had brought some entirely new concept to his mind. He went over to her and patted her head gently. "You have taught *me* something tonight. I had forgotten the Holy Scriptures."

She looked up at him, her gray eyes glistening, as if she were a flower and he were the sun. In that moment he remembered Sarah. Abruptly he took the child's hand and raised her from the chair. "Come, you must go to bed. It's getting late. Tomorrow we will talk again."

She nodded and reached up to kiss him on the cheek.

After she had left, Vera and Leo came into the dining alcove and sat down opposite him.

"You heard?" he asked anxiously.

"Of course," they answered together. Vera took a pair of socks that needed mending out of her sewing bag. "Don't let it disturb you," she said placidly. "Girls are very emotional at her age. They like to dramatize everything. She loved the whole scene."

"I had forgotten how vulnerable the young are," Andor said almost to himself, still remembering Sarah.

"Vulnerable they are, because they are ignorant," Leo agreed. "That's why they are surprised and upset by new circumstances. But you and I"—he shook his head wearily—"we are no longer young, but we are still vulnerable, not because we are ignorant, but because we know too much."

Andor looked at him sharply, startled to hear such an admission from Leo. He got up and went to the little card table by the window. "I think we need some relaxation. How about a game of pinochle?"

"Why not? Come and play, Vera," he said to his wife. "Leave the socks. Tomorrow I'll just wear another hole, so why bother?"

31

Rudy Tabor sat hunched over the desk in his small white-washed study, his pudgy fingers pecking rapidly at the keys of an old German portable typewriter. He was writing his third novel since coming to Tel Aviv. Like the others, it was about war and humanity; he hoped it would be as successful. The first two had received acclaim all over western Europe. To some of his friends it had seemed strange that a man almost sixty should begin a new career, but when he and his wife came to Israel he decided not to go back into the newspaper business, for there were crucial things about life he wanted to say, unhampered by the restrictions and deadlines imposed by a daily newspaper. When his wife died the following spring, he was even more certain he had taken the right course. In his simple study with its wealth of books he had already collected here in Israel, he could be at peace; he was serene, if not happy. It was his great pleasure to watch the younger people creating a new nation. In the cities they were building factories and office buildings, shops and hotels, while the desert areas, barren for so long, were being forced by brave and determined men and women to turn green and fruitful again, as they had been so many hundreds of years ago.

Last summer the Chief of Staff of the Army had summoned him to his office. There were four thousand Hungarians serving then in the Israeli Army, the general said, and he and his officers needed some way to communicate with them until they learned Hebrew; some of his subordinates thought a Hungarian-language daily newspaper was the answer. A single sheet would be sufficient, mimeographed. He had summoned Mr. Tabor because, after all, he was president of the Hungarian Settlers' Society and a former newspaper publisher, an ideal combination; he was a singularly appropriate man for the job. Would Mr. Tabor undertake it, on behalf of his Hungarian friends and the new nation?

As the young general spoke, all at once Rudy felt old and tired. But how could he say no? Of course he would do it, he told the general. So began his emergence out of a semiretreat from the world. At first his life changed very little. His routine was the same except for the telephone contacts he made, mostly with government and army officials who gave him the bulletins they wished him to use. In the cool of the early morning he would work on his novel. About noon he prepared the material for the little mimeographed paper, and shortly afterward a messenger arrived to pick it up. Later in the afternoon an elderly immigrant woman from Hungary came to clean the apartment and he went for a walk, to see what was new, stopping for coffee in one of the sidewalk cafés along Dizengoff Street, where he would always find some of his former compatriots. Often his route was down Allenby Road with its hundreds of attractive shop windows. The bookstores especially attracted him, for almost every day there were new publications either from the presses of Israeli publishers or from Europe and America. Occasionally he walked down to the seashore and stood looking out over the Mediterranean. For him the sea had paradoxical powers; it was calming and stimulating, both at the same time. It gave a man perspective, staring out over that vast body of water, when one thought of how many different civilizations the Mediterranean had seen come and go and how many different ways of life were followed right now by nations of people living along its shores—the descendants of the ancient Greeks and Romans, Slavs, Arabs, Jews, Spaniards and their colonial people—there was no other sea on earth like it. Occasionally with a friend who had a car he would visit a kibbutz or drive through the Judean hills. It was a quiet life, and it suited him now. When the sun began to go down, he would return to the typewriter until the housekeeper announced that his supper was ready.

This night, as she stood in the doorway saying she was ready to serve him, he replied, "I'll be there in less than two minutes." He finished the sentence he was typing and got up. Just then the telephone rang. He reached over the desk and picked up the receiver.

"Andor!" he said happily. ". . . Yes, I'll be delighted to see you. How about eight o'clock? . . . Yes, I'll be there."

At ten minutes to eight he left his apartment on Amsterdam Street and walked leisurely north to the Horvaths', enjoying the cool evening breeze from the sea. It was refreshing after the heat of the afternoon.

"How good to see you, Rudy!" Andor pumped his hand enthusiastically. Because of the time he spent in Jerusalem, he did not see his shrewd, tough old acquaintance as much as he would have liked.

Jessica kissed him lightly on the cheek. "Ah," Rudy said, his eyes twinkling, "that is what I really came for."

Andor led him to the sofa, and Jessica moved quietly out of the room. "Rudy," he began tentatively, "I need your help."

The older man's grin was good-naturedly mocking. "Since when? In Budapest it was always the other way around."

"Since now, Rudy. I'm serious."

"All right. I'll be serious, too. What's your problem?" He adjusted his bulk to a more comfortable position.

"I want you to do for all the Hungarian immigrants what you've been doing for those in the Army. A little more. We need a daily Hungarian-language paper, not just a mimeographed sheet."

"Impossible!" Rudy shook his head emphatically. "I'm too old to begin such a business again." He started to rise.

"Please don't close your mind before you hear me out." Andor laid a restraining hand on his friend's arm. "You know that less than a third of our former compatriots can understand Hebrew. They are learning, but it takes time, especially for the older ones. In the meantime my office and the other government departments have no way to reach them; we can't make them understand what we are doing and why. We need their co-operation for their own sake as well as ours. Don't turn me down. You're the only one who can do it."

Rudy threw up his hands. "Even if I were willing to take on such a heavy burden, there are a thousand problems. I would need linotype machines and a steady supply of paper—"

"I'll get them for you, and everything else you'll need."

Rudy raised his eyebrows skeptically.

"I promise."

"Also, I will need journalists, men who can make the paper lively and interesting enough so people will buy it and pay attention to what it says."

Andor felt a small spurt of encouragement as Rudy changed the "would" to "will." Aloud he said, "Come now, you know there are dozens of competent Zionist intellectuals among the Hungarians here."

For several moments Rudy was silent, speculatively running his heavy forefinger over his lips, his small eyes screwed up in concentration. Finally he said, "I'll do it, on one condition: that *you* write me three articles a week."

It was Andor's turn to be taken aback, but his hesitation was brief. "Signed?" he asked.

"Of course, signed! You're a good journalist, Andor. You are also Director of Rationing, and we can use the prestige of that office. It won't do you any harm personally, either. But I'm sure you thought of that." He glanced out of the corner of his eye at his friend, and they both smiled knowingly.

"It occurred to me," Andor admitted.

Rudy chuckled and slapped him on the back. "You're going to be a great politician here in Israel."

Jessica came in with a tray of refreshments. "You are just in time," Rudy said to her. "Your husband and I have an important announcement to make. We are going to set up a Hungarian-language newspaper. I shall be the publisher, he the star columnist."

She looked from one beaming face to the other. "You are both to be congratulated," she said tactfully.

From the decanter on the tray Andor poured sweet Israeli wine into three glasses. "To the success of our new venture!" he said as they put the glasses to their lips.

After Rudy had left, Andor swept Jessica into his arms. "It's another step toward the Cabinet, darling," he said happily, pressing her closer to him. Suddenly he stood stock-still, then tilted her head so that her

sapphire eyes looked into his. "Have I told you today that I love you?"
She shook her head playfully.

"Then I tell you now, I love you very much."

She ran her fingers lightly over his cheekbones, then back to the
nape of his neck, drawing his head down so that his lips met hers.

Within a month the Hungarian *Gazette* was being published again. It
was small compared to the old Budapest journal, and it was on poor-
quality paper, but the Hungarian population of Israel welcomed it
eagerly. Andor, delighted at the reception of his articles, worked diligently to keep them both interesting and provocative, thus increasing
his popularity as well as his prestige. Now, on the nights when he was in
Jerusalem, he would eat his dinner at nine or nine-thirty and then spend
several hours writing. If Deborah and Hannah pleaded, he would talk
or play cards with them until their bedtime. On such nights he wouldn't
get to sleep until two or three in the morning. It was an exhausting schedule, one result of which was that he developed the ability to sleep almost
anywhere and in any position as soon as he relaxed. Sometimes Vera
found him in the chair next to Deborah's bed, a storybook on his chest,
both he and the child fast asleep. But there was a more gratifying result.
Other newspapers and many of the magazines began to ask him to con-
tribute articles, and soon his opinions on everything from the cooking-
oil ration to comparative political philosophies were being read not
only by the Hungarian colony but by subscribers to a wide variety of
publications.

Near the end of the year he was elected president of the Hungarian
Settlers' Society, to succeed Rudy Tabor, who had now served the maximum number of terms permitted by the constitution. There was an
initiation ceremony in the ballroom of the Sharon Hotel at Herzliya, a
sea-coast resort just north of Tel Aviv. Andor and Jessica were on the
dais with Rudy, Leo and Vera, and other officers of the society and
their wives. Below them at a sea of tables covered with white linen cloths
and decorated with masses of flowers sat three hundred members of the
society, with their guests, including Andor's sister, Rena, and her husband, Sam. All were dressed in their best clothes, eagerly anticipating
the entertainment that was to follow the swearing-in. Andor stood up
modestly, and Rudy conferred the title on him to the applause of the
audience and the flashing of photographers' bulbs. As soon as the ceremony was concluded, a covey of newspaper reporters crowded around
the dais, besieging Andor with questions. Rudy rapped on a glass for

quiet. "One question at a time, gentlemen," he pleaded. Directly in front of him was a spare, sallow-complexioned man in his early forties, with an impatient manner. "You first," Rudy said, pointing to him.

The man turned to Andor, fixing him with a gaunt-eyed stare. "What did you do to save Hungarian Jews, Mr. Horvath?" His voice became shrill. "Why did you save only the important ones?"

The people at the tables had begun to talk among themselves, but the shrill voice asking the blunt questions silenced them all as they waited for the answers. An elderly man at a table near the rear of the room stood up and shouted, "Yes, what did you do to save them?" Another voice screamed, "Get off the stage, Horvath!" Andor's defenders tried to shout them down. It was several minutes before Leo and Rudy, with the help of some of the hotel staff, managed to usher the hecklers out of the room and restore order.

The waiters began serving dinner, and soon most of the Hungarian immigrants were eating and talking and laughing as if nothing extraordinary had happened. Some, like Leo, dismissed the episode with a shrug, saying, "Always there are a few who aren't happy unless they make trouble." To Rena and Sam, who had rushed up to the dais, Leo said, "Please go back to your places. Everything is okay."

But Andor was pale, and he remained exceptionally quiet during the rest of the evening. Once Jessica put her hand on his arm comfortingly, but he seemed not to notice, so she decided it was better to leave him alone. She was sure that eventually he would put the whole episode in its proper perspective. Nevertheless, as they drove Rudy home later, he continued to be silent and preoccupied, looking intently at the road ahead. The older man sat in the back seat, distressed. He was certain, as Jessica was, that proverbs and platitudes wouldn't help. They were nearing Amsterdam Street when Andor, still staring straight ahead, asked him, "Who was the reporter who started all the trouble?"

"His name is Chorin, László Chorin. From Szeged, I think."

"Where does he work?" As he asked the question, Andor brought the car to a halt at the curb, turned in his seat, and faced Rudy.

"On the Tel Aviv *Morning News*. He's new." Rudy made a disparaging gesture with his hand. "Oh, Andor, forget it! He's probably just an ambitious man trying to draw attention to himself by starting a controversy. You must get used to the fact that as your political position gets more important you'll be attacked by all kinds of cranks and unscrupulous people."

"I know that, and I can deal with Chorin and his kind. But it was the others . . ." His voice trailed away until it was almost inaudible. "How ungrateful they are for all I tried to do. Every time I walked into an SS office I wondered if I would come out the door standing up—if I would come out alive."

"Since when do you expect gratitude from people?" Rudy barked.

Andor grinned ruefully. "You think I'm a fool." It was not a question but a statement. "Perhaps you're right. But I can't help the way I feel."

Rudy shook his head sadly. "I know, and I'm sorry, because you will hurt yourself." He kissed Jessica on the cheek and got out of the car. *"Shalom,"* he said, and disappeared into the building.

The following day was Monday, and Andor was in Jerusalem. All the newspapers that afternoon printed some version of the previous night's incident at the ceremony; those supporting one or another of the parties making up the government coalition were sympathetic. The political opposition was not, among them the Tel Aviv *Morning News*. Besides a news story describing the disturbance at the meeting there was an article on the editorial page signed by László Chorin, boldly titled, "The Quisling," which said in part:

> Last night a traitor among us was given a post of honor. When this reporter and a few others peacefully attempted to question the justice of this act, they were abruptly ejected from the premises. . . .

Andor's hand shook with anger as he laid down the paper. He was so incensed that he failed to see Nira standing beside his desk until she spoke.

"The Minister wants to see you in his office. Right now."

He looked up and saw a strange expression on her face. Who knew what she had heard? How eager everyone was to pass on bad news, he thought bitterly. "Do you know who I was in Hungary, Nira?" he asked quietly.

"I heard you were a big Zionist," she said tentatively.

"So I was. But that's only a small part of the story. You don't really know anything about me. These"—he slapped the paper containing Chorin's article with the back of his hand—"are all lies," he said, and walked hurriedly out of the office.

"I don't believe them, Mr. Horvath; really I don't," she murmured at his retreating figure, but he didn't hear.

The Minister of Supply and Rationing, along with other key figures in the government, had decided that the wisest course would be to ignore the article. They felt the language was so unrestrained and the charges so obviously untrue that no one would take them seriously. In their view either Chorin was a psychopath or he was being used by someone in an attempt to embarrass the government. Whichever it was, it was better to ignore him. Accordingly the Minister was instructed to urge Andor not to use his column in the Hungarian *Gazette* to refute the charges or to make any counterattack, despite his justifiable anger.

"Of course the charges are all fabrications," the Minister said. "If we thought for a minute they were true—" He left the sentence unfinished, but his queer smile and the gesture of his hand indicated that it would probably be the end of Andor's political career. After a pause he added, "We must act with restraint. If we say nothing, I am sure the matter will be dropped and forgotten."

But this tactic did not succeed. Week after week Chorin repeated his charges, embellishing them with anecdotes about Andor and various Nazi personalities. At the same time a whispering campaign began; its origin was nebulous, but its effect was like a great silken web slowly woven to form a soft but inescapable trap. Even Andor's friends began to ask why he did nothing about Chorin. Then one day the following article appeared in the Tel Aviv *Morning News* under Chorin's name:

Andor Horvath collaborated with the Nazis, willfully preparing the ground for the mass murder of Hungarian Jewry. He acted with complete awareness of the consequences of his behavior. He deliberately sacrificed the mass of Hungarian Jewry to save a group of less than 1,700 friends and relatives on the Bergen-Belsen rescue train. Horvath poses as the savior of Hungarian Jews, but out of the country's 800,000 Jews, 650,000 were killed in a systematic program of annihilation carried out during the final period of World War II, when the Germans were in desperate straits. . . . Nevertheless, Horvath, of all the Hungarian Jewish leaders, remained immutably loyal to the "German line," despite its dreadful consequences. . . .

Is it conceivable that 500,000 people could have been taken to Auschwitz, as they were, if they had not been deluded? If they had known, they would have attacked their would-be murderers with whatever weapons they could find, even their hands, before they were forced into the gas chambers. Yet we are told that almost half a million went to their death like sheep to the slaughter. Why?

During the war Andor Horvath was the leader of the Budapest Rescue Committee, the most powerful Jewish organization in Hungary, which was supported by funds from Jewish organizations the world over. . . . When the deportations were going full speed, he had almost daily contact with Otto Wedemeyer, the Nazi colonel in charge of the Judenkommando. . . . The Nazis took him personally, and his friends, under their protection during the deportations. Despite the fact that he was a Jew, they let him travel freely through Germany during the crucial months near the end of the war.

Though he knew well the operations of the German Army and its officers, he was not sent to an extermination camp, like his less fortunate brothers. Why? The answer is simple: so he could provide his Nazi friends with an alibi after the war. And that is exactly what he did. After the war he deliberately saved a notorious war criminal, Colonel Franz Weber, head of the SS Economic Division and close associate of Heinrich Himmler.

But why should a Jew, even this one, save a Nazi *after* the war? It is reasonable to ask. The answer: because this Jew shared a guilty secret with the German Weber. As head of the Economic Division of the SS in Budapest, Weber forced money from Jews at every opportunity. He was the receiver of monies paid for the rescue of the Bergen-Belsen hostages. . . . Horvath was his partner in this looting, and shared the profits. . . .

Mr. Horvath is now a respected and prominent member of the government of the people for whom he showed so little compassion, whose suffering, unequaled anywhere in the world by any other people, he callously disregarded to gain his own ends. Are we to accept this state of affairs blindly, docilely, as our ill-starred dead brethren in Hungary once accepted their fate? If we do, we will follow a new path to disaster in this young nation. . . .

Two days later Chorin wrote:

The silence from Mr. Horvath and his associates in the government is ominous. They hope that we will forget . . . in the hustle and bustle of everyday life, in our strenuous efforts to cope with the shortages and inconveniences, the long workdays, the constant problems of food and shelter and military defense as Israel grows, but *they are mistaken; we will not forget!*

"I've had enough," Andor said aloud to himself as he read this new attack. He threw the paper on the desk and walked down the hall, past the astounded secretary of the Minister in the outer office, and into the presence of the Minister himself.

"The time has come to do something," he cried.

The Minister raised his eyebrows slightly.

"I can no longer sit still—"

"But you can at least sit down."

Andor sat on the edge of the nearest chair. "Did you see today's *Morning News?*"

"Of course."

"Then you must agree that is is necessary for me to take some action." Without waiting for a reply he rushed on: "I have tried to be patient, but I cannot continue to let this diabolical man damage my career—or the reputation of the party," he added hastily.

The Minister smiled thinly. "What do you have in mind?"

"I want to sue him. For libel. For damages. Catch him in his lies under oath."

The Minister rubbed his chin reflectively. "Yes, the time certainly has come for action, but a lawsuit . . . You know that lawyers have a saying, 'If someone calls your sister a prostitute, don't argue with him because by the time you have proved that you don't even have a sister, it's too late—the whole world knows your sister is a prostitute.'"

Andor laughed grimly. "I'm even worse off than you suggest. I *have* a sister." His expression became more serious. "I'm aware that I will open myself to attack and injury, like everyone else who brings charges into a courtroom, but I'm sure that I have more to lose by inaction than action. It may sound naïve, but I believe that in a court justice will prevail."

"You realize, of course, that if you file suit you will have to resign for the duration of the court proceedings, as much as I will hate to lose you."

"Yes, and that troubles me."

The Minister sighed. "You can think of no better way to fight Chorin than a suit for damages?"

Andor shifted uneasily in his chair. "Yes," he said slowly, "I can."

"Well, what is it? Say it. You know you can be frank with me."

"A better way would be for the government prosecutor to instigate a *criminal* libel action against Chorin."

The Minister's calm face took on a look of surprise.

Andor went on: "This would strengthen my position and make it clear that the government will not tolerate a deliberate smearing of any of its agencies."

The Minister weighed Andor's suggestion silently. Finally he said, "It will have to be given very careful consideration. All the possible repercussions will have to be calculated."

354

32

The Trial: First Day

"The case of the State of Israel against László Chorin . . .
Violation of Paragraph 201 (1) of the Criminal Law ordinance . . ."
intoned the squat little clerk with the black mustache, his voice rever-
berating in the high-ceilinged room so that it almost drowned out the
sounds of the shifting, murmuring spectators.

It was the morning after the Passover holiday. The courtroom was
full. Most of the spectators were friends of the accused and of the com-
plaining witness, but there were also many merely curious men and
women, drawn here by the knowledge that this was a case concerning
the holocaust in Europe and therefore of interest because it had connection with their own experience. No photographers were allowed inside the courtroom, but there were perhaps a dozen reporters with pads
and sharpened pencils listening intently for sensations.

The Jerusalem District Courtroom was not large, but like most court-
rooms, it had a very high ceiling, beneath which the people who played
out their tragic or comic roles seemed insignificant, dwarfed in the vast
space above their heads. There were eight sets of french windows on
three sides of the room, and in the center of the fourth side a platform
on which was the judge's bench and next to it the witness box. The
entire room was paneled in dark wood to a height of eight feet. Above
that the walls were of white plaster. From the whitewashed ceiling hung
two fans with enormous blades. When the press of people began to
raise the temperature, the fans were turned on. The soft whir of the
slowly turning blades provided an accompaniment to the activity in the
courtroom.

Beneath the fans hung several lamps on metal chains that were
lighted despite the glare of sunlight that came through the east windows.
At the rear of the room were five rows of wooden benches for spectators.
Between them and the judge's dais were two long tables and two benches
for opposing lawyers and their clients. Slightly above them, but below
the judge, was a small platform for the court stenographer and the other
attendants. On this platform stood an old-fashioned kerosene stove. The
west windows looked out onto a court shaded by evergreen and euca-
lyptus trees.

Andor, sitting at the prosecution's table, was confident and at ease as the preliminary legal proceedings got under way. There was no doubt in his mind that Chorin was guilty of malicious slander and would quickly be proved guilty. Alongside him, Reuven Weiss, the Attorney General, bent over some papers, occasionally turning one slowly. He was of medium build, with receding brown hair, about forty-five, a refugee from Germany; a man of enormous inner strength and an unfailing manner of outer equanimity.

At the defense table Chorin extracted a pill from a small white box and signaled to an attendant for a glass of water. To Andor he looked even gaunter than he had the night at the Herzliya hotel. His skin was pallid, and his hands trembled as he grasped the glass that was handed to him and lifted it to his lips. Just behind him, in the first row of spectators, sat his wife, a dark, vibrant woman in her early forties who leaned forward every few minutes and said something to which Chorin nodded affirmatively. Once, seeing drops of perspiration on his forehead, she gave him a handkerchief. Dutifully he wiped his face and returned the handkerchief to her, at the same time brushing her renewed attentions aside with a brusque wave of his hand. Then he turned and murmured something to his lawyer, whose glance as he looked up from his notes inadvertently met Andor's. For the first time Andor felt a twinge of apprehension as he stared into the clear gray eyes of the defense attorney.

The young lawyer met his gaze for a long moment, then, as if having satisfied himself, turned his attention to what Chorin was saying. Andor continued to watch the strong, rather stocky figure, as if in the scrutiny he might learn something useful about him. Not much was known about Yaacov Ben-Nathan, except that he was a *sabra,* born in Israel; that he had been a brilliant student at the university, a member of the disbanded terrorist Irgun Zwei Leumi, and had handled only a few cases before this one, none of great public interest. It remained to be seen what kind of opponent he would be. Andor shrugged and glanced back at Chorin, who seemed about to collapse. It was difficult to reconcile the vicious words in the *Morning News* with the author. The contrast puzzled Andor but didn't worry him.

In fact, nothing at this point really worried him. Even the selection of the judge who would decide the case was to his liking. In contrast to Yaacov Ben-Nathan, Judge Daniel Lehmann was widely known. He had been born in Austria, had survived Mauthausen, and had been one of the ablest criminal lawyers in the new country before his appointment to the bench. He had an awesome presence. Looking up at the tall, black-robed figure, Andor was impressed by the abundant wayward blond hair, one lock of which hung over his right temple, the finely drawn light brows that shadowed the piercing blue eyes, the straight, rather too long nose, the even, relaxed mouth that never seemed to smile, and the powerful chin.

The big mahogany wall clock to Andor's right chimed ten o'clock as Weiss rose to make his opening statement. He described the four charges against Chorin: that he had accused Andor Horvath of (1) preparing the ground for the mass murder of Hungarian Jewry, (2) collaborating with the Germans, (3) testifying at the Nuremberg Tribunal to save a Nazi war criminal, and (4) sharing Jewish wealth with a Nazi.

Ben-Nathan's opening statement was a fervently delivered declaration that all the accusations his client had made in print against Andor Horvath would be proved, and that Chorin had acted in good faith, without malice, and in the interest of all his people in his attempt to obtain justice for those who had survived and retribution for those who had perished.

When he had finished, Judge Lehmann addressed Weiss. "Is the state ready to proceed?"

The Attorney General stood. "We are ready, your honor."

"Call your first witness."

"I call Andor Horvath."

Andor approached the witness box, was sworn in, and stood complacently, ready to testify.

After opening questions that established Andor's identity and position in the government, Weiss went back to the beginning. "You were the chairman of the Budapest Rescue Committee in Hungary during the latter part of World War II, Mr. Horvath?"

"I was."

"Will you tell the court the nature of this organization and how it was formed, please?"

"In the late spring of 1941 some of my friends and I heard rumors that in addition to the fighting on several fronts there was another war going on, a secret war against the Jews which was never mentioned in reports of the German Army that we received in Budapest. In the Hungarian Army there were some anti-Nazi officers who told us about the start of the mass murder of Jews. In August we heard that thirty thousand so-called Polish Jews had been expelled from Hungary. Two months later we learned that most of them had been shot to death. So we called a meeting of Zionist leaders and of former Hungarian Jewish representatives in the Parliament. I gave them all the information we had. The Zionists present proposed formation of a secret defense organization that would be ready to resist any attempt to exterminate Hungarian Jews. The non-Zionist leaders rejected the entire idea. They didn't believe in the extermination story. They said my figures were exaggerated. They said Hungarian Jews should do nothing illegal. They were sure Prince Regent Horthy could handle the situation and that he wouldn't abandon our people to the Germans.

"In 1942 the death camps of Auschwitz and Treblinka were established. Jewish refugees from Poland and Slovakia began to arrive in Hungary, and their presence created a great many problems—food, shelter, and means of livelihood. A small group of Zionist leaders—I was one of them—decided to help these people. We collected money, forged papers to help them move freely, and found work for them. Official Jewish bodies refused to give us any money, saying the existence of almost a million Hungarian Jews shouldn't be endangered by so small a number of refugees. Even the Palestine Immigration Office of the Jewish Agency in Budapest refused to give us any of the money it received."

Judge Lehmann, who had been listening with calm and sympathetic attention, furrowed his light brows and leaned forward. "Mr. Horvath, are you saying that the Palestine Immigration Office rejected your requests for funds to help refugees?" There was a note of incredulity in his voice.

"Yes, your honor."

"Did the Palestine Office at any time assist you with funds when the situation in Hungary became desperate?"

"No, it did not."

Lehmann's pale brows shot up in surprise. Then he leaned back again. "Go on with your story, please."

"One of our members, Erno Gábor, succeeded in sending a letter from me to the Jewish Agency in Istanbul with a report of the situation in Budapest and the rest of eastern Europe, and a request for help. As a result, the Agency established a committee in Istanbul and we kept in fairly regular contact almost until the end of the war. The committee answered our appeal for help by sending us at first a small sum of money, then when we confirmed that it had been received, even larger sums. Our group expanded. In January 1943 we decided to establish in a formal, though illegal, way an Assistance and Rescue Committee in

Budapest. I was made chairman, Erno Gábor was deputy chairman; the three other main roles were given to Arthur Gruen, Alex Peto, and Joseph Nagel. Secretary Teller handled problems concerning women and children. Our aims were to help Jews who had already arrived in Budapest from Poland and Slovakia and to rescue from those countries Jews who were in danger of losing their lives. Representatives of the refugees from Poland and Slovakia joined the Committee, and representatives of the chalutzim. With the money we now received we organized a band of smugglers whom we sent to Poland to look for Jews and bring them to Hungary, and we organized a network of people inside Hungary who helped with their transportation after they crossed our frontier."

In the afternoon Andor took the stand again and at Weiss's direction described his activities after the Germans occupied Hungary. He explained his negotiations with Captain Erich von Klaussen, occasionally at Weiss's prompting pointing out the precarious position in which he and his Committee had placed themselves in these dealings. From the bench Judge Lehmann continued to listen in respectful sympathy.

The crowded courtroom grew still warmer as the day lengthened, and the slow whirring of the fan blades created a drowsy atmosphere. Even Chorin seemed in torpor most of the time. Occasionally he removed another white pill from the little box and swallowed it. For a while he peered nervously at Andor in the witness box, frequently whispering in an agitated manner to Ben-Nathan, whose only reply was either a negative shake of the head or a noncommittal shrug. Not once did the attorney for the defense take his eyes from Andor, even when Chorin was talking to him. He absorbed every intonation, every gesture, every change of posture. Nothing escaped him.

By four o'clock Andor had finished the story of Wedemeyer's offer to release a million Jews in exchange for ten thousand trucks, and at this appropriate point court was adjourned.

As he and Jessica left the room with Weiss, people elbowed each other to shake his hand. In the courtyard photographers jostled the crowd out of the way so they could take pictures of the principals, especially Andor. He smiled and waved when they asked him to, but to the reporters' persistent questions he made no reply. Taking Jessica's arm and waving a final time, he helped her into the car with Weiss and they drove off.

33

The Trial: Second Day

The next morning Andor resumed his testimony. In well-modulated diplomatic language he repeated the story of Wedemeyer's offer to free a hundred Jews for each truck the Germans received, of his own attempt to persuade the Germans to accept money instead, of Erno Gábor's trip to Istanbul, the haggling with Wedemeyer, the increased persecution of the Jews, and the Committee's appeal to Wedemeyer to give some evidence of good will, which resulted in the Bergen-Belsen train.

While Ben-Nathan's cold gray eyes continued to study him, a young assistant for the defense sat beside Ben-Nathan taking abundant notes.

By the end of the day Andor had explained that in August 1944 he had told Wedemeyer the United Relief Organization was willing to deposit twenty million Swiss francs in a Swiss bank, to be made available to the Germans if they carried out the Istanbul agreement. An advance of five million francs was immediately put on deposit. With a deprecating smile he told the court he had tricked the Germans; they had never received the money.

At that a contemptuous grunt escaped Ben-Nathan. Judge Lehmann glared at him, and for the first time the young lawyer dropped his glance to the notes his assistant had placed before him.

To substantiate Andor's testimony Weiss introduced in evidence several documents: letters from the International Red Cross and the United States State Department, and a memorandum from Himmler written in January 1945, attesting to the validity of the negotiations with the United Relief Organization.

That night and the next morning the press publicized Andor's success on the stand. They left no doubt he was a man of stature. Public interest in the case was ballooning. Everything was going so well that Andor decided Jessica should return to Tel Aviv. "You'll be more comfortable at home than sitting on a hard bench in a hot, cramped courtroom all day," he told her as they lay in bed that night. "Of course I'll miss you, but we'll have the weekend together. I'll be home Friday, and I promise to tell you everything that has happened."

"Do you really think there is nothing more to worry about?" she asked fearfully.

"Chorin hasn't a chance. The trial will be over in a week. At the most ten days, you'll see." He was full of confidence.

"All right then, I'll go," she said slowly, but there was still reluctance in her tone.

"Good. Leo will drive you tomorrow." He turned off the lamp and drew her to him, kissing her ear gently and then more urgently.

34

The Trial: Third Day

The press of people who wanted to get into the courtroom to witness the proceedings was bone-crushing. Several hundred were turned away, but not before many others had cheered Andor, slapped him on the back, and pumped his hand. He was a hero. So handsome, too, the women said. He was jubilant as he took his place next to the Attorney General. The climate of triumph touched even Reuven Weiss, though he was exceedingly careful not to show any premature assurance of victory. As he had done the two days before, he called his chief witness to the box.

"Mr. Horvath," he began, "when you left Bregenz, Switzerland, in December 1944, where did you go?"

"To Vienna, because I learned that the Russians had surrounded Budapest and it was no longer possible to get in or out."

"Will you describe your activities during this period, please."

"On December 30, 1944, I arrived in Vienna. Colonel Franz Weber was there, too, with part of his headquarters. Through him I received a room at the Grand Hotel." Andor went on to say that he met Himmler in March 1945 and as a result of his activities Himmler ordered the Gestapo to cease the extermination of Vienna's Jews. Himmler appointed him a special commissioner of concentration camps for the Reich, with instructions to alleviate the conditions of Jews there and prevent their extermination. "Himmler also told me that he no longer wanted money for saving Jews and that money already received would be returned after the war." He added that under pressure from him Colonel Weber traveled to several concentration camps to be certain

Himmler's orders were carried out. Because of his own role, he said (with what Ben-Nathan thought was pretentious modesty) the camps at Bergen-Belsen and Theresienstadt were hastily surrendered to the Allies, with the result that the lives of many Jews were saved.

"And when this task with the camps was finished, what did you do?"

"It was April by then, and the war was nearly over. The Germans wanted to get out of Vienna and back to the Reich. I was offered transportation by car to Switzerland with Colonel Walter Heinemann and I accepted it. He left me at the Swiss border. I remained in Switzerland for almost two years, until passage for Palestine was available for me and my wife."

Weiss then asked if he had any connection or contact with the Germans during his Swiss residence or afterward.

Andor shifted his weight from one foot to the other and gazed at the ceiling a long time before replying. In 1947, he said, he became a special adviser to the prosecution at the Nuremberg trials. The next year, after moving to Palestine, he returned to Nuremberg to give more testimony.

"Is the defendant's charge true that you went to Nuremberg in order to help Colonel Franz Weber?"

"It is a complete lie that I helped Weber. I gave no testimony nor affidavit in Weber's favor."

Weiss lowered his head as Andor finished his answer, and then raised it slowly. "Are you a man of wealth or property, Mr. Horvath?"

Andor's face broke into a wry grin, but his tone was polite. "All I have is debts. Even my apartment was bought for me by friends when I arrived here—for which I was very grateful," he added with a humble smile.

"Did you ever make any accounting of the money and valuables received by you as head of the Budapest Rescue Committee to ransom the Jews of Hungary from the Nazis?"

"On behalf of the Committee I submitted a financial statement to the 1946 Zionist Congress and to the United Relief Organization in Switzerland in 1947."

"Thank you, Mr. Horvath." Weiss returned to his seat and glanced at Ben-Nathan, who was still taking the measure of the man in the witness box.

Judge Lehmann looked at his watch and said, "Since it is now five minutes to twelve, we will recess for lunch." He banged the gavel. "Court is adjourned until one-thirty this afternoon."

Andor stepped down into the milling, admiring throng. He felt tired, and his legs ached, but he put on a smiling face.

"You are still under oath, Mr. Horvath," Judge Lehmann said as Andor took his place in the witness box at the opening of the afternoon session. Then he turned to the defense attorney. "You may cross-examine."

Ben-Nathan rose slowly, a yellow pencil gripped in his right fist, though he had not written a line since the trial began. His voice was even and pleasant as he asked, "When did you first appeal to Istanbul, Mr. Horvath?"

"In 1942."

"When were you notified about the existence of the Rescue Committee there?"

"In January 1943, I heard about the formation of the Committee."

"And in 1941 and '42 you did not know of the existence of this Committee?"

"No."

"You insist that as a result of your efforts this Committee was established?"

"I am ready to take back the words 'as a result.' After our appeal the Committee was established."

"And I tell you, Mr. Horvath, that you have a compulsion to attribute every attempt at rescue to your own activities!" Ben-Nathan flung the words out.

"I deny the assertion with contempt. I said 'as a result' because I could have made a mistake. This was my impression, and that of my colleagues in Budapest. We may have erred." Andor's face was flushed with anger. Such presumption from an upstart, he thought indignantly. Weiss shot him a warning look that said "Take it easy."

Ben-Nathan paced slowly in front of the witness box, and his voice became soft again.

"Is it true, Mr. Horvath, that no non-Zionist Jews were on your Committee?"

"True."

"Is it also true that the non-Zionists, the Orthodox, and the neologists constituted the great majority of the Hungarian Jews?"

"True."

"Is it also true that you and your Committee were not members of the Jewish Council during the German occupation?"

"Yes, that's true."

"And that Hugo Mayer was a member of the Jewish Council?"

"Yes."

"Is it true that everywhere in Hungary the contact between Germans and Jews was maintained through the Jewish Councils?"

"Yes."

"Did you know that Mayer negotiated with Von Klaussen?"

"Yes."

"How long did their negotiations last?"

"Not very long. Their last meeting was in August 1944. They met only several times."

"Nevertheless, how long did their contact last?"

"As far as I know, from March to August, but it was a superficial contact."

"Even at the beginning?"

"No, not at the beginning, but—"

"So it was not superficial?"

"Well—"

"Isn't it true that their close contact stopped because your Committee asked Mayer to stop it?"

"No. It is not true."

"And I tell you that you made him understand it was not desirable."

"That is an exaggeration."

"How do you explain the fact that the contact between them stopped then?"

"It stopped because the Germans invited us and not him to continue the negotiations."

"I repeat that you made Mayer understand he should drop this close contact."

"That's not true."

"And if Mayer himself says so?"

"Then he's mistaken and doesn't remember well."

Ben-Nathan stared silently at the witness as he lightly tapped his yellow pencil against the palm of his left hand. After what seemed like a long time he suddenly said, "Did Colonel Weber ask you or expect you to provide an alibi for him after the war?"

"He may have expected it," Andor answered coldly.

"But you did not live up to his expectations? You gave him no help, is that right?"

"None whatsoever."

"Do you agree that it would have been a national crime for anyone to have interceded on behalf of a Nazi officer?"

"Yes, of course."

Abruptly the defense counsel turned his back on the witness and addressed the bench, declaring, "No more questions at this time. Mr. Horvath will be called as a witness for the defense later."

There was a surprised expression on Judge Lehmann's face and an immediate buzz of conversation among the spectators. The judge rapped the gavel and called for order. Then he told Andor to step down.

The next witness for the prosecution gave his name as Saul Kazin. He was a massive, dark-haired man with a pale complexion who walked with a limber stride to the box. In reply to Weiss's first question he stated in a firm, rather brusque manner that he was a member of the Defense Ministry and a former representative of the Jewish Agency in Istanbul. In 1944 he had been a member of the Istanbul Rescue Committee. He recounted briefly the work of the Istanbul Committee in bringing ten thousand Jews out of Europe and in rescuing thousands of others by supplying them with forged papers and helping them flee from German-dominated areas.

"During this time was your Committee in communication with the Rescue Committee in Budapest?" Weiss asked.

"Yes, we communicated with them by letter concerning routine matters and by courier on matters that were confidential. We also maintained contact through citizens of neutral countries, through the diplomatic channels of neutral nations, and through agents who worked for both the Allies and the Germans."

"And on May 19, 1944, did you receive an important communication from the Budapest Rescue Committee?"

"Yes, the Istanbul Committee received a telegram, signed by Andor Horvath, stating that Erno Gábor would arrive shortly with an offer from Colonel Wedemeyer of the Judenkommando. Mr. Gábor arrived, accompanied by Mr. Max Franck, and explained the offer verbally. He also brought a letter endorsing the proposal from the Budapest Rescue Committee. It stipulated we had two weeks in which to decide whether or not to accept the offer."

"What was your Committee's reaction to the proposal?"

"At first we thought it was some diabolical trick. We were sure the Germans believed the Americans and the English would refuse to receive the Jewish envoy and thereby hoped to show it was not only Germany but also England and the United States who wanted the Jews to be exterminated. We also suspected that the Germans wanted to cause disunity among the Allies."

"Nevertheless, you accepted the proposal?"

"We decided we couldn't refuse any proposal that offered the slightest hope of saving our people, so we asked the Jewish Agency Executive in Palestine to cable Horvath that the offer was being seriously considered."

"What happened when Mr. Gábor and Mr. Franck arrived in Istanbul?"

"Two members of our Committee, Mr. Hyman Brodkin and myself, were sent to meet them."

"Then what happened?"

"The Turks, acting under pressure from the British, ordered both of them expelled to the Bulgarian border. But we bribed the authorities and the order was revoked. Still the Turks refused to give visas to them; they gave them only permission to stay in the country, which had to be renewed almost every day. One day, while their papers were being renewed, Franck asked permission to go to Palestine, and it was granted."

"What action did the Istanbul Committee then take concerning the proposal Mr. Gábor had brought?"

"We cabled the Agency Executive in Jerusalem and asked that Mr. Avner Sachs, the Political Secretary, come to Istanbul to talk to Gábor, but the Turks refused to let Mr. Sachs enter their country. Mr. Sachs then sent instructions that Gábor return to Budapest and say that the offer was being discussed and a decision would be made very soon. The Agency had decided that he should go back with an agreement providing payment in money, but not in goods. It was my job to persuade Gábor to return to Budapest."

"Did Gábor agree to go?"

"No. He said he couldn't return without Franck, but by now Franck was somewhere in Palestine. He also said he couldn't return with empty hands. He and his family would be killed and the Jews of Hungary would be sent to extermination camps."

"What did you do then?"

"We pressed the British, and they finally agreed that Gábor could go to Jerusalem to talk to the Agency Executive."

"And did Mr. Gábor go to Jerusalem?"

"He and I started out for Jerusalem, but just before the train reached Aleppo, on the Syrian border, our passports were examined by a British official."

"Did you and Mr. Gábor reach Jerusalem?"

"No. Gábor was arrested in Aleppo."

"By whom?"

"I didn't know at the time, but later I learned that the British had him under house arrest in Cairo."

"Did Mr. Sachs get an opportunity to speak to Mr. Gábor?"

"Mr. Sachs went to the Syrian border and after a day's delay was permitted to visit Gábor in the presence of a British intelligence agent."

"Did you see Mr. Gábor again?"

"Not until he was released, several months later."

"Were you able to persuade the British to free Gábor?"

"No. He was taken to a villa in Cairo and remained there under house arrest until sometime in October, when he was taken to Jerusalem by British intelligence and released there. He died of a heart attack about a month later, after futilely trying to get the British to let him go back to Budapest."

"He was no longer reluctant to go back with empty hands?"

"He felt his mission had been destroyed by the British. I don't think he cared about his own life; I think he just didn't want his wife to be alone in that terror in Budapest. He wanted to keep his word about coming back."

"During this time did your Committee and the Agency continue to negotiate with the Germans?"

"Just before the two weeks were up, our Committee received a cable from Horvath stating that if Gábor didn't return with a provisional agreement the destruction of the Jews would be speeded up. We replied that the Germans were making acceptance of the proposal difficult by continuing the deportations. We asked them to show their good faith by agreeing to release two thousand Jews as a token shipment to a neutral country."

"What was the reaction from Budapest?"

"We received two cables from Horvath. The first asked that Gábor return immediately with a provisional agreement. The Nazis would not stop the deportations until they received it. The second said Wedemeyer had implied he would release some Jews when, and only when, he had the agreement in his hands."

"What did the Committee do then?"

"Together with the Agency Executive they decided to make the greatest possible effort to persuade the Western Allies to accept Wedemeyer's proposal, and Mr. Sachs went to London for this purpose."

"What was the result of Mr. Sachs's trip?"

"The British flatly rejected the whole idea."

"That's all, Mr. Kazin, thank you." Weiss turned to Ben-Nathan. "Your witness," he said.

The defense attorney approached the witness box and in a tone as brusque and authoritative as Kazin's had been began, "Mr. Kazin, you have stated that the British authorities in Jerusalem and Istanbul assured you that Mr. Gábor would be permitted to travel to Jerusalem and return from Jerusalem freely. Is that true?"

"Yes."

"You accepted assurances from the British in Jerusalem even though it was common knowledge that the High Commissioner was undermining your rescue operation?"

"The Turks harassed Gábor every day by asking him whether he preferred being expelled to the Bulgarian border or to Palestine. If he was expelled to the Bulgarian border, it would mean the failure of his mission because the Germans would know about it immediately and it would be clear to them that if the Istanbul Rescue Committee didn't have enough influence to get a Turkish visa for Gábor it certainly didn't have enough influence to persuade the British to accept Wedemeyer's offer. But if Gábor went to Palestine, there was a chance he would be permitted to return with a provisional agreement."

"Wasn't it plain to you that the British granted Mr. Gábor a visa to Palestine but persuaded the Turks to refuse one to Mr. Sachs to go to Istanbul because they wanted Mr. Gábor on their own grounds, so they could arrest him?"

"That wasn't at all a foregone conclusion."

"Mr Kazin, tell the court, please, the circumstances of Mr. Gábor's arrest."

"On the trip from Istanbul to Jerusalem we had to change trains in Aleppo, so when the train pulled into the Aleppo station I left the compartment I shared with Gábor to call a porter. I stood on the platform outside our compartment and saw Gábor show the porter a rack containing our suitcases. The porter returned to the platform with the suitcases. When I looked up a half minute later, I saw that Gábor had disappeared from the compartment."

"Did anyone pass you to enter the train during this half minute?"

"No one."

"What did you do then?"

"I jumped on the train and ran to the compartment. It was empty. I suspected that Gábor had been arrested. I ran through the train, looking into each compartment and the lavatory, but I didn't see him."

"What did you do when you couldn't find Gábor?"

"I took the train to Jerusalem to report to the Agency Executive."

"Mr. Kazin, you have testified that you were a member of the Istanbul Rescue Committee and a representative of the Jewish Agency in that city, but publicly you were known as a journalist. Is that correct?"

"I was a journalist, but my activities for the Agency didn't include any specific duties that weren't public knowledge."

"Really?" Ben-Nathan's tone was sarcastic. "What were your duties for the Agency, Mr. Kazin?"

"My main task was collecting information from Jewish refugees and others about the enemy."

"Isn't the truth that you were working for British intelligence and that the actual collecting of information was left to your assistant?"

"Absolutely not!"

"Your primary objective was to work for the British and only after that for the Jewish people!"

"That's a lie! Our first objective was to fight the White Paper of 1939 and the limitations on Jewish immigration to Palestine."

"But the Political Department of the Jewish Agency co-operated with the British, didn't it?"

"Of course. They did what any organization in a country at war with Germany would have done."

"Wasn't the official British policy to obstruct all your rescue operations?"

"That was their official policy, but some British officials were sympathetic to us."

"Mr. Kazin, you have testified that the Agency's Political Department, through Mr. Avner Sachs, informed the British of Wedemeyer's offer of a million Jews for ten thousand trucks."

"Yes, since the proposal could not be put into operation without their agreement and aid."

"And the British rejected this proposal."

"Yes."

"They did more than reject it. Didn't they undermine the entire deal by broadcasting it and implying that it would mean supplying materials to the Nazis?"

"Yes."

"Yet your Istanbul Rescue Committee and the Agency continued to help Horvath and the Committee in Budapest pursue now fruitless negotiations with Wedemeyer, negotiations that could only help the Nazis without helping the Jews."

"We tried to stall, to string them along. We did what we thought we *had* to do."

"How is it that Max Franck, a known Nazi agent, who arrived in the German diplomatic plane with Gábor, is now employed by the Agency and has never been brought to trial?"

Kazin shrugged. "Franck could never be called an admirable man; he worked for both sides. But he aided our cause enough to compensate for his other activities."

"I suggest that you don't want to bring him to trial because you are afraid he will open his mouth."

"He has already opened his mouth. It is remarkable when he closes it."

Several spectators guffawed. Judge Lehmann brought the gavel down hard and threatened to eject the next person who laughed.

Ben-Nathan rubbed his hand over his bristly black hair and stared at the stone floor. Then he looked up at Kazin.

"Did you, as representative of the Agency in Istanbul, inform the Budapest Rescue Committee that parachutists Ely Farber, Martin Klein, and Naomi Loeb were going to be dropped over Yugoslavia and from there would go to Hungary?"

Lehmann raised his eyebrows at this question and looked to Weiss, expecting him to object since this ground had not been covered in examination. But the Attorney General only returned his look noncommittally and waited for Kazin's reply.

"Yes," Kazin answered evenly, determined not to lose his temper again. "We sent the Committee a letter by courier in March 1944."

"And the Committee strongly objected to your sending the parachutists."

"No. We never received any reply from them. I don't know for sure that the letter ever reached them."

Ben-Nathan went to the defense table and picked up a typewritten sheet. "I would like to introduce in evidence this copy of a report to the Jewish Agency Executive, signed by the witness, supporting the assertion that Andor Horvath did indeed object to the arrival of the parachutists." The paper was accepted in evidence, and then Ben-Nathan handed it to Kazin. "Will you look at this report, signed by yourself, and tell me again that Horvath did not object?"

Kazin looked at it perfunctorily and seemed unimpressed. "Horvath

objected—but that was some time after the parachutists had arrived and
been arrested. We never received any objections *before* they got there."
He put a large forefinger beneath the numerals at the bottom of the
page. "This report is dated December 12, 1944, and nowhere does
it deal with events that occurred before July. The parachutists arrived
in Budapest in June."

Ben-Nathan gazed at him stonily. "I didn't ask you *when* Horvath
objected, only *if* he objected. And the truth is that he did object, is it
not?"

"But—"

"Yes or no, Mr. Kazin."

"I have already said so," Kazin snapped.

Ben-Nathan retrieved the report and started to return to his seat,
then abruptly turned around and said, "Did you know that Mr. Gábor,
before he died, accused your Rescue Committee of being responsible
for the death of thousands of Jews?"

"No, I didn't know it. But even if he did say so, there was no justification for such a charge. We did everything possible to save our people."

"No more questions."

The judge excused Kazin and adjourned the court.

35

The Trial: Fourth Day

Isaac Singer was a smooth and dispassionate witness. As he
stood in the box, the early-morning rays of the sun fell across his hawk-
like face, breaking into planes and angles that made his craggy features
even sharper. In monotone replies to Weiss's questions he related that
the Swiss branch of the United Relief Organization had been ordered
by its American headquarters to tell the Germans that the money to
rescue the Jews was available in a Swiss bank—as in fact it was—but not
to pay the ransom. This policy of stalling was the one the late Edward
Schoen followed in his negotiations with Andor Horvath and the German emissaries. Horvath, he added, repeatedly pressed Schoen to pay
the Germans when there seemed to him no other way to save the Jews.
But Horvath didn't seem to understand that Schoen couldn't do this.

Nevertheless, Schoen's postwar report to the U.R.O.'s American headquarters stated that as a result of these negotiations and Horvath's part in them, 1,679 Hungarian Jews had been sent to safety in Switzerland, the Budpest ghetto had been saved from destruction, and exterminations in the concentration camps throughout German-held territories were halted.

When this recital was over, Singer watched with detachment as the lawyers exchanged places. Ben-Nathan moved toward him with barely concealed animosity.

"Mr. Singer, during your wartime service with the U.R.O. were you aware that the United States State Department, under pressure from the British Foreign Office, opposed any effective program to rescue the Jews of Europe?"

Singer's thick gray-black brows slowly rose, and he regarded Ben-Nathan condescendingly for a moment. "No," he said quietly, "I was not aware of any such pressure or any such effect."

Animosity crept into Ben-Nathan's voice. "Wasn't it true that the British Foreign Office, the United States State Department, and several Jewish organizations, including the U.R.O. and the Jewish Agency, joined in a conspiracy of silence concerning the extermination of the Jews in Europe? And wasn't Andor Horvath a central figure in that conspiracy?"

Weiss jumped to his feet. "Objection! The case is turning into a trial against the Agency and the U.R.O. The accused has become the accuser!"

Judge Lehmann's tone was severe as he asked Ben-Nathan, "Are you going to substantiate this charge?"

The defense attorney hesitated briefly, then with his usual aplomb replied, "I withdraw the charge for the present and ask the witness instead, as a former member of the U.R.O., can you tell the court why so few people in the Allied countries knew about the rescue activities of your Committee?"

"The U.R.O. chose to conduct its operations without publicity; our people felt there was a great advantage in keeping our personnel and work as quiet as possible. Other groups sought publicity in the press and radio. Still others believed bribery was the most successful method of rescue. It was a matter of one's point of view."

"But now that the score is in and you know that six million Jews died in the holocaust, do you still feel justified in your silence?"

Singer gazed at Ben-Nathan squarely, and his sharp features became granitelike. "We saved many lives. What we did was significant. Unfortunately what we failed to do was also significant."

Ben-Nathan, surprised by this concession, said pleasantly, "Thank you, Mr. Singer. No more questions."

"Call Martin Klein," said Weiss.

The former parachutist moved with an easy gait to the witness box, a tall, blond-haired, muscular figure, still lithe, the well-proportioned features of his face enhanced now by a look of maturity. At Weiss's request he carefully recited the story of his wartime venture from Cairo to Budapest to organize rescue work on behalf of the Jewish Agency and to engage in military operations for the Allies. He told of his own and Ely's surrender to the Germans and of Naomi's execution.

Weiss moved from the prosecution table, against which he had been leaning, closer to the witness box. "When did you first think of surrender?"

"After Horvath explained to us about the negotiations with Wedemeyer and after we had been followed by the Hungarian security police. Ely began to think that our being in Hungary was likely to do more harm than good. The rescue train might be delayed, and other reprisals might be taken against the Jews. So Ely decided to go to the Gestapo. He and Horvath made up a story he would tell them. He would say he was an agent of the Jewish Agency and was in Budapest to discuss the ransom offer that Erno Gábor had taken to Istanbul. But the Gestapo didn't believe him. They tortured him to get him to confess the true reason for his mission—though they apparently already knew it, because they had captured Naomi and our fourth officer, Jaffee," he added bitterly. "They threatened Horvath that Ely would be executed unless I turned myself in. Horvath came to the Columbus Street camp, where I was hiding, and told me this. He said the Gestapo had threatened to send the rescue train to Auschwitz instead of to Bergen-Belsen."

An expression of pain twisted Martin's handsome face. "My parents were scheduled to go on it, so I felt I had no alternative but to surrender."

"Thank you, Mr. Klein." Weiss nodded to Ben-Nathan.

"Mr. Klein," the defense attorney began, "you have testified that you voluntarily surrendered to the Gestapo because your superior officer had been tortured and threatened with death, because your parents were promised places on a rescue train, and because Wedemeyer threatened to send that train to Auschwitz if you didn't. How did you know all these things? You heard them from Horvath, didn't you?"

"Yes."

"You had no firsthand knowledge of these things."

"No, but everything he said turned out to be true."

"But you heard them only from him and you believed them."

"Yes."

"Did it occur to you that he had his own private reasons for operating the way he did—reasons that had no connection with saving the great mass of Hungarian Jews?"

"No, it didn't! And if you had been there, you would understand why. He was constantly in danger. Even while Ely was being tortured, Horvath himself was under arrest."

Ben-Nathan smiled scornfully. "Until he agreed to deliver you."

Martin, his face red to his blond hairline, choked with fury. He swung around to face the bench. "Your honor, I request permission not to answer this charge. My reply would offend the dignity of the court."

Lehmann fixed a look of stern gravity on him. "You will answer the charge, yes or no."

"No!" he yelled, rage and frustration sending a tremor through him. "No more questions."

Martin marched from the box, his face still flushed, and took his seat beside Rachel. She reached over and held his hand. The cool touch of her calmed him a little.

At one-thirty the courtroom was again jammed, and there was a scuffle among the spectators over the last vacant seats in the back row, but the guards moved in quickly to settle the bickering.

"Rachel Klein, please," called Weiss.

Rachel squeezed Martin's hand affectionately and felt the answering pressure of his, then she rose and walked to the front of the room, holding herself tightly to keep down the dreadful panic rising within her. They were going to ask her about those terrible days, and they had no right. They had no right! As she took her place in the witness box, the sweating mass of faces—friendly, curious, contemptuous, hostile, cold, leering—loomed before her like a hydra-headed monster. She had an impulse to push them away, but a feeling of weakness came over her. She looked frantically among them for Martin. He smiled reassuringly as her eyes found his.

She was sworn in, and Weiss began, "Mrs. Klein, you are the wife of Martin Klein, the previous witness?"

"Yes."

374

"Your maiden name was Rachel Teller, and as Rachel Teller you were a member of the Budapest Rescue Committee?"

"I was not a member of the Committee. I was just the secretary."

"Will you tell the court briefly about your work, please."

In a low voice she described her activities in wartime Budapest and her relationship with Andor and the other Committee members. The harsh experiences she related seemed incongruous with her voluptuous body, the soft, full curves of her mouth, the burnished curly hair, and the velvet-deep brown eyes.

Lehmann leaned closer to hear her and once gently requested that she speak a little louder.

When she had finished, Weiss asked, "Were you ever arrested by the Hungarians?"

"Yes. They arrested me after they learned that Martin Klein and Ely Farber were in Budapest. They wanted to know all about the parachutists' mission and what Andor Horvath was planning with them. They told me they knew Ely had been arrested by the Germans and asked me where Martin was hiding."

"Did you tell them?"

"I couldn't tell them. I didn't know. I didn't even know Ely had been arrested. But they didn't believe me. They burned my feet with cigarettes to help me 'remember.'" She shuddered at the memory. Several spectators gasped.

"What happened after that, Mrs. Klein?" Weiss prodded mildly.

"After about three hours they were convinced I had no information of use to them, so they released me. As soon as I left the prison, I tried to get in touch with Mr. Horvath. I telephoned his apartment, then the office in Sip utca. Finally I went to the Columbus camp. There Leo Strauss told me that earlier in the morning he had seen Mr. Horvath and Martin get into a Gestapo car just outside the gate and drive away."

"Did Mr. Strauss say Klein had decided to surrender?"

"He said he didn't know anything except what he had seen: Captain Mueller of the Gestapo escorting Mr. Horvath and Martin into the car and then ordering the driver to start."

"Thank you, Mrs. Klein."

Ben-Nathan approached the box slowly. In a compassionate, almost admiring tone he began, "Mrs. Klein, you were a loyal secretary of the Rescue Committee for several years, is that correct?"

"Yes."

"You were also personally devoted to Mr. Horvath. You came from

375

Pécs, the same town as he did, and you knew him before you joined the Committee?"

"Yes. Our families had known each other since my childhood."

"You approved of his negotiations with Wedemeyer and took part in the organization of the rescue train?"

"Of course."

"Yet there came a time when you no longer could accept the things he was doing?"

"I don't know what you mean."

Ben-Nathan abruptly dropped his soft demeanor and rasped, "I mean you resented the fact that Horvath pressured Farber and Klein into sacrificing themselves so that he could rescue his own friends on the Bergen-Belsen train."

"Objection!" Weiss was on his feet. "Defense counsel's charges are irrelevant and immaterial, besides touching on matters not covered in examination."

Ben-Nathan approached the bench. "I ask the court's indulgence. I am trying to show that even the most loyal of Horvath's followers came to doubt his wisdom, if not his motives."

"Is it your intention to show that this witness's actions proved a lack of trust of her superior?" Lehmann asked.

"Yes, your honor."

"In that case I will overrule the objection."

Ben-Nathan turned back to the witness. "Now, Mrs. Klein, will you answer the question, please. Did you resent the fact that Horvath had persuaded Farber and Klein to surrender to the Gestapo and that they were now under the shadow of the executioner?"

"I didn't resent it. I thought he had done what he believed necessary, and I respected his judgment."

"You respected his judgment so much you conspired with Joseph Nagel, a member of the Committee—behind Horvath's back—to rescue the two men?"

Rachel bit her lip to keep it from trembling. "I didn't want them to be sentenced to death."

"You didn't want these two men to die, but you didn't care that 1,679 people being held on ice in Bergen-Belsen might be sent to Auschwitz because of your actions?" Without waiting for a reply he said, "That's all, Mrs. Klein," then turned on his heel and walked to his seat.

Weiss rose. "I have a couple of questions on re-examination. Mrs. Klein," he said gently, regret and apology in his eyes as he looked into hers, "you knew Ely Farber long before he arrived in Budapest in 1944, didn't you? You knew him in Pécs before the war."

"Yes, I knew him in Pécs." Her voice was low and unsteady.

Martin watched her intently, but she didn't look at him. Please, he begged her silently, *please* don't show the whole world you still love him. Knowing this had been his private agony all these years; he couldn't bear for everyone else to know, too. He swallowed against the terrible constriction in his throat and stared hard at her, willing her with all his being to meet his gaze, but she only stood with lowered eyes, looking at no one.

"You were going to marry Ely Farber and go to Palestine with him, weren't you?" Weiss asked.

"Yes." Her voice was barely a whisper.

"Were you still in love with Farber when he came to Budapest in the spring of 1944?"

Rachel's expression begged the prosecutor not to insist on a reply.

"Please answer the question, Mrs. Klein."

Tears filled the velvet eyes. "Yes, I was still in love with him."

"That was the real reason you engineered the escape, wasn't it? Because you couldn't let the man you loved die, not because you thought Mr. Horvath had done anything wrong. Isn't that true?"

"Yes, I did it because I loved him. That was the only reason."

36

The Trial: Fifth Day

Joe Nagel stood in the witness box reluctantly, the usual fanatic look on his sharp dark features overlaid with an expression of sullenness. Nevertheless, his replies to Weiss's questions were rapid, coherent, and detailed. He told the court that he had organized the first "hike" from Poland to Slovakia in 1941. Later he went from Slovakia to Hungary with the aid of Hungarian counterespionage agents and members of Andor's underground organization to urge resistance and plan escape among the Jews. But with the exception of the chalutzim, the youth movement, and the Zionists it was impossible to make the Jews understand the fate that awaited them, even after the Germans entered Hungary in March 1944. Immediately after the occupation he began a program to obtain arms on a large scale, he explained, but he and his colleagues found that they could buy few pistols, and these only at exorbitant prices. Later the underground managed to acquire several hundred side arms, a sub-machine gun, and some hand grenades. They also established five bunkers, or resistance headquarters, in Budapest.

"When did all this activity take place?" Weiss asked.

"In the summer and fall of 1944."

"With Mr. Horvath's knowledge and approval?"

"With his knowledge and approval."

"Mr. Nagel, it has been charged in this courtroom that other members of the Committee disliked Mr. Horvath's tactics as leader. Did you approve of his dealings with Wedemeyer and Gábor's mission?"

"The Committee discussed Wedemeyer's offer, and everyone agreed that we couldn't afford to turn it down."

"Did you really think the Nazis were bargaining in good faith?"

"No, but we couldn't be sure. We felt that by negotiating we might be able to stall off the threatened deportations until the war ended. The Germans were no longer very strong by the time they occupied Hungary. They were losing the war."

"Did you trust Mr. Horvath to represent properly the interests of the Committee in his dealings with Wedemeyer and the other Germans?"

"I trusted him fully."

"Thank you, Mr. Nagel."

"Mr. Nagel," Ben-Nathan began tartly, "during the Committee's discussions about Wedemeyer's proposition didn't you object that it was wrong to deal with Nazis and supply them with goods?"

Joe wet his lips with his tongue. "I may have, but in the end I realized that we couldn't reject the slightest chance to save our people."

"Weren't you aware that the price the Nazis were demanding for these negotiations was that the Rescue Committee allay the fears of the Jewish population and keep them quiet?"

"No. Nobody had to keep them quiet. The Hungarian Jews refused to believe they were going to be murdered. If you tried to warn someone, he would brush you off as a nuisance. If you insisted, he would call you crazy."

"Did you ever try to warn anyone?"

"Frequently, usually without success. When Horvath heard from Von Klaussen that the Jews in the provinces were going to be put into ghettos, I went to the community in Szeged and offered forged papers and transportation to anyone who wanted to escape to Rumania, and also I offered to hide anyone who wanted to remain in Hungary. A couple of men threatened to report me to the Jewish Council as a troublemaker. Others threatened me with bodily harm if I didn't stop spreading what they called 'terrible lies.' I went to other towns and offered help, but my reception was the same almost everywhere. The people didn't believe the Nazis would kill them, and when the time came they went willingly into the ghettos."

"Now, Mr. Nagel, you have testified that you made purchases of weapons and defense materials with Mr. Horvath's knowledge and approval. But he didn't associate himself in any way with these purchases, did he? He didn't supervise them or connect himself in any way with them."

"He didn't supervise them. He couldn't possibly supervise everything that was done by the Committee and the underground."

"Nevertheless, he kept apart from these activities, so that the Nazis couldn't connect him with them if they discovered them."

"Well, it would have been stupid if he had openly engaged in buying weapons, wouldn't it?"

Ben-Nathan wheeled around to the judge. "I ask the court to direct the witness to answer the question."

"The witness will answer the question," Lehmann ordered.

Joe glared at Ben-Nathan. "I don't know what his reason was. The direction of the operation was left to me."

"And this operation took place in the summer and fall of 1944. In other words, you waited until several months after the Germans had occupied the country to set up a defense organization. Wasn't that too late?"

"Of course it was late, but I've already explained that only a handful of us were willing to be realistic about our situation before the occupation." He snorted, and then added indignantly, "We worked to save Jews, and now we must submit to questioning as if we had committed a crime."

Ben-Nathan ignored the complaint and continued, "Mrs. Klein has said that in trying to rescue Farber and Klein she conspired against the interests of Mr. Horvath and the people at Bergen-Belsen because of love. You conspired against them also, in the same plot." His voice became sarcastic. "Were you in love, too? Or," he shouted, "was it because you knew Horvath was willing to sell out all the rest of the Jews

379

to the Nazis, even his old acquaintance Farber, to save his friends, his family, and a few other important Zionists?"

Joe's face became livid. "You're twisting the whole thing! I was young and hotheaded, and I was impatient with talk and negotiations. Talk was all right for Horvath. He could persuade the Nazis with words. I wanted to act. I thought between us we could accomplish everything. I didn't intend to sabotage Horvath's negotiations."

"Isn't it true that in the presence of others you recently called Mr. Horvath 'an extraordinary swine'?"

Joe shrugged. "I call a lot of people swine if I don't agree with them."

There was an outburst of laughter among the spectators. Judge Lehmann banged his gavel.

"Give me a straightforward answer. Did you call Horvath a swine or not?"

"Yes."

"Wasn't this the same occasion on which Mr. Kazin told you that everyone connected with the Bergen-Belsen affair should be stood against a wall and shot?"

The cords in Joe's neck bulged. "Those who act make mistakes," he shouted. "Those who do nothing make no mistakes. Mr. Kazin made a mistake."

"Those who act make mistakes." Ben-Nathan repeated the words, nodding to indicate that they sounded reasonable. "Would you say that Mr. Horvath also made mistakes?"

Weiss stood immediately. "Objection!"

"I withdraw the question," Ben-Nathan said quickly, and began a new tack. "Mr. Nagel, you went to Switzerland in 1945?"

"Yes."

"Did you see Mr. Horvath there?"

"No."

"Isn't it true that he asked you to meet him and you refused?"

"Yes, I refused. I was busy trying to make a living and to get a certificate to Palestine."

"Wasn't the real reason that you felt Horvath had sacrificed all the rest of Hungarian Jewry, even the parachutists, to save his friends?"

"No!"

"Do you deny there was deep antagonism between you?"

Joe wet his lips again and hesitated. "We had our differences," he answered reluctantly. "But they were differences of personality."

"For instance?"

Maybe he did deliberately hand over Ely Farber. Maybe he did turn his back on Naomi and let them kill her. Just the same, he saved many lives. Those people who stone him now are the same ones who either did nothing except save their own skins or didn't criticize others who just saved their own skins."

He took out an enormous handkerchief and mopped his damp face. "I hope that answers your question," he said bitterly to Ben-Nathan.

The courtroom was still, its occupants dumfounded at this two-edged description of Andor Horvath.

"That answers it very well, thank you," the defense attorney replied. "There is just one point to clear up. Would you say that sacrificing the parachutists was the act of a traitor or a hero?"

Joe looked at him as if the question were idiotic. "To call Horvath a traitor is mean and vile. Was he a hero? I don't know. If you mean by a hero a person who is ready to sacrifice his life for others, then he was a hero."

"Yet this hero, Andor Horvath, is alive, here with us"—the defense attorney pointed to Andor, sitting at the prosecution's table—"and 650,-000 Hungarian Jews he appointed himself to save are dead, aren't they, Mr. Nagel?" Without waiting for a reply he turned his back to the witness and snapped, "No more questions."

The judge excused Joe and he stepped down, his head lowered as he walked passed Andor, who gazed after him with a melancholy smile.

When the afternoon session began, Alex Peto was called. The dark sunken eyes in his gaunt face were sad as he placed his thin hand on the volume of Scriptures. He began his testimony by saying that he had been a member of the Budapest Rescue Committee and the leader of Haganah in Hungary in March 1944 and that the day the Germans moved into the country he was arrested by the Gestapo and charged with organizing resistance against the Third Reich. He described his imprisonment in Auschwitz and then his transfer to Mauthausen. His lips quivered as he told of the murders at the Austrian camp—how hundreds were shoved into gas chambers or shot, or thrown from roof tops, or dismembered by dogs, or pierced by hypodermic needles.

He told of Franz Weber's visit to Mauthausen and of his own release at the hunting lodge.

"Did Colonel Weber give you two suitcases and ask you to give them to Horvath?"

"Yes."

"Will you tell the court why Weber gave them to you, what was in them, and what you subsequently did with them?"

"Weber gave me the suitcases and said, 'This is what I got for organizing the rescue train that reached Switzerland. I promised Horvath I would return it if at all possible.' Well, I accepted the suitcases but I didn't know where Horvath was, and I was afraid to keep the valuables in my possession for very long because they might be stolen, so a short time later I went to the American C.I.D. intelligence center at Bad Ischl and told all about the suitcases. A Jewish-American officer opened the suitcases. They were filled with gold and jewels."

"Was that the first time you saw what was in them?"

"Yes."

"Did you and the American officer count the money or estimate the value of the contents?"

"No. I just turned them over to him."

"Did you ever see the suitcases or their contents again?"

"No."

"That's all. Thank you, Mr. Peto."

Ben-Nathan rose to cross-examine. "Mr. Peto, do you have any idea what the contents of those suitcases were worth?"

"When I came to Israel, I heard that they were worth from eighty to a hundred thousand dollars."

"From whom did you hear this?"

"It was the gossip in some circles. I don't remember from whom exactly."

"In these circles did you ever hear that the contents might have been worth not eighty thousand dollars but two million?"

"No."

"Did you hear any more about the suitcases before you came to Israel?"

"Yes. A couple of days after I left Bad Ischl I went to Salzburg and started to work with the Committee for Jewish Displaced Persons, which had its headquarters at the Hoter-Ishay. After some time a Jewish-American colonel named Frankel appeared in my office. He said he was from the U.R.O. He told me the U.R.O. had the suitcases and asked me to tell my story. I explained the whole affair to him."

"Then what happened?"

"I finally got to Switzerland and saw Horvath. I went over the whole story with him. We had a great deal of difficulty finding out what happened to the suitcases, but after much investigation we learned that they had been turned over to the Jewish Agency in Palestine."

"And that the contents were worth about eighty to a hundred thousand dollars."

"I learned that later, yes."

"Did it occur to you that part of the contents might have been stolen before they reached Palestine?"

"No. Of course, it's possible, since they passed through many hands, but I had no real reason to think so."

"Did it occur to you that Weber might have given the bulk of the two million dollars to Horvath before he gave you the suitcases; that the real motive for giving you the suitcases was to make Weber look good to the Allies while he and Horvath divided up the main part of this Jewish wealth?"

"No! Horvath is an honorable man. He never stole a penny."

Ben-Nathan threw up his hands in mock exasperation. "Then we are faced with two alternatives—either Weber and Horvath took the money or the American officers took it." He paused, then asked, "Do you think that Weber, as well as Horvath, is an honorable man?"

"He was kind to me. That's all I know. And he gave me the money and the jewels. He didn't have to."

"Come, Mr. Peto, you thought more of him than that." He turned to the bench. "Your honor, I have here a copy of a letter of recommendation, to the Allied commander at Weissenbach, on behalf of Colonel Franz Weber, dated May 8, 1945. It is signed by Alex Peto. I wish to introduce it as evidence." The letter was processed, and then Ben-Nathan handed it to Alex: "Do you remember writing this letter, Mr. Peto?"

Alex glanced over it warily and gave it back to the lawyer. "Yes."

Ben-Nathan tapped the letter briefly with two fingers. "There is a great deal of praise here for Weber's good deeds in saving Jews. How did you learn of these good deeds? Wasn't it from Weber himself and no one else?"

Alex lowered his head. "Yes, but—" he began just above a whisper.

"That's all, Mr. Peto."

Weiss rose immediately. "Mr. Peto, you wrote that letter on May 8, 1945, just a few days after you had been released from Mauthausen. Isn't that true?"

Alex raised his head painfully and answered with grave dignity, "Yes."

"At that time, after thirteen months in two death camps, what was your mental and physical condition?"

"I was a living corpse"—in spite of himself he felt a tremor shake his body—"and this man Weber, whatever his motives, was the only person in more than a year who seemed to be aware that I was human . . ."

"Thank you, Mr. Peto."

Since it was nearly four o'clock and the next day was Shabbat, Judge Lehmann adjourned court until Sunday. Without stopping to discuss the day's session with Weiss or even to talk to Alex, Andor hurried out of the courtroom and started toward his car, parked in the Russian Compound near the courtyard, intent on getting to Tel Aviv as quickly as possible. But several of the reporters who were clustered around Alex, seeing Andor leaving the grounds, ran after him, calling out their questions. He ignored them. What he needed now was the sight and the touch and the scent of Jessica. He started the car impatiently, pressed the gas pedal to the floor, and sped toward the winding road from Jerusalem to the sea.

37

The Trial: Sixth Day

The first witness was a former member of the Slovak underground, who described his dealings with Andor Horvath. He said he had met Horvath only twice. The first time Horvath gave him ten thousand Swiss francs for underground work. Several months later Horvath appeared at his bunker in Slovakia and said he had come from Hungary with an SS officer, a Lieutenant Colonel Heinemann, and that he, the Slovak, was to go to the Bratislava station and try to trick the stationmaster into halting a deportation train that was scheduled to leave that day. The attempt failed.

"What was your feeling toward Mr. Horvath?" Weiss asked.

"I had the greatest respect for him."

"Thank you," Weiss said, and returned to his chair.

Ben-Nathan rose lethargically. "No questions," he said in a bored monotone.

Young Rabbi Vogeler was called to the box. Serenely, without emphasis or emotion, he related how in his house in Nagybathely his name was called out with several others who were told they and their families were to leave Hungary. He explained that he asked to stay behind with his congregation but the request was refused. He described in detail life at Bergen-Belsen and the trip to Switzerland.

"Were you a friend of Mr. Horvath?" Weiss asked.

"No. I met him only after we reached Switzerland—at a party in his honor arranged by those who had been rescued."

"Did any of the other members of your congregation who were on the rescue train know Mr. Horvath personally?"

"Not until we reached Switzerland."

"Were most of the people on the rescue train his friends or members of his family?"

"So far as I could tell, no."

"How was Mr. Horvath honored at this party you mentioned?"

"Toasts were drunk to him, and he was presented with a testimonial book."

Weiss went back to the table and picked up a volume three or four times the size of an ordinary book. "Is this the testimonial?" he asked, handing it to Vogeler, who recognized it immediately.

"Yes."

The Attorney General retrieved the book and offered it in evidence, handing it up to the judge, who, scrutinizing it, read aloud, "'the deliverer of Hungarian Jewry.' That is extravagant praise," he murmured, handing the volume back to Weiss. "The clerk will record the testimonial in evidence." Then to Weiss he said, "You may continue."

"So, Rabbi," Weiss concluded, raising his voice in order that no one in the courtroom would miss the point, "this great honor was conferred on Mr. Horvath by people many of whom knew him only through his brave and daring rescue of them."

"Yes, that's true."

"Thank you, Rabbi."

Ben-Nathan approached the witness box with obvious deference. "Rabbi Vogeler, why did you want to stay with the members of your congregation?"

"They needed me. My place was with them." His plain features took on a sad look. "It was almost unbearable to be separated from them at that time."

Ben-Nathan's voice became more businesslike. "Rabbi, did you know how your name happened to be on the list of rescuees?"

"I had no idea."

"Did you then know or do you now know who compiled the lists on which your name and the names of your congregation members appeared?"

"No."

"Weren't you sufficiently curious to ask someone—Leo Strauss, the head of the rescue group, or Mr. Horvath when you met him in Switzerland?"

"No."

"Rabbi, we have seen the elaborate testimonial, with words of such great praise for Mr. Horvath. But tell the court, what were the feelings the people of the train displayed toward Mr. Horvath in talking about him to each other when he was not present."

"The deepest gratitude and admiration."

"Were those your feelings—and are they now?" Ben-Nathan's acrid tone made his implication plain.

Vogeler looked disconcerted and glanced appealingly at Weiss, but the Attorney General was already on his feet. "Your honor—" he protested to Lehmann.

"I withdraw the question," Ben-Nathan said hastily. "That's all, Rabbi. Thank you."

The next witness was Marvin Ravitch, a man in his middle thirties, of medium height and medium build, with a face that was difficult to distinguish in a crowd and easy to forget once it was seen. He had been one of the underground workers for the Budapest Rescue Committee. His task, he said, was to obtain ration cards by illegal means for refugees from Slovakia, and to provide sleeping quarters and work for them. When the Germans moved into Budapest, the Rescue Committee made him head of their Documents Center. It was also his job at this time to provide Jews with the proper papers so those who wished to could live through the dangerous time as Christians.

"I was an expert at obtaining forged papers," he added. The pride in his voice was palpable. "But our task was doubly difficult because the Jews of Hungary didn't believe they were going to be murdered."

"Did you ever try to warn them?" Weiss asked.

"Many times, but they wouldn't listen. Once when I went to a ghetto an old man stoned me and yelled that I was possessed of a dybbuk. The Lord would not let the Jewish people die, he said." Ravitch smiled bitterly at the recollection. "He caused such an uproar that several people threatened to call the Gestapo unless I left. That was the kind of madness there was in those days."

"Did you respect Andor Horvath as a leader—did you and the others who worked for him and the Committee think he was a good leader?"

"Yes. He was a man with great courage. Fearless. We valued that quality. He played a very dangerous role. Not one of the rest of us could have done it."

"Thank you, Mr. Ravitch. Your witness," Weiss said to Ben-Nathan.

The defense attorney went straight to the heart of the matter. "Mr. Ravitch, you have stated under oath that you respected Mr. Horvath as a leader."

"Yes."

"But you and the other chalutzim who worked for the Rescue Committee had differences with Mr. Horvath, did you not? And these differences were so great that you and your friends preferred the leadership of Joseph Nagel—"

"No!" Ravitch interrupted brusquely. "We were loyal to Horvath—in spite of occasional differences," he added grudgingly.

"Serious differences?"

"All differences at such a critical time are serious."

"Tell us about those differences, Mr. Ravitch."

"Well"—he rubbed the side of his nose speculatively with a forefinger —"Mr. Horvath was not a very democratic man. He was an individualist, an egocentric, with great confidence in himself. He was an actor. I mean, the truth was not always on his lips. But to understand him and the way he was you have to understand the situation in Hungary then. At that time the most important attribute a man could have was a thief's honor. Horvath had it. This was a time when our best friends were men of the underworld, who could be bought and bribed; the worst men in Budapest, but they became our most useful friends. It's hard to understand this now, and some people taunt the Hungarian Jews with the example of the resistance in Poland. The fight in the Warsaw ghetto is simple to understand. Historically it is very nice. Everyone understands heroism. But resistance was only one of several possible ways of surviving under the Nazis. Resistance is born of desperation. Horvath's way with the Nazis and our way of illegal action was a more complicated and in some respects a more difficult way. A less"—he searched for an appropriate word—"a less *photogenic* way."

"Are you saying you approved of Horvath's dealings with the Nazis?"

Ravitch looked annoyed and his voice took on a weary, irritated quality, as if he were trying to explain something very simple to a stupid man. "As chalutzim, our goal was to save as many Jews as possible. That was Horvath's goal, too. I believe our way of illegal action was

389

better and cheaper and more honorable, but I'm convinced it was necessary for Horvath to deal with the Nazis."

"Even to collaborating with them?"

"He never collaborated!" Ravitch said hotly, but almost immediately calmed himself and tried to explain. "Horvath was always arranging things"—he made a vague gesture with his hands—"making compromises. He was a fixer. But he never made any money out of this," Ravitch added quickly. "He had no interest in money, though he liked some of the things money bought. He went through hell in Budapest because he imagined that after the war he would be the hero of the Jewish people."

A superior smile flitted across Ben-Nathan's face. "But obviously he is not the hero of the Jewish people"—the smile became a scowl—"because he didn't care about them, because the truth is that he saved himself and a handful of important individuals by selling out the rest of the Jews to the Nazis!"

"Objection!" shouted Weiss. "Defense counsel is engaging in pejorative oratory."

From under his pale brows Judge Lehmann's blue eyes peered coldly at Ben-Nathan. "The court admonishes defense counsel to confine himself to proper questioning of the witness."

Ben-Nathan apologized and addressed Ravitch again. "A few minutes ago you said Mr. Horvath was not a very democratic man. What did you mean by that?"

Ravitch looked uncomfortable. He obviously regretted having made the statement. "Well . . ." He rubbed the side of his nose again. "It was just that he always wanted the best of everything—the best food, the best wines, cigarettes, and clothes. He thought he was entitled to them. He felt he was better than most people."

"And this attitude of Horvath's caused resentment among the chalutzim and others who worked for the Rescue Committee?"

"Some resentment, yes."

"Why, Mr. Ravitch? Was it because most of the other Jews didn't have enough to eat or a real bed to sleep in, while Horvath lived like a prince?"

"I didn't say that!"

But Ben-Nathan had already started to his seat. "No more questions."

38

The Trial: Seventh Day

Leo Strauss was as self-assured and ebullient as usual. He stood confidently, his large body almost seeming to overflow the witness box as he told the court about the formation of the rescue train, the camp on Columbus utca, the stay at Bergen-Belsen, and finally the passage to safety in Switzerland.

It was midmorning before Ben-Nathan took over to cross-examine. He made a strong probing attack, for it was as plain to him as to the rest of the courtroom that he had a formidable witness. But Leo remained unruffled, and the defense attorney was unable to get him to change any part of his story, though he hammered again and again, from every angle, at the selection of people from Pécs for the rescue train.

Several times Leo repeated that in the case of Pécs the Rescue Committee in Budapest sent no list of persons marked for rescue. All he received, he insisted, was a letter from Horvath instructing him that the Zionists, the chalutzim, and the Orthodox were all to have places and wherever possible he was not to separate families.

"Do you have this letter?" Ben-Nathan asked.

"No, in all the moving it has been lost."

"Then we have only your word that there was no list?"

"You have my word and the word of the other three men who made up the selection committee, if you want to subpoena them. But if you are asserting there was a list, Mr. Ben-Nathan, it is up to you to produce it."

Ben-Nathan wheeled around to Judge Lehmann. "Your honor, will you instruct the witness to restrict himself to answering the questions put to him?"

The judge leaned forward. "Mr. Strauss, you will answer defense counsel's questions and not indulge in gratuitous comments," he ordered, but his tone was mild. "You may proceed," he said to Ben-Nathan, casting a frigid look at him.

"Thank you, your honor. Now, Mr. Strauss," Ben-Nathan resumed, "on this list that you say the four-man committee made up, were there a large number of Mr. Horvath's relatives?"

"I don't know what you mean by 'a large number.' Some of his relatives were on the list."

"Was the number as large as fifteen or sixteen?"

Leo shrugged. "It might have been. I don't remember the exact number."

"Didn't Mr. Horvath indicate to you in some unofficial way that his relatives were to be put on the list?"

"He did not. But after all, he was the originator of the whole project, and naturally the rest of the committee and I assumed he wanted his family to be saved. Wouldn't you?"

"I am asking the questions here, Mr. Strauss!" For a few seconds Ben-Nathan paced the floor in front of the witness box, then in a calmer voice began again. "How many members of your family went on the train?"

"Five, besides myself: my wife and two daughters, and brother and his wife."

"Was there any other family besides Horvath's that had as many as fifteen of its members on the rescue train?"

"I think so."

"But you are not sure."

"I'm not sure."

"Wasn't there a great deal of bitterness against Horvath in Pécs over the selection of who should be rescued? Didn't many people feel the selection was unfair?"

"Of course. The people who were not chosen thought the selection was unfair. They blamed Horvath for not rescuing them, but they didn't blame the Nazis for placing them in a situation where they had to be rescued."

Ben-Nathan continued to insist that the selection was unfair, but he was unable to wring any further concession from Leo and the exchange ended in a deadlock. That was the end of the cross-examination.

Weiss rose to re-examine. "Mr. Strauss, during the Nazi occupation many men from Pécs were sent to work camps in other parts of Hungary, weren't they?"

"Yes."

"Were any of them from Mr. Horvath's family?"

"Yes, there were three cousins and an uncle. One of them died at Kenyérmező."

"Thank you, that's all."

"Call your next witness," Judge Lehmann ordered Weiss as the afternoon session began.

"I call Hermann Richter." From the last row of spectators a little white-haired man rose and nervously made his way down the aisle to the witness box. "Mr. Richter will be my last witness, your honor," Weiss announced.

In his seat next to Ben-Nathan, László Chorin paled with fright and surprise as he heard Richter's name, his large myopic eyes like those of a startled fawn. Ben-Nathan's expression revealed nothing, but he bent close to his client and engaged in a whispered conversation with him. Chorin continued to stare at the little man approaching the witness box. This was the first time since the trial began that he had shown any interest in the proceedings. Usually he sat motionless, dully staring ahead, except when he swallowed the familiar white pills. Sometimes he even appeared to be dozing. He was the forgotten man of the trial. No one in the courtroom had referred to him. Even the press had virtually ignored him in favor of the more colorful personalities and the feuds, intrigues, escapades, and heroism of the war years in Hungary. Now, however, Chorin looked not only alert but alarmed, and the reporters took note.

Hermann Richter was sworn in, and in a rapid, uneven manner, his wrinkled hands trembling, he related that he had known Chorin in Budapest before the war. "I was a rich man in those days. I owned one of the largest stove factories in Hungary." His weak blue eyes lighted up as he said it. "Then in 1937 I was made head of the Jewish community in my suburb. Soon after this I received a telephone call from Mr. Chorin. He was then the publisher of the newspaper the *New Israel*. He asked to see me because he said he had something I would be interested in. The next day he came to my office with two men and showed me the typewritten copy for a newspaper article he had written about me—"

"Objection!" shouted Ben-Nathan. "This line of questioning is irrelevant to the case before the court. The defendant's past activities have no bearing on whether or not Andor Horvath is guilty of collaboration with the Nazis."

"Your honor," said Weiss, "Andor Horvath is not on trial here despite defense counsel's persistent attempts to make it seem so. The defendant is László Chorin, and it most certainly is relevant to this case that he is a convicted liar and blackmailer. In his opening statement to the court defense counsel asserted that Mr. Chorin made his published accusations against Andor Horvath in the interests of truth and justice

—and without malice. We assert that the defendant has a history of acting with malice, out of not good but bad motives."

"The objection is overruled," Judge Lehmann pronounced. "You may proceed," he said to Weiss.

The Attorney General addressed the witness again. "Mr. Richter, what kind of an article did Mr. Chorin show you that he had written about you?"

"A defamatory article." Richter's voice quavered with agitation. "It made of me a bohemian, a chaser of women—somebody unfit to be the head of the community."

"Were these allegations substantiated?"

"Chorin said he had witnesses who would swear I had been at the local whorehouse. He pointed to the two men with him. Then he said that if I would pay him a 'reasonable' amount—say fifty thousand pengö—he wouldn't publish the article."

"What was your answer to him?"

"At first I was indignant, but Chorin only laughed. He said he was sorry but he had to do it, his paper was losing money and he had to get it somewhere. Then he added that it was a small price to pay for 'saving' my reputation. So I told him I had to think it over and would let him know my decision. But after he left, I went straight to the police and they set a trap for him. I paid Chorin the money in marked bills, while two detectives watched without him seeing them. They arrested him, I pressed charges, and the case went to court."

"What was the result?"

"The court found him guilty of attempted blackmail, and he was sentenced to four months in prison."

Weiss allowed himself a thin sidewise grin at Ben-Nathan, then turned back to the witness. "That's all, Mr. Richter. Thank you."

"You're welcome," the little man answered emphatically, obviously pleased with his role in the proceedings.

Ben-Nathan rose wearily. "No questions."

Chorin turned on him, gesticulating wildly as the judge dismissed Richter. The little white-haired man stepped out of the witness box and started back to his seat in the rear, looking neither to the right nor left.

Ben-Nathan laid a calming hand on Chorin's arm, but he wouldn't be pacified.

"Look! Look at him, the bastard! He can't face me!" he yelled as Richter passed the defense table.

Judge Lehmann's gavel banged repeatedly, but nobody paid any attention.

Richter made an about-face and stared into Chorin's blazing countenance with contempt. "I spit on you!" he yelled back, and expectorated vigorously on the courtroom floor.

By this time the courtroom was in an uproar. The judge swiftly dispatched two guards to restrain the offenders. When order was finally restored, he placed charges of contempt against both Chorin and Richter and once more sternly threatened to clear the room if there were any further disruptions. Then he turned to Weiss. "Do you wish to recall any witness?"

"No, sir. The state rests."

He looked at his watch. It was three-thirty. "Very well, court is adjourned until nine o'clock tomorrow morning, at which time we shall hear the case for the defense."

39

The Trial: Eighth Day

László Chorin stood at attention as the president of the court addressed him. His dark blue suit hung loosely on his emaciated frame, and his thin fingers reached out to grip the polished mahogany of the defense table in front of him for support. Beside him Ben-Nathan coolly surveyed the scene, his gray eyes unfathomable.

"You understand, Mr. Chorin," the judge was saying, "that under Israeli law you, the defendant, have three alternatives in presenting your case. The first is that you may testify under oath. This requires that you submit to cross-examination by the prosecution; the second alternative is to be silent; the third is to make a declaration, in which case there is no cross-examination. Which do you choose?"

Chorin glanced down at Ben-Nathan, whose impatient nod urged him to proceed as they had planned. He looked back at the judge. "I choose to make a declaration, your honor." There were mutterings of disappointment from some of the press in the rear, but they died away almost immediately.

"Very well," Judge Lehmann replied. "You may proceed."

Chorin picked up several typewritten sheets from the desk, and in a high, rather monotonous voice started to read.

He began with his own life story. He had been born in Budapest, had graduated from the university, and then became a journalist. During the holocaust he had lost forty-six of the forty-seven members of his immediate family. He himself had served in a labor battalion and later had fought in the final battle for Budapest, receiving a head injury when a shell exploded near his bunker. He condemned those Jews who had collaborated even in the slightest degree with the Nazis. That was why he had concentrated his journalistic fire on Andor Horvath, whom he considered the archenemy of Hungarian Jewry.

He spoke in a thin voice that was difficult for everyone to understand. Every ear in the courtroom was strained to catch his words. The spectators in the five rows of benches bent forward, some of them even cupping hands to their ears so as not to miss anything. Andor stared at him intently, his own eyes narrow, his fists clenched in his lap. Weiss looked over his papers. Ben-Nathan watched his witness dispassionately, apparently satisfied with the way he was reading his statement.

"I am not an old man," Chorin said, "but I have only a short time to live. I am ill. Very ill. However, during the few years that my doctor tells me I have left, I wish to live at peace with myself. I would, of course, like to have the power to bring back to life the dead—all our dear, dead people who lost their lives so needlessly in Hungary. But I am not an idiot. I know that this is impossible. So what can I do to justify the fact that I myself escaped death? I thought a long time about it and finally made my decision. I knew that it was my duty to my brothers and sisters, to my cousins and aunts and uncles—to all the members of my family who went to their deaths—as well as to the hundreds of thousands of other Hungarians who were murdered—it was my duty to reveal the truth about how they died, and why they died, and who was responsible. That is the reason I wrote the articles in the Tel Aviv *Morning News* about the extermination. That is the reason I stand here today. I am not the accused. Not really. I am the accuser. I accuse Andor Horvath of murder—of the murder of all the Jews of Hungary!"

As he finished and slumped into his chair, confusion swept the courtroom. Andor's friends began to shout imprecations against Chorin. A few of Chorin's friends applauded. Judge Lehmann banged his gavel angrily. Ben-Nathan signaled to a court attendant for a glass of water for his client. Weiss spoke placatingly to Andor, whose face was bright red with suppressed fury. It was several minutes before quiet was re-stored and Judge Lehmann asked, "Is the defense ready to continue?"

"We are, your honor." Ben-Nathan rose.

"Call your first witness."

"I call Maximilian Franck."

The bald-headed little man, his rotund body encased in an obviously expensive dark gray wool suit, rose in the spectators' section, a wide, toothy grin on his pudgy face, his black eyes gleaming with pleasure as he saw everyone staring at him. Several men waved to him as he moved to the front of the room, and he waved back. Judge Lehmann glared at him ominously as he took the oath and then stepped into the witness box, but Max was still grinning at his friends and didn't notice.

After the routine opening questions Ben-Nathan led him to state that he had begun working for the Hungarian Secret Service in 1942 and that his job was to discover the identities of German agents whose activities were causing unrest in Hungary.

"Did you know Andor Horvath at this time?"

"No. Erno Gábor introduced me to him in 1943."

"And after that you worked for the Budapest Rescue Committee, in addition to working for the Hungarian Secret Service?"

Max's chest expanded with pride. "Of course! I played a very im-portant part in the rescue work. Eight times I went to Istanbul with messages from the Committee and brought back money to Budapest."

"Andor Horvath was the head of the Rescue Committee?" Max nod-ded. "So he was an important man then?"

"Nah. There were plenty of others doing rescue work besides Horvath." The disdain in Max's voice was plain. "He wasn't more important than anybody else—until the *Germans* came in. After that Horvath began to negotiate with them. *Then* he was a big shot. They even gave him special identity papers to make sure he wouldn't be arrested."

"Did you ever receive special papers?"

"Naturally not. So I was arrested twice by the Gestapo."

"Did Horvath see the German officials often during the time he was negotiating with them?"

"Every day, almost. And at night he played cards with them."

"He played cards with them?"

"Yes, with Wedemeyer and the other higher-ups, he played cards."

Ben-Nathan paced before the witness box, his head lowered, his hands behind his back, letting the full implication of those words fill the courtroom. Then he turned back to the witness. "Did you ever meet Otto Wedemeyer or Walter Heinemann?"

"I met Heinemann several times. Colonel Wedemeyer I met only once, when I was called to his office and told that I had to go to Istanbul with Gábor."

"Did you know the purpose of this trip?"

"Colonel Heinemann explained it to me later. He said the Germans had offered to open negotiations for a separate peace with the Western Allies and that Wedemeyer's offer to save Jews was a cover-up for the peace negotiations. I told Heinemann I didn't think the West would make a peace without the Soviet Union."

"What was the result of your conversation?"

"Heinemann led me to believe that Gábor's mission wasn't taken seriously by the Germans because if the Germans made peace they would put an end to the extermination of the Jews. If they didn't make peace, nothing would save the Jews."

"Nevertheless, you went to Istanbul with Mr. Gábor on May 19, 1944. Tell the court what happened there."

Max explained that he and Erno drove with Heinemann to Vienna and left from there in a German plane. In Istanbul they went to the Pera Palace Hotel, each to a separate room. "A few minutes later a man who said he was an American agent came to my room, and we discussed Heinemann's separate peace proposal for several hours."

"Was the American impressed by this proposal?"

"I don't know. He spent most of the night questioning me."

"Did you see him again?"

"No. The next day the Turks wanted to expel both Gábor and me to the Bulgarian border, but I had some influential friends in the country"—he smiled slyly—"and with their help I received permission to be sent to Jerusalem."

"Did you get to Jerusalem?"

"No. When the train stopped at Aleppo, on the Syrian border, I was arrested by British intelligence and taken to Cairo, where I was imprisoned until May of 1945."

"Did you see Mr. Gábor again?"

"No. When I left for Jerusalem, he was still in Istanbul, as far as I knew. Later, when I was in prison, I heard that he was in Cairo under house arrest in another part of the city."

"And that was the end of the mission?"

"As far as I know, that was the end."

"No more questions." Ben-Nathan went back to his seat.

Weiss opened his cross-examination by saying, "Mr. Franck, when you were released from the prison in Cairo, where did you go?"

Max looked uncomfortable. "To Turkey."

"You went of your own volition back to Turkey?"

"You know I was expelled," Max answered peevishly.

"You were expelled to Turkey. What happened to you there?"

"I don't know what you mean, what happened?"

"Weren't you tried for smuggling and for spying for the Allies?"

"They were trumped-up charges."

"Nevertheless, you were convicted on both counts, were you not? And you were fined for the smuggling and sentenced to four years for spying."

Max blinked nervously. "Yes, but—"

"That's all, Mr. Franck. You've answered the question. Now let's go back to Hungary. You testified that you joined the Hungarian Secret Service in 1942 to help ferret out German agents in the country."

"Yes."

"Wasn't the real reason that you had a two-year sentence for smuggling hanging over your head and you were promised that you could avoid serving it if you worked for the Secret Service?"

"That's a lie!" A flash of crimson covered Max's round face and drops of perspiration appeared on his upper lip.

"But you *had* been convicted twice before 1942 for smuggling."

The pudgy figure shifted resentfully in the witness box.

"Answer the question."

"Yes!"

Weiss walked slowly away from the witness box and back toward Max again. "Mr. Franck, you testified that Mr. Horvath had special papers issued by the Gestapo to protect him and that you had no papers. How did you protect yourself? Wasn't it by working for the Gestapo?"

"No!"

"I tell you that you worked for the Gestapo not to save Jews but for money. Isn't it true that you worked for the Gestapo, the Hungarians, and the Jewish Agency, and you told each of them you worked only for them?"

Max was choleric. He waved his arms frantically, shouting, "You have no right to vilify me, God will punish you for what you're saying." He choked and fell against the enclosure.

Ben-Nathan stood immediately. "Your honor, the witness is obviously distraught as a result of this trying experience. I request a recess to allow him to regain his composure."

Judge Lehmann turned to Max. "Would you like a recess, Mr. Franck?"

With this solicitude Max partially recovered. "No, but I would like a glass of water."

The judge motioned to an attendant, who brought the water. Max gulped it and wiped his red face with a large white linen handkerchief. "I'm ready to go on now," he announced.

"You may proceed, Counselor," the judge said to Weiss.

"Mr. Franck, you stated that Mr. Horvath played cards with the Gestapo," Weiss began. "But that was a lie, wasn't it? There wasn't a word of truth in it."

"Of course it's true. I swear it. He played cards with them several times a week—and usually lost. Once he lost almost twenty thousand dollars."

"How do you know?"

"It was common gossip. Everybody knew."

"I tell you you knew because *you* played cards with the Gestapo." Max shifted his squat body tiredly.

"Didn't you?" Weiss barked.

"Yes."

The prosecutor again moved away from the witness box and, in a quiet voice once more, asked, "When you were released from the Turkish prison in 1948 where did you go?"

"To Israel."

"This is your home?"

"Yes."

"But you aren't a citizen. You are still listed as a tourist. Can you tell us why?"

The plump dapper figure seemed to shrink. "When I applied for citizenship shortly after I arrived here, the Israel authorities told me I was not welcome in this country," he mumbled dejectedly.

"That's all, Mr. Franck." Weiss's tone of dismissal was peremptory.

During the afternoon Ben-Nathan called several witnesses, all survivors of Auschwitz. The first was an accountant from Debrecen, the second a lawyer from Pécs, and the third a merchant from Mukačevo. All three testified that the Jewish communities in their cities were completely unaware of the exterminations in Auschwitz and were never informed by the Rescue Committee in Budapest of their imminent danger, despite the fact that telephone communications with the capital still existed in April and May. So they allowed themselves to be herded into ghettos and later, willingly, even eagerly, boarded the death trains, believing the lie the Germans had spread, that they were going to an internment camp for the duration of the war and that those who arrived there first would get the best living quarters and jobs. When they reached Auschwitz, the terrible reality overwhelmed them. Had they known what was going to happen to them, they would have made another choice; they would have revolted. The merchant from Mukačevo, a city less than three miles from the Rumanian border, declared that escape to that country would have been relatively easy.

Weiss cross-examined them only briefly. From each man he drew the admission that their statements were based on hindsight knowledge and that, in fact, it was always easy to be wise after the event.

The day's last witness was Miriam Berg. She was still slender and elegant, even in the plain dark cotton dress she wore. In a low, sweet voice, her pale eyes filled with sadness, she told of her imprisonment with Naomi and of their experiences under custody.

"Did you do anything after your release on behalf of your sister?" Ben-Nathan asked coldly.

"Oh yes," Miriam said quickly. "I was told that Andor Horvath was the one person who could help me. I was told that he had a great deal of influence with the Nazis and that he knew something about the parachutists. They said I must see Andor Horvath, so I tried."

"Did you ever succeed in seeing him?"

"Never!"

"How often did you try?"

"At least half a dozen times."

"Did you go to his office?"

"Yes, and I also tried several times to see him at his apartment."

"Do you mean to tell the court that Andor Horvath refused to see you?"

"I was never able to see him."

"Did he know that you wanted to see him about your sister?"

"Of course. I told his secretary many times." She paused, then added softly, without any trace of recrimination, "He just refused to see me."

"Did his secretary give any reason?"

"She always said he was busy, working on extremely important matters."

"Did you have any idea what these important matters were?"

"She gave me to understand that they had to do with saving Jews."

"But your sister Naomi was Jewish, was she not?"

"Of course." Miriam's quite soft voice was creating a new mood in the courtroom. From the judge's bench to the back row of spectators there was a somber hush as Ben-Nathan turned to Weiss and said, "Your witness."

The prosecutor rose slowly and with a slight bow said, "I have nothing to ask. Thank you, Mrs. Berg."

40

The Trial: Ninth Day

Ben-Nathan introduced in evidence a record of the proceedings of the Twenty-second World Zionist Congress, reading aloud several excerpts commending Andor Horvath for his work in saving Jewish lives. Then he called Abraham Kossuth to the witness box.

Kossuth had been the head of the Palestine Immigration Office in Budapest during the war. He was a sturdy man of medium height, about fifty, with a head of sparse brown hair mixed with gray, and large thick features. His suit was baggy and wrinkled. There was a somber, determined expression on his face as he took the oath and answered Ben-Nathan's questions.

"During your years as head of the Palestine Immigration Office, did you know Andor Horvath?" the defense attorney asked him.

"Yes, I knew him well. We met many times to discuss Jewish emigration and the distribution of the certificates the British sent us through the Jewish Agency."

"Tell the court about those meetings, please."

"Well, as soon as Horvath became head of the Rescue Committee he began to pressure me and my assistants to give him more and more certificates to Palestine for favored individuals—"

"What kinds of individuals?"

"Mostly Zionists, chalutzim, some friends of his, and important people who were eager to get out of Hungary."

"Did you give in to this pressure?"

"I tried to be fair—to distribute certificates among all groups—the

Orthodox, Neologs, and the Zionists, regardless of how rich or important they were."

"Did your attitude cause friction between you and Mr. Horvath?"

"Yes. He tried to tell me how to run my office. He was always interfering."

"Did this interference increase in the spring of 1944, after the Germans occupied Hungary?"

"Yes. I heard that Horvath had begun negotiations with them, and one day when he came to see me I asked him about it. He told me a little about Wedemeyer's proposal, but he said it was unlikely the Germans would permit mass emigration of Jews from Hungary, therefore it was important to keep my office operating so that we could at least get legal immigration certificates. Later, on another visit, he said that the Germans were demanding certain things in return for allowing Hungarian Jews to emigrate, but he refused to tell me what those things were. He said it was a Reich secret. In the meantime he continued to demand certificates for people *he* thought should get them."

"What did you think of the proposition when you did learn what the Germans wanted?"

"I thought it was a deception, and I said so to my Zionist acquaintances and to members of the Jewish Council. I told them the Bergen-Belsen rescue train was a clever trick to weaken the Hungarian Jews by encouraging many community leaders and Zionists to board the train. Without these leaders there was little chance that the thousands of Jews left behind would revolt, as they had in Warsaw. The Nazis also wished to create bitterness among the Jews by encouraging competition for places on the rescue train."

"Did you tell this to Horvath?"

"Yes, but he only answered that Wedemeyer had shown his good will by agreeing to allow fifteen hundred people to go on the train instead of the original few hundred Wedemeyer had offered. That made Horvath think that if he appeased them he might be able to set up another rescue train, and then another."

"Did you have other differences of opinion with Horvath?"

"Yes. In mid-June the Jews who were still in Budapest began to receive post cards written by people presumably in work camps. I saw some of them. The messages were all alike: the writer was in good health, he was working, and he didn't want for anything. I mentioned this similarity to Horvath and told him he should warn the people who received the cards that their relatives and friends had probably been forced to write these messages; that they had probably been taken to Auschwitz. But he refused to warn them."

"Since you didn't approve of Horvath's activities, did you do anything to counteract them?"

"Several things. On June 19, I sent a report on the exterminations in Auschwitz to the JA representative in Switzerland. This report was published in Swiss newspapers a few days later. As a result the Pope appealed to the Hungarian Government to stop the actions against the Jews, and the United States threatened to retaliate against the Hungarians if the exterminations were not halted. So on July 2 the Hungarian Government declared that the deportations had been stopped. That wasn't true, but they were stopped by July 7. After this I implied in my reports to the JA representative in Switzerland that Horvath was being used by the Nazis. Finally in August I requested that the Agency stop sending funds to Horvath since they were only being used to destroy the Jews. I also requested permission not to deal with the Budapest Rescue Committee any more."

"Were your requests granted?"

"No. Instead I was discharged by the Agency."

"Why?"

"I wasn't given any reason."

"Did you feel that the Palestine Immigration Office, under your direction, had done a good job of saving Jews?"

"Yes. We supplied passports to approximately ninety thousand people. About eighty thousand of them were given to us by Switzerland, four thousand by Sweden, fifteen hundred by the Vatican, and about seven hundred by Portugal."

"Yet, in spite of this, you were discharged. Do you feel Horvath was in any way responsible for your dismissal?"

"Yes. He tried several times to sabotage the work of my office. The continuation of my policy of public appeal and rescue through diplomatic channels in the Palestine office might have destroyed his deal with the Nazis."

"In 1944 did you believe Horvath was making serious mistakes, or did you think he had evil intentions?"

"Horvath thought the Germans were very powerful when they occupied Hungary and that negotiating with them was the best way to save the Jews. But after it was obvious to everyone that they were losing the war, he still continued to negotiate with them. He knew he was doing the wrong thing, but he wanted to justify his past activities, irrespective of the consequences. In that sense he had bad intentions."

"Are you saying that Horvath collaborated with the Nazis?"

Kossuth hesitated. "Well, he worked with them long after he knew the deal was dead, so I guess you could say he collaborated."

Judge Lehmann's pale eyebrows shot up.

Weiss leaped to his feet. "Objection! Your honor, I ask that the witness' last remark be stricken from the record. It is, by the witness' own admission, an unsubstantiated 'guess.' A man's reputation, perhaps his entire career, is at stake in this courtroom."

"The witness' last remark will be stricken," the judge ruled; then he addressed Kossuth: "I caution you to use the utmost care and accuracy in your language. The court is not interested in guesses. Now, Mr. Kossuth, tell the court: what is your definition of a collaborator?"

Weiss sat up alertly as he heard the question. It surprised and worried him. On Ben-Nathan's young face there was the hint of a grin and an unmistakable look of gratification.

"A collaborator is a person who works with the enemy against the interests of his own people," Kossuth replied.

"Do you think that a person who has worked with the Nazis to save Jews and has been unsuccessful is a collaborator?" Lehmann continued.

"No. But if a person has worked with them knowing they were exploiting him for their own ends, then he is a collaborator. I am convinced that this is what Andor Horvath did."

For the first time Judge Lehmann looked weary. "Do you have any more questions of this witness, Counselor?" he asked Ben-Nathan.

"No, sir."

"Then we will recess for the noon hour."

"Mr. Kossuth," the Attorney General began when court reconvened at one-thirty, "you have shown a compulsion to credit every successful rescue operation to your own efforts."

Kossuth looked nettled. "I have no such compulsion. I freely admit that many other people were engaged in successful rescue work, but Horvath was not one of them. He used his energy to frustrate the work of others, including the Palestine Immigration Office."

"Even if that is true, how does it prove that Andor Horvath worked for the Germans, as you have charged?"

"He was helping those who followed the Nazi line."

"Are you aware that the accusations you are making against Mr. Horvath are extremely grave?"

"Yes."

"But what you have said in this courtroom indicates only that he didn't work with you. It doesn't in any way show that he collaborated with the Nazis."

"Then I'll make the connection clear. If the Jews had organized resistance, the Hungarians would have helped them, because the Hungarians, while they were passively anti-Semitic and wanted restrictions on Jews in business and professions like law and medicine, they didn't welcome the deportations."

"Mr. Kossuth, you know very well that it would have been impossible to carry out the deportations if the great majority of Hungarian people had been against such a policy."

Kossuth's large features took on a grim, tight expression. "I dispute that. The truth is that the Germans didn't want the Hungarians to learn of the deportations until they were an accomplished fact. So they carried out the deportations as quickly as possible. But in the meantime they needed a man who could keep the Jews calm and quiet. A man like Horvath." He spat out the name. "Many thousands of Jews—maybe even a hundred thousand—might have been saved if Horvath had stopped collaborating with the Nazis in the early summer of 1944 and worked with me to get help from the outside world."

"This is all conjecture, based on contrary-to-fact suppositions." Weiss's voice had a disparaging tone. "It has absolutely nothing to do with what actually took place in Hungary."

"I deny that. And the proof of my statements is that the deportations were stopped in July as a result of the memorandum on Auschwitz which I sent to Switzerland, the same memorandum that was printed in most of the western European and American newspapers. I insist that if Horvath had placed his funds and political connections at my disposal, much more could have been done, and much earlier. Early enough to save the Jews of Hungary."

"Mr. Kossuth, you have insisted on predicting the outcome of situations that never existed, thereby putting yourself in a very favorable light. Let's examine a real situation in which you made a prediction. On October 13, 1944, you sent a letter to the Agency Executive harshly disapproving of the Bergen-Belsen rescue train, didn't you?"

Kossuth bit his lip and hesitated.

"I can introduce a copy of the letter in evidence if that will refresh your memory."

Kossuth glowered at him from under shaggy gray-brown brows. "It's not necessary. I wrote such a letter."

"You also said in this letter that you didn't think the train would ever reach Switzerland."

"Yes."

"But it did reach Switzerland, didn't it?"

Kossuth sighed audibly. "Yes."

"Yet on the basis of this faulty prediction you also asked in this letter of October 13 that Mr. Horvath be dismissed as head of the Rescue Committee."

Kossuth's chin dropped to his chest. What he mumbled was not audible.

"But you never told anyone that Mr. Horvath was in the service of the Nazis."

"That's not true!" Kossuth's head snapped up. "I told lots of people."

"What did they say—that you had lost your senses?"

"No. They believed me, but they were afraid of Horvath, so they didn't do anything about it. Most of the Zionists who didn't board the rescue train felt the same way about Horvath as I did."

"Isn't there another explanation for your attitude toward Andor Horvath—that you were humiliated and angry because you weren't chosen to be a member of the Budapest Rescue Committee?"

"That's ridiculous!"

"No further questions." Weiss went back to his seat. Andor immediately leaned over and whispered, "Did he hurt us?"

Weiss shook his head. "Not much."

Kossuth stepped from the box with a heavy, shuffling tread, his expression grimmer than before.

The mahogany clock on the wall chimed four times.

"Is the defense prepared to continue its case tomorrow morning?" Lehmann asked.

Ben-Nathan replied "Yes" and said Andor Horvath would appear. "He will be our last witness, your honor."

"Very well. Court is adjourned until nine o'clock tomorrow morning."

People began to leave. Outside, in the crowded corridor, half a dozen reporters lay in wait for Andor. As he appeared, they pressed about him, firing questions as people continued to stream out of the courtroom. By the time the last reporter had left, there were only two men and a woman standing at the far end of the corridor, engaged in low-toned conversation. Andor started to leave, but at that moment Ben-Nathan came out of the deserted courtroom alone. The men acknowledged each other with a nod. Then Andor offered his hand to the young lawyer. "Mr. Ben-Nathan," he smiled, "I'm told that the greatest danger to my reputation is the fact that you'll have me in the box tomorrow. I've been told that your examination can be stronger than the examinations at Nuremberg."

It was said half in jest, a polite compliment to an opponent. But Ben-Nathan didn't smile back. He said earnestly, "If you answer me one question, you won't have to worry about your reputation, Mr. Horvath."

"All right, I will. What is it?" Andor replied, still keeping a light tone.

"You were a leader of eight hundred thousand Jews. No one really knows what happened. But they were gassed and you are alive. Years have passed. You've returned to the free world, leaving them behind. Let's not judge what you did under horrible pressure. Let's examine what you did later, in the free world."

Andor listened tolerantly, trying to maintain a pleasant expression, wondering when the lawyer would get to the point.

"I read in the press two days ago that you said, 'Owing to grave mistakes of the Jewish Agency, hundreds of thousands of Jews weren't saved.'"

Andor nodded.

Ben-Nathan regarded him incredulously. "I would understand if you called for a public inquiry into the JA's policy. I would understand if you moved to Hawaii and started life all over again, trying to forget it all. I could even understand if you came to Israel, opened a small business, and began a new kind of life. Any of these things would be only human and understandable. But to say that you think the Jewish Agency, the present leadership of this country, is responsible for the debacle and then to run back into the midst of this leadership . . . How can you do it? If you can explain this, I'll quit the case."

Andor had to admire him. He was shrewd, quick, aggressive, and tough. But he was also a *sabra,* and he hadn't seen the cold, stench-filled, starving ghettos, the screaming terror in the deportation trains, the smoking chimneys of the crematoria, the insane panic of refugees fleeing from the crushing heels of the SS. He was young, too, and he didn't know much about mistakes. He hadn't lived long enough to make very many, and he hadn't been important enough to make big ones.

"Yaacov," he said gently, addressing the young man by his first name, "what you ask isn't a simple question. But I'll answer it, someday, when the case is over, maybe when we have coffee together. Then I'll tell you the whole story."

"Give me a plain, logical answer now or there'll be no coffee after the case," Ben-Nathan snapped. Andor shook his head ruefully. Ben-Nathan lit a cigarette, blew out a cloud of smoke, and then added persuasively, "I won't use it against you if you give me a simple answer now, out of court."

Andor laughed, but it was a bitter sound. Once again he shook his head, then walked down the corridor and out into the courtyard.

At dinner that evening in the small alcove of the Strauss's apartment he ate absent-mindedly, hardly noticing what Vera put on his plate. The girls chattered with Leo about school, but Vera watched Andor.

"Something is wrong with the *kreplach?*" she asked him finally.

He looked startled. "No—no, it's fine, delicious."

"So since when do you have to chew for five minutes on each one?"

"Vera!" Leo reprimanded her, for the first time noticing the preoccupied expression of his friend.

"I'm *sorry,*" she said huffily, glaring at her husband. "I'm only asking is something wrong. It's so terrible to ask?"

"That's enough!" Leo turned to Hannah and Debbie. "Come, girls, finish your supper and go inside. No more talking."

When they had left, Vera cleared the table and silently served coffee to the two men. Then she left, too.

"Something bad happened today?" Leo asked, blowing on his coffee to cool it.

"I think so." Andor told him about the conversation with Ben-Nathan. "You know, he's clever and very ambitious. It's all over him. That's bad enough, but there's more. He's something of a fanatic. This isn't just a case he's got to win because it will make him a big lawyer; it's a cause. He's convinced I'm a dangerous villain, and I think he'll do anything he can to destroy me."

"And you think he can?" Leo scoffed. "So he wants to be a big shot. Does that make him one? He's a *nebbishe,* a nothing, a little smart-aleck lawyer. Why are you worrying?"

Andor grinned. "You know me, Leo. I'm sure I'm cleverer than he is. Just the same," he added soberly, "he makes me uneasy."

Leo got up and clapped him on the back. "Come, take your mind off Chorin and Ben-Nathan and the Nazis for a while. Let's play cards. We'll see who's the cleverest in this house tonight." He took a deck of cards out of the serving table and then paused. "You know, I owe Vera two pounds from last time. Should we ask her to play? Such a bluffer she is, we both might be broke by tomorrow."

In spite of himself, Andor laughed.

41

The Trial: Tenth Day

The morning sky was dismal and dark. Intermittently rain drizzled outside the tall french windows of the courthouse. Ben-Nathan, his black robe billowing about his stocky frame, looked dour as he shifted papers on his table and conferred with his assistant.

Judge Lehmann appeared, and the session began. Ben-Nathan rose to wind up the case for the defense and called Andor Horvath. Andor, handsome and well tailored as always, moved easily and with assurance to the witness box, his misgivings of the previous day gone. This morning he felt renewed and strong. Ben-Nathan seemed very young and not at all dangerous as he began. "Mr. Horvath, when were you interrogated by the Israel police about your activities in Pécs?"

"Three years ago."

"Do you know why they waited until just three years ago?"

"No."

"Don't you know that precisely at that time the Nazi Collaborators Law was passed?"

"I knew that the law was passed."

"And you took no interest in the connection between the law and your interrogation?"

"I took no interest in the subject at all." Andor's manner was good-humored and polite, with just the right touch of hauteur to make Ben-Nathan and his questions seem trivial.

"I tell you that the officer questioned you concerning the charge that because of your activities the people in the Pécs ghetto didn't try to escape across the border to Yugoslavia."

"That's not true."

"Mr. Horvath, you knew the fate that awaited the Jews of Hungary, but did you warn them? Did you urge them to escape? What did you tell them during your visits to the provinces?"

"I told them the situation was grave."

"Did you tell anyone in Pécs what you knew about Auschwitz?"

"I had no certain knowledge. I had only suspicions. Of course I told the people in Pécs about them. I told everyone. But I couldn't say to my friends, 'All of you will be sent to Auschwitz and exterminated.' I had no such information. I could only tell them there was a danger of deportation and deportation meant extermination and therefore they must do everything to save as many Jews as possible. I said this during my last visit."

"After the deportation had begun and it became clear that the trains were going to Auschwitz, did you tell anyone in Pécs about it?"

"Then I had no more contact with Pécs. But I did speak on the telephone with my father-in-law, and whatever I could say on the phone I told him. I said the situation was very bad, and he knew what that meant. After all, we had discussed the possibility of deportation and extermination."

"The court wishes to question the witness," Judge Lehmann said. "Mr. Horvath," the judge began, "at the end of April you had information that gas chambers and crematoria were being prepared in Auschwitz for the Hungarian Jews. And you also knew that Slovakia had agreed to allow passage of the trains to Auschwitz through that country. How can you say you didn't know?"

Andor was dismayed. What did Lehmann think he had been, a prophet? But he kept his tone calm and pleasant. "These were rumors, and I had no way of telling whether they were true or false. Such information was whispered about, but there was also contradictory information."

"But Gábor left Budapest on May 19, and he told the Agency representatives in Istanbul that twelve thousand Jews were being sent to Auschwitz every day."

"I don't know why he said that."

"On the strength of the meeting with Wedemeyer."

"But Wedemeyer told us he would wait two weeks."

"Two weeks later then, and at a rate of twelve thousand a day."

"I don't know how Gábor knew about the rate."

"But he said it in Istanbul—and you knew it, too."

"I had doubts at the end of May. Until then I thought, maybe not, not in such numbers."

"But as of the middle of May you knew that every day closed trains were going—this you knew?"

411

"Yes."

"Then why didn't you let the Jews of Pécs know what you knew?"

"All that I knew I told them as long as I could communicate with them."

"Then why didn't all the Jews of Pécs know about it?"

"You're asking my opinion? Well, I think that my colleagues in Pécs, including my father-in-law, didn't do everything that it was possible for them to do. They should have, perhaps, speeded up not only escape operations but warnings. Perhaps they feared it might have been dangerous to spread rumors among the public."

Judge Lehmann gazed at him somberly. "That is the only reason you can think of?"

"Yes, the only one that seems logical."

The judge looked to Ben-Nathan. "You may resume your examination, Counselor."

For the rest of the morning Ben-Nathan pulled apart the answers Andor had given the judge, but Andor refused to withdraw or change them. In the afternoon he attacked from another angle.

"Mr. Horvath," he began, "did your Committee have a representative in the Pécs ghetto?"

"No."

"Was Philip Kemeny in the ghetto?"

"Yes."

"Isn't it true that he went out of the ghetto on several occasions?"

"I don't know."

"Try to remember. I repeat: he went out of the ghetto on several occasions, to the hospital in the city."

Andor shot him an irritated look. "I assume that's correct."

"Did Kemeny take part in composing the list for the Bergen-Belsen rescue train?"

"As far as I know, no."

"Who did?"

"I understand it was a four-member committee: Leo Strauss and three other men."

"The three others were members of the Pécs Jewish Council?"

"Yes."

"Isn't it true that taking three hundred eighty out of several thousand in the city caused bitterness and tragedy?"

"Yes."

"Isn't it true that a letter you sent to Strauss constituted the basis of selection?"

"Yes."

"What principles did you lay down to Strauss for composing the list?"

"The principles were: 1. public figures, both Zionist and non-Zionist; 2. wives and children of those who had already been deported; 3. workers of official Jewish and Zionist institutions."

"Did your father-in-law, Philip Kemeny, speak to you about the list?"

"As I have testified, I had short telephone conversations with Mr. Kemeny. He asked me on the phone whether there was a possibility of rescuing some of the Jews in Pécs. But we didn't talk about the composition of a list at all. I received only one request from him—to include Rabbi Jesse Gershon. Except for this one we mentioned no names."

"Mr. Kemeny didn't mention the members of his family?"

"He was my late wife's father. He didn't need to recommend the members of his family. He knew they would be included."

"How many members of *your* family were included from Pécs?"

"Fourteen."

"Who were they?"

"My father-in-law, my sister, her child and husband, his two sisters-in-law with two children each, two brothers-in-law of my father-in-law, each with one child. They went on the train, but before the train started for the Columbus utca camp in Budapest, my mother's sisters, with five other members of her family, had already been sent to Auschwitz."

"Did you have other relatives in Pécs who had not been deported?"

"Yes."

"And your father-in-law?"

"I don't think so."

"How many of the Gábor family went on the train?"

"I don't know exactly. About five or six, as far as I remember."

"And the families of the other members of your Committee?"

"The other members of the Committee had no relatives in Pécs, as far as I can remember."

"Try to remember, Mr. Horvath. Apart from the fourteen relatives you mentioned, were there any other of your relatives who went on the train?"

"I don't remember any others."

"And of the other members of the Committee?"

"Arthur Gruen's wife and children."

"Can you mention any of your friends?"

"The Wallach family, the Levins, Leon Wechsler with his father and sister."

"Did you have any more friends on the list?"

"Some. I grew up in Pécs with the Zionists, and I was friendly with many of them."

"There were, then, a large number of your friends on the list?"

"I suppose you could say there were a large number."

"Mr. Horvath, is it true that when the rescue train left Pécs for Budapest, most of the people in the ghetto had already been deported to Auschwitz?"

"Yes."

"And while several thousand Jews were being sent from Pécs to their deaths, the four members of the committee were busy composing a list of a few hundred who were to be rescued?"

"I don't know that they were busy with this *alone,* but they were busy with this."

"And they didn't advise the Jews to resist with arms, or even passively?"

"I didn't hear of it."

"How can you explain the fact that there were more people on the rescue train from Pécs than from any of the other provincial towns?"

"It didn't depend on me."

"And I tell you that you asked for it especially from Wedemeyer."

"No. I did not."

"Did you demand that the Jews of Pécs pay for their places on the train?"

"Their property had been confiscated before this, so they didn't pay. But in Budapest we asked for and received payment from the wealthy."

Ben-Nathan led him to describe in detail exactly how places on the train were sold and how he had arranged with Hugo Mayer for the latter to get money from the wealthy Orthodox people of Budapest who wanted to board it. Then he asked, "Weren't you afraid that the Bergen-Belsen train would be regarded by the Germans as your tacit approval of the deportations?"

Andor snorted contemptuously. "My answer is that the Germans didn't give a damn for this 'approval.'"

42

The Trial: Eleventh Day

Because the morning newspapers had said that Andor Horvath would be questioned next about the parachutists, every seat in the courtroom was taken long before Judge Lehmann rapped his gavel and opened the eleventh day of the trial. Ben-Nathan began his examination by asking, "Mr. Horvath, will you agree with me that the parachutists Farber and Klein and their companions came to Hungary to organize a resistance to the Germans and to engage in rescue and sabotage?"

"Yes."

"And you delivered them up to the Gestapo."

"No. I didn't give them up but I gave myself up, because their arrival was known the moment they crossed the border. My problem was whether to try to protect them and myself by going to the Gestapo and informing the Germans of their presence before they asked me about it. I decided to do this after Klein disappeared because I was afraid that he had been captured by the Hungarians. All this happened a week before the departure of the Bergen-Belsen train, while the rescue of Jews from the provincial ghettos was taking place."

"When the parachutists came to Hungary, was one of their tasks to meet with the Gestapo?"

"I don't know that they had any such task."

"Wasn't it clear to you that after such a meeting Farber wouldn't be able to organize resistance to the Germans in Hungary?"

"No. It wasn't clear at all. Even after meeting with the Gestapo it was possible, in principle, to organize resistance, though the possibility was slim."

"Did you know that Klein was an idealistic boy?"

"And how!"

"Who went with him when he gave himself up?"

"One or two members of the Committee."

"I tell you it was you who went!"

Andor hesitated. "I don't remember exactly, it's been several years, but I accept the responsibility." He felt no compunction about lying to Ben-Nathan. It was almost like the times he had lied to Wedemeyer.

His life and the lives of others had been at stake then. Now his integrity and honor were at stake. If he lost them, he might as well be dead. This young fanatic before him would be no sorrier than Wedemeyer would have been to see him dead, despite the fact that one was a Jew and the other had been a Nazi. That was the irony of it. Each hated the other and both hated him.

"Did you know that Farber ordered Klein to leave the country and that he agreed to go?" Ben-Nathan barked, rousing Andor from his reverie.

"Yes, I, too, wondered whether to give Klein an opportunity to go on the rescue train or to advise him to stay. Both possibilities involved dangers. I decided to advise him to stay, because I couldn't be sure the Germans wouldn't search the train and find him. And there was no other way to leave the country at that time."

"You mean it was you who demanded that Klein stay?"

"I didn't demand it from him. I advised him."

"Did you want to take him to the Gestapo as well?"

"It's possible that one of my intentions was to take him to the Gestapo to convince them that he didn't run away, that he had come to Hungary for the purpose of rescue in connection with Gábor's mission, as we had explained to them."

"And what if I tell you that there is a well-founded assumption that Klein was arrested a few steps from the Columbus utca camp?"

"That's a romantic version of what happened, but an untrue one. Klein gave himself up at Gestapo headquarters." That wasn't exactly a lie, he thought. It depended on how you looked at it. It was a fact that Mueller hadn't actually arrested the boy.

"And you accompanied him there."

"Maybe I accompanied him."

"Mr. Horvath, when did you first learn of Naomi Loeb's presence in Hungary?"

"As well as I can remember, in October 1944."

"Did you know that Naomi arrived in Hungary before the other two parachutists?"

"Now I know. But Farber and Klein, when they came to see me, didn't tell me that she was a member of their group. They kept it secret. I wish they had told me."

"Who told you Naomi was in the country?"

"Rachel Teller, who is now married to Klein. She told me Naomi's sister visited her and told her that she had received a note from Naomi in prison. Joe Nagel, Rachel, and I discussed possible ways of helping her. We decided to find out from the Hungarian authorities if there was any chance of releasing Naomi, together with Farber and Klein, for whom we had already tried to find a way out. If we failed there, we would go to the Germans. We also decided to learn whether Naomi had a lawyer and if not, to give her financial or other assistance, so she would have legal representation."

"Did you appoint a lawyer for her?"

"As far as I can remember, yes. He was a Hungarian lawyer, a young army man."

"What was his name?"

"I don't remember. I think one of my workers contacted him."

"Do you know whether the lawyer visited Naomi?"

"I'm not sure."

"Did you ask your worker whether the lawyer visited her?"

"Of course. As far as I can remember, he said that the lawyer told him he had visited Naomi."

"Did you ask when?"

"No."

"Did you ask how many times he saw her?"

"No."

"Did you ask if she had sent any message to you?"

"No."

"Did you ask whether she was tortured?"

"No."

"Did you ask whether she had anything to eat?"

"No."

"I tell you, Mr. Horvath, that you took absolutely no interest in Naomi's fate!"

"That's not true! I didn't have to ask anyone about it. I knew that being imprisoned wasn't comfortable and pleasant."

"Did you see the lawyer yourself?"

"No. The legal handling of the matter was not in my hands. I handled the political negotiations."

"Mr. Horvath, I suggest you refresh your memory. You didn't appoint a lawyer for Naomi at all."

"You are mistaken. We did appoint a lawyer for her."

"Did you ever meet Mrs. Miriam Berg, Naomi's sister?"

"No. She never asked to see me, as far as I know. She could have seen me like any other Jew who came to see me. My door was open."

"Did you have a secretary?"

"Yes."

"Was it necessary to go through your secretary in order to see you?"

"Not always. Hundreds of people saw me. Why didn't she come to me?"

"And if I tell you she asked for an interview through your secretary?"

"If that had been so, my secretary would have told me."

"Did you send a package to Naomi?"

"Sending packages to Naomi was a matter handled by Rachel. As far as I remember, she told me that packages were sent both to Naomi and the two other parachutists."

"Whom did you contact in your effort to get Naomi released?"

"I spoke to two Hungarians: Dr. Sigray in the Ministry of Defense, and Lieutenant Colonel of the Police Ravasz. Among the Germans, I spoke to Colonel Heinemann, his deputy, and with someone from the German counterintelligence."

"Did you visit Naomi in prison?"

"I asked Ravasz for permission and he refused. He refused to give me permission to visit Farber and Klein, too, although I insisted."

"Why did you especially insist on visiting Farber and Klein?"

"Because I knew both of them officially. Officially I knew nothing of Naomi. She was arrested on the border as a spy, and the other two came to me and told me they had come on a rescue mission."

"And I tell you, Mr. Horvath, that you didn't want any contact with a British spy or with her sister!"

"That's not true."

"Is it true, Mr. Horvath, that Naomi Loeb was a British soldier besides being an emissary of the Jewish Agency?"

"Yes."

"Then why didn't you appeal to the Swiss Legation, which represented British interests in Hungary?"

"I appealed to the Red Cross, not to the Swiss Legation. I don't remember the considerations any more."

"What was the result of your appeal to the Red Cross?"

"I attempted to arrange a meeting between the Red Cross representative and Lieutenant Colonel Ravasz."

"I asked you what the *result* of your appeal was, Mr. Horvath."

"Before I managed to arrange the meeting, Naomi was executed."

During the afternoon session Ben-Nathan continued to go over and over the misadventures of Ely, Martin, and Naomi. As the day wore on, his voice became loud and strident. Andor, unable to recall all the minutiae of events that had occurred so long ago, sometimes gave answers that sounded vague and evasive. He was relieved when the session ended. The next day was Shabbat. He would go home to Jessica immediately. With her he could rest, he would have time to think, too, and refresh his memory.

43

The Trial: Twelfth Day

The trial resumed on Sunday. Most of the day's session was given to Andor's financial negotiations with the Germans, Ben-Nathan pressing him to recount each transaction in detail, beginning with the first payments to Braun and Klaussen, down to the last payment made to Weber. When Andor stepped down from the witness box at four o'clock, he felt enervated; his head throbbed and his legs were leaden weights. He had been standing in the box for three days, and despite yesterday's rest the effects of physical exhaustion and Ben-Nathan's hammerlike questioning were beginning to show. He looked thinner, and there were faint gray shadows beneath his eyes. Still his spirit was high. He regarded his ordeal as a contest of will, strength, and intelligence between Ben-Nathan and himself. His old, implacable assurance that he would emerge the winner in any such contest still buoyed him up. Nevertheless, he had never been a man who confused foolhardiness with courage; he decided that tomorrow morning he would ask for a chair. Ben-Nathan was young and could stand all day, declaiming and waving his arms about. He, Andor, didn't have to, and he intended to take advantage of that fact, he told himself as he left the courtroom.

When he entered the apartment, Leo regarded him curiously. "You don't feel well?"

"I feel fine, fine. Just a little tired."

"What you need is a drink." Leo's brisk cheerfulness disguised the concern he felt at seeing his friend's dull eyes and pale drawn face. He went to the buffet and poured brandy into two glasses from the large decanter.

"An excellent idea," Andor said as he accepted the glass Leo held out to him. Suddenly the room seemed to whirl around him. Vaguely, far away, he heard Leo shouting. He felt his body grow weak and his legs give way. A strong arm grabbed him, and then there was nothing, only a bottomless blackness.

He woke up in his bed in the small guest room. A strange elderly doctor with delicate hands was bending over him with a stethoscope. Leo was standing on the other side of the bed nervously chain smoking.

The doctor slid the instrument down from his ears so that it hung about his neck. "Don't worry," he said reassuringly to Andor, "your heart is all right." He put the stethoscope into his bag and snapped it shut. "But you should rest in bed for a couple of days. I'll prescribe some medication. If you take it, in a few days you'll be completely well again."

"Please"—Andor forced himself up to a sitting position, although the effort made him break out into a sweat—"please, Doctor, fix me up so that I can be in court tomorrow. I don't want them to have the pleasure of my absence." He spoke the words bitterly.

He was pleading, something Leo had never seen him do before. It hurt Leo to see his dearest friend so reduced. Damn Ben-Nathan! What did he know? Nothing! Nothing but his ambition and the stories told by revengeful, jealous people who didn't have one small fraction of Andor's brains or courage. Leo's hands itched. What a pleasure it would be to wipe the cocksure expression off Ben-Nathan's face and shut that loud, accusing voice. But he pressed back his anger and instead echoed Andor's plea. "You can fix him up, can't you, Doctor?" he urged, sadly aware that his friend was at the edge of a precipice and that to be a whole man again, to be the old Andor, he had to appear in the witness box the next morning.

The doctor hesitated, then seemed to understand, and nodded his wizened head to mean a reluctant yes. He wrote a prescription and gave it to Leo. "See that he takes one every three hours."

Leo had the prescription filled immediately after the doctor left and gave the first pill to Andor, saying, "Vera and I are going out later. There is a meeting of the Hungarian Settlers' Society tonight, remember? Tabor will take over for you. I want to hear what's going on. Tomorrow I'll tell you all the gossip. In the meantime you rest. Hannah and Debbie are here. If you need anything, they'll bring it to you."

Andor reached out and patted Leo's hand gratefully. Almost at once he was asleep.

Some time later he was awakened by voices that seemed to be coming from the living room. One of them was Hannah's, thin and girlish, high and querulous with anger. The other was a boisterous, resentful male voice he didn't recognize. Their words were piercing staccato sounds to which his closed door was no barrier.

"You have no right to say such terrible things. You don't know what you're saying," Hannah cried.

"*You* don't know," the male voice flung back at her. "You're fooled because he's so handsome. Anyone who's so good-looking must be virtuous and intelligent and brave." The sarcasm was heavy. "Well, you'll find out. He's a liar and a cheat, a Nazi-lover, a murderer who doesn't deserve to live."

"You're just jealous." It was a shout. "You're just a boy and you're jealous of a real man."

By this time Andor was fully awake. He lumbered out of bed, pulled on a robe, and went into the living room. "What's going on here?" he demanded.

Embarrassment and contrition flooded Hannah's face. She rushed to him. "Uncle Andor, I'm sorry. We didn't mean to wake you. Here"— she extended her arm—"let me help you back to bed."

He brushed her aside and gazed at the youth. The boy was about nineteen, tall, thin, fair-haired, with a ruddy complexion that showed a few pockmarks, a sharp nose, and a thin, hungry mouth. He stared back at Andor defiantly. "Who is this young man?" Andor asked Hannah.

"My name is Chaim Glazer," the youth said.

Andor sat down on the sofa and lit a cigarette, inhaling deeply and continuing to survey the boy, who stood sullenly before him. He had a haunted, driven look, Andor thought, trying to keep his own expression impassive. "I take it you were discussing me?" he said to Chaim.

"Yes." The answer was flat and unrelenting.

Hannah moved nervously to Andor's side. "He didn't mean everything he said. He's lived in Israel all his life. He doesn't know what it was like in Europe."

"She's mistaken, Mr. Horvath." The boy's acid-sharp voice cut across Hannah's. "I meant every word."

"How dare you talk like that!" she screamed at him. She picked up his schoolbooks from the buffet and thrust them at him. "Get out of here!" One of them fell, open, on the floor.

Andor drew Hannah down beside him and gently smoothed her dark brown hair. "Don't, Hannah dear! It doesn't become you. The young man is entitled to his opinion." He turned to Chaim, who had reluctantly bent down to pick up the fallen book. "But you aren't entitled to try to force your opinions on other people—at least not in the home of my friends," he said. For a moment Chaim glared at him with impotent fury, then stalked out of the apartment, slamming the door behind him. Hannah threw her arms around Andor and began to cry.

"What's the matter with you *now?*" a petulant, childish voice asked from the doorway. Debbie was standing there, squinting beneath the bright light, barefooted, in rumpled blue pajamas, her dark hair tumbling over her shoulders.

"Go back to sleep," Hannah ordered her impatiently.

"I can't sleep. You make too much noise." She rubbed her eyes irritably. "Where's Chaim?"

"He's gone. Go back to bed, Debbie," Andor urged.

But now she was wide awake and eager for company. "I'm hungry." She padded to the kitchen and returned with a large chunk of *challah*. "Do you know what that Chaim told me?" she asked Hannah between bites, hoping to prolong her stay.

"I can't imagine."

"He said he and his friends had a plan to destroy all of Israel's enemies. He said it was their mission."

"Oh, he just likes to talk like a big man. Finish your *challah* and go back to bed," Hannah replied casually, but there was a cold feeling around her heart.

44

The Trial: Thirteenth Day

The next morning Andor felt better. As the early sun cast a cheerful brightness over the staid courtroom, the nightmarish quality of the previous night's experiences faded away. His request for a chair had been granted, so he sat comfortably in the witness box as Ben-Nathan introduced several documents in evidence and then asked his first question.

"When you went to the Swiss border for the last time with Colonel Heinemann, why didn't you take the treasure with you?"

"The explanation is simple. We went to Theresienstadt on April 16.

That was a week before the Americans and the Russians met. It was certain that I would be able to go from Theresienstadt to the border then, but twenty-four hours after I crossed into Switzerland the border was closed. If I had left Berlin a day later I would have had to remain in Theresienstadt, and I didn't want to take the responsibility of the treasure since I didn't know what might happen to me."

"Why did Weber give the treasure to Alex Peto?"

"Weber didn't want to leave the money in Berlin, so he took it with him. Afterwards, he rescued Peto, and probably wanted to make an additional gesture so that a better impression would be left of him. Meanwhile he didn't reach the border, was left in German territory, surrounded by Allied troops, and assumed that it would be worse for him to be left with the money."

"Did you see the treasure in Weber's hands?"

"No, but I knew that he went around with suitcases full of valuables."

"Did you ever speak to Weber about giving up the treasure?"

"Yes. He said that he wanted to give it up and that perhaps I should take it, but I advised him that the best thing would be to hide it."

"How much did you give Weber's office in Hungary?"

"According to our calculations of five pengö to the dollar, we paid more than two million dollars; according to the German calculation of ten pengö to the dollar it was one million dollars, together with the other valuables."

"But, Mr. Horvath," Judge Lehmann broke in, lifting a document from the desk, "you wrote to the Jewish Agency's Financial Department, in this letter which Defense Counsel previously introduced, that 'we are pleased to announce that the valuables given by the Committee to the Germans in Budapest were not exploited by the Germans.' Does that mean that the valuables were returned in full?"

"That I don't know. I assume Weber returned everything. Alex Peto arrived in Switzerland and told me that Weber had given him two suitcases."

The judge picked up another document. "There is the report by the Jewish Agency investigator, too. He writes that the valuables returned are worth $65,000 at the most. It seems clear to him that Weber gave Peto only a small part of those valuables. Do you agree with this conclusion?"

"I am under oath here, and I want to tell the truth. Either Weber didn't return all the treasure or the investigator was not accurate in his estimation."

"What do you say to the investigator's conclusion that there is no basis for any claim that the jewels disappeared while they were with the Americans?"

"Neither the investigator nor I have proof. We are both assuming and estimating."

Judge Lehmann's expression was inscrutable. He nodded curtly to Ben-Nathan, and the defense attorney rose. "Mr. Horvath, on what basis did Himmler issue the order for stopping the exterminations?"

"As a result of the talk Weber had with the American, Cornelius Trench, Edward Schoen, and myself."

"I tell you that if Himmler issued such an order it wasn't as a result of this talk but because he was surrounded by the American, Russian, and other armies."

"It is lack of knowledge to say that."

"You attribute this order to yourself because you are a megalomaniac."

Turning toward the judge, Andor said, "I am not a megalomaniac, but Mr. Ben-Nathan is ignorant of historical facts."

"So, according to you your demands were more important in this case than the strategic situation of the Germans?"

"I have no doubt."

"According to you, Weber's interference helped to save Jews?"

"That's right."

"And Himmler's interference, too, helped to save Jews?"

"Yes."

"And Himmler did it out of positive humane motives, in your opinion?"

"No. I don't think so."

"Why don't you think so?"

"Because of his past."

Ben-Nathan walked to the defense table and leaned against it. "How many times did you cross the border from Austria to Switzerland?" he asked in a casual tone.

"A few times."

"How many times did the Germans search you on the border?"

"Twice."

"So there were times when you weren't searched?"

"Yes."

Ben-Nathan moved away from the table toward Andor. "How do you explain the fact that they let you cross the border without a search?" he demanded sharply.

"A superficial search was conducted every time, but a thorough search took place only twice."

"How many times did they search your pockets?"

"Only twice."

"So most of the times when you went to and from Switzerland you crossed the border without the Germans searching you?"

"I went back and forth without the Germans searching me."

"How did it happen that they didn't search you? Did they have such trust in you?"

"When they searched me the second time, I complained to Weber, and he gave instructions at the border to let me cross without being searched."

"So Weber had the power to influence both German intelligence and counterintelligence?"

"I understood he had influence on the border post and on German counterintelligence also."

"Go on."

"Near the bridge at St. Margrethen the German border police had a small office. In it was a sergeant who was authorized to allow people to pass, with or without a search. I became aware that Weber had influence over that sergeant."

"And a border sergeant accepted instructions in wartime from a senior officer unknown to him?"

"There was a standing order to let me pass without a search."

"The same sergeant was always there?"

"Usually the same sergeant. Sometimes there were others."

"And they, too, let you pass?"

"They, too."

"You often took money across the Swiss-German frontier?"

"Yes."

"How did you transfer it?"

"I tied it around my waist, under my shirt."

"Then you went to Vienna with money."

"Yes."

"What passport did you have?"

"A passport issued by the German Legation in Budapest."

"What nationality was stamped on it?"

"Nationality 'Unknown.' Apparently this was the maximum they were willing to give me."

"Did you get a visa so that you could return to Budapest?"

"I don't remember."

"Did you have an Austrian visa?"

"No."

"How could you go to Vienna without a visa?"

"My passport was German."

"Where is your passport? Can you show it to the court?"

"I don't know whether I still have it. I didn't look for it."

A sardonic smile played about Ben-Nathan's mouth. "That historic passport, with which you crossed Europe during the occupation, you can't find?"

"Perhaps I lost it."

"Why didn't you return by air to Budapest when you found you couldn't go by train?"

"Weber warned me it would be dangerous."

"You, who risked your life all the time, were suddenly afraid of flying?"

"I wasn't afraid to die in the hands of the Germans, but I didn't want to die in the hands of the Russians as a German."

Ben-Nathan stared at him hard for a moment, then asked quietly, "What did you do in Vienna?"

"I supplied the hospital with medicines and utensils."

"Was there no one else who could have done it?"

"Not at that time."

"How many Jews were then in Vienna?"

"A hundred and sixty."

"And in Budapest there were eighty to ninety thousand?"

"Yes."

Ben-Nathan paused, his head lowered, allowing the significance of the figures to be felt. Then he turned to Andor again. "Is it true that as a man who saw many Nazi crimes you were an important witness against the leading Nazis?"

"I was a witness against some of the Nazi leaders, those who handled the exterminations."

"Did Weber ever tell you that you knew too much?"

"Yes. That was when I spoke to him about the atrocities against the Jews."

"You knew a lot about the Nazis and their crimes, yet they released you, to return to Switzerland, a free country."

"They had no choice."

"Why? Because Weber asked for it?"

"Weber asked for it."

426

Again Ben-Nathan paused while this sank in. Judge Lehmann's face was ashen and grave. Weiss gazed at a paper before him. There was utter stillness in the courtroom, except for the soft whirring of the overhead fan. A few minutes later the midday recess was ordered.

"Mr. Horvath," the defense attorney began, as the afternoon session opened, "Weber was appointed supreme commissioner for all the concentration camps in the spring of 1945. Would you agree that in no camp was there an improved treatment of the people, despite Weber's appointment?"

"The question is too general."

"Why?"

"Because it was different in different cases."

"Were there instances where Jews in camps were treated in an improved manner?"

"You didn't ask me about Jews."

"We are talking only about Jews."

"There weren't only Jews in the camps."

"Let's go to the Bergen-Belsen camp. I tell you that the Jews' situation in that camp was never improved."

"That's not true."

"When was it improved?"

"I don't know whether it was improved or not."

"It was disastrous from beginning to end?"

"Judging by the results, it was disastrous."

"And in Theresienstadt there was no improvement?"

"There, too, the situation remained as it had been."

"Yet the order to stop the killing and oppression of Jews in Theresienstadt was given by Colonel Heinemann in your presence?"

"Yes."

"Wasn't it clear to you that he was doing it to create an alibi for himself?"

"I didn't get that impression."

"Where did you go from Vienna?"

"To Berlin."

"Where did you stay in Berlin?"

"In the apartment of one of Weber's aides."

"What was his name?"

"I don't remember."

"How long did you stay there?"

"Four or five days."

"What did you do in Berlin?"

"I sat in the flat and waited for the meetings with Weber. I also thought that a meeting with Himmler would take place, but it didn't."

"You had already been presented to Himmler in February 1945 in Vienna, hadn't you?"

"Yes."

"What was the reason for that meeting?"

Andor shrugged irritably. "I don't know. Himmler may have wanted to use me for an alibi, or to contact the Allies. Maybe he was just curious to see how I looked."

"I suggest that Weber brought you to Himmler to show him what his Jew looked like."

Andor pounded the ledge of the box with his fist and turned to the judge. "I will not submit to the slurs of Mr. Ben-Nathan."

The judge's face was grim as he replied, "I realize this is an explosive case, Mr. Horvath, but you will control your emotions in the courtroom. Defense counsel," he added, turning a severe look in Ben-Nathan's direction, "will confine himself to proper examination and not indulge in unproved insinuations."

"Where did you eat?" Ben-Nathan continued.

"In the apartment."

"Who prepared your food?"

"The wife of Weber's aide."

"Did you pay her for the food and lodging?"

"No."

"You lived on the Germans, Mr. Horvath."

"That's a lie. I lived on my own account. I paid Weber in Vienna for the general expenses of my stay in Germany."

"Did Weber ask you to give evidence in his favor after the war?"

"Only once he hinted at an alibi."

"When was that?"

"During the last days of the war, on the way from Hamburg to Berlin, in the woods, when we took a walk, around the fourteenth of April."

"And apart from this once, Weber never spoke to you about an alibi and never asked you to give evidence in his favor if there was a trial, nor to do favors for him after the war?"

"No. Never."

"What is your opinion of Weber?"

"Weber was a thief, like all Nazis, but on a smaller scale."

"And you did nothing to fulfill the promise you made him that you would help him after the war."

"Nothing whatsoever."

"May I have Exhibit 31?" Ben-Nathan asked. A court attendant handed him a document the prosecution had introduced in evidence early in the trial—a long report Andor had made to the Jewish Agency containing dozens of pages of facts and figures. Ben-Nathan flicked the pages until he found what he wanted. Then, speaking slowly and forcefully, he said, "I read from page seven of this report by Mr. Horvath to his superiors the following sentence, 'Franz Weber was an SS colonel who served as a representative of Himmler during our rescue work. He was released from prison in Nuremberg by the occupational forces due to my personal intervention.'"

There was not a sound in the courtroom as he put the document down on the table and turned to face Andor.

"What do you have to say about this statement?"

"It was a stupid remark, I admit. Boasting, perhaps. I am guilty of careless phrasing in the report, that is all."

"You still contend you took no initiative whatsoever in keeping your promise to help Weber?"

"None whatsoever."

"You did not testify at Nuremberg on his behalf?"

"No."

"You gave no affidavit for him?"

"No."

"Mr. Horvath, I now tell you that you did *not* lie when you boasted in your report to the Jewish Agency that you were the one who saved Weber. *That* was the truth. You *did* save him!"

Andor glared back at the lawyer, too angry for the moment to speak.

"You still agree," Ben-Nathan went on, "as you have already testified, that to intercede for a high SS officer, such as Weber, would have been a national crime?"

"Yes."

Ben-Nathan picked up a piece of paper from his desk. "I read you Document 2957 of the International Military Tribunal at Nuremberg, submitted to that court by one Andor Horvath under the date of August 4, 1947. You were in Nuremberg that day, Mr. Horvath, were you not?"

"Yes. I believe I left August 5."

"This affidavit reads as follows: 'I, the undersigned, Andor Horvath, wish to make the following statement concerning former SS officer Franz

Weber. As a result of negotiations in 1944–45, I, as representative of the Jewish Agency and chief of the illegal Jewish Rescue Committee in Budapest, helped save the lives of tens of thousands of Jews and inmates of concentration camps. The negotiations between Franz Weber and me were carried out in financial and economic terms in the most serious and effective attempt to obstruct the Nazis' program of total annihilation of the Jews at German hands, as prescribed by Adolf Hitler. Weber was one of the very few SS leaders who had the courage to oppose the program of extermination and try to save human lives. . . .'"

In an icy voice the lawyer went on reading the detailed, eulogistic account of Weber's activities and ended, " 'I have no doubt that Weber's intentions were good, and in my opinion he deserves the fullest possible consideration when his case is judged by Allied or German authorities. I make this statement not only in my own name, but also on behalf of the Jewish Agency. Signed, Andor Horvath, official of the Jewish Agency.' "

He started to put the document on his desk, but before he did, he reread the final sentence. "I make this statement not only in my own name, but also on behalf of the Jewish Agency." Then he wheeled on Andor.

"Who authorized you to make this statement as a representative of the Agency?"

"Saul Kazin in the Istanbul office."

"Do you have any written evidence of this authorization?"

"There was no written authorization. It was oral."

"And if I tell you that Mr. Kazin denies ever authorizing you to represent the Agency in this matter?"

Andor hesitated. "Well, even if he denies it, I *was* representing the Agency in negotiations with the Germans. Should I consider that immediately after the war ended I no longer represented them in the same matters?"

"Mr. Horvath, I submit that you dishonestly used the weight the name of the Jewish Agency carried to give a malicious, false affidavit in favor of a war criminal to save him from trial at Nuremberg. You knew that Weber's purpose was never to save the lives of Jews but to achieve Nazi aims for the benefit of the Nazi regime. You knew the Nuremberg Tribunal would never believe Weber's lies, so you helped him by exploiting the Jewish Agency. Why, Mr. Horvath?"

"I have already explained my action."

"There was no reason other than the one you have already given?"

430

"No."

"I tell you that there *was* another reason—that you owed Weber a personal debt. You admitted it in a letter to Alex Peto. In your own words, 'I was saved because Weber spread his protecting wings over me!'"

Andor's rigid tenseness that had characterized his testimony earlier fell away. Gazing straight into Ben-Nathan's fierce gray eyes, he said evenly, "If I did right or wrong making the statement for Weber, only my conscience can decide, and my conscience is as untroubled today as it was then."

Several spectators hissed. A few applauded. Ben-Nathan raised his voice above the noise. "I suggest, Mr. Horvath, that your conscience is as elastic as rubber."

Judge Lehmann, his lips compressed to a thin, angry line, banged the gavel until the disturbance subsided, then, casting a look of exasperation at Ben-Nathan, said, "You may resume, Counselor."

"I have no more questions, your honor."

"Prosecution may cross-examine."

Weiss rose and approached the witness box. "Mr. Horvath, was your statement on behalf of Weber true?"

"Yes, it was entirely true."

"Why are you so sure?"

"Most of the time during the last year of the war I—and only I—was in a position to say whether or not Weber helped the Jews, because I and I alone was a witness from the beginning to the end of his activities."

"Would you make the same statement for Weber today?"

"Yes!" Andor paused, then added with a rueful smile, "But I would omit reference to the JA unless I had written authorization."

"The defense has made a strong point of the fact that you made a positive statement *for* a Nazi officer. Did you make any statement *against* others?"

"In September 1945, I made a sworn statement that included accusations against scores of German and Hungarian war criminals whose activities I knew about. As far as I know, that was the first time the War Crimes Office in Nuremberg was given a clear picture of the atrocious deeds of the Nazis. My statement was used against Goering and his aides. Besides making the statement, I assisted in the investigation to find Wedemeyer after he had disappeared."

"Do you now, in view of all that has happened since, regret having negotiated with the Nazis?"

"No. Mr. Ben-Nathan has created a distorted picture in this courtroom of a certain period and certain activities that I am proud of. I maintained my dignity as a man and as a Jew in my dealings with Wedemeyer and other Nazis until the end. I am one of the few Jews remaining alive who was given the opportunity to see Nazi brutality at first hand, to judge both the Nazis and those who in various ways saved Jews. My only ambition during those terrible years was to save as many Jews as possible. Unfortunately soon after the occupation it became obvious that there was no hope of saving all Hungarian Jews. The other members of the Rescue Committee and I had to decide immediately whether we should try to save at least some. For me there was only one answer."

"Thank you, Mr. Horvath." Weiss returned to his seat.

The judge looked to Ben-Nathan. "No questions on redirect," the defense attorney said, rising. "The defense rests, your honor."

Andor stepped down. It was over, finally. He mopped his damp forehead. As he slumped into the vacant chair beside Weiss, Judge Lehmann asked, "May I assume that the State will be ready to present its summation in the morning?"

The Attorney General nodded.

"Court is adjourned."

That evening in the Strauss apartment nothing was said about the trial during dinner, but as soon as the girls had gone to their room to do their schoolwork and Vera was in the kitchen washing dishes, Leo began.

"I can't understand you, Andor. You let yourself into a fine trap today, yah?"

"What do you mean?"

"You know very well. Your mistake wasn't giving an affidavit for Weber. In return for all he did, you promised him you would help get his name cleared after the war and you kept him waiting two long years for the help. That was the mistake you made. Keeping him waiting. Not giving him the affidavit right away. Keeping him waiting."

Andor snapped back resentfully, "Did you expect me to say this in court—that I was sorry I kept him waiting?"

"I did not expect you to make acrobatics in court. I expected you to tell the truth."

"I did."

"Andor, you are not in court now. You know damn well you didn't tell the truth." Leo's face was florid as he paced back and forth, declaiming. Sometimes he would stop in front of Andor's chair and shake a finger in his friend's face. "You should never have tried to cover things up. You should have said, 'I gave the man a promise and I am an honorable Jew, so I kept the promise.' "

"But Ben-Nathan was trying to trap me. I *had* to play what you call acrobatics with him, otherwise—"

Leo stopped him. "Foolishness! For a man so intelligent as you, I am ashamed of you. You cannot beat a man like Ben-Nathan at his own game. Your best defense from the beginning was the truth. You should have said, 'Yes, this man Weber was SS, but he never did believe in a Nazi victory and he worked with me to help save Jews, and so I made a promise to him that after the war I would see that the truth was told about how much he helped us.' "

"But to say this in court— In court they were trying to crucify me. Do you think—"

"I think in court they were all Jews and they all know the Talmud. You should have reminded them of Joshua and the two agents he sent to spy out the Promised Land and how when they were detected by the enemy they took refuge in the house of Rahab, the harlot, and they made a promise to her that if she would conceal them, when the army of Joshua came she would be saved. You know the rest of the story, Andor. You know that the Jewish belief in the importance of keeping a promise was so strong that Joshua issued an order that whatever else was done, Rahab the Prostitute must be saved, because a Jewish promise had been made to her. Surely you recall, Andor, that one third of the order of the day was devoted to this common harlot. Why? In order to emphasize that it is always the duty of the Jewish nation and the Jewish people to keep their promises. So everything was destroyed and many people were killed, but Rahab and her property were left untouched. You could have reminded the court that fifty per cent of the report in the Talmud on what happened is devoted to a description of how the Jewish people kept their word to this common prostitute."

Andor tried to stop him, but Leo waved aside the interruption.

"You should have told the court that you had a good precedent for what you did. In the Talmud story it was Rahab the Harlot. In Europe it was Weber the Nazi. You made this Nazi a promise, for good reasons: to save the lives of some of our people. Naturally you were obligated to keep your promise. If you had made this defense, everyone would have respected you—the lawyers, the judge, the journalists, the public. No one would have been able to argue with you. Instead, look at the trouble you made for yourself. You let them trap you in a lie. Not one lie but many lies."

Leo was still talking when Andor excused himself, saying he was very tired and must go to bed.

45

The Trial: Fourteenth Day

The next morning Attorney General Weiss was calm, dignified, and self-assured as he began his closing argument to the bench and a crowded courtroom, but his words were often sharp. Most of the time he faced the bench, but occasionally he would turn and point to Andor when he referred to him by name.

"This is an extraordinary case. It is one in which the defendant, László Chorin, has accused a fellow Jew, Andor Horvath, of one of the most treacherous and cowardly crimes punishable in Israel: collaboration. This state, which refuses to impose the death sentence even on those who commit the most heinous crimes, regards death as the only proper punishment for collaboration with the Nazis. If László Chorin's charge is false—and it is false—then *he* has committed a crime for which there is no possible atonement.

"The one issue in this trial concerns the motives of Andor Horvath, not his errors or poor judgment. The defense has established no justification for the acts of the accused, and in fact it could not, for there never was any justification. Andor Horvath always was and still is as loyal and righteous a Jew as any one of us, whatever his mistakes may have been, and defense counsel knows it.

"So the defense has brought out every error, every wrong judgment that Horvath made or someone else thought he made. A whole series of petty, peevish complaints based on jealousy, envy, and retribution for the deaths of loved ones whom no one could possibly have saved has been recited in this courtroom. For the rest, all the court has heard has been circumstantial evidence against Horvath. In spite of this it has been plain that he saved the lives of many of his people in the face of the hostility and disloyalty of some of his colleagues. Horvath's achievement is something for which he should be commended, but instead he has been vilified.

434

"The tactics of defense counsel have been disgraceful. He has persistently worked to pervert these proceedings so that the accused would become not László Chorin but Andor Horvath. He has pressed from witnesses every possible gripe against Horvath and forced him to defend himself against them here, publicly, without preparation and without advice of counsel.

"And what has been the result of all this trickery? Has he proved that Andor Horvath sold out his people to the enemy? No. He has proved nothing except that according to his own criteria Andor Horvath was not a good leader. But did that give Chorin the right to call him a collaborator? Can this court allow a man in Horvath's position who perhaps made mistakes to be publicly and irresponsibly accused of the dastardly crime of collaboration?

"A man of integrity and accomplishment has been slandered. Let us examine the defense's charges against Horvath that compose this slander. When we have finished, it will be clear that the accused is without justification, that his acts were willful and malicious.

"The first charge is that Andor Horvath co-operated with the Nazis to achieve their pernicious goals. But no one has said in this courtroom that his early dealings with the Nazis were not intended to help the Jews. When did his intentions change? Never! The Bergen-Belsen rescue train proved that he was succeeding. Was it moral to save a small group of people while the majority were threatened with deportation? Yes, once the majority couldn't be saved. If the rescue train hadn't left Hungary, its passengers would have been deported and murdered. The fate of the majority would have been no different if they had died.

"When the Nazis moved into Hungary, the Budapest Rescue Committee knew that there was no hope of saving everyone. Nevertheless, it decided to try to open negotiations. Horvath, as the leader, was given the task of negotiating, a task that required superhuman courage and ingenuity. Because he accepted this dangerous role, every one of us should be grateful to him. He could have gone into hiding or escaped abroad. If he had been killed, no one would have sullied his name. But he stayed to fight for his people, and so left himself vulnerable to vicious attacks.

"The second charge is that the thousands of Jews in Pécs would have escaped if they had been warned of their danger. Maybe. The court has not heard one word to prove that Horvath, directly or indirectly, was involved in the failure to warn the Pécs ghetto. In any case it wasn't his job to warn them. It was the duty of the Jewish Council to advise them.

But each Jewish Council tried to calm its people. They thought, perhaps wrongly, that they should quiet them, not awaken them to action. Here in the safety of this country we cannot judge their decision.

"It is true that Horvath favored residents of this ghetto over others, since 388 persons from Pécs—among them his father-in-law, relatives, and friends—boarded the rescue train. He couldn't have called himself a man if he had done anything else. Everyone tries to save his loved ones first. Anyone who denies it is a hypocrite.

"The defense has implied that the Nazis needed Horvath's help to have massacred so much of Hungarian Jewry with such speed and efficiency. The fact is that the Nazis were neither interested in nor demanded nor used the help of Andor Horvath in slaughtering Hungarian Jews. They held all the strategic positions in the country and could manage very well without help, as they had elsewhere.

"Nevertheless, wasn't it the primary duty of everyone to save as many people as possible? Of course. If there had been a revolt, would a greater number have been saved? No. It was more likely that no one would have been saved.

"But was it even possible to start a revolt? Of the six million Jews who were killed, 5.9 million boarded death transports without resistance. Revolts like the one in the Warsaw ghetto were rare. And even there those who took up arms faced the opposition of the majority.

"Andor Horvath's job was to save without discrimination. But this was impossible, for anyone not given a place on the Bergen-Belsen train was being discriminated against. His duty was to save as many persons as he could. But it is wrong to say he sacrificed the many to save the few, for the truth is that all were doomed.

"Even if Horvath hadn't warned the people, hadn't organized a revolt, did this make him the partner of murderers? Had his action or inaction caused the slaughter?

"The only reason the Nazis took Horvath under their protection was to extort money from him. They wanted a man—or men—who had access to foreign sources of money. To annihilate these people would be to cut off the source of money. The Rescue Committee knew that without money to bribe the Nazis they could get no concessions. The Germans needed money so much that they ignored the fact, which they knew through their intelligence service, that these funds were also being used to finance an underground and other anti-Nazi activities. They ignored it, too, because they considered the Committee incapable of organizing any widespread anti-Nazi resistance.

"As for the third charge, that Horvath played cards with the Nazis, this only makes him worthy of our deepest compassion, for it shows how far he was willing to go to continue the negotiations in behalf of the Jews.

"The fourth charge, the implication that Horvath—or anyone connected with the Jewish Agency—handed Erno Gábor over to the British and thus spiked his mission, stands without one iota of evidence to confirm it. The defense made the insinuation only to soil the name of the Jewish Agency for political purposes. Mr. Avner Sachs treated Gábor's mission with extreme gravity and flew to London to present it to the late Chaim Weizmann. But the British and the Americans regarded the offer as a blatant attempt at extortion. This was the reason for its failure. They did not, nor could anyone, believe that Wedemeyer would keep his word.

"Concerning the fifth charge, that Horvath didn't warn the outside world and that the Yishuv played down news of the exterminations, I give it the lie." He picked up several yellowed copies of the newspaper *Davar* and proceeded to quote headlines in issues beginning with January 1943. "This was before the Nazis overran Hungary. In the month that they did, March 1944, *Davar* reported that 3.5 million Jews had already been killed.

"The sixth charge, that Horvath didn't do everything he could to save parachutists Ely Farber and Naomi Loeb or that he induced Martin Klein to report to the Gestapo, has not been substantiated by any local witness. But even if we assume that Horvath did induce Klein to turn himself in, does this prove that he was a traitor? No. It only proves that he was a human being with human weaknesses.

"He was absolutely justified in exerting moral pressure on the parachutists to surrender to the Gestapo so he could continue his rescue work. He acted with the best intentions, honestly and courageously. He believed with his whole heart that Farber's surrender would save not only the Rescue Committee and its negotiations but also Farber himself. He was willing to face a military court and death if one of the parachutists had refused to surrender freely.

"As for Naomi Loeb, today we know who she was. But did Horvath know in the summer of 1944? The court has heard no evidence that he knew, or could have known, that Naomi was a brave and daring girl with a rebellious spirit. Nevertheless, the defense could offer no more than speculation that Horvath hadn't acted to save her.

"The seventh charge is that Horvath traveled freely in Germany and Europe. He has admitted it without hesitation. It must be clear to even

437

the most biased spectator that such freedom was necessary to his work.

"He has also admitted the eighth accusation, that he wrote a favorable affidavit for SS Franz Weber. His action was dictated by his conscience, and his conscience told him that Weber had risked his own life to save Jews. As for signing the affidavit in the name of the JA, his explanation that he received oral authorization should be accepted. If Mr. Kazin had denied giving the authorization, why hadn't defense counsel called on him to substantiate this charge? Horvath represented the Agency in his negotiations with the Nazis during the war. Why should he have assumed that this right had been withdrawn afterward?"

Weiss supported Andor's contention that Weber had helped the Jews by detailing several occasions on which rescues were effected owing to Weber's actions. Weber, he said, was instrumental in securing the arrival of the Bergen-Belsen train in Switzerland, he had helped to save 85,000 Budapest Jews, and his hasty surrender of the extermination camps to the advancing Allied armies had saved thousands. It wasn't important if Weber had done these things to put himself in a favorable light. His motives might have been based on arrant hypocrisy, but the objective truth was that he had had the audacity to circumvent instructions from his superiors and so halt the massacre. The fact that during the last weeks of the war many Nazis were trying to provide themselves with alibis and Horvath—like other Jews—tried to exploit this desire in order to save Jews by dealing with these Nazis, among them Himmler himself, was no indication that he betrayed his people or that he collaborated with the enemy.

The ninth charge, that Weber gave Horvath part of the Bergen-Belsen ransom, Weiss dismissed as being utterly unsubstantiated.

"It has been shown by one witness after another," he went on, "that Horvath's decisions were the best possible under devastating circumstances. But even if this were not so, has any man in such a position of serious and overwhelming responsibility committed no errors of judgment? That the Nazis intended to use Horvath for their own ends and granted him special privileges in no way proves that he was derelict in his duty toward his people, nor does it indicate criminal collaboration with the Nazis, as the defense has charged.

"During those terrible days in Budapest in 1944, facing a depraved beast of prey without a modicum of compassion, all those brave souls who worked to rescue their fellow Jews from death transcended their human frailties and their own desire to live. They rose to great heights of selfless service to their people. Among them was Andor Horvath, whose whole being was motivated by only one desire: to save Jews any way he could. It is shameful that ten years afterward, ignorance, hatred, and a thirst for wrongful retribution have brought him into this courtroom. Perhaps mistakes were made in Hungary. But who here now, in the safety of Israel, can judge with impunity the actions of those who daily lived with death so many years ago in another land?

"There is no more monstrous defamation than that which the accused, László Chorin, has foisted upon Andor Horvath, and the defense has offered no basis on which the charges of libel brought against Chorin can be refuted. The accused stands convicted by the facts. Defense counsel has presented not a single ameliorating fact to lessen his dastardly crime. In spite of defense counsel's emotionalism, I am certain the court will find the charge of libel proved by the facts."

While the Attorney General had been speaking, his confident tone and his arguments gradually obliterated from Andor's mind all trace of the embarrassment he had suffered in the courtroom the previous day, as well as the sting of the reprimand he had had from Leo. By the time court adjourned for the day, he was in an ebullient mood. Dinner was a festive affair. Vera cooked a plump chicken in the Hungarian style and made *palashinken* for dessert. For the first time in months Andor ate with appetite. He was gallant and gay, as in the old days, Leo thought happily, telling stories that kept Hannah and Deborah giggling with amusement.

When it came time for bed, Debbie begged him to read to her. It was the first time she had dared to ask since the trial began, and she held her breath waiting for the answer.

"Certainly. Why not?" Andor said. "Tonight we will read from Sholom Alecheim—after you put on your pajamas."

"You shouldn't tire yourself," Leo warned as he and Andor left the table and went into the living room. "Even if you're finished testifying, you want to make a good impression in court tomorrow."

"What good impression? I'm not going to court tomorrow. Should I give Ben-Nathan the pleasure of seeing me listen to his lies about me? Never. I hope the place is empty. Let him hear his words bounce off the walls." He lit a cigarette and inhaled with deep satisfaction. "I'm going to sleep late tomorrow," he said dreamily, harking back to another time and another way of life. "You know, it is really a primitive custom to get up at dawn and go to bed right after dark. As a civilization advances, this is one of the first practices people abandon, and I intend—"

"You are so sure the verdict will be favorable?" Leo interrupted tentatively.

"Of course. Aren't you?"

"Well, it depends on many people, this verdict—on you and Weiss, and a little bit on me, and your other friends who testified, on Chorin and Ben-Nathan, but most of all it depends on Lehmann, and who knows what he's thinking?" He paused and then went on almost apologetically, "I think the decision will be in your favor; it's just that I don't like to say I'm *sure* of anything unless I can make it happen myself."

"What you need is more faith, Leo," Andor said heartily. "There is a basic justice in the world. Don't look so astounded. There is; it isn't naïve to say so. And this justice will eventually triumph. For two thousand years our people have had no home. They have been wanderers, guests, visitors—tolerated, abused, or oppressed in strange lands, a third of us finally murdered. But out of that terrible history a new destiny has been created for us. Who can say that it would have happened if the past had been different? So it is with me. The verdict will be the expiation for everything that has been done against me these past months."

"I'm ready! I'm ready!" Debbie, clad in pajamas, raced into the room carrying the book by Sholom Alecheim. "I want to hear this one," she said, opening the book and pointing with a plump little forefinger to the illustration of a dark-haired young woman standing beside a cypress tree. "She's very beautiful, isn't she?" There was a note of wistfulness in her voice.

Andor picked her up and kissed her. "Not as beautiful as you will be when you grow up," he said, and carried her to her bed.

From the living room Leo listened as Andor read. He was troubled. Andor was so positive. How could he be? Or was it maybe that he had to be, that the alternative was unthinkable? Leo had a nagging feeling that his friend's certainty of justice was based less on faith than on a fear he refused to acknowledge. What would happen to him if the verdict was unfavorable? Leo himself shrank from thinking about it and listened once more to Andor.

The next night the newspapers carried extensive accounts of Ben-Nathan's summation. Leo had the sheets spread all over the sofa, reading aloud choice excerpts to the assembled family and Andor. He picked up one and read: "'This morning Mr. Yaacov Ben-Nathan began his summation in the Chorin libel trial. He launched into a diatribe against Mr. Andor Horvath and all those who had given him the "go ahead," as well as against the Attorney General, Mr. Reuven Weiss. Neither

Mr. Weiss nor Mr. Horvath was present . . .' And so forth, and so forth."

Leo skipped a few sentences, then read, " 'The courtroom was so jammed that Judge Lehmann ordered the police to remove all those who were standing. People had begun to arrive outside the courthouse at 7 A.M., two hours before the session was scheduled to begin. Mr. Ben-Nathan's opening remarks were moderate, giving no hint of the violently emotional words that were to come. He said that the eyes of Israel were upon the courtroom, looking to it for a just verdict. The court had a great national, historic, and moral responsibility in this case.' And so forth, and so forth," Leo muttered, glancing farther down the page, and then reading again, " 'Mr. Horvath had "willfully" lied during the trial, had concealed evidence, and should be tried as a war criminal, Mr. Ben-Nathan said.

" ' "For the past several weeks," the defense attorney continued, "a new attitude has been evident in the press and among certain groups of people: Why dig up the past? Will it bring the dead back to life? Won't it hurt all of us? Shouldn't we stick together? We're all in the same boat. Won't this damage our prestige among other nations? My answer is that the truth must be known, no matter what the repercussions. We *are* opening a wound. But we must cut into it to remove the infection that is festering there. If we do not, we shall all be contaminated by it.

" ' "The Attorney General has said that it is impossible to judge from the safety of Israel the hell that was Hungary in those days. But dozens of people have been judged here since the law about Nazi collaborators was passed. The little fish have been tried. Should we allow the whales to go free?" The defense attorney said he had done everything possible to put himself in the place of those who had survived the holocaust and to see it through their eyes.' And so forth, and so forth.

" ' "Mr. Horvath's star rose with blinding brilliance," Mr. Ben-Nathan said, "as the star of Hungarian Jewry descended, fading to extinction. This was no accident of history; it was the result of a well-laid plan." ' "

"And so forth, and so forth," Andor said, mimicking his friend. "Leo, forget it. The court isn't going to be misled by such a stupid appeal to emotions. The oldest trick that lawyers know, when they have a weak case, is to attack the man and forget the case. It works on juries, but not judges; not on a shrewd one like Lehmann, anyway."

Leo knew it would do no good to argue with him, so he sighed, piled the papers on one corner of the sofa, and listened with some misgiving while Andor and the girls made plans for a celebration when the verdict was announced.

"We're going to have a dinner party at the King David Hotel," Andor promised them. "The best of everything on the menu!"

Hannah and Debbie squealed with delight, hugging each other, then Andor, as they pictured themselves in the stately dining room, filled with sophisticated people, the gleaming silverware on spotless white table-cloths, the deferential waiters, and the lovely, lovely things they would order to eat. Even Vera was caught up in the gaiety.

46

The Verdict

The courtroom was more jammed than ever. Everyone was sweltering in the late June heat. Martin, Rachel, Joe and Alex were all there. Rudy Tabor sat in the first row with Jessica. She was exceedingly pale, and her sapphire eyes seemed enormous. In her nervousness she had pinned her abundant black hair back from her face in the old, severe way. She had tried to share Andor's optimism, but the burgeoning fear within her had withered it. She sat now with her hands tightly clasped, hoping that the fear didn't show. Her eyes never left Andor, who was in his usual place at the prosecution table beside Weiss. Behind Jessica and Rudy sat Andor's sister, Rena, and her husband, Sam. She nervously pulled on a handkerchief, twisting it into a roll over and over, as Sam anxiously watched her. Every few minutes he patted her hand, and she would force a weak smile. Two rows farther back sat the Strausses, Leo perspiring copiously, impatient for the proceedings to begin. Even Moshe Hahn was there, busily greeting and gossiping with everyone he knew. All of Israel's daily and weekly publications were represented in the press section. In the corridor men and women jostled and shoved trying to gain admittance. Police officers, struggling to keep order, finally had to turn hundreds away. But Chaim Glazer wasn't one of them. He had been there since 7 A.M., and he had a choice seat in the front row of the spectators' section, on the side that enabled him to see Andor's face from a 45-degree angle. The young man was certain that Chorin would be exonerated, and he didn't want to miss the intense pleasure of seeing

Horvath's expression when the verdict was announced. He sat eagerly taking in the whole scene, his eyes bright and his cheeks flushed.

It was nine-thirty when the bailiff and his staff were finally able to create order in the courtroom and the session got under way. Judge Lehmann, his face lined with fatigue and his brow ruffled, took his place on the bench, in his right hand a thick sheaf of papers. Everyone looked at him expectantly. As he began to read the verdict, his voice was somber. The words seemed to come out almost reluctantly. He began by reviewing the background of wartime events in Hungary. For the first few minutes there was general restlessness among the spectators, but as he began describing the catastrophe that had overtaken the Hungarian Jews, absolute quiet fell over the crowded room. The noise of people waiting outside in the corridor in the futile hope of being admitted in case someone left was the sole distraction.

Ben-Nathan listened impassively. Beside him Chorin was in his usual lethargic state, his lids half closed. On the other side of the room, Weiss seemed in deep thought, hardly looking at the judge. Andor, eager to hear the declaration of Chorin's guilt, found it difficult to restrain his intensity. He shifted restively and began to draw on the back of an envelope caricatures of Ben-Nathan that made him look like a strutting cock.

Judge Lehmann paused to drink from a glass of water on his desk, then continued in the same heavy, low-pitched tones. He analyzed the evidence given by the witnesses. On the basis of their testimony, he said, he found László Chorin not guilty on three of the four counts of libel of which he was accused. He found that Andor Horvath had, in fact, collaborated with the Nazis, had prepared the ground for the mass murder of Hungarian Jewry, and had aided a Nazi war criminal to escape proper punishment. On the fourth charge, of sharing the ransom with a Nazi, the court found that this accusation had not been substantiated and Chorin was therefore guilty of libel on this count and was fined one pound. Mr. Horvath, the judge ended, had betrayed the trust of the Hungarian Jews. He had sold his soul to the devil.

Andor was stunned. The faces that swarmed around him were a kaleidoscopic blur. The melange of voices that filled the room as court was adjourned created a cacophony that almost split his eardrums. Vaguely he was aware of Jessica beside him. Weiss, looking old and tired, was trying to tell him that everything was not lost; they would appeal.

Gradually things came back into focus. He saw Joe Nagel, alone, hurrying from the room, his head down. "You bastard!" he thought bitterly. "You helped do this to me!"

In the rear the Strausses stood disconsolately. "Let's go home, girls," Leo said.

Hannah stared at her father, aghast. "Aren't you even going to speak to him?"

"No. He wants to be alone. I know him. And I don't want to make him eat his words."

The Strausses trudged out despondently. Chaim Glazer noticed their sorrow with pleasure. As he looked back at Andor, who was now surrounded by reporters and solicitous friends, he muttered angrily, "This isn't punishment enough; they ought to put *you* on trial now!"

From some fathomless resource Andor gathered the courage to declare, with seeming equanimity, to the reporters who pressed around him, "For me this verdict is just the beginning of a struggle for justice. Naturally I am shocked by it. I believe the court has made some serious errors in interpreting the facts. It is almost impossible to understand how the court could have put such a contrary interpretation on the bravery, self-sacrifice, and accomplishments of those who devoted themselves to rescuing others. I intend to do everything in my power to clear my name. In the last analysis I am sure justice will triumph."

He barely managed to utter the last sentence. He felt he had to get away before he fell apart in the presence of all of them. He brushed off the rest of the questions, roughly took Jessica's arm, and led her out of the room, elbowing aside the loitering groups of spectators. A few people tried to shake his hand and assure him that their good opinion of him was unchanged. But some looked at him contemptuously, and a plump, untidy woman with gray hair stepped in front of him and shouted, "Nazi Horvath! They finally caught up with you, didn't they?" A policeman escorted the woman out of the building, but the words seared Andor. He wanted to flee. It took all his strength for him to move out of the building at his normal deliberate pace and to maintain his habitual proud posture. Skillfully he guided Jessica through the crowd to their car.

Jaffa Road was crowded with bicycles, busses, trucks, and private cars; progress through the city was slow. Despite the heat, Andor had all the windows of the car closed, but several times when they had to stop because of traffic jams pedestrians who recognized him from newspaper pictures pressed their faces against the windows, staring and telling each other his name, to Andor's intense annoyance. But finally they were on the road to Tel Aviv and he was able to make good time, for traffic was thinning out by now.

Jessica knew better than to try to engage him in conversation. She sat at her side of the front seat, pensively gazing out of the window. Although she had traveled the Jerusalem-Tel Aviv road many times, she never tired of the scenery. Today it helped divert her thoughts from the tragedy of the courtroom. The Arab villages on the approaches to Jerusalem were still picturesque, although they had begun to fall into ruin now that they were deserted. The weather had almost obliterated the pale blue color superstitious Palestinian Arabs painted their houses as protection against the evil eye. When they passed Castel, the site of the ancient Roman fortress that had guarded the approaches to Jerusalem, Jessica noticed that a new marker had been put up by the side of the road. Andor was driving too fast for her to read all the words, but she did see that it called attention to the bitter fighting there during the War of Liberation.

As the road twisted through the steep hills in the Sha'ar-Hagai district, she noticed that a fresh coat of red-brown rustproof paint had recently been sprayed on the several dozen burned-out skeletons of trucks and armored cars that had been left along the roadside as a war memorial, just where they were shot up in 1948 while trying to run food and medical supplies to besieged Jerusalem through the gantlet of Arab forces that commanded the hills on both sides of the road. Some of the metal carcasses were upside down, and their wheels were slowly being turned by the soft breeze blowing through the valley.

Occasionally Jessica glanced out of the corner of her eye at Andor. His jaw was tight-set, and his eyes seemed to be staring not just at the roadway ahead, but trying to peer far into the future. In her compassion, in her understanding of what he was suffering, she put one hand on his arm. As a slight acknowledgment of the gesture, a ghost of a smile crossed his face. She pressed his arm gently, then withdrew her hand.

About halfway to Tel Aviv, near the place where legend says the great Samson was born, they had to slow down because of the cars streaming into their road from the main artery down to the Negev Desert, but soon they picked up speed again and before long were on the outskirts of Ramla, the twelve-hundred-year-old town that had been an important resting place for pilgrims on their way to Jerusalem in the time of the Crusaders.

"Andor, you've taken the wrong road!" she exclaimed as he turned off sharply to the right.

For the first time since leaving the courtroom he spoke. "No, I haven't. We're not going home."

Jessica spun around in her seat to study his face, a little frightened by his abruptness but trying to keep her tone calm. "It's all right, darling, but where are we going?"

"I don't know yet, but we're not going home."

As much as this was out of character for him, she understood and said nothing more. In Tel Aviv there would be more reporters, well-meaning friends, and perhaps a few people like the woman who had shouted "Nazi!" at him in the courtroom.

The road he had taken led more than a hundred kilometers due north to Haifa and then across Galilee to the frontier of Lebanon, but where he intended to stop she still had no idea, and she realized that he might not have either.

As they were passing Lydda Airport, a foreign plane with strange markings was taking off. The reverberations of its engines churned up the air. Andor let his eyes wander from the road and stared at the plane. She wondered what he was thinking. Did he really want to stay and fight to clear his name, or would he like to be in that plane, going off forever to some faraway place? She wanted to ask, but she dared not.

As they approached Petah-Tikva, the oldest Jewish settlement in Israel, now grown into a thriving town, Jessica recalled that the name means "Door of Hope." She wanted to say something to her dejected husband about the adversities the founders of Petah-Tikva had overcome—malaria, blight, drought, marauders—but she kept her silence.

As they approached the Half-Way House, where they had often stopped for refreshments, as was the custom among those who traveled frequently between Tel Aviv and Haifa, she realized how hungry she was. It had been a long time since their early breakfast. But the number of automobiles in the parking lot kept her from speaking.

A few minutes before they passed through the town of Hadera, with its remnant of an old Arab caravanserai, they both saw a sign pointing to the left, to Caesarea, the city founded by King Herod and named for Augustus Caesar. For five hundred years it had been the Roman capital of Palestine. Jessica wanted to suggest that they detour long enough to look at the great ancient harbor, but again she restrained herself.

It was not long before they saw the sparkling Mediterranean on their left, while on their right the foothills of Mount Carmel began to take shape. Jessica knew that the main highway led directly into the industrial district of Haifa, along the water's edge, past docks and factories and the most spectacular grain elevator in the world. But as they approached the city, Andor took a sharp turn to the right and they began to climb at a steep angle.

Haifa is like a layer cake, built on three levels. The middle layer, Hadar Hacarmel, is the area of shops and homes. On the top layer are hotels, sanitariums, schools, pleasant parks, several museums, and a zoological garden. They were heading for the summit, and Jessica was delighted. If any place could take Andor's mind off his troubles, it was this mountaintop. High places and wide expanses of water gave people perspective, and this was what he needed more than anything else.

As the car turned around hairpin bends, the harbor, the ships, and the city below were first on his side and then on hers. Each minute they seemed smaller and more remote.

"There's the golden dome of the Persian temple!" Jessica suddenly exclaimed. "What *is* it called, Andor?" Her exuberance was stronger now than her self-discipline.

"Bahai," he said flatly.

"Yes, the Bahai shrine. I love that golden dome. For Haifa it's like a jewel tucked in a lady's hair."

They were on a wide street running parallel with the water when Andor stopped at the entrance to a small hotel. "You wait in the car," he said. "I'll be out in a minute."

While he was gone, she arranged her hair and studied the surroundings. This was a street of substantial villas, each with a garden or the promise of one. In little more than a minute Andor returned and said, "I think this one will be all right. There aren't many people here."

She followed him up the several steps into the modest lobby. The manager greeted her and led them up two flights of stairs. "Wait until you see the surprise I have for you, madame," he said to Jessica with a pleasant smile as they walked down a long hallway.

The room was dark, because a Venetian blind hung over the large window. But when the manager raised it, the place was flooded with light. Jessica looked down on the glorious panorama of Haifa and clapped her hands in joy. "Andor, isn't it wonderful!" she said ecstatically, trying to implant in him the exhilaration she felt.

"It's our best room," the manager said proudly. "We often rent it to newlyweds."

Andor walked to the window and lowered the blind with a swift gesture that sent it clattering down to the sill. The room was in darkness again. "What time is dinner?" he asked brusquely.

Jessica looked crestfallen.

The manager glanced at his watch. "We eat early here. Dinner will be served in an hour. You'll hear the bell."

They had just finished bathing and dressing when the bell sounded. Although they had a table to themselves, the dining room was too small for any private conversation. The tables were jammed together, and it seemed to be the custom for everyone to talk to everyone else. Most of the dozen or so people in the room stared at Andor and Jessica from the moment they entered. Occasionally they heard a few words of low-toned conversation that made them sure the other guests were discussing the verdict. During the meal Andor spoke only when it was necessary to instruct the waitress. After dinner they followed the other guests into a comfortable-looking sitting room and were settling back with the evening newspapers when someone turned up the volume of the radio that had been providing soft background music.

"Kol Israel now brings you the latest news," the announcer said. With a rapid glance at Jessica, Andor indicated that they should leave. They were halfway up the first flight of stairs when they heard the announcer add, "In Jerusalem District Court today László Chorin was found not guilty on three counts of libel and guilty on the fourth. Judge Lehmann, in a verdict unusual for its strong language, accused Andor Horvath, former Director of Rationing, of having sold his soul to the devil, and of . . ."

By this time they were near the second landing, and the rest of the man's words were inaudible, but the damage had been done. Andor's face was pinched with pain again, as it had been when he originally heard the verdict.

As soon as they were in their room and the door was locked behind them, he dropped wearily on the large bed and let out a sigh that seemed to come from the depths of his soul.

All afternoon Jessica had wanted to comfort him; now she could put aside the desire no longer. Moving quietly to the bed beside him, she stroked his hair softly, then kissed the back of his neck. "Andor darling, it will come out all right. It's impossible that the courts or the people— or anyone with a grain of sense—will condemn you. You must have faith, as you have always had. This is no time to lose your belief in yourself, my darling."

Her plea had exactly the opposite effect to what she intended. Andor covered his face with his hands and began to sob. She could feel him trembling violently beside her. She was alarmed and perplexed. Until now he had always been the master of his emotions. She put her arms around him and held him as tightly as she could. "Andor, it's going to be all right. Faith, my darling," she murmured urgently. "Don't lose faith in the man I adore. You must be strong, beloved."

When they raised the Venetian blind and threw open the doors that led onto their small balcony, the moon was already high. The harbor was dotted with ships, most of them shining white. The water sparkled. Lights in houses and along the streets winding up the mountain speckled the scene as if with stardust.

"It's magnificent, Andor!" Jessica whispered, slipping her hand into his as she said a silent prayer that somehow he would be able to survive what had happened.

47

For weeks after the verdict Andor seemed to be in a daze. He was still shaken by the court's decision, refusing to face the fact of it, though he was continually besieged by proof that it had been no dream. Each morning the postman brought a bundle of letters, some of consolation and compassion, many of denunciation, usually unsigned. There were disquieting telephone calls, especially at night. They were infuriating, but the very act of hanging up the receiver always put an end to the incident. Letters were worse. Andor would read each one two or three times, and with each reading the letter seemed more offensive. Then it would lie on his desk and he might pick it up days later and become disturbed all over again. Jessica suggested that he destroy the letters after reading them the first time, but he shook his head in emphatic refusal. The thought occurred to her that he was taking perverse pleasure in his misery, but she decided that this wasn't true: he simply was unable to comprehend what had happened to him.

Friends telephoned, inviting them for dinner, for tea, to the theater, to play cards. At first Jessica consulted him about each invitation, but his "no" was so consistent that after a while she got into the habit of saying it herself for both of them.

Before long Andor stopped going out of the apartment at all, even for a walk after dark. "When I pass a café or a lighted shop, people always stare at me," he complained to Jessica. "They stare as if they were looking at an animal in a cage. Well, maybe I *am* an animal in a cage. Sometimes that's exactly the way I feel!"

Jessica knew that he missed the ebullience of Leo Strauss, whom he never saw any more because Leo's business kept him in Jerusalem. Even more he missed the warm relationship with Hannah and Deborah. In all the years of their marriage Jessica and Andor had never discussed having children. She was certain that if she could produce children ten or twelve years old at birth, Andor would be delighted to have as many as she wanted. He was not the sort of a man who could ever put up with the household annoyances of a small baby. He needed a child of his own—perhaps more than one—but less to be adored than to adore, more to feed his need of respect and love. When Andor was in his blackest moods, she was often tempted to write to Leo and Vera and suggest that Hannah and Deborah come and stay with them in Tel Aviv for a few weeks, but she knew they would have to sleep on a cot in Andor's small study, and the resulting clutter without a doubt would annoy him as much as the girls' presence might brighten his life.

Rudy Tabor was the only person who was really welcome. He was understanding enough not to come too often and adroit enough never to force the conversation. If Andor seemed eager to discuss the trial, Rudy would lean back in his chair and listen, seldom offering his own opinions. Because he knew Andor had stopped reading the newspapers, he kept him informed with anecdotes about events in the world at large, in Israel in particular, and in the Hungarian colony.

When the libel suit had been filed, Andor had not only resigned as Director of Rationing, virtually by request, but he had stopped writing his column for the Hungarian *Gazette,* despite Rudy's violent objection. One evening several weeks after the verdict, as Rudy was sipping *barack* in the Horvath living room, he winked at Jessica and said to Andor, "Do you remember the night, right in this room, that you persuaded me to start the *Gazette?*"

Andor nodded mechanically, his thoughts obviously on something else.

"Well, I've got a proposition for *you* now. I'm getting old. I can't carry on the *Gazette* forever. I want you to take over." Observing Andor's negative expression, he added hastily, "Not all at once. Gradually. Kahane, the night editor, has just resigned. He's leaving at the end of next week for a job in one of the ministries. My suggestion, Andor, is that you take his job now. Let's see how you like being an editor again."

Andor made no reply. Hunched over in his chair, he gazed dolefully at the carpet. Rudy sipped his *barack* again. After a long silence Jessica urged softly, "Try it, Andor. You used to like to work at night. It would be a good way to return . . ."

Rudy leaned over and patted her arm affectionately, then addressed Andor briskly: "You'd start at four in the afternoon and be home by eleven or eleven-thirty. Midnight at the latest."

Andor continued to be apathetic, nevertheless Rudy managed to extract a promise that he would consider it seriously. The next week, the morning of the day Kahane was to leave, Rudy telephoned. "Andor, help me out; take the job temporarily, at least."

In this way Andor Horvath resumed his journalistic career. After a few days it was plain to both Jessica and Rudy that the new job was good therapy. Working at the newspaper, Andor was compelled to fill his mind with something besides bitter thoughts.

"If only nothing else happens!" Jessica kept saying to herself prayerfully.

She always waited up for him. Together they would have brandy and coffee while he told her what he had done that evening.

After he had been on the *Gazette* for a week, Jessica greeted him one night with the news that Rena had telephoned. "She and Sam are coming here on Shabbat." Seeing the disappointment on his face, she added quickly, "Darling, there wasn't anything I could say. After all, Rena is your only sister. How can I make flimsy excuses that you don't want to see her?"

Jessica spent most of Friday cooking and cleaning the apartment in preparation for the guests. The next day Sam and Rena arrived about noon. It was the first time the family had been together since the end of the trial. Everyone was exaggeratedly cheerful, making no reference to the verdict. They gossiped about mutual friends and discussed the current wave of fedayeen raids from the Gaza strip. They were all pretending and they knew it. The tension in the atmosphere was palpable.

"How is your job?" Andor asked Sam, trying to make casual conversation.

Rena gasped, then jumped from her chair, tears welling in her eyes, and started to run from the room.

Andor, appalled, rushed to her and seized her by the shoulders. "All I asked was how is Sam's job. What's wrong with that?"

"Rena, please—" Sam begged, annoyance and dismay in his voice.

She ignored him and wrested herself free of her brother's grasp. "If you listen to Sam, he'll tell you some nice lies, but I'll tell you the truth," she cried venomously. "I'm tired of pretending so your precious pride will be saved."

Jessica paled and gripped the arms of her chair.

"Sam was fired because he's your brother-in-law. Now when he looks for work anywhere, they say to him, 'Surely your influential brother-in-law can get you a job!' And that's not all. Dan doesn't have a single friend. Every day he comes home from school in tears because the other children call him names. They tell him his uncle is a Nazi-lover. He cries himself to sleep at night. Your nephew!" She began to wail. "What's going to happen to us? What are we going to do? How are we going to live? It's your fault, Andor. You and your goddamn Nazis! It would be better if they had killed us with all the others. Better if we were dead!" Her sobs were choking her.

"Rena!"

That was all Sam said in reprimand, but the explosive word was the culmination of years of futile struggling to keep his wife alive, normal, and happy.

Andor stood facing her, immobile and silent, a figure of complete despair. Jessica moved to her. Whispering words of comfort, she led Rena toward the bedroom. At first she resisted, then all at once became limp and tractable, her anger spent, her energy gone. But at the doorway she turned and said to her brother in half apology, "It doesn't really make any difference. We're all going to die anyway." The two women disappeared into the bedroom. Several minutes later Jessica returned. Andor was standing at the window, staring, unseeing, at the scene below. Sam was sitting disconsolately in a corner chair.

"She's asleep, and I don't think we should wake her up, even for dinner." She hesitated, fearful of saying something that might make the situation worse for her husband.

Seeing her plight, Sam said, "Please don't take it so to heart, Andor. She's never recovered from Bergen-Belsen. One of her troubles is that she gets so little sleep. She still has nightmares, and she's afraid of being alone. Even when I'm right beside her she feels alone if I'm asleep, so I can't go to sleep until she does. If she doesn't feel sleepy, I tell her stories, talk to her, anything to take her mind off her fears. She's very distraught. Make allowances for her. But don't be hurt. Try to forget what she said."

Andor looked searchingly at his gentle brother-in-law. Until now he had thought of himself as the only victim of the tragedy. But Rena's outburst had made him realize that the problem was not so simple and that the victims were numerous. Suddenly he was overwhelmed with pity for them. Putting his arm around Sam, he said affectionately, "I think what you and I need is some *barack*. Not one of those polite little drinks, but a big one!"

Jessica hurried from the room to get glasses. She was relieved that the scene was over, but she had a sinking premonition that the bitterness of this Shabbat would be with them for a long time to come.

48

It had been a tiring night. As sometimes happens in the best-run newsroom, everything seemed to go wrong. An article by the Minister of Agriculture that was supposed to be delivered at 6 P.M. did not arrive at the *Gazette* office until almost ten, and it was twice the length the Minister had said it would be. One of the Linotype machines developed trouble an hour before they were supposed to put the paper to bed. And every headline Andor wrote was either a character too short or too long to fit. But finally the last form was locked up and placed on the press, and the next morning's edition of the *Gazette* began to roll. An ink-smeared apprentice ran up from the pressroom to the editorial office with the first copy. Carefully Andor looked over every headline, every important article, even the advertising, to be certain no errors had crept in. Then he turned out the light over his desk, put on his hat, shouted "O.K." to the foreman as he passed the door of the pressroom, and left the building, with the rumble of machinery still echoing in his ears.

He looked at his watch as he walked to his car. They were a half hour late, because of all the complications, but they would still get their papers on the early morning busses out of the city. That was what was important.

It was one of those steaming August nights when everything hung limp. Even driving at sixty kilometers an hour brought no relief, for the air that beat on Andor's face through the open windows was hot and sticky. Budapest had never been like this. When he had thought of Mediterranean cities before coming to Israel, he had mistakenly assumed that seaports always got some relief from offshore breezes. But tonight in Tel Aviv the air was oppressively still and heavy, sea or no sea.

As he circled around the Habimah Theater he saw that the lights were still on, which meant the janitors were cleaning up after the evening's performance. The offering had been a play by Sophocles, which was receiving an excellent review in tomorrow's *Gazette*. From the Habimah he drove down Dizengoff Street until he came to the city's brightest, gayest area of cafés, night clubs, and cinemas. The sidewalk tables, five or six rows deep, were still crowded, though it was past midnight. He had a strong desire to park the car and relax for a few minutes at one of the vacant tables, but he resisted the temptation. During the two months he had been editing the paper, he had not broken his resolve to keep out of the public eye. It was not that he was a changed man. He was still a cosmopolite. But to be just one of the great throng, or, worse, to be singled out and treated with either contempt or condescension, was more than he could bear.

Sighing, he drove on, telling himself that perhaps before long things would be different. The Attorney General was preparing his appeal. He had urged Andor not to rush him. There were, he said, many serious judicial errors in Judge Lehmann's verdict, and every one of them must be pointed out and documented. Only in this way would they be certain of victory. But it would take time, and Andor must be patient. Patient! Patience was not one of his virtues. Daring? Yes. Courage? He knew he had it, in good measure. Ability? Who else could have twisted the Nazis around one finger the way he had? But he was in an uncomfortable position now. He had to sit back and wait while lesser men went through their technicalities. Of course, the Supreme Court would reverse Judge Lehmann's absurd decision. And as soon as it did, he would start where he had been forced to leave off. He still could make a great political career for himself. He would capitalize on all that had happened. He would ridicule his opponents and make them look as stupid to the public as they really were. He would establish himself as the savior of at least some of the condemned people of Europe. All he needed was the decision of the Supreme Court. He was certain what that decision would be. If he could only be patient!

He swung his car from the wide avenue into a cross street and headed for the Street of the Palms. He was later than usual and Jessica would be a little worried, but thank God she never became panicky. She was all that a woman ought to be—calm in moments of crisis, comforting when things went wrong, silent when he needed solitude, beautifully passionate when they came together. Tonight he felt a longing for her —her smooth arms, her lush, resilient body, the excitement he felt when he held her close. How warm and responsive she was! How fortunate he'd been to see her that day in the camp on Columbus utca . . .

He parked the car in its usual place, directly in front of the entrance to his apartment house. Since no one else in the building had an automobile, the place was almost always vacant. He turned off the ignition and the lights, holding the brass ring with its assortment of keys to car, office, apartment, and bank box in his right hand as he picked up his brief case with the left, slammed the car door, and started up the short concrete sidewalk from the curbing to the apartment-house door. It seemed a little cooler now.

"Stop!"

Andor obeyed, not because it was a command, but because the speaker had stepped in front of him and was blocking his path.

"Don't you remember me, Horvath?"

The voice was high-pitched and excited. Andor stared hard into the face of the young man who stood before him, trying to make out his features in the dim light from the single street lamp in the middle of the block. It was an unattractive countenance, thin and twisted with hatred, yet the eyes were bright.

Suddenly it came to him. "Yes," he said angrily, "I recognize you. You're the one who was so obnoxious at the Strausses' apartment in Jerusalem, months ago. What are you doing here in Tel Aviv, and by what right do you block my way?"

"I want to have a little talk with you." It was almost a whine of false cordiality. "And my name, if you have forgotten, is Chaim Glazer." He gripped Andor's right coat lapel with his left hand and in a commanding voice added, "Remember it!"

Andor shook him off contemptuously. "You may make an appointment with me by calling my office," he replied, starting for the apartment entrance. "I am not accustomed to holding conferences at this hour of the night."

"You held conferences with the Nazis in Budapest at all hours of the day and the night, didn't you?"

"You don't know anything about it. Now get along or—"

"I know one thing, Horvath. You are responsible for the murder of the Jews of Hungary. You could have saved them, but you didn't. You sent them to die so you could be a big shot with your friends. You are evil!" His voice began to rise hysterically. "You are an enemy of our people and you must be punished."

Again Andor started to step around him, snapping, "I have no intention of standing here listening to the insults of a fanatic. You'd better leave now, or I'll call the police."

"The police? What do I care about the police? What could they do to me? Put me in prison? Kill me? I don't care about life. There are some things more important than life, like loyalty and honor, but you don't know about things like that."

"Move out of my way!"

"Not yet, Horvath. I've come here to pay a debt I owe to my people. Especially to the hundreds of thousands who were slaughtered in Hungary by the Nazis. I know that this is why I was born, so I could carry out my mission in life. Most of the executioners of our Jewish brothers have been killed, one way or another. Those who are still alive will be hunted down. Then they, too, will die. So will you, because you are the beast who betrayed the Jews of Hungary. In the name of the six hundred thousand murdered Jews of Hungary . . ."

Jessica had been uneasy for the past quarter hour. Andor had never been more than a few minutes late. Twice she had gone out on the balcony to see if he was coming. She had just opened the french doors to go out again when she heard two sharp explosions. They sounded like revolver shots. A second later she heard a clatter, like coins or keys striking the concrete, and then a dull thud. She ran out and leaned over the balcony rail. A small automobile was starting up noisily. A man ran from the other side of the street and bent over a motionless figure lying on the sidewalk halfway between the curbing and the apartment-house entrance.

"Call an ambulance!" he shouted as people began to peer over balconies.

Jessica knew. She turned and raced through the apartment and down the stairs to the entrance. Several people were standing by the body. She pushed them aside, fell to her knees, and took one of Andor's hands in her own. A dark spot on his white shirt front was spreading. She put an ear to his lips. He was breathing, but he was unconscious. Frantically she began to talk to him, without considering that he couldn't hear her.

"Andor darling, be brave and strong. Andor, please live. Live for me!"

It seemed like hours before the ambulance arrived. Two men lifted him gently onto a stretcher. There was an immense dark pool on the sidewalk. The intern said Jessica could go along, but at the hospital she was not permitted in the emergency operating room. All she could do was pace the corridor. After a half hour a police officer arrived and asked her for a statement, but there was almost nothing she could tell him. He said that a man who had been walking on the opposite side of the Street of the Palms fortunately had obtained the license number of the car in which Mr. Horvath's assailant had fled. Also, he had been able to give a good description of the young man. Solicitously, the officer added, "Don't worry, Mrs. Horvath, before the night is over we'll catch him."

Catch him! After the officer left, Jessica went back to pacing the hallway, repeating his words over and over to herself. "Catch him," what good would that do? What they must do now was save Andor's life. If he lived, she would take him far, far away. Maybe to America or Australia. Maybe to an island somewhere. To a place remote from all this terrible backwash of the war. To some place where the name Andor Horvath would mean nothing. To some place where they had never even heard of Wedemeyer or Weber. Preferably to some place where there were no Jews. Just people. People who had never been branded, like cattle, so they could always be picked out. People who had never suffered. People who had no religion or cultural heritage to enrich their lives but at the same time to condemn them to eternal torture. As she walked wearily back and forth in the strange, empty corridor and whispered these words to herself, she glanced frequently at the door to the operating room, wondering what was happening behind it. Wondering yet afraid that any moment they might come out and tell her.

At last the door opened and a white-robed surgeon appeared. He seemed exhausted as he slowly removed his rubber gloves. "Your husband is on the way to his room, Mrs. Horvath," he said. "You can go up and see him, but it will be at least an hour before he gets over the effect of the anesthetic."

"How is he, Doctor?" she asked with painful anxiety.

For a moment the surgeon was silent, carefully gazing at her before he decided what to say. His eyes were kind and compassionate, but she read the answer in them even before he spoke. "We removed two bullets. They were lodged in the right lung, and there is a great danger of hemorrhage. Mrs. Horvath, I must tell you that your husband's chances of recovery are slight. In fact, he may not even regain consciousness."

Rudy Tabor was sitting with her beside the bed several hours later when an intern and a nurse each took one corner of the top sheet and slowly pulled it over his face. Then they led Jessica from the room, holding onto her arms in case she collapsed. Rudy followed silently.

She said nothing as they went down in the elevator and walked through the waiting room. But once on the outside, she stopped, grasped the old man's arm in a viselike grip, and said, "Rudy, Andor is dead!" as if she were announcing something he didn't know.

"Yes, Jessica," he replied gently.

"I can't believe it." The words were said in a deep monotone. They had a flat, dead sound.

Rudy tried to kindle in her a desire for revenge that would rouse her out of her stupefying grief. "The boy who fired the shots has been arrested," he said briskly. "I heard just a half hour ago that they caught him and he has already confessed."

Lethargically Jessica turned her stone-cold face to him. "Of what importance is that?"

49

Day after day Jessica went monotonously through the motions of living, her actions mechanical, her thoughts hidden behind an impenetrable mask. She hardly seemed aware of what she was doing. She moved about in a daze, possessed by a melancholia that pervaded her entire being. Occasionally when she looked into a mirror through force of habit, she stared blankly at the face that looked back at her. She answered telephone calls in a lifeless monotone, giving only monosyllabic replies to questions. She opened the considerable number of letters that arrived each day but read them as if they were addressed to someone else. Her only real link with life was Rudy Tabor, who came each afternoon on his way back to the *Gazette* office after lunch. She made coffee for him and then sat, politely quiet, while he tried to interest her in the world beyond her own door. But he got little reaction from her, even to his reports about Chaim Glazer.

The picture of the young murderer that Rudy pieced together for her from the newspapers and what he had learned from the police was of a confused and unstable youth driven by strange ideas and dangerous compulsions. Although he didn't belong to any organized group, Glazer had been meeting often with seven other men, all in their early twenties, who shared his fanaticism. Under police questioning Glazer and his friends had confessed having a vague plan for a series of political murders. They insisted they were motivated only by ethical and spiritual ideas. They had agreed that anyone guilty of "Horvathism"—their word for political corruption—was not entitled to "walk among the living." After murdering Horvath, they planned to eliminate several officials of the Jewish Agency whose names had come up in the libel trial. They knew well the methods of the Stern Gang, which had been responsible for the assassination of Count Bernadotte and Lord Moyne, and of the Irgun, the terrorist organization that had blown up one wing of the King David Hotel in Jerusalem. With both these groups now disbanded, they believed that it was the duty of younger men to revive terrorism as a political weapon. Rudy said it had not yet been decided whether to put any of Glazer's companions on trial as accessories. It was certain that Glazer himself, having confessed, would be found guilty after a quick trial and given a long prison sentence.

But Jessica was indifferent to the entire matter. She only hoped, she said, that they wouldn't call her as a witness at the murder trial.

One day as Rudy sat back sipping his coffee, she suddenly blurted out, "I'm going to have a baby."

He stammered for a moment before the words rushed out. "Why, that's fine, Jessica. Wonderful! I'm so happy for you." After waiting for her to say something more, he added, "Did Andor know?"

"No. It is almost three months, but I wasn't sure until a few weeks ago, so I didn't tell him."

"This will give a new purpose to your life, Jessica," Rudy said paternally.

She gave him a harsh look. "What you really mean is that I will bring into the world one more poor innocent creature to be despised."

"Jessica, you mustn't say such a thing!"

"Can't we ever be really honest? Andor was despised and you know it. His child will be despised, too. He will always be known as the child of the man who sold his soul to the devil."

"You have reason to be bitter," Rudy said softly, "but soon the appeal will be heard and I am as sure as I have ever been of anything that the District Court's decision will be reversed and Andor's name will be cleared."

Still in her dull monotone she replied, "I wish I could be so optimistic. But just think of all the people who are against us. There are the families of all the Hungarian Jews Andor didn't succeed in saving. I understand how they feel. It's natural that they should be bitter when they see us walking down the street and think of their own dear dead.

"Then there are Chorin's friends. He has a following that thinks he is a brave crusader." A crooked smile creased her soft features. "And the friends of Ben-Nathan. He's a shrewd man and he's won over a great many people with his emotional oratory, and he's convinced them that Andor really was a collaborator."

Rudy tried to interrupt, but she went on talking. "And don't forget those who read the verdict and say to themselves that the learned judge who listened to all the evidence should know whether Andor was guilty or not. In the face of all this, how can I be hopeful?"

Rudy moved his bulk forward in his chair. He caught Jessica's gaze and held it. "My dear, dear girl," he chided her gently, "you are so bitter that you aren't being reasonable. First, Hungarian Jews here in Israel are much more divided about Andor than you believe. I know them. Sure they argue the case. They will argue it as long as there are two of them with the breath to speak. But the very fact that they argue proves that opinion is divided. Don't you see that?"

He drained the last few drops of his coffee and then went on. "You say Chorin has a following. Of course. But very damaging evidence was introduced against him at the trial. He may have some friends, but he had many, many critics and bitter enemies, even before he made such an unfair attack on Andor.

"As for Ben-Nathan—and this also applies to Chorin—it is well known by lawyers and newspapermen all over the world that if you attack someone too viciously, even if everyone knows he is guilty, people feel sorry for him and take his side. This happened in Andor's case. Many Israelis who weren't at all certain whether Andor did right or wrong came to his support because Chorin and Ben-Nathan were ruthless in their treatment of him.

"As for the mass of Israelis, I am sure many more were influenced by the prosecution's case than by Ben-Nathan's defense, and that they think Andor was right in saving as many of our people as he could, by the methods he used. They give him credit. But what has finally swayed most of the others was Glazer's fiendish act."

Jessica looked down at her own lap.

"You know as well as I do, Jessica, that our people don't like terrorism. They have been the victims of too much of it. When you and I and Andor first came here, we saw Jewish terrorists in action. What they did is no secret. They argue now that without it the British never would have left here and we never would have got our state. Maybe, but I tell you the great majority of Israelis do not condone violence, even when it is used against people who are standing between us and our great dream. When violence is let loose by Jew against Jew, it is even less excusable in the eyes of our people. That is why most Israelis are angry about the assassination."

He looked into Jessica's face to see if he had changed her mind, but she was unimpressed. With a sigh he leaned back and concluded, "I hope the Supreme Court's decision is handed down before your baby is born, because I am positive it will wipe away the stain that has been put temporarily on the name the child will bear."

As Rudy looked at his watch and got up to go, Jessica gave him a pale smile and kissed his cheek gratefully. "You are a very good friend. I could not have lived through these last weeks without you."

He took her hand and pressed it to his lips.

After the door was closed behind him, she murmured, "But that doesn't mean I believe anything you say."

A sharp pain shot through her stomach and she sat down quickly. Closing her eyes, waiting for the pain to go, she thought back to the night in the little hilltop hotel at Haifa.

"You were conceived in sorrow," she whispered grimly to the growing fetus within her; "you will be born in sorrow."

50

The Chorin libel case and the Glazer murder trial were in the Israeli courts at the same time, the appeal of the prosecution in the libel case being considered by five justices of the Supreme Court in Jerusalem, the murder case by three judges of the District Court in Tel Aviv.

It took only a few days for the district judges to hear the evidence against Chaim Glazer and to decide, unanimously, that he was guilty of premeditated murder and should be given the maximum punishment under the law—life imprisonment. At no time during the trial did the young defendant express any regret for what he had done. Instead, he seemed to enjoy being the center of so much attention, and when he was led from the Tel Aviv courtroom after the sentencing he smiled and bowed slightly to the crowd of spectators, much as an actor taking a curtain call.

Although Israel's Supreme Court hearings were always held in the largest courtroom in Jerusalem, no case in the short history of the state had ever drawn much of a crowd, due to the nature of the proceedings. After the filing of an appeal, opposing counsel had the privilege of presenting written briefs to the court and then were given the right to argue verbally before the bench. Because witnesses were not normally called, and because the arguments in most cases hinged on legal technicalities, there was never much public interest.

The Chorin-Horvath case was an exception. On the first day the spectators began arriving several hours before the start of the session. Soon after the doors were opened, every seat was occupied and a long waiting line circled through the hallway and down a flight of stairs. Extreme security measures were taken at the entrance of the court building and of the courtroom. Everyone seeking admittance was subjected to six different examinations, including a body search for concealed weapons. Brief cases were emptied out on a table, parcels were examined, identity cards checked, and a written list made of each person's name, address, and occupation.

While they waited for the first day's hearing to begin, the spectators did their own arguing of the case, the pitch of their voices giving an indication of the intensity of their feelings. In the hallway several impromptu debates grew so acrimonious that police officers had to intervene. By the time the bailiff called the court to order and the five black-robed justices filed in, an atmosphere of intense dramatic expectancy had been generated.

Attorney General Weiss was the first to address the bench. After a technical preamble he launched immediately into his attack on Judge Lehmann's verdict.

"No court anywhere, neither in Israel nor abroad, has ever perpetrated so great an injustice as that of the Jerusalem District Court in the case now under review," he declared sternly, half facing the bench, half facing the spectators. "Some of the arguments advanced in the verdict border on absurdity."

The presiding justice leaned forward and in a reproving tone said, "Is there not a more fitting phrase?"

Weiss half smiled at the reprimand and said, "I do not want to besmirch the name of the District Court, for I know that Judge Lehmann wrote his judgment with blood and sweat, with an honest heart and the best of intentions, but the facts are that the judgment is studded with the rage which the court seemed to feel against Andor Horvath. It reads like a Dickens novel with all the characters either coal-black or pure white."

After pausing for a drink of water he went on. "In actual fact Andor Horvath made many mistakes during his short career as head of the Budapest Rescue Committee, but he was a man who acted in good faith, honestly, humanely, and with superhuman courage and valor. For what he did, every one of us should be deeply grateful."

Picking up a copy of the verdict from the table, he continued, "Judge Lehmann in his findings used a parable of his own creation to demonstrate what he called 'the infamy of Andor Horvath.' He said, 'Armed soldiers are asleep in a camp. A strong force surrounds the camp, intending to kill everyone. They contact the guard, telling him, "If you do not arouse those in the camp, we will save you and a few of your friends." The guard does not arouse his comrades, and thus saves himself and some of his friends.'"

There was complete silence in the courtroom. Many of the spectators were leaning forward in their seats so as not to miss a word, for this was the best-known passage in the verdict. For months it had been used in private and public arguments, in newspaper editorials, and in political speeches, to confound Horvath's defenders. To many Israelis it had seemed to present an unanswerable condemnation.

"May I point out to the court," Weiss went on, "that there is no equation between the facts in our case and the facts in Judge Lehmann's parable. Andor Horvath was not a guard in a camp, but a parliamentarian, sent by those in the camp to negotiate with the enemy. Besides, Hungarian Jewry was not an armed camp sleeping on its weapons, as in the parable. The Jews in Pécs, for example, were in a ghetto, without arms, without food, with few clothes, without hope, on the threshold of complete despair."

As Weiss paused, a buzz of whispering swept the courtroom.

"The lower court has stated that it was better to die with honor than to adopt the path taken by Horvath," Weiss continued. "But I ask this court if it was not the duty of Horvath, or any other leader, to try to save as many persons as possible, rather than to lead them to their death? If there had been a revolt, would more lives have been saved? Of course not. No one would have been saved.

"We must ask ourselves whether it was possible for Andor Horvath or anyone else to lead a revolt in Hungary. Six million of our people were exterminated in Europe; 5,900,000 of them boarded the death transports without resistance. Revolts such as the one in the Warsaw ghetto were rare, and even in Warsaw those taking up arms faced the wrath of the majority, for it is not human or natural for people to throw away their lives in what they know in advance is a completely futile revolt—an enterprise without even the slightest possibility of success.

"Andor Horvath is criticized by the lower court for not having warned his people in Hungary of the fate that awaited them. But if he had told them, would they have believed? No, for human nature is such that each person has the confidence that the other will be killed and that somehow he himself will escape. Soldiers in all armies believe this. Otherwise war would be impossible."

By the time the court was recessed for lunch, Weiss had raised so many fundamental philosophical and ethical questions that the spectators began arguing them with each other even before they were out of the courtroom. No matter how the five justices might decide the case, these were questions for which there would never be definitive answers. That was why, day after day, interest in the case grew more intense. Even those who had no direct involvement in what had happened to Hungarian Jewry became intellectually concerned because the issues were so basic. That was why there was never a vacant seat in the courtroom and why the country's newspapers devoted so many columns each day to the case.

Weiss presented no new evidence, but for six consecutive days he reviewed the case, seeking to convince the five justices that the lower court had misinterpreted the evidence.

On Sunday of the second week, as Yaacov Ben-Nathan arose from his chair at the defense table to begin his arguments, he appeared confident, self-possessed, and brimming with optimism. During the original trial he had tried to impress the District Court with the idea that Andor Horvath was part of a deeply entrenched and exceedingly corrupt Establishment, while he and his client were men of noble principle, engaged in an altruistic crusade to expose the secret machinations of those sinister forces. Some spectators had looked on him as a Sancho Panza, tilting against windmills, and yet he had impressed many who either disliked the Establishment for other reasons or who instinctively were inclined to side with any idealistic-sounding minority campaign. But now the situation was reversed. Judge Lehmann's decision had given respectability and standing to Ben-Nathan's client and had gone even further than the defense attorney himself had ever gone in branding Horvath a colleague of the devil. As Ben-Nathan now began to speak, he no longer appeared to anyone as a Sancho Panza, but rather as a military commander safely entrenched behind the walls of a fortress he had just captured, defying the enemy to try to retake it.

"It is impossible to clear Andor Horvath without clearing Himmler," he declared dramatically, "and it is impossible to clear Himmler without clearing Hitler. We have already, to the satisfaction of the lower court, proved that Horvath deliberately tried to annihilate Hungarian Jewry. He was enslaved by the Nazis. He became their victim, the tool of all their planning. As the bodies of others were burned to cinders at Auschwitz, so was the soul of Andor Horvath burned to cinders by his Nazi masters. He began to work with them with the best of intentions, but gradually he became enmeshed in the cogs of the Nazi machine. He was led to this collaboration by his abject pessimism, his feeling that all was lost, and his nonbelief that resistance could be effective. He relegated eight hundred thousand living persons to annihilation. He reconciled himself to the idea that they were doomed. Their names were stricken from the rolls of the living so he could save his friends and relatives. The cold facts, denuded of emotionalism, led Judge Lehmann to draw his conclusions about Andor Horvath the man."

One of the justices bent forward and said, "In a criminal trial, such as this is, it is forbidden to consider the character of the person."

Ben-Nathan nodded, then went on, changing his angle of attack only slightly. "None of Horvath's lies on the witness stand were accidental. They were skillful, logical, a combination of half-truths blended with outright falsehoods. However, in the end he was trapped by his own lies, for his lies did not hang together."

At the start of the next day's session Ben-Nathan asked for permission to introduce some new evidence. He said that since the original trial he had been in touch with a man who had been head of investigations for the American Prosecution Office at Nuremberg and who was ready to testify that Colonel Weber had been acquitted of war crimes because of the evidence given in his favor at Nuremberg by Andor Horvath. The lawyer said he would also like to introduce a letter Horvath had written to a Jewish Agency official boasting that Colonel Weber had been released "owing to my personal intervention." Also, he wished to present documentary proof that Horvath had intervened at Nuremberg on behalf of Captain Klaussen. The court denied all three requests.

The second day's appearance of Ben-Nathan was enlivened by an exchange between him and one of the justices, who said, "Defense counsel has declared that no leader has a right to sacrifice his followers without their knowledge. Let me ask defense counsel, assuming that there is no way open for a leader but to save 1,680 persons, and he concentrated all his efforts on doing this, and by so doing this he did not aid the Nazis, would you still brand him as a collaborator?"

Ben-Nathan refused to enter the trap. "I would brand him the worst possible criminal," he replied acidly. "No man has the right, not even under the most despicable totalitarian regime, to say, 'I know that they —my followers—are doomed,' and then to decide their fate for them. No one has the right to prevent them from taking their own decision in such a matter."

The justice replied, "Let us assume that this person had warned them and they paid no heed, would you still call this person a criminal?"

Ben-Nathan turned to face the bench directly. "Without entering into the discussion of hypothetical questions, I repeat: no man has the right to decide for his followers that the situation is lost. Nor has he the right to impose his belief in this matter on eight hundred thousand persons, even if he wants to save 1,680."

The justice: "This is the focal point. Did those in the ghettos of Hungary know what fate awaited them?"

Ben-Nathan: "Twenty witnesses appeared in the lower court and testified that they did not know. Horvath even admitted that they went like sheep to the slaughter, and if there were those who knew and refused to believe, it was the duty of the leaders to drive home the truth. Leadership carries with it responsibility to warn one's followers."

After five days of argument by Ben-Nathan, the Attorney General was given the right to make a final plea.

"I beg the court to consider," he began, "that Andor Horvath never had any despicable motives. He never desired to help the Germans. He negotiated with them only to save lives and further his rescue work. The worst that can be said about him is that he may have committed errors of judgment. He has been criticized by those who had personal grievances against him for being a bohemian and a dilettante, for not taking his colleagues more into his confidence, for behaving sometimes in an arrogant manner, but no one who really knew him ever thought of Andor Horvath as a Quisling, not even his bitterest foes."

Then, picking up a sheaf of papers from his desk, the Attorney General dropped his defense of Horvath and launched into an offensive against Chorin. "Let us remember that the defendant in this case is not Andor Horvath, but a man who wrote most scurrilously about many people. If the court will recall some of the words of Chorin's newspaper articles attacking Horvath, it will become clear that he did not write in good faith, but in a spirit of slanderous vindictiveness. This charge of criminal libel was brought against him under the laws of the State of Israel, which forbid such attacks, unless the facts on which they are based and the allegations that are made are beyond any reasonable doubt. May I remind the court that just before the libel action was filed the defendant in a newspaper article wrote: 'The stench of a corpse assails my nostrils . . . this will be the best of funerals . . . Andor Horvath must be liquidated. . . .'

"Gentlemen of the court, Andor Horvath *has* been liquidated. There is nothing we can do to bring him back to life. But we have a solemn duty to perform. In a spirit of strict legality, scrupulous fairness, and unwavering devotion to justice, we must see that the terrible wrong that was committed by the judgment of the lower court is righted. I ask your honors to reverse that decision and to find László Chorin guilty of criminal libel under Paragraph 201 (1) of the Criminal Law ordinance, as charged in the indictment."

When Jessica's time came she went to a nursing home on the outskirts of Tel Aviv and there one early morning gave birth to a baby boy. Rudy Tabor, one of the few who knew of her confinement, was informed by a nurse when he telephoned late that day that the mother would not be well enough to have visitors at least before the next afternoon. It was actually two days later before he finally was permitted to see her. As he entered the room with his hat in one hand and a small bouquet in the other, Jessica had just finished nursing her child. Looking down into its minuscule face, Rudy spontaneously said, without even thinking whether it was a tactful remark, "Already he looks exactly like Andor!"

"Yes," Jessica said, with a disembodied voice, "I think so, too. I suppose that should make me happy, but somehow it doesn't. It frightens me. He's a perfect baby, the doctor said. Perfect in every way. The doctor said I should be very proud. But—Rudy, I'm frightened!" Tears welled up in her eyes, and she reached out for his hand. Her own hand was moist with perspiration, and he noticed that her forehead was, too. He held her hand firmly, trying to give her strength through his fingers.

"Rudy, he's such a sweet child. I couldn't stand for him to be despised!"

Early one morning of the next week, Rudy received a message from the hospital that Jessica had been given permission to go home at noon that day; would he be so good as to arrange for transportation? He took his housekeeper immediately to the Horvath apartment to clean, dust, and polish everything in the three rooms and then to set a luncheon table with two places. As she began work, he went out shopping and in Tel Aviv's best delicatessen bought a market basket full of delicacies he knew Jessica liked, and on the way back to the Street of the Palms stopped in a florist shop and selected enough flowers to fill half a dozen large vases. By the time he reached the Horvath apartment again, a blue and white crib he had ordered had arrived. He and the housekeeper arranged the flowers together. At half past eleven he gave the apartment a final inspection and then left to find a taxi.

It was almost an hour later when he returned with Jessica, who climbed the stairs slowly, for she had only begun to regain her strength. Rudy followed, carrying carefully a small bundle swaddled in white wool. For the first time since the night of Andor's death he saw a pleasant smile cross Jessica's face as she opened the apartment door and noticed the roomful of flowers, the carefully set table, and the sparkling polish his housekeeper had given to the apartment.

"Rudy, you're an angel!" she said as she turned and kissed him affectionately on one cheek. Then she took the white bundle from him, saying, "Sit down and pour each of us a drink. I'll be back as soon as I settle the little one."

When she returned to the room, there was a tear in the corner of each eye. "The crib is lovely, Rudy. *Köszönöm szépen*. I only wish Andor were here to see his son asleep in it. The child will probably grow up to wish that I had never brought him into the world, but right now he looks so serene and so—so—so untouched by evil."

They drank a toast in imported *barack* and then sampled some of the delicacies Rudy had found in the delicatessen. Jessica noticed that he frequently looked at his watch, so finally she said, "I know I have taken a great deal of your time today, Rudy. You go along whenever you feel you must go."

"No! No!" he replied quickly. "It's just that at two o'clock you and I have a date."

Jessica sighed. "I'm sorry to disappoint you, after all you've done, but I couldn't move out of the apartment this afternoon if my life depended on it."

"You don't have to move from that chair, Jessica. It's almost two now. Do you mind if I turn on the radio?"

A little perplexed, she said, "No, of course not."

As he turned up the volume, they heard the last strains of a symphony and then the announcer said, in Hebrew, "This is Kol Israel calling. We now bring you the news." The voice paused and Jessica looked at the gray-haired man opposite her with bewilderment. He pointed to the radio as the announcer went on, "This morning in Jerusalem the Supreme Court announced its decision in the appeal filed by the Attorney General against the District Court's verdict in the László Chorin libel case. The lower court had found that Andor Horvath had in fact collaborated with the Nazis, and had prepared the ground for the mass murder of Hungarian Jewry, and had testified for Standartenführer Franz Weber, a notorious war criminal, and it ruled that in making these accusations against Horvath, László Chorin had not been guilty of criminal libel."

Rudy was sitting back comfortably in his chair puffing on his pipe, but Jessica was leaning forward, nervously clasping and unclasping her hands. The announcer paused and then continued. "Today in the Supreme Court all five justices concurred in finding that Andor Horvath had actually testified for Franz Weber, Nazi war criminal, as the lower court had declared, and the five justices therefore rejected the appeal of the Attorney General for a reversal in this connection."

As the announcer paused again, Jessica began to cry, softly.

"However," the announcer continued, "all five justices also concurred in finding that Andor Horvath did not prepare the ground for the mass murder of Hungarian Jewry, as had been charged in the newspaper articles by László Chorin, and four of the five justices agreed that there also was no basis for Chorin's charge that Horvath had collaborated with the Nazis. Thus the highest court in the State of Israel has removed from the name of Andor Horvath the stigma of having been a traitor to his own people, by reversing the finding of the lower court.

After declaring the defendant, László Chorin, guilty of criminal libel, the court retired briefly to consider the question of sentence. The Attorney General had asked for a prison term. Defense counsel had entered a plea for mercy, on the ground that his client was seriously ill. When the justices returned to the bench, the president of the court announced imposition of a one-year suspended sentence but declared that if Chorin committed a felony or published libelous material during the next three years, the suspension would be lifted and he would be required to serve the prison term. Chorin was also ordered to pay five hundred Israeli pounds as court costs. In a moment we will have additional news from the Jerusalem courtroom. In the meantime here are highlights of news from around the world."

Rudy walked over to the radio and turned down the volume so the announcer's voice was just audible. Then he returned to the table, took one of Jessica's hands, kissed her finger tips, looked into her face, and said, "Now, my child, maybe you have learned to listen to an old man. I've been telling you for months that this is the way it would turn out, but you wouldn't believe me, would you?"

Jessica was biting her lower lip to control herself. "Rudy, it's wonderful. I know I should be happy. This really does clear his name, doesn't it?"

"My child, they couldn't have said it any plainer. I can quote the exact words back to you. 'Thus the highest court in the State of Israel has removed from the name of Andor Horvath the stigma of having been a traitor to his own people.'"

He walked back to the radio and turned up the volume just as the announcer was saying, ". . . and that concludes a résumé of news from around the world. Now here are more details from the courtroom in Jerusalem, where, as we have already announced, László Chorin has been given a one-year suspended prison sentence after being found guilty of criminal libel, and the name of Andor Horvath has been cleared of charges that he collaborated with the Nazis or that he aided in any way the destruction of Hungarian Jewry. Each of the justices wrote his own judgment. We bring you now a few excerpts from these five opinions.

"Justice Abramson: 'We must ask ourselves how many Hungarian Jews would have survived if Andor Horvath had not existed.'

"Justice Carmel: 'Horvath was criticized for saving fourteen members of his own family. No one can blame a man for seeking to save his own family. It would be abnormal if he did not. But it should be further noted that more than one hundred other relatives of Andor Horvath remained behind to die in the death camps.'

"Justice Havilio: 'Andor Horvath kept the Bergen-Belsen train a secret from the majority of the eight hundred thousand Hungarian Jews in order not to create riots among those who could not board it and also in order to hide it from the Hungarians, for the train never would have left if the Hungarians had learned about it.'

"Justice Magnes: 'The agreement between Horvath and the Nazis to save a trainload of notables, as they were called in the trial, was not a final act but the beginning of a heartbreaking drama, a cruel game of hopes and despairs in which Horvath was involved during the months of the total annihilation and until the train reached safety.'

"Justice Yadin: 'It is easy now, in an atmosphere of calm and tranquillity, to pass judgment on the right or wrong of an individual's behavior ten years ago, but in ruling on this appeal, we have tried to project ourselves back to the horrible days of 1944–45 and to realize that nothing then was normal, that there was chaos on all sides, that the established order had collapsed, that many human beings were living like wild animals, that death was raining down from the sky by day and by night, that armies were collapsing, that the civilian population was cold, hungry, sick, and helpless, that morale was gone, and under such conditions decisions had to be taken quickly, often without the possibility of consultation with anyone. In this situation a man with no concern at all for his own safety or well-being did what he could, by the only method available to him, to save some of his fellow men. To send such a man to his grave with the brand on his forehead put there by the lower court was patently unjust, and therefore we have reversed that decision.' "

As the broadcast terminated, Rudy snapped off the radio and turned back to Jessica.

"Now, my dear girl, I must leave you. I shall keep in touch with you by telephone, and from time to time, as long as I am permitted to remain in this mixed-up world, I shall look in on you. But it's up to you now. You must carry on. You must raise that son of yours to be a man of high principles and to be fearless when he thinks he's right. There is no reason, with your training, he should not someday have the career here in Israel that his father aspired to have."

Jessica rose slowly to her feet to see her guest to the door, then suddenly threw herself into the old man's arms, sobbing, "I promise, Rudy. I promise to try. To the best of my ability I'll try!"

This tremendous panoramic novel tells the story of the Jews who were caught in Hungary during the last two years of World War II. The central character is Andor Horvath, a courageous negotiator who tried desperately to stop the deportations and cremations and who succeeded in bargaining with the Nazis for a few thousand Jewish lives. But this is a book with many characters and many plots which shows how Jews were lulled into a sense of false security, how they were methodically liquidated at Auschwitz, how Horvath arranged for the famous rescue train which eventually brought 1,659 Jews